Kingston Libraries

On line Services

www.kingston.gov.uk/libraries

Renew a book (5 times)   Request a book
Change of address   Email a branch
Library news and updates   Get your pin
Search the catalogues   Access free reference sites

020 8547 5006

New Malden Library
48 Kingston Road
New Malden
KT3 3LY
020 8547 5006

D1380360

KT 2344916 0

TERRY GOODKIND

SIEGE OF STONE

SISTER OF DARKNESS

THE NICCI CHRONICLES
3

HEAD
ZEUS

First published in the UK in 2018 by Head of Zeus Ltd
This paperback edition published in the UK in 2019 by Head of Zeus Ltd

9 7 5 3 1 2 4 6 8

A catalogue record for this book is available from
the British Library.

ISBN (PB): 9781786691736
ISBN (E): 9781786691705

Typeset by Adrian McLaughlin

Printed and bound in Great Britain by
CPI Group (UK) Ltd, Croydon CR0 4YY

Head of Zeus Ltd
First Floor East
5–8 Hardwick Street
London EC1R 4RG

WWW.HEADOFZEUS.COM

SIEGE OF STONE

CHAPTER 1

The city of Ildakar continued to burn, even though the violent revolt had run its course. Riled up by the rebel leader Mirrormask, the city's downtrodden had torn apart the prosperous neighborhoods. Arena warriors, tradesmen, and gifted nobles battled one another with every weapon and resource at their disposal.

As Nicci worked alongside Nathan Rahl to quell the worst of the destruction, she knew the unrest was far from over, but Ildakar's woes were no longer her problem to solve. Nicci had helped bring freedom to the oppressed city, and now these people would have to rebuild their own society—nobles and slaves, gifted wizards and everyday laborers. In order for a city to function, all the parts need to work together.

Back in the D'Haran Empire, Richard was likely facing the same turmoil, but on a grander scale. It was Nicci's job to spread Lord Rahl's message of freedom to the entire Old World, not just one city, and she and her companions were anxious to move on to other destinations.

In the last hours of the exhausting night, though, Ildakar remained her priority. She shouted orders, calling the people together to fight a fire that roared out of control in a silk merchant's warehouse. Flames licked up the wooden walls and shattered the window glass, then spilled out of the upper windows. Ildakar was famed for fine silks, created by gifted craftsmen in the spinners' guild. Now hundreds of bolts of valuable cloth went up in flames, sending a sour smell of smoke into the air.

"We have to get this fire under control before it spreads to other buildings." Nicci swept her piercing blue gaze across the bedraggled crowd, assessing them as fighters, as helpers. Many of them wore clothes spattered with blood and grimy with soot, while others looked battered and disheveled from fighting one another or trying to put out the scattered fires. "This is not a time to choose who benefits most."

Rendell, one of the older house slaves who had joined Mirror-mask's revolt, rallied several of his comrades. "We destroyed the water basins so Sovrena Thora couldn't spy on us, but we can still use the water from the aqueducts." He ran to a nearby wall where a public fountain had been smashed. Together, he and several companions used metal bars to break the cap that blocked the fountain pipe, and a silvery ribbon of liquid sluiced out. "Buckets! We need buckets!"

From nearby shops and homes, people emerged with pails and tubs. Together they collected the spraying water and rushed to throw it on the fire in the silk warehouse.

The cavernous building had become a blazing furnace. Flames erupted through a hole in the tile roof, and sparks shot through the air like night wisps. Dawn would arrive in an hour or two, but for now, the orange glow of burning lit the sky.

Flaming tatters of silk wafted through the air toward the nearby rooftops. Nicci summoned her gift and created a river of wind that drove the sparks away from nearby roofs before they could catch fire. The embers swept higher, twirling like orange stars against the deep darkness, until they extinguished themselves.

The wizard Nathan stood beside her, his long white hair tangled from the night's struggles. He showed no lack of confidence, and he smiled as he took a step forward. "Now that I have my gift back, Sorceress, it's time to get a little more practice with magic."

So long stripped of his gift, Nathan reveled in having his abilities back. That was one reward he had received from the wizards of Ildakar, though the fleshmancer had been forced to rip out Nathan's heart and give him a new one from the dying Chief Handler Ivan. A horrific process, but that had cured his problem at last.

As Rendell and his companions continued their bucket brigade, pouring water on the flames at the street level, Nathan blasted open a second fountain at a nearby intersection so that more water gushed into the streets. He called upon the flow, tugging the stream like a liquid whip, looping it in the air. The manipulated water rose above the warehouse roof, then struck down like a viper. The column of water poured through the open roof and onto the roaring flames. Nathan pulled more water from the aqueducts to continue the deluge. With a whistling hiss, a mist of steam sprayed out, overwhelming the black smoke. The flames began to sputter and withdraw from the warehouse windows.

Nicci formed a wall of air to surround the broken walls where the flames tried to escape.

Nathan flexed his fingers, as if feeling the tingle of magic through them. "It's quite exhilarating to be able to do that again!"

The warehouse owner watched the destruction of his goods, his face sagging with dismay. The man had a lush brown beard and overly curled locks of long hair. He wore layers of colorful silk robes that were now rumpled from the night's ordeal. "All of my silk, all of my wealth. The slaves destroyed it!"

"The fire destroyed it," Nicci said. "The nobles and merchants are as much to blame for the uprising as the slaves."

Rendell handed the distraught merchant a wooden bucket full of water. "If you want to save part of what you have, then pitch in and help with the rest of us."

The merchant held the bucket and looked helplessly at the team of people pouring load after load of water on the now-dying fires.

"This isn't our warehouse," Rendell scolded him in a stern voice. "We're doing this to save Ildakar." He nudged the reluctant man into motion.

The dazed merchant squared his shoulders and got in line with the workers, filling the bucket at the nearest gushing pipe. "For Ildakar," he muttered, as if to convince himself.

The legendary city had hidden beneath the shroud of eternity for fifteen centuries. During that time, Sovrena Thora had tried to build her perfect society, which had become more grim and stagnant over the years. Thora and the other gifted nobles had been oblivious to the explosive situation they were creating. Thora's own husband, Wizard Commander Maxim, had exploited that situation, fashioning himself into a rebel leader and trying to destroy the city just because he was tired of it. But his guise of Mirrormask had been exposed, and Maxim had fled the city at the height of the revolt. Thora was also overthrown, turned to stone by members of her own duma—just like the hundreds of thousands of stone soldiers that had laid siege to Ildakar fifteen centuries earlier.

"Nicci!" called a familiar voice. Bannon Farmer, who had journeyed with them across the Old World, ran to them with his long ginger hair flying wild. The young man had gained some muscle during his travels, but Nicci noticed how fit Bannon's physique had become from his training as an arena fighter. He was still shirtless from escaping the combat pits, and he carried his unremarkable sword, Sturdy.

He stopped in front of them, breathing hard with alarm. "Three spiny wolves are loose in Potter's Alley, and they've killed nine people already. Some citizens have blocked them, but they can't kill those beasts." He held up his sword. "And I can't do it by myself."

"You are not by yourself, boy," said a wiry young woman who trotted up beside him. She wore a black leather wrap around her waist, and another enfolded her breasts. Her short light brown hair stuck out in spiky strands. Her body was marked with protective runes that had been branded into her skin during her training to become a morazeth, a ruthless female warrior. Lila had put Bannon through harsh training to become an arena warrior, but after the revolt, she now offered her grudging cooperation to help.

"Spiny wolves were bred to slaughter humans," Nathan said. The fleshmancers of Ildakar had altered fearsome wild wolves, added muscles, arched their backs, extended their teeth.

Bannon said, "They were turned loose by escaping slaves, but now we have to take care of them before they hurt anyone else."

"Tonight, we take care of everything," Nicci said. "Lead on, Bannon Farmer."

The tall young man trotted off, while Lila darted after him. The group ran past shuttered shops, overturned cobbler's benches, a ransacked grocer's stall, and finally into the alley where several potters had set up their wheels along with shelves to display their wares. At the end of the street, near a shared, smoke-stained kiln, anxious people armed with sticks stood together, barely managing to hold three spiny wolves at bay. Several men already lay dead on the ground, their chests torn open, their throats mangled.

Behind the cornered wolves, Nicci heard the wails of two young children and their mother trapped in a small potter's shop. The door of old planks was too flimsy to offer much protection. One of the spiny wolves growled at the whimpering children and smashed at the door with a large paw, splintering the supports, but the jabbing spears and shovels kept the animals preoccupied.

Rushing toward the end of the street, Nicci snatched up a glazed pot from a nearby shelf and hurled it with perfect aim, shattering it against the skull of a wolf. The three beasts snarled, and the reluctant defenders backed away in fear. Nicci strode forward, palms on the daggers at her waist, while Nathan, Bannon, and Lila joined her.

She saw a flash of tawny fur, heard a familiar growl, and Mrra bounded up beside her. Nicci's sister panther had prowled the streets of Ildakar after being released from the combat pits. Now Mrra was free, and because of her bond with Nicci, she didn't attack the humans in the city.

Unlike the sand panther, these three wolves could never be captured and tamed, and Nicci had no intention of letting them terrorize or kill more people. She glanced at Bannon and Nathan. "We need to make this quick. Don't let them suffer. They are monsters through no fault of their own."

Lila nodded. "Yes, we have other work to do this night."

Using her gift, Nicci would have reached out and simply stopped their hearts as the swiftest and most merciful way to end the threat, but the spiny wolves were branded with protective runes that rendered them invulnerable to direct magical attacks. She would have to kill them in a more straightforward way. Nicci drew her two daggers, Nathan held out his ornate sword, Bannon raised Sturdy, and Lila grasped a short sword.

The growling beasts knew their true enemies. They moved together as a pack and lunged. Nicci wielded a knife in each hand, slashing and stabbing. The wolves' fangs glistened with ribbons of silver drool as they tried to tear into her, but she drove her left dagger up, plunging it into one creature's throat, and then stabbed the other blade into its heart. Mrra dove on top of the beast, driving it to the ground.

The spiny wolf weighed twice as much as Nicci did, and its sheer momentum forced her to the street, still thrashing. Its paw tore a long wound in her bare arm, but she pushed the knives deeper. The wolf jerked and twitched. Suddenly, its head rolled free as Bannon decapitated it with a stroke of his sword.

Nicci shoved the rank-smelling wolf carcass off of her and found herself soaked with the creature's blood. She yanked her knives loose, and blood ran down her wrists. She pulled herself up to see if Nathan needed help, but the wizard stood victorious over another beast, his ornate sword wet and red. He wiped the blade on its matted fur. Bannon and Lila had killed the third wolf.

Nicci gathered her composure. Dust and gravel clung to her bloodstained black dress, and sticky blood coated her fingers. She wiped her daggers clean on the wolf fur and sheathed them. Mrra came to stand beside her, twitching her long tail.

In the huddled shack next to the potter's shop, two little girls and their mother yanked the flimsy door open and rushed out, sobbing, into the arms of a broad-chested man. The crowd cheered, calling out her name: "Nicci! Nicci!"

At the beginning of this violent night, these same people had shouted for Mirrormask, yet Nicci had been a more dedicated leader of their uprising. "Nicci, we continue the fight!" cried a voice. "You helped show us."

"We've got to free ourselves from the nobles of Ildakar!" called another.

She turned to see two burly slaves wearing the drab garments of workers from the yaxen slaughter yards. Proudly, the men carried blood-soaked sacks, as if they held trophies. One man with a burn scar on his forehead strutted forward. He glanced down at the dead spiny wolves. "You killed those arena animals and you helped make the city safe. Meanwhile, we continue to fight our true enemies."

The bloody sacks made Nicci uneasy. "And do you know your true enemies?"

The two defiant slaves walked up to her, ignoring Bannon and Nathan, while the other people in Potter's Alley backed toward their shops. Opening their stained sacks, the men dumped the heads of four nobles onto the street. The dead faces wore frozen grimaces, their eyes still open. The neck stumps were ragged and still bloody. "These were cruel masters," said the gruff man with the burn scar. "They beat their slaves, treated them badly."

"They might have been gifted, but they were still vulnerable." The second man chuckled. A few others in Potter's Alley cheered, though most seemed shaken and nauseated by their own ordeal.

The scarred man said, "Even though Mirrormask deceived us, his words were valid. We will have our revenge, and we have you to help us, Nicci. We demand justice before we rebuild Ildakar. The slaves must be the ones who rule the city now."

Before Nicci could speak, Nathan expressed his own troubled thoughts. "Dear spirits, you will all have to rule together to build something stronger for Ildakar. If you kill all the nobles and make yourselves the new ruling class, you'll be as cruel and corrupt as they were."

"Never!" sneered the scarred man, insulted by Nathan's suggestion. He kicked one severed head with his foot, and it bounced down the street like a ball in a game of Ja'La.

"The wizard is right," Nicci said. "I make no excuse for the corrupt nobles—I know what Thora and Maxim did. But Ildakar is your city, so don't waste the opportunity. You have work to do, hard work, while I have my own mission, given to me by Lord Rahl himself." She shook her head. "My companions and I have spent far too much time in Ildakar already."

Even though the two burly, blood-flecked slaves looked cowed by her rebuke, they remained unrepentant as they stared at the four severed heads. Nicci was sure there would be much more killing before this unrest settled.

She couldn't save the whole city; she knew that. Nicci would not become their new sovrena and impose her own rule. "You're free now. Understand what that means. The people of Ildakar will have to make their rules and live with the consequences of their behavior."

"I'm afraid that's the cost of true freedom," Nathan agreed. "There might be lean and painful times ahead, but it's the only way you can truly value what you build."

After the long and violent night, the sun began to rise on a new Ildakar. The sacrificial pyramid had been destroyed, along with all the bloodworking apparatus that Thora would have used to create a new shroud of eternity. The legendary city was now permanently a part of the real world.

Lila stood silent, looking at the dead wolves. Bannon said with his usual optimism, "This turmoil will settle down soon enough. People will see reason. They want to make a nice life for themselves."

"They simply need to remember how, dear boy," Nathan said, sounding reassuring.

An alarm went up as the dawn brightened. Sentries on the high walls that blocked off the city shouted, first one outcry and then dozens. Loud warning bells began to clang.

Lila looked up, frowning. "Those are invasion bells. They haven't been rung in centuries."

"What threat could be coming from out there?" Nicci asked, remembering the broad, empty valley bounded by a line of dry hills on either side.

As the alarms grew louder and more urgent, the group hurried toward the outer wall. Mrra loped along behind them. High Captain Stuart of the Ildakaran city guard met them at the base of the wall, his face ashen. "They're moving. After all this time . . . they're moving!"

"Who?" Bannon asked. "What?"

Nicci pushed past Stuart and bounded up the stone stairs to the top of the high wall. The others followed her up to the battlements and stared westward toward the foothills and distant mountains. When she and her companions had crossed the wide valley, they encountered a huge army of statue warriors once led by General Utros, a besieging army that had nearly brought down Ildakar before the city's wizards worked a petrification spell that turned them all to stone.

Now, by the smoky light of dawn, Nicci saw that the huge stone army was stirring. The long-petrified soldiers began to move with a purpose, forming ranks against Ildakar.

CHAPTER 2

From the top of the defensive wall, Nathan gazed at the enormous petrified army. "Dear spirits, that is not a sight I expected."

Bannon paled and struggled to contain his gasp. Lila stood at his side, stern and defiant.

When they had first encountered the statue figures, Nathan studied them with the interest of an avid historian, examining their armor, their weapons, their ancient expressions frozen in a moment of assumed victory over the great city of Ildakar. From his centuries of reading and learning, Nathan knew the history of General Utros and how the immense army had attempted to conquer the Old World in the name of his emperor, Kurgan. But after Nathan, Nicci, and Bannon entered the legendary city and found themselves caught up in the turmoil, he had barely given the petrified army another thought.

Flushed, High Captain Stuart stared at the siege force approaching the walls. "Our city has enough problems after last night's uprising. My guards are still putting out fires, capturing combat animals, and stopping looters. But this . . ."

Nicci's expression was shrewd and analytical. "What made

the ancient soldiers come alive again, and why now? This is not an accident."

Bannon leaned over the wall to get a better view. "Remember, the one named Ulrich woke up when I was out there with Amos, Jed, and Brock. The spell wore off, and he was just one confused warrior among so many thousands." The young man's voice became sadder. "Ulrich asked us for help, but they threw him into the combat arena. Chief Handler Ivan killed him."

"He was a hard target to kill because his body was still partly stone, his skin much tougher than normal," Nicci reminded them, focusing on the threat rather than the sad story. "And Ulrich was only one man, just a foot soldier. This is an army of many thousands."

Nathan's throat went dry as the realization sank in, and he glanced over at Stuart. "I would suggest, High Captain, that you close and barricade the gates and have the gifted add reinforcement spells. Mount Ildakar's outer defenses."

Stuart ran off, shouting for wizards and gatekeepers.

During Nathan's time here, Elsa, a charming member of the duma, had helped him understand just how impregnable Ildakar was—or should have been. After fifteen hundred years behind the shroud of eternity, though, he wasn't convinced the city had maintained those defenses. The duma members were overconfident, complacent in their isolation. The shroud had taken Ildakar outside the normal flow of time to where no army or magic could touch them.

Now, though, the shroud was destroyed and Ildakar could not hide. The city was stuck in the real world, and the petrification spell that neutralized the enemy army had failed. He knew that Wizard Commander Maxim had cast the spell in the first place, and the man had fled the city in disgrace. Had Maxim somehow dissolved his own spell, released the statue army as some kind of last treachery?

Nathan tossed his shoulder-length white hair and tried to

sound confident for the benefit of the others crowded at the top of the wall. "We'll have to rely on our own defenses." After the events of the previous night and the destruction of the sacrificial pyramid, no amount of blood magic would bring the shroud back.

Bannon stared at the swarm of distant moving figures. "So many of them! Sweet Sea Mother, it's like a hundred anthills, all ready to go to war."

"If they were ants, we would stomp them," Lila said. She seemed to like the idea.

Resigned, Nathan turned to Nicci. "Well, Sorceress, it doesn't appear that we'll be leaving immediately."

Bustling in her purple robes, Elsa climbed the stairs to the top of the wall. "Ah, there you are, Nathan! I wanted to be sure you didn't save the city without me, now that you have your gift back." Her eyes twinkled with admiration. "After seeing what you did to the giant Ixax warrior, I have no doubt you could wipe out that entire army single-handedly."

"Thanks for your faith in me, my dear, but it will take a little more than that." Nathan felt a warmth in his chest that had nothing to do with the new heart of Ivan beating inside him.

Ildakar's defenses consisted of more than just these immense walls blocking the city from the plain. Millennia ago, the wizards of Ildakar had altered the landscape, raising a huge swath of land along the Killraven River. From the river side, Ildakar ended abruptly on a bluff that loomed high above the water. The magical upheaval also spread out the river channel, creating labyrinthine lowlands for countless miles downstream. The surrounding swamps were an intimidating defense, with their tangle of shallow waterways and monstrous swamp creatures created by Ildakaran fleshmancers.

The most direct access to the city came from across the plain. Centuries ago, General Utros had led his overwhelming army from that direction and filled the valley with his soldiers as he laid siege to the city.

Worried, Bannon narrowed his hazel eyes. "We're trapped in here."

"We are safe in Ildakar, boy," Lila corrected him. "This city has never fallen."

He shook his head. "What about all the escaped slaves who already fled out into the hills? And there were hunters, yaxen herders, and other travelers out there, without protection."

"They can run and hide, if they know what's good for them," Nathan said. "I'll save my worries for us."

From the top of the wall, they watched in concerned silence as the ancient soldiers formed lines like game pieces arranged on a broad strategy board. With a muffled, distant clatter of weapons, shields, and heavy boots, the enemy vanguard began marching forward.

"According to history, General Utros trained his people well," Nathan said. "He was an efficient, powerful commander, and it was through his military genius that Emperor Kurgan conquered much of the Old World. Although Kurgan wasn't a great leader himself, he was feared because of Utros."

The front ranks trudged forward, only a few hundred at first, determined to reach the walls, but Nathan doubted they could do anything against the defenses. He tapped his chin as he scrutinized the countless ancient warriors on the open plain. "Look at them. They seem disoriented."

Nicci gave her assessment. "I think this is an initial sortie to investigate. They may not understand what happened to them any more than we do. We can take advantage of their confusion."

"I wish we could see what they're doing," Elsa said, shading her eyes. The shadows of sunrise still sprawled across the open plain, blurring the details.

Still feeling twinges of pain from the scar in his chest, Nathan called upon his gift. The heart of a wizard—Ivan's heart—continued to beat, circulating his blood, strengthening his Han. He spread his fingers, holding his hands straight in front of him as if pushing against an invisible wall. "This may help us see them better." He pinched the air and swirled his hands, as if rolling out dough on a table, stretching it. "Air is transparent, but if I fold it and curve it, I can make a kind of lens."

An imaginary window rippled in front of him as he distorted the air. He sharpened the view, focused the image. Images hovered in the air before them as the ethereal lens magnified their oncoming foe.

Seen up close, the ancient soldiers wore flat expressions, and their skin was pale and chalky. Curved helmets covered the sides of their faces, and they wore leather shirts with many small metal plates sewn in place. Carrying thick swords, spiked maces, and long spears, rank after rank passed through the focal point of Nathan's magical lens. Emperor Kurgan's flame symbol stood out prominently on shirts and shields.

A chill went down Nathan's back, coupled with a hint of awe. For so long he had studied records in the Palace of the Prophets, reading half of the library just so he could understand history, but these once-petrified warriors were no longer history. These men were alive, and they meant to attack Ildakar.

A full five centuries before Nathan himself was born, one of the most powerful leaders in the Old World had been Emperor Kurgan, called Iron Fang because of the artificial tooth that was his fearsome affectation. Iron Fang owed his success to the military genius of General Utros, who served his emperor with utter loyalty—except that Utros had secretly fallen in love with Kurgan's wife, Empress Majel. Utros had gone off to conquer the legendary city of Ildakar, but he never returned, and now Nathan knew it was because the wizards of Ildakar had turned his army to stone.

Meanwhile, Emperor Kurgan was a bitter, capricious leader, not capable of ruling the lands Utros had conquered for him. In the general's absence, when the volatile leader discovered evidence of his wife's affair, Kurgan had skinned Majel alive in public and fed her still-living body to ravenous beetles, even though she wailed and repented, claiming she was still loyal to her husband and emperor.

When Iron Fang's restless people saw the horrors he inflicted upon their beloved empress, they rose up and overthrew him, then dragged the man's body through the streets, and the great but fragile empire broke apart into squabbling kingdoms. . . .

Now, as Nathan watched through his shimmering air lens, he marveled at the countless soldiers, all of whom still thought they were marching for Emperor Kurgan. They couldn't possibly know how much time had passed.

But he wasn't worried about the long-dead emperor. He muttered, "General Utros was always the greatest threat. He's right here, and he is the one we should fear."

The first ranks of enemy soldiers marched forward, their lines disorganized, and then they began to yell, a horrifying, hollow sound that boomed louder and louder. The thunder of their footfalls crashed across the grassy plain as they closed in on Ildakar.

Long ago, deep trenches had been dug around the outer walls, moats filled with spikes and sharp rocks, but over the centuries those trenches had become weathered and overgrown, as the people of Ildakar grew lax. Now hundreds of soldiers made their way up to the thick stone walls that loomed over their heads.

"What are they going to do?" Bannon asked, peering down at the hordes pressing against the wall.

"We'll see soon enough," Nathan said.

The enemy soldiers formed lines along the stone barrier, two or three deep. When they pressed close, they raised their gauntleted hands and pounded against the blocks, shouting with their cave-wind voices, hammering and hammering on the walls.

Before long, the first line stepped back, letting the second ranks replace them and continue the pounding. Several minutes later, they backed off to allow the third line forward. The monotonous pounding echoed throughout Ildakar, a nonstop rumble.

Elsa stood next to Nathan, nervous. "Our walls will hold," she said. It sounded like a prayer.

For now, Nathan thought, but did not say it aloud.

CHAPTER 3

W hen he awoke, the world had changed.

General Utros, commanding the grand army of Emperor Kurgan, had reached the city of Ildakar, his target. The army should have been an unstoppable force. Hundreds of thousands of conscripted warriors from across Iron Fang's empire had laid siege to the legendary city, the true prize of these southern lands, and he meant to crack it open like the rind of a ripe pomegranate so they could feast on the sweet treasure within.

On that cold, clear day, with his ranks of soldiers filling the plain, Utros had faced the high walls of the city. He noted the beautiful towers, the stair-stepped districts, the crowded buildings and enameled tile rooftops that shone like the scales on a dragon's back. He would conquer it in the name of his sworn emperor.

His innumerable soldiers were restless, but Utros would try to prevent the men from ruining too much, knowing the city's value. He wanted to keep his reputation as well as this prize. A peaceful conquest benefited Utros as much as the people of Ildakar. Once the army breached the walls, though, even the strictest discipline could never stop the ransacking.

The conquest would not be simple or straightforward. This was *Ildakar*.

Facing his goal, he had stood bare-armed in the cold afternoon sunlight, feeling the chill of oncoming winter. He stared, always calculating, searching for any chink of weakness. His thoughts were one continuous war-council meeting in his head. Utros had advisors, particularly the beautiful twin sorceresses, Ava and Ruva, but he always made up his own mind. He had already developed several schemes to bring down Ildakar.

Then wizards had appeared on the high walls, a large group of them in colorful silken robes, working some kind of magic. He had heard of the powerfully gifted here in Ildakar, but Utros was not afraid of them.

Unexpectedly, he had felt his body stiffen with a sudden weight around and inside him. He could barely think as some horrific power washed over his form, seized him, hardened around him like drying clay. The sounds grew muffled in his ears, and the last thing he heard were outcries of dismay from thousands of throats, his soldiers shouting in confusion as they froze in place.

Outside his imposing command tent, Ava and Ruva turned white, as if they had become statues. His vision dimmed, focusing down into a pinpoint, like the bull's-eye on an archer's target, and the last thing he saw was the city of Ildakar, taunting him.

Utros knew nothing for an unknown period, nor did he experience the passage of time.

An instant or an eternity later, the bright afternoon suddenly switched to predawn darkness. For a moment, he thought he had gone blind. A crackling sound, like ice breaking on a pond, rattled all around him. A buzzing rang in his ears, as if the thoughts had been dammed up inside his brain and now were unleashed all at once.

Utros found himself still looking at Ildakar, but the details had changed. The lights of the city glowed into the night, washing out stars overhead, but a haze of dawn rose straight ahead of him to the east.

Before he even moved, his thoughts searched for possibilities and explanations. General Utros did not take brash, uncalculated action. He had the largest and best-equipped military force in the world, and he'd already conquered most of the continent for Iron Fang, but the army's greatest asset was his mind.

The air around him felt much warmer than the cold afternoon he remembered only a moment ago. Instead of a crisp winter, this was early autumn at best, which meant the better part of a year had passed. How could that be? The grasses were brown and dry, but wildly overgrown around him, and that simply couldn't be true. In their relentless siege, his huge army had trampled the entire plain into barren dirt.

Utros took a step forward and instantly felt an unnatural stiffness in his skin, the tightness in his arms, his neck, his face. His body, which had always been so limber and strong, felt like a grinding wheel that had sat for too long without grease.

He looked at his bare arms and the oddly tarnished copper wrist guards marked with Kurgan's flame. His flesh tone had a chalky cast. He poked his biceps with an exploratory fingertip and found that the skin itself was tougher than normal, as if infused with half-hardened clay. He felt the pressure of his fingertip, but the delicate sensitivity of his skin was gone. Utros flexed his arm, felt his elbow grudgingly bend. His muscles bulged like boulders.

He touched his face, felt the full beard there, the square jaw, the prominent cleft in his chin that even the beard could not cover. He felt the smooth waxiness of the burn scar across the left half of his face, but it no longer ached. He remembered when his captive silver dragon had escaped, destroyed part of the camp, and burned him with the searing acid of dragon fire. Now the scar felt smooth, with even less sensitivity than before.

Around him, Utros heard gasps of astonishment, murmured

questions that rose to shouts. He turned to look at his entire camp, only to find that it was gone!

Countless thousands of warriors milled about. The soldiers had been in position, some posted as sentries, most gathered in clusters according to their assigned companies. Hundreds upon hundreds of tents had covered the plain, along with wagons, horses, pickets, big bonfires.

And now . . . nothing.

He remembered his large command tent, the bright and defiant banners of Iron Fang, the grain stockpiles, the armorers' tents, the sword-sharpening stations, the fletchers' camp. All had vanished. Nothing remained but the people themselves, pale and stiff, still wearing their armor, carrying their swords and shields. Some horses wandered around loose, their corrals and paddocks gone.

"Keeper and spirits," he said under his breath. "What has happened to us?"

The confused army was like a cloud of swirling gnats, but the general concentrated hard, as if in a trance. With total focus, he could dampen the sounds across the camp. He doubted anyone in his army knew more about the situation than he did, but he had to learn their circumstances.

Utros took a few steps. His body felt as if it was still partially stone, not entirely thawed back into soft flesh. He still wore his leather vest, studded with rectangular metal plates for extra protection, and his fearsome helmet adorned with the horns cut off a monster bull that Ildakar had unleashed on them. He remembered the day that beast had charged through the camp, wreaking havoc. Utros had killed the monster himself and taken the horns as trophies.

He turned to his two willowy sorceresses, who were just as confused as he. Ava and Ruva were shapely and slender, clad in blue gowns that fit tight around their narrow waists, emphasizing their ample breasts. The twins looked identical, but Utros knew them as well as he knew his own hands, and he had used his hands to study every inch of their bodies. They gave him strength, but not sex.

Now, he needed that strength.

Ava and Ruva were pale, their skin showing less warmth than a corpse's. The two were completely hairless, through their own fastidious efforts, using razor-sharp knives to scrape smooth their scalps, their eyebrows, even the thatch between their legs. Ava and Ruva took care of each other. In normal times, they painted their creamy exposed skin with swirls and designs that helped channel the gift they possessed.

In the brightening dawn, the women stared at each other and turned to Utros, their expressions full of questions. Without speaking, he joined them, and both folded around him, touching their bodies to his. He felt the shared strength grow.

As the confusion increased across the camp, Utros said to his sorceresses, "We have to learn what happened." The grumbling outcries began to shift, uncertain and fearful. "I need to tell the soldiers something."

"Then we will have to lie, because we know nothing," said Ruva. "Yet."

Ava disagreed. "We know it was a spell, a powerful one. And we can be sure the wizards of Ildakar wielded it against us."

Ruva touched the general's face, ran her palm along his beard, his scarred cheek. It seemed a loving caress, but she was investigating. Ava reached out to do the same thing to her sister. "Stone. We've been turned to stone."

"And back," said Ruva.

"Not all the way back. We are still flesh and blood, but there's a hardness throughout." Utros glared at the walled city backlit by the rising sun. Now that his shock was dissipating into a sea of questions, he noticed subtle changes in Ildakar. Some of the buildings inside were burned, and tendrils of greasy smoke smeared the sky.

He said, "Their wizards petrified us with some kind of spell, but the magic they would need to immobilize so many

22

thousands of warriors is beyond my comprehension." He gestured toward the raised city above the river. "Look at Ildakar now. Something's happened there. Those fires . . . maybe there has been a civil war."

"Could that be what awakened us?" Ruva asked.

Ava said, "Maybe the wizard who cast the stone spell is dead, so the magic faded."

Thousands of his front ranks, responding to their desperate confusion, marched forward to throw themselves against the wall and the gates in what seemed to be a futile gesture.

"They are angry," Ruva said.

"Let them be angry," Utros said.

His men had been trained so well they could mount an assault in their sleep. As they crashed toward the walls now in an instinctive reaction, Utros knew there was no purpose to the charge, but he wouldn't call them back. He did not like unplanned operations, but the sortie would occupy them for a time and give him a chance to decide what to do. If his entire army had been petrified for months or even years, he needed to know more.

His thoughts spun along different paths, suggesting answers and tracing consequences. He couldn't explain why all the tents, campfires, and supplies had vanished. He remembered vividly how the entire plain had been trampled by so many soldiers, all the machinery and materials that accompanied such a huge military operation.

In the previous week, his army had endured three days of cold rain and even an early-season snow. The ground had been a nightmare of muck that should have frozen each night, but all the campfires and troops kept it churned into a mess. Smoke from tens of thousands of fires made the air heavy and bitter. Simply to provide firewood, crews had stripped the hills of trees for miles around, but the distant forest looked thick and healthy now. The landscape had recovered completely.

He began to suspect that more than a few seasons had passed. How was that possible?

"General Utros," said a familiar gruff voice, his battle-scarred first commander, Enoch. Enoch had been with Utros since early in the general's career. Though ten years older and bearing the scars of many more engagements, Enoch was entirely faithful to Utros. He was a man who understood tactics and quickly grasped the plans his leader gave him, but not so ambitious that he had anything to prove. Enoch did not seek glory for himself, because serving General Utros was entirely sufficient for him. His loyalty to Emperor Kurgan was secondary. The first commander also looked pale and chalky, still partially stone.

"What happened, General? Something changed, something terrible."

Utros stood straight. "You know as much as I do, for the moment, First Commander. Ildakar attacked us with some kind of spell."

Enoch frowned, thinking of his specific duty. "Until we learn what's happened, sir, confusion among the ranks will grow, and that will destroy our military discipline."

The general knew the complexities of managing such a huge force, even under the best of conditions. "Do you think the men will be frightened enough to abandon the siege? Is their confusion such that they'll panic and scatter?"

Shocked by the suggestion, Enoch gave him a disappointed grimace. "Of course not, General. They will never desert. Each man is yours, heart and soul. But they'll look to you for explanations. You have to give them something before too long."

Utros's smile was muted by his skin's stiffness. "Send messengers among the troops and tell them to wait for word from me." As he scanned the crowded ranks, he noted the few loose horses. "Send riders throughout the valley, have them inform each company that General Utros still leads them and that we will be victorious. I will avenge whatever needs to be avenged."

Enoch nodded. "They already know that, sir."

"Tell them anyway. First I need to assess our situation." Before Enoch could depart, Utros snapped more instructions. "It appears we've lost everything, so we have to act swiftly. Don't show panic, don't even let the men consider the implications, but we have no camp, no firewood, no shelter. If storms should come, we need to have tents. Send crews into the hills to cut down trees, bring supplies back, hunt food. Have them use their swords and battle-axes if necessary." He knew that the streams across the valley would provide plentiful water, but his soldiers needed a great deal more.

He looked behind him, dismayed again to see the empty space that had held his large tent. "I need a new command headquarters erected immediately. If they can't find any fabric for a tent, then have them use wood to build a structure." He placed his hands on his hips, and the orders continued to flow. Enoch received them all in silence. "Also, launch raiding parties, a hundred of them with twenty men each. Have them ride in all directions and scout what lies around us. Find cities and towns, where they can commandeer the supplies and tools we no longer have."

Enoch made a mental note of every instruction. "Yes, General."

After Utros dismissed him, Ava and Ruva stood close, silent and calculating. The soldiers milled about, but none dared to approach, not yet. They were awed by General Utros, even though he wasn't a cruel or ruthless commander, as Iron Fang was a ruthless emperor.

No wonder sweet Majel had needed a soft touch, love and compassion, even if it meant the two of them were betraying Kurgan in their hearts.

Utros longed to see her again. It had been half a year since he'd been home to Orogang, the capital of the empire. It seemed like ages since he'd touched Majel's soft skin, run his fingers through her lush hair, kissed her sweet lips.

25

He locked those thoughts in a separate mental compartment. Often as he drifted off to sleep at night, Utros would open that cabinet in his mind to review and rejoice in his times with her. Now, though, he couldn't afford the distraction. He felt a genuine urgency, which he hoped his soldiers didn't realize yet. They didn't have much time.

With so many thousands of fighters filling the plain outside of Ildakar, entirely without supplies, they would all understand the urgency as soon as they began to starve.

CHAPTER 4

As the awakened soldiers continued to pound on the walls of Ildakar, Nicci judged that the city had time, but perhaps not much. Such constant battering might damage the defenses, though the gifted wizards could summon strengthening spells to keep the stone solid.

The watchers on the high wall didn't need Nathan's air lens to see the immensity of the enemy out there. When she served Jagang, Nicci had traveled with the huge armies of the Imperial Order, which had spent decades conquering the Old World, eventually moving north and crossing into the New World. But she had never seen an army such as this.

She turned to the kind sorceress Elsa, who stood nearby, deeply worried. Other duma members had not yet arrived at the wall, but Nicci knew they had to begin their work soon. "After the revolt last night, the people of Ildakar must work out their political differences, rebuild the city, and strengthen its leadership." She nodded toward the immense siege force moving toward the city. "Even with their simmering resentments, the factions of Ildakar have a common enemy. Now is the time you can forge a permanent internal peace, make your city strong enough to defeat General Utros. I'd suggest you use this opportunity to solve your problems."

Elsa remained troubled. "If that's what the people really want."

Barking orders to the city guard, High Captain Stuart ordered standard siege defenses, using boulders, sharp projectiles, boiling oil, and flaming arrows against the soldiers below. From their high strategic position, they could bombard the attackers with no risk to themselves.

Nicci knew the defenses were in good hands, for now. "Call an emergency meeting in the ruling tower. The duma has been torn apart, but you have to establish a new one. It's a time of crisis, Elsa. You, Quentin, and Damon still sit on the council, but we have to rally all of Ildakar's gifted."

Elsa said, "We should have added more wizards to the duma a long time ago, ever since the sorceress Lani was turned to stone. We need them more than ever with Wizard Commander Maxim gone, Andre and Ivan both dead, Thora defeated, and Renn off on that fool's quest to find the Cliffwall archive."

Nathan rubbed the center of his chest. "Chief Handler Ivan's heart still lives within me. I am as gifted and powerful as I ever was, so let's count our blessings. We'll work together to defend Ildakar."

Bannon frowned, considering. His skin looked paler than usual, which emphasized his freckles. "The revolt still isn't over in the city. If you have a war council, you can't call only the gifted nobles. They were part of the problem. You need to listen to the rebels and the freed slaves, as well as the arena warriors. If it comes to a real fight, those are the best soldiers Ildakar has."

Lila shot him a glance. "And the morazeth, boy. We are the best fighters."

Nathan raised a hand to stall further debate. "It is not a competition. Everyone will defend Ildakar in their own way. I agree with you, dear Elsa. The duma needs to appoint replacement members as soon as possible, and someone has to lead the city, now that we're at war."

Gliding past Nicci, Mrra placed her feline head between the crenellations and peered out at the awakening army in the morning light. The panther growled at the booming of the hardened fists.

When Nicci and her companions entered the main chamber of the ruling tower, the two stone sorceresses had awakened and were locked in battle.

Sovrena Thora, whom Nicci despised, had been punished for her abuse of the people of Ildakar. Rather than being executed, Thora had suffered the same fate as Utros's army, cursed by the stone spell. After pronouncing her sentence, Elsa, Quentin, and Damon had petrified her, leaving Thora a defiant statue in the ruling chamber.

The only other sorceress who had suffered that fate was Lani, after her failed challenge to Thora's rule, centuries ago. Nicci had never seen Lani as anything other than a stone figure.

Now both women were reanimated and attacking each other on the open floor in the ruling tower. Nicci recognized Lani's broad shoulders, the squarish yet pretty face, and the long locks of hair that had been marble before, but were now the color of smoked honey. The revived sorceress threw herself upon Thora, who looked just as furious. The dissolution of the stone spell that had thawed General Utros's army must have also released these two from their fates.

Hearing the clash of the physical battle, Nicci rushed into the ruling chamber with Nathan and Elsa close behind, calling for the two sorceresses to stop fighting. The wizards Damon and Quentin came in, accompanied by other powerful wizards, who had answered the call for the war council.

The floor of the ruling chamber was made of blue marble, a lake of polished stone in front of the raised platform that had held thrones for the sovrena and the wizard commander. In a long gown of green silk, Thora grappled with Lani. The women, whose skin remained pale and grayish, battled with spells and physical blows, as well. Thora and Lani used fists and claws, but their tough skin deflected the damage.

As Nicci strode forward, commanding the women to stop, Lila dashed past her and leaped into the fray. Together, Nicci and the morazeth physically separated the two sorceresses. Lani and Thora both seemed confused, furious, and unsure of what had happened, but knowing their hatred for each other.

Nicci's implacable glare made Thora hesitate, while the young morazeth held Lani back. With a sneer, Lani turned from Thora and softened in surrender as she recognized the familiar faces of Elsa, Damon, Quentin. "I know you are on my side. Where is the wizard commander?" She looked more intently. "And where's Renn? Has something happened to my dear Renn?"

"We all have a great many questions," Nathan said in an erudite voice, "and not enough answers."

"Not enough time either," Nicci said. "The petrification spell has dissipated, not just here but also with the hundreds of thousands of warriors outside the wall. The army of General Utros has awakened."

The words were like a blow to the two women, and they fell awkwardly silent.

Nathan stepped in, looking at Quentin and Damon. "We've called the duma so we can decide how best to fight."

Lani stared daggers at her rival. "I cannot serve on the duma if Thora is also a member. The sovrena has corrupted and destroyed Ildakar."

Nicci broke in, "Thora is no longer sovrena, nor is she a member of the council. She betrayed Ildakar and will continue to pay the price."

"Ildakar is my city!" Thora said. "Maxim is the one who destroyed it by inciting rebellion before he fled the city. I wouldn't be surprised if he unraveled the stone spell himself, just so Ildakar could suffer." She spun on Nicci. "And you, too—you are to blame for the uprising and all the destruction it caused."

"Now, the revolt was a long time coming," Nathan explained. "You planted the seeds, and your oppression nurtured all that violence. Don't complain about the bitter harvest."

"Enough about the revolt and the unruly slaves," said a man with long, grayish-yellow hair braided down the left side of his face. "Our city is under siege. After fifteen centuries, Emperor Kurgan's army is now pounding at our walls again. If we bicker about petty things, we may as well throw open the gates to the enemy."

Nicci looked over at the stranger, deciding that she liked the man's hard-line attitude. Elsa leaned close and whispered to her, "That is Oron, a powerful wizard. He leads the skinners' guild. He has been suggested as a duma member, but the sovrena never allowed any replacement, fearing that new members might overthrow her."

Bannon added, "I think Lord Oron is Brock's father. I saw him once when Amos, Jed, and Brock took me around the city."

"I hope he's more worthy than his son," Nicci muttered. Brock and his two companions had been a bad influence on Bannon, taking advantage of him and setting him up to be captured for the combat pits.

Though she knew that Ildakar was not her responsibility, Nicci stepped to the middle of the blue marble tiles. Someone had to set this meeting on track. "We must convene the duma and get to work." She gestured for the gifted members, even Lani, to take their places at the curved side tables.

Also in the crowded audience, the military commanders and other high-level spectators found places, along with angry slaves and workers. High Captain Stuart and two city guards took Sovrena Thora into custody and pulled her aside. She remained defiant, though she was still convicted and a prisoner. As the people muttered and listened, Nicci, Nathan, and Elsa told everyone about the movement of the enormous enemy army.

Concerned merchants and gifted nobles argued, expressing their dissatisfaction. They seemed far more concerned about the unrest in the city. "What about the rebels and the damage they caused?" demanded a member of the silk spinners' guild. "Are we supposed to just forget about that? Some of those unruly bastards have murdered nobles, chopping off their heads!"

Members of the lower classes also spoke up. Rendell, still soot-stained from fighting the fire at the silk warehouse, raised his voice over the chatter. "How can we overlook all the damage the nobles have caused? For generations they've harmed us. What about our blood that's been spilled?"

"Does cutting off a few heads make up for all that?" Nathan asked. "I sincerely doubt it."

"Only fools would keep arguing while an enemy army pounds on their walls," Nicci said, impatient. "Concentrate on the real problem. Everyone in the city needs to know how to fight General Utros. That is the most important thing."

Quentin cleared his throat and spoke up. He was a dark-skinned wizard with smoky-gray hair. Deep lines on his face emphasized his habitual frown. "Long ago, Ildakar had more powerful wizards than we do today. Fleshmancer Andre created the three giant Ixax warriors, which were never unleashed. Wizard Commander Maxim developed and cast the stone spell that petrified the entire siege army. It took all of our population, at the cost of a great many lives, to work the blood magic that protected us all behind the shroud of eternity."

Damon stood beside his friend, adding his voice to Quentin's. Damon was a thin-faced, olive-skinned man with drooping mustaches that dangled on either side of his mouth. "If we couldn't defeat General Utros before, what chance do we have now?"

As grumbling ricocheted around the chamber, Nicci raised her voice. "Ildakar's situation has changed dramatically, but that doesn't mean the city is weaker." She swept her intense blue gaze across the audience. "I am here now, as is Nathan Rahl. We bring new ideas, new magic, and new ways of fighting."

"And I am back, too," Lani said.

"But the enemy army is different, as well," Bannon interjected. "Those aren't normal soldiers. Remember when Ulrich woke up, he was still partly stone and very hard to kill. Now there are many thousands more just like him out beyond the wall." He held his sword, turning the discolored blade from side to side. "I don't think our weapons will be enough against them."

"We'll fight with our magic, and for that we need to rebuild the duma," said Oron. "We've lost too many of our wizards already."

"And Thora," said Elsa in a stern tone. "She's been banished from the duma and will not be allowed to serve."

"No matter how much you need me?" Thora sneered in a voice like frozen vinegar.

"No matter how much you think we need you," Lani said. "If the stone spell no longer works, then I propose the guards place you in a dungeon cell with warding runes around the door so you can't use your magic to break loose."

Quentin nodded, anxious to move on to other business. "That should work for now. We can decide what to do with the sovrena after this crisis."

Damon said, "I propose we add Oron to the duma. His name has come up before, and he has demonstrated his worth and ability many times." He stroked his mustaches. "We don't have time for a drawn-out process."

"I agree," Quentin said. "We need wizards and we need a full council. Oron can be a provisional member."

"Agreed," Lani said.

Beaming, Oron tossed the thick blond braid over his shoulder. "I will be proud to serve."

"That's not enough," Elsa called out. "We need a new sovrena,

33

and no one is more powerful than Nicci. Let us acclaim her as the new sovrena of Ildakar."

Even as the voices built, Nicci shouted over them. "No! My companions and I will help you, because we're trapped here as well, but you have to help yourselves. This isn't my city. It's yours."

"It's *my* city," Thora said. "No matter what you do to me, *I* built Ildakar. No one cares more about the city than I do, and I will not see it fall."

"You won't see anything at all." Lani gestured for High Captain Stuart and his guards to remove her from the ruling chamber and take her to the dungeons beneath the tower. Disgraced and defeated, the former sovrena walked stiffly away.

Nicci was glad that Wizard Commander Maxim had fled the city. He was gone now, perhaps even captured by the awakened stone army. Regardless, he was no longer her concern.

CHAPTER 5

When Adessa thought about Wizard Commander Maxim, she longed to hold his head in her hands.

The morazeth leader possessed the singular focus that only the very patient, or the very obsessed, could have. Maxim's face was at the center of her thoughts: the narrow nose, the dark goatee, the thick brown hair. She longed to slide her fingers through that hair, grasp it tightly while ignoring the clumps of blood.

She wanted to stare into Maxim's brown eyes as they turned glassy with death, then lift the head from his bloody shoulders as his body collapsed to the ground. She would hold her trophy high with blood still dripping from his neck, and she would smile as his face went slack, forever erasing his pompous sneer.

Adessa was determined to hunt down and kill the wizard commander for what he had done to Ildakar. That was her mission, and as leader of the morazeth, she refused to fail.

She had sprinted from her beloved city during the night of the revolt, clad only in high-laced fighting sandals, a black leather wrap around her waist and across her breasts. Her bare skin was toughened from a life of combat and branded with protective spell runes. She knew each symbol intimately, remembered the trainer pressing a red-hot iron onto her arm, her inner thigh, her back. Each rune was a gift bought with pain, unparalleled protection against magic. She recalled the heat that sizzled and smoked as the trainer held the branding iron in place longer than was necessary, because he relished the wince on her face, the hiss of burning flesh. After earning the first few symbols, Adessa had learned not to give him that reaction, to ignore the pain. So long ago . . .

Each such branding mark made her stronger, if she was strong enough to receive it. Unworthy morazeth candidates who whimpered or flinched were rejected, some of them executed outright, others allowed to die in the combat arena or, worst of all, sent down to the ranks of slaves to live out their days in public humiliation. Most of those failed women took their own lives within weeks.

When Sovrena Thora had personally dispatched her to kill Maxim, Adessa had wasted no time gathering supplies or preparing a pack. Instead, she had just left the chaos in the streets—the wild slaves giddy with their undeserved liberation, the burning buildings, the prowling arena animals—and had run beyond the city walls to find Mirrormask before he escaped.

If Sovrena Thora had asked her, Adessa would have stayed behind to fight the rebels all night and not count the cost in blood, because a traitor's blood was small coin indeed. But her mission was to bring back Maxim's head and throw it like a melon on the floor before the sovrena. If necessary, Adessa would spend the rest of her life achieving that aim.

Fleet of foot, Adessa had run beyond the walls into the dark night. After a lifetime of hard training and brutal combat, she was strong. She had a sharpened short sword, a dagger in a sheath at her right hip, a spiked gauntlet on her left hand, and her bonded agile knife, whose pinprick could unleash a world of pain in a victim.

Those were only the obvious weapons. Adessa herself was the real weapon, and she also had the added power of life magic within her, the strength of the growing baby she had absorbed from her own womb, reclaiming the life she had created. Adessa would be more than a match for the wizard commander, as soon as she caught him.

In the darkness outside the city, Adessa had discovered his tracks, and once she knew the general direction Maxim had taken, she loped across the open grasses, heading to the hills in the south, following him.

Maxim had always been an aloof, lazy man, pampered because of his powerful position in Ildakar. With her senses heightened because of the life magic, she could easily spot the broken grass blades, the stir of weeds, the stink of his passage. Maxim didn't realize how many oils and perfumes he wore. When surrounded by the city's smells, he never gave a thought to it, but now his trail left a lingering aroma, which Adessa could easily track.

Just before dawn in the hills to the south of the city, she came upon an obvious mark on the slope, a place where Maxim had cleared away grass to expose raw dirt. Using a dagger, the wizard commander had gouged a complex spell-form in the soil. She stared at the design, but couldn't recognize the magic he had worked. From the residual tingle, though, she sensed it was powerful.

Kneeling, she touched the moistened clumps of dirt that ran along the main lines and studied the red-black smear on her fingertips. This was not just mud, but dirt mixed with blood. Seeing no human or animal carcass nearby, she realized that Maxim must have shed his own blood to work the spell. A wizard's blood, which was potent indeed. She wondered what magic he had unleashed.

Wary, she looked around, listening to the predawn noises, the restless stir of wind and grasses, creatures prowling in the last hour of night. Did Maxim know she was hunting him?

Had he cast some sort of camouflage spell that would deflect her pursuit? No, this spell-form was something else.

Maxim's magic didn't concern her. Anything other than finding and killing him had no bearing on her life. She saw the tracks where he had left his bloody spell-form and headed south into the hills along the uplift above the Killraven River. She realized he was heading toward the swamps that stretched for miles downstream.

Adessa set her face with grim determination. Maybe he thought he could hide there. She wouldn't let him.

In ancient times, the Killraven River was one of the main waterways in the Old World. Ildakar had originally been a river port, a bustling trade center that received barge traffic from the many communities in the mountains upriver and from the estuary that spilled into the sea to the south.

In the wizard wars three thousand years ago and the Midwar fifteen centuries later, the wizards of Ildakar had defended their city by reshaping the landscape. They had lifted the land into impregnable cliffs that rose high above the river, while unleashing the Killraven from its banks to flood the lowlands, creating treacherous defensive swamps. Long ago, those duma members had not given a thought to the consequences of their actions. Many thriving villages had been ruined and displaced in the floods, but Ildakar was safe from attack.

She continued to hunt for two days, following the line of hills as the uplift gradually sank back to river level. She left Ildakar far behind, pursuing her quarry. The pampered wizard commander kept up a surprisingly swift pace.

Adessa made her way into the flooded lowlands full of gnarled, knobby trees balanced in the muck, where she found it more difficult to follow his trail. She picked her way across hummocks of grass, spotty islands of solid ground amid soggy puddles. At first, the stable path was obvious, and she could tell where Maxim had gone, but soon she faced thousands of options, a step left or right, over this puddle or that. She experienced a thrill upon finding a deep footprint in the mud where the wizard commander had stumbled.

The swamp simmered, grew more sinister. Silvery webs strung between the branches were large enough to catch the buzzing dragonflies, leather-winged moths, or even small birds. Hanging in wait, round spiders with bodies the size of an apple hung like black fruit. One of the spiders dropped onto Adessa's bare shoulder, and she crushed it with her palm, splattering ichor and smearing away its sharp, twitching legs. She wondered how the wizard commander would survive out here. If one of the swamp monsters killed Maxim before she got her chance, Adessa would be very angry.

She worked her way along, always pursuing, searching for any mark of his passage before the swamp erased it. She lost the trail for more than a day, which forced her to backtrack and retrace her own faded footprints, looking for any sign. Adessa scoured the hummocks, looked through the knobby tree roots, fought her way among vines, splashed through the muck, thrashed the high razor-edged grasses, searching for any hint of where he had gone. The wizard commander had vanished.

At first she was confident, but after circling the obvious routes for hours without any sign, she began to feel desperation. She could not fail! She dared not return to Sovrena Thora without the man's severed head. She ranged wider, stopping to meditate, extending all her senses, looking for any hint of his passage. Maxim was a weak and inexperienced man, and she could not let him best her. She couldn't.

Adessa's face was splattered with mud, her short dark hair clumped with perspiration. She pushed her way across a thicket, slashing spiderwebs with her dagger. When she crashed out into an open grassy area, she came upon the swamp dragon.

The fierce armored reptile was low to the ground. It had spiny ridges along its back, an elongated snout filled with fangs that could snap down on prey and crush bones, rip flesh. The swamp dragon's head was raised, its jaws open, its slitted eyes dull and turned to stone.

The monster had been petrified. The creature must have tried to attack Wizard Commander Maxim, and he had unleashed his stone spell. The swamp dragon stood as a fierce-looking statue in the grass and muck.

Adessa smiled. She was on the right track again. This was a reminder of the creatures she might face in the swamps, but she was not afraid. As a morazeth, she was the most dangerous thing out here.

Adessa extended her senses and picked up the path again. Now she knew where she was going. She continued to hunt.

CHAPTER 6

General Utros had lost all but the most rudimentary tools, but he did have inexhaustible manpower, and his soldiers had complete devotion to serve the needs of their commander. He did not waste any time.

Within a day of their awakening, though the displaced army still reeled in confusion, First Commander Enoch sent teams into the hills to cut trees with sharpened battle-axes, to strip and haul the logs down onto the plain, where they chopped them into structural beams. With furious effort, the men erected a dozen command structures, with the largest headquarters for General Utros and the twin sorceresses. The workers created wooden buildings with sturdy walls, logs cemented with mud, thatched roofs of thin branches lashed with long grasses.

Though the awakened soldiers were oddly numb and impervious to the chill that had set in the night before, Utros insisted on building up the camp, pulling together as many normal trappings as possible. Though it was mainly symbolic, his fighters had nothing else to cling to.

Situated in the center of the plain, his headquarters structure was a rectangular building with a high roof, lit by daylight through open windows, as well as two braziers inside that held low fires. The rudimentary building was not as comfortable as his old lavishly appointed command tent, but after campaigning for Iron Fang across the wilderness, Utros was no stranger to austerity. This would do.

He sat inside the structure now, inhaling the wafting smoke from the braziers, basking in the orange-red glow of embers mixed with pungent herbs. With hewn logs, the soldiers had constructed benches and a long, rough table where Utros could conduct his war councils, but as of yet he had no maps, no paper or ink for messages, not even any fresh clothes. He hoped his scouting teams would soon find outlying towns where they could procure basic supplies.

For now, Utros sat on a sturdy bench at the head of the long table. With regimented thoughts, he contemplated Ildakar, his army, and his war. Ava and Ruva were with him, close and alluring, their skin as smooth as marble. Many times, he had watched the two stand naked inside the dim shelter, using razor-sharp knives to scrape every inch of their skin. The only mark that marred their perfect bodies was the ugly mirror-image scar on the outside of their legs, where their bodies had once been fused together from birth.

The paint that now swirled and colored their skin was faded and flaking, but neither of the two women looked weak. They were patient. They were strong. They counted on Utros to get them what they needed as soon as he could.

And he intended to do so.

The foremost ranks of his soldiers continued to pound on the impregnable walls of Ildakar, showing their might. Given enough time and men, and their hardened fists, they might actually batter their way through the thick stone. A tiny acorn growing in a crack could split apart a boulder.

From atop the walls, the defenders of Ildakar pelted the soldiers, dropping missiles on them: rocks, bricks, chamber pots. They poured down burning oil, which covered the fighters and sent them away screaming. But the projectiles caused little damage to the hardened warriors, and the actual casualties were remarkably few. The flaming oil seared them and their armor, but Utros had seen burn victims before. The fire didn't have nearly the same effect on the partly solidified flesh. Maybe his vast army was no longer entirely human, but their stiff skin made them more invincible. As a commander, he could make use of that fact.

Hour after hour, lieutenants appeared at his headquarters, delivering reports in an efficient military fashion, as they had been trained to do. The officers described the disposition of the troops, the status of the awakening camp. Utros absorbed the information, memorizing the words because he had no paper on which to write notes. The twin sorceresses also listened intently.

When the vast army had marched across the Old World, crossing over the sheer mountains and covering miles each day at a forced pace, they knew how to set up huge camps along the way.

Now, one of his senior lieutenants stood before him at the far end of the table. Ava and Ruva stared with intense eyes, like two vultures waiting for a dying horse to perish so they could feed. The well-trained lieutenant ignored them and fixed his gaze on the general.

"We spread out the camp, sir. The valley itself shows none of the damage that our army caused on our march to Ildakar and the siege, before we turned to stone. I've dispatched a hundred squads for the usual labors, clearing spots for campsites even though we have no blankets or tents, excavating midden trenches. They're digging enough latrines to serve so many men, thousands of pits." He looked away, a frown on his pale, hard face.

Utros rested his elbows on the rough surface of his table. "What is the problem, Lieutenant? Report." Dealing with the bodily functions of hundreds of thousands of soldiers was no laughing matter. Without efficient sanitation, the giant camp would become a cesspit, and diseases such as dysentery and the plague would spread. Utros knew that such debilitating sicknesses killed more soldiers than any enemy's sword. "You still have spades. You have plenty of space to dig the pits?"

"The latrines are complete, General, but . . ."

Ava and Ruva stared at him. Utros grew impatient. "Speak! I've faced countless enemies and huge opposing armies. What could possibly be problematic about waste pits?"

"They haven't been used, sir," the lieutenant admitted.

Utros drew his broad brows together. "What do you mean, they haven't been used?"

"No one has so far . . . needed them, sir. They haven't . . ."

"Are they using the bushes?" Utros demanded.

"I've asked, sir, but no one claims to have felt the need. I confess, I haven't myself, not even to . . . not even, you know, to piss."

Of all the grand questions Utros had faced, this had never entered his mind. As he was about to growl another question, he realized that he himself had felt no need in the past day and a half.

And that led to another realization. His teams had made makeshift basins, delivered water from the streams across the valley. Utros had plenty of water here in his command structure, but he couldn't recall whether he had needed to drink. "We've been petrified for an unknown time, and we've neither eaten nor drunk anything. Our bodies haven't felt any such call."

A knock came at the door as someone else arrived. Utros turned to the latrine commander, who backed toward the door. "It was merely an observation, sir. I felt you should know."

"So noted. Thank you."

The next visitors sickened Utros. He'd seen bloody violence in his many battles, had witnessed the most appalling injuries and torments, but this was beyond anything he had seen before.

Ava and Ruva lurched to their feet from the side bench. Even the subcommander looked sickened as he led four soldiers into the command structure.

The glow from the braziers and the slanted daylight through the windows lit the horrifically mangled faces of two blind, staggering soldiers. They still wore their armor, but their faces looked like chewed raw meat. Their noses were gone, their eyes gouged out. One man's ear had been smashed off. Their teeth had been battered, and only jagged stubs protruded from their gums like shards of pottery. Their breath came in wet, sucking sounds through ragged mouth holes.

The third man had an arm shattered off at the elbow, and his ragged, bloody stump dripped onto the ground, though a leather belt had been cinched around it in a makeshift tourniquet. The fourth victim had a mangled crotch, as if someone had used a dull axe to chop away at his groin, striking off his privates and leaving torn flesh on his thighs. The victims moaned with the abject misery of their inexplicable wounds.

"We found dozens like this, General," said the subcommander. "They're alive and awake, and yet they've been mutilated. I can't understand how it happened. It is malicious, senseless damage."

Utros tried not to show his revulsion. His thoughts spun in different possibilities, looping around until he finally understood. "They were attacked while they were petrified and helpless. Some cruel person smashed off their features and left them horribly damaged."

The general remembered when his army had swept through conquered cities, ransacking them. They would tear down the capital buildings, burn the temples, and destroy the statues, because General Utros would allow no god other than Emperor Kurgan. Yes, the Keeper dominated the underworld behind the veil, but here in this world, Iron Fang must be the one they feared and worshiped. If the conquering soldiers found revered statues of their leaders, they would batter the faces until they were nothing more than chipped stone.

Seeing the mangled wreckage of these soldiers, the broken arms, the maliciously destroyed groin, he knew someone had done the same thing, vandalizing the stone figures in his petrified army. But these weren't just statues. These had been real men, loyal men, and Utros felt enraged.

"It is one more thing we will avenge when we invade Ildakar," he said. "Tend these poor men, care for them however you can." He wasn't sure if the moaning, agonized victims could hear him. "You have already paid a tremendous price, and for that I am eternally grateful. I vow that Ildakar will pay a greater price than you've suffered."

After they departed, Utros needed a moment to compose himself. He looked up with relief when First Commander Enoch entered, his rugged face showing a hint of satisfaction. Utros gave a lopsided smile with his scarred face. "Enoch, I hope you have a good report. I've heard enough details about latrines and campsites and mutilated soldiers."

Enoch seemed pleased. "Yes, General. We finally have some answers."

Three armored soldiers wrestled a pair of captives through the open door, a man and a woman. They were middle-aged, but bent with the years added by a lifetime of hard labor. They wore patchwork leather, wool, and fur garments. The couple huddled close to each other, but the soldiers pushed them into the dim room. The woman stumbled, and the man caught her arm, holding her upright. They trembled as they stood in front of the table.

The first commander stepped off to the left. "Our scouts found these two camped in a high meadow. They are animal herders tending fifty creatures called yaxen."

"Yes, sir," said the captive man, trying to sound helpful and cooperative. "We're yaxen herders, just simple people. We pasture the animals and bring them in to sell at Ildakar or to other towns in the mountains."

Utros was glad to have real witnesses, a man and woman

who had not been petrified for years. "Then you have vital information for us. You know what's been happening in the world."

Ava and Ruva glided forward to regard the captives in predatory silence, their eyes boring into the shivering man and woman.

Enoch said, "We captured their animals as well, sir. Scouts are herding them back to camp right now, so we'll have some food supply. Enough for our officers, maybe."

"Good thinking, First Commander." Utros steepled his fingers as he leaned over the table. He spoke in a calm voice, hoping the captives would not need to be coerced. "Tell us about the lands around us. Apart from Ildakar, where are the nearest towns and cities? Who are the leaders?"

"My lord, we are simply yaxen herders! We don't know anything," said the man.

Utros added an edge to his voice. "You may address me as '*sir*,' not 'my lord.' I serve Emperor Kurgan, and I will be the judge of how much you know."

The woman sputtered. "Emperor Kurgan? But, my lord . . . but, sir, he's been dead for ages. He—"

Utros pounded his fist on the table, not sure he wanted to hear what she had to say. "What are your names? Let's start with simple information first."

The man reached out to touch the woman's arm. "My name is Boyle. This is Irma, my wife. We've herded yaxen all our lives. Our two children are grown up and now they live in a mountain town to the north."

"What is it called?" Utros asked.

"The town? Why, it's . . . Stravera, my lo— . . . sir," said Boyle. "Stravera. It's the nearest large town."

Irma cleared her throat. "Many of the other villages grew over the centuries after Ildakar disappeared, but now that the city has come back, we have a new market for our yaxen."

Utros frowned. "What do you mean, now that Ildakar has come back?"

"Why, the whole city vanished for centuries, sir, disappeared behind the shroud of eternity. And your army . . . sir, it was turned to stone, too. Thousands and thousands of statues. They were there all my life, many lifetimes. There are legends about where you came from, but we were never sure," Irma said.

Boyle broke in, "We'd take our yaxen to the high pastures in the summer and then down to the plain as the weather grew colder. We'd camp among the stone soldiers year after year. I think I may even have seen one that looked like you, sir, and . . . and the ladies." He glanced at Ava and Ruva.

"Explain these legends. How were we turned into statues?"

"Why, everyone knows that, sir," said Boyle, indignant.

The twin sorceresses quivered like serpents preparing to strike. Utros said, "If we knew the answer, we wouldn't need to question you. Speak!"

"Why, sir, when the army of General Utros came to lay siege to the city, the wizards of Ildakar worked a powerful spell to turn them all to stone," said Irma.

"After that," Boyle continued, "the wizards knew that Ildakar would keep being a target for outsiders, so they worked more magic and swept away the entire city for more than a thousand years. Only in the past couple of decades did the magic fade. The city reappeared after all that time, so we started selling them our meat and pelts again."

"Then why did my army awaken just yesterday?" Utros asked.

Boyle and Irma were confused. Their mouths opened and closed, but no answers came forth. They looked at each other, and Utros saw an undercurrent of caring and mutual protection flash between them. That was a weapon he could use.

"We've been up in the hills. We didn't even know you were awake, until your soldiers captured us. Always before, we just saw the statues," Boyle said. "That's all."

The general did not expect subtle explanations of magic from these two. "Tell us where to find Stravera and also describe the other cities in the area. As herders, you must know where they are."

"We know of a few," Irma said, "but I've never been farther than Stravera or down here to Ildakar, not in all my life."

"Our two sons live in Stravera," Boyle said. "Why would we need to go farther? The yaxen have all the pasturage they need."

Utros didn't think they were lying, but, to be sure, he asked the questions again, pressing for more details.

Because he sensed their vulnerability, he had Enoch snap Irma's two little fingers, a brittle hollow-branch sound that was much more delicate than her shrill wail of pain. Boyle babbled and repeated his information, and the threat of breaking more of his wife's fingers finally elicited the names of four more mountain and river towns that Boyle had heard of, but never visited.

"Thank you," the general finally said, looking at the sobbing old woman, the ashen and wrung-out man. "You have been most helpful." He turned to the two sorceresses. "Do you think they've divulged everything they know?"

Irma cried, "We have, my lord!"

"I assure you, General! I swear!" Boyle insisted.

"Very well. I believe you." He nodded, and Ava and Ruva glided close to the two terrified yaxen herders.

"Can we . . . can we go now?" Boyle stammered. "We're worth nothing to you as prisoners. No one will ransom us."

"We're nobodies," Irma insisted, holding up her mangled hands. Her broken fingers drooped.

The sorceresses caressed the air around them in strange gestures, circling the two whimpering captives like hungry wolves. "You've given all you can," Ava said in a soothing voice. "You no longer need to take up space in this world."

Ruva leaned closer, drawing upon her gift. The twins were linked, their gestures in a perfectly symmetrical synchronicity. "Fold yourself up now, so we can put you away."

Boyle and Irma twisted and jerked, not comprehending what

was happening. Against their volition, their arms bent upward, pressing flat against their chests. They leaned over at the waist, bending at an impossible angle until their vertebrae cracked like brittle branches.

Boyle screamed as he bent his legs at the knees and then bent again in the middle of his femurs, breaking himself, folding down. His shoulders cracked and crunched, collapsing in like a wilting flower. Beside him, Irma continued to fold herself again and again. Like old blankets, the two human forms were creased and then folded, then folded repeatedly into a smaller and smaller package. Finally, their necks snapped and the screaming stopped. But the pop and crack of breaking bones continued as the two layered themselves into compact packages of dense, dripping flesh on the floor of the headquarters. The entire process took several noisy minutes.

"You may remove them," General Utros said to Enoch. "Call me when the herd of yaxen is brought in. Tonight, we'll have our first feast since awakening."

All fifty of the shaggy animals were slaughtered at the edge of the camp. Because supplies would be lean for some time, the butchers were careful to save all the blood, to strip off the hides, to keep the offal, the bones, anything that might be useful. The pelts could be used for blankets or tent walls, the sinews dried as lines, the guts made into bowstrings, everything else boiled into large vats of soup.

The meat was roasted on huge bonfires, and although there wasn't nearly enough to feed thousands of troops, Utros divided the feast among his top-level commanders and their lieutenants. The fifty yaxen provided enough meat to feed more than a thousand when judiciously rationed. Utros had made up his mind to take no more than the others.

He stood before the bonfire, inhaling the savory smells of haunches and joints searing over the flames. Meat juices dripped into the embers. The commanders pressed forward to be served.

Because of the tension and confusion, as well as the rigorous work he had to do, Utros had driven away all thoughts of food for more than a day, but he knew he had to have nourishment. He accepted a small serving of the fresh meat and made sure Ava and Ruva were also fed.

Feeling the heat of the large fire, even with dulled senses, he stood next to the twins and First Commander Enoch. They all took bites of the steaming meat, but the food felt oddly leaden in Utros's mouth. He had often relished rare, dripping meat fresh from the hunt. He'd eaten countless meals of game cooked over a fire.

Now, though, he felt queasy. When he tried to swallow, his body rebelled. He didn't want to eat. He couldn't taste the meat. He felt sickened, and saw that his other commanders had the same reaction. One man even spat out his first mouthful, looking confused and embarrassed.

Enoch said, "Maybe you should give my serving to some of the men, General. I . . . I'm not hungry."

Utros realized that neither was he. Genuinely perplexed, he looked around, saw that no one was eating the meat. All the slaughtered carcasses would go to waste. More details circulated in his head as he tried to understand, pieces fitting into place, even though they made no sense. He remembered no one drinking the water, no one using the latrines. Many supplies had gone untouched, though they were available to the soldiers.

His body craved no nourishment. The stone spell had preserved him for centuries, and it had not entirely let go. He stared toward Ildakar as the realization dawned on him. He dumped his meat on the ground and felt nothing. The others grew alarmed as they came to the same conclusion.

Utros smiled, understanding what an enormous blessing he had just discovered.

Maybe he wouldn't need to feed his giant army after all.

CHAPTER 7

Bannon felt uneasy when he and Lila returned to the fighting pits near the combat arena. The place held only terrible memories for him, but that was where the hundreds of seasoned warriors wanted to gather. That was where they felt at home, where they had learned to fight for the entertainment of the people of Ildakar. Now they had to defend the city that had enslaved them. Everyone could see the enormous military force outside.

Bannon had rested after the night of the uprising, but he couldn't relax. The city was under siege and he, too, might have to fight for Ildakar, a place he had never dreamed of calling his own. The awakened stone army filled the plain, and for three days now they had battered the walls, with little effect. General Utros had sent no ultimatum, no emissary, but Ildakar needed to be ready.

Lila remained by his side, though he didn't understand why she stayed so close to him. He couldn't forget how many times she had browbeaten him, challenged him, ground him under her heel as she imposed exhausting, painful training so he could fight against some desperate warrior or hungry beast in the arena. Now Lila seemed to consider him her friend, or at least her special project, though he had not asked for her company.

For these training exercises, Lila had called more than two dozen surviving morazeth to help prepare the warriors for what might be a far more terrible fight. The hard-bitten women seemed to be composed of tightly wound springs, hard leather, and sharp edges. The morazeth served their city without question, without deviation, and did not accept that their roles had changed despite the uprising. Ildakar was still Ildakar. Though the arena warriors outnumbered the morazeth by nearly ten to one in the training areas, they showed clear deference to the women.

The fighters had returned to the combat pits to rearm themselves. Many of them, including Bannon, had helped Mirrormask's cause during the bloody revolt, but now, faced with the ancient army trapping them inside, the various parties had come to an uneasy, though unresolved, truce. The downtrodden slaves still felt generations-long enmity for their former masters, but most of these warriors recognized the common enemy. Once they defeated General Utros, they would continue their philosophical argument and reshape the government, if anyone remained alive. Bannon hoped to be gone by then.

In the tunnels near the arena, many hollowed-out grottoes had been painstakingly converted into combat rings, training floors, and sunken pits where warriors could face off against each other. Bannon had sparred with Lila many times here, once even with the captive sand panther Mrra.

With Ildakar under siege, the fighters gathered as if for a daily training session, but they realized how much more was at stake. They were muscular, scarred, flinty-eyed—survivors all. Many wore only loincloths, though some had donned leather chest armor. They chose sharpened staves, square knouts, curved hooks, short swords, whatever weapons made them most comfortable.

Lila stood in the torch-lit grotto holding a whip in one hand, a short sword in the other. At her hip, she also had her agile knife, its small handle engraved with spell runes, the tiny pointed blade capable of delivering a burst of enormous pain. Bannon had felt its sting himself when Lila had used it to control him, to punish him, to drive him to fight harder. Now she disregarded how she had treated him, seemed to think he didn't even remember.

Lila raked her hard gaze over the gathered warriors. The rest of the morazeth stood in their places looking just as beautiful, just as deadly. Bannon had watched them train other warriors, and he knew some of their names—Kedra, Lyesse, Marla, Thorn, Genda, Ricia—but none of them had given him "special" attention, like Lila.

"While we wait for General Utros to make his next move, we will train you into the best fighters possible. We may have to prepare you for war," Lila said, stepping into the role of leader. "Adessa is gone. Some saw her leave Ildakar on the night of the uprising, perhaps on a mission of her own. If she's not here, she's no longer our concern. My sisters and I will continue to harden you. For Ildakar."

Bannon spoke up. "We're not training to fight for the entertainment of the gifted nobles. None of us are. I want that understood." He looked around at the other warriors. "But we have to be ready to fight against the army outside. That's our real enemy."

"Of course, boy," Lila said with a mocking smile. "Do you believe battling those ancient soldiers will be less demanding than arena combat? Don't be ridiculous. A fight to the death is a fight to the death, whether it's on the arena sands or out on the battlefield. I want you to have the skills to survive either."

The other morazeth squared their shoulders, lifted their weapons, and faced the countless opponents. Lila continued, "Today my sisters and I will fight our utmost to help you survive in a real war. The few of you who die immediately in a battle will be of no benefit to our city." She looked at Bannon as the other fighters shifted restlessly. "And I intend for you to survive, boy. I'd be greatly disappointed if you got yourself killed too soon on the battlefield."

"So would I," Bannon said, without any trace of humor. He raised Sturdy, swung the sword to loosen his arms. As a farm boy, he had worked in the cabbage fields, the son of an embittered man who drank too much and couldn't control his violent tendencies. The man had beaten Bannon, but unleashed the worst of his temper on his battered wife; he'd finally clubbed her to death, because Bannon hadn't been there to stop the vile man. His father had been hanged for his crimes, but Bannon took no satisfaction from it.

Feeling the darkness in him, he bunched his muscles, squeezed his grip on the hilt. He didn't care about the cold morazeth or the warriors who fought in the arena because it was their job. Rather, his anger flared when he thought of how he wanted to kill his father, how he had failed to save his mother. Crouching, he swept the blade through the air, letting the violence simmer inside him, but not letting it boil into uncontrollable rage. Sometimes in the heat of battle, Bannon had a tendency to fly into a blood fury and forget where he was, simply fighting and killing, without returning to himself for a long time. Now, he kept the anger under control as he imagined facing the giant ancient army outside the walls.

Even adding these hundreds of warriors to the ranks of the city guard, he didn't know how they could make a dent in the vast siege.

A blade clanged against his own, startling him from his thoughts, and he whirled, instinctively bringing up Sturdy in defense. Lila smashed hard with her short sword, intentionally catching the guard at the end of his blade so as not to hurt him. Bannon backed away, crouching into a defensive stance. "I wasn't ready."

She laughed. "So you think General Utros will send a polite notice when he intends to attack you?" She struck again, swinging her sword while cracking the whip with her other hand.

Bannon couldn't afford to be distracted now. He parried her attack, blocked her sword, and ducked beneath her snaking whip. The torch-lit training grotto was large, with plenty of places for combat. Lila and Bannon sparred near one of the shallower pits. Five feet down, the bottom was raked sand mixed with ashes to absorb spilled blood.

"We need to give these others room to fight, boy," she said, then raised her voice. "All of you, battle my sisters! Fight against one another, and fight for your lives, because your survival may well depend on what you learn from us and from each other. Kedra! Thorn! Lyesse! Assign opponents."

As the other morazeth separated training candidates, Bannon looked at the smooth side of the pit. "I don't think—"

Lila slammed her shoulder into him, shoving him backward. He stumbled, tried to regain his balance, but she dove at him and knocked him over the edge. They both landed hard on the soft sand below, the young woman on top of his chest, pinning him down.

He thrust her to the side as he got into a fighting stance. As Lila rolled, she laughed, "You have to do better than that, boy, if you want to earn your reward from me tonight."

"It's not a reward." He thought of the times she'd claimed his body, plying him with just a hint of softness along with a hungry lust that his body couldn't help but respond to. "I'm free now. I'm not your pet. I'm not your captive."

"Freedom just makes you stubborn," she retorted, "and disappointing. I don't like to be disappointed." She attacked him with a flurry of sword maneuvers, lashing her whip. Bannon concentrated on meeting her blows.

Above, in the main training chambers, Genda, Ricia, Marla, and the other morazeth plunged into a melee with their selected opponents. Shouts and outcries echoed along the rough stone walls, ringing down the tunnels. To Bannon, it sounded like all-out war, but he knew it was merely practice combat. Although the morazeth imposed ruthless violence upon their trainees, he understood that they all shared the single-minded goal of protecting Ildakar.

"Sweet Sea Mother," he panted as Lila threw herself upon him again. He fought faster, pushed her back, struck a ringing blow that made her short sword shudder, and she lashed out with her whip, trying to catch him, but close quarters rendered the long whip ineffective. He reached out, grabbed the braided leather, and yanked hard, making her stumble toward him. He let go and in a swift blinding motion, seized her wrist instead, pulling her even closer to him.

She pressed her face close to his, smiling. "So, you want me now? Are you trying to take me right here on the sands? That would be exhilarating! Maybe I'd even let you. You've done well today."

He shoved her away. "You tormented me. You battered me. How can you think we'll just be lovers?"

She looked confused. "I trained you as I was commanded to do. I taught you the skills you needed, and I made you a much better fighter than ever before. I saved your life, or at least extended it. How can you resent that?"

He felt exasperated. "I resent being imprisoned, being forced to fight. I was never part of Ildakar. I just wanted to save Ian. He was my friend, and you all corrupted him, made him forget about his life."

"He was the champion." Lila was just as baffled. "We revered him. Adessa even took him as her lover. She might have let herself conceive a child by him. What more could a man want?"

"What more?" Bannon spat on the sand. He backed away, keeping his sword raised in a defensive position. "I wanted to make my own choices. I didn't want to be in the combat arena. I didn't want to be trained by you."

She looked down at his sword, his well-muscled arms, his

lean and wiry form. "But you still have me to thank for it. How do you resent me?"

They were panting, drenched in sweat. He knew he had fought well. Lila had parried his blows, pressed forward, and he had pushed back. He was almost, *almost* good enough to fight her to a stalemate. But now she backed away, troubled by his reaction. "I find you strange, boy. This is what I am. I did as I was instructed. What more could you want of me? Someday you will appreciate what I gave you."

He was grateful for the swordplay that Nathan Rahl had taught him. He had learned the basics of fighting on the deck of the *Wavewalker*. Before then, he had simply swung the blade from side to side, trying to get close enough to hit some reckless enemy, but Nathan showed him skill and finesse.

It was true, though, that Lila had honed him into a real fighter. He had been forced into one-on-one combat with Ian, his former best friend, who had become a bloodthirsty killer with cold and leaden eyes. The champion fought not one whit below his ability, even against Bannon, who had been forced to use every flicker of skill to save his own life, and just barely. Ian had struck him in the head with the side of a knout, rendering him unconscious rather than killing him. Bannon was sure his friend had done it on purpose, but if Bannon had let his guard falter for even a heartbeat during combat, he would be dead now. He was sure of it.

"I can't forget what you did to me," he said. "I'm sorry, Lila. I know who you are. I can't blame a viper for biting me, but the venom can still make me sick."

She chuckled. "You compare me to a viper now? I was hoping for something more romantic." She narrowed her eyes and hardened her voice. "Boy—"

"My name is *Bannon*. Until you think of me as a person, I can't think of you as anything but a snake."

She laughed again. "As you wish, Bannon—I'll remember that from time to time, when you earn it. But understand that my morazeth sisters and I have always fought for the good of Ildakar, and that hasn't changed. Everyone in the city has the same enemy, and only a fool would hold a grudge in a situation like this. Fight the army of Utros, not me." She lowered her voice. "Then you'll find that we both deserve our rewards."

Bannon pondered that, worried that she might use his moment of distraction to attack him. He knew that what she said was correct. "All right, I'll put aside my grudge against you and the morazeth. For the time being."

She smiled, a genuine smile, and when she did she was quite beautiful.

The morazeth and the combat arenas had been an integral part of Ildakaran society during their many centuries hidden beneath the shroud. Lila had not been malicious, though it had felt so at the time. She had no emotional attachment, was simply doing her job. When she presented him with a "reward" of her body and expected him to take as much pleasure as she did, she meant it. On those evenings, Lila had wrapped herself around him with wild abandon, not as a power play, but as a woman with a man. Considering how much battering she had inflicted on him, the reward had not been entirely unpleasant.

"Everyone here has to put aside their grudges, as you say. And we have to train to be deadly fighters." He thrust Sturdy into the sand, indicating he was done with their sparring for now. Around them in the other combat pits, the battles continued.

Lila rubbed her arms, touched a sore spot from where he had dealt her a blow with the flat of his blade. He studied her slender form, the lean muscles, the spell markings on her skin. She was beautiful like a wild thing.

No grudges . . .

He thought again of Ian on Chiriya Island, an innocent lad who had been captured by Norukai slavers. Ian had sacrificed himself so Bannon could get away. . . . Bannon had watched the hideous raiders club his dear friend into unconsciousness.

They had tied Ian up and sailed away, eventually selling him in the slave market of Ildakar.

Of all the things he hated, Bannon loathed the Norukai raiders the most. Perhaps he could find a way to forgive, or at least ignore, what the morazeth had done, and perhaps those women could make up for their past by saving the city from the new siege.

But Bannon could never forget nor forgive the Norukai. That was a grudge he would hold until the end of time.

CHAPTER 8

Waves crashed like war hammers against the black cliffs, as if the serpent god were angry or restless, but the Norukai were accustomed to storms and high seas. The harsh waters and treacherous channels between the islands heated the blood of the Norukai, strengthened them.

The air was damp and cold inside King Grieve's enormous Bastion, which towered over the main Norukai island. Built from perfectly fitted black stones, its impregnable square walls were even more intimidating than the sharp reef spires that protruded from the foaming surf below.

A fire roared in the cavernous hearth of his throne room, fed with logs delivered by lumber ships that razed the coast. The Norukai were feared as raiders, destroyers, slavers, but on their rocky islands, wood was a commodity as valuable as gold and less unruly than defiant captives. The large fire in the throne room burned constantly against the persistent damp chill.

King Grieve wore a sleeveless scaled vest made from the skin of a wolf shark that he had wrestled into submission, hauling it up onto the rocks and gutting it while it was still alive. His arm muscles were enormous from hard work and from killing.

The Norukai king needed to be stronger than all of his people, and Grieve often demonstrated the fact, although it was difficult to coerce anyone to fight him, because any challenger knew he or she would die.

He clenched his fists as he sat on his blocky throne, staring at the hot, bright fire. Grieve's knuckles had been inset with curved iron plates. One blow from his fist would crush an opponent's skull and drop him like a clubbed spearfish. Grieve liked to do that, although it ended the fun of a duel all too soon.

Outside the Bastion, the howling wind tried to force its way inside. Breezes clawed at reinforced glass, rattled the panes. Even with the windows closed and barred, he could hear the crashing surf. Stone buildings covered any flat space on the island, huddling against the persistent wind.

Even as rain streaked through the air, people continued their daily business. Women were still out planting herbs and succulents in cracks in the cliffs, using every small patch of fertile land. Goat herders grazed their animals among the mosses and lichens. Fishermen came in with their catch, braving the waves. Grieve would feast on fresh fish, as he did each night, while most of the catch was salted and preserved, or pressed into tanks with cabbage and vinegar that could ferment during the worst of the stormy season.

Out in the narrow harbor sheltered by high cliffs, wood-and-iron docks held the larger serpent ships that came in to deliver the plunder from Norukai raids. His people were not so weak as to worry about the weather, and this was just a small storm.

As he listened to the wind and thought about war, Grieve heard the clang of iron bells from the harbor cliffs. Sentries hammered the long hollow cylinders to announce the approach of a ship. It was not an alarm, because no one would dare attack the Norukai archipelago, a hundred islands on the charts and others too small to be worth recording. Each one was a fortress.

The iron bells rang to spread word that some raiding party or explorer had returned to the harbor.

Grieve scratched his cheek, felt the long gash scar that ran from the corner of his lips to the back of his jaw—an intentional cut that had widened his mouth, the skin sewn up to leave his face looking serpentlike. Tattooed scales on his skin did even more to honor the serpent god. The king had other enhancements to his body, bone spines implanted in his shoulders, a sharpened hook through his left nostril. Rather than a belt, he wrapped an iron chain around his waist, and over the course of his life, Grieve had added one link for each man he had killed in personal combat. Now the chain belt circled his waist more than three times.

Grieve frowned at the white sticklike figure that pranced in front of the fireplace. The great hearth looked like the mouth of a dragon ready to breathe fire at the shaman who hovered there absorbing the warmth. He leaned so close to the flames that his albino skin reddened.

Hearing the bells, the pale figure cocked his head and jittered his arms. "It's Captain Kor! Captain Kor has returned."

"How do you know that, Chalk? It could be anyone."

"I know. The bells ring in my head. The voices tell me what I can't see with my own eyes, and my eyes see what I can't imagine." Squirming with energy, the shaman left the roaring fire and danced across the cold stone floor. "It's Captain Kor, I know it."

Those who saw Chalk for the first time often cringed, but Grieve saw only his friend. Chalk was naked except for a loincloth of stitched-together fish hides. His own skin was ghostly pale, as it had been since birth. His family had called him an abomination, shunned him.

His body was covered with countless small scars, where his skin had been ravaged with innumerable fish bites. When Grieve was a teen, his father King Stern ordered young Chalk to be thrown into a pool infested with man-eating razorfish.

Their fangs tore his tender skin, drawing blood, tasting his flesh. But for some unknown reason, except that it was a blessing from the serpent god, the razorfish did not devour him. Young Grieve had dragged Chalk out of the pool and suffered savage bites while saving him.

The fish had eaten any soft and tender flesh: Chalk's ears, part of his lips, his eyelids, his privates. The young albino recovered, thanks to Grieve's tending—but he was never the same.

As a young man, Grieve had sensed Chalk's power. King Stern was disgusted with the outcast, but Grieve befriended the scarred and half-mad youth, listened to his babblings. The horrific ordeal had awakened some strange manifestation of the gift in him, some kind of premonition.

Chalk had foreseen many things and even told Grieve when to challenge and kill his father. Since then, the albino had been at his side as his shaman and advisor. Even though Grieve often questioned his bizarre pronouncements and tried to clarify what Chalk saw in order to make the predictions useful, he never actually doubted the veracity of what the shaman knew.

"Are you certain it's Captain Kor?" he repeated, knowing Chalk would not change his answer.

"It is Kor. Three ships. He's back. I know it, my Grieve! King Grieve! They'll all grieve!" He chattered the refrain like a mantra. He hopped from one foot to the other. "You'll see. Listen to the bells. The ships will dock soon. Kor will come up, and he'll tell you about your new war."

"What war? I haven't decided on a war."

"You will, and you will know."

Grieve crossed his arms over his sharkskin vest and leaned back in the throne. The storm continued to whistle and howl, and cold rain slashed against the glass windows. "If you're correct, I'll give you a treat."

"More fish? Can I have more fish for my tank? I like the pretty fish."

64

"We'll see," Grieve said. "But if you're wrong, I'll find a suitable punishment."

Chalk skittered away, holding up his hands, touching his rough skin. "Don't feed me to the fishes. Not the fishes. Not again. I am your Chalk. You are my Grieve. King Grieve. They'll all grieve!"

The look of abject terror on the shaman's face gave the king pause, and he spoke in a softer voice. "You know better. I would never feed you to the fishes."

"Not to the serpent god either. Don't chain me to the cliffs."

"Not that either. You're too valuable, and you're my friend."

"Grieve's friend," Chalk said in a quiet whimper. "They'll all grieve."

Trusting Chalk's prediction, he knew that Captain Kor would come bearing a report of what he had seen at the city of Ildakar. Grieve looked forward to the news. Maybe Chalk would be right about the war, too.

In a bellowing voice, Grieve called for five slaves, who rushed into his throne room. With jerky movements they shuffled reverently toward the throne, two women and three men. During their training, many of the slaves serving in the Bastion had bones broken and then set improperly as a reminder. Grieve kept the slaves he needed here, while some were pressed into service throughout the Norukai islands, and the more valuable ones were sold. Anyone here in the Bastion was replaceable and worthless.

Grieve growled at them. "Prepare a meal to welcome our brave Captain Kor back so he can report on his expedition. Do we have enough fresh fish in the kitchens, or must I slaughter one of you so we feast on human flesh again?"

"A celebration!" Chalk cried, excited by the possibility.

Moaning, the slaves skittered backward. "We have fish, King Grieve," said the oldest male slave, a man who had survived for nearly ten years in service. "Smoked fish and fresh fish. You need never resort to human flesh again."

"What if I enjoy it?" Grieve asked, partly meaning it, but mostly to intimidate them. "One gets tired of fish. I like other kinds of meat."

"I'll have the kitchen prepare fish," said the older slave. *Emmett,* yes, that was his name. The man always seemed to be here, though Grieve paid little attention to him. He wondered how adept the slave must be. Emmett was a survivor. Grieve didn't normally like survivors, since that type often caused trouble. Maybe he would execute the man and roast him after all, though seeing Emmett's gnarled hands and wrinkled face, the king suspected his flesh would be stringy and bitter. No, it was not worth the effort. He'd let the old man continue in service.

Chalk scuttled back to the hearth to warm himself. He jabbered about different kinds of fish, the small ones he kept in his tank as well as some of the large ones, poisonous creatures with spines, even one that could release a jolt like lightning. The tank was an indulgence Grieve allowed his shaman and friend.

By the time food was prepared and brought in on stone trays, three burly Norukai men marched through the smoke-stained wooden doors and into the throne room. Grieve recognized Captain Kor by the pointed shark's tooth implanted in his shaved scalp. Each of the Norukai had their mouths slashed, their lips and faces altered to honor the serpent god.

Grieve leaned forward on his blocky throne, his chest broad, his arms bunched, the bone spines poking several inches above his shoulders. King Grieve never required simpering bows of obeisance from his bravest warriors or raiding captains. He preferred to earn their honor, loyalty, and respect through actions, not empty gestures. The remaining Norukai were Yorik and Lars, captains of the other two ships on the slave-trading mission.

"I told you it was Kor," Chalk said. "He came back from his expedition. Kor, Kor, there will be war!"

The three new arrivals kept their attention on the intimidating king on his high throne. The scarred shaman made them nervous.

"Tell me what you found, Captain Kor," Grieve said. "Your report may make us launch our newest conquest. It's about time."

Kor looked determined. "With three serpent ships we sailed far south to where the river spills into the sea, then we made our way up the estuary as before, like trading ships, carrying a load of nearly two hundred slaves. We picked up more along the way."

"Good," Grieve said. "I thought the coastal towns down south were picked clean, just like their forests. Our raids will concentrate on the northern coast from now on."

Kor bowed. "Or maybe we have a better target for conquest. We've traded with Ildakar over the years, although the city appears and disappears. The wizards hide behind some magical shroud, but they are growing lax and I know there is unrest in their streets. Somehow, one of our own went missing the last night, and we never found his body."

"Dar," Lars and Yorik both grumbled.

Grieve stiffened. "Those perfumed fops killed one of our Norukai?"

Yorik spoke up. "We can't be sure, my king. Dar frequented the whorehouses in Ildakar, and then one day he was gone. He could have been drunk and gotten himself robbed and killed in an alley."

"We could use it as an excuse for Norukai retaliation on the city, if that is what you wish," Kor said. "We could avenge Dar."

"I don't want excuses. I loathe excuses." Grieve clacked his iron-studded knuckles together. "If we mean to declare war, then we'll simply attack."

"Ildakar is our destiny," Chalk said. "My Grieve. King Grieve. They'll all grieve!"

The king shushed the shaman. Chalk continued his antics,

but placed a hand over his own mouth as if to hold the words in.

"Captain Kor, what do you think about conquering Ildakar?"

"It is a wise idea," the Norukai captain said. "Our ship is filled with kegs of their bloodwine and crates of preserved meat from a creature called a yaxen. The Ildakarans produce fine silks and lavish furs extracted from laboratories and businesses right inside the city. The city welcomed us. They are open to more trade." Kor smiled with his gashed mouth. "We just need to get inside when their shroud is down, and we can surprise them. From what I have seen, they require days of preparation and the shedding of much blood before they can make themselves disappear again. We would have plenty of opportunity to attack and plunder. The city is a treasure chest of jewels and potential slaves."

"And wine," Lars interjected.

Kor continued, "The people are weak, although many of their wizards are greatly gifted."

"Wizards?" Chalk cried. "Magic can be defeated. The serpent god knows how. Chalk knows how."

Grieve turned to him. "How can magic be defeated?"

"I don't know yet. But I will." Chalk retreated to the warmth of the fire where he hunched, rubbing his hands in front of the flames, staring into the embers as if looking for the answer. "I will know when it's time to know."

When the platters of food arrived, Kor, Yorik, and Lars took seats at the long table and King Grieve sat before the largest platter at the head of the table. He tore into the roasted fish with his bare fingers, peeling the flaky meat from the curved bones.

"First, send that yaxen meat to the Bastion. I'm weary of fish, and I don't like goat. Meanwhile, I will plan for war. I have a hundred new serpent ships being built across our islands, and I won't depart until at least fifty of them are finished. Ildakar has been there for thousands of years. It'll wait another few months. They will fall to us, regardless."

Kor sucked on fish bones, tossed a roasted head aside. "I don't want to wait for months, my king. That trade mission taxed my patience, and I ache for the feel of fresh spilled blood. Give me something else to do."

Since Kor had just finished a calm journey, perhaps a good battle would satisfy him. "I've been considering a raid anyway. I'll dispatch you north. Take your ships and attack the town called Renda Bay. They somehow defeated our ships the last time we raided, and they must learn their lesson."

"A lesson!" Chalk said. "Gut them, burn them."

Grieve said, "Leave the town empty, with nothing but ghosts."

"Ghosts!" the shaman said, touching his pockmarked skin. "Like me." Alone among Norukai adults, Chalk did not have a slashed mouth. His lips extended only to the normal reaches of his cheeks, except for where the fish had torn shreds away.

Kor nodded so deeply it was almost a bow. "I accept this raid with gratitude, King Grieve."

The king had punished the previous captain who was defeated by the small fishing town. That man had been chained to the cliffs and fed to the serpent god, so his blood could strengthen the sea serpent, and the serpent in turn would protect and strengthen the Norukai race.

"Don't fail," Grieve warned.

"Don't doubt me," Kor replied.

The king found the answer satisfying, and he finished his platter of fish, already imagining the taste of the promised yaxen meat.

CHAPTER 9

"I am a wizard of Ildakar," Renn said, puffing himself up as he faced Prelate Verna in the grand foyer of the Cliffwall archive. The stranger's face was florid, his cheeks a little jowly, but sagging from weeks of hard travel. He swirled maroon robes around him.

Verna remained unruffled as she crossed her arms over her chest and stepped forward to meet the stranger. Despite his bluster, the self-proclaimed wizard flicked his eyes nervously from her to General Zimmer, intimidated by the grandeur of the portico, the columns, the marble floors inside the enormous cliff overhang. She could sense the gift in him, but she also thought that if she challenged him, his bravado would deflate like a wineskin that had sprung a leak.

"And I am the prelate of the Sisters of the Light," Verna said. "This Cliffwall archive is a priceless library of profound magical lore, available to gifted scholars who come seeking knowledge, with certain restrictions."

"It is not available to those who demand," General Zimmer growled. The burly military man had dark hair and a square jaw that showed a shadow of whiskers even though he had scraped his cheeks smooth only a few hours ago.

Renn sputtered, fidgeted, and sniffed. "You must not be aware of the archive's origin. The lore in Cliffwall belongs to Ildakar." He struggled not to sound condescending. "We are grateful that you people have been stewards of the knowledge in the interim, but my city was instrumental in creating the archive long ago, before Emperor Sulachan purged all magical records."

Ten soldiers wearing unfamiliar Ildakaran military uniforms stood behind Renn, glancing uncertainly at the wizard. Their captain said, "Renn, sir, maybe we should not be so—"

The portly wizard waved him to silence.

Hearing the rising voices, Cliffwall scholars ventured into the grand foyer. They wore comfortable wool and linen garments and soft sandals, showing little difference between the diligent archivists and the recall-enhanced memmers.

Verna calmed herself with a common exercise, inhaling and exhaling slowly. "I am aware of Cliffwall's history, though Ildakar's name isn't as prominent in the archives as you might think. My Sisters of the Light are visitors here, too. We've come to study the library and to guard the dangerous knowledge from those who might abuse it."

Other curious Sisters came into the large chamber, including Sisters Eldine and Rhoda and the fresh-faced novice Amber. Verna saw owlish Scholar-Archivist Franklin enter the foyer alongside the lead memmer, Gloria, a plump and determined-looking woman. Franklin wore an uncertain, welcoming smile. "Cliffwall has been hidden for thousands of years, and the camouflage shroud was only recently dispelled. Our knowledge is meant for all who deserve it."

Verna remained cautious. "The unwise and unschooled use of this powerful lore has already caused several disasters, and so we must be cautious. General Zimmer and his D'Haran soldiers have sworn to protect the archive." She narrowed her eyes. "If such powerful magic were to fall into the wrong hands, or even untrained hands, another catastrophe might occur."

Renn huffed. "As a wizard of Ildakar, my rank and abilities exceed those of anyone at Cliffwall. I'll take over here."

"No, you will not," said Franklin. "I am responsible for the material in Cliffwall." He was normally a quiet, soft-spoken man more comfortable with books than with people, but his ire had been sparked by the wizard's pompous attitude.

With a huff, Gloria stepped next to the scholar-archivist. "And I represent the memmers, who have imprinted thousands of volumes in our minds. We've maintained the information in Cliffwall for millennia, and we will not surrender it."

Verna restored the edge to her voice as more scholars stood up to the party from Ildakar. "The Sisters of the Light are also gifted. You'll find us to be powerful enemies, all of us . . . if you choose to make enemies." She gestured toward the increasing numbers of scholars gathering there. "Many of us have been studying ancient spells. If it came down to a battle, I'm sure they would love to practice what they've learned."

Renn was flustered, and his florid face turned a brighter red. "But . . . but, I'm a wizard of Ildakar!" He paused, as if those words should make them tremble. "Sovrena Thora sent me on a mission to find this archive." He glanced at the group of soldiers who had accompanied him. "And I have to . . ."

"You have found it." Verna stood her ground, but didn't try to provoke him further. "But the books stay where they can be protected."

Nine more armed D'Haran guards entered the foyer, climbing up from the cliffside after the intruders. Though these were only a fraction of General Zimmer's force, they already exceeded the Ildakaran guard. Zimmer put his hand to the hilt of his sword, and the other D'Haran soldiers did the same, threatening. The tension in the room escalated.

The leader of the Ildakaran guard escort interrupted calmly as a flustered Renn wrestled for words. "We've had a long and arduous journey over the mountains. I am Captain Trevor, leader of the wizard's escort. Maybe we should learn more about each other before we argue?"

Quiet and introspective Franklin spoke up. "We haven't even finished cataloging the material yet. We don't know the books that exist here in the archive, and our entire library of prophecy was destroyed in a, uh, magical mishap, when a student named Elbert activated a Weeping Stone spell he could not control. All those prophecy books . . ."

Verna muttered with a sigh, "Prophecy books were no longer relevant anyway, just wasted paper."

Renn looked from side to side, his thoughts spinning. Obviously, his arrival had not turned out the way he had imagined it after his long journey. "I want to see the archive."

"The books will remain here," General Zimmer said firmly.

Renn's shoulders slumped in defeat. "I don't think Thora would even appreciate all this knowledge. She always mocked me and dear Lani for how we spent our time reading and learning." The flustered wizard lowered his voice so that Verna barely heard his last words. "Maybe she doesn't deserve it." His entire attitude seemed to change. He deflated, as she thought he might.

Verna took a step forward and spoke in a calm voice. "You've had a long journey, and tempers and patience are frayed. Let us get to know one another, as Captain Trevor says. We're just as anxious to learn about Ildakar as you are to know more about Cliffwall."

Gloria spoke up. "The kitchens are making cauldrons of lentil and sausage soup and fresh baked bread. Perhaps we can continue to talk over lunch?"

Renn's eyes widened at the mention of food, and Verna could almost see him drool. The escort soldiers also perked up, looking eager.

Zimmer spoke to Captain Trevor and the nine bedraggled Ildakaran soldiers. "We have a military camp in the valley, with provisions and a place for your men to stay. Soldiers always have stories to exchange, so long as they're not enemies."

Trevor responded with a smile. "Yes, so long as they're not enemies, General. For now, let's proceed on that assumption." He addressed his men. "We'll go make camp and relax. The meadows by the stream looked better than any camp we've had since leaving Ildakar."

Renn seemed reluctant to be left alone in Cliffwall, but he forced himself to relax. "The lentil soup does sound very good indeed." The pretentious wizard had begun the conversation with escalating demands, but he seemed out of his depth. Verna could tell from the lines in Renn's face and the barely concealed rips in his maroon robes that he must have had a difficult trek overland.

As General Zimmer led Trevor and the soldiers back down the steep cliffside path to the military camp, the prelate asked the visiting wizard, "How did you even know to look for Cliffwall? We didn't realize word had spread to the far points of the Old World."

Renn said, "We had recent visitors, strangers from far away, and a young swordsman named Bannon blurted out the location of Cliffwall. He was traveling with a powerless wizard named Nathan Rahl and a blond sorceress named Nicci."

Verna caught her breath. "You've seen Nathan and Nicci?"

"Yes, do you know them? They are in Ildakar, working with the wizards' duma."

Curious, Verna led him deeper into the archive. "In that case, we have much to talk about."

As large bowls of steaming lentil soup were ladled out and shared around the table, intent scholars clustered around Wizard Renn, full of questions. Verna looked at Rhoda, Eldine, Amber, and her companion Sisters, all of whom listened eagerly.

She had known that Nicci and Nathan were traveling the Old World, since they had sent back records of their adventures by courier. In one such message, delivered by a pair of young scholars from Cliffwall, Nicci had called for soldiers and gifted scholars to help defend the ancient archive of dangerous knowledge. The people at Cliffwall had countless volumes of powerful magic but almost no instruction in how to use it.

After reading Nicci's request, Verna had joined General Zimmer and more than a hundred D'Haran soldiers on a journey south. Much of the Old World was an unmarked map, a landscape of mysteries, undiscovered cities, and peoples. Even though the ancient wizard wars were over, the Imperial Order defeated, and Sulachan and his undead army crushed by Lord Rahl, there were still many risks in the unruly continent.

On their search for Cliffwall, Verna and her companions had come upon the coastal town of Renda Bay, which had been plagued by ferocious raiders that ransacked and burned villages. General Zimmer had left part of his expeditionary force there with instructions for Amber's brother Captain Norcross to help Renda Bay drive off the Norukai slavers if they should return.

It was just one step in building the defenses of the Old World as part of the expanding D'Haran Empire. Complete security would take a long time, Verna knew, but as the Cliffwall scholars often quoted, "A book is read one page at a time, a shelf is read one book at a time, a library is read one shelf at a time." Verna hoped Norcross and the people of Renda Bay would be safe and secure, but she did know that three large sailing ships had remained anchored there as a defense.

Cliffwall had suffered terrible tragedies when their naive scholars dabbled with magical lore, accidentally unleashing destruction when they didn't know what they were doing. Verna could only imagine how much worse it would be if a tyrant like Emperor Jagang were to get his hands on such lore and actively use it as a weapon.

As soon as they had arrived at the Cliffwall canyon, the D'Haran soldiers studied its defenses. The archive had been built inside an alcove high up on a sheer cliff, which made the place relatively secure, but Zimmer planned even more rigorous defenses, barricades and battlements. Even though the entrance to the enclosed canyon was difficult to find, Zimmer wanted to increase guards. Such prominent defenses had caused consternation among the scholars, but they had already seen the devastation of the Lifedrinker and the monstrous uncontrolled sorceress Victoria.

Now Renn scooped soup into his mouth, ravenous. "I'm used to feasts in Ildakar. Roast yaxen, fine desserts, candied fruits." He slurped another mouthful and wiped his lips with soft, warm bread. "This would be considered food for the lower classes, even for slaves. I never knew it could be so delicious!"

"We eat what the valley provides," Gloria said. "We've had to be self-sufficient for a long time. Cliffwall has little contact with the outside world."

Franklin added, "Here in the canyon we have orchards, crops, flocks of sheep. Notice the minced lamb in your soup?"

"Delicious," Renn repeated. He seemed satisfied now, and his arrogance was gone. With a sigh, he looked around the table. "I'd like to stay here for a while—on behalf of Ildakar, of course."

"Why exactly does Ildakar need all this magical knowledge?" Verna asked. "In ancient times, wizards hid the books here so Sulachan couldn't destroy them. We don't want to create another ruthless tyrant."

"Oh, the wizards of Ildakar would never become tyrants! They would never misuse . . ." He paused. "Well, Sovrena Thora did send me here because she wanted to control the power. And Wizard Commander Maxim has already unleashed some dramatic spells to protect our city." He scratched his cheek. "By the Keeper's beard, I'm actually not certain why they'd want all this knowledge." He lowered his voice. "I'm not convinced they should have it."

He chewed on a roll, silent for a moment, then continued,

"Maybe they didn't care. It is possible they never believed I would find Cliffwall at all. I had only sketchy directions, very few supplies. Captain Trevor and his men had never led a long expedition, nor were they trained in wilderness survival. They were just city guards. . . . We had a difficult time and lost three of our men on the way. It was only through luck that we even found Cliffwall, and just in time."

His expression darkened, and he seemed preoccupied. "Sovrena Thora sent me into that mess. I wonder if she was trying to get rid of me. Thora never forgave me after Lani challenged her rule." He scratched his neck, patted his potbelly. "I was younger then. Some might even have called me handsome, but after Thora turned Lani to stone, I just didn't . . ."

Renn shook his head. "I am still a loyal citizen of Ildakar, but the city is not the sovrena. After all those centuries under the shroud of eternity, Thora herself might have become stunted, like a tree trying to grow inside a glass bottle." He reached across the table to grab the large serving bowl and ladled more lentil soup for himself. "Yes, I've decided to stay here and learn more. Maybe the Cliffwall archives should remain exactly where they are."

Verna nodded, somewhat relieved. Beside her, always attentive, Amber listened to everything but held her questions back. The prelate said, "Cliffwall has a lot of information, and so do you, Wizard Renn. We want to hear all about Ildakar, and any news you can tell us of Nicci and Nathan."

CHAPTER 10

Trapped inside the walls of the city, Mrra was restless. The sand panther prowled among the buildings, the streets, wanting to hunt, wanting to run. She controlled herself, even though she longed to kill something.

Through her spell bond with the animal, Nicci had felt just as caged while she worked with the rebels in the catacombs beneath the city. Now, with the ancient army of General Utros besieging Ildakar, the trapped feeling increased.

The people were reinforcing their defenses to stand against a long siege, and Nicci wondered how long Utros and his troops could last. What did he want? It had been three full days since the army awakened, and the ancient soldiers were still rebuilding their camp, preparing to press against the impregnable city.

Night had fallen, and the monotonous pounding on the stone walls continued. Years ago, when the Imperial Order had begun its northern march to conquer the New World, Emperor Jagang required that drums be beaten relentlessly, all day and all night, whenever he intended to visit a city. It made the population tremble in anticipation, even if Jagang took months to arrive. This hammering sounded similar, and since Utros had many thousands of soldiers, he could maintain the barrage for a very long time.

At night, Nicci remained in her spacious guest quarters in the grand villa. With both Maxim and Thora gone, Nicci kept her rooms, as did Nathan and Bannon.

Restless, Mrra wanted to prowl through the dark streets to hunt rats, to jump from rooftop to rooftop for the joy of stretching her muscles. Nicci refused to leash the panther or lock her inside a cage. Mrra understood that she couldn't attack people the way the spiny wolves had done, but Nicci never forgot that the sand panther was a wild animal. If the big cat felt cornered or provoked, she would lash out. She needed to roam free through the grassy hills, needed to hunt in the forests. But how could Nicci let her out there with the enormous army lying in wait?

She sat in on the edge of the broad bed, the silken curtains wafting in the breeze. In addition to the distant pounding, she could hear the quiet sounds of the city, the nobles in their mansions, the cacophony of taverns and street vendors, the silk yaxen whorehouses, people playing music as Ildakar tried to maintain its normal life, even with the ancient army pressing on the gates.

Mrra paced inside the bedchamber, brushing her tawny fur against Nicci's knees. Nicci reached down to scratch behind the sand panther's ears. Purring contentedly, Mrra circled the room and stood on the open balcony, where she pricked her ears to listen to the sounds outside. She sniffed, twitched her whiskers, then returned for more scratching. Nicci could feel her longing to be free, no matter how many enemy soldiers were out there.

"You wouldn't be safe," Nicci said. What were General Utros and his army doing? What were they planning? Why hadn't he sent a representative to discuss terms?

Mrra growled as if to insist that life wasn't safe in Ildakar either. Nicci felt the animal's sharp claws and tightly wound reflexes, and knew full well that she could take care of herself. Though their spell bond was sharpest in dreams, Nicci could communicate with Mrra clearly. They understood each other.

Then Nicci straightened with the realization that having the big cat outside and running free could be useful to Ildakar. Mrra could be her secret eyes where she couldn't see. What would serve as a better spy than a predator who could glide through the night unseen?

Nicci leaned forward and put her hands on either side of the large feline head. The golden eyes looked up, meeting hers. "The enemy army is out there. We can see their camp, but that's not enough for me to make plans. Will you show me what you see? If I let you loose, will you be careful? Will you watch out for yourself?"

The sand panther's tail thrashed. Nicci made up her mind.

"Stay to the hills, take shelter in the trees, but you can also prowl. I want you to see them, so I can see through your eyes." Nicci gave a thin smile. "Be my spy against General Utros."

Lashing her tail, Mrra padded to the door of the chamber and out into the halls of the villa. Nicci felt her pulse racing and knew the panther was excited. "Let's go. I'll find one of the smaller gates to let you out, away from where the soldiers are hammering the wall." Her brow furrowed. "You might actually be safer out there than we are in here."

Even though the ancient soldiers concentrated their attack near the towering main gate, Ildakar had smaller access points near the cliff drop-off to the river, traveler's entrances and secret gates for merchants farther down the wall. Nicci and Mrra wound their way through the streets, listening to night birds and prowling house cats that stalked along the gutters. Mrra padded ahead as they worked their way to the northern end of the wall, where it curved around and abruptly met the edge of the sheer bluff.

Nicci found a low door cleverly hidden, covered with stone, exactly where she had been told to expect it. She released her gift and worked the magic to undo the latch. No scout from Utros's army could ever find these concealed entries. When the spell lock released, she swung the person-sized gate inward. A flood of moist air swept in, wafting up from the Killraven River below and the grassy hills stretching around the plain.

Mrra's tan body tensed with anticipation. Nicci placed a hand on the panther's broad shoulders, also feeling the cat's exhilaration. "I wish I could go with you, but my place is here in Ildakar—for now." She bent down and wrapped her arms around the big panther's body. Mrra rumbled with a purr, then licked Nicci's cheek with a raspy tongue.

"Go," Nicci said. "I'll be with you. I'm your sister panther."

Mrra bounded through the gate and loped out into the hills, vanishing into the night shadows. Nicci felt an ache in her heart, hoping it wouldn't be the last time she saw the sand panther. She knew how dangerous it would be out there, but Mrra was dangerous, too.

Nicci stared across the valley at the countless campfires of the siege army, blazing bonfires that would have required an entire hillside of trees just to supply the wood. The fires looked like red, winking eyes of hungry spirits, a pack of heart hounds unleashed from the underworld.

Each campfire represented enough enemy warriors to overwhelm a village. If all of these ancient fighters were turned loose to pillage the Old World, they might well conquer the entire continent. Nicci had to contain them here, somehow. She stared for a long moment at the fires, hearing the distant noises of the immeasurably large enemy force.

Mrra roamed free out there now, but as Nicci stood at the gate, she was the one who felt trapped.

Long after midnight, back in her own quarters, Nicci tried to catch a few hours of sleep, knowing she needed the energy. She didn't want to dream, didn't want to think, but as she drifted off, her consciousness flew free and she found herself inside her sand panther's mind.

Mrra was overjoyed to run wild. She had felt so crushed inside the city, and now she bounded along for the sheer joy of it, feeling her forepaws on the crisp grasses, her hind legs pushing her forward. The big cat was meant to be loose in the wilderness, even though she'd been raised by handlers in Ildakar, bred and trained to be a vicious fighter, to kill enemies in the combat arena. Mrra's skin had been branded with countless runes to protect against a magical attack.

What free panther needed to fear magic?

Mrra and the two sister panthers in her first *troka* had broken loose from the chief handler's cages. They had escaped Ildakar and fled across the countryside, roaming aimlessly until they encountered Nicci and her companions near Cliffwall. The three big cats had fought the humans, as they had been trained to do, but Nicci and the others killed her two sister panthers and nearly killed Mrra. The sharing of blood during Nicci's healing had forged the spell bond, making her a new sister panther. Now, Mrra would have it no other way.

Unleashed, she ran into the hills, stalked among the trees, stirred up night birds, smelled animals in the underbrush. She also sensed other arena beasts that had escaped during the revolt in Ildakar, but Mrra didn't attack them. She didn't even hunt for fresh meat, not yet. She was hungry, but more hungry for her freedom.

In spite of her joy, Mrra also understood what Nicci needed. Her sister panther had asked her to prowl around the outskirts of the camp, to observe the huge army so that her sister could see through sharp feline eyes.

In the villa, as Nicci tossed and turned on silken sheets, her blue eyes closed but flickering back and forth, she looked in all directions in her dreams. Mrra and Nicci both saw the magnitude of the threat that Ildakar faced.

CHAPTER 11

In his command headquarters late at night, General Utros lay awake with two naked women pressed against him. Ava and Ruva were motionless, but he knew they weren't asleep. He could feel their skin against his, smooth but cold, harder than the soft feminine curves he was used to touching. His own skin was just as tough, the nerve endings muffled like a voice shouting from a great distance.

Ruva stirred and, through the intangible connection with her twin sister, Ava also shifted. Lying still, with the sorceresses on either side of him, Utros stared up at the crosshatched roof and thought of the one woman he truly wanted, the passions that still stirred in his stony heart. He didn't love these faithful twins, but they gave him what he needed.

Majel had given him so much more.

In his mind, she was far away in the capital city of Orogang with Emperor Kurgan, the man to whom Utros had sworn his loyalty. And though he still felt bound by that oath, Utros was torn by his passions and his dogged insistence on serving both, even if it ripped him apart and destroyed everything.

If the two yaxen herders could be believed, Majel was now

separated from him by much more than distance. He had seen the lovely empress only a few months ago, according to his memories. Was it possible that he and his army had been petrified for centuries? That the beautiful and passionate woman was long dead? He couldn't bear such news, if it was true. He had to know, but here on this broad plain, far from Orogang and the rest of Iron Fang's empire, how could he learn the truth?

If Majel was dead and Emperor Kurgan was no more than the dust of history's bones, what was he fighting for?

Utros locked away those worries in a separate section of his mind, like damming a stream. The trapped thoughts and concerns would flood him unless he found real answers.

Outside the headquarters, he heard the camp stirring. The wooden structure had been raised quickly, using rough-hewn logs and branches. His soldiers had done their tasks well, given their minimal resources. They always served him without question, and Utros never disappointed them either. He was their commander.

On his years-long military march, he'd become accustomed to traveling with a fine tent, a place with furs and hangings, council tables spread with maps and battle plans. He wanted to keep Ava and Ruva content, and now he held the two women in his bed, one beefy arm around each as if to crush them against his body and squeeze their energy into him. They lay together beneath a freshly cured yaxen pelt. It wasn't the same as fine woven blankets or slick sheets from the palace in Orogang, but it was a first step.

The thin mattress was stuffed with dried grasses. Under other circumstances it would have felt prickly and uncom-fortable, but his hardened skin didn't notice such minor things. The smoke from the braziers curled upward, escaping through the gaps in the crisscrossed roof. The dull red glow of burning charcoal and incense bathed the structure in comforting light. The smoke was thick, but Utros could barely smell it. The two sorceresses had added special herbs to the braziers, which sometimes gave him visions and revelations. Now, his dusty lungs seemed dulled to the effects.

But he didn't need visions. Utros had his mind, and he could make plans.

Scouting parties had returned to the great camp with supplies, having ransacked the homes of a few settlers in the hills, woodcutters, a lone prospector, two men with mules bringing a load of goods to Stravera, all of whom had confirmed the information provided by the yaxen herders Boyle and Irma.

Before long, a raiding party would find the large town itself and bring back more vital tools and materials.

His invincible army would make the world tremble. Utros had swept across the land and seized an entire continent in the name of Iron Fang because he had sworn to do so, and the general always kept his promises.

Now he felt like a beggar. His vast army, though still powerful, was little more than a collection of refugees. The soldiers had no tents and nothing to eat, even if they no longer had an appetite. The glorious city of Ildakar stood before them, huge and impregnable, mocking the army with its wealth and its way of life.

Utros had to know the truth of what had happened to his army. He needed to know what he was required to do next, and he had to understand the answers before his countless soldiers began to realize that their commander might be facing doubts.

"I know you're awake," he said aloud. "Both of you."

Ava pulled away from him, propping herself up on an elbow. Ruva held herself against his broad chest, as if trying to reassure him with the pliability of her breasts, nipples that were hard from the lingering effects of the stone spell, not from arousal. She, too, pulled away.

Lying on his back, he continued to speak. "We have to find out what has happened to Ildakar, what's happened to the empire. Whom do we serve now?"

"We serve Iron Fang," said Ruva, "as always."

"But what if Iron Fang is nothing more than a skeleton in a crypt, or a memory in a history book?"

The women remained quiet for a moment before Ava said, "Then you serve yourself, as we have always served you."

"I don't serve myself," Utros snapped. "I am not a petty tyrant. I don't do this for my own aggrandizement."

"You may not, beloved Utros," said Ruva, "but we serve you. We only supported Kurgan because he is the leader you chose to serve. All your soldiers fight for you, not for Iron Fang. You earned their loyalty. You led them to glory. Iron Fang is merely a tick on the ear of a dog, drinking blood and growing bloated."

Utros sat up, tossing the heavy yaxen hide aside. "Kurgan is my emperor. If you spoke such words in Orogang, your tongues would be ripped out and burned on skewers before you."

"We are not in Orogang," said Ava. "You know that this empire was built because of you, not Kurgan."

Ruva said, "The emperor doesn't deserve you, beloved Utros, but my sister and I respect you, so we serve your wishes."

"Cast some spell or show me visions so I can understand my place in the world. I'll fight ruthlessly to defend what I must, but not if I don't know!"

"You already know." Ava slid out of the bed and walked over to the brazier, tossing more dried leaves into the coals so that the smoke thickened. She waved her hands, making the fumes drift toward Utros and her sister. The general caught the sweet tang of the herbs. "The yaxen herders already told you the answers. Don't you believe them?"

Utros sighed. "I don't want to believe them. You say that I'm the heart of this army, but I draw my strength only because I serve my emperor."

And I have betrayed him with his wife . . . the woman I love.

"I may be strong, and I may have led these soldiers to many

victories," he said, "but without my emperor, I am like a door without a hinge. He is my commander."

Ava returned to the bed and sat next to him. She began to caress his chest, while Ruva stroked his back. They touched his cheeks, the smooth skin and the dragon-burn scar.

All he could think of was beautiful Majel with her long black hair, streaked with reddish highlights when the sunshine struck her. Her almond-shaped brown eyes, her tanned skin that was more beautiful than gold, her kisses, her sighs, her moans as he held her, taking her with ferocity in his tent like an animal in heat. And then after that passion was sated, a longer, slower lovemaking as they sang a song with their bodies, a secret song that Emperor Kurgan could never hear. . . .

"Our magic is given to you," said Ava, lying down and draping her leg over his, while Ruva touched his thigh, then wrapped herself around him as well. They were trying to tangle themselves in a knot of bodies and cold flesh. They had painted their smooth, hairless skin with fresh, bright colors again, but he could not see the details in the dimness of the smoky fires.

"We will give you everything, beloved Utros, if we can."

"As you always have," the general said in a soft voice, and then he responded to their touch.

The sisters had given him their devotion, their love, their energy, their faith, since they were teenage girls. They'd been considered oddities, revered in a small mountain town, which was one of the first conquests General Utros had made in expanding Iron Fang's empire. Ava and Ruva had been born even closer than normal twins. Their bodies were fused, their legs melded like two soft candles pressed together.

The babies might have died or been cast out by superstitious villagers, but their father took a terrible chance while they were still infants. As their mother wept in despair, the father had taken his sharpest skinning knife and placed the two connected infant girls on a table. He had cut them apart, hacking through the skin and fused bone that was like an intertwined tree.

He had broken them apart, splitting their fused legs; then he wrapped the wounds that bled and bled. Their wounds became severely infected. The shrieking babies had faltered, becoming sicker and sicker.

Then they had died. The spirits of the two innocent infants went to the underworld and actually faced the Keeper. Their hearts stopped, but for only a few minutes. Somehow the village healer managed to revive them. The father stood there, his face sagging, horrified at what he had done. But the girls lived. They had been snatched away from the Keeper.

But He had touched them.

Though each had a horrific matching scar on her leg, the girls were strong, and they healed. They tested each other. They grew up and learned how to walk and run so that they barely showed even a limp. But they did not hide their scars; they flaunted them, wearing short shifts, growing up aloof and beautiful.

When they were ten, the Keeper claimed the debt they had taken from him by killing both their mother and father in a terrible coughing plague, leaving the odd twins to raise themselves. The village feared Ava and Ruva, but their real magic hadn't manifested until their blood courses came, at the age of thirteen. The young sorceresses lived in the cottage their father had built, and they terrified the villagers. They did no work, but simply claimed whatever food they wished, the clothing they needed, by walking into other houses and rifling through wardrobes and shelves, walking off with what was their due. The townspeople were too frightened to argue with them.

When Utros's armies marched into their village, the soldiers pillaging and ransacking, the town leader begged the twin sorceresses to help. Ava and Ruva merely scoffed at him, then walked through the startled ranks of soldiers and presented themselves before General Utros.

"You need us with you," Ruva had said.

"Why?" Utros had demanded, not understanding who the

twins were, although he had seen the odd sparkle and offset gaze in their faces.

"You'll know, sooner or later."

Utros had indeed taken the twins as his own, though not as lovers. They were too young, and even though they grew to be quite beautiful, he never changed his mind. When he asked Ava and Ruva what he should do with their village, if he should subdue it in the name of Emperor Kurgan, they advised him to make a gesture that could not be misread by other villages in line to be conquered. So he killed all the townspeople and burned the buildings, then spread the word. He'd been a brash young commander then, and the sacrifice of that one town caused fifteen others within a day's ride to surrender immediately to the banner of Iron Fang.

Utros never took credit for his victory, always insisted that Kurgan deserved the power and the glory, which meant that the emperor also received the blame and the fear. Utros moved on, conquering land after land. . . .

"We will help you fight," said Ruva now, whispering close to his face in the dim command structure. "My sister and I know many spells, but for simple information, there is a more straightforward way."

"I know," he said. It had been several days since his army had awakened, and their siege was firmly in place. He remembered when this military force had first arrived at Ildakar. They had just recovered from the disastrous attack of the wild silver dragon they intended to unleash against the city.

Even without the dragon, Utros had brought his ranks to fill the plain and let Ildakar tremble before the unspoken threat for two days before he had marched up to the city gates to demand their surrender. He'd known they wouldn't concede immediately, but he could starve and strangle them over time.

He hadn't expected the wizards of Ildakar to turn his army to stone for centuries.

Those events seemed like only a week ago in his own mind.

"I've made my decision," he said. "We'll demand to speak with their representatives. Our next step depends on how Ildakar responds." He smiled, then reached up to stroke his stiff beard and the patchy scar on his left cheek. "After we talk with them, I will plan how to tear down the city."

CHAPTER 12

The next morning, Nicci awoke refreshed from dreams of running free and wild while also assessing the siege army. Now her thoughts assembled the details of the huge encampment she had seen through Mrra's eyes.

She joined Nathan as he emerged from his own quarters dressed in trim white wizard's robes enhanced with gold stitching on the cuffs and collar. After he had freed himself from his long confinement in the Palace of the Prophets, Nathan Rahl had preferred fine ruffled shirts and tight pants, high boots, wide belts, but on their journey he'd been stripped of his magic for so long, and now that he could use his gift again, he had decided to look like a wizard.

"Shall we solve this problem today, Sorceress?" he said with a quirk of his lips. "Save Ildakar and dispel the enemy army so we can be on our way again?"

Nicci set her jaw as they emerged from under the trellises of sweet-smelling vine flowers. "Yes, that would be a good idea."

She had never shied away from difficult tasks. Even without the threat of the ancient army, Ildakaran society had many raw wounds that needed to heal. Many in Ildakar were selfish and aloof, takers who thought only of their own needs and nothing of the hard work, the blood and sweat of those who supplied them. But she had also met many strong and worthy citizens, including the followers of Mirrormask. Though the rebel leader himself had been a sham, the freed slave Rendell had shown particular wisdom and bravery, and Nicci was also sure that numerous merchants and lesser nobles would be worth preserving. Yes, parts of Ildakar had to be saved.

When she'd led conquests for the Imperial Order, Nicci had viewed Jagang's entire army, from the commanders to the foot soldiers, as *tools,* nothing more. She herself had been raised under the poison philosophy of the Order, blind to the good in people. During her lifetime, Nicci's tragedies and pain had turned her heart to black ice, and when her love for Richard Rahl thawed that ice and helped her see the truth, she herself had become the tool, the weapon that Richard required.

Nicci had felt only satisfaction when she killed Jagang, but that cold determination was tested to its limits when she was forced to murder the innocent girl Thistle so she could obtain the poison she needed to save the world.

That had been a prediction written by the witch woman Red in Nathan's life book. *And the Sorceress must save the world.* The witch woman's other premonition had guided a powerless Nathan over the high mountain pass of Kol Adair to Ildakar, where he had found the heart of a wizard to restore his lost gift.

Nicci had always made her own choices, pursued her own goals, rather than following the capricious winds of prophecy, but she took the life-book pronouncement seriously. *And the Sorceress must save the world.*

In order to win here in Ildakar, she needed to find her heart of black ice again. She would use her skills to save the city and defeat General Utros. The fight would require the resources, the weapons, the magic, and the manpower of the entire city, from powerful wizards down to the common people. She hoped they were willing to pay the cost for their freedom.

Outside the grand villa, the sound of the army hammering on the walls was a monotonous background noise that thrummed through the streets, but Nicci barely noticed it after several days.

When the pounding abruptly stopped, the unexpected silence was as loud as a scream.

Nathan nearly stumbled on the fine gravel path as he walked alongside her. "Dear spirits!" He scanned the skies, gazing past the city to the tiny dots of soldiers on the plain.

Nicci narrowed her eyes, listening to the sudden quiet. "I don't like this."

Nathan forced an unconvincing smile. "Maybe it means Utros has decided to surrender."

"Neither of us is that much of a fool," Nicci said, hurrying toward the wall.

When they reached the towering main gates, High Captain Stuart was barking orders for his sentry soldiers to be ready for an attack, but the ancient soldiers had withdrawn beyond the fallen moats. Stuart rushed over to Nicci and Nathan. "Some sort of signal came from the center of the army. The soldiers stopped their pounding and marched back."

From the high battlements, Nicci peered over the wall, noticing the chipped outer surface of the huge blocks at the base. The endless pounding had marred the stone, gouged divots and small cracks, but the gifted wizards had reinforced the blocks with strengthening spells. At the base of the barrier, she saw smoke stains, pools of oil, scattered boulders, and other missiles that had killed hundreds of the enemy, whose bodies had been hauled away.

Out on the plain, General Utros's army spread apart with eerie coordination, the ranks forming an open path for a single man to ride forward. He sat astride a chalky war mount that plodded forward like a plow horse instead of a charger. The rider wore leather armor with broad shoulder plates, a blocky helmet, and a wide curved sword at his side, but he did not draw it. He rode at a methodical pace up to the enormous gates, where he stopped.

From the high parapet, Nicci looked down. The man was a craggy-faced veteran, an older warrior who exuded power and efficiency. He stared up at them for a long moment while High Captain Stuart and the wall guards muttered, waiting for the representative to say something.

Finally, the scarred veteran raised a gauntleted fist and shouted, "In the name of General Utros and on behalf of the almighty Iron Fang, Emperor Kurgan, we demand to speak with a representative of Ildakar. We will negotiate how much damage your city must suffer before you surrender." He waited.

The wall guards whispered to one another, glancing at Stuart, who in turn waited for Nicci and Nathan. None of the other duma members had yet arrived at the wall.

Nathan furrowed his brow and called down at the man on the horse, "So, you're not General Utros, then? You are just a lackey."

The armored man's expression twisted, then returned to stony frankness. "I am First Commander Enoch. I speak for Utros, and Utros speaks for Emperor Kurgan. We will withdraw our forces so you can send us your negotiator. We guarantee the safety of your representative. The general wishes to be sensible, until you give him reason not to be."

Enoch wheeled his horse around and rode back out to where he disappeared among the countless enemy soldiers.

Without the firm hand of the sovrena or wizard commander, the duma members were disorganized. For centuries under the shroud, their city business had been aimless, but now that they faced a terrible crisis, the council members weren't sure who would make such an important decision, or even who would speak for Ildakar. No one seemed eager to volunteer.

Nicci and Nathan sat among them, impatient. The duma members Elsa, Damon, Quentin, and the half-petrified Lani discussed Utros's ultimatum among themselves. Oron, the newest member of the duma, had the most to say. "We have no choice but to speak with Utros. It's the only way we can get information."

"It's the only way to resolve this," Damon agreed. "What if he offers tolerable terms?"

"But we can't send our most powerful people out there," Quentin said. "What if it's a trick? If General Utros holds us hostage, our city will be that much weaker."

"He gave us his word, promised the safety of our representative," Elsa said. "That army has pounded on our walls for days, but this is the first we've heard from the general. Aren't we obligated to find out what he wants?"

Oron agreed, resting his chin on a bunched fist. "It'll buy us time until we figure out how to drive them off, or how we can all escape."

"Escape?" Nathan said with a snort. "Dear spirits, there must be half a million people in this city. You mean to send them all out, down the bluffs with ropes and ladders, to sail away down the river? That would be impossible."

"Not evacuation," Quentin said. "We were thinking of other alternatives."

Nicci said, "General Utros may know nothing about what happened to him. They just awakened after being turned to stone for centuries. He might not realize how much time has passed."

Lani nodded. "I myself didn't notice any passage of time when I was petrified. Maybe he doesn't know that his emperor is long dead."

"His entire siege is pointless," Elsa said. "Maybe we can make him see that. Will he see reason?"

"He'll be the desperate one. This city has been self-sufficient for a long time, and we can withstand a siege indefinitely, but all those soldiers need to be fed," Quentin pointed out. "Hundreds of thousands of soldiers without supplies. We can just wait until they all starve. We have the advantage here."

Oron laughed, a cold twisted sound. "We should send our best orator. If Utros has no emperor to serve, we can recruit his army for Ildakar."

"Then *we* would have to feed them," Elsa said. "Even if they agreed to cease hostilities, how could the city support countless thousands more people?"

"It was not a serious suggestion," Damon said.

Nathan wore a puzzled look. "No, that's an important point. It's been days already. Surely, they haven't eaten since they awakened. There should be panic, mass desertions, yet they seem well disciplined. How can there be hundreds of thousands of soldiers without food or shelter?"

Lani had a confused expression of her own. "I haven't felt the need to eat or drink since I awakened." She touched her chalky skin. "Part of the spell still lingers. Maybe they don't need food."

"If that's true, they can maintain the siege forever," Nicci said.

Damon groaned. "I wish we could simply raise the shroud again and go about our business as before, when Ildakar was at peace."

"Ildakar was never at peace," Nathan muttered. "You just didn't see it."

Nicci pulled the conversation back to the point. "Once Utros knows that Iron Fang is long dead, that the empire itself has crumbled, he should realize his siege serves no purpose. Someone should be able to convince him of this."

"Who would go out there and tell him?" Quentin asked. "I certainly won't volunteer. I don't trust those bloodthirsty soldiers not to kill our representative and launch the severed head over our walls."

"Why not send Thora to do it?" Damon asked. "Let her take the risk. She insists she only wants the best for Ildakar, and she's expendable."

This provoked loud, angry muttering. "We cannot trust her," Lani said, with surprising venom. "Not at all."

Nicci hardened her voice, disappointed in them. "You are the members of the duma. Will none of you go and face General Utros for the sake of your city? You will not walk out there and parley with your greatest enemy?"

Elsa sighed and seemed to be deep in thought. Damon and Quentin looked to Oron, as if expecting the new duma member to accept the challenge, but he merely picked at his fingernails with a small dagger.

"Enough of this foolishness," Nicci said. She had walked among enemy armies before, had seen the worst the Imperial Order could do. "It must be done." She glanced at Nathan. "Will you accompany me, Wizard? You and I can speak for Lord Rahl as well."

"Of course," he said with a wistful smile. "I spent centuries studying history. If nothing else, I'd be delighted to meet the legendary General Utros himself."

CHAPTER 13

The gates of Ildakar opened with a slow, grinding groan. All the locking spells and protective wards had been removed by the wizards working together to release their defenses. The towering slabs of reinforced wood began to creak apart on mammoth hinges.

Nicci's blond hair flowed loose in the breeze that stole through the widening gap. Her clean black dress fit her form perfectly. Nathan was beside her, an equally striking figure, with his pale hair brushed to a silky luster and his gold-trimmed white wizard's robes that made him look powerful and imposing.

The thirty-foot-tall gates of Ildakar weighed innumerable tons. They were primarily an architectural flourish, kept open only during times of complete peace and security. "We could have left through the merchants' door," Nicci said, glancing at the much smaller entrance at the bottom of the great gates.

"But far less impressive," Nathan said, "and this is a time when we need to impress them. We are not skulking about like mice, ready to scurry back into a hole. This is Ildakar, and I want to show General Utros that we are worthy of its reputation. We're not afraid."

When the doors swung wide with ponderous majesty, Nicci gazed across the expansive plain. Countless enemy soldiers waited for them at a safe distance from the wall, having retreated to give the emissaries freedom to leave the city without fear of a surprise ambush.

Nathan stroked his cleanly shaven chin. "I've studied General Utros a great deal, and he is an honorable, respected man. He'll abide by the terms he offered." His lips quirked in a smile. "I'm anxious to meet a man who stepped right out of the history scrolls. I have many questions about the Midwar, about Iron Fang, about his unique battle tactics that brought him victory after victory." Before stepping forward, he looked through the gate at the giant army waiting for them. "But I suppose that discussion will have to wait until such time as his troops aren't trying to tear down the city and destroy us all."

"We'll inform the general how the world has changed since he and all his people were turned to stone." Nicci lifted her chin. "Once he knows the full story, and his changed situation, if he's such a great commander he may embrace the new D'Haran Empire. If he devotes his military genius to the service of Lord Rahl, then Utros will have a true purpose to serve, and we will have an incomparable ally."

Nathan chuckled. "Or they could be too angry to listen to reason, knowing they've been stone for centuries and have lost everything from their past."

"That's also a possibility," Nicci said.

Nathan's expression darkened. "I have no doubt Utros will be greatly disturbed to learn what happened to the Empress Majel. She was his lover and . . . it didn't end well for her."

Bannon hurried up behind them, anxious, his long ginger hair bound with a strip of leather. He wore a loose brown Ildakaran shirt, dark trousers, fresh boots. "I'm coming with you, too. I'll protect you if the general's soldiers try any treachery."

At another time, Nicci would have scoffed at the young man's offer, but Bannon had proven his bravery before, although his exuberance and naïveté could sometimes be problematic. Still, his presence would not gain them any additional safety.

As gently as he could, Nathan replied, "The two of us will be sufficient, my boy. We're counting on you to protect the city of Ildakar if we should fail."

Though Bannon obviously didn't believe him, he stepped back with a solemn nod. The duma members and curious citizens of Ildakar gathered around watching, hopeful, but letting Nicci and Nathan take the risks.

When the doors had opened to their full extent, she and Nathan set off beyond the city walls and headed toward the battlefield. Nicci looked ahead at the swarms of soldiers separated into ordered regiments. Tens of thousands of soldiers lined themselves up like an honor guard, creating a clear path to the general's command headquarters.

The two of them walked side by side at a confident pace. Lining the path, the ancient warriors stood shoulder-to-shoulder. Some held new makeshift banners that fluttered in the breezes, displaying Kurgan's flame symbol. The enemy soldiers stared straight ahead with implacable expressions, as if they had become statues again. Nicci assessed their helmets, their leather vests covered with metal plates, round bosses, flared shoulder plates. Each face had a dusty gray complexion, indicating that not all of the stone spell had faded away. She knew these men would be tough to kill.

When the first one, Ulrich, had accidentally awakened, she wished the duma had spent more time studying his hardened skin to discover weaknesses, but the nobles had been eager to throw him into the combat arena. It was just another one of the duma's demonstrably bad decisions.

Nathan muttered, "These look like very worthy fighters."

"Our only concern is General Utros. If we can change his mind, then we won't need to worry about the rest of his army."

The two reluctant emissaries walked along the clear path, not hurrying. Nicci found the eerie silence of the gigantic army noteworthy. The army camps of the Imperial Order had been a ruckus of constant activity—chopping wood and grinding steel, clanging practice swords, the screams of captives, the coarse laughter of gambling men, shouted orders from lieutenants and captains. The army of Utros seemed ominously subdued.

They approached a wooden building constructed of rough-hewn logs decorated with paints, makeshift fabric banners, scavenged materials, since the army's possessions and equipment had deteriorated over the centuries.

Four guards stood outside the door of the headquarters, and a tall, weathered man whom Nicci recognized as First Commander Enoch emerged from the structure. "The general is ready to see you," Enoch said.

Nicci replied, "We're eager to resolve this matter, so he can take his army and be on his way."

The battle-scarred veteran looked from Nathan to Nicci. "You are the leaders of Ildakar? The wizard commander and the sovrena?"

Nathan chuckled. "No, not at all. The city's leadership has changed since your last encounter."

"We are visitors to Ildakar, but your siege has trapped us here," Nicci said in a crisp voice. "We've come to speak for the city, as neutral representatives." She looked past Enoch into the headquarters. "Are we supposed to discuss terms with you, or with General Utros himself?"

Enoch gestured them inside. With the wind blowing their hair around them, Nicci and Nathan entered the crude but sturdy structure, which was lit by open windows. Pungent smoke wafted from braziers on either side of the main room.

General Utros sat stiff-backed in a sturdy wooden chair at a table. He was a substantial man with broad shoulders and a powerful chest. He had a neatly trimmed gray-brown beard, except for a waxy patch on his left cheek, where a smooth scar showed the remnants of a serious burn.

On a rough bench beside him sat two striking women in

gossamer gowns that clung to their curves. They were obviously twins, their heads entirely shaved, their skin painted. Nicci could sense the gift emanating from them and realized the twins were sorceresses.

She and Nathan stopped before the table and pointedly waited for the general to speak first. Utros remained in his chair, but gave them his full attention. "I command the army that will conquer Ildakar. Your fate depends on how reasonable the city can be."

Nicci ignored the twin women and spoke only to the general. "We've heard that you are a wise man, General Utros. Let us see you prove your wisdom. Do you even know what's happened to you and your army? How much time has passed? What was the fate of Emperor Kurgan and Empress Majel?"

The general seemed angry, leaning forward slightly. "I have heard wildly impossible stories."

Nathan intervened, speaking in a conciliatory voice. "Now, we haven't even finished introductions yet! This is the sorceress Nicci, and I am the wizard Nathan Rahl. I was once a powerful prophet, too, but prophecy is entirely gone now." He sighed and brushed down the front of his white robes. "I'm not sure you knew that. So much has changed in the world. . . ." He gestured, acknowledging the two sorceresses. "As you will come to see, the underpinnings of magic are fundamentally altered. Before we begin, let me tell you about the state of the world. There's much you need to know before you can make a wise decision on what to do with your army."

Utros frowned with a mixture of skepticism and anger.

Nathan placed his hands together and spoke as if he were lecturing to gathered students. "Over the centuries I've fancied myself something of a historian, so I can fill in the gaps for you. And yes, I know much about you, General Utros. Your exploits are legendary. As you've probably guessed, your entire army was petrified by a spell from Ildakar. Your ranks stood as stone figures exposed to the elements for fifteen hundred years."

He paused to let the number sink in. "I'm afraid everything you knew is gone, General. Kurgan's empire is dust."

The two smooth-skinned sorceresses muttered to each other. Utros grew stern and troubled, leaning forward in his sturdy chair. "So we have heard, but the idea is preposterous. We've seen no proof."

"What more proof do you need?" Nicci interrupted in a firm voice. "Where are your tents? Your camp? Your supplies? Everything disintegrated with the passage of time. Centuries have gone by, and history has left you behind. All that you knew has changed." She hardened her expression. "Surely you realize your bodies have a lingering infusion of stone, because the spell hasn't entirely worn off. Accept what you know is true."

As Utros growled, Nathan intervened again, folding his hands together with a small, polite bow. "If I may, Sorceress? Your own conquests are legendary, General. Speaking as a scholar, I'm impressed to talk with such an imposing personage. You are seen as a seminal figure in military history, until you and your army disappeared. Now we know what happened to you. Nevertheless, your battlefield tactics and your conquests have been studied for more than a thousand years."

Utros remained determined. "I'm not interested in your flattery, Wizard. I conquered those lands for my emperor. I serve Iron Fang, and he ordered me to seize Ildakar. I intend to do so. I would never betray him."

Nicci scoffed. "Oh? Now that's an interesting comment, considering you took his wife as your lover. Wasn't that a betrayal?"

Utros shot to his feet, looming before them in his half-stone body. "That was different! Majel loved me." His eyes flicked back and forth, a gray gaze that struck Nicci, then went back to Nathan. "How can you even know this? It is impossible."

Nathan explained, "We know because *history* knows, dear general, just as history knows everything. All was revealed as Kurgan's empire crumbled. You and Empress Majel weren't as discreet as you thought with your affair, and this is a terrible story that was told to students for centuries. After conquering much of the Old World, your army marched away from Orogang, ordered by Iron Fang to capture Ildakar. But then you and your armies vanished, as did Ildakar itself. The complete disappearance of such a vast army was a mystery that historians have debated for centuries."

Utros knotted his hands as he gripped the edge of the rough-hewn table. On one corner rested his imposing helmet, adorned with curved bull horns. "But what about my emperor? And . . . Majel? What do you think you know? What happened to her? And to the empire?"

Nathan sniffed. "Alas, I'm afraid that without your military to hold it together, Kurgan's empire crumbled. It didn't last a decade after you were gone. The man you served, and betrayed, is long dead."

Nicci spoke into the silence. "There is a new emperor now, a worthy master for you to serve. His name is Richard Rahl, and we are working to consolidate these lands under the rules of fairness and freedom. That's why Nathan and I came to Ildakar, only to find ourselves caught in this unnecessary conflict. Lord Rahl is a new, worthy master for a great and honorable military leader like yourself. We hope you and your army will agree to serve him."

"I serve Emperor Kurgan," Utros insisted.

"And we serve you, General Utros," said the two sorceresses in strange harmony, shifting on their bench.

He glanced at them. "These are Ava and Ruva, my advisors and powerful sorceresses. We don't fear any magic Ildakar brings against us."

"What you seem to fear is the truth," Nicci said. "Emperor Kurgan is gone, nearly forgotten. Join the D'Haran Empire as one of Lord Rahl's greatest generals. You no longer need to conquer Ildakar."

"I need to conquer Ildakar, because I swore to do so," Utros said stubbornly. "Kurgan is my emperor, not this upstart Lord Rahl, who is nothing more than a name to me."

"I assure you, Lord Rahl is much more than a name," Nicci said with a hint of threat in her tone. "And he is alive and powerful, unlike Iron Fang and your murdered lover."

Incensed, Utros said, "Murdered? How did she . . . they die? What happened to them?"

"It didn't end well, I'm afraid." Nathan continued telling his story. "Iron Fang's own people rose up and overthrew him. The mobs killed him because of what he did to . . ." He hesitated. "It's rather unpleasant, General. Are you sure you want to hear the full details?"

"What did Kurgan do?" Utros demanded. Then the lines on his face softened. "What of Majel?"

"The emperor executed her," Nicci said, using the words like a barbed lash. "When Kurgan discovered Majel's love for you, he skinned her alive in public. Then while she slowly died, dripping blood in the city square of Orogang, he placed flesh beetles on her body, and they burrowed inside her. I understand she screamed for days."

"No!" Utros cried. "Emperor Kurgan wouldn't . . ." His words trailed off as he realized that the story sounded all too probable.

"That is the man to whom you swear your loyalty," Nicci reminded him.

"The story is true, I'm afraid," Nathan said. "If you knew Emperor Kurgan as you say you do, then you'll believe me. Was he not violent and mercurial? What do you think he would have done once he found out about Majel's betrayal? With his bravest general?"

"It wasn't a betrayal!" Utros cried in a hoarse voice. "She still loved him, but she also loved me. I gave her what her husband could not, and I also gave the emperor what he could not achieve on his own. I loved her, but remained loyal to him."

"History has already been written, General," Nathan said.

"Both Majel and Kurgan are spirits now, and the veil has been permanently sealed. No spirits can ever return from the underworld." He explained Richard's star shift and how he had ended prophecy and healed the breach forever.

Utros bunched his fists into boulders, but he somehow contained his rage. "I don't believe you."

"You know in your heart that we're not lying to you," Nathan said. "How else do you explain what you see and feel?"

The sorceresses rose from their bench. One of the women said, "Perhaps we'll hold these two, beloved Utros, and peel the truth from them, just to be sure."

"You could try." Nicci returned their glare. "But I wouldn't recommend it."

Nathan said, "You promised us safe passage, General. Are the legends not true about your honor?"

"Go from here!" Utros shouted. "Return to your city walls, while I consider how best to tear them down. I will conquer Ildakar, as I swore to do. It doesn't matter if Emperor Kurgan is gone. I have my mission, and I must succeed. That's all I need to know." He pounded a fist on his table hard enough that the fresh wood splintered. His horned helmet slid to the ground. "Go!"

Nicci and Nathan withdrew as First Commander Enoch pushed them out into the open air again. The sudden gust of wind caught Nicci's long blond hair. Thousands of soldiers framed the way for them to return to the gates of Ildakar.

CHAPTER 14

Grieve observed from the high wall of the Bastion, pleased by the progress.

Captain Kor's raiding vessels took only four days to reprovision for the raid against Renda Bay, and soon they were ready to launch from the main island, joined by three more serpent ships. Kor's previous expedition to Ildakar was secretly to identify the vulnerabilities of the great city for possible invasion.

This time, Kor had a more standard Norukai mission, and King Grieve had different expectations. The raiders would sweep into the defiant fishing village, capture as many slaves as they could, and fill their ships with walking meat to be sold at various markets. Captains Kor, Lars, and Yorik would kill any captives that wouldn't fit on the boats, and then the rest of Renda Bay would burn. It would be a profound lesson to the rest of the world.

For the raid, Kor took several hundred seasoned Norukai warriors, scarred muscular men and brutish dangerous women, but they needed the rest of the room on the ships for the captives they would take.

After the misty storm passed, Grieve drew a deep breath

on the high open battlements, studying the fanged mouth of the harbor. The six serpent ships were a swirl of activity as the raiders piled aboard. The broad-beamed ships with long oars and distinctive midnight-blue sails would strike fear along the coast. Each ship's prow bore a ferocious carving of the serpent god, guiding the raiders to victory.

Watching the expedition prepare to depart, Grieve longed to go on a raid again himself. He remembered the ecstatic younger days when King Stern had sent him out to toughen him, to temper him with blood, or let him die on the battlefield if he wasn't good enough. That was the fate of failures.

Salty wind whipped around the Bastion's rooftop, but the sky was a bright blue, the waters relatively calm. Though Chalk liked to remain inside by the fire, today's sunlight was bright enough that the pale-skinned shaman joined him, hopping about and burning energy to keep himself warm.

"Renda Bay, Renda Bay!" he said. "Don't think about Renda Bay."

"Why shouldn't I? Kor will destroy the town, then we never need worry about them again."

Grieve reached into his yawning mouth, scratched out a morsel of the yaxen meat he'd eaten for his midday meal. Grieve liked the taste much more than tiresome fish or gristly goat. Yet another reason that he needed to conquer Ildakar.

"Renda Bay, Renda Bay!" Chalk rubbed his hands together as he looked over the battlement, gaping down at the six serpent ships tied up to the docks far below. The shaman was so awkward and reckless that he nearly fell over the edge, but he kept himself in place with a scrawny arm. "The war is with Ildakar, my Grieve, King Grieve! They'll all grieve! Ildakar, not Renda Bay."

"Kor will destroy Renda Bay and come back in time for the war. We are still building our ships."

"Renda Bay!" Sounding like a crow, Chalk shook his scarred head and scuttled backward without speaking further. The skin of his shoulders, his arms, his back was pockmarked from the bites of hungry razorfish.

The Norukai king heeded Chalk's visions, but the shaman was also eccentric, damaged. Patchy hair grew in bristly clumps around his head, wherever the follicles could poke through the scar tissue. Chalk swiped his knuckles across drool that leaked from his damaged lip. He stood in the sunlight and turned his face to the sky, bathing his bare skin in the warmth.

Even though the terrifying past ordeal had given Chalk his ability to see visions, Grieve still resented his father for allowing it. Grieve had been too young then to defy King Stern, and he had barely known Chalk, certainly not well enough to give his life to save the strange creature. After pulling the albino from the pool filled with razorfish, young Grieve had wrapped the torn and mutilated boy in sailcloth and tended him.

The other Norukai had assumed the freak was dead, but young Grieve rowed him across the inlet to a small neighboring island, little more than a hummock of rocks and grasses that poked like a stump above the waves. That was where the blind old fish woman kept her cottage, a woman whom many Norukai used as a healer, especially when their slashed mouths grew infected after the ritual cutting. The old woman was an expert in scars.

Grieve took Chalk to her and, using all the power of command he had learned from his father, told the old woman to save the boy. Without arguing, she coated Chalk's torn skin with greasy, foul-smelling ointments made from guano and fish liver, and she wrapped the albino with strips of cloth, encasing the entire body like a cocoon.

Grieve couldn't let King Stern or any other Norukai know that he tried to save the misfit they had meant to sacrifice. He secretly rowed over to the fish woman's island every day and watched Chalk recover. Finally, when the scarred pale boy was conscious enough to speak, he gazed at Grieve with his oddly shifted eyes. "Don't kill your father yet," Chalk said, out of context, speaking from nowhere. "Let me tell you when it's time. I will know."

Grieve responded with only silence, staring at the blind fish woman, who pretended not to have heard. Until then, Grieve had never even considered killing his father. The idea of ruling the Norukai islands had felt so far in the future, but Chalk seemed absolutely certain. Grieve had felt gooseflesh crawl up his back and arms. He *believed* that Chalk would know and would tell him.

And he had.

Over the years he had visited the hundred main islands that formed the Norukai archipelago, as well as the coastline that the raiders pillaged and stripped of its resources. They forced slaves to cut down the forests, leaving the hillsides bare after seizing the wood, and they used slaves to mine in the mountains for iron, gold, and silver. But Grieve had always wanted more. Now, he intended to get it.

He agreed with the shaman's prediction and Captain Kor's assessment of Ildakar. If they took over the legendary city, that would plunge a knife through the heart of the Old World. From there, the Norukai could spread in all directions, up and down the Killraven River, blockade the estuary, swarm up the coast all the way to Tanimura and beyond.

Thousands of years ago, the Norukai tribes had been wild and fierce. They fought in countless tribal wars, leaving wreckage and sorrow in their wake. But while they ravaged the land, the Norukai were not organized enough to be invincible. When Sulachan's powerful empire rose, the tribes were hunted down because they proved to be uncontrollable. When they refused to swear loyalty to Sulachan, the emperor ordered the extinction of the entire people. His armies drove the Norukai to the sea, and they retreated to countless defensible islands. The death toll on both sides was immense.

In the millennia since, the Norukai grew powerful again and took their slow revenge. But it was too slow.

Such impatience was one of the reasons that convinced Grieve to overthrow King Stern. And now his father's skull, picked clean by the fishes, rested as a centerpiece in Chalk's glass-walled tank in the throne room where he kept his favorite specimens.

Grieve and Chalk had become friends, and the albino shaman was devoted to his savior. Grieve had slain nine rude Norukai warriors who made the mistake of laughing at the strange young man, and after that, the other Norukai left Chalk alone, showing a grudging respect for Grieve, if not the odd shaman.

The king insisted on leaving Chalk behind when he went out on raids, even though he valued the shaman's visions. Chalk was not a fighter, and Grieve knew that sometimes the walking meat could become violent. Whenever Grieve came home scarred with battle wounds, his friend was overjoyed to see him safe.

Once, before a typical raid, the shaman was inexplicably terrified. Grieve intended to accompany four ships south to raid a mining village they had not preyed upon for fifteen years. The children they'd left alive would be grown up now, the population fat and lazy. It should have been a simple raid, but Chalk begged Grieve to stay home. He wouldn't explain why, but he grew more frantic, his jagged voice shrill. "Don't go, don't go!"

Grieve would never admit he was afraid, but Chalk's insistence chilled him. The other Norukai were puzzled as to why he would back out of the raid, but he owed them no explanation. When one brutish female warrior, Atta, laughed too loud and pressed too hard, Grieve broke her nose and shattered her cheekbone, injuring her so severely that she had to stay home from the raid as well.

Grieve learned later of a tremendous storm that had swamped the raiding expedition. Three of the ships were sunk outright, and the last one attempted to limp home, only to be set upon by vicious selka. The undersea creatures tore the vessel apart, and only three survivors were found in the wreckage. If Grieve had gone along on the raid, he would have died.

From that point on, he always listened to Chalk, even if he didn't understand his mysterious predictions.

Now, in the harbor below, iron bells rang out, the clangor ricocheting along the cliffs louder than the roar of the ocean and the whistle of the wind. The six serpent ships set their dark sails and engaged their weather spells to catch the wind. Muscular Norukai manned the oars to drive the vessels like knives out of the narrow, protected harbor. The iron bells continued to ring.

"Renda Bay, Renda Bay!" Chalk scuttled up to him again. "Plan for Ildakar, and the whole world, my Grieve, King Grieve! They'll all grieve."

"I'm building my fleet," he said. "We won't invade until our fighters are ready. Our navy will be like a school of sharks."

As Kor's raiding vessels sailed away from the main island, Grieve shaded his eyes and gazed across the water to the misty hummocks of other islands dotting the sea, with barely navigable passageways through the reefs. On the leeward side of the islands, long docks had been built where more ships were being constructed, in addition to all the serpent ships that already existed. Grieve had ordered the nearest mainland stripped of lumber, the tallest trees seized for masts, with other logs to be sawn into hull planks. Ribs curved along the keels, growing into fearsome serpent ships, dozens and dozens of them.

Each island had its own master wood carver, and skilled artisans used knives and chisels to fashion a distinctive figurehead, a unique representation of the serpent god for the bow of each ship, one great vessel for every main island. Thirty new warships had already been completed in the past two weeks, with fifty more under construction and dozens more planned. From the top of the Bastion, Grieve heard the distant hum of activity as Norukai shipbuilders took advantage of the good weather to make swift progress.

King Stern had taken far too long to launch his war against the mainland, and young Grieve had lost patience. When Chalk told him it was time, Grieve hadn't hesitated. He had challenged and killed his father. Stern hadn't led the Norukai to the glory they deserved, but Grieve would.

Now, as he surveyed his extensive, growing navy across the water, he knew it was only a matter of time.

"They'll all grieve," he muttered to himself, and Chalk grinned.

CHAPTER 15

I nside his headquarters structure, General Utros brooded in
darkness, wrestling with disbelief and dread certainty. The
sun fell behind the western hills in the direction of Kol Adair,
but even before darkness gathered, Utros pulled the shutters
closed. Inside the dim, stuffy building, Ava and Ruva built up
the hot coals in the braziers, filling the shadows with orange
fire, and then acrid herbs. The smoke that swirled around the
enclosed room had a bitter smell, but not as bitter as what
Utros had learned.

With so many small kingdoms and principalities in turmoil
after his armies smashed them, news would have taken a long
time to travel across the Old World. Could it be that Utros had
conquered the continent, crossed over the mountain passes and
placed Ildakar under siege, in the name of an empire that had
already crumbled? How could history be so cruel? How could
time have abandoned him after so many unparalleled triumphs?

And yet, in his heart, he believed what Nathan and Nicci
had told him. He could not deny the evidence.

For now, with the door and windows closed, with guards
stationed outside so that no subcommander would enter with

a report, Utros kept only the sorceresses with him, but even their powerful magic could not drive away his doubts.

Iron Fang was truly gone, his empire crumbled into dust by the march of time. Empress Majel, beautiful Majel, was also dead in the most horrible way imaginable. Utros would have mourned his beloved in any case, but to know that her own husband had flayed the skin from her creamy shoulders, her rounded breasts, her flat stomach, her smooth thighs . . .

Utros squeezed his eyes shut, picturing Majel's classically beautiful face, and those shimmering dark eyes that had gazed on him with so much love and forbidden passion. When they were together, she had felt such joy to be held in the arms of someone who wanted to love her, rather than possess her.

And then she'd been killed by the man she married, killed by the man to whom Utros had sworn his loyalty.

He was also the man Utros and Majel had both betrayed.

"Can it be true?" he asked aloud, looking at Ava and Ruva. He seemed to be pleading with the sorceresses to tell him otherwise.

The sisters had freshly painted faces, their cheeks swirled with scarlet and yellow, their necks adorned with a smear of indigo, outlined in crimson. "How can it be false?" Ava said. "You feel it, beloved Utros. You know you do."

Ruva added, "I could not cast a spell to verify the truth when the emissaries were here, but I saw no doubt or deceit in their eyes."

Ava took a step closer. "Emperor Kurgan is certainly gone, but our loyalty is not. You are, and have always been, our leader. Those hundreds of thousands of soldiers follow your commands, no matter who is emperor."

"As I follow my emperor's commands," Utros said, struggling with his own loyalty. "When we departed from Orogang, I swore to complete my mission, and I did not need to receive any further instructions from Iron Fang. Even with this damnable stone spell, how is anything changed, just because more time has passed? I still have to conquer Ildakar."

"The city must fall, if that is what you need," Ava added. "Your soldiers will do what they swore to do. For you."

Ruva's voice picked up so swiftly that the twins seemed to speak the same thoughts. "And after Ildakar falls, you can set yourself up as its military leader, a new ruler for a modern empire."

Utros was troubled by the thought. "No, that would make me feel an even greater traitor." The image of Majel flashed before his eyes, and he set it gently aside in a different part of his mind. "I am a military man, not a power-hungry despot. I don't do this for me."

"But your army needs a leader," Ruva said. "Command them. Do what you know you must."

"Perhaps you're right." He wrestled with his fists, knotted his fingers, twisted his arms, trying to limber up his stiffened skin. "I am a hunter, and I have my eyes on the game I intend to kill. Before I worry about how I'll preserve the meat for winter and distribute it among the storehouses, first I must kill the prey."

"Ildakar," said the women in unison.

Utros closed his eyes, blocking them out, setting aside all distractions. Ava and Ruva likely thought he was making military plans in his well-ordered mind, mentally positioning groups of soldiers, dispatching huge companies in different directions to overwhelm the surrounding lands. His forces could bottle up Ildakar and press upon the walls, which would perpetuate the terror inside the city, even if Ildakar's magic-enhanced barriers held against the attack.

But Utros couldn't stop thinking about Majel. His stony expression masked his disgust at how she had died, so much blood and pain. He should have been there with her. He should have saved her, but he couldn't imagine how their love had been exposed. What had he and Majel done wrong? They had been so careful! What was their mistake?

Though he longed to write his thoughts every day, he had sent Majel only a very few letters, which he asked her to burn as soon as she read them. Even if she did keep them, who would dare rummage through the private possessions of an empress? And no courier would break the seal to read the letters.

But what if Iron Fang had questioned why a military courier would bear a secret sealed message from his general to his wife? Had Kurgan intercepted and read one of his letters? The courier was sworn to deliver it only to its intended recipient, but would a courier defy a direct order from his emperor? No.

Utros knew his ruler all too well. Kurgan was the man who sat upon the throne in Orogang, but he was capricious and reckless. What Nicci and Nathan had said about how history viewed Iron Fang was correct. Emperor Kurgan had achieved greatness only because of the victories and wise leadership of his greatest military leader. *Utros* had conquered the Old World, and Iron Fang had been left to rule it, despite his inability to administer such a vast realm.

Perhaps Kurgan had understood that himself. Maybe he'd felt inadequate, jealous of his talented general. He would have realized in his heart that the victories belonged to Utros, and his army and his citizens knew that also. When the volatile ruler discovered he was an inadequate lover as well as leader, Kurgan would not have been able to endure it. It was another victory General Utros had won over him. Iron Fang would have exacted his revenge on someone weaker than he, a person whom Utros loved. *Majel.*

Yes, he could very well believe Kurgan had skinned his own wife alive, then fed her still-living body to flesh beetles.

Utros winced, struggling to bear the vivid portrait his fears painted for him. Had Majel cried out his name, holding on to her love for him even as her body was torn apart? Or had she begged her vile husband for forgiveness, denouncing her betrayal and swearing her loyalty to him again? It would have done her no good.

Utros knew the clash of honor and need in her soul. He himself could barely stand the constant tug of war between his loyalties. He had made a sacred vow to serve Emperor Kurgan, and that was the core of his being, and yet his heart had gone over to Majel. How could he reconcile that? Loyalty or love? So long as Kurgan hadn't learned of their passion for each other, Utros was able to compartmentalize his duty to Iron Fang as separate from his love for Majel.

But now, if his beloved was murdered and their affair revealed, and if the very empire had fallen, how could Utros balance anything? What was his reason to exist? What about his orders, his mission to bring down Ildakar?

He squeezed his eyes closed and felt the tears burn there. He remained deep in thought until he purged the emotions, turned them into stone so that they crumbled into dust within his heart.

Finally, he opened his eyes to find Ava and Ruva waiting intensely, their eyes locked on his face. He couldn't even hear them breathe.

Utros said, "We still have to bring down Ildakar. I must complete my orders." He thought about how he had challenged the legendary city fifteen centuries ago. "The wizards of Ildakar were very powerful once, but if the stone spell has faded, then we know their magic is weaker than it was before." He narrowed his eyes at them. "And yours is still strong, I hope."

Ava and Ruva nodded. "We have the gift as before, and now we are enhanced with the strength of stone, as well as flesh and blood. That makes us more powerful."

Ruva added, "We know secrets that others don't." Outside the headquarters, twilight thickened, but the brazier light remained a dull, throbbing orange. "Nicci and Nathan may have inadvertently left something behind, something we can use against them," Ava said.

Her twin smiled. "Yes, they were not careful. They don't suspect the power that resides in every scrap of themselves. But we do."

Before the two representatives had arrived for the parley, the sorceresses had tended to each other, using a knife to scrape their eyebrows, scalps, arms and legs, every patch of skin, removing the tiniest bit of hair, which they burned in the braziers. Then they clipped their nails, also feeding each bit to the fire. They had made sure that not the slightest speck of their bodies could be found by an enemy.

But Nicci and Nathan were careless.

Ava and Ruva intensely scoured every place where the sorceress and the wizard had stood. The women crawled about, scanning the rugs on the floor, the edge of the door, any place the two visitors had touched. Utros didn't ask why. They were searching for something.

Ava combed her fingers over the rough wood of the doorframe, squinting in the light of the braziers. Then, with a cry of triumph, she produced a single golden hair caught on a splinter in the wood and snapped off. Their faces filled with delight and anticipation, the two sorceresses inspected the fine yellow strand, which obviously belonged to Nicci.

"Now we have what we need." Ruva's eyes shone.

"Nicci may be a powerful opponent with great magic of her own," Ava said. "But she is a fool to leave us a weapon such as this. My sister and I would never make such a terrible mistake."

Holding the strand, Ruva carried it close to the brazier so the ruddy light sparkled along its delicate length. The hair looked as fine and ephemeral as a spiderweb. She dangled it over the glowing coals, and her sister bent close, both of them looking hungrily at the single hair.

Utros could sense the magic building between them. Though he didn't have the gift himself, he had watched the twins perform for him before. They would not let him down.

Ava lifted the strand high. "We have a day or two of preparations to make, but with this single golden hair, we can work great magic. And we can target Nicci."

CHAPTER 16

N ow that Nathan had looked General Utros in the eye, he realized the ancient commander would never withdraw his siege. He had seen the determination in the legendary leader's eyes and his refusal to give up. With everything else lost to him, the siege was all Utros had left.

After Ildakar closed the gates and sealed itself tight again, the duma would spend days debating the reports he and Nicci had brought. Nathan knew in his heart that the city needed some other means to fight back. No straightforward clash was going to defeat the gigantic army.

"We have to find another way out of this siege, my dear," he said to Elsa as they walked together the following day. "And considering the legendary glory of Ildakar, I'm sure its gifted citizens can come up with unexpected magic. It might not be another petrification spell, but surely they can offer something."

"Oh, we will." Elsa was a handsome woman with a smooth face, a little too broad to be delicate. Her warm brown eyes were filled with intelligence and humor as well as patience, and she had certainly been patient with Nathan, especially when he couldn't use his gift. She had helped nurse him back to health after Fleshmancer Andre replaced his flawed heart with that of the dying Chief Handler Ivan. Nathan felt a twinge in his chest, a flare of pain along the scar. *Thump, thump. Thump, thump.* But the new heart was strong, his gift was restored, and Nathan was a wizard again.

"When Utros first came against us with his army, the wizards experimented with many types of magic," Elsa said. "They didn't fear the effects of their power and paid little heed to the consequences. They wanted to protect Ildakar, no matter the cost."

The two of them walked along the edge of the bluff that dropped in a sheer cliff to the river below. The uneven rock face was dotted with a succession of platforms and walkways that led into tunnels for supplies brought up from the river. She gestured farther downstream, toward the tangled swamps that infested the land to the south. "Look there, the ancient wizards flooded the river valley and turned it into a deadly swamp."

Elsa wore a purple silk robe, which was comfortable rather than extravagant. Even as a duma member, she wasn't concerned with the pomp and finery of her position. She had always been considerate, trying to strengthen the society of Ildakar, keeping others content. She had owned household slaves, but treated them well. She even purchased extra servants she didn't really need, just to keep them from the combat pits or other reprehensible jobs.

After Mirrormask's uprising, Elsa had spoken to her restless household slaves, riled up by the mob mentality sweeping through Ildakar. That night, Elsa herself had been covered with dust, ash, and blood from fighting alongside Nathan and Nicci to defeat the cruel sovrena. She had told her own servants they could go where they wished, but she hoped they would stay here in their home. Most of them had remained.

Knowing Elsa's gift, Nathan asked, "Is there any way we can use your transference magic to defend ourselves? Or to attack General Utros?"

"It's always possible." She stroked her chin in an unconscious imitation of his mannerism. He found it endearing. "I could put an anchor rune here in Ildakar, but in order to work the transference magic, the complementary symbol has to be at the target. For example, I could draw a rune next to a roaring fire inside my villa and then transfer that heat and make General Utros burst into flame." She paused. "But someone would have to draw the corresponding rune on his chest. I don't think he'd stand still for that."

"I doubt it. Still, let's use our imaginations. Think beyond the usual possibilities. Maybe there's something else."

They watched a barge arrive from upriver filled with crates, casks, and sacks, food supplies that Ildakar would need, because of the renewed siege. Ildakaran workers climbed down the walkways and staggered platforms to meet the barge at the docks. The river workers appeared tiny at the base of the bluff as they unloaded the cargo. Straining laborers pulled on ropes, turned cranks, and lifted the heavy containers up the cliff to platforms and receiving tunnels.

"We'll send word up and down the river," Elsa said. "Ildakar needs all the supplies other villages can provide, and we'll pay dearly for it."

"The city can last quite some time against a siege," Nathan said. "You were self-sufficient under the shroud for all those centuries."

Elsa nodded. "But as you said, the underpinnings of magic have changed. The petrification spell faded away. The changes from Richard Rahl's star shift are only beginning to show their repercussions throughout the world."

Nathan's new heart twitched, as if reacting to the suggestion. "At least the breach in the veil to the underworld is sealed, and we no longer need to worry about the Keeper or an undead army."

Elsa said, "We have enough enemies in the real world."

As they walked, she told him about her life in Ildakar. She had been happily married to a wizard named Derek, a kind man with a strong gift and an interest in crafts and music. Derek had demonstrated genuine magic when he played his lute, which could produce music more moving than any spell.

After years of marriage, Elsa had teased him about his growing potbelly, and Derek had responded by telling her it was to make sure her love for him was genuine. Then one night Derek had choked to death on a fish bone after dining late in his quarters. No one had been there to help him, and Elsa found him the next morning. She had mourned his loss for the better part of a century, but now she was able to tell stories of her lost husband with a wistful smile and a sparkle in her eyes.

Having listened to her tragic tale, Nathan asked, "And you took no other husband, not with all the other nobles and wizards in the city?"

She glanced shyly at him. "I never found a man who could match Derek's kindness or his charming interests." She made a dismissive gesture with her hands. "I'm no longer a flighty young woman looking for the excitement of romance. I have a good life as it is."

Nathan self-consciously stroked his white hair behind his shoulder. "Ah, my dear, I'm sure you still have that flighty young woman in you somewhere. I can see it behind your eyes and in your shy smile."

She turned away, but not before he saw the flush on her cheeks.

Elsa mentioned ancient vaults in the lower levels of Ildakar, which had been used as chambers and laboratories by the earliest wizards. "The gifted were more powerful in those days. They developed magic so terrible that they were afraid to use it. At the time, there was no need for it."

Nathan thought briefly of the powerful magical lore in the Cliffwall archive, but Cliffwall was far out of their reach now. "It appears we *do* have the need at present. If you have any suggestions . . ."

"There are places here in Ildakar that no one has thought

about in more than a thousand years," Elsa said. "Behind the shroud of eternity, we didn't face any outside dangers, and we never dreamed the stone army would reawaken."

"Do you remember where some of these places are?" Nathan asked.

She led him down one sloping street to the next, emerging into broader open areas, marketplaces, stockyards, warehouses, the sprawling districts of noisy, smelly crafts, such as blacksmiths and tanners. Elsa and Nathan greeted carpenters who were sawing logs, furniture makers busy at their craft, despite the siege outside. Weavers stood outdoors by their huge looms, making fabric with intricate patterns that might have been magical, or just decorative.

Some workers looked at the two strangers with suspicion, but Nathan gave them a warm wave. Elsa led him past roughhousing children, a barking dog, a smith snipping thin strips of iron and pounding them into nails, which he tossed into a wooden bucket.

Where the city met the plain, large sandstone hummocks like weathered tan bunkers were all that remained of crumbling old structures that had once been the towers of weathermancers and astronomers. After the gifted had moved up to the higher levels of the city, these ancient buildings had become storage silos, communal dwellings where workers lived, or simply piles of scrap material to be reused. Some of the sandstone hummocks had stone doors leading to inner chambers, still sealed.

"This one here." Elsa took him to a sandstone island that had been the foundation of a grand building weathered away long ago. She found the door bricked shut. "It was a vault of some kind. Only the most important wizards were granted access, but I could never find any record as to what it was exactly."

"Then shall we find out?" Nathan paused in front of the bricked-up barricade, touching the solid blocks with his slender fingers. They seemed as impregnable as the base rock itself. "I see one problem, however."

Elsa touched the thick stone next to Nathan, letting her fingers brush against his. "That's easily enough solved."

Nathan stepped back. "I can unleash my gift and blast this open."

"Yes you could, but let's not resort to that. I'll use my transference magic instead." She went to the nailsmith, who ceased his loud hammering when Elsa asked if she could borrow a bucket of water.

Handing her an empty wooden pail, he pointed to a trough. "Anything to help Ildakar," he said, with no apparent irony.

Nathan filled the bucket for her and carried it to the bricked-up barricade. "Do you mean to splash water on the blocks and make them dissolve?"

"Of course not." She dipped her finger into the water and drew a symbol on the side of the bucket. Before the pattern could run or evaporate, Elsa dipped her finger again and drew a larger version of the symbol on the solid barricade. "There, anchor rune and corresponding rune. Watch."

When she completed the design, the bucket trembled. The surface of the water rippled with concentric rings that shuddered inward, then reflected outward. The stone barricade also shifted.

The water in the bucket grew murky, muddy, silty. The stone blocks in the barricade softened and slumped. The mortar holding them together ran like liquid, while the water in the pail solidified into cement. The bricks loosened, several of them dropping to the ground.

When her magic was complete, Elsa said, "Now, just knock them aside."

"Remarkable." Nathan pressed his palm against the stones and shoved. With alarming ease, the blocks tumbled inward to expose the large inner vault. "That was far simpler than I expected. It seems transference magic is quite effective, if one knows how and when to use it."

With the barricade gone, Nathan and Elsa entered, each

calling up a globe of light in the palm of a hand to illuminate the chamber. They found themselves in a cool shadowy place that smelled damp, with a tang of metal, not just rust but the indefinable undertone of silver and brass. Instead of a store of magical devices or a great library of secret spells, though, the chamber held only a low circular wall in the center of the room, like a well. That was the source of the odd smell.

Elsa frowned. "I was hoping for more. Is it another water source? Why would they keep it enclosed and hidden?"

Nathan felt a chill, and with it a sense of exhilaration. "I've seen something like this before. That's not just a well. It's a sliph."

Nathan gave only hints of what he and Elsa had found as he persuaded Nicci to accompany them with all due haste. "Even with my gift restored, this discovery does me no good, Sorceress, because it requires both Additive and Subtractive Magic. You will be the one who has to use it."

Entering the newly unsealed chamber, Nicci stepped forward and ignited her own light as she studied the low circular wall. Damon, Quentin, and the pale sorceress Lani had also joined them, curious about the find that had sparked such enthusiasm from Nathan.

"What is it?" Damon asked, glancing at Elsa. He seemed skeptical. "What could possibly be so exciting about finding a hole?"

"It is more than a hole," Nicci said, stepping forward. She could feel the possibilities rise within her. "It's a sliph well, a kind of transportation network."

Lani frowned. "What is a sliph? I've never heard of it."

"The sliph is—was—a woman transformed into a creature of great power. Anyone who has both Additive and Subtractive Magic can travel great distances in the sliph, in almost no time. I have used it before."

"Do you think this sliph is still alive?" Nathan asked. "Can you travel through it?"

Nicci placed her hands on the stone rim and peered down into the moist, metallic-scented depths. The well seemed to have no bottom, no standing water, just an emptiness that went on forever. She sensed no stirring, heard no noise. "I have experienced two different sliphs before, and this could be one of those, or another one entirely. Ildakar is far from any other destination I know of. This could be part of a separate sliph network with destinations throughout the Old World."

Thoughts circled in her mind. Could she perhaps travel back to the People's Palace to tell Richard and the entire D'Haran Empire about the ancient army? For now, Ildakar was isolated, under siege, and far from any help.

"Maybe once I see what Utros intends to do to Ildakar, I will travel and spread a warning to other cities."

CHAPTER 17

Much as he'd come to despise the city of Ildakar, Wizard Commander Maxim began to reconsider leaving civilization behind. On his fifth day out in the treacherous swamps, he was bedraggled, wet, muddy, and hungry. Clouds of bloodthirsty insects were constantly on the attack.

As he crashed through thornbushes and razor-edged sawgrass, Maxim used his gift to disentangle himself from a ropy spiderweb. He reached a mound of mossy dirt, rotten branches, and clumps of reeds. With resignation, he realized this was likely the best spot he would find to camp.

His black pantaloons were rumpled and muddy, but at least the tough Ildakaran silk had not torn. His yaxen leather boots kept his feet dry, except when he plunged up to his knees in the muck, and then water ran inside.

He paced around the disappointingly small island and listened to the burble and splash of creatures moving through the sluggish waters. He dragged together slimy fallen branches covered with moss, making a pile of sodden wood for his fire. It would take great mastery of the gift to keep himself dry and warm throughout the night, but he was one of the most powerful wizards in Ildakar. He could certainly manage a campfire.

He arranged the rotting wood in a haphazard stack, giving up on finesse. With a wave of his hand, he released his gift into the branches and logs, and flashed the moisture into steam, which hissed out and dried the wood. He sent a spark into the middle, careful not to explode the whole pile into a conflagration. Soon enough he had a crackling, popping fire as the darkness deepened.

Claiming another log for a makeshift seat, he brushed away the rough bark before settling down. It would be another uncomfortable night. He thought longingly of the spacious beds in his grand villa in Ildakar. He could have slept on silky sheets, feeling cool breezes wafting through the windows, no doubt sated from sex with one of his many partners in the pleasure parties.

Or, he might have lain beside the cold and venomous Thora, whose icy demeanor extended beyond her flesh and deep into her spirit. Maxim shuddered now and leaned closer to his fire. No, even this was better than being with her.

Nearly two thousand years ago, his love for Thora had been genuine. Thoughts of her consumed his emotions, his actions. They'd been inseparable, loving each other with a passion that even minstrels could not adequately chronicle. Together, the sovrena and wizard commander had built great magic to rule the city they had claimed, like guardians. Thora had dreamed of shaping the perfect society, every slave, every worker, every merchant serving Ildakar in their own way.

That had been Thora's dream, and because Maxim's mind was dulled by love, he had let his wife have her way. The thought sickened him now as the night swamp buzzed around him. He couldn't believe how gullible he had been. Maxim was such a powerful wizard himself, why had his heart been so weak? He could have stood up for himself and shaped Ildakar according to his wishes, rather than hers. At the time, he'd been a fool to think that was what he really wanted. And maybe it had been, but desires changed, needs changed, and Maxim's interests had waned. Ildakar had been his greatest triumph, but over centuries of stagnation, he'd grown bored with it.

When fighting the siege of General Utros, Maxim and Thora had been united with the other wizards of Ildakar. Such triumphant days, days with purpose! Even a passion that burns so bright, however, will eventually run out of fuel. The greatest love could not last forever; that was simply human nature.

Thora had a perfect body, a face whose beauty went beyond the ability of sculptors to capture, but her once-sweet kisses had grown tasteless, the soft curves of her body and her warm flesh felt like an old worn garment. His adoration for her turned to scorn.

The city of Ildakar, built upon the map of dreams that Thora had drawn, became bitter and stale. Most citizens didn't even notice the changes. Ildakar was like a beautiful porcelain vase, shot throughout with countless hairline cracks. Maxim wanted to smash it.

He had become Mirrormask, toying with unrest among the slaves and lower classes, feeding their doubts and anger. It had been a delightful exercise, which amused him for some time. The downtrodden people had been so hungry for a savior, a hero, and by playing a mysterious gray-robed figure who hid behind a reflective mask, Maxim had given them what they longed for.

At first it was a game, and Maxim enjoyed duping the needy people. But as his plan grew more complex, he realized he had stumbled on a way to undermine the foundations of the nobles, the duma members, the arrogant wizards—and especially Thora. The entire city was dry tinder, and he supplied the spark.

The revolt had been his finest hour. He watched the slaves unleash the combat animals, rile up the arena warriors, and run wild through the streets. Maxim had felt an erotic thrill to see his plans come to fruition, aided by the charismatic sorceress Nicci, who truly believed in the goal.

Maxim had succeeded, and Thora had been deposed, but

he fled Ildakar, not wanting to become a victim of its internal collapse. Adding more fire so he could be sure the great city would crumble, he undid the unique petrification spell he had developed, so that the countless soldiers in the ancient siege could awaken. How he wished he could simply sit back to watch events unfold!

Instead, he was alone and miserable in these swamps, though the misery was of his own making. Sitting on his moss-covered log in front of the snapping campfire, Maxim used his gift to dispel the water from his clothes and cleanse himself so that he felt more comfortable. Yes, he had the power to control his environment. He didn't have a lavish, silk-covered bed in the grand villa, but he would survive. In fact, he thought of himself as the king of this entire swamp, a domain of mud and bugs and scaly creatures.

At least he was a king, and this was a new beginning.

Uprooting a green willow stick from the edge of the hummock, Maxim probed in the sluggish water and found a large bottom-feeding fish. With a release of his gift, he stopped its minuscule heart. Seconds later, the dead fish floated belly up, within reach. Maxim pulled it out of the water, gutted it, and threaded the willow twig down its mouth so he could roast it over the fire for his dinner.

He sat in silence listening to the ominous, yet comforting, hum of night creatures. He heard a heavy splash and cracking branches, but knew the large predators wouldn't bother him— or if they did, they would regret it.

He watched the fish skin blacken, curl, and slough off, leaving pale meat that clung to the bones. The buzzing whine of bloodsucking insects swept around his head, drawn not to the scent of the roasting fish, but to him. When one of the large gnats bit his neck, he flinched. With an annoyed thought, he conjured his petrification spell and cast it out in waves so that all the flying, biting insects turned to tiny grains of stone and dropped out of the air. Now he would have peace long enough to eat his meal, but more of the pests would soon come to plague him.

Maxim's thoughts drifted as he chewed the tender fish. He reminded himself, again, that living with Thora had been worse than this.

Suddenly, out of the shadowy night thickets, a demon appeared—a woman. Adessa, the morazeth leader. He saw murder in her eyes.

She had a lithe body, a hard-bitten expression, and a weapon in each hand, a short sword and a dagger. Her exposed skin glistened in the orange light of the campfire, covered not only with branded runes, but with scratches, welts, and swollen insect bites.

The sight of her was so incongruous, Maxim could only gasp.

"I've been sent to kill you." Adessa slashed with her short sword, cutting branches and shrubs out of the way so she could lunge toward him.

Maxim scrambled back from his campfire, blurting out, "What are you doing? I forbid this! I am your wizard commander."

She charged toward him without speaking another word. A different warrior might have let out a bloodcurdling yell, but Adessa was a silent killing machine.

Maxim reacted instinctively, releasing his gift to hurl a ball of fire at her, but the protective morazeth runes made the flames ripple harmlessly aside. She swung her sword at him as he jumped over the log, and the blade struck the mossy wood with a loud thunk.

She stumbled on a soft divot in the muck, and Maxim sent his magic into the campfire, blowing it up in a surge of flame. The fire didn't burn the protected warrior woman, but the sheer flash of light and heat made her reel backward, giving him a chance to dart away.

Maxim plunged across the hummock and sloshed into the muddy water. Adessa leaped right through the surging flames, and her hard and merciless eyes glittered in the sparks of the blaze. "Sovrena Thora has ordered me to kill you and bring back your head. I will not fail."

He had seen Adessa fight many times, had watched her defeat Nicci in the ruling chamber after the sorceress challenged Thora, and he had seen Adessa fight her warrior trainees or slay powerful monsters in exhibition bouts in the arena. She seemed to enjoy it. Maxim could never fight her in that way. He wouldn't survive.

He lashed out with a fist of wind, tried to knock her backward, but the runes on her skin protected her. Instead, he used the wind to rip branches loose and hurl them at her like clubs. She battered them away, striding toward him as if he were a yaxen caught in a slaughterhouse pen.

Maxim ran through the watery channel, struggling in the soft mud, sinking up to his knees. Adessa had little difficulty running after him.

With a burst of magic, he made the water boil behind him. Steam curled up, blinding Adessa. He couldn't concentrate on manipulating his gift while he fled for his life. He was the wizard commander! He could resist, he could delay her, but he knew that Adessa was relentless, and she was a morazeth. He didn't know what he could do, where he could hide.

In the end, the swamp saved him. As Maxim churned through the muddy water, splashing steam and tearing up bushes and vines to throw at her, Adessa kept coming, paying no attention to the other dangers in her environment.

But two large swamp dragons lay in wait among the reeds, ready to lunge out at unsuspecting marsh deer or wild boars. The armored lizards scuttled toward the morazeth with jaws that could snap a tree in half.

Maxim sprang onto another hummock and swung himself over a fallen tree while Adessa turned to face the unexpected swamp dragons. She hacked with her sword, and the blade struck sparks off their gray-green hides. The first swamp dragon snapped at her, driving her backward. The second dragon closed in, lunging for her leg, but Adessa jumped up with an angry snarl of her own. She concentrated on fighting the pair of giant lizards.

Maxim spared only a glance for her as he ran off into the night. He didn't expect the swamp dragons to kill her—Adessa was too skilled a fighter for that—but the monsters would keep her busy long enough to give him a chance to escape.

Now that he knew the morazeth was hunting him, he would never let down his guard again.

CHAPTER 18

Though the city and the people had betrayed her, Thora still believed that Ildakar was hers. Its wealth, its legend, its very soul and society endured because of *her,* no one else. She had stood in the ruling tower and surveyed the sweeping buildings, the levels of society from the outer walls to the pinnacle of the plateau. She had ruled it all, protected it all.

And Ildakar had turned on her. They didn't appreciate what she had done for them as sovrena, how much they owed her for their very existence. If Utros and his invaders now ransacked Ildakar because the people had no powerful leader, then maybe they would understand. She hoped they would realize their mistake before it was too late.

The stone walls of the cell surrounded Thora like a throttling grip. She clenched her fist, felt her stiff knuckles and fingers bend according to her command, but the lingering taint of stone was still inside her because of the damnable spell that Elsa, Damon, and Quentin had hurled upon her.

This small, unlit dungeon deep in the bowels of the bluff left her alone in darkness with her dark thoughts. The door was sturdy wood half a foot thick, mounted to the jamb by three iron hinges riveted with long metal pins that had rusted in place. A heavy deadbolt and an imposing wooden crossbar held the door shut.

Sovrena Thora knew these dungeons, because over the centuries she had dispatched complaining nobles and restless citizens down here. The incarceration had been for their punishment, sometimes for their own good, always for the good of Ildakar. And now she was trapped inside, just like one of them.

Thora was the most powerful sorceress the city had ever produced. Her rule had endured for more than fifteen centuries. With her gift, she should have been able to blast away the door or shatter the stone walls, but wizards had warded these cells long ago. The wooden door and the surrounding stones were chiseled with protective runes that nullified any magical attacks she might unleash, just like the symbols branded onto the combat animals or the morazeth.

She thought briefly of faithful Adessa and knew the morazeth leader would find and kill the despised Maxim, as ordered. Thora wished she could witness the execution herself, because her hatred for her husband went beyond even her anger at falling from grace and becoming a prisoner now. Thora resolved to be returned to her rightful place in Ildakar by the time Adessa brought back Maxim's head.

Alone in the dark cell, she hardened her fist, felt her way across the blackness until she reached the wall where only the vaguest gray blur penetrated the small, barred window in the door. Even the tunnels were unlit, since no one would waste wood or transference magic on burning torches down here. The darkness and gloom were part of Thora's punishment, but she refused to consider it a punishment. The darkness was her friend now, a place where she could contemplate her situation and make the necessary plans.

She pressed her palm against the cold, smooth stone. She felt the slime of algae thriving in the shadows, but the sensations were muted, her nerves dulled by the heaviness in her flesh. Her once-sensitive fingers were clumsy as she traced the surface, so she squeezed her hands into hard fists and pounded on the stone block just like the half-petrified soldiers of General Utros continually hammered the city's outer walls.

With the muffled thud of the impact, she felt only a distant echo of pain. Curious, she struck with her other hand, harder, but despite her pounding, the solid blocks held fast, her dungeon secure. With one last slam of her knuckles, she stepped back. If she'd been entirely human, she would have battered her hands bloody, but she just felt a dull throbbing, with no real damage done to her hands or to the wall.

She needed to get out of here. Ildakar would fall without her.

Maxim was responsible for this current turmoil, but she blamed the treacherous duma members who had overthrown her, convicted her, cast the stone spell, especially the meddling sorceress Nicci, who had been the catalyst for so much disruption. Nicci and her impotent wizard companion had come to Ildakar seeking help, claiming to be nothing more than travelers with a message from the D'Haran Empire, but Thora had suspected them from the beginning. Nicci really wanted to become the next sovrena, to take Ildakar for her own.

Now the outside sorceress had the city, and Thora was locked in a dungeon while Nicci and the others faced an invincible army from the past. Thora knew that parts of Ildakar remained loyal to her. In the darkness, she envisioned the glorious buildings, terraced gardens, orchards and olive groves that she herself had built. Such a marvelous, perfect city.

A flash of anger heated her face. By the Keeper, how she wanted Nicci and the other traitors to fail and die horribly! Thora pounded uselessly on the stone wall again.

She worked her way around the cell and encountered a low stone bench whose front corner had broken away. The jagged edges had been smoothed by the worrying, sweaty, even bloody fingers of other desperate prisoners over the centuries.

The sovrena had a narrow waist, delicate features, and thin, graceful arms. She never considered herself weak, but she did not rely on physical combat when she fought an enemy. Even though her body felt heavy and dull with lingering stone, she did feel the gift still burning in her heart. She held out her hand and summoned magic, lighting a small flame, which winked into existence like a bobbing candle in her open palm.

The cheery flame was a bright glimmer of hope, casting a yellow glow around the walls. Now that she could see the details of her confined prison, she noted the spell runes around the doorway. Even though she knew it was useless, she summoned a larger blast of fire and hurled it against the wall, but the flames merely splattered and scorched the slime into a foul-smelling stain. Her fire curled around and ricocheted from one protected wall to another. Thora flinched as the flames lashed back and struck her, too, but her hardened skin protected her before the fire flickered away into a dull glow.

In wonder, Thora rubbed her arms where the flames had touched her. She felt a tingle, saw a scorch mark on her gray-white skin, but she rubbed it away. There was no damage to herself, nor to the cell. It was no use. She couldn't get out, no matter how badly the people of Ildakar needed her to save them.

She spent the next hour hating Maxim for what he had done, for his plan to turn the slaves against the very city that nurtured them and asked only their devotion in return. How those weak people had whined at the injustice, at the hard work they had to perform, without seeing that she herself suffered more for Ildakar than any of them did! No one was more aware of the painful cost of their prosperity than Thora was. The slaves had sore muscles, perhaps, and some even lost their lives, but what was the cost of a few lives to build a civilization that endured for millennia? She despised those who refused to make the sacrifice for the greater good of Ildakar. *She* had certainly given everything.

Then Maxim had uprooted the underpinnings of her beautiful society. She'd loved him long ago, and now she couldn't understand how she had been such a fool. Was she just young and naive, driven by the heat of romance and lust? Over centuries of sharing his bed, then sharing the beds of many others, Thora had learned that lust could be easily satisfied without surrendering her heart, or even common sense. She had wasted the best years of her youth on Maxim, letting him cheat on her, learning of it, forgiving him. She had turned her heart to stone long before any petrification spell, realizing how worthless he was. But the wizard commander was too powerful to be discarded, and she had kept him as her husband, in name only, a figurehead.

Now, Thora realized she might have overestimated his power. She had been in awe of his great petrification spell, just as she had been instrumental in the great bloodworking that formed the shroud of eternity. She could do it all herself, though. She didn't need him.

It was clear that Maxim's magic must be waning if the stone army had awakened. No wonder he had fled. But perhaps Thora's gift was also fading. The shroud of eternity had dissipated over the years before they had brought it down entirely. She had been willing to work the final blood magic to restore the shroud permanently, but would it truly have endured?

The underpinnings of magic had changed, the fundamental rules of the world altered in ways she didn't understand. Nicci had offered an explanation, although Thora didn't entirely believe her about what Richard Rahl had done. But, Utros and his army had indeed awakened, and Thora herself had revived from the petrification spell. Yes, much was changing, and she had to use that to her advantage.

Maxim hadn't needed magic to create his revolution among the gullible lower classes, to turn those mindless animals, *human* animals, loose to destroy her city. The rebels followed him, all the while cheering for a foolish dream they had not earned.

As anger and frustration welled within her, Thora lashed out again, opened her fingers to slam a trembling quake of magic against the wall like a mastiff battering the sides of a cage, but the spell runes deflected her onslaught, and the magic dissipated without any effect.

Thora sank back and let the flicker of fire die in her hands. She gripped the chipped stone bench and listened to the resounding silence again.

Darkness made the time pass interminably, and she didn't know how long she waited before she saw the light brighten in the corridor outside. She heard heavy footsteps, hard boots, the jangle of keys. She heard gruff voices, saw shadows outside the barred window.

With a scraping sound, the crossbar slid aside as it was removed from its metal rests, followed by a squeak and clank as the deadbolt shot back. The hinges protested as two burly guards pushed the door open. Light poured into the cell, making silhouettes of the two men from their torches, but Thora's eyes adjusted.

One man, with black stubble on his chin and a helmet askew on his wide head, wore an ill-fitting armored vest taken from the city guard. He obviously wasn't accustomed to such a uniform. With a pang, she remembered how dashing High Captain Avery had looked when he guarded Thora and also served as her lover. But Avery had been slaughtered in the streets by Mirrormask's rebels, and Thora knew it was no accident. Maxim—Mirrormask—had done it just to spite her, out of an acid twinge of jealousy.

These two guards were obviously rebel slaves who now felt important, having taken unearned uniforms. The first man looked at Thora with a hungry sneer and spoke in a blunt voice that made her doubt the extent of his vocabulary. "We've come to you again, Sovrena. Are you lonely yet? You might be partly stone, but your skin looks smooth enough. If we spread your legs, would you be soft and wet where it counts?"

"I doubt you would be hard enough to find out," she retorted.

The second guard snickered at the insult.

Thora continued, "Or maybe I would crush your soft little member, like between two stones."

Struggling for words, the gruff guard proved that he did not, indeed, have much vocabulary.

The second guard carried a tray with hard bread, a cup of water, and a small bowl of gruel. "We brought your food, but if the siege lasts longer, we might have to cut off prisoner rations."

Thora wasn't hungry. Even though this was the third time guards had brought food, she'd never felt the need to eat or drink. The water did nothing for her and the food just felt leaden in her stomach. When the guard approached, she smashed the meal out of his hands, and her hardened fist split the tray down the middle. The guards scampered backward as the broken dishes clattered to the cell floor, uncertain of what she could do.

"I don't want any rations," she said. "I want my freedom."

"That's beyond our ability to give, Sovrena," said the second guard.

Still stinging from her insult, the first guard said, "We'll leave you with your own company. And the dark. And the rats." He huffed. "You can think about me in your dreams."

The second guard looked at her with scorn. "I liked it better when you were a statue in the ruling tower. It's what you deserved." He looked down at the broken tray and crockery. "No more rations for you. We'll save the food for the good people of Ildakar."

With a grunt of effort, the guards pulled the door shut. Keys turned in the lock, and the deadbolt slid into place again. They rammed the crossbar onto its rests.

The men departed, extinguishing the torches behind them. She sat on the stone bench in darkness again, extended her hand, and called forth the magical fire, playing with the flame as it bobbed and danced in her palm.

CHAPTER 19

From behind the safety of the high walls, Bannon watched. He wanted to fight, wanted to *do something,* but how could even the entire city stand against such an enormous enemy?

His greatest hurt, though, came from the night of the revolt and the terrible circumstances that had built up to so much violence. His thoughts turned to the treacherous young men who had claimed to be his friends. False friends. His heart was torn by what had been done to him. Amos, Jed, and Brock had set him up and done nothing to save him, hadn't even bothered to tell Nicci or Nathan what happened when he was captured and dragged down into the training pits. Yes, he had survived the ordeal—scarred, and maybe even stronger for it— but how could friends do that to him?

The answer was obvious: they had never been friends at all.

When Lila recently sparred with him, she had urged him to put aside his grudges. In order for Ildakar to endure this crisis, the city could not tear itself apart. The besieging army was dangerous enough to force them to set aside their differences.

Jed and Brock, though . . . their actions were malicious. Led by Amos, they had taken the young and naive outsider under their wing to show him their city, but they had done it only to trick him, to mock him. But Bannon was not just some gullible fool.

Now he strapped on his sword and shored up his courage, knowing he couldn't avoid this any longer. It was time he confronted the two surviving young men and made them understand what they had done.

His fingers clenched around Sturdy's leather-wrapped grip, his forearm bunched, and he could feel the ripple of hard muscles—muscles that had grown strong from hand-to-hand fighting and wrestling, from swinging weapons. Bannon was strong in his heart and mind, too.

He left the grand villa and made his way to the headquarters of the skinners' guild and Lord Oron, the newest member of the duma, who was Brock's father. The young man paid no attention to the tightly packed grapevines on narrow terraces along the steep hillsides or the clustered orchards of dwarf fruit trees. A few workers were out picking grapes, harvesting apples, plucking green olives from the trees. Much of the work had simply been abandoned after the uprising. The freed slaves were indignant and many refused their responsibilities. "Let the nobles get blisters picking crops for a change."

Others, though, understood that if the city were to survive this siege, they would need all the food Ildakar could produce. Former slaves would starve just as quickly as nobles did. Those who went back to work did so by their own choice, out of responsibility rather than oppression. Their families, at least, would have something to eat.

Bannon wore simple clothes, feeling uncomfortable in a fur-lined cape or billowing pantaloons, which were the height of Ildakaran fashion. Despite his many adventures, in his heart he still thought of himself as a farm boy from Chiriya Island. He would never lose that core.

Amos, Jed, and Brock had considered him to be beneath

144

them, but they nevertheless dragged him to the silk yaxen dachas, trying to get him to partake of the pleasure women along with them. At first he was sure they were teasing him, or maybe the three really wanted to make Bannon just like them. Silk yaxen were women created and trained to be nothing more than beautiful bodies to serve the pleasure of their customers. They supposedly couldn't think, couldn't feel, but Bannon had always felt sorry for them.

Amos had treated the silk yaxen Melody the worst. On the night of the revolt, he had raped her, slapped her, bruised her, and she finally responded, using a shard of broken glass to slash his throat. That same night, seven other silk yaxen had killed their abusive customers. Afterward, they reverted to their meek and pliable state, not denying their crimes, but passively accepting them. With all the other turmoil going on in Ildakar, Bannon wasn't sure the women would ever be called to account for their crimes. Justice had indeed been served in its own way. He couldn't help but think of how his own mother had been beaten and murdered by his father.

But Jed and Brock had never faced what they had done to him, never admitted their own responsibility. Did they feel sorry at all?

He approached Oron's mansion, which was connected to a long outbuilding where the skinners' guild conducted their operations. He drew on all the strength he had developed since leaving Chiriya, since joining Nicci and Nathan on their long journey. Though Bannon didn't know what he expected from Jed and Brock, he needed to do this for himself.

No one answered when he rang the small brass gong outside the mansion's entry. Hearing activity inside, he tentatively pushed open the door and was surprised to see several servants lounging in comfortable chairs and sprawled on a divan. "Excuse me. Didn't you hear me knock?"

The servants sneered at Bannon. A middle-aged man propped himself up on an elbow on the divan. He wore a slave shirt of drab rough-spun cloth, but he had piled silken sheets, fur-lined cloaks, and scavenged jewels around himself. "Keeper's crotch! Lord Oron can answer his own damned door. Why should we do anything to help you?"

Bannon was unsettled by their attitude. "Because I fought beside you during the revolt. I escaped from the combat pits and helped stop the great bloodletting at the pyramid."

"Then, what do you need with Oron?" one man grumbled.

"Are you here to kill him?" said another slave, sounding hopeful. "If so, maybe we will help."

"No, I'm not here to kill him. He is a powerful wizard," Bannon said in disbelief. "Ildakar will need his gift to fight General Utros." He frowned at them. "And we'll need your help, too. Every fighter, to defend the city."

"We've given enough to Ildakar," said the man on the divan, resting his feet on the fine fabric. "Now, it's time the city gave back to us."

Exasperated, Bannon didn't want to continue the argument. "I'm just here to speak to Oron's son, Brock."

The slave on the divan gestured toward the rear of the mansion. "Out back. They're in the animal buildings. Since many of the slaves refuse to do skinning anymore, Oron has to do it himself."

The slave in the chair chuckled. "It's about time he got his hands bloody in a real way. He's making Brock and that other boy Jed pitch in. Beware if you go there, since he might press you into service, too. Those pelts won't take care of themselves, and a lot of skinning needs to be done or else the animals will collapse under their own fur."

"I . . . I'll keep that in mind." He swallowed hard. *Sweet Sea Mother!*

As he headed toward the kitchens in the rear of the mansion, one of the slaves called, "If you're hungry, there's plenty of food in the pantries. Eat it before some gifted noble does."

"I'm not hungry," He hurried through the kitchens, where

the ovens were cold and the cabinets were open, ransacked for food. Spilled flour and half-eaten fruit lay discarded on the floor and the counters. One matronly woman had curled up in a corner, snoring loudly in the company of two empty bottles of bloodwine.

Bannon passed through a breezeway outside, following a path of crushed sparkling stone that led to a large low structure with shallowly sloped roofs and propped-open windows. Sounds wafted out, stirring, rattling, grunting, along with bone-chilling wails of animal pain. He paused, having second thoughts; then he remembered how Amos and his friends had laughed at him when the Norukai captains beat him senseless at the yaxen slaughterhouse. Bruised and broken, he had barely survived that attack, and then he'd been given over to Adessa so she could train him to die in the arena. His supposed friends had promised they would help him. They never did, and he would have died.

Pushing open the door, Bannon entered a giant outbuilding crowded with penned animals, the source of all the fine furs worn by the gifted nobles. The stench hit him first, coppery blood, pungent feces, the foul musk of terror exuded by dying animals. Two aisles of cages ran the length of the building, with more cages along the outer walls. Long, flat worktables had shallow gutters that led to drains in the floor. Eight harried, blood-spattered workers toiled at the skinning tables.

Oron was there, his face and his chest flecked with red. He wore a blood-smeared apron over a silken shirt that was now ruined. His long faded-yellow hair was matted, tied back and smeared with gore. He barked orders at the workers, whom Bannon realized were minor nobles. "If we don't skin these animals now, the fur will stop growing. Our guild depends on this! If the lazy slaves won't do their duty, we nobles have to pick up the slack . . . as always." He sounded weary and disgusted.

Oron walked down the line of tables and cages. "Now that

I am a duma member, my obligations have increased tenfold. I need to count on other guild members." He turned to a queasy-looking young man. "And you too, son. Your life has been far too easy. It's time to get your hands bloody."

Bannon hadn't at first recognized Brock, because the young man's face was smeared with blood, his short, dark hair crusty, his hands covered with red up to his elbows. "I always did what I could," Brock said in a whining tone.

Bannon finally saw what they were actually doing and stumbled backward in shock. The skinners would open one of the cages, reach in, and grasp the ruff of a squealing animal. The unnatural creatures had broad, squat bodies with stubby heads and stumplike, useless legs that flailed as the workers dragged them out. The animals looked like swollen, living pillows made of fur. Their heads were small, like a turtle's, and the entire body was covered with a rich, thick pelt, some spotted, others streaked with ash gray. These were not normal animals, Bannon realized, but creatures shaped by fleshmancers, made for a terrible painful purpose.

No one noticed Bannon as he stood speechless inside the door. He watched as another reticent young man—Jed, he realized—grabbed an animal with rusty fur. He dropped the flailing, squeaking creature on the skinning table in front of him. He had a short, razor-sharp knife.

"We're doing what we can, sir," Jed said defensively. He pushed the struggling creature down and held it by the back of the neck as he jabbed with the point of the knife, slicing its shoulder. He cut across its short forelegs and all the way around its body. The creature mewled and screeched in pain. Jed dug with the knife, grabbed the edge of the pelt, and ripped it up. He pulled off a wide swatch of fur and set it aside for scraping while the whimpering creature twitched and bled. Though skinned alive, it was not dead, but naked, its pelt torn off.

"How long until this grows back?" Jed asked as he tossed the skinned animal back into the cage.

Oron said, "The ones that survive will have a fresh new pelt in three weeks, ready for harvesting again."

The skinners worked one cage at a time, grabbing the animals, stripping them of their pelts, and returning them to their cages.

Bannon's stomach clenched with nausea. There were hundreds of trapped animals. "This is horrible. You're all horrible!" The others looked up, startled by his arrival. The young man shook his head, trembling. "This whole city is horrible."

Oron barked at him, "Good, we could use more help. There's a lot of work to do and too many lazy people refusing to do it."

"You're torturing those poor things," Bannon groaned. He had always loved animals.

Oron let out an impatient snort. "Where do you think fur comes from? There's always a dark underside to what society needs. Do you eat meat? You can't have a yaxen steak without killing the yaxen. Or maybe you'd rather live naked and eat plants."

Fighting back the urge to vomit, he gathered his courage and strode to where Jed and Brock were working shoulder-to-shoulder, covered in blood. Seeing him, Jed quirked his lips in a sarcastic smile. "We wondered what had happened to you. Did you enjoy playing with Adessa in the training pits?"

"I survived. I learned a lot about myself and I learned the truth about you."

Brock grabbed another animal out of a cage, a gray-speckled one this time, and slammed it on the table in the smear of blood left behind from the previous creature he had skinned. "If you're our friend, help out with some of the work here."

"You weren't my friends," Bannon said. "You only wanted to laugh at me. But I'm stronger now. I know who you are."

"It wasn't us," Jed said. "It was Amos. We just followed him."

"That still makes you participants. You could have told Nicci or Nathan what happened to me after I was captured,

149

but you wanted me down there in the pits." His hand drifted toward his sword, though he had no intention of killing them. Still, Jed and Brock flinched as if afraid of what the young man would do. It was a strange sensation to see them fear him, but Bannon didn't back down. "Amos beat and abused poor Melody, and she killed him. You two were lucky on the night of the revolt."

"We hid for our own protection," Brock said. "It was the right thing to do."

Jed somehow managed to sound indignant. "Amos is dead. He was the son of the wizard commander and the sovrena."

"And they'll be the only two who mourn him," Bannon retorted. "But the sovrena is locked in a dungeon, and the wizard commander fled the city." Anger and disgust welled up within him. It wasn't the same thing as the blood rage he often encountered. He felt strong. He needed to say these things aloud.

Still working, Brock sliced into the fur animal, peeled up the pelt. Bannon nearly retched.

Oron interrupted, looking at his son with scorn rather than pride. "Brock has lived with his pampered delusions for centuries. That's my own fault as his father. He needs to live up to his name as the son of a duma member. He needs to work and make himself worthy."

Insulted, Brock continued his bloody task. The mewling animal lay raw and skinned on the table, twitching but unable to escape. Brock growled, "We fought for the city. How many times did we go outside and smash the stone warriors? No one else in Ildakar did so. If the rest of the people in this city had done as much to damage the stone army, we wouldn't be under siege right now. They would all be destroyed already."

"Yes, you were very brave, vandalizing statues," Bannon said. "You said you wanted to fight against General Utros for what he had done in the past. Well, now you can truly fight. The city is under real siege, and the army is alive again. If we have to

150

go to battle for Ildakar, will you be on the front lines?" He lifted his chin in challenge, though he nearly gagged from the stench inside the outbuilding.

Jed and Brock muttered, looking away. "We've already done our part."

Oron spoke in a firm tone. "You need to make something of yourself, son. I worked for centuries to build my power and influence, and now I'm finally a member of the duma. You need to prove yourself worthy, too. Jed's mother feels the same. Lady Olgya said as much to me." He looked up, hardening his gaze. "I'll expect you to meet your obligations when the time comes. General Utros isn't bound to agree to peace anytime soon."

"We . . . we won't need to go to battle," Brock insisted. "The wizards' duma will find a way to end the siege."

Oron opened a cage and brought out a black-furred animal, which squirmed and twisted in the air. "We'll try, but if it comes to a real fight, you will need to help save Ildakar, too." He pressed the creature down on the stained table in front of him. He glanced at Bannon and snapped an order. "You, boy, put on a smock. Take up a knife. We could use your help."

Instead, Bannon walked away. "No. I'll leave you to the work you were born to do."

CHAPTER 20

As darkness settled again over Ildakar, Nicci pondered the unsatisfying meeting with General Utros as well as how she might use the sliph whose well Nathan and Elsa had discovered in the ruins. One way or another, she was determined to save Ildakar.

The ancient army had made no move in two days, but their mere presence was intimidating. Utros had too much to digest, too much to accept about what had happened, but she hoped he would understand the truth of the situation, realize that his effort was not only unnecessary but pointless. Ildakar had the resources to withstand a siege for years, decades, centuries.

Nicci thought it would be most beneficial to wait, for now, but she doubted the legendary general would abandon the goal of overthrowing Ildakar. His duty remained as unyielding as stone. Nicci understood his obsession, because she felt the same way about her own promise to Richard. If some courier had told her that Lord Rahl was gone, or if she awoke from a spell sleep to find that centuries had passed, would she abandon her duty to the D'Haran Empire?

Never.

She and Nathan had certainly planted questions and doubts in the general's mind, but he was a man who followed orders, and his loyalty was legendary. He had conquered the continent on the basis of Iron Fang's command, but he would not be reckless either. She hoped he would ask for another parley with them, soon.

From the high vantage near the ruling tower, Nicci looked out at the night-shadowed streets of Ildakar after dark, the tense people in their homes waiting for resolution. At least the pounding on the walls had stopped, but the silence did not give the city any peace.

When they had walked into the middle of the huge enemy camp, Nicci and Nathan trusted in the general's legendary honor. But what was he planning now? How did he think he could breach the city's defenses or fight the many gifted who would defend the city?

As she watched the blackness and the vault of stars overhead, Nathan emerged from the grand villa to join her, dressed in his ruffled shirt, black trousers, and boots instead of his white wizard's robes. He even carried his ornate sword, as if to remind himself how much he enjoyed being an adventurer as well as a wizard. He looked up at the unrecognizable constellations, a vault of night like another kind of shroud. "Out to gaze at the stars, Sorceress? They've changed, but someday they will become familiar to us."

After the star shift, Nicci had paid little attention to the patterns in the sky. "If General Utros is as honorable a man as your history claims he is, I hope we can find a way to save Ildakar and also let him save face. We can resolve this, if he wants to."

The sparkle in Nathan's expression was unsettling to her. "You wear your optimism as easily as you wear that black dress, and it fits you just as well. Next thing, you may be creating rainbows out of the ruling tower."

He was teasing her, but she was not amused. "I was a Sister

of the Dark and I gave myself over to the Keeper, then I served the dream walker Jagang. I brought enough despair to the world before Richard showed me a different way to succeed through cooperation, friendship, and faith. He opened my eyes to the stain of the Imperial Order and made me realize how I myself had been spreading that poison." Her voice grew softer. "Richard taught me hope, and that's a lesson I don't ever intend to forget."

She walked along the path that led past other lighted villas toward the immense sacrificial pyramid, Ildakar's center of power. That structure was where the bloodworking apparatus had been set up, where hundreds of slaves would have been massacred to raise the shroud of eternity, but Nicci, Nathan, and other rebels had defeated Sovrena Thora and ruined the structure.

Nicci felt drawn to the place now. If the pyramid was the heart of Ildakar's magic, she wondered if she could use that magic against the siege.

The wizard realized where she was going. "Elsa and I have climbed through the rubble already looking for any viable remnants. Alas, we found nothing that would be of use to us."

Nicci didn't slow her pace. "We have to keep searching. You found the well of the sliph. Who knows what else Ildakar holds?"

"Elsa and I completed our search of the other sealed ruins, but I'm afraid all we found was a lot more dust." The wizard frowned. "A barrel of forgotten apples that must have been there for centuries, tools and bits of iron-hard leather in what was once a cobbler's shop. Nothing, alas, that would make Utros tremble in his sleep."

Jogging footsteps crunched on the path behind them, and she turned to see Bannon, his long red hair loose, his shirt untucked as he ran with his sword in hand. Grinning, the young man called, "Where are you going? Let me join you, in case it's dangerous."

Nathan gave him a paternal smile. "We will risk it ourselves, my boy."

Bannon was out of breath but excited. "Today I went to see Jed and Brock. Believe me, I had words with them." He huffed.

Nicci frowned as they reached the largest stone blocks at the base of the pyramid. She had never liked the two young men or their ringleader Amos, knowing how badly they had treated Bannon, who was desperate for friendship. Since the first time she had rescued him from robbers in a Tanimura alley, she had felt responsible for him. She had held little hope that the eager young man would amount to anything or survive this long, but he'd surprised her after all. She admitted that he had proven himself useful in some of their adventures.

"I would probably have killed them both for what they did," she said. "But you have your own way of fighting your battles."

"Let me come with you now," Bannon suggested, sounding altogether too excited. "Maybe I'll offer some ideas. A different perspective."

Nicci kept walking into the wreckage of the pyramid, letting him tag along. "You've earned it. You fought well many times, and you helped us free the slaves."

Bannon blushed. "You aren't often generous with your compliments, Sorceress. Thank you."

"It was a fact," Nicci said, "not meant as a compliment."

Nathan patted him on the shoulder. "Now we have to save the city from the siege. Any ideas are welcome."

They worked their way up the broken stairsteps, layer upon layer. The apex had been blasted away in the battle, leaving huge chunks of rubble all around.

Nathan mused aloud, "I wonder how many people were sacrificed here over the centuries when Ildakar was trapped beneath the shroud. How much blood did they spill just to keep the shroud intact?"

Nicci spread her fingers and concentrated. "I feel nothing.

The magic here is dead." She closed her eyes and continued searching for any hint of the gift, but shook her head. "Nothing."

Nathan concurred.

Then she felt a strange tingle emanating from herself, like a probing unwelcome finger inside her, a touch that stretched to her spine, then climbed to the back of her neck. Her head began to throb, her scalp crawled.

"Wait, there's something else, something powerful." Feeling the energy increase, she looked around in growing alarm. Her blond hair crackled with static electricity, wafting gently around her. She took a step higher on the pyramid steps. Overhead, the stars were diamond bright, and the lights of the city shone out like thousands of eyes.

Something wasn't right.

Nathan frowned as he sensed the change in the air, too. "My dear sorceress, are you certain you're not summoning it?"

"Not intentionally, but it's coming to me." Her long hair crackled and thrashed about as if in a brewing storm. She clutched a handful, wrapping her fingers around the golden strands. It seemed like something alive.

To her astonishment, she watched her hair *grow* between her fingertips. The blond locks lengthened like mad weeds. All around her head, the hair writhed out like living threads in a voluminous mane. She grabbed at it, but the strands whipped like probing tentacles. Her hair kept growing, out of control. She clawed at it, tugged, but the hair fought back.

Stepping forward with his sword, Bannon cried desperately, "What can we do?"

Nicci tugged hard on her own hair as it tried to wrap around her like a strangler's garrote. The golden strands thrashed at her, already longer than her waist, some strands down to her knees, wrapping around her like ropes, twisting and clumping together. The hair wound around her arm like thin chains as she reached up to tug at it. Another clump circled her neck, wrapping tight and cutting off her flow of air.

Nicci struggled, choking. With one hand, she snatched the dagger at her right hip and hacked at the hair around her neck, severing a long clump, which she threw to the ground. More hair tightened around her wrist until she thought her bones would break.

Diving in to help her, Nathan swung his ornate sword, cutting at the thrashing strands. "Your hair is quite beautiful, but I'm afraid it has to go." He hacked hard, lopping off a long hank of strands that continued writhing like worms, even when they were severed from her head.

Bannon sliced with his sharpened sword, careful not to hurt her, and then the hair lashed out at him, too.

When she shouted, another tentacle of strands dove into her mouth, thrusting down her throat. Gagging, she bit down with her teeth, grinding until she cut it off. She slashed with her knife, cutting her other wrist free, but more hair looped around her waist and lashed her legs together, drawing tight until she collapsed to the stone step of the pyramid. She sawed with her dagger, hacking off another hank of hair.

Still, it continued to grow like an infestation. Her hair struck out to snare Bannon's sword arm. He yelped and fought back but couldn't free his wrist. He tugged against her violent hair, while more locks lashed out to catch his leg, winding around his left boot, and dragging him closer to the main mass. He couldn't even swing his sword. "Help! Sweet Sea Mother."

Nathan chopped more strands of hair, then sliced the locks that had captured Bannon. The young man staggered away, stumbling on the steps.

Nicci kept cutting, throwing severed handfuls of hair to the ground. Even so, the cut strands flopped and squirmed in search of more targets. They slithered forward to wrap around Nathan's boots.

No matter how much they cut, Nicci's hair kept growing, long past her feet, wrapping around and around her like a cocoon. Already exhausted, she realized she couldn't succeed by hacking more away. She had to find a different answer, a smarter solution. She needed to turn her magic against the attacker, somehow.

Though she could barely breathe, her entire body caught in a strangling vise, she called upon her gift, unleashed fire that threw lightning around her skin. The blast singed and curled her hair, burning it away, but it grew back in seconds and wrapped around her again.

Nicci could barely move her arms. Concentrating hard, she could feel the power of the magic attacking her, and the lightning strike left a tracery in her own aura, like an intrusive vine growing throughout her Han. The magic was centered on her hair, attacking her hair. She could feel it.

There must be some vulnerability, a window through her defenses that she had not detected. But, no . . . it wasn't all her hair, it was just *one strand* of hair! Yes, that was the focal point, the link that her attacker was using, one hair, out of countless strands.

The locks wound tighter, crushing her ribs, squeezing her waist, cutting off all circulation in her legs. She collapsed to the ground, like a fly wrapped up in a spider's web. She had stopped struggling, stopped cutting, in order to concentrate. It was her only chance.

Dimly, she heard Nathan yelling at her, demanding that she not give up, but Nicci would never give up.

She sent her thoughts out, tracing her Han just as the Sisters had taught her. At last she found the single connection that tied the evil magic to her like a fisherman's hook and line. That was what connected the spell to her!

She had to find it, break it. She followed her thoughts, closed her eyes, paying no attention to the fact that she couldn't breathe, that her bones creaked, about to crush inward. Fighting to move her trapped fingers, she stirred through the wild, combative strands, working upward, trying to reach her scalp. She followed the bright line inside her mind, the key single strand, a broken hair. The other half of that blond strand was somewhere else, in the hands of her enemy, an evil wizard or sorceress.

Twin sorceresses!

Nicci found the hair, just a short strand that had not grown fantastically like all the others. This was the strand that bound the spell to her, half still connected to her head, the other half in the hands of her enemies. She couldn't separate that single hair from the thicker strands all around it, but she twisted the clump of hair with her fingers and gave a sharp yank, ripping out a bloody swatch—which included the single broken strand.

Once she pulled that strand out by the root, the spell connection was broken. The evil magic recoiled like a taut rope suddenly cut. Her ravening hair curled, then fell limp. The bindings sagged around her body, giving her a chance to heave a huge breath, filling her lungs. Her ribs ached and several were likely cracked. Her throat was bruised from the strangling locks.

Yelling her name, Nathan and Bannon cut at her hair, tearing the severed strands away from her face and her mouth, freeing her.

She breathed heavily and blinked her blue eyes up at her two companions. "Thank you."

Bannon clawed the dead ropes of hair from himself, untangled his legs, kicked the mass away. He looked around warily and tugged his hair back, as if afraid his own ginger locks might also spring into deadly life. "What caused that, Sorceress? Was it some wild magic still left in the pyramid?"

"No." Nicci turned her cold gaze toward Nathan.

The wizard looked exhausted and battered, confused. "Dear spirits, then what—"

"You know what it was. General Utros doesn't want to negotiate. His two pet sorceresses attacked me, tried to murder me. There will be no honorable solution." She brushed strands from her black dress as she stood in a pile of curled, blond hair. "And now, I am angry."

CHAPTER 21

After being attacked by the sorceresses' twisted spell, Nicci spent the following day with Nathan and the duma members, deep in angry discussions about how to respond to the threat of General Utros.

Bannon was not part of that debate, and instead he went into the city the next morning, accompanied by Lila. Even with an ancient army camped outside the walls, he knew that Ildakar had more than one enemy, and the city's populace would have to fight together. The revolt was over, but not settled, and when the duma called upon them to make extreme sacrifices, the lower classes would not forget their generations of oppression under the gifted nobles. He himself had been held prisoner in the combat pits, and his friend Ian had been transformed from an idealistic boy into a killing machine.

As he headed down into the lower levels of the city, he didn't invite Lila along, but she accompanied him nevertheless. Her skin was marked with countless protective runes, but she had an animal sensuality that was as terrifying as it was attractive.

She fell into place beside him. "Where are we going today,

boy?" She sized up his loose shirt, the sword he carried at his side. "Are we going out to fight?"

"My name is Bannon," he reminded her. "I'm going to the old slave market." He glanced over at her, narrowing his hazel eyes. "You're a morazeth. The former slaves there won't look kindly upon you."

Her step didn't falter. "I'm not expecting hugs or smiles, but you've proved that you need protection. I go with you."

Bannon sniffed and kept walking. "I can take care of myself."

"I can take care of you, too. It's the best way to be sure. I would consider it my own failing if I let you get killed by some thug in an alley."

Knowing he couldn't convince her otherwise, Bannon headed to the open market. He thought back to the day the three Norukai serpent ships had arrived on the Killraven River, carrying more than a hundred and fifty captives for the slave market. *Walking meat,* the Norukai called them. Bannon had watched the sickening spectacle as the nobles bid on slaves like silk merchants haggling over bolts of cloth, and then the sovrena and the wizard commander had preempted the bids to buy the entire lot for their grand bloodworking.

Even though the slaves had freed themselves, they were not in a forgiving mood. They were bottled up inside the walls of Ildakar, forced to defend their city alongside the nobles who had oppressed them.

Bannon and Lila passed under an arched gate into the open square with stepped stone seats on the outer perimeter, where noble bidders had once sat to inspect the captives for sale. He had expected the slave market to be mostly empty after the uprising, but instead the place was a bustling bazaar, with tents and awnings, colorful Ildakaran silk stretched across wooden frames. Intricate tapestries were spread on the flagstones like rugs, likely torn from the walls of noble villas. Bannon saw chattering families around cook fires, grim-looking people in ragged tunics or drab brown robes, while others flaunted expensive finery looted from their masters' dwellings.

After Mirrormask's revolt, many of the freed lower classes abandoned their former domiciles and formed a community of their own, scorning the old order and old duties. But everyone needed to work in some capacity to keep the city functioning, to harvest the food they required in order to withstand the siege. Some citizens understood their duty, while others seemed reluctant to help any of the upper classes they still resented. Several more nobles had been surreptitiously murdered in the past few days.

As Bannon entered the square, hundreds of eyes turned toward him. He felt like a trespasser, but many of the slaves knew him on sight. He had fought at their side during the uprising, and he had been with them on the top of the plateau, freeing the sacrificial victims.

But mixed in with the general hubbub of conversation, he heard a grumble directed at Lila, though she seemed deaf to it. She walked ahead of Bannon as if clearing the way for him. She looked around and frowned. "Is this what you wanted to see, boy?" She raised her voice, scolding the former slaves who had occupied the slave market. "This is not your home. This is a public square. You shouldn't be living here."

"We don't listen to any morazeth," grumbled one man, his hand clenching a sturdy wooden pole that supported a stolen tapestry. "This is our home now. We no longer serve the nobles in their villas."

"This is our city, too," said an older woman who washed clothes in a fountain, and then spread them on the sunlit flagstones to dry.

Two laughing boys ran past, chasing each other, but they stopped to stare at Lila. When she stared back at them, they fled in terror.

"Yes, this is your city," Lila repeated, "and you have responsibilities, too. You must help defend Ildakar against enemies."

"Against *all* enemies," said the man gripping the wooden pole.

Bannon came forward, trying to make peace. "We know that your society has to change. Nicci and Nathan will help when they talk to the duma members."

"We have no one to speak for us," grumbled the woman as she slopped a wet, soapy rag onto the flagstones.

Bannon searched for words. He was just a former cabbage farmer, not a politician, and he didn't know how to fix social injustices. More people began to gather around them like a mob closing in. There were enough potential opponents here to tear Lila apart, but the morazeth would probably kill half of them before they took her down. She stood as still as a stone warrior.

Bannon raised a hand, realizing that now *he* was protecting *her*. "It'll take time. You've already made your point. Your grievances are still valid."

Lila seemed oblivious to her danger. A couple of people took flaming brands from the cook fires, and another man found a makeshift wooden club. She didn't flinch as they approached.

Bannon's voice grew more urgent. "Look at how much has changed in such a short time. The wizard commander is gone, the sovrena is in a dungeon. You've made progress. Don't destroy it by some foolish action. We all have to fight against General Utros."

"The morazeth bitches should be in dungeons, too," said a young man with a crippled arm. "Think of what they did to those arena fighters, what they did to you, Bannon! I was at your side when we freed the victims up at the pyramid."

"How can you stand with *her*?" sneered the woman washing clothes, shooting a glare at Lila. "Didn't she beat you? Break you?"

"It's not as simple as that," Bannon said, his voice uncertain.

Lila turned her glare on the people who had made their makeshift settlement in the slave market. "You live in Ildakar and you've seen the thousands of enemy soldiers outside the walls. Our true battle is against General Utros, our common enemy. Once he is defeated and the city is safe, then we can discuss the niceties of equality and representative rule. But right now we're at war, and we need all fighters."

Her tone of voice did not appease them. One man was braiding long leather thongs into what would become a bull-whip. He spoke up. "Over the last few years, lots of escaped slaves slipped out the city and made new lives for themselves in Stravera and other mountain towns. I stayed, but what if that was a mistake? The sooner Ildakar falls, maybe the better it is for us."

Someone else said, "We should just leave the city and join General Utros."

Now Lila was incensed. "Then you are truly the enemies of Ildakar and should be killed here and now."

"Lila!" Bannon cried out, afraid the mob would swarm forward. "Sweet Sea Mother, don't you see where you are?"

"Yes, I am among potential traitors."

Then a young man's voice broke in, surprising them. "I don't care what's been done to us by some arrogant nobles. Ildakar is still our city. Do we want to *earn* our new place in it, or not? What would Mirrormask say?"

"Mirrormask betrayed us, too," grunted the man with the bullwhip.

Bannon turned to see a ragamuffin figure with unruly hair, a boy no older than fourteen in a rough-spun tunic and flimsy sandals. Oddly, the boy's skin, his face, his hair all had a pale powdery appearance, a hint of gray on his flesh. Bannon suddenly recognized him. "I know you—you're the yaxen herder, the boy caught working for Mirrormask."

"I planted mirror shards, as a symbol, and then I was caught by the morazeth." The boy snorted at Lila. "I think *she* was one of them, but they all look alike to me."

"As you look alike to us," Lila said.

Bannon remembered the day Adessa and other morazeth had dragged this captive young man into the ruling tower. The boy had confessed his involvement with the rebels, and Wizard Commander Maxim had worked the stone spell on him before the boy could confess any details. Since Maxim himself was Mirrormask, Bannon understood now why the wizard commander had needed to silence the captive boy.

He said, "You do know that Mirrormask was lying to you? Using the unrest of the lower classes for his own purposes, not for your good."

The boy looked downcast. "That doesn't mean his words weren't true. We staged the revolt for our own reasons, not for his."

Clearly angry, Lila placed her hands on the black wrap around her waist, touching the agile knife that could inflict incredible pain on others. "Ildakar is your city, no matter what. Will you fight for it, or will you shirk your duties and complain?"

Bannon stepped closer to the half-stone yaxen herder. "They placed you as a statue in the slave market to warn others against resisting the nobles."

"And how did that work?" the young boy snorted. "I'm Timothy. Everyone here knows me." He gave a stiff grin. "In some ways, becoming a statue was the greatest thing that ever happened to me." He turned around, and Bannon realized that the freed slaves camped in the broad market did indeed defer to him.

Timothy raised his voice to all of them. "I agree with the morazeth in this. Ildakar is our city. We fought too hard to be free, and now that we have much of what we wanted, would you just give it up?"

Bannon stood closer to the boy. "We're all fighting for the same thing, really, and judging by the size of the army out there, we'll need all the help we can get."

Timothy stared uncertainly at Bannon for a long time. "I've heard of you. I know what you did breaking the warriors free, fighting alongside Nicci." But he shook his head at Lila. "Since I worked for Mirrormask, I accepted that I'd probably be caught someday, but that didn't stop me from spreading messages, helping recruit others to fight for the cause."

"And we found you," Lila said, "and so many others."

"Still, we won," Timothy said with a shrug. He seemed young, happy-go-lucky, and determined, as if he had iron inside of him as well as stone. "I'll agree to fight for Ildakar, and so will all these people—but only if we have part of the city once we win."

Remembering the vast army outside, the pounding stone fists that made the thick walls echo and tremble, Bannon wasn't sure anything would remain unless they won, and soon.

"We need an *army*," Lila said in a haughty voice, "not muttering slaves who hide under tents in the city square."

Timothy crossed his arms over his hardened chest. "I'll fight, but only if I can be part of a real army. It's better than herding yaxen."

Lila stepped very close to him, intimidating, but the boy didn't back down. "You're just a scrawny wisp of a child. What would you do for our army? Trip some of Utros's soldiers?"

He gazed right back at her, mirroring her defiance. "I'll fight."

"You could never be a real fighter. How could you inflict any damage?" In a lightning strike, Lila backhanded him hard across his chest.

Surprisingly, her knuckles cracked against his tough skin. The blow would have knocked anyone else backward, but Timothy remained sturdy, as if anchored to the flagstones.

Shocked, the morazeth looked at her stinging hand. Her knuckles were bloody.

Timothy chuckled and offhandedly struck her in return. Lila wasn't expecting the blow, and she staggered from the impact. She blinked in amazement, then turned to the street scamp with greater respect. "Maybe we can make fighters out of you after all."

"Teach me how to fight, and I'll show you what I can do," said Timothy.

The freed slaves in their camp looked up from cook fires, while others emerged from silken tents.

Lila gave a small smile, glancing at Bannon. "I could train him into an adequate fighter. Let me teach you, Timothy. I'll take you under my wing."

"Teach all of us how to fight," the young man said, "or it's no bargain at all."

The morazeth considered, while the freed slaves muttered. They respected Timothy for the ordeal he had gone through, and now he was forcing them to put their unrest, their dissatisfaction, and their complaints into real action.

Bannon felt strangely relieved. "We'll be happy to have you as part of Ildakar's defenses. We need every fighter right now."

CHAPTER 22

The high windows in the ruling chamber were open to let the breezes and city noises waft in, along with the renewed drumbeat of fists pounding against the wall. Nicci sat by herself, her blond hair ragged and uneven, roughly shorn after the spell attack.

Quentin looked down at a long strip of paper spread out on his table, where he had written lists. He raised his voice to get the attention of the duma members. "What is our next order of business?"

Damon sat beside Quentin, peering down at ledgers as if searching for some number in a long-forgotten accounting. Oron sat in another seat wearing a fur-lined cape and a fur-collared shirt. He used a stubby knife to scrape beneath his fingernails, removing the residue of blood. Beside him on the stone bench perched a short-statured woman, Olgya, who ran the silk spinners' guild, another new duma member. Her round eyes were highlighted with crow's-feet. Her long, straight brown hair was shot with lines of pale gray, as if infused with strands of raw silk and gathered in clumps tied with bright silk ribbons. She was also Jed's mother.

The meeting had droned on with very little progress, and Nicci was growing impatient. High Captain Stuart presented a long list of new defenders who had been recruited from the arena fighters, along with hundreds of volunteer militia members, citizens of Ildakar willing to fight. "With such a large population, we will have a formidable army if we choose to attack the general's forces," he said. "Given the right circumstances, our numbers might even match theirs."

"A full-fledged military offensive on our part could certainly cause a great deal of damage," Damon said. "And think of Ildakar's gifted! Utros has only two sorceresses, while we have many powerful wizards."

"Who would lead such a strike?" Oron asked.

Glancing at the unoccupied thrones of the wizard commander and sovrena, Oron spoke up. "Sooner or later we have to choose new leaders. We dare not let these duma meetings become tedious arguments, as they were for centuries. We are under siege—we need more than a committee!"

Nicci rose to her feet and self-consciously ran her hand through her ragged hair. "Before choosing leaders, we must finish—no, *you* must finish—filling the vacancies in the duma, and your ruling council cannot be composed only of Ildakaran nobles, as it was before." She nodded a signal to High Captain Stuart, who ran into the hall to fetch the person waiting outside the ruling chamber.

"We already invited you and the wizard Nathan to formally join us," said the stony sorceress Lani. "You two are the best candidates, and we need your gift to help us fight. Why not agree to become members of the council?"

"We will not join your duma," Nicci insisted. "We are not part of your city. You have to make your own decisions—fair decisions, for all the people." She softened her voice, showing a small amount of conciliation. "But we will help."

Damon sighed. "Then whom do you suggest? We have other gifted people in Ildakar, but nobody who has our standing."

"Did you learn nothing from the recent uprising?" Nicci snapped. "Freedom and a stable society must be built from all sides. You require a duma representing the citizens of Ildakar—all people. Your city is home to more than just wizards, more than nobles, and you can't restrict the duma to nobles. You need representatives from the merchants, the lower classes, even the slaves."

They all turned as Rendell entered, a reliable and determined older man who had helped nurse Nicci back to health after her battle with Thora. All the former followers of Mirrormask respected him. "Welcome, Rendell. I would like everyone here to consider you as the next member of the duma. Every group in the city must have a voice."

Elsa looked puzzled, while the expression on Lani's stony face was unreadable, but Quentin, Damon, and Olgya frowned. Oron snorted. "He's a slave! We're trying to save Ildakar."

"There are other ways to save the city," Nicci said, "and Ildakar will be better able to save itself if you give *all* your people the same goal. If Rendell has a seat on the council, he can speak on behalf of the lower classes. As you saw on the night of the revolt, they can be ruthless fighters. Imagine what they could do against enemy soldiers."

Quentin blew a loud breath out through his nostrils. "A slave does not belong in the duma. Haven't those animals already killed enough nobles? I heard another one was beheaded yesterday. How can you think of rewarding them?"

Rendell stepped forward, indignant and speaking loudly for himself. "I'm not a slave. I am free now, and I am a citizen. I represent many thousands of people who could just as easily become your worst nightmare."

"He threatens another revolt!" Olgya cried. "While the city is under siege!"

"Several nobles have been murdered by the rabble in recent days," Oron said. "How can we trust someone like him?"

Rendell looked deeply saddened. "I'll speak with them,

demand that they stop their unrest for now. I can redirect their anger, if you will listen to our grievances and let us be a part of this city in a meaningful way."

Quentin scowled. "Why would we need them?"

Nicci spun to face the dark-skinned wizard. "Are you all deaf? He offered you a large fighting force, and all you have to do is treat them fairly. Did you not just suggest launching an attack on the siege army?"

"We can't turn down their help," Elsa said. "For many centuries we've asked the slaves to maintain Ildakar. This city is their home, too. Give those people a voice, and they may fight passionately to protect Ildakar. We should let Rendell be a provisional member of the new duma, just to control the unrest."

"If General Utros breaks down the walls and tears apart the city, we'll all be dead," Oron said with a continued scowl. "I'd rather Rendell's people died fighting enemy soldiers instead of murdering us in our beds." He shrugged. "Throw the slaves this little bone so we no longer need to worry about them."

An insulted expression crossed Rendell's face, but before he could speak, Nicci stepped out onto the blue marble floor. "That is a start, but not good enough. The duma must also include merchants, tradesmen. All of Ildakar needs to feel they are heard. If you do this, then after the siege is broken you will have a solid foundation for your city. You may even make Ildakar into the perfect society that Sovrena Thora imagined she was creating."

"I still think it's risky," Quentin grumbled.

"And foolish," Damon added.

"It's not foolish." Lani rose from the stone bench near Nathan and Elsa. "Many things will have to change now that Sovrena Thora has been overthrown." She turned to face the former slave. "I, too, welcome Rendell to the duma."

"I cast my vote in favor," Nathan added, "if my vote counts."

"Good enough," said Oron.

Olgya fiddled with one of her braids, then tossed it over her shoulder. "I suppose it doesn't make much difference. Now can we move on to more important business?"

Outvoted, Damon and Quentin sat down and shrugged. "It's done for now," Quentin said, "and I hope we haven't made a mistake."

"The duma has made mistakes before," Lani pointed out. "That's why we're in trouble now. If Thora hadn't sent my dear Renn away on a fool's mission, we'd have another strong wizard in the fight against Utros." Her long sigh sounded hollow through her partially petrified lips. "I hope he's all right out there. . . ."

Nicci spoke again, addressing the duma. "This isn't just an administrative meeting, but a war council. We have to make decisions. What are we going to do, now that the general's sorceresses have attacked here?" She swept her blue gaze across the members, touched her ragged hair. "How will you respond?"

"What options do we have?" Damon asked.

Elsa leaned forward, placed her elbows on the stone table. "All options? Well, we can annihilate Utros and his army . . . which doesn't seem likely. Or we can drive them away, scatter them to other lands."

"Even if we could break the siege and drive them away, it would only turn them loose on the rest of the Old World," Nicci said. "And my responsibility is greater than just this one city."

Elsa raised a third finger. "I'm just listing all options, however unpalatable they may be. Another possibility is that Ildakar can simply surrender, open its gates and let the city be overrun."

Amid the shocked whispers around the tables, Lani said, "I'd rather not make that choice."

Elsa smiled. "So, I think our best option is the fourth one." She glanced at Nathan. "We find some way to negotiate a peace. That is the general's best option, too. What is he still fighting for? What purpose does this siege serve? He no longer even has an emperor."

Nicci said, "He does not seem to be in a mind-set for negotiating. His sorceresses attacked me."

"If we prove our strength, then he'll listen," said Oron. "I say we make a focused attack, target one section of his army, and give him a black eye. Show him what we can do and threaten much worse if he isn't reasonable." He sniffed. "We are not to be trifled with."

"Those are all the choices I can think of," Elsa said.

The duma members talked among themselves, considering, but Quentin interjected, "You are forgetting one other option." He glanced at Damon, who nodded. Obviously they had discussed this before.

The dark-haired wizard stroked his drooping mustaches and said, "We know how to work the blood magic. It's been done before. We could rebuild the apparatus, make the spell-forms, and find enough volunteers for sacrifice." He paused to let everyone realize what he was saying. "If we raised the shroud of eternity again and took Ildakar out of time, we would all be safe and protected forever." He smiled. "We'd never need to worry about General Utros again."

When the duma meeting broke for an uncomfortable recess, Nicci went to the top of the high ruling tower, where she had a view of the huge army on the expansive plain. She watched the enemy ranks drilling, like game pieces on a vast board.

When Emperor Jagang had practiced his strategy, the big tyrant found ways to amuse himself and to hone his skills. As the Imperial Order consolidated the Old World and moved north to conquer D'Hara, he would play his game of har'kur, forcing Nicci to serve as his opponent, as Death's Mistress. Back then, though he abused her, she had tried to please him, believing in the cause of the Order.

In a large clearing in camp, Jagang's soldiers would scribe

lines in the turf with their spears, and then assemble the playing pieces—slaves who represented the parts of various armies. As Nicci and Emperor Jagang sat together on a wooden observation tower, they would command the game pieces to move across the field. The slaves had no choice but to go where they were told. If Nicci lost a move, Jagang's soldiers would stride forward with their halberds and hack off the head of the losing piece.

Once, one of Jagang's game pieces, doomed after Nicci made a bold move, had tried to run from the playing field, only to be skewered with spears. By the rules laid down by Jagang himself, the fleeing piece meant that his side forfeited the game. In a rage, Jagang had ordered all of Nicci's pieces slaughtered as well as his own. The evil dream walker had not known how to lose. Afterward, he looked at the slaughtered slaves and huffed. "Let that be a lesson. In war sometimes unpredictable disasters happen."

Now, as Nicci watched the ancient army, she wished one of those unpredictable disasters would befall General Utros.

Nathan emerged into the tower's rooftop gardens. Under the open sky, there were hedges in planters, jasmine shrubs, and dwarf citrus trees. Songbirds flitted around without fear now that the hair-fine nets Sovrena Thora had strung around the roof were gone.

Nathan smiled. "I don't mean to disturb your thoughts, Sorceress. Have you found a brilliant solution to overthrow the enemy army?"

"I am still thinking." It was in these peaceful high gardens that Wizard Commander Maxim had secretly encouraged her to challenge the sovrena's corrupt rule. "The duma has to make their own decisions. I am not their leader, and neither are you."

Nathan stroked his chin. "Agreed, but I am not convinced a surprise military offensive against an army of that size will be as effective as the wizards think it will be." He mused, "We could send another negotiating party to Utros. Do we have any reason to believe the general might be willing to listen, now that he's had time to consider the reality of his situation? Maybe his bluster was just a tactic. We did defeat his sorceresses and prove our strength."

"And now we know we cannot trust him." Nicci breathed cold air through her nostrils and peered into the distance. "He attacked me, Nathan. I can't let that go unchallenged. I want to find a way to make him *hurt,* and if the duma intends to launch a strike with all of their gifted and a great many soldiers, maybe we could succeed, if we targeted a specific part of his army and hit him without any forewarning."

Humming, the wizard extended his arms in front of his chest, palms outward. Spreading his fingers, he sketched a rectangle in the air, pinched his fingertips, and used his gift to create a distance-viewing lens. The army of General Utros sprang into sharp clarity in front of them, and as Nathan shifted his hands, so did the view, to show thousands of soldiers like individual armies drilling. Smaller parties rode out into the hills on scouting or raiding expeditions.

Nicci raised a hand. "Go back. What was that?"

They watched a group of more than a thousand soldiers marching westward into the hills, a powerful invading force toward the mountains. Another large army marched north into the thick forests and the mining areas in the hills, while a third expeditionary force moved south toward the Killraven River and the lowlands.

Nathan frowned. "He is shrinking his siege force."

Nicci was deeply concerned. "Very few cities could withstand even one of those splinter armies. Imagine all those enemy soldiers arriving at Cliffwall, or Renda Bay, or one of the larger cities along the coast like Larrikan Shores or Serrimundi. General Utros could threaten the entire Old World." She squeezed her fists, feeling the chill in her heart, the black ice forming there. She couldn't stop thinking of what Richard had commanded her and Nathan to do. "We can't let that happen. We have to work with the wizards here, keep Utros occupied."

Nathan waved his hands, and the shimmering view dissolved. He spoke in a softer voice. "I have the utmost confidence in your ability to save us. After all, you must save the entire world. It was foretold in my life book."

"I don't trust the word of a witch woman, and prophecy is gone. You know that better than anyone. Why should we believe it?"

Rather than arguing, Nathan brought out the book, as if to offer proof of what Red had written. He opened the leather-bound volume and flipped forward from where he had added journal entries of their adventures, from the Dark Lands to the Old World, down beyond the Phantom Coast and now over the mountains to Ildakar. He stopped at the first page to read the lines that both he and Nicci knew well.

Kol Adair lies far to the south in the Old World. From there, the Wizard will behold what he needs to make himself whole again. And the Sorceress must save the world.

Shortly after Richard dispatched them as his roving ambassadors, they had encountered Red in her wilderness of skulls, deep in the Dark Lands. Nathan asked her to create a life book for him, wanting his own story preserved, and the strange witch woman had complied, but not in the way he expected.

Nathan held out the book now, touching it with his long finger. "We can't dismiss the words entirely, Sorceress. Even though we didn't know what this meant at the time, Red was absolutely correct. I have the heart of a wizard now, I have my gift back, but you, my dear Nicci, still need to save the world." He tapped the page. "It's written."

Nicci took the book from him, closed it. "Prophecy is gone, as I said."

"It need not be a prophecy," Nathan replied, taking the book back. "Maybe it's just good advice. 'And the Sorceress must save the world.'"

They continued to watch separate contingents marching from the plain toward unknown destinations. Nicci didn't disagree with the words Red had written, whether or not she believed the premonition. "I'll save the world, for my own reasons."

"That is always best. And I'll help you in any way I can."

CHAPTER 23

I n the Cliffwall archive, Verna spent the morning inside a library chamber, drinking hot tea and studying the books that the scholars had delivered to her. Two other Sisters of the Light, Rhoda and Eldine, scrutinized volumes, whispering as they compared notes. Novice Amber cheerfully carried in a stack of ledgers, blowing dust off the embossed leather cover of the top volume.

"Here's another catalog, Prelate." She deposited the armful on the table, rattling Verna's cup of tea. "These refer mainly to maps and descriptions. The scholar archivist is still trying to pull the right listings because many books contain more than one subject."

Verna looked at the open volume in front of her and traced her fingertip down the lines of titles. Many were written in the expansive hand of Scholar-Archivist Simon, who had spent a decade compiling the catalogs, but the new entries were written by Franklin, whose penmanship was much tighter, more efficient.

The prelate looked up at Amber. "The titles listed here contain legends of magical creatures, abominations that were developed as weapons in the ancient wizard wars. The sliphs, for instance." Verna shook her head at the long list. "And here, two entire volumes on the dangers of succubi! Those creatures were turned loose in the Old World to seduce and destroy men and thereby weaken armies that stood against the enemy wizards." She pursed her lips in a frown. "I expect it's quite salacious reading."

Amber blushed, and Verna wondered how experienced the pretty young girl might be in romance or sex. Turning the page in the dusty old book, Verna recalled being so youthful, but that was more than a century and a half ago, when she and Warren were the same age, trying to keep a professional boundary around their growing affection for each other. When Verna left the Palace of the Prophets in search of Richard Rahl, she had aged during those decades, while Warren remained as young as ever. Dear Warren . . . she missed him so much.

She flipped a page back, looked at more listings. "Here, they have three books about the selka, one of them a log from an ancient warship captain."

Amber leaned close. "The selka?"

"Humans transformed into water-breathing creatures that dwell in the oceans. They could battle an enemy navy from beneath the hulls."

The young girl gave a visible shudder. "We are far from the ocean, here, Prelate. I don't think I'd like to see them." She frowned with worry. "I hope my brother's all right. He's still at Renda Bay. Do you think the selka might attack the village?"

"Captain Norcross is building defenses for a much more likely enemy, child," Verna said. "Lose sleep over Norukai raiders rather than the selka." She realized her words offered the girl little reassurance.

The young scholars Oliver and Peretta entered the study room. Although they had lived all their lives in the Cliffwall canyons, these two had volunteered at Nicci's request to embark on a long journey to deliver a report for Lord Rahl.

They had found Verna and General Zimmer in Tanimura and led them back here. The two shy, diligent scholars were glad to be back home in their sanctuary, but that journey had changed them. Verna could see a restless glint in their eyes, an appreciation of the adventure they'd experienced. The prelate supposed it wouldn't be long before the two wanted to explore the world again.

"We brought books on healing lore," said Peretta. She was a thin, large-eyed girl with a mop of dark curly hair. "I've memorized them all, but I thought you might like to have a look."

"Healing spells are always appreciated," Verna said, "and always useful."

"It's just a *list* of the books, not the actual spells," Oliver corrected, squinting at the volumes he carried. Though he was young, he had spent so many years poring over illegible writing, faded ink, and crumbling pages that his vision was already waning. "A complete catalog is the first part of understanding the knowledge available to us." He let out a tired sigh. "We're working as hard as we can, but Franklin estimates we still have a decade or more before we even complete our list of the titles in Cliffwall."

"The Sisters will help however we can," Verna said, accepting the books from each of them. "When I first set foot in here, I looked forward to studying the amazing knowledge." She paused, then smiled. "Now it seems we may spend years reading mere lists of books and none of the content."

Oliver said, "Knowledge is one thing, Prelate, but *knowing* what you know is an overlooked skill."

"I know what I know," Peretta said with a sniff. "All memmers do." She flushed in embarrassment. "I'm sorry, I didn't mean to sound arrogant. My gift of remembering is a virtue, but you all have skills as well." She flashed a quick apologetic glance at her friend. "Oliver is very smart."

He responded with a shy laugh. "To me, these books are a

great adventure of discovery. Once you learn something, it's even more important to share your knowledge." He looked warmly at her. The two of them had spent so much time together in the wilderness that they'd formed a close bond, maybe even a romantic one.

"Unless we know what we know, we'll never be able to find what we need." Verna reached into the pocket of her robe and withdrew a small glazed figurine of a toad. It was just a memento, a cute decoration that she had found when searching the ruins of the Palace of the Prophets. The toad figurine had no significance, as far as she could tell, although she thought it might have belonged to Sister Armina back in the palace. Now the toad was just a reminder of better days. Verna liked to have it there, silently watching their busy work.

Amber picked it up, and smiled at the figurine with delight before placing it back on the study table. "I remember when we found this."

Renn bustled in, looking fresh now that he had rested comfortably for several days. He was dressed in clean gray scholar's robes instead of his maroon silk garments, which badly needed mending after his long journey.

He strolled up to the study tables piled with books. "I must admit, Prelate, I am impressed with this archive. I've always loved books and the knowledge they contain. For centuries I devoted myself to reading the libraries in Ildakar, then reading them again so I could understand the nuances. Beneath the shroud of eternity I had plenty of time! But all these books in Cliffwall"—he clucked his tongue against his teeth—"it is like a river of knowledge. How could I possibly have time to read them all?"

Verna realized that good meals and a polite welcome had softened the blustery, arrogant wizard. "Now that you've seen the vast number of books here, Renn, I hope you no longer consider packing them on a mule and carrying them back to Ildakar."

Renn scoffed. "By the Keeper's beard, that was never a realistic goal. My city is so far away, I don't relish making that journey again. I don't see the point! The cooks and bakers you have here in Cliffwall are quite talented. I don't think I'll ever get tired of that mutton and currant pie they made last night." He patted his rounded stomach.

Verna raised her eyebrows. "So, Captain Trevor and his nine men are not plotting to overthrow the archive, conquer General Zimmer and his D'Haran soldiers, and steal all the tomes?"

Renn blew air through his lips. "Oh, I think that would be far too much trouble, however much Sovrena Thora might like to get her hands on these records." He sank heavily onto the bench beside Verna, looking curiously at the odd toad figurine. He picked up one of the books and scanned the titles about legendary succubi. "Hmm, interesting. I don't think we've ever had a succubus in Ildakar."

He read for a few moments, then glanced up at Verna, more serious now. "Ildakar is truly a beautiful city, Prelate, as glorious as the legends would have you believe, but Cliffwall is a fine place, too. I admire what the people have done, and I've never seen anything like those memmers."

Standing beside the table, young Peretta smiled proudly. "There has never been anything like the memmers."

Distractedly, Renn picked up another volume. "Rather than hauling so many fragile and ancient books on a rigorous cross-country journey, it would make far more sense if I just brought a few scholars and memmers back to Ildakar with me, so they could at least convey the extent of the knowledge here."

Brightening, Oliver glanced at Peretta. "That could be arranged. And I'd like to go along."

"I would definitely like to see Ildakar," Peretta added.

Surprised at their eager reaction to his offhand suggestion, Renn raised a pudgy hand. "Oh, I'm not suggesting that yet! I will need much more time to recover from our arduous trek." He looked away. "And I'd want to be careful, since I am not entirely certain what Sovrena Thora might intend with this powerful knowledge. I'm a duma member, and therefore loyal to Ildakar, but the sovrena did many objectionable things. She turned my beloved Lani to stone." He paused for a moment. "And all her bloodworkings, how she treated the ungifted, her scorn for those weaker than her. I was *ashamed* of what Thora did."

Verna closed the volume in front of her and sipped her tea, which had grown cold. "Good thing Nicci and Nathan are there to keep her under control. I don't believe either of them would suffer a tyrant."

Renn chuckled at the thought. "Yes, I've seen the lovely Nicci, the flash of anger in her eyes, so blue! The wizards of Ildakar did grow complacent over a millennium and a half, but Nicci challenged their daily assumptions. I don't expect Thora likes it." He sighed. "Ah, I wish Nicci had been there when Lani battled the sovrena centuries ago. If they worked together, those two could certainly have overthrown Thora."

Amber looked confused. "And you want to give the sovrena all the magic in this archive? Why would you do that?"

"Now, now, it was what she ordered me to do, but maybe it's high time I stop listening to everything Thora says." He sniffed, looked at the toad figurine again, and slid it aside. "Ildakar was a beautiful city. Lani and I had a good life together. You should have seen her call the songbirds. They would flock around her, chirping, singing." He sighed. "But eventually, when Thora executed a slave for stealing some jewels she knew her own son Amos had taken, Lani couldn't tolerate the injustice. She challenged the sovrena."

His eyes filled with tears and he turned away. "Lani was powerful and dear, but compassionate, while Thora was ruthless. She defeated my poor Lani, petrified her, and then kept her statue in the ruling chamber for all to see the price of defiance." He wiped a hand across his eyes and distracted himself by opening another book, squinting down at the words. "What is this? An entire list of cures for flatulence? Is that vital magical lore?"

Verna said, "If one suffers from the affliction, the cure would seem very important indeed."

"And the person's family and neighbors would appreciate it as well," Rhoda commented from the adjacent table, eliciting chuckles among the scholars.

Renn returned to his ponderings, ignoring the studies of intestinal maladies. "The sovrena always doubted me because I cared so much for Lani. Yes, I was the weakest gifted duma member, and she always held a threat over me. I knew she'd petrify me too if I didn't support her cruel rulings. I should not have agreed, but I didn't have any choice." He tapped his fingers on the table. "I now suppose she sent me on this wild and pointless quest just to get rid of me. She never expected me to find Cliffwall, maybe never believed it even existed. She gave me only a dozen escort soldiers to fight all the dangers we might encounter on a long and arduous journey across unknown lands." He shook his head. "I suppose Captain Trevor and I could find our way back to Ildakar, but why would we want to?"

"I would like to know what Nicci and Nathan are doing," Verna suggested.

"You have a point, but let's wait a little while longer, shall we? I'd like a few more nights in a dry bed with a warm blanket."

General Zimmer and his fifty men camped in dozens of neat tents erected in the pastures alongside the stream. The Cliffwall farmers tended fields of grain, families weeded their vegetable gardens, shepherds watched their flocks near orchards of nut and fruit trees. Though far from home, the D'Haran soldiers were relaxed, feeling safe after their long journey from Tanimura.

Despite the protection of the high rock walls, the narrow canyon entrance, and the isolation of the plateau, Zimmer didn't let himself relax. He had explored up and down the main canyon, studied the tributaries of streams and side canyons through the high desert. He insisted that his fifty D'Haran soldiers keep their swords sharpened, their armor clean, their eyes alert. He did not intend to be caught unawares.

General Zimmer was young to hold such a high rank, but harsh experiences had aged him well beyond his years. He'd been promoted only because so many superior officers had been slain in the brutal battles against the ravenous undead armies that surged across the Dark Lands, driven by the resurrected Emperor Sulachan. Zimmer had faced death himself, been splashed with the blood of countless enemies, and he had also led vicious commando strikes down in the Old World against the army of the Imperial Order. He recalled his previous commanders, his brave mentors who had fallen under the gnashing teeth of a horrific enemy no one should have had to face.

Now, in the bucolic setting of the Cliffwall canyon, birds chirped in the orchards, and the sun shone in a blue sky. It was easy to be lulled into forgetting the true dangers of the world, but Zimmer never let down his guard.

Trevor, the captain of the Ildakaran escort, stepped up to him, still wearing his chest armor, short sword, and high boots. "My men are rested, General—and restless. Although this is a peaceful place, as we hoped, I don't want my guards to get fat. They were unprepared for the journey from Ildakar. That's why I lost three of my men." He cleared his throat, ashamed. "I'd like to keep the other nine men sharp. Would you allow them to train with your troops? Spar with them? Maybe we could learn from your men, and vice versa."

Zimmer looked skeptically at him. "It seems to me, Captain Trevor, that only a week ago, your handful of men were intent on conquering Cliffwall."

The other commander looked away, embarrassed. Trevor appeared much younger now that the mud and dust of travel had been washed away, the stubble shaved from his cheeks.

185

"There's not much chance of that, General, as you know full well." He lowered his voice in a conspiratorial tone. "Renn is a wizard of Ildakar, and they tend to begin a conversation with bluster, but that's all it is."

Zimmer remained wary. "And by training with your men, you want us to teach you our D'Haran fighting techniques? What if you turn them against us?"

Trevor shrugged. "I could say the same. My men would also teach you our methods of fighting. Surely there's something we could learn from one another?" He frowned as a thought occurred to him. "Are my nine men prisoners? Are we being held here?"

Instead of answering immediately, Zimmer considered his words. "If you left Cliffwall, I suppose I could let you aimlessly wander the wilderness again." He raised his eyebrows. "If that's what you'd really like?"

Trevor coughed and fidgeted. "No, I don't think that would be necessary. I'd rather make friends than enemies. Ildakar has faced enough enemies in the past."

Zimmer kept his voice stern. "Then maybe your wizards should learn about diplomacy. It would be remarkably beneficial for both sides." He looked at the young captain's face, saw true earnestness there. The other nine Ildakaran guards were relieved to have been welcomed in Cliffwall. He relented and said, "I, too, would rather have Ildakar as an ally than as an enemy. Even I have heard legends of the city, and I'd like to see it someday. Lord Rahl wants to consolidate the Old World." He clapped a hand on Trevor's shoulder. "Your city can have its independence, so long as you don't become aggressive invaders."

"That doesn't seem too much to ask for a strong empire and a life of peace," said Trevor.

Zimmer walked alongside the captain as they went to the line of D'Haran soldiers. "In that case, let's include your men in today's drills. Show us your techniques, and we'll forge a bond that will make us all stronger."

CHAPTER 24

Captain Norcross was pleased with how rapidly the defenses of Renda Bay were improving. The people in the seaside town were fishermen, boatbuilders, weavers, farmers, and tradesmen, and they had been preyed upon by the Norukai for far too long.

Thanks to the fortifications the D'Haran soldiers were installing, Renda Bay was now less vulnerable, but the village was not a garrison. These people would fight to defend their homes, but they were not a hardened army. They bore plenty of scars, however, and after Nicci and Nathan had fought with them to drive off the hideous slavers during the last raid, the town's heart had changed. The people decided to stop letting themselves be victims. Renda Bay had increased lookouts, sent out coastal patrols, rebuilt their town, and added defenses.

Then the D'Haran expeditionary force arrived, and Norcross had stricter orders from General Zimmer. The young captain and his soldiers stayed behind while the others went to Cliffwall. They swore to protect the fishing village against threats, but Norcross knew that even fifty brave soldiers wouldn't be enough to fight against the violent Norukai.

He stood at the harbor's edge in midmorning, after the day's mist had burned off and the fishing boats had gone out for their catch. The seasonal redfin run was nearly over, and the people were busy salting and smoking their catch for the cold months. The flocks of sheep and goats that grazed in the hills were growing fat for the winter slaughter, while others provided wool, milk, and cheese.

The people of Renda Bay worked day and night with Norcross's men, building towers and defensive walls so the town would be ready whenever the raiders returned. From his training, Norcross understood siege defenses, battle tactics, offensive weapons. Though he was not an engineer himself, three of his officers knew how to construct catapults and spiked archery towers, along with some surprises that could be used against raiders from the sea.

The young captain would not let his people rest until the town was safe. Even though the morning was peaceful and sunny, with a salty chill in the air, every person in Renda Bay knew that any day, rain or shine, could bring an attack from the ominous serpent ships.

Thaddeus, the town leader since his predecessor had been slain in the last Norukai raid, joined Captain Norcross to inspect the construction of the new towers that rose high above the harbor, one on each side of the river mouth. Built out of stone blocks brought from quarries down the coast, the massive guard towers weren't pretty, but they were nearly finished, with wooden platforms behind defensive crenellations, so that the guardians of Renda Bay could fire upon invading ships that attempted to enter the harbor. Three large cargo ships remained just outside the bay, like large guard dogs.

"How soon will we be ready?" Thaddeus asked, wiping his brow. "I'll lose sleep every night until our defenses are finished."

"We will be ready the moment we have to be," Norcross said. "We're ready now, and we will fight back if we are attacked. Each day's efforts simply make us more prepared."

Thaddeus nodded slowly. He was a broad-faced man with a reddish-brown beard and facial worry lines that hadn't been there a month ago. "We can't stop until the Norukai learn to leave us alone."

The young captain continued to reassure him. "My men belong to the D'Haran army, and that means something, but if it comes to a battle, we'll need everyone from Renda Bay to do their part, from a teenage farm boy swinging a rake to a grandmother striking with a cast-iron pan. Don't underestimate anyone fighting for their home and for freedom."

Thaddeus turned to look across the mouth of the river to a nearby hillside, and his expression grew sad. "If we had learned how to fight earlier, there wouldn't be so many wooden markers in our graveyard."

On the day after General Zimmer, Prelate Verna, and the other half of the expeditionary force departed for Cliffwall, young Norcross had accompanied the town leader to Renda Bay's cemetery. Permanent stone markers memorialized the fallen over the years, but an even greater number of wooden posts, each carved with a name, signified a loved one who was not dead but captured by the Norukai slavers, clubbed senseless and dragged aboard the serpent ships.

Norcross had said, "Your cemetery should be a place for old, contented grandparents who died fat in their beds, surrounded by family. Not this."

Thaddeus let out a wistful sigh. "Yes, that would be best."

Amid the construction noises of bricklayers and carpenters in the lookout towers, blacksmiths continued their work, producing loud clangs as they fashioned sword blades, spear-heads, and metal spikes. Norcross perked up as he heard a different sort of clang in the distance. He shaded his eyes to look beyond the shore wall and out toward the open sea. One of the stonemasons on top of the southern tower began waving, shouting down to those below. "There's a boat coming back. Seems to be in a hurry."

Norcross and Thaddeus hurried up the tower steps to the top platform. Even though the construction wasn't yet finished, the defenders had stocked the towers with baskets of pitch-tipped arrows, piles of large round stones, rows of unstrung bows. On each side of the river, a large siege engine stood in place, giant catapults made with beams from whole tree trunks, strung with thick ropes, fastened with heavy iron springs. Baskets at the end of the throwing arms could hold boulders covered in pitch and set aflame.

From the tower platform, Norcross spotted a lone fishing boat tacking back and forth at full sail as it raced into Renda Bay. A distant tinny sound rang through the air, the fisherman aboard the boat banging on a metal pot to sound an alarm.

Norcross frowned, wishing the boat could sail more swiftly. "Alert the townspeople. We should get ready. There's something not right about this."

Thaddeus gave the orders, and runners raced down the tower steps and sent out a call through the streets of Renda Bay. The D'Haran soldiers pulled back from the work sites and gathered their armor and weapons, pulling on thick leather shirts and donning swords. More townspeople came running in from the hills and outlying homes.

Though the fishing boat raced toward the harbor as swiftly as the errant winds could bring it, Thaddeus identified the broad-beamed and sturdy fishing vessel long before it came to shore. "That's the *Daisy*. Kenneth looks like he's running from a storm."

Norcross kept staring. "There's no storm. It's something else."

Kenneth sailed swiftly toward the harbor. The bearded, shaggy-haired fisherman stood at the *Daisy*'s bow, trying to raise an alarm with his banging. Norcross remembered when Kenneth had intercepted the three sailing ships that carried General Zimmer's expeditionary force down from Serrimundi.

The D'Haran ships were commandeered merchant vessels that had sailed through uncharted waters along the coastline, guided by Oliver and Peretta, the two young scholars from Cliffwall. The ships were led by Captains Mills, Straker, and Donell. At the moment, the three D'Haran vessels were anchored just outside the mouth of Renda Bay, too large for the shallow harbor to accommodate. Right now, with their sails furled, the ships were manned only by a skeleton crew who preferred to sleep on deck rather than in shared rooms in town. The three captains insisted on remaining aboard, unless they were called to important duties on shore.

By the time the *Daisy* reached the mouth of the harbor, with Kenneth shouting at the top of his lungs, Norcross had spotted the terrifying forms coming over the horizon, sleek attack ships with midnight-blue sails.

Beside him, Thaddeus swallowed audibly. "Those are serpent ships. The Norukai."

Captain Norcross watched the sails appear, one serpent ship after another, six in all.

Thaddeus said in a low, shaken voice, "That's twice as many as the last raid, and even with the help of the sorceress Nicci, we barely drove them away. How can we fight six serpent ships?"

"We'll show you how," Norcross said, his voice hard as iron. "We made plans day after day. We prepared the people, trained them. Your defenses are stronger now."

"But, we're not ready," Thaddeus said.

"You are ready. Dear spirits, you have no other choice."

Thaddeus turned and ran down the stairs of the lookout tower.

Norcross shouted for his D'Haran soldiers to gather in front of the piers and prepare to defend the town. He had only fifty soldiers. "Each one of you will have to be a commander," he called out. "Take some villagers under your wing. You know that we have surprises for the Norukai this time. Let's drive them away and convince them never to attack Renda Bay again."

His men cheered, understanding the dire threat they faced. They didn't doubt his confidence.

For his own part, Norcross felt very young and inexperienced. He was barely twenty-five years old and wasn't ready for such a responsibility. He'd fought only twice in great battles. Now, he had a mere handful of men, each of them just as inexperienced and probably just as frightened as he was, and a large population of villagers who had been bruised and terrified many times before.

But none of them had another option. They had to be ready.

Norcross remembered that General Zimmer had also been young, promoted far beyond his ability or expectation, but Zimmer had shouldered his responsibility and become a genuinely inspiring leader. Now, Norcross understood that concept more than he'd ever wanted to. He wouldn't let his general down, or Lord Rahl.

The *Daisy* docked in the first open slip on the pier. Kenneth threw down the hawser to one of the stanchions, quickly tied off the boat, and leaped onto the dock. His footfalls thundered as he ran to meet the soldiers. "Did you see them? Six serpent ships! They're close behind me."

"This town is ready to face them," Norcross said. "We're pulling together our defenses. Thanks to you, Kenneth. Your warning gave us an extra hour to prepare."

Town leader Thaddeus stood beside Norcross, trying to match the D'Haran captain's confidence. "Renda Bay will not be a victim again, not under my watch. The Norukai might expect us to be plump little lambs, but we know how to fight now."

Soldiers rushed to prepare the siege engines. Workers filled carts with rocks and barrels of oil, then ran down the streets of Renda Bay and out onto the piers. More rowboats pulled out to the three anchored sailing ships led by Captains Mills, Straker, and Donell, which were now preparing for war. Village defenders stormed up to the high towers on either side of the river mouth.

Loud bells rang throughout Renda Bay in case anyone had remained unaware of the impending attack. Norcross stared out past the end of the piers, watching the ominous ships approach.

"We're ready for you," he muttered under his breath. "Come and learn your lesson."

The nautical magic invoked from the serpent god pushed against the midnight sails, stretching the fabric and driving the Norukai vessels toward Renda Bay. The lookout on Kor's ship had spotted the fishing vessel and snarled a challenge. Kor had shifted course to race after the fishing boat in hot pursuit, but somehow the man from Renda Bay either had magic of his own, the special favor of the Sea Mother, or just unexpected skills. His boat caught the right breezes, tacked from north to south, covering distance across the waves even faster than the raiding ships could. As the fishing boat dwindled toward the shore, the serpent ships could see Renda Bay not far ahead.

His first mate, a burly man with tattoos on his arms and neck, gripped the railing. "He will warn them, Kor. We shouldn't have let him escape."

"I didn't *let* him escape," Kor retorted. "Perhaps you'd like to swim after him, chase the sea serpents, then wreck the boat before he can deliver his warning?"

The first mate backed away. "No, Captain." On normal voyages, such a challenge was an insult. Kor could have punched him, broken his jaw, and thrown the man overboard, but right now he needed every fighter. He would let the man die in the raid if he was meant to die.

In the two serpent ships immediately behind him, Lars and Yorik sent up signal flags, preparing for the wild raid. There was no military strategy. The raiding vessels would simply crash into Renda Bay, and the Norukai would attack with landing boats. Some would wade to shore, run along the piers, and set fire to any intact structures. They would kill or capture every person they could. Anyone too worthless to be a slave would be slain outright.

This was a raid to acquire more walking meat to be sold elsewhere down the coast, but it was also meant to send a message. Kor had his orders from King Grieve. Renda Bay was to be left a lifeless ruin, with black smoke rising high into the sky for all other coastal towns to see.

Kor leaned forward at the prow, admiring the carved serpent head enhanced with iron spikes for ramming ships. Kor had seen the real serpent god himself, three times, and knew that no carving could match the majesty or the terror of the immense creature, but Kor and his fighters would inspire their own terror. Renda Bay didn't need to fear the serpent god. They needed to fear the Norukai.

On the shore, villagers scurried about like terrified ants. Kor's lips twitched in an imitation of a smile on his slashed cheeks. Salt spray crashed from the prow of the raiding ship. He narrowed his eyes as he looked at the helpless town. He felt hungry.

CHAPTER 25

After sunset the following day, General Utros surveyed his vast camp and his countless soldiers. The warriors lit campfires, not because they needed the warmth or to cook meals that they wouldn't eat, but because it was part of their routine, as it had been since ancient times. Such a colossal army needed campfires as a symbol of camaraderie. In addition to the other effects of the petrification spell, Utros had noticed that his night vision and that of his soldiers was severely diminished, just like the sensitivity of his skin. He could see the fires blazing bright and defiant, but the shadows seemed to be deeper than before.

Over the days since awakening, as the news spread about how much time had passed and that Iron Fang's empire had fallen long ago, a ripple of despair went through the countless soldiers. Utros spent the day walking among the troops, telling them that even though everything they knew was gone, they were still *his* army. "As my soldiers, you are always with your true family, and I will lead you."

He wore his helmet with the horns of the monstrous bull, looking powerful, but he could feel the shock of his men, their sadness. He understood their disbelief, but he could do nothing to help them. He, too, had lost everything. Majel . . .

Utros spoke to the squads, stepping up to just a few sullen, dutiful warriors, but others gathered closer to hear.

"I can't bring them back, not any of them," he said. "Time has stolen our families, our friends, our loves and our lives from us." He paused. "No, not time—the wizards of Ildakar stole them from us. They placed this spell on us." He clenched his partially hardened arm. "They are to blame."

Utros saw the grief and loss in their expressive eyes, the inability to shed tears the way they normally had. The reality sank in, and these soldiers, so many thousands of them, had only their duty and their loyalty—to *him*. "I can't bring you the past. I can't bring any of them back. But I can bring you hope and duty. Our reality is now centered on capturing Ildakar, as we swore to do when we left Orogang so many centuries ago." He drew a deep breath, felt his lungs expand. "And that is what we will accomplish."

At first the dutiful cheers were halfhearted, but slowly the soldiers pulled themselves up with the new realization and their new purpose. Later that night, under a common banner, soldiers gathered around the big fires and told stories about their families, now long lost to the ravages of time. His troops would reminisce about their loves, their children, the homes they would never see again. But they would complete their mission. For him. Utros knew it.

His warriors came to accept their fate. What choice did they have? They had always followed Utros, and he had never let them down. So long as he convinced them of his vision, they would continue to serve him. But even he didn't have a complete plan.

First Commander Enoch reported after sending scouts along the wall of the city, then up into the hills and along the cliff that plunged down to the river. He did not seem optimistic. "It is possible, by traveling far from these plains, to find a way down to the river, but it widens into swamps, which seem impassable. If we did send troops along the water to the base of the bluffs below Ildakar, we would still have to scale the cliffs to get into the city." Enoch frowned. "It does not seem a good strategy, General. The Ildakarans have defenses there, too, and we have no boats, no means to attack from the water. I think our siege at the walls may be the best option. Ildakar can't withstand us forever."

Utros listened, absorbing the information. "I'll continue to work on a plan, First Commander. Bring me any other intelligence you gather. There must be a way." Enoch gave a formal bow, then departed.

Despite his reassurances, Utros had only a limited amount of time to find his clarity of purpose, because the army's questions would become too loud for any answers he might offer. His orders from Emperor Kurgan were fifteen centuries old, and the mercurial ruler himself had been overthrown by his own people because of his cruelty.

Long ago, Utros had taken a vow of loyalty to Iron Fang, yet there was also Majel, and his love for her had been as strong as a boulder diverting a fast-flowing stream. Somehow, in the compartments of his mind, Utros managed to separate those conflicting loyalties. He held them like the opposite poles of two lodestones, both attracting and repelling, and it was only through rigid determination that he could hold both in his mind at the same time.

As he studied the campfires dotting the valley, he felt a chill rather than warmth. Kurgan was gone—and Majel was gone. Iron Fang could no longer advise him or give him new orders, and he couldn't hear the beautiful voice of his beloved. Both were in the underworld now, their spirits with the Keeper. Utros could never speak with either of them again.

In ancient times, there had been rumors of a fraying of the veil, occasional ways for spirits to return to the world of the living, if only briefly, but Richard Rahl's star shift had sealed the breach forever, if Nicci and Nathan could be believed. Never again would spirits be able to pass from the underworld.

His leader and his lover were both lost to him forever, and Utros was on his own. Even surrounded by hundreds of thousands of loyal soldiers, and the sorceresses who served him with their bodies and their magic, Utros felt entirely alone. . . .

From the doorway, he turned to the inside of the head-quarters, where the two braziers glowed red. Ava and Ruva stood waiting for him in gauzy gowns that clung to their curves. Freshly shaved and painted, the twins watched him in silence, letting him have his thoughts, but they seemed to read his mind.

"We remember the magic we have been taught, beloved Utros," said Ava.

"All the stolen books we studied in the cities we conquered," Ruva said.

Utros closed the wooden doorway behind him. "I have never doubted it." He could smell the dizzying smoke from the braziers. "But if what the representatives of Ildakar claim is true, the underpinnings of magic have changed. Your most powerful spells may not work anymore."

Ava held up a finger, studied it, then stroked her sister's cheek. "Or at least not in the same way."

Ruva closed her eyes and let out a sigh of pleasure from the touch. "That also means we may have different opportunities. Magic might function in ways we never considered before."

Utros ran his palm over his scarred cheek. "Maybe you can find a spell that will turn Ildakar's stone walls to dust, and then we can simply march through the city streets."

"An interesting possibility." Ruva reached across to stroke her sister's face in a reciprocal gesture. "But that's not what you want most, beloved Utros." The twins stared intently at him.

Ava said, "We know what you want, and it will strengthen your heart."

"Strengthening your heart will strengthen your army," Ruva added.

Utros frowned. "What do you mean?"

"You know exactly what happened to your dear Majel, the woman to whom you gave your heart and your soul," Ava said, "while your mind and your skills were sworn to Emperor Kurgan. Absolute loyalty and absolute love, tugging against each other."

Ruva nodded. "Before you can accept your place in this time, you need to speak to Iron Fang. And to Majel."

The general's heart ached. "That is true, but they're long dead. The only way I can speak to them is if I go to the underworld, and I am not ready to die yet."

"Maybe there's another way," the twins said in eerie unison.

Ruva took a half step closer, and the ruddy light from the braziers painted its own patterns on her skin. "We've studied what the sorceress Nicci said. We cast webs, made probes with our magic. We sacrificed small creatures, and that blood allowed us to tease out answers."

Ava said, "The underworld is indeed sealed, and there's no way we can exploit a breach or a weak point. You cannot travel beyond the veil, nor can we bring back the spirit of Majel or Iron Fang."

Ruva and Ava crept closer until they were nearly touching him, but they stopped, letting him sense their presence. "It might be possible that you can still *observe* through the veil, however. You can look in on the underworld and find those spirits."

Utros blinked. "You mean just to communicate, not to bring them back? I hadn't considered the idea. That would be excellent."

"My sister and I have discovered a way to make a window, a lens to let you look through the veil. You could see the spirits of Majel and Kurgan. You could talk with them."

"I could speak with her," Utros said, his voice dropping to a husky whisper. "I could say . . ." He drew a breath and straightened, restoring his professional demeanor. "I could brief Emperor Kurgan and receive further orders from him, learn what he really wants me to do, so many centuries after I laid siege to Ildakar." Utros felt his heart grow lighter for the first time since awakening. "Yes, do it. That is my command."

"There are complex preparations to make," said Ava. "In order to create such a lens, we need a special kind of glass."

Ruva added, "And that will require special ingredients, difficult ingredients."

"Whatever you need, I'll see that you have it," Utros said.

The sorceresses had no doubt. "The molten glass needs to be mixed with the blood of innocent children. Those pure sacrifices will delight the Keeper, and then with our magic we'll be able to see through the veil."

Utros spoke quickly. "I'll instruct First Commander Enoch to find innocent children and take their blood. Of the many scouting parties I sent into the hills, surely they've located some villages that can be harvested."

Ava and Ruva pressed themselves against him, wrapping their arms around his solid body. He felt their curves, the solidity of their skin and bodies, their firm breasts. "Let's sleep now and share our power," they said.

Utros felt a clarity and an optimism that had been long gone. Ava and Ruva peeled off their garments and then removed the general's armored vest, his sword, his dagger, his greaves, his belt. While her sister completed the work of undressing Utros, Ruva added more pungent herbs to the braziers, filling the chamber with thin, aromatic smoke.

Together, they all lay naked and entwined on the low, makeshift bed. It was not to share bodily warmth, for their toughened flesh had little of that, and it was not to share passion, though Utros knew the twin sorceresses held a fire of love for him in their hearts. This was to share strength, as they had done many times during his conquests across the Old World.

Utros held the beautiful twins, stroked their smooth cold skin, following the curves of their backs, their buttocks, while their fingertips traced imaginary spell designs across his chest and down his legs. As he lay there, all he could think about was the chance to see and speak with Majel again, even from beyond the wall of death.

CHAPTER 26

The stair-stepped spectator benches of Ildakar's combat arena rose on all sides of Nicci as she walked out onto the raked sands along with Nathan, Elsa, and all the powerful gifted members of the duma. The council had at last made a decision, and they planned to go on the offensive.

The seats were filled with thousands of people, crowded shoulder-to-shoulder. Nicci saw a blur of faces, lower classes in drab clothes in the bottom tiers, merchants in the better seats, nobles in the prominent observation towers safest from the violence and bloodshed. Though the huge arena was filled to capacity, Nicci knew this was only a fraction of Ildakar's population. Yes, the city did indeed have the potential to create a formidable army.

Though she had her doubts about the duma's plan, Nicci would help them achieve victory. She just needed them to define their goal properly. Nathan was also committed.

The duma members walked forward, leaving footprints on the same ground where countless warriors and combat animals had died. The loud background murmur fell to a hush as the ruling council stood to address the large audience. Even

Rendell, the newest official duma member, stood among them. The lower classes, the workers, and the freed slaves would see him there and understand that something had fundamentally changed in the city's power structure. If they succeeded, the duma would convince the people of Ildakar to direct their violence outward, against the army of General Utros.

Nicci spotted Bannon in the lower tiers, giving his silent encouragement. The young man wore a common shirt and had tied his hair back. Lila sat beside him, as if she were his personal guard, reminding Nicci of how the Mord-Sith always stationed themselves close to Richard.

Quentin, Damon, and Elsa stood silent beside the reawakened Lani, and the new gifted duma members Oron and Olgya. Nicci and Nathan remained with the council, and although many Ildakarans looked to the two of them as outside heroes, Nicci insisted on letting the city's own representatives speak. Without the wizard commander or the sovrena, though, the duma had no clear spokesperson.

After building the crowd's anticipation, Elsa finally stepped forward. She enhanced her voice so that all could hear. "People of Ildakar, all *citizens* of Ildakar, we face the enemy you have feared for fifteen centuries. That ancient army is now awake again and outside your walls."

Oron spoke up. "And we are like yaxen in a pen awaiting the slaughter, unless we do something." He stepped forward, made his voice even louder. "I for one do not intend to wait for that. We must prove our might, show that we can be a formidable foe and push back against the enemy. Ildakar has many powerful gifted, and our magic is stronger than anything General Utros can command."

"We also have countless fighters," Lani said. "Look at all of you! We call on anyone who can take up arms, train for battle, and help us deal a resounding blow to our ancient enemy." She looked around the tiers at the pale faces, the bright Ildakaran silks, the earthy garments of workers and former slaves. "We have our city guard, our morazeth, our arena warriors. Together, we have an *army*, the army of Ildakar."

The people began to mutter and cheer, and Nicci saw Bannon applauding. She felt her own resolve hardening. She had traveled too far and fought too hard in the name of Lord Rahl. She could not let an enemy from the dusts of time win against an equally legendary city. Rather, she wanted Ildakar to become one of the capitals of the new D'Haran Empire. But in order for that to happen, Nicci had to save them first.

She thought of the blood that had been spilled on these arena sands, unwilling warriors cut to pieces by opponents or torn by combat beasts. There was much to dislike about this twisted city, but there was also much worth salvaging. If these people could be convinced to follow the sensible rules of Lord Rahl, Ildakar would be a powerful ally.

She made up her mind and raised her voice. The enthused crowd fell silent, wanting to hear what Nicci had to say. "The enemy believes we're cowering behind our walls, just waiting. They think we have no way to fight them. They think our magic is weak because the stone spell faded." She waited a beat. "We'll show them that is not true."

Nicci knew how to rally these diverse people, the many factions that disliked one another, the angry rebels who still held their grudges. "We must have warriors, but we know you aren't all soldiers. Ildakar also needs material support, whatever the city can give. Swordsmiths must create weapons, blades, spears. Fletchers must make many arrows. We need armor and shields." She swept her gaze across the former slaves in their tiers, the tradesmen, the merchants, even the gifted nobles in the high levels. "The recent uprising nearly tore Ildakar apart, but this is a chance for you to heal those wounds. I urge you to fight for your city instead of against one another."

Oron gave her a respectful nod and added, "Our best hope is in a surprise attack. Let us train our fighters, gather our gifted. When we are ready, we'll mass our army just behind the walls where the enemy can't see us, then we will attack late at night, a strike as swift and deadly as a lightning bolt, and then return to safety behind our walls." He extended a hand, pointing to the spectators in the stands. "We have to do a great deal of damage in order to make our point."

Nicci focused on the sea of faces in the tiered seats. The buzz of conversation grew louder in the arena, accompanied by the percussive beat of clapping hands and stomping feet.

CHAPTER 27

The six Norukai vessels arrowed toward the harbor, their rows of oars like the legs of a centipede on the water.

Running along the docks, Captain Norcross shouted orders. He had spent many nights alone at a candlelit desk drawing up scenarios, imagining defenses against the hideous raiders. He had consulted with his fellow D'Haran soldiers, and together they had come up with many ideas, some of them ingenious, some impractical. Norcross had decided to implement everything he could. He didn't have magic, but he did have tactics.

Now he raced to the end of the southern pier, watching his three large cargo ships move into position, ready to close like pincers around the oncoming Norukai. On the largest ship, helmed by Captain Mills, Norcross could see armed sailors crowding the rail on the starboard side. Bright pinpoints of light sparkled as a dozen archers lit pitch-covered arrows and loosed a volley that rained down on the first oncoming raider.

The Norukai scurried to extinguish the fire on the deck, but several arrows struck the dark sail, which went up in flames. Three of the raiders were killed by the burning arrows, and their crewmates quickly dumped them over the side.

The other five serpent ships pressed forward like hungry predators. Loud, bass drumbeats echoed from the raiding vessels, and Norukai warriors crowded the sides, eager to fight with swords, spears, and battle-axes. They chanted an inhuman-sounding howl.

Out on the water, bright wooden buoys marked positions. The Norukai paid them no heed, but the D'Haran engineers had practiced, setting their aim and their range, and the buoys marked the specific strike points. When the serpent ships approached the line, Norcross fought back a smile. "Catapults!" he shouted, and other soldiers picked up the order. "Catapults!" They knew exactly how and when to fire the giant boulders resting in the cradles.

Soldiers turned the heavy cranks on the siege machines, winding the cables and ratcheting the gears. Ropes groaned and long wooden beams creaked as they cocked back the catapult's arm. Muscular fishermen loaded a boulder into the cradle, doused it with pitch, then ignited the missile. When a Norukai serpent ship passed the first marker buoy, Captain Norcross gave a signal, and the catapult loosed its stone. With a liberating snap and crash, the arm heaved upward and launched its burden. The giant flaming stone tumbled like a comet through the air.

Aboard the serpent ship, the Norukai shouted in sudden terror as the burning boulder smashed the hull. The people of Renda Bay cheered, seeing the tremendous damage. The crippled enemy ship veered to the south as the raiders struggled to regain control and put out the fires.

Meanwhile, the first vessel that had been peppered by flaming arrows also burned. The sail was nearly consumed, and now the fire spread to the decks and climbed the masts.

As raiders approached the watchtowers at the mouth of the harbor, the Norukai responded with their own fire arrows like a rain of shooting stars. Some defenders raised shields to cover their heads, but others had no such armor. Dozens of people fell, skewered as they fled for shelter.

Norcross felt isolated at the end of the pier with arrows pattering around him, thunking into the wooden boards.

The four intact serpent ships pressed in, relentless. The first raiding vessel ground up against the base of one of the lookout towers at the mouth of the harbor. Its carved figurehead smashed the head of the piers. Norukai boiled off the decks, some leaping into the water, others dropping onto the piers and surging forward.

Seeing them for the first time, Norcross was appalled. The raiders were as hideous as he had been led to believe, their mouths slashed and tattooed to look like serpent jaws, their bodies studded with spikes and horns implanted in their skin. They were monsters as terrifying as Emperor Sulachan's undead armies, which Norcross had seen only once.

Another serpent ship crashed against the opposite pier and disgorged its army of invaders.

At the top of the twin watchtowers, the defenders shot arrows and hurled rocks down upon the raiders. From their high vantage, they should be able to massacre these invaders. Even so, Norcross felt sick as he drew his sword and ran to fight hand-to-hand. The scarred slavers didn't seem to care how many they would lose.

U sually during raids, Kor's warriors were like wolves chasing fat and stupid sheep, but now he saw that Renda Bay would be more of a challenge. The people were putting up a real fight and they had built unexpected defenses.

Kor let out a rumbling hiss deep in his throat. The villagers would still lose, but it would be a test for his raiders, and the Norukai liked to be tested. Harsh challenges made them stronger, just as their bleak windswept islands made them hungrier for conquest. Renda Bay's resistance would only bring about greater retribution, and that was fine with Kor.

A flaming boulder from the second catapult hurtled through

the air after the crack-smash of its released arm. The giant stone whistled overhead, and the Norukai crew on the target ship—Yorik's vessel—used their oars in a furious but futile attempt to shift course. The projectile clipped the top of the mast, shattered the yardarm, and made the sail collapse.

Kor's ship cruised into the small harbor, passing one of the new stone watchtowers. His vessel ground up against the nearest pier, and his fighters threw ropes to lash the vessel into place. Norukai warriors leaped from the decks and ran wildly down the docks with weapons raised.

Within minutes, they encountered a force of trained soldiers that stood against them—real soldiers, not simpering villagers, with armor and good swords. Kor resolved to claim those swords, even if he had to pry them from the bloody hands of fallen warriors.

Howling raiders slammed into the soldiers in a spray of blood and a crash of steel. These outside soldiers, strangers to Renda Bay, were well trained and not easily frightened. With some surprise, Kor watched several of his own warriors fall, cut down by the combat skills of their unexpected opponents. Dead Norukai bodies were roughly kicked into the water to get them out of the way.

For his own weapon, Kor preferred a long-handled axe with a rounded stone club on the opposite end. He swung it one-handed as he bounded onto the pier, striking viciously, left and right. He hit the first soldier who faced him, smashing his axe brutally against the steel sword. The soldier's wrist snapped, and the man reeled away as he gaped at the strange angle of his arm, the protruding bone. Kor swung the weapon again, bashing him in the face with the rounded end. For good measure, he turned the weapon around and sank the axe blade with a wet, meaty impact into the defender's chest. With his boot, Kor stomped on the fallen man's ribs to yank his weapon free.

Screams of pain, howls of anger, and the clash of weapons

made a deafening clamor all around him. To Kor it sounded like music.

From the watchtowers above, defenders hurled rocks and sharp javelins while archers fired a rain of arrows. Kor saw seven of his fellows drop in an instant, arrows protruding like spikes from their bodies, and he spun just in time so that an arrow merely struck his shoulder instead of his heart. When he reached back and ripped it free, the barbed arrowhead tore a wide gash in his flesh, but Kor didn't feel pain. He was in a battle mind-set now.

The first wave of Norukai stormed down the length of the pier and into the town. Many of the homes, freshly rebuilt after the last fiery raid, were burning again, ignited by fire arrows. The defenders formed a cordon to stop the raiders from entering the town. They held swords, spears, even rakes and shovels, and their expressions were grim, determined. This was no scattered, panicked flock of cowards. The people of Renda Bay had been trained, and this surprised him. But they would all still die.

The Norukai smashed into the defenders, wielding their axes and spears. The townspeople tried to stand their ground, but they fell like harvested grain. And yet the rest of them kept fighting.

One of the officers on the opposite side of the water, a captain of some sort, shouted orders as the fifth and sixth serpent ships pushed into the mouth of the harbor, their impatient crews eager to attack. But on either side of the bay, the villagers worked huge cranks and chains, raising some unexpected weapon submerged beneath the water. Kor swung his sword instinctively to deflect the blow of a bearded fisherman who attacked him with a boat hook, but he was preoccupied with what was happening in the water. He punched the fisherman in the face, kicked him off the dock, and turned his attention back to watch.

A deadly rake of sharp metal shafts, spears lined up on a rotating hinge that had been sunk beneath the shallow harbor, began to turn, rising to the surface. Kor had never seen such a thing before. The long, deadly spikes lifted out of the water, angled directly toward the oncoming serpent ship.

Kor saw what was going to happen, but could do nothing about it. "No!" he roared. "Change course!"

The serpent ship pushed forward at full speed, driven by the coordinated sweep of the oars. On deck, several Norukai screamed a warning, and the men at the oars flailed, disorganized, but they couldn't react quickly enough. Momentum drove the vessel ahead, and the hull rammed itself upon the parallel spikes.

Even from where he stood, Kor heard grinding and splintering as the metal points gutted the serpent ship like a fish. Nearly a hundred Norukai warriors leaped overboard, and several of them were impaled on the spikes as well. The ship was destroyed, its keel shattered, and within minutes its hold flooded, although the sharp spikes held the wreck up like a slaughtered goat hung on a meat hook.

Other raiders charged down the docks into the town, while longboats scraped up on the stony shore. Even before they landed, the Norukai men and women tossed torches onto docked fishing boats. Abandoning their vessels and splashing ashore, the burly raiders raced up the shingle to keep attacking.

Kor led his own party, killing townspeople and armored soldiers as he swept his battle-axe from side to side. He pushed deeper into the streets.

Hundreds more villagers emerged from their hiding places, bursting out of buildings where they had lain in wait. In moments, the defenders doubled in number, making the invaders' charge falter.

Astonished, Kor howled in wordless rage. This was supposed to be a slave raid, a punitive attack to avenge the previous failure of weaker Norukai. His mission was to leave no one alive, no structure standing, but now three of his ships were already destroyed, two of them still in flames. The people of Renda Bay were not fleeing in terror. Instead, they surrounded the raiders and blocked off their escape.

He saw one of his best fighters, his own first mate, jabbing and stabbing with his spear. He killed three Renda Bay villagers, but six more closed in on him. They caught the first mate's spear with a boat hook, drove it to the ground, and broke the shaft. The first mate fought back with both fists, his scarred jaw flapping open and closed as he snarled, as if he meant to snatch them with his teeth.

The Renda Bay townspeople knocked him to his knees, then stabbed and clubbed him to death. In that moment, as he watched the man fall, Kor began to feel fear. For the first time in his life, he sensed that he was going to lose.

Outside the harbor, Yorik's ship was listing to the side, trying to limp away as its hull filled with water after being damaged by the catapult missile. Five landing boats full of scarred raiders ready to die fighting had already launched from the sinking ship.

The three large sailing ships outside the harbor, vessels of a type he had not seen before, closed in with inexorable momentum. Fully under sail, the three-masted ships came after the Norukai landing boats, and from their high decks, the sailors shot countless arrows and killed all the warriors who had been trying to escape. The nearest cargo ship scraped against the damaged serpent vessel, their hulls colliding. The sailors aboard leaped over the rail, swarming the deck of the damaged Norukai ship.

Kor spun about to look at the larger disaster, not just the bodies of those he had killed lying around him. Twenty more Renda Bay defenders charged down the street toward him. They didn't look terrified at all. Rather, their eyes showed a bloodlust that Kor had previously seen only on the Norukai.

Backing away, looking for a defensible position, he glanced to the other side of the harbor, saw the professional soldiers forming a blockade, marching forward with their swords and spears to trap twenty Norukai who had no place to run. The raiders fought viciously, but failed, and their bodies dropped into the water.

Sweeping his eyes across the battlefield, Kor made a quick count. He had lost three of his six serpent ships, and two-thirds of his warriors were likely dead. It was simply not possible! If other towns learned to stand up like this, the Norukai could face defeat after defeat.

This was something entirely unexpected. Kor could not accept the idea that the Norukai were being defeated by a fishing village!

He saw Lars and Yorik, still alive, struggling to pull their crews together on the three remaining ships, and Kor knew he had to withdraw with what remaining fighters he had, with the ships that could still sail. King Grieve needed to know what had happened here. In a hoarse voice, he bellowed the signal that all Norukai dreaded to hear, a signal that had rarely been used in many centuries.

A retreat.

Kor shouted for any Norukai fighters who could break away to rush back to their ships. He would lead them from Renda Bay and back out into open water so they could limp back to the main Norukai islands.

His raiders were burned and bruised, and the fire in their hearts had been snuffed out. It might be better if he just stayed and died here, because once he reported his failure to the king, Kor would surely be sacrificed to the serpent god. But he couldn't think of that. He had to save his warriors so they could return and fight again with greater frenzy. For vengeance.

King Grieve had to know of this terrible and disturbing new threat, even if it cost Kor his life.

He decapitated a burly villager who swung a sharpened spade at him. Kor didn't even watch his victim fall as he sprinted back, hoping he could survive long enough to reach his own ship.

CHAPTER 28

Behind the walls of Ildakar, Nicci worked day and night to rally the city's defenders, to arm them and train them for the surprise strike, now that the duma had set their plans in motion. Since the insidious attack from his twin sorceresses, the city had received no word from General Utros, no ultimatums, no requests. Nicci was sure the ancient general was building some strategy of his own, but she hoped Ildakar would strike first, taking him unawares.

Even while she slept, Nicci gathered information through Mrra, roaming in her dreams with the spell-bonded sand panther. She glided through the shadows and studied the enemy troops. When she felt bold enough, the big cat even prowled among the troops, nothing more than a tawny blur. Mrra didn't understand the human details of what she saw, but through her eyes Nicci could assess their camp, their numbers, supplies, and weapons, and she could see where their weaknesses were.

Using feline senses, she could tell that these ancient warriors were not entirely human. They didn't smell right, and their warm blood and flesh was cooler than a normal person's.

The following morning, Nicci delivered a report to the

duma of what she and Mrra had seen. Nathan wasn't there, claiming that he wanted to investigate another idea.

In the meeting, Lady Olgya said, "My guild has crafted enough special silk to make protective cloaks for twenty gifted nobles, who will lead the charge in a few nights. Our worms are spinning themselves into exhaustion. The fleshmancers adapted and strengthened them, but they cannot go faster."

Nicci knew the preparations couldn't simply continue forever. "General Utros is sure to move soon, and we have to strike first, or we will lose our element of surprise."

"Preparations continue throughout the city, and this will be a significant offensive," said Damon. "Our fighters are gathering, training. Arms are being distributed. It will take at least three more days before we can hope to be ready to move."

"I've ordered guards posted at every gate, even the low shepherds' doors," Quentin said. "And they've been reinforced with spells. The walls are secure."

Oron frowned. "I'm more concerned about our former slaves who were willing to murder innocent nobles and burn down the city. Even with Rendell now elected to the duma, are all the slaves as committed as we are? What is to stop one of those traitors from slipping outside and selling information to the enemy?"

Upset, Rendell rose from his stone bench. "We are sworn to protect Ildakar as much as you are. The slaves fought for justice, but they can see a better future here. I think I've gotten through to them. Once we rebuild the city, it will be partly theirs. Why would they betray us now?"

Nicci narrowed her blue eyes. "I understand your passion, Rendell, but I don't believe everyone is so altruistic. We don't dare let a whisper get out to General Utros."

"Our greatest weapon is surprise, and we must not give it up," Lani said. "We've made our plan, and we need to launch everything in this attack, cause as much damage as possible. We have to convince Utros that we are strong enough to defeat him."

The duma members responded with confidence and enthusiasm. Nicci hoped they were right.

I nside the fleshmancer's silent, empty villa, Nathan stepped forward, feeling the weight of dangerous magic in the air.

The two Ixax warriors towered above the rubble. Stone support columns had broken like giant tree trunks, toppling amid fragments of the shattered ceiling and collapsed walls. The weight of the entire building had fallen on top of the motionless behemoths, leaving smears of dust and splinters of stone on their armor, but causing no real damage to the titans. The remaining pair stood ready, as they had done for more than fifteen centuries, trapped and unable to move. But aware.

Approaching the two giant figures alone, Nathan stared at them with awe and a thrill of fear, but even though he knew what horrific damage their unleashed comrade had caused, he allowed himself a small glimmer of hope. The wizard's high leather boots crunched on the broken stone strewn across the cracked tiles.

Somewhere, buried under the fresh dust and debris was a large red stain, now dried—all that remained of Andre, splattered blood, pummeled flesh, and splintered bone, after the lone awakened Ixax had released his fury. No one had bothered to clean the mess, since all of the fleshmancer's servants and apprentices had abandoned him during the uprising.

With the tip of his boot, Nathan kicked over a stone, exposing a wiry blood-encrusted hank of hair, next to a curved yellowish fragment, part of the fleshmancer's skull. "Dear spirits," he muttered. He couldn't deny that Andre had gotten what he deserved after tormenting the three Ixax for centuries. . . .

The single released Ixax warrior had broken through the fleshmancer's magical defenses. Andre had created the titans to defend Ildakar, but they had never been put to use. Out of boredom, he had spent centuries pestering them, tormenting them. No wonder the released giant had created havoc in Ildakar before Nathan managed to destroy it. The whole situation was regrettable.

Now all of Ildakar was preparing to launch a surprise attack on the ancient army. The council had given the people a goal, a hope for real success, although Nathan thought their hope was based more on enthusiasm than on true military strategy. Maybe General Utros would be fooled, and maybe the Ildakaran defenders would cause some real damage. Or, the military genius might surprise them in turn. After reading so much history, Nathan would not underestimate Utros.

He hoped to increase the city's chances by finding a weapon unlike any the ancient army had ever seen. Could the Ixax warriors serve that purpose? Could they be controlled?

He stepped over a toppled column and stood before the two armored titans, each fifteen feet tall. They couldn't speak, but they would listen.

Gathering his courage, remembering how he had faced the one enraged Ixax that had nearly destroyed him, he studied the giants. With his fresh wizard's robes and his white hair, he did look impressive, like someone in command. The silence was tense and ominous, but Nathan confidently stared at the two mammoth figures.

When he cleared his throat, the sound seemed excessively loud. "Hello!" As soon as the word left his lips, he realized how foolish it sounded. "My name is Nathan Rahl. I'm a wizard, but not from Ildakar. I have traveled here from far-off lands."

The two Ixax didn't tremble, didn't move. The binding spell prevented them. Thick iron helmets encased their heads, leaving only an eye slit. Thick metal armor wrapped their bodies, thickened at the shoulders, while chest plates were studded with rounded bosses, engraved with the sun-and-lightning symbol of Ildakar. Their massive arms were bare, with pebbled skin like concrete studded with gravel. Their hands were covered with huge gauntlets reinforced with iron knobs and sharp spikes.

Each Ixax wore a terrible sword as tall as a man. Their legs were like oak trunks, rippled with sculpted muscles. Their boots could crush boulders. Through the slit in their helmets, round staring eyes the size of pomegranates peered out, crackling with magic. Andre's corrupt fleshmancy had taken three mere foot soldiers who had volunteered to defend their beloved city and transformed them into . . . this.

"I'm sorry for what was done to you," Nathan said. He hoped they could hear him, hoped they would listen. "I know you didn't expect this when you offered yourselves, but Ildakar truly needs you now."

The silence continued to hang over them like a cloak. He couldn't even hear the Ixax warriors breathing. Did they need to breathe?

But he sensed a subtle change. Inside their massive helmets, the blazing yellow gaze shifted slightly, their focus changing from an endless stare. A chill went down Nathan's back, and he felt certain that their attention had turned to him. "Fleshmancer Andre did this to you, and he's paid for the torment he inflicted. You might have seen that with your own eyes."

On the night of Mirrormask's uprising, one—and only one—of the Ixax had been awakened, and that juggernaut smashed the entire villa, killed Andre, and rampaged through Ildakar. Only Nathan had been able to stop it.

Two of the Ixax remained.

"You were created to defend Ildakar," he said. "I know what was originally in your hearts. You were brave soldiers, but Ildakar is still under threat. General Utros holds the city under siege. Ildakar still needs you." He drew a deep breath. "Even though the city—no, not the *city*, just some bad people—did you wrong."

He tried to see through the helmet slits, thought he saw the bright eyes tinged with fury and madness. Nathan pressed on, wondering how many centuries it had been since anyone had spoken to the giant warriors with kindness and compassion.

"I understand just a little of how you must feel. I was held prisoner, too, for a thousand years. The Sisters of the Light locked me in the Palace of the Prophets because they were afraid of me, just like many Ildakarans are afraid of you. I was a prophet, you see, and prophecy can be very dangerous." He began to pace, relaxing a little. He rubbed the scar on his chest, feeling his heart beat, feeling the restored gift inside him.

He remembered when he was just a young boy as the beginnings of his gift manifested in vivid nightmares, the confusion as his prophecy began to show itself. He was descended from the line of Rahl, so his gift was no surprise, but he hadn't known what to do.

He could not forget the day when the Sisters had sought him out, as they did all gifted young men. Young Nathan had grown desperate as his headaches grew worse, along with confusion and fear about the incomprehensible prophecies haunting him. The Sisters had made promises, which were mostly lies, and he had gone with them, submitting to the Rada'Han, the iron collar around his neck that allowed them to control him. That iron collar was different from the immense confinement that held the Ixax warriors. Even so, he understood . . .

"I will come and speak to you again," Nathan said in a soothing voice. "Your sacrifice is not wasted, and we may well need you. Ildakar hasn't forgotten you, believe me." He ran his fingers in a nervous gesture down his long hair and felt a prickle of sweat on his face. "We still need you, both of you. Truly we do."

He paused for an awkward moment, hoping he could get through to them eventually, before it was too late.

The look on Rendell's face told Nicci how disturbed and angry he was as he met her outside the grand villa. "Come with me." He swallowed hard as he led her along the streets down from the top of the plateau. "The duma members will know soon enough, but maybe you and I can avert a bloodbath. This should not have happened." He sounded sickened.

Nicci followed the former slave to a secluded area down tangled alleys and shaded with tall trees. These were lavish whorehouses that served the wealthy, though the dachas had been frequented less since the night of the uprising, when the beautiful silk yaxen had killed some of their abusive customers.

Nicci saw frightened faces in doorways as they passed, many of them wearing the drab clothes of the lower classes, slaves who refused to go back to work. Many of them had commandeered lavish vacation homes and expensive villas, driving out the nobles who no longer had as much power as before.

Rendell still hadn't explained the reason for his anger and alarm, but Nicci's uneasiness grew. "Why do you think I can help in this?"

The former slave turned to her with a worn expression. "Because you fought for us, Nicci. You led us on the night of the revolt, helped us gain our freedom, when Mirrormask betrayed us." His eyes looked mournful. "Maybe they will listen to you—and me—and make this bloodshed stop."

He led her around a corner to a marble-pillared villa, one of the most expensive silk yaxen dachas. Ten people had gathered around garbed in grays and browns, muttering to one another. At the front of the dacha, a man's head rested on a post. His eyes were open and glazed, his mouth slack, his beard curled in fancy ringlets, his wavy hair meticulously coiffed, but caked with blood. From a nearby pillar, his headless body was suspended upside down by a rope tied around his ankles. Written in the noble's own blood were the words our turn, splashed across the white marble.

Nicci's stomach tightened, and her jaws clenched with anger.

Rendell said in a hoarse voice, "We must make it stop! All of Ildakar will turn against us if we don't."

Nicci demanded, "Who is the dead man? Do you know his name?"

"Lord Aubur. I received a message this morning that said justice had been served and a monster had been taken care of." Rendell shook his head, dismayed. "I didn't ask for this. It can only make things worse!"

Among those standing outside the dacha were five beautiful women dressed in filmy gowns. The silk yaxen stared blank-faced, unaffected by the grisly sight.

"Lord Aubur owned three silk yaxen dachas," Rendell continued. "I heard that he treated the women poorly, but no worse than most."

Nicci studied their impassive expressions, but saw no blood spatter on their creamy skin. "Did these women kill their own master?"

Rendell pressed his lips together. "I don't think so, but they will be blamed. I know that no silk yaxen could have written me the note I received. Most of them cannot read or write."

Nicci felt the turmoil build within her. She knew nothing about this Lord Aubur, nor did she care about any whoremaster, but she did know that the already tense society was only being made worse by continued internal violence. "Ildakar has much healing to do, but you'll never build a better society if your people continue to murder the very ones you need to make peace with."

Rendell groaned. "I know! And the fact that I now have a seat on the duma means that we have taken a step forward. This is the tenth beheading of a noble since the night of the uprising. There are those among the lower classes who want to kill them all and purge the city."

The five silk yaxen continued to stare at the headless body, but the other spectators drifted away.

Nicci fumed. "If you kill all the gifted in the city, then who will help defend you against General Utros? Have your people not looked outside the walls? The duma is planning to launch a major attack as soon as we've armed and trained ourselves. If the former slaves are so thirsty for blood, then tell them to fight the enemy that threatens all of us!"

"You have to help me make them see, Nicci," Rendell pleaded. "They called out your name on the night of the revolt. They know you didn't abandon them like Mirrormask did. They will listen to you."

"I have said it again and again. This is not my city! Saving and rebuilding Ildakar has to come from within."

Rendell looked away from the bloody body and the severed head. "Sometimes they need a little help. I know how we can spread the word."

Leaving the site of the murder, they moved along the familiar streets to what had previously been the slave market. Nicci despised the place after the one time she had watched cheering Ildakaran nobles bidding over the "walking meat." The market was now occupied by hundreds of liberated slaves who no longer wanted to live in hovels in the lower levels of the city. Reunited family units and new friends congregated here.

When they saw Rendell and recognized Nicci, they cheered, but Rendell raised his hands to demand their attention. The murmurs died down from hundreds of people who gathered around cook fires and under makeshift awnings.

"You think you have your freedom," Rendell said, his voice rough and angry. "You think you won, but some among you are trying to destroy our only chance. You are pointing a knife straight at our own hearts!" He paused. "Another noble has been killed."

"We are free," called out one gruff man. He had a scar on his face and was dressed in the clothes of a worker in the yaxen slaughter yards. Nicci recognized the man from the night of the fires after she had fought the spiny wolves. He and his partner had proudly presented her with the severed heads of four nobles they had killed.

"You haven't earned your freedom," Nicci said in a low, dangerous voice. "There is a cost for freedom, and it often comes in blood. But not just any blood. You cannot keep spilling it indiscriminately."

The people muttered. They had expected congratulations, not scolding from these two people they considered heroes.

Rendell looked beseechingly at the crowd. "You all know I have a place on the duma council. Before long we'll include others from the lower classes, not just gifted nobles but tradesmen, workers, even more slaves like myself. We have to work for equal representation."

"We have to finish purging the disease that makes Ildakar sick," said the scarred man in a challenging tone. He turned his head so that his voice boomed out to the crowd. "You all know what they did to us. Justice must be served."

"And peace has to be arranged!" Rendell said. "Many nobles have been murdered."

"Not murdered—executed!" said the gruff man. "For crimes committed against us."

"By what trial and what authority?" Nicci demanded. "You hated how the powerful nobles abused you. Now you want to do the same? Ildakar is still under siege, and we have to fight the ancient army, together. We need every person, every noble, every slave, every tradesman. The city has to be strong, not tearing itself apart from within."

"Lord Aubur deserved what happened to him," insisted the gruff man. "We all know what he did to the silk yaxen."

Since neither Nicci nor Rendell had mentioned the victim's name, it was plain that this man had been involved. She stepped closer to him. "This new murder will touch a spark to the tinderbox of the duma members. Do you know how much work it was to get them to accept Rendell on the council? You will erase all the progress we've made. Are you fools?"

The people muttered, looking embarrassed. Timothy, the young half-stone yaxen herder, came forward. "We are a long way from evening the score. We thought you would fight on our side for justice, Nicci."

Nicci turned to the young man who had once been a statue. "Every victim sees justice in a different way. Your actions make the nobles feel like victims, and so they will retaliate." She gestured to the crowds around the slave market, the makeshift tents, the piles of plundered supplies from noble villas. "It will take the best of my ability to convince the hard-line duma members not to simply come here and burn you out. The city guard could surround this square with torches and swords and slaughter all of you in revenge for what one man did to Lord Aubur." She glared at the gruff man who seemed to take such pride in his executions. "All because some of you couldn't wait for revenge."

"We all want revenge," said the gruff man with a twisted smile. "One piece at a time."

"I thought you wanted justice, not revenge," Nicci said. "And justice requires an accounting. You declared Aubur guilty and beheaded him because you thought you were his judge, and now the nobles will want your blood in repayment for his. You've kept the wheel turning, round and round."

"It's a step in the right direction." The scarred man crossed his beefy arms over his chest, refusing to back down. "I thought you'd be pleased after all those words you said when you led us against Sovrena Thora. I thought you were on our side. I thought you stood against evil."

"Evil takes many forms, including self-justification. Hard justice is how we stop this cycle. You are the one who killed Lord Aubur. You know it. We all know it." She took a step closer to the man. The other people in the square shifted uneasily.

The murderer squared his shoulders and faced Nicci. Though she was smaller in stature, she was far more powerful.

"This is how I make the accounting," she said. "Afterward, I'll convince the duma that the guilty man has paid for his crimes, and no further retaliation is necessary." Her voice boomed out to all those gathered in the market. "But it must end here. No more nobles can be attacked if you ever hope to find equal footing in Ildakar. Do you understand?"

The scarred man snorted. "I'll go and talk to them myself,

give them a piece of my mind." He still did not comprehend his danger. "I'll make them see. I'll—"

Nicci reached out with her gift and, with barely a thought, stopped the man's heart. His eyes bulged. He twitched, then toppled like a felled yaxen on the tiles of the slave market, stone dead.

As the people gasped, Nicci looked to Rendell, who swallowed hard, then nodded. Rendell said to the crowd, "I speak to you as a member of the duma. We can't play favorites. If we want equality, then we have to be equal, with equal rules. If we want freedom, we have to pay the price of our freedom. If we want our part of Ildakar, we have to *be* a part of Ildakar."

Nicci spoke into the stunned silence. "That means you have to fight for Ildakar, too. When we attack the general's army, we will need as many fighters as we can possibly have. We'll give you training, weapons, and armor if you help in the assault. If you are going to shed blood for your freedom, then make sure it's the right blood."

The frightened people were cowed into nervous shifting.

"When the duma members find out about the murder of Lord Aubur, Rendell and I will inform them the matter is over." Nicci paused long enough to sweep her intense gaze across them all, saw that her words had made an impact. The dead man lay sprawled on the flagstones, and no one came closer to him.

Nicci gave a quick nod. "Good. Then, as I said, the matter is over."

CHAPTER 29

Bannon had fought battles before, but he had never gone to full-scale war. Now, he stepped out onto the combat arena sands at night, gripping Sturdy in his sweaty palm. Lila and the other morazeth had trained him with clubs, knives, and fists, but he preferred his sword. With its discolored steel, unadorned pommel, and flat blade guard, the sword didn't look like much, but neither did Bannon. Appearances could be deceiving.

When a weapon cleaved an enemy in two, what difference did it make if the steel was bright or tarnished?

In the cool evening air he wore nothing but a fighting girdle around his waist and the kind of combat sandals preferred by Ildakaran warriors. Soon enough, the rigors of fighting would warm him. Even though he was confident in his skills, the thought of rushing out with only his sword against thousands of half-petrified warriors sent a chill down his spine.

As the duma's plans proceeded, the fighters would keep practicing, honing their skills for the massive surprise attack. Around the top ring of the arena, blazing crystalline torches glowed like blue-white suns against the darkness, illuminating the arena. Sixty of the best warriors, along with officers of the city guard, emerged from the arched gates to the open sands, carrying their practice swords, staves, and spears. The Ildakar arena sometimes presented nighttime exhibitions, melees with dozens of fighters that resulted in an exciting slaughter. Tonight, the patchwork army of defenders would practice deep into the darkness.

Bannon had tied his long hair back so it wouldn't get in his way while fighting. Lila had suggested he chop off his locks, as Nicci had. "An enemy can grab your hair, boy, yank it, throw you off balance, even snap your neck."

Thinking of Nicci's spell-possessed hair made him shiver, but he shook his head. "I haven't cut my hair since I left Chiriya Island. I won't lose that part of who I am."

"Then you might lose your head."

"I'll try not to."

Lila's expression was hard, but he could see the softness behind her eyes. "See that you don't, for my sake if nothing else."

Facing the warriors on the field, Lila and six other morazeth held their weapons of choice. The branded runes that covered their skin protected them against magic but not traditional weapons, and Utros and the ancient soldiers would fight with real weapons instead of spells. The women remained fixated on defending Ildakar. To them, their purpose had not changed. An opponent was an opponent.

Bannon had talked to many of the arena warriors, asking if they resented the morazeth for the abuses done to them, but most seasoned warriors already had their independence beaten out of them over the years. He remembered how wholeheartedly loyal Ian, Ildakar's champion, had been to Adessa, but she had killed him on the night of the revolt. For that, Bannon could never forgive the morazeth leader, any more than he could forgive the Norukai slavers.

But Lila . . . He slowly, reluctantly, began to understand the young woman's mind-set. Her harsh and painful tutelage had made him a far better fighter, and those skills might save him when he fought against a real enemy.

Now, the morazeth women drew their weapons. Lila held a short sword in one hand, a whip in the other, while others held wooden fighting staves, long hooks, tall pikes. Genda, a squarish, stocky fighter, wore metal-studded gloves on each hand and prepared to fight with her fists alone.

Lila called, "There is no excuse for failure. When we attack General Utros and his army, don't embarrass me by getting killed." She meant no humor in her statement, though some of the city guard chuckled nervously. The arena warriors did not. "You will fight and you will learn. And if you do well enough in real battle, you may not need to fight Utros again."

"We'll make them sting, ha ha!" called a bright young voice.

Bannon turned to see Timothy, whose rough-spun slave clothes had been replaced with a fighter's girded waistcloth. The scamp wore no shirt and gripped a short sword that looked too big for him. His skin was gray-white from the lingering stone effect, and when he swung his sword, his movements were slow and his joints stiff, but the grin on his face was real.

Lila seemed impressed. "I expect every one of you to be at least as brave and strong as a lowly yaxen herder."

Some of the fighters affirmed that they were, while others, particularly the haughty city guard members, grumbled at the boy's arrogance.

"We'll fight beside you, Timothy," Bannon said.

The seven morazeth trainers divided the fighters into squads, so that the smaller teams could spar against one another.

"Out in the combat field," Lila said, "you won't have a well-mannered arena fight. If you don't watch your back while battling one enemy, another might thrust a spear through your heart. Don't expect rules, don't expect honor." She strode among them, glaring at those who didn't show sufficient confidence. "And I don't expect you to fight with neat rules either. A real battle is not a game, and the winners don't receive ribbons or trophies, though some of you might receive a pleasurable reward from one of our beautiful morazeth." She waited, sure she had their attention. "You are responsible for protecting our city and preserving our freedom."

"And do we have freedom now?" asked one of the household slaves, a muscular man who had volunteered for training.

"You have more freedom than you had before," Lila answered. "And if General Utros is defeated, you will be in a position to demand more."

The former slave rested the point of his sword in the sand and stood with his legs spread, facing Lila, who came forward to meet his challenge. He said, "I could have had complete freedom if I'd slipped away one night. Many others ran from Ildakar, and now they have full lives far from here. Some mountain villages like Stravera accept runaway slaves. When my friend Garth ran off, he begged me to go with him, but I listened to Mirrormask instead. I stayed behind to overthrow Ildakar for the freedom of all." He grimaced. "Now look at us! The entire city is imprisoned. I should have left when I had the chance."

Lila stepped so close to him that her flesh nearly touched his. "Do you think you could escape now? Why not slip out at night, tiptoe through the thousands of enemy soldiers? Be my guest."

"I'll stay," the man grumbled. "And I'll fight. I already made up my mind. The sorceress convinced me."

Lila stepped back. "Good, then you'll be my first opponent tonight." She glanced to the side. "Bannon, you train Timothy. Break the yaxen herder if you can."

Genda let out a loud shrill whistle, and all the fighters stood at attention. Kedra, Lyesse, Marla, Thorn, and Ricia took up their positions, facing groups of opponents. When Genda whistled a second time, the battle was unleashed.

The arena rang with wooden staves striking armor, hardened

gloves smacking against flesh, steel crashing against steel. Big Genda struck her opponent in the chest with a steel-mesh fist and knocked him back onto the soft sand.

Without hesitation, Timothy swung his short sword at Bannon, laughing as he attacked. Bannon lifted Sturdy to deflect the blow, and he smiled as well, seeing the scamp's eager fury. Timothy flailed his sword from side to side with no finesse, and Bannon easily countered each thrust, each parry. He couldn't help but think of his own clumsy abilities when he had first bought Sturdy from a Tanimura swordsmith. Vowing never to be defenseless again, he'd used his last coins to buy the weapon, but he hadn't really known how to fight.

Timothy drove at him with such energy that Bannon took a step back. He met every blow, countering the boy's energy, but all too often the yaxen herder left himself wide open. As soon as Bannon saw a chance, he struck hard, crashing the flat of the blade on the boy's shoulder. He checked his blow at the last instant, not wanting to injure Timothy, but to his amazement his steel merely glanced off the bare shoulder, as if it had struck a hard surface. Bannon hesitated in surprise, and his young opponent charged forward, smashing Sturdy so hard that Bannon nearly dropped the weapon.

Timothy let out a cry of joy. "I could have killed you, Bannon Farmer! Beware of a worthy opponent like myself."

Bannon slipped under the boy's short sword and again struck his scrawny arm with the flat of his blade. "And I could have cut off your arm."

"Could you? My skin is better protection than any armor you've ever worn. Besides, I have two arms, and by the Keeper's beard, I could keep fighting even if I lost one."

Around them, the loud combat continued, punctuated with yelps of pain as fighters suffered blunted blows from the morazeth. One arena veteran, a man with scars on his skin and face, seemed uninspired in his fighting. His morazeth opponent, Ricia, knocked him to the ground and placed her sword against his chest. "Aren't you interested? When you fail, you will die. Remember that when you fight the enemy soldiers."

The veteran's face turned ruddy. He picked himself up from the combat sands, brushing himself off where dust clung to his sweat and blood. "I make no excuses, Ricia." Letting out a growl, he fought with renewed energy.

Bannon kept sparring with Timothy, although perspiration dripped down his face and his muscles ached. The scamp was reckless and full of energy, and after Bannon suffered several bruises, he decided to stop going easy on the young man. "You're careless," he warned, and slapped the flat of his sword against the boy's hardened thigh.

"We need to take risks!" Timothy said. "How else are a thousand of us going to fight tens of thousands of enemies? Or more?"

Bannon didn't have an answer for that, so instead, he just fought harder.

A man's voice spoke out from the arched entry at the edge of the arena. "I brought two more for you to train."

Genda whistled again, and the fighting stuttered to a halt. The grunts, clangs, and clatters faded into heaving breaths, coughs, and groans of pain.

Lord Oron nudged two young men ahead of him. "My son Brock and his friend Jed will do their duty to fight for Ildakar. Lady Olgya and I have encouraged them to volunteer for the upcoming offensive."

Bannon wiped sweat from his face as he stared at the once-haughty young men. He wondered if his harsh words in the skinning house had had any effect on them. They wore colorful silk jerkins sashed at the waist, Brock dressed in crimson, Jed in forest green. Both wore black pantaloons and polished boots, and each carried a gleaming sword, fresh from the city armory. Clearly, the weapons had never been used in battle or even practice.

As the trainees looked at them, a few snickered or muttered.

Jed and Brock stumbled forward, uncertain. Brock turned back to his father. "But we're gifted. We should be testing our skills in magic. Train us!"

"You could have been doing that all these years," Oron said, "but it's also good to learn how to fight for yourselves." With a brusque gesture, he forced them to join the other sweaty trainees.

Lila came forward. "Those two should strip down if they intend to fight. This isn't a pleasure party or a banquet, and we wouldn't want to stain those fine silks."

Oron made no move to join the two newcomers on the training field. "These new silks might protect them. Jed's mother says the fabric may be impervious to blows." He frowned at the boys, showing his impatience. "Jed and Brock are pleased to test the garments against your weapons."

The two young men fidgeted nervously.

Bannon nudged Timothy, and he and the young yaxen herder went to meet the pair. "We'll train with Jed and Brock, and we'll go easy on them for now."

The two young nobles responded with arrogance, as if Bannon and the young scamp were far beneath them.

"Oh, show them no mercy," Oron said with an iron smile. "General Utros certainly won't." The lord tossed his yellow braid behind him as he stalked out of the arena.

Bannon and Timothy faced the newcomers, who drew their pristine swords. Genda let out her shrill whistle again, and the fighting commenced.

When Bannon met the nervous gaze of Jed and Brock, he remembered how he'd berated them for what they had done to him, but he doubted his words had changed their attitude. Brock and Jed certainly hadn't apologized to him.

"We're all on the same side now, Bannon Farmer," Jed said grudgingly, "for Ildakar."

Brock added, "If we defeat General Utros, then you and your friends can leave. It can't be too soon for me."

"I would like nothing more than that," Bannon said. He was genuinely tired of this legendary city.

"Enough talk!" Timothy ran forward, swinging his sword and startling Brock, who reeled back. He tried to bring up his own blade in defense, but the scamp was too wild. Timothy's sword struck Brock on the left biceps, and Bannon feared he would cleave the young noble's arm right off with the first blow, but the silk fabric held like tough, fine chain mail. Even so, the hard blow elicited a scream from Brock, who staggered away clutching his bruised arm. Timothy drove in for the kill, looking as if he meant it.

Jed ran to defend his friend, intercepting the yaxen herder. Bannon and the scamp fought together, testing the two nobles as they regained their footing and helped each other.

"This isn't how I wanted to fight," Jed whined.

"I've seen you fight," Bannon said bitterly. "You went out to smash the faces of statue soldiers who couldn't even move."

Still wincing, barely able to bend his bruised arm, Brock said, "We damaged hundreds of them, and that's hundreds more enemy soldiers than you fought, Bannon Farmer."

"We should have destroyed thousands more," Jed said.

"I'll grant you that, but now you have to stand against soldiers who can actually fight back."

CHAPTER 30

S logging through the muck, her skin covered with insect
bites and slime, Adessa used her dagger to hack at a thorn
vine that hung in her path. The plant's tendrils recoiled when
her blade severed them, leaking greenish sap, like blood.
These mindless hazards kept her from her real prey, Wizard
Commander Maxim.

One of the thorn vines actively slashed at her like a whip.
The sharp spines glistened with diamondlike drops of venom.
One of the thorns caught Adessa on the arm, slicing across
her skin, and she whirled and slashed once, twice, severing the
tentacle from its base and letting the twitching tendril fall into
the muddy swamp beside her.

She looked at the scratch and saw that her skin was already
inflamed. Without hesitation, she used the dagger to slice her
own arm, turning the scratch into a profusely bleeding cut. She
squeezed and milked it to make the flowing blood flush out
the poison. She sheathed the dagger and now used her sword
to chop away the rest of the attacking vines, then pressed
forward, following Maxim's faint trail.

She had confronted him only once, that night at his camp

when he'd distracted her with magic and left her to fight a pair of swamp dragons. While Maxim vanished into the wilderness, she battled the large lizards for half an hour before finally dispatching them. She hadn't found him again since.

Now Adessa's work would be more difficult, because he knew that Thora had sent her on this mission to kill him, and he knew how deadly the morazeth were, especially her.

As she searched for his trail, she pondered what her sisters were doing back in Ildakar. She assumed they had quelled the unrest and saved the sovrena. Adessa had faith in them, and she would worry about her own task. When she brought back the wizard commander's head, she would once again concern herself with Ildakar.

Alert for more attacking vines, she picked her way through the swamp, studying broken twigs, crushed grasses, old footprints in the soft muck. She knew Maxim was a day or more ahead of her. Fortunately for Adessa, even though he was a powerful wizard, the man was not particularly good at covering his tracks.

She continued, cautious in the hazy light that penetrated the leaves overhead. She didn't want her scorn for Maxim to let her make mistakes. Yesterday, she had gotten off on a wrong trail and followed what turned out to be a young black bear, which had bolted into the underbrush. She realized that Maxim had gone a different direction entirely. Several wasted hours later, she finally found where she'd gone astray. Now she was after him again. She moved along, eyes to the ground, scanning around her for spiderwebs, attacking vines, or swamp dragons lying in wait.

Back in the city, Maxim had been an aloof man. Despite his rank, he treated Ildakar with disrespect, and now Adessa knew that Maxim was Mirrormask, a traitor who had fomented the rebellion among the slaves, causing untold harm to the city. Even without the sovrena's orders, Adessa was convinced that the wizard commander had to die for his crimes.

She was devoted to Ildakar and always had been. Adessa had been born centuries after the shroud of eternity was put in place, and she had grown up hearing legends of outside enemies, but never seeing any threat beyond the unrest within Ildakar itself.

As a girl, Adessa had shown great physical prowess in rough-and-tumble games that nobles watched for amusement. She had been recruited by three morazeth who came to her parents' home one day and paid them gold from the Ildakaran treasury. More importantly, they convinced Adessa's mother and father, and the girl herself, that joining them was the greatest honor their beloved city could bestow. Agreeing wholeheartedly, Adessa promised to become the best morazeth Ildakar had known, but her father had chastised her for bragging. "You don't have to be the best. Being a morazeth is enough."

She had joined other girls her age, begun combat sparring. From the very first day, it was more exhausting and painful than anything she'd ever experienced. At first, the recruits treated one another as friends, but when the girls didn't fight hard enough, or strive with all their might to hurt their opponents—their comrades—other morazeth would come in with clubs, gang up on the entire team, and beat them senseless until the girls understood. Or at least most of them did.

Two of the new trainees died in the first week. By the second month, Adessa killed one of them herself, a young girl who had tried to make friends, but showed a core of weakness. After Adessa did that, she'd been rewarded with the first protective rune branded on her upper arm.

She remembered the expressionless morazeth standing close, nodding encouragement, whispering, watching as the training leader removed a white-hot branding iron from an intense brazier fire. Adessa braced herself, knowing that if she cried out, she would be punished for her weakness. She thought she was prepared, but nothing had readied her for the searing bolt of heat that screamed through her skin, into her nerves, until it exploded in her mind. Adessa gritted her teeth and made no sound, listened to the sickening sizzle, smelled the burning meat of her own arm. The pain lasted forever, but it was done as swiftly as the morazeth could manage. Someone splashed a bucket of cold water on her arm and another doused her eyes to wash away any hint of tears that might have leaked out of her squeezed lids.

"It's all right," said the training leader, replacing the still-smoking brand in the brazier. "You can faint now."

With her trainer's permission, Adessa collapsed.

Over the years, each branded mark had been just as painful, but Adessa never screamed, never flinched, never cried. And now, her skin was a complete leatherwork of art. No part of her was vulnerable to a magical attack.

Adessa was proud of the ancient tradition, a carefully bonded society of women warriors, guardians. According to very old legends, some morazeth had gone north as mercenaries, but they were long departed, and if any of their teachings survived, the women must have changed dramatically in the intervening millennia. Adessa and the morazeth of Ildakar remained unwavering.

Now when darkness fell in the swamps and Adessa could no longer be sure of her path, she found a place to camp, resting on the ground against a wide tree trunk beneath dangling beards of moss. She let herself doze, her senses alert for any creature that might consider her an easy meal. As she sat motionless, she heard a rustle in the grasses. She peered out from behind the mossy veil to see a serpent as thick around as her thigh gliding through the underbrush.

When the snake broke through the reeds, sensing Adessa, it rose up to reveal not one serpent head, but three of them branched like a trident from its neck, tasting the air with black tongues. Each had only a single eye, and when they struck forward, the three mouths yawned open to reveal curved fangs.

Adessa prepared to fight. Even with three heads, a snake was just a snake. She felt no fear.

The central head plunged down to strike her, but she ducked to the side, letting the fangs sink into the moss-covered tree trunk. In the instant it was trapped, Adessa struck off its head with her sword, and dark blood spurted out of the stump.

The other two serpent heads attacked. The thick main body rolled forward, rising up as the remaining pair of heads lashed out. She lifted her sword overhead and brought it down with a single stroke, splitting the snake at the juncture of the last two heads. The sharp blade cut down along its spine, and the snake flopped in two halves like a split ribbon. The separated heads, not knowing they were dead, kept trying to bite her. She continued sawing downward and finally cut through the snake's heart, or one of its hearts, and its entire body collapsed.

Adessa grimaced in disgust as she found herself covered with serpent blood as well as insect bites, mud, and sweat. Standing over the dead hulk of the snake, she used her dagger to skin off the scaly hide. Snake meat, even raw, was nourishment.

As she chewed on the moist reptilian flesh, Adessa withdrew into her makeshift shelter again, resting, pondering. She still felt the blood magic from the unborn infant within her, enhancing her senses and powers, and she knew that boost would last until she tracked down and killed Maxim.

But she had to sustain herself. She made sure she drank enough water, ate enough food, to keep her body strong. Over the years, she had given the same admonishment to all trainees in the combat arena. Adessa had never thought of the fighters as slaves, but as her pets, and pets needed to be disciplined.

Now, in the dark buzzing swamp, she recalled the champions she had made and the lovers she had rewarded over the years. When she was finished with them, those men were completely loyal to her, wrapped around her finger even when she sent them into the combat arena to die. Many had been kidnapped from outside villages, taken when they were young and broken, sold by Norukai raiders, or born of other slaves inside the city.

Ian, her last champion, her last lover, had been a devoted young man who never disappointed her, always defended her, until the end, when that outsider Bannon had made him remember his past. Though Bannon seemed a weak and naive young man, he created hair-fine cracks in Ian's armor of duty and eventually turned her champion against her.

Adessa still didn't understand what she had done wrong. She had taken Ian into her bed and had shown him true passion, primal lovemaking like the rutting of wild animals. His pleasure had been so great he nearly fell unconscious after satisfying himself. Adessa had even let herself grow fond of him, sometimes holding his sweaty body against hers after he was sated and after she, too, had let herself release that inner thunder of pleasure. She'd let him plant his child in her, and Adessa had felt it growing, the energy of the unborn part of her.

If not for the uprising, she would have given birth to Ian's baby, but Ian had betrayed her, and so she killed him. Instead, that child growing within her had proven to be a powerful resource, an innocent life. In addition to the protective runes that covered her skin, Adessa now had that blood magic, the *life magic* of the unborn child, a sacrifice as potent as any slave on the great pyramid. As a woman she had given life, and as a morazeth she took it back.

Now, as the hours of the night crawled along, she sat against the mossy bark of the tree, sensed the emptiness in her womb and compared it to the fresh strength throughout her muscles.

She waited several hours for the moon to rise, and under the silvery light, she emerged and sprinted off again in pursuit of her quarry.

CHAPTER 31

Sitting inside her dark dungeon cell, Sovrena Thora wished she could become a statue again and let time slide past until this nonsense was over. Since her hardened body had no need to eat or drink, the guards had stopped bothering to deliver her meals.

The dank cell remained silent, a stillness so deep that when she concentrated Thora could hear the delicate movement of spider legs. She once heard a rat skitter across the floor until it found a hole somewhere and escaped. No vermin had any interest in her partially petrified body.

After hearing the rat, she ignited a small flame in her hand and spent hours inspecting her chamber, touching each stone block from floor to ceiling. Eventually she discovered a small chink in the stone that made a crack just wide enough for a skinny rat. It wouldn't help her escape at all.

It maddened her most that she had no idea what was happening in Ildakar. What foolishness were the dithering duma members undertaking, what irreparable damage? By now Nicci and Nathan had likely taken over the duma, named themselves sovrena and wizard commander, even though they didn't belong in Ildakar. Thora had spent centuries building her perfect city and the interloper Nicci had been here for what? A month?

The city Thora loved so much was disintegrating while she was trapped in here. She didn't know whether it was day or night outside.

After an interminable time, she heard movement in the corridor, saw bright light seeping through the small barred opening. The diversion piqued her interest, and she crept to the door, listening to footsteps. She assumed it was the rude guards again, street rabble who had no business wearing the city uniform.

The footsteps sounded slower than a normal gait, like a warrior weighed down with armor. Since she was the only prisoner in these dungeons, and since the protective runes around the door kept her from attacking with magic, Thora wondered why anyone would need such protection against her.

A person approached the door, and she heard the rattle of a heavy key in the lock. The crossbar slid aside and the hinges creaked. The door opened, allowing more light to stream in from the corridor. Facing her visitor, Thora was astonished to see the sorceress Lani, the woman who had challenged her and lost, who had spent centuries as a statue to serve as a warning for other would-be challengers.

Now, the two rivals stared at each other. Thora could feel hatred emanating from her. "I came to speak with you, Thora," Lani finally said, refusing to use her lost title. "Much needs to be said."

Thora wasn't impressed. "You came to gloat."

"Not everyone is like you." Lani remained at the door, and Thora made no move toward her. Although Thora was a greater sorceress than the other woman would ever be, Lani was not weak. Nevertheless, the spell runes would stifle any attack Thora might release.

Lani continued, "I remember Ildakar from before, and I

241

see the city now. Back then, I challenged you because I saw the damage you were doing. I'm appalled at how much worse you've made it. Thank the spirits we can begin rebuilding now, with you and Maxim out of the way."

"I *preserved* Ildakar! I love Ildakar," Thora sneered. "You were always weak, just a follower, calling your birds, playing with water and scrying magic." She sniffed. "I learned from you. I kept cages of larks as my own pretty pets, and with your scrying spells I was able to spy on the unrest in my city."

"It's no longer your city," Lani said.

"That may be true now, but the people know what I did for them. Soon enough they'll realize that Ildakar will fall without me."

The other woman suddenly changed the subject. "What did you do to Renn?" Quiet, intelligent Lani had contented herself with the weak wizard, not the best choice for a partner, although Renn had indeed been more handsome back then.

Now Thora realized what had really brought the woman here. "He's gone on a fool's errand, and I doubt we'll ever see him again. I wouldn't expect him to succeed."

"I know you sent him to find Cliffwall," Lani replied, "but what did you *do* to him in the intervening centuries? You hurt him, didn't you? He was such a wise man, full of ideas, a scholar, a historian. He and I would spend hours together studying ancient spell books to hone our gifts."

"Yes, I remember how sweet it was," Thora scoffed. "When you two went to bed together, did you tuck ancient books under your pillows for added romance?"

Lani looked annoyed. "Just because we refused to take part in your pleasure parties doesn't mean we didn't experience our own love. You dispatched my poor Renn into the wild without preparation. How could he survive such a journey?"

"That depends entirely on his own abilities," Thora said.

"In that case, I have confidence in him. And when Renn does come back and rejoin us, the duma will be even stronger. We'll rebuild Ildakar together and make this city into a perfect society for all, not just for your selfish pleasure."

Thora found herself offended by the lies. "There was nothing selfish about my rule of Ildakar. Everything I did as sovrena was to make the city great. The people will realize that in time. I'll wait." The flickering flame in her palm suddenly flared brighter. "The only reason you're outside that door instead of me is because of an accident. Three other duma members betrayed me, and my husband betrayed all of us. You had no hand in this victory."

Lani responded with a small smile. "A victory by accident is still a victory, and you're still in the dungeon where you can do no further harm."

Her smug words enraged Thora. She bunched her stony muscles, gritted her teeth, and felt power building within her, but she knew she couldn't release her gift. "I want to save my city, and you'll soon see that you need my help. The people will appreciate me."

"They appreciate their freedom more," said Lani. "We voted in new duma members, not just Oron and Olgya, but also a representative of the freed slaves who can speak for the lower classes. There will be merchant duma members to help determine Ildakar's future. Together, we are one united population with a common enemy, General Utros. Someday all those people you hurt might be willing to forgive you, but not now."

Thora remained silent, and her stiff skin helped to mask her angry expression. She used words she knew would cut Lani deeply. "After I defeated you and turned you to stone, Renn was a broken man. He still served on the duma, but he was weak, listless. He would look at your statue and sometimes weep. A pathetic little man, but I kept him because he did as he was told. I could have taken him as my lover anytime. Renn was entirely mine. He barely cared for himself. He gained weight, his clothes were shabby and ill fitting. Even you wouldn't want him now."

"I'll decide that when I see him again." Lani stepped away

from the door, finished with her confrontation. "I don't think I'll ever see you again, though. If we leave you here in the cell forever, maybe Ildakar will heal."

She pushed the heavy door shut and slammed the crossbar into place. Keys rattled in the lock, and Lani extinguished the bright torches even before she left the corridors.

In darkness and silence again, Thora felt helpless, furious. She had given her entire life to creating the legend of Ildakar, and now it was all being stolen from her. She could do nothing about it.

Thora stood in front of the barricaded door. She called up the magic within her, flared the flame so she could study her stone block walls yet again. She knew the protective runes were powerful. She had crafted many of them herself long ago. No spell of hers could ever break them.

Though she knew no one could hear her, Thora let out a loud scream of frustration. The sound echoed throughout the corridors, bouncing back on the stone walls of her cell. Unleashing all the power in her half-petrified body, she swung her fist and pounded the stone blocks that held the door in place. Her skin was hard and could feel no pain, and this time she didn't care. She could mangle her hand if she wanted, because it would heal.

Fury turned her fist into a battering ram. When she smashed the offending blocks, she felt the thunderous impact and heard a *crack*. Thora stepped away in surprise, holding up her hand to illuminate the chamber. Her stone fists were barely damaged, but when she looked at the blocks around the door, she saw a fracture in one stone. She had done that?

This wasn't magic. It was sheer, brute force. Her anger and her hardened body were powerful enough to break stone! She wondered how much damage she could do.

With a growing sense of wonder, she ran her hardened fingers along the crack, noting how her blow had damaged the spell rune. Even if direct magic could not break her free, maybe her body could produce enough force to do it. She looked at her barely damaged knuckles and considered.

This was very interesting indeed, and Thora had all the time in the world.

CHAPTER 32

After Renn settled in at Cliffwall, he would sit for hours with scholars who gathered around him as he held court. Verna listened to the stories, though she doubted some of his descriptions.

Renn waxed poetic about Ildakar, wistfully talking about the things he missed. "The city has fountains on every level, and so many statues! The sculptors of Ildakar are master artisans, shaping solid marble as if it were soft clay." He heaved a sigh. "And our terraced orchards produce the most delicious little apples you've ever tasted, lovely for making apple wine."

He had trimmed his beard, combed and oiled his brown hair after the hard days of traveling. In the intervening weeks Renn had indulged in Cliffwall's hospitality, and now his cheeks were round again, the shadows gone from under his eyes. He was relaxed and loquacious.

As Verna listened to him talk, she hoped to learn more about Nicci and Nathan, and how they were promoting Lord Rahl's expectations for peace, freedom, and prosperity. Beside her, Amber listened intently, as if she were in a class about secure binding webs taught by the Sisters of the Light. When

Renn waxed poetic about Ildakar, his most attentive listeners were Oliver and Peretta. The two young scholars had explored enough of the world to know that there was much more to see.

"And how far away is Ildakar? Exactly?" Oliver inquired. "How long would it take us to go there? If we wanted to travel, I mean."

Renn nibbled on a crumbly biscuit from a plate beside his chair, then brushed crumbs from his restored maroon robes. "Oh, it is very far, a terrible journey. We took weeks of hard marching to find Cliffwall."

Peretta's face pinched with concentration. "But you didn't know where you were going. Surely it wouldn't be so hard to find the route *back*? Oliver and I crossed half the Old World in that amount of time."

"Well, uh," Renn fumbled, then wiped his mouth, "the landscape is rugged, trackless for the most part. We had great tribulations and difficulties."

"We had a few of those ourselves," Oliver admitted. "Still, I'd like to see Ildakar with my own eyes."

Verna was surprised that the wizard looked downcast, not at all excited by the prospect of going home. "Yes, very understandable. Captain Trevor and I did see some spectacular terrain, but . . ." He dropped his voice, uncertain. "There's a chance we will never find Ildakar because it is no longer there. The sovrena and the wizard commander were planning to raise the shroud of eternity again, and if they did, I will be forever outside." He sounded professorial again. "It isn't dissimilar to the camouflage shroud that hid this archive for all those centuries."

Verna spoke up. "Cliffwall's camouflage shroud is down permanently. In fact, if we could find a way to put it back in place, then the archives would never fall into the wrong hands." The gathered scholars muttered at her suggestion, but Verna casually brushed her curly gray-brown hair away from her ears. "It may be the only way to keep it entirely safe."

Amber looked to her in alarm. "But if we did that, none of us could study the archives. There's so much here to learn, Prelate." Her face grew flushed.

"I meant only as a last desperate measure to protect the archive." Verna tried to calm them. "General Zimmer always likes to be prepared."

In the confined canyon, Zimmer drilled his soldiers every day, keeping them in good fighting shape. Trevor and his Ildakaran guards joined in the efforts. So far, they had heard no rumors of any great army like Jagang's sweeping across the Old World, but Zimmer would never let down his guard.

Gloria and Franklin walked into the chamber, overhearing the last part of the conversation. Gloria said, "I would object to that strenuously, Prelate. Our knowledge belongs to all people. We can't seal the archive again."

Franklin said, "In ancient times we had to protect this lore from Emperor Sulachan, but now it should be available to all gifted students, for the benefit of humanity."

"And not just to Ildakar." Gloria narrowed her eyes as she looked at Renn.

The wizard had finished the last biscuit on his plate. "I agree. The knowledge should be shared with all, under certain restrictions. Sovrena Thora might have selfish uses, but there are many gifted among the duma members and the noble classes of Ildakar. I can just imagine how my Lani and I would have adored the opportunity to study here!" He flashed a wistful smile. "Opening the Cliffwall archive could be the start of a new golden age. We could bring back a time of wizards, like in the ancient history books."

"We're just starting to learn here," said Franklin. "Many of our scholars know some basic spells, but it'll take centuries before we have a firm grasp on what the archive even holds. We don't want to be rash." He lowered his voice. "We learned that lesson already."

Verna spoke up. "Nicci made her concerns clear when she

asked for representatives to come and help protect the archive. The knowledge in Cliffwall is dangerous, and it should be guarded against abuse." She looked at the gathered listeners. "But there is more to our mission. We serve Lord Rahl in D'Hara, and his rule will bring strength and happiness to the Old World. We also need to build alliances. With Nicci and Nathan already there in Ildakar, maybe that city can become one of our strongest allies."

Renn nodded sagely. "I hope someday you can visit my city for yourselves, and then you'll see that my stories don't do it justice."

Verna made up her mind. "Yes, we should see it. What is wrong with now?" Oliver and Peretta lit up at the suggestion, and young Amber smiled with excitement. Verna continued, "Everything Renn says should inspire us. As Sisters of the Light we seek knowledge. We have to go to Ildakar."

Sisters Rhoda and Eldine looked just as interested in the prospect. The group of Sisters had departed from Tanimura seeking a new purpose for their order now that prophecy was gone and the Palace of the Prophets destroyed, and they all hoped to find their calling here in Cliffwall. Long ago, the Sisters had vowed to train and protect young men with the gift, and now all these apprentices needed to learn their true potential.

Verna nodded firmly to herself. "Yes, we should go to Ildakar and see if we can help. Nathan Rahl is a powerful wizard and a former prophet, and Nicci is . . . *Nicci*. She was Death's Mistress."

Renn's eyebrows shot up; he looked uncomfortable. "I found both of them most impressive, but . . ." He hesitated, scratched his cheek again.

"We're going," Oliver insisted, touching his young companion's arm, "both Peretta and I. Nicci and Nathan might need us."

The memmer girl didn't even glance at him. "Of course we

are. We can help find the path, even though we've never gone there before. We're good at it."

Renn was startled, thinking hard. "It will be a difficult trek back over the mountains. We aren't prepared—"

"We'll be better supplied this time," Verna said. "General Zimmer can accompany us with a contingent of his troops, and of course Captain Trevor knows the way now. It will be a much easier expedition."

Seeing the eager audience in the room, Renn let his shoulders sag. "I suppose I'm ready to go back, too, so long as we have a well-equipped expedition. Couldn't we rest and recover for just a few more days?"

"A few more days," Verna agreed. "We have plans to make and supplies to pack. We'll gather whatever maps remain in Cliffwall, so we can find the best route." She looked forward to seeing the legendary city and to reuniting with Nicci and Nathan. In times past, she had chased Nathan all over the land after he escaped from the Palace of the Prophets. Before that she had spent years searching for Richard Rahl, knowing that a new war wizard had been born in the world. A trip from Cliffwall to Ildakar didn't seem like such an arduous journey. In fact, Verna felt confident.

She looked around the room, sensing the excitement among the scholars. She nodded at Renn. "We will all go see this city of wizards."

CHAPTER 33

As he led his hundred handpicked soldiers into the hills beyond Ildakar, First Commander Enoch thought of the early days when he had marched with General Utros. They had carried Iron Fang's banner, but every soldier knew they were really fighting for Utros. The imperial palace in Orogang was far away, and Emperor Kurgan had little bearing on their lives. Utros, though, was always with them.

Enoch had met the emperor only once, at a military gala with bright pennants and bold fanfares. General Utros had vowed to make the unruly lands bow to Iron Fang, and Enoch had promised to help his commander succeed. He and his loyal men would give their sweat, their strength, their skill, and even their lives to make that happen.

During that brief celebration, Enoch had not been impressed with Kurgan as a person. The emperor valued affectations—gaudy clothes, jewels, and monuments—more than leading his people. Enoch had wondered how such a man could rule the lands Utros intended to conquer for him, but the first commander would follow the orders of his general, one mission at a time.

Such as this one.

Utros told him the vital resource his sorceresses required to create a lens that could see through the veil to the underworld. The very thought sent a chill down Enoch's spine. He had listened and nodded, but offered no opinion. His team would obtain what Ava and Ruva needed, as his general ordered.

Now Enoch and a hundred soldiers moved at a steady pace through the forested hills to the north. Because the half-petrified warriors needed neither food, water, nor rest, they could march at a constant pace. They searched the untracked woods for paths that would lead them to the mountain town of Stravera.

Scouting parties had already combed the vicinity and ransacked a few isolated homes they found, but now Enoch and his company needed to find a large town that would have enough children to fulfill the general's demand.

His troops wound through the forest of oak and pine, picking their way among the deadfall. The company came upon a swath of downed trees on a hillside, dead pines toppled by a windstorm. Such an obstacle would have been an impenetrable barrier for a normal army, the protruding branches like spears to gut or castrate an unwary man. But Enoch's hardened troops simply marched through the debris, crushing the dry wood into splinters, grinding the deadfall underfoot.

The marching soldiers passed into a sparser forest, then climbed a ridge from which they could look back at the hills that enclosed the broad valley. Enoch's scouts found a clear footpath, and he ordered the soldiers to follow the trail single file into the mountains. Soon, the path widened and became a discernible road that surely led to a large settlement.

As they continued along the road, they spotted a man far ahead, leading an old nag by a halter rope. The man shaded his eyes to stare at them and seemed unable to understand the presence of so many armed men marching down the road. Pressing his straw hat to his head, the man ran, yanking on the halter and forcing the stubborn old nag to trot after him.

First Commander Enoch nodded to his troops. "That's the direction we go. Follow that man."

The soldiers marched forward at a brisker pace. Their footfalls became synchronized even without a drummer to call them into a formal rhythm. As they continued, roads converged in the forested hills, leading to the town.

Stravera had several hundred homes, shops, and a smithy near a stream that ran out of the hills. A sawmill had been built on the creek, powered by a waterwheel. The blacksmith's forge sent smoke into the air. In the center of town, an open market had tables and stalls displaying fabrics, fruits, vegetables, meats, a wicker basket filled with eggs. Many had abandoned their homes and run from the approach of the company, but more than a hundred villagers stood in the marketplace with makeshift weapons, already alerted by the man with the old nag. Enoch saw, though, that they posed no threat.

He strode up to the nervous but defiant villagers. Behind him, the column marched in perfect formation and stopped in place when the first commander raised his hand. Without speaking, he looked at the people of Stravera, noticing the hodgepodge of clothing styles, hair colors, pale freckled skin or dark skin. The town was a mix of peoples from many lands.

One man with olive skin and blue-black twists of hair seemed to be their leader. He was broad-shouldered and well muscled from a life of hard work. To give his arms freedom of movement, he had cut the sleeves from his brown shirt. From the smear of soot on his face and arms, his blunt fingers and dark-stained nails, Enoch suspected he was the town's blacksmith.

"Is this Stravera?" he asked.

The villagers held their breath as the blacksmith took a step forward. "Yes, this is the free town we built with our own hands. My name is Garth, and I will speak for these people today." His brow was hooded. "Most of our people are slaves who escaped from Ildakar. But you aren't from Ildakar. Your uniforms, the whole look of you . . . you're from somewhere else."

"I am First Commander Enoch of the army of General Utros. We laid siege to the city in the name of Emperor Kurgan, to make Ildakar swear allegiance to him. Surely you've heard of us?"

The people muttered in astonishment.

"That was centuries ago. The stone army awakened?" Garth seemed excited. "I recognize your armor now. Then you're also enemies of Ildakar, as we are? That city needed to be humbled." Garth looked to his fellow villagers. "We are no friends of those people. The nobles enslaved us, tortured us, killed our families." He walked forward to greet Enoch, who hadn't moved. "You awakened from the stone spell, yet you still look pale. How can you move?"

"The spell faded enough, and our entire army is ready to bring down the walls of Ildakar."

Garth looked insistent, fighting hard not to show his fear. "We are not your enemy, none of us. After the shroud dissipated, we built our own sanctuary here in Stravera. We should be allies. I would like nothing more than to see the wizards' duma and those gifted nobles fall. Perhaps we can help you in the fight?"

"We came to Stravera because we needed assistance," Enoch said. "Over the course of time, most of our supplies and equipment crumbled into dust, and when we awakened we had nothing left." He turned slowly, narrowing his eyes as he studied the stalls, the smithy, the merchant shops. "Stravera has certain things that we require."

Garth gave a nervous nod. "We will help as we can, but we don't have much." He regretted his words the moment he spoke them. "I saw the size of your stone army when I ran away from Ildakar. We can't possibly feed such a force. All those thousands! We have barely enough—"

Enoch raised his hand. "We don't require your food. What I need—what *General Utros* needs—are some basic supplies. To start, we could use several wagons, perhaps four."

"That can be done," Garth said, relieved as he barked

orders to the villagers. He was trying hard to be cooperative, anxious about the armed force that could easily take whatever they wanted anyway.

"And barrels," Enoch said. "Empty barrels. Six will do."

"We . . . we have barrels of wine, if you need that. And kegs of beer, brewed right here in the town."

"No wine or beer. Just the empty barrels. We need them to contain something else."

"Of course, of course." Garth wiped sweat from his brow. His long blue-black locks hung down over his face. "In the name of the spirits, we'll help you bring freedom to Ildakar."

Townspeople brought four empty wagons from the stables, and Enoch approved of their sturdy wheels. A mule had been hitched to the front of each one. Other villagers rolled large barrels out into the town square to be loaded into the wagon beds.

All this time Enoch's soldiers hadn't so much as stirred, as if they had turned to stone again. They just waited, intimidating by their very presence.

Garth couldn't stop talking. "There may be other ways we can help. We want to see the walls of Ildakar broken down and the people set free. The slaves are forced to follow the whims of the nobles, but there is great unrest. When I escaped, a man named Mirrormask was rallying the lower classes. He would be a powerful ally to your cause. I could send word into the city, perhaps trigger an uprising?" He smiled. "Ildakar will fall from within, even as your army breaks down the walls. It would be an easy victory."

"I shall consider the idea," Enoch said. "Though that is not the way our general defeats an enemy."

By the time the wagons and the empty barrels were ready, Enoch had enough time to think. The gigantic camp was so squalid because their tents, tools, and supplies had decayed into nothing. He nodded toward the stream. "I see you have a sawmill. We will need much lumber so we can rebuild our command structures. And fabrics—we'll take your cloth for tents and banners." He nodded to himself, remembering that all of their colorful battle flags had long vanished.

The townspeople seemed more nervous now, but they couldn't deny the request. In a thinner voice, Garth called for the supplies to be brought and loaded in the wagons.

"And tools," Enoch continued. "We have almost nothing. We'll need mallets, saws, hammers, nails, prybars."

Finally the town leader balked. "Please, First Commander. That would devastate Stravera."

"Serving the army of General Utros is not always easy." He put an edge in his voice. These people would be broken one way or another, whether willingly or by force.

"But our future . . ." Garth pleaded. "I am merely saying it will be hard, by the spirits." He scratched his thick hair, sweating profusely.

"Do you have any children?" Enoch asked.

"Children?" Garth seemed surprised by the question. "Why yes, I have two young sons and a daughter, just a baby."

"Good. Are there many other children in Stravera?"

"Any town has children," the blacksmith replied, growing more suspicious. "Two infants born just last week. In our school, twenty children are learning their numbers and letters. As slaves, few of us had any education, and we want to make up for that lack."

"Twenty, that's good," Enoch said. "I am especially interested in the babies you mentioned." Although he didn't know anything about magic, he suspected that infants might have the most potent blood. "We will need all of them. Bring them forth."

The people of Stravera gasped, either not understanding, or not believing.

"Your children! Now!" Enoch roared. "Bring all of them. I expect to see twenty and at least three babes."

Now his hundred soldiers marched forward, closing ranks on either side of their first commander. The townspeople began to wail, some tried to slip away. Two of Enoch's soldiers grabbed a young woman who attempted to flee. With heavy swords, they cut her down right there, and her bleeding body sprawled in the village square. The townspeople moaned, but when they didn't move fast enough, Enoch barked, "Kill another one."

Two soldiers grabbed a skinny, long-haired man who struggled and squirmed. They didn't bother to use their weapons this time, but simply broke the man, smashing him against their hardened knees and snapping his spine, neck, and arms with a succession of loud cracking noises.

The villagers did as they were commanded, and soon a group of confused children were dragged out of homes amid much weeping and begging. The children varied from toddlers to young teenagers, many of them shivering. Some wore rags, while others dressed in fine clothes likely stolen in their flight from Ildakar.

While he waited, Enoch spotted a paddock used for goats. He had his men turn the goats loose so they could herd the children into the small corral instead. The three babies were placed into the arms of young girls, who also huddled inside the pen.

Garth grew more and more upset when he saw the boys and girls locked inside the fence. "Enough! You can't take everything."

"We won't take everything," Enoch said, looking at the adults gathered there in dismay. "We don't need you at all."

The people of Stravera tried to re-form their desperate defensive line, but Enoch gave orders to his soldiers, and the slaughter began. No matter how determined the townspeople were, they were no match for one hundred well-trained warriors with swords.

After more than twenty villagers had been slain, Garth dropped to his knees, raising his hands and demanding to know why. Enoch left him alive until the other villagers were all dead, and then the first commander beheaded him.

Inside the corral, the children screamed and wept. Some just stood in shock. Ten guards surrounded the paddock to ensure that none of the boys or girls tried to flee.

"Do we need to tie them?" asked one soldier. "They will slow our march if we drag them through the forest back to camp."

"We don't need to bring them with us," Enoch said. He commanded that the six empty barrels be brought into the corral with the trapped children. "We only need their blood. Six barrels should be enough to hold it all."

The return trip took two days. His men had ransacked Stravera for all the supplies and equipment they could use. They found many valuable and useful items—rope, utensils, nails, knives, nets, leather, and furs. The soldiers emptied Stravera, taking another two wagons to hold it all. They toiled out of the mountains, and when the road dwindled to nothing, they cut away fallen trees to clear a more permanent path back to the valley.

The caravan finally returned to camp at dusk, crossing the tinder-dry hills. The rustling grasses were crushed under the wagon wheels as the beasts of burden plodded along. When First Commander Enoch reported to his general, he stood proud.

Utros and the two painted sorceresses stepped outside to meet him. Ava and Ruva smiled at the sight of the wagon full of stained barrels. The twins touched the wooden staves, looking at the sticky red on their fingertips.

"Now we have exactly what we need," Ruva said.

CHAPTER 34

In the hours before the surprise attack, the Ildakaran fighters gathered in the lower levels near the supply buildings, storehouses, granaries, and the yaxen slaughter yards. High Captain Stuart brought five hundred of his city guard, all wearing chest armor and carrying short swords. Stuart wore a red pauldron on his shoulder to show his rank, just as his predecessor had done. Hundreds of the earnest arena fighters had no interest in ranks, and there were also countless volunteers from the lower classes who had scrounged up weapons and were ready to join the unexpected strike against the siege army.

From across Ildakar, families pulled swords out of storage, heirlooms that had never seen battle, while others carried new-forged weapons produced by the overworked smithies. Blacksmiths turned out hundreds of iron-headed clubs, hard wooden handles topped with metal spheres and spikes, and the ragtag fighters adopted them quickly. Such blunt, deadly weapons might do better than sharp blades against an enemy with hardened skin, and they required far less training, needing only anger, energy, and an arm to wield them.

Nathan joined Nicci near the gates as night began to fall. The dashing wizard wore black travel pants and boots beneath his white robes, as if he couldn't decide which identity he preferred, adventurer or wizard. They watched the new Ildakaran army congregate.

"Dear spirits, it is going to be a fight." Nathan cocked his eyebrows. "I hope the duma's confidence is warranted. It will be a surprise all right, but I'm not certain about this idea of attacking such a huge army."

"We are only attacking a defined portion of the camp, the large companies closest to the walls and against the hills," Nicci said. "As long as we keep to our goal with a focused strike, cause as much damage as possible, and return behind the walls before the rest of the ancient army can rally, we might succeed." She hardened her voice. "I plan to cause plenty of damage of my own."

As they stood together, Nathan responded with a skeptical smile, noting her raggedly shorn hair. "Are you not just doing this out of anger because the sorceresses attacked you?"

"I never do anything merely out of anger," she said. "But anger is a useful motivator. I have an enemy. All of Ildakar has an enemy. If General Utros defeats this city, then I'm convinced he will move on and threaten the rest of the Old World and then D'Hara. Therefore, we have to stop them here. Our goals align with the duma's."

"Indeed they do." Nathan chuckled. "When dear Richard turned us loose in the Old World, I'm not sure this is what he expected."

"The rest is going to depend on General Utros," Nicci said.

Elsa worked her way through the crowd to join them. She wore a distracted, worried look. "I set up several transference runes here in the city, anchor spell-forms that I can use once we get out on the battlefield." She smiled. "It should be quite a surprise."

Hundreds of arena warriors joined the congregating army, well muscled and scantily armored because they liked the freedom of movement. They carried whatever weapons they had preferred during their exhibition battles. A group of fierce-looking morazeth walked among them, and Nicci was glad they fought on the same side now. The branded runes would protect the women against magical attacks, but their main fight would be against Utros's thousands of hardened warriors.

Lila followed as Bannon came toward them. He carried one of the iron-tipped cudgels, but his sword also hung at his side. "We're ready to fight." He looked at the ever-growing crowd of armed defenders. "We all are."

Nathan clucked his tongue. "Dear boy, this is not a game. It's going to be hard, very hard."

"But, we will do it," Bannon said.

"Yes, we will. Let's go out and fight!" said Timothy, who held a short sword in one hand and an iron-tipped cudgel in the other. "Nobody beat me during training, and no one will beat me during the attack."

A far less enthusiastic Jed and Brock also joined the group, each wearing one of the colorful new silk cloaks provided by Lady Olgya. Neither of the brash young men seemed like much of a warrior to Nicci.

As the darkness deepened, the thousands of troops gathered, restless. From outside the walls, the enemy army could not see any of the preparations. After days of tense silence, Nicci doubted Utros would suspect this surprise move late at night. They would march out at midnight.

As the fighters organized into ranks, they received water and food. They talked among themselves, bragging about their prowess, shoring up their own bravery, while some were justifiably nervous. Most had never faced a real battle before. Nicci watched their excitement build as the duma members made their own preparations, spoke with High Captain Stuart, surveyed the large numbers of angry troops. The wizards and sorceresses of Ildakar would unleash the greatest destructive powers as part of this sortie.

She remembered other nights before Jagang's army would launch full attacks. He would let his soldiers get drunk, gamble, go into the pleasure tents and abuse the slave women. Jagang didn't care what his soldiers did, so long as they won the following day.

Nicci preferred more discipline. These people were fighting for Ildakar, and she had advised the duma to carefully time the charge for when their enthusiasm was at its peak but before impatience and doubts could set in.

At midnight, without pounding drums or sounding horns, the wizards removed the locking spells from the towering main gate. It took four men working together to roll back the enormous crossbar. The duma members gathered, swollen with their own magic, anger, and maybe too much confidence.

Nicci mounted the bay charger that had been provided for her, and she turned in the saddle, holding the reins. She looked impressive in front of the troops. The other powerful duma members also rode sturdy horses from Ildakar's stables, but the long-isolated city did not have enough mounts for an entire cavalry, only for the commanders of the city guard and wealthy, gifted nobles.

The duma members were focused on one another, staring toward the enormous gate, but the aloof council was not good at rallying its people. Nicci knew how vital that was, and after a restless moment, she raised her voice. A hush fell over the thousands of fighters. "We will charge out and attack our enemies. We must strike hard, cause as much damage as possible, and ransack their camp. This blow will send them reeling."

Although she didn't want to alert the enemy army, she couldn't stop the troops from responding with a resounding cheer. Quentin, Damon, and Oron turned toward her, giving an appreciative nod. Lani and Olgya were also mounted, ready to fight. Only Elsa remained on foot, near Nathan.

She drew a deep breath and continued, "Tonight Ildakar fights together, slaves, arena warriors, city guards, gifted nobles.

Everyone has a stake in this." Nicci didn't explain her own reasons or Nathan's, but she would do her best to lead by example. The Ildakaran defenders could rebuild their city once they were free. First, General Utros had to be defeated.

"Follow us," Quentin shouted to all of them. "We've waited fifteen hundred years to fight this enemy."

The soldiers roared their readiness to do battle, "For Ildakar!"

The huge gates swung open on titanic hinges, and the army surged like a storm out onto the moonlit battlefield.

CHAPTER 35

T he defenders of Ildakar were filled with energy, anger, and a sense of invincibility. Finally unleashed, they yelled and ran forward, holding cudgels, swords, spears. They intended to leave General Utros reeling. Riding at the forefront, ready to lash out with their gift, the duma members were confident, full of energy.

As planned, the army rushed headlong to the targeted enemy ranks near the boundary hills. The front lines of eager arena warriors and city guards ran out, holding their weapons high and howling at the unsuspecting army camped beyond the walls. At the forefront, Nicci rode on her bay horse, one slender arm upraised. With her uneven blond hair, she looked like a vengeful spirit in the starlight.

Since Elsa had never ridden a horse, much less into battle, she had stubbornly insisted her horse be given to a more appropriate fighter. Seeing her reluctance, Nathan also decided to fight on foot. "I'll stand with you, my dear. We'll be powerful enough together. Now that I have my gift back, I can defend you against the rigors of the battlefield."

She looked at him skeptically. "I don't need your protection,

Nathan. Why don't we fight together, so we can cause twice as much harm to the enemy?"

"That sounds like a fine idea."

They were swept along with the tide of fighters.

Nathan felt grand, as if marching with Richard Rahl's army again. In that moment he had no doubt the united defenders would deal a painful blow to the ancient army, yet he was pragmatic enough to know that the feeling would be short-lived as soon as the two forces actually collided.

Elsa did not look particularly athletic, but she was resilient and had great stamina. She kept pace with Nathan as they ran along with the foot soldiers. His ornate sword was in its scabbard at his side, because he intended to fight as a wizard for now. He held his left hand open, fingers cupped, as his magic brewed to a boiling point.

Utros's army had scattered countless campfires up to the dry grassy hills, which looked like a swarm of red demonic eyes, each representing hundreds of enemy soldiers. Nathan caught his breath as the sheer numbers began to sink in. "I have fought desperate battles before, but never against quite such an overwhelming force."

"You've never fought with *me* before, Nathan." Elsa raised her voice against the racket of the charging army. "We will show them how it's done."

After studying the arrangement of the enemy warriors from the city walls, the duma members had all agreed on targeting their strike against only the companies encamped on the northern side of the valley. They would hit there.

As the Ildakaran defenders rushed into the first clash, the ancient army stirred with a clatter of weapons and shouted orders. The response of the huge military force was not quite the panic and clamor Nathan had hoped for. The well-disciplined enemy soldiers formed ranks, lining up alongside their subcommanders to defend their entrenched positions. The alarm spread as criers raced from company to company, informing them of the surprise sortie. More torches were lit, and the outcry grew louder.

In the distance, Nathan could make out the wooden headquarters where he and Nicci had met with Utros, but this unexpected strike would be much closer than that, limited to the troops camped nearest the walls.

He could see Nicci riding at the lead, summoning a storm. She called down searing bolts of lightning that exploded among the foremost ranks of the enemy. A second bolt skittered sideways to rip through a line of makeshift tents and hurl ten warriors into the air like chaff caught in a crosswind. Her lightning was mixed with blue-black spikes as Nicci called upon her Subtractive Magic as well as more conventional Additive Magic.

Alongside her, Oron, Damon, and Quentin also used their gift, summoning catapults of condensed wind, lashing storm gales so powerful they bowled over lines of Utros's soldiers in formation.

Wild with exuberance, the defenders ran forward. "For Ildakar!"

The first lines of the ancient army crowded shoulder-to-shoulder as they made a stand, holding their shields, raising antique swords to block the charge. Ildakaran fighters crashed into them, running at full speed and unable to stop. Nathan saw members of the city guard, arena fighters, even Bannon and the morazeth Lila throw themselves into the clash. Sluggish ancient soldiers defended themselves against the flurry of iron-tipped cudgels. The din erupted like an avalanche.

"We dare not let ourselves fall behind, my dear," Nathan called to Elsa, summoning a globe of wizard's fire in his hand. He held his fire, waiting for Nicci and the other duma members to ride ahead so he had a clearer shot. Elsa created a ball of conventional fire, unable to match a wizard's power, but her flames would burn just as well.

Nathan lobbed his first fireball far over the front ranks of

266

enemy soldiers, careful not to let any of the incinerating fire splash back on Ildakaran forces. The intense magical blaze erupted behind them, engulfing nearly a hundred ancient warriors. They screamed and staggered, collapsing into greasy ash.

Elsa hurled her own fireball, which exploded behind Nathan's strike. Her flames caused less damage than wizard's fire, but the blast scattered the confused enemy. Overall, the effect was quite impressive.

As he built his attack, Nathan called upon his gift, feeling the Han in his new heart strong within him with remnants of Chief Handler Ivan's anger. He disliked feeling the insidious touch of that other wizard inside him, but he used the anger and darkness to create an even larger ball of wizard's fire that exploded and drove back hundreds of the ancient warriors.

Ildakaran soldiers, furious but undisciplined, spread out as they struck the enemy ranks, like water splashing around rocks in a stream. They fought hundreds of individual opponents and began to crack through the swiftly organized enemy ranks.

Nicci's lightning danced across Utros's defenses, while the other wizards continued their magical attacks. Elsa set countless tents alight with her fire, burning lines of enemy soldiers who tried to flee. Nathan found reserves of energy inside him, called another ball of wizard's fire, and blasted dozens more. Even though each strike drove back entire lines of General Utros's troops, he knew the Ildakaran sortie couldn't hope to make more than a dent in the overall ancient force.

Nathan realized he had to think bigger, find a way to cause more substantial damage, not just a hundred enemies at a time. As the remnants of his wizard's fire continued to rush through the targeted part of the camp, starting secondary fires, he realized something that he and Elsa could easily do, and it might affect a much larger part of the besieging army. "The hills! The dry hills." He gestured toward the brown slopes at the edge of the valley. "It's a tinderbox! We can start a blaze that will sweep across the army."

She immediately understood. "They'll never be able to fight it." Reaching out both hands, she used her gift to ignite fire there and build it. But while she was concentrating, a burly enemy soldier lunged forward with a curved sword to cleave her in two.

"No!" Nathan shoved with his other hand, making a shield of air that smashed the enemy off his feet and knocked his curved sword away. The warrior crashed to the ground, but Nathan was so incensed at the threat to Elsa that he slammed down hard with a fist of air and crushed the enemy's chest and face.

Elsa gasped, thanking Nathan before she threw the next sphere of fire that had materialized in her hand, tossing it as far as she could toward the dry hills.

Nathan summoned more wizard's fire, one ball in each hand, and launched them both. Blazing, alive with destruction, they arced like comets high into the night, so bright they illuminated the battlefield below. Elsa's fireball struck first, erupting into a spray of sparks and igniting another swatch of grasses, while Nathan's more powerful fire impacted higher on the hillside.

At first, the enemy soldiers paid little attention to the spreading grass fire, but Nathan was pleased to see the flames catch and build into a conflagration. Blazing curtains raced up the hillside and burned down toward the encamped army. He grinned at her. "Yes, indeed, that was a good idea."

"Follow me, Nathan. I may need your help for something else." Elsa ran deeper into the camp, away from the primary fighting. "I have more magic we can use."

He saw where she was going. The ancient army was rapidly growing stronger as more soldiers from deeper in the camp gathered their weapons and ran toward the fight. Nathan had hoped to hit these separated ranks hard before too many reinforcements arrived. "Not there. We can't—"

"We will," she said. "It's transference magic. Remember, I prepared for this."

Elsa ran with surprising speed, and Nathan couldn't leave her to fight all by herself. "Whatever you say. We did promise to protect each other."

Elsa reached a large trampled area that had been a section of campsites. She studied the ground, as if hunting for something buried there. She extended an index finger, pointed at the turf, and began to run in a strange, drunkard's circle.

Nathan caught up with her, panting. "What are you doing? How can I help?"

"Keep me safe. Don't let those soldiers attack me until I finish drawing my pattern on the ground."

"What pattern?"

"This transference rune."

As she bustled along, Elsa's extended finger released a thin trail of power like an invisible knife that cut a line on the ground, scribing a complex design. She ran to and fro, swirling her finger, adding a flourish to the lines in the dirt.

"It's a spell-form," Nathan cried.

"A transference rune," Elsa said. "I showed you before."

A force of more than two hundred ancient warriors charged toward him and Elsa. He realized that the partially stone warriors seemed not to see well in the darkness away from the main campfires, but they could surround their targets. Many carried torches, bright firebrands snatched from their own blazes.

"Here they come," Nathan said. "I hope you've thought this through."

"Yes, in great detail. I etched the corresponding rune on a cistern in Ildakar that holds nearly a thousand barrels of water."

Not trying to guess what she meant to do, he summoned more wizard's fire and bowled over the front ranks of charging soldiers. The fiery explosion wiped out the first fifteen, but hundreds more came. Needing to give Elsa time, he called wind and a blast of lightning to delay their attack.

"Almost finished, Nathan." Elsa pointed to her intricate

design that covered a large area on the ground. As the ancient warriors charged forward, Nathan saw he and Elsa would be engulfed at any moment. "Ah, there!" she said.

As the soldiers ran into the open area that Elsa had inscribed, she jabbed down at the ground, made a final connecting line that completed the transference rune, and linked the spell.

In that instant, all the water from the distant cistern suddenly occupied what had been solid ground, and hundreds of charging enemy soldiers found themselves in a slurry of thin mud and clinging quicksand. Rank after rank tumbled and plunged in up to their waists and shoulders, mired and helpless as if the ground had swallowed them up.

Nathan let out a heavy sigh. "I should never have doubted you, my dear."

Elsa looked at her handiwork, all the enemy soldiers rendered helpless in an instant, and then glanced back at the hills where the grass fire continued to surge. "No, Nathan, you shouldn't have doubted me."

CHAPTER 36

During his training on the *Wavewalker*, as a naive young man, Bannon had learned to fight with his sword, prancing across the ship's deck as Nathan showed him true skills. He had never imagined facing such impossible numbers of enemies. Now he did.

He ran forward along with hundreds of fighters into the enemy ranks, reminding himself that they were only targeting a small portion of the huge camp. It should be something they could accomplish. These ancient warriors would have been extraordinary foes under normal circumstances, but now, to make matters worse, they were also partially stone.

Beside him, Lila didn't seem intimidated at all. She threw herself into the fight.

Utros's army formed orderly ranks for defense, while the Ildakaran warriors were independent and wild, turning any military response into a melee. Through sheer momentum and energy, their first charge crashed into the enemy's hastily erected defenses, shuddering the line. Once the city's surge broke the front ranks, each clash came down to single combat.

Bannon steeled himself and rushed into the fray, holding

his iron-tipped club in one hand and Sturdy in the other. His discolored blade met the downsweep of a curved scimitar, and the ringing impact sent a shock wave down his arm. He grunted, but held firm as he swung the iron club in his opposite hand, bashing his opponent's chest. The blow did little apparent damage, but it forced the soldier back two steps. Bannon pressed forward and swung with Sturdy, chopping the base of his opponent's neck. The impact felt like an axe hitting solid wood, but the blade cut through even the hardened skin. The enemy toppled to the ground.

"That was good, boy," Lila called to him, her lips pulled back in a hard grin. "Now do it a dozen more times, and we'll make some progress." With a feral hiss, she leaped forward, wielding an iron club in each hand. The muscles on her bare thighs rippled as she sprang, battering and clubbing. She moved from one opponent to the next, smashing hard. The ancient soldiers reeled, but they kept coming back.

Thorn, Genda, Ricia, and the other morazeth women fought in a cluster, selecting targets to strike and destroy. The ancient warriors were powerful, but their stony bodies made them sluggish, while the more nimble morazeth struck, retreated, and struck again, like angry vipers. The women ranged ahead, setting an example for all the arena warriors they had trained.

The morazeth were whirlwinds, and Lila glanced over her shoulder as she sprinted ahead. "Follow closely, boy! I'll damage them, and you finish them off."

"I'm trying." Bannon swung the heavy club in his left hand, breaking the face of an ancient warrior. His sword arm already ached from hammering enemy soldiers, smashing their armor, damaging their skin.

Jed and Brock fought clumsily nearby, shoulder-to-shoulder. Their silk cloaks offered some protection as enemy soldiers pummeled them, but the bright colors made them targets. The two men battled defensively, not seeking targets, just trying to survive.

On the other hand, Timothy was exhilarated. The young yaxen herder had trained with a sword in practice sessions, but now seemed much happier with his club, which he swung with reckless glee. The enemy soldiers were startled to encounter such a wild fighter who also had a chalky, hard complexion like theirs.

Leading the more organized city guard, High Captain Stuart bellowed orders. One of his guards blew a golden horn, rallying the uniformed soldiers into a singular attack against the forward contingent of the enemy. The crash of the Ildakaran guard against ancient soldiers resounded like a thunderclap.

In the loud, violent frenzy, Bannon couldn't keep up with Lila and the morazeth. He spent all his time defending himself against oncoming warriors, thousands of them. His sword cut into the breastplate of a bearded soldier, but that did not deflect the enemy's charge. As the bearded opponent swung his scimitar for a killing blow, young Timothy sprang in and hammered the man on the back of the helmet. The enemy soldier grunted and crashed to his knees. Timothy made a "be my guest" gesture to Bannon, who swung his sword to chop the soldier's neck.

The fighting grew more frenetic on the battlefield, the sounds deafening. Riding ahead on horseback, Nicci and the wizards of Ildakar unleashed magic in volleys of rock-hard wind and slashes of lightning. In a different part of the battle, Nathan and Elsa hurled fireballs, intentionally setting the dry, grassy hills ablaze with strategic fires.

Then Bannon saw a tan blur out of the corner of his eye as Mrra darted in. The powerful sand panther crashed into an ancient warrior, mauled his hardened skin, then sprang away to attack another, dodging blows from enemy swords. Mrra raked the prey with her claws, tearing their armor and doing some damage to their hardened skin. Her golden feline eyes met Bannon's for an instant, and then she streaked off.

Jed and Brock fought back-to-back, their faces tense and terrified.

Timothy ran in, challenging two large warriors. Foolishly thinking himself invincible, he struck right and left with his iron clubs until the two hardened soldiers turned on him. They swung their heavy swords and sent Timothy reeling. The cocky grin on his face faltered.

"Watch out!" Bannon yelled. "Get away from them."

Instead, Timothy swung his clubs even harder. "For Ildakar!" He smashed the arm of one of his opponents. The other soldier struck the yaxen herder from the side, spinning him around. Because his half-petrified skin made him resistant to the damage, Timothy recovered, but his enemies had the same protection. From behind him, a third warrior struck the boy hard with the flat of his blade, stunning him.

Bannon fought an enemy of his own. Slashing and pounding, he tried to dispatch the man quickly so he could help the young scamp, but his opponent was more skilled than he expected. Bannon needed all of his concentration just to stay alive.

Timothy flailed his clubs and kept the three enemies at bay for a moment, until a fourth soldier joined them. They all pressed around the boy, raising swords and clubs. One carried a massive mace. In a concerted, horrifying effort they pummeled Timothy, and his defenses faltered. A heavy blow from the mace shattered his arm. Even though it was half stone, the bone broke, as did the skin.

The ancient soldiers took turns: one hammered Timothy, then stepped back while a second dealt another blow, and a third drove him to the ground. The yaxen herder was broken, his shoulder smashed, red and white, like a bleeding statue. He sobbed, "For Ildakar!"

Bannon finally killed his enemy. His lungs burned and his arms trembled from the effort, but he lurched after the trapped boy. "Timothy!"

On his knees, the young yaxen herder could no longer hold his clubs. The four enemies kept hammering their victim into the bloody mud of the battleground.

Bannon arrived too late. More burly soldiers trapped him. In desperation, he looked ahead and saw that Lila and the other morazeth had pulled out of reach, fighting wildly and slaying countless opponents. He shouted for Lila, but the clamor drowned out his words.

Jed and Brock were also surrounded, fighting for their lives. As clashes continued around them, hundreds of one-on-one duels, he saw that many enemy warriors had fallen, but it seemed that half of the Ildakarans lay dead as well.

General Utros had roused his army, responding with a vicious counteroffensive. Thousands of reinforcements came from the other side of the valley. The Ildakaran attackers were driven back as the enemy numbers flooded in.

Bannon backed closer to Jed and Brock, forced to fight alongside them. He feared they didn't stand a chance. He pushed away the ache and exhaustion and understood that this would be his last fight.

Remembering Timothy's defiance in the face of despair, Bannon yelled, "For Ildakar!" He looked at Jed and Brock. They were sweating, terrified, flailing their iron-tipped clubs— the same weapons they had used to bash motionless statues as a prank. The two young men didn't echo his battle cry.

Feeling his blood boil with the battle rage that sometimes came upon him, Bannon prepared to fight to the last. He yelled again, this time without words as the enemy warriors closed in, and he lost himself in the combat.

CHAPTER 37

The grass fires set by Nathan and Elsa burned out of control. As Nicci attacked with her own lightning and aggressive storm winds, she watched the flames leap from the tall grasses to gnarled live oaks in the hills. The burn line hooked down toward the rear of General Utros's camp, spreading faster than any man could run. The reawakened army had a few hundred tents scattered among the dispersed companies of soldiers. Nicci watched the brush fire catch on the tents, setting them ablaze.

The legendary general emerged from his headquarters, bellowing orders as the grass fires spread and became a greater threat than the Ildakaran attack. He commanded thousands of his soldiers to fight the blaze, which threatened to engulf the entire valley. The ancient army had plenty of men to spare, though, so the firefighting efforts didn't ease the pressure on the Ildakaran defenders.

Nicci, feeling drained after drawing on so much of her magic, nevertheless summoned another wall of lightning. The jagged bolts blasted the ground, hurling several hundred enemy warriors away, trapping them between the fire line and the lightning. Most of the hardened soldiers chose to face the blazing grass, staggering about with their armor and bodies smoking.

Nicci unleashed more lightning. She could see that the Ildakaran army was indeed having a destructive effect on the segment of the camp they had targeted. The duma members reveled in the mayhem, but for her it was a bittersweet victory. She knew Utros could recover from whatever damage the Ildakarans did here tonight.

The city guard and arena warriors, who fought with conventional weapons, were being slaughtered by the hundreds. Utros's army could lose fighters all day and suffer no great harm, but these initial Ildakar forces had only a few thousand in the first place.

Nicci's bay charger whinnied, unnerved by the carnage and noise, but she gripped the reins to steady her mount. Riding next to her, Oron lifted his chin in a haughty gesture. "How much longer can we sustain this attack? Our people are dying everywhere."

Nicci conjured a whirlwind that spun like a rampaging monster, ripping up ranks of enemy soldiers before she grew too exhausted to sustain it. "I think we've made our point."

Following her example, Oron called a storm, icy wind and rain that tumbled across the vast camp. Nearby, Quentin and Damon conjured similar storms, disrupting the forward charge of five hundred enemy warriors. Olgya sparked fire and drew strands of lightning through the air.

The sortie had gone on for nearly two hours, and General Utros and his soldiers had begun to form a full-fledged defense. Massive reinforcements were coming in from outside the targeted ranks. The duma's surprise attack had concentrated on the northern end of the valley, but after the calls to arms, the bulk of General Utros's army was converging on the main fight. Ildakar's defenders would have to withdraw soon, or they would be overwhelmed.

Also hardened with lingering stone, the sorceress Lani strode into the fray. She wore no armor, just her pale blue robes. The enemy soldiers recognized her as a powerful, gifted opponent, and four of them ran toward her, shouting, their curved swords raised. Lani paid them no heed as she prepared her own attack. Nicci destroyed a group of the oncoming warriors with a blast of lightning to give Lani more time, and the other sorceress didn't even flinch. Instead, she knelt on the ground, alone, and raised both pale, hard fists. Chanting unintelligible words, she brought her fists down like a blacksmith hammering an anvil.

Bright light splashed around her hands, dazzling Nicci, and the resounding impact sent a shock wave through the ground. The battlefield lurched like a bucking horse. Lani remained on her knees at the center point of her quake, while charging troops were flung to the ground all around her. A jagged fissure split the earth, tearing the ground apart.

As the shock wave died away, Nicci held on to her horse, impressed by what Lani had just unleashed, though it had only pushed the hordes back temporarily. Still, a delay was all they needed right now, to give the Ildakaran army a chance to return to safety behind the walls. Though she longed to keep fighting, Nicci recognized the great losses they were suffering.

"Wizards, duma members!" She amplified her voice with the gift. "We've done all we can. Back to the city walls!" Fanfares sounded from the remnants of the city guard, and High Captain Stuart shouted to his troops. The morazeth continued to fight as they withdrew, while blood-spattered arena warriors dispatched a few more opponents as they fell back.

Nicci watched Mrra leap in among the enemy soldiers, wreaking havoc. The big panther was still full of energy, but Nicci saw several wounds in her rune-marked pelt. She sent a thought to her sister panther, not sure she would get through in the heat of a killing frenzy, but she urged Mrra to retreat, to flee from the spreading grass fires and find a place in the forest where the cat could be safe.

Fearing the Ildakarans might slip through their fingers, Utros's army shouted an eerie battle cry. More soldiers arrived just in time to reinforce the damaged front ranks. Nicci saw the enemy ranks grow stronger by the minute and knew the Ildakarans had little time to get away. She wheeled her horse about and shouted to Oron, Damon, Olgya, and Quentin. "All of you, use your gift to push them back. We need to buy time for the retreating army."

Not far away, the city of Ildakar was bright in the moonlight. Torches and braziers burned on the top of the high wall from which a crew of sentries watched the battle below. The gifted duma members called their magic again. Oron summoned a hailstorm that pelted the hardened warriors. Nathan and Elsa hurled fireballs against the swelling hordes of enemy fighters.

General Utros was too far away to join the actual fight himself, but Nicci saw him ordering his soldiers to form a tight line to protect his headquarters and a large supply wagon from the encroaching grass fires. His twin sorceresses, pale and beautiful in the firelight, conjured their own magic, manipulating winds to divert the fire. Ancient soldiers lined up to form a human barricade, physically blocking the flames from reaching the headquarters, the wagon, and a set of large barrels. The warriors screamed as the flames rushed upon them, but they stood firm and endured, deflecting the blaze.

"Once more, Lani! Shake the ground!" Nicci cried.

The half-stone sorceress dropped to her knees again, focused her gift, and produced an impact that knocked back the enemy army.

Taking advantage of any respite, the Ildakaran army retreated toward the city. They had decimated the enemy ranks they had targeted, and they had to escape before they, too, were killed. Nathan and Elsa joined them, flinging more fire for good measure. Nicci still found the energy to summon her own wizard's fire, which she exploded into the nearest line of relentless soldiers.

Utros's army continued to close in.

Nathan and Elsa were running, but couldn't keep up. Nicci rode close on her charger. "Wizard, take my hand! Join me on horseback."

"Not without Elsa!"

"I can't carry both of you," Nicci said.

Then Damon rode up. "Ride with me, Elsa. You did well tonight. All the duma members did."

"Well, then I accept your offer," Nathan said, swinging up onto the bay charger behind Nicci.

She yelled a retreat again, but the Ildakaran fighters needed no further encouragement. "We've made our mark on them tonight, and Utros will know that we can hurt him." She allowed herself a hard, personal smile. "We'll make an even grander plan for our next attack."

With Nathan situating himself in the saddle behind her, pressing against her back, Nicci drove her horse at a gallop. Elsa mounted behind Damon, and they rode after. The weary and battered soldiers raced toward the giant open gates. With some relief, Nicci sensed that Mrra had loped away into the wilderness, fleeing the fire and escaping safely.

But even with the apparent success of their mission, there were far too few of the original fighters returning to Ildakar. Far too few.

The enemy army pursued them, giving the survivors a surge of energy. Crowds flooded through the high gates, and Nicci glanced behind her, wondering how many Ildakaran soldiers would be trapped outside. She didn't like to abandon the fighters who had followed the duma's plan and offered to fight for their city, but very few were still out there battling the ancient army. Most of those left behind had already fallen in combat. These hundreds rushing through the gates were all that remained.

Nathan leaned close as they galloped through the high gates. When most of the soldiers had stumbled through, the sentries inside worked the huge wheels, cranking the thick ropes to pull the enormous gates shut. As the gap closed, a few stragglers scrambled in, tripping and sprawling to the cobbled streets. One young man, bleeding profusely from an arm wound, picked up a woman who had stumbled, and they limped off to the side and collapsed together. The last of the party careered through the closing gap.

The immense gate ground shut with a thunderous boom. Shouting workers shifted crossbars the size of trees into place just in time as the ponderous Utros army slammed into the walls. The half-petrified soldiers began their implacable pounding again, like constant thunder.

From her mount, Nicci surveyed the exhausted and chattering fighters. Some were jubilant, others moaning in pain, still others shuddering with long-delayed terror. Behind her, Nathan said, "Dear spirits, what a battle that was!"

Nicci let out a long breath. "Yes, but we tested them, and we tested ourselves. Ildakar proved its mettle, and we damaged Utros."

She was surprised to see Lila alone. The morazeth looked bedraggled, covered with soot and blood, her spiky hair damp with perspiration.

Nathan's breathing hitched. "They hurt us as well, Sorceress. We'll be a long time counting our losses." He paused to look around, and his eyes fixed on Lila, who seemed forlorn. His voice cracked as he pointed out what Nicci should have realized immediately. "And Bannon is gone."

CHAPTER 38

When he saw only three ships from Captain Kor's raiding party return to the Norukai islands, King Grieve saw no cause for rejoicing. He'd intended to host a celebratory feast, possibly even serving some of the delicious yaxen meat to the victorious captains.

Instead, he felt anger rise within him. Something had gone terribly wrong.

In the previous raid of Renda Bay, the villagers had found new ways to fight, even using a powerful sorceress. The previous captain had been foolish and overconfident. Chalk had never liked the man, which meant that King Grieve never liked him, and he returned from Renda Bay with excuses for his failure. Any Norukai should know not to come back alive from such defeat. Without remorse, Grieve had fed the captain to the serpent god.

Kor's raid, though, with twice as many ships and fighters, should have avenged that ignominious loss.

Now, the cylindrical iron bells tolled a mournful clamor, which the king could hear even up in the Bastion. Grieve snapped his extended jaws open, feeling the scar tissue along his cut lips. He gnashed his teeth, as if he meant to tear out Kor's throat and grind his spine into dust. Bunching his fists, he clacked the iron plates in his knuckles together.

Chalk squatted in front of the fireplace to warm himself by the flames, hunching forward on the hearth. When the bells rang out, the shaman sprang to his feet. "A sad mission, a terrible mission, my king. Renda Bay!"

With growing anger, Grieve left his throne room and climbed the steps to the Bastion's high rooftop so he could watch. Chalk scampered after him.

At the second landing above, a door opened and a slave emerged carrying a stack of folded blankets. She took one look at King Grieve's expression and fled back into the corridors. Grieve would remember her. He had seen her face, and he would punish her later. For now, though, Captain Kor would be the one to receive the brunt of his anger.

Out on the windswept rooftop, Grieve strode to the battlements, placed his massive hands on the pocked stone and gazed down the sheer wall to the narrow protected harbor, watching the three battered serpent ships pull in from the sea. The vessels looked damaged. One of the midnight-blue sails hung in tatters. The other two sails were also damaged, but had been crudely repaired with wide crisscrossed rope stitches. The extended oars guided the ships past the dangerous rocks, toward the docks.

Grieve grumbled something incomprehensible, just a noise to express his displeasure. Chalk leaned close, his naked, scarred skin brushing Grieve's muscled arm. "Renda Bay, Renda Bay!"

"Don't worry about Renda Bay. After this, I will destroy Renda Bay," said Grieve, "just as I will destroy those weaklings who failed their mission."

"Maybe," Chalk said. "Maybe."

Grieve sent a summons for the leaders of the three ships to be brought to him as soon as they docked. It remained to be seen whether Kor had been foolish enough to come back alive.

While the ships were gone, Chalk had experienced exciting, violent dreams. He had foreseen Norukai conquests, which he described to his king, though the murky foretellings were often difficult to comprehend. That was the problem with the shaman's babbling. Nevertheless, Grieve had come to expect victory for his people.

Kor's obvious defeat made the bile rise in his throat. He gripped the rough block where salt air and harsh weather had scrubbed the stone. Chalk scuttled from one overlook to the next, peering down the cliffs to the waves crashing against the rocks.

Grieve could see the hulking shadows of dozens of other islands in the distance, some of them shrouded in mist. His empire held more than a hundred islands, maybe a thousand— no Norukai king had ever counted—but even those numerous islands weren't enough. His father, King Stern, had strengthened the Norukai, but his vision for their future had been dim and shortsighted. Grieve had no choice but to kill him, at Chalk's insistence.

The coastal raids had increased as their fleet of serpent ships grew larger, with many Norukai warriors called upon to prove themselves to their new king. But that was only the beginning. Chalk had premonitions, and Grieve had grand dreams. Together, they knew how to implement the future.

In some of the raided towns, the Norukai had seen statues of local heroes, revered leaders, military geniuses. The raiders tore them all down, taking joy in destroying them. Someday, though, King Grieve wanted statues built of him, gigantic stone figures so that people would never forget him. He sacrificed regularly to the serpent god, and now the blood of the Norukai race was strong, just as the great sea serpents were strong.

Fifteen more warships had been completed in the ten days since Captain Kor sailed off on his raid. Other missions had returned to the islands bearing treasure, slaves, and supplies, along with information about the rest of the Old World. Grieve kept careful charts, mapping out the lands yet to conquer. Sometimes he would sit alone and relish the territories, like a starving man considering what he would eat first at a banquet.

If he was going to conquer the world, he could not allow defeats to shame him.

He watched in grim silence as the three battered ships tied up to the piers. Chalk hung over the edge of the Bastion, stretching out his long, skinny arm to grasp at gulls that circled halfway down the wall. Grieve grabbed his friend's shoulder, steadied him. "Come Chalk, back to the throne room. I have work to do as king."

"Yes, my Grieve. King Grieve! They'll all grieve."

"Kor will certainly grieve." He turned away from the fresh, cold air and stalked into the shelter of the Bastion again.

Waiting, the king sat on his imposing throne. More logs had been thrown onto the fire to make it an inferno hot enough to incinerate living victims. Grieve was considering that as punishment. It depended on the excuses Kor made.

The glass-walled tank that held Chalk's pet fish as well as the picked-clean skull of his father rested on a stone shelf behind the throne. Grieve could turn and look at it if he chose, but now he stared forward as Kor entered the large chamber. Preoccupied with the fish tank, Chalk paid little attention to the tension in the room. He tapped the glass with his finger and watched the little forms dart away, only to return seconds later.

Kor, along with equally sullen-looking Lars and Yorik, plodded into the throne room. They wore sharkskin vests, and their knives were thrust into the belts at their waists. They also wore iron manacles, even though the king had not commanded it. The three men entered alone, without a guard escort.

Grieve leaned forward on his blocky throne, feeling the bone spines implanted in his shoulders. He rested a hand on the iron chain wrapped around his waist. "I didn't think you would be foolish enough to return defeated. You would have been better off to cut your own throats."

"Maybe, but we are Norukai, and we are not afraid," Kor said. "We could have killed ourselves rather than face your wrath, but that would be stealing from our king. Only King Grieve has the right to our lives." He raised his hands, holding up the heavy manacles. "We placed ourselves in chains to surrender to you. I would rather have you kill me than take the coward's way out."

He dropped to his knees, as did the other two captains. Tattoos on Kor's face mimicked the scales of the serpent god, and a sharp implanted tooth poked out of his shaved scalp like a tusk. Lars and Yorik also bowed their heads, letting the iron chains rattle on the floor.

King Grieve rose from his throne and stepped forward, his boots making loud sounds down the stone steps to the polished floor. He loomed over the kneeling men.

Chalk skidded over, abandoning his fish tank. He pranced a weaving path, circling Kor, then Lars and Yorik. "Grieve! You'll all grieve!"

The three defeated captains remained submissive, their heads bowed. "You may kill us now," Kor said. His shoulder muscles bunched, and the tendons in his neck stood out.

"I decide how and when to take your lives!" Grieve bellowed. "First, make me understand how a small village like Renda Bay could defeat the Norukai not once, but twice! Did they have another sorceress?"

"They had defenses and an army, King Grieve. Since the previous raid, they have built up fortifications in preparation for our return."

Grieve snorted. "No one can prepare for the fury of the Norukai."

"They were . . . good warriors," Lars said, sounding ashamed.

"And you were not? The Norukai weren't sufficient?"

"They had warships of their own," Kor said. "Siege defenses

at the mouth of the harbor, and a great many armed soldiers. They weren't just fishermen."

Grieve flashed a glare at Chalk. "You said we would take over the world! And one fishing village manages to stand against us?"

Chalk was oblivious to the king's rage. "Don't worry about one fishing village, my Grieve. It's insignificant. Just a village."

"If they defeated us, they are not insignificant."

"They are, they are!" Chalk said, standing behind Kor. "Not important!"

Grieve glowered at the still-hunched captains. "We'll launch a dozen serpent ships . . . no, twenty. We'll send our might north and crush Renda Bay, punish them for the shame they brought upon the Norukai."

"No, no!" Chalk shouted. "I dreamed it. Not Renda Bay."

King Grieve quelled his anger, surprised at his shaman's outburst. Kor, Lars, and Yorik continued to stare at the floor, exposing their necks and waiting for Grieve's heavy blade to strike the heads from their shoulders.

The king glowered at Chalk. "Are you saying I'll never take Renda Bay? That I should ignore them and let them have their victory?"

"It's not a victory. It doesn't matter." The pale man rushed up to the king and stared at him. His lips sagged, lumpy with scars, but his eyes were earnest. "We need the cities. Big cities! That's where your victories must be. Listen to me, my Grieve, King Grieve. We'll all grieve!" He ran over to the fireplace and stared into the flames.

Grieve waited in awkward silence, and the humiliated captains didn't move.

The shaman reached his hands into the fireplace until his fingers nearly grasped the fire. "I see it. The cities, the Old World, the whole continent!" He turned back toward the throne and shook his head. Drool came from the mangled corner of his mouth. "Not a little fishing village, my Grieve. You must go to

Ildakar. Send all your ships. Conquer that city. Ildakar should be your capital."

Grieve considered. "Ildakar would make a fitting capital."

Captain Kor finally raised his head. "Yes, it would, my king. I offer no excuses. I meant to capture the people and burn Renda Bay to the ground, but it was only a gesture. They have just a handful of people in fishing boats, but Ildakar is one of the grandest cities on the continent. It is a fitting place from which to rule a vast Norukai empire."

Grieve sneered at him. "You couldn't even take a fishing village, and you mean to conquer Ildakar?"

"Not just Ildakar," Chalk said, frenetic with energy. "All cities, many cities! Big cities, old cities. I know their names. I've seen them in my dreams. Serrimundi, Larrikan Shores, Tanimura, Skald's Keep, Effren . . . so many more, my thoughts are dizzy. You must conquer them all, King Grieve."

The king wrestled with his need to punish these weaklings. Kor continued to look up at him, not pleading. His expression was strong and fierce, enhanced by the hideous scarification. "Listen to your shaman, my king. Ildakar is a worthy center of your empire. I've given you all the information I can report. Use it wisely." He bowed his head again. "Our lives are yours to take."

Grieve stewed, wanting to lash out to demonstrate his power over these captains. He was tempted to seize all their crew and feed them one at a time to pools of razorfish. He gnashed his teeth again, knowing that now was not the time to sacrifice so many warriors. But he could not doubt his shaman.

The Norukai were restless, and with their many wives, they had given birth to numerous children, a whole new generation of warriors that needed a continent to conquer. And King Grieve would deliver it.

He stepped over to the glass-walled tank, from which his father's eyeless skull stared out of the murky water where the fish swam. He could be vengeful, or he could be strategic. From his maps, he envisioned the path of his conquest, how once he took Ildakar, the Norukai could spread up the Killraven River, then inland over the mountains, while more naval attacks struck the major cities on the coast. They could conquer the entire continent, and then the Norukai would no longer need to raid and pillage. No matter how glorious they were, raiders were nothing more than violent scavengers. King Grieve wanted an empire of his own.

He turned back to the three captains. "Your lives are mine, and I command your execution."

The Norukai men sagged, but braced themselves.

Grieve continued, "But I will be the one to decide the time of your execution—especially you, Captain Kor. You are the greatest failure." He crossed his meaty arms over his chest. "Look at me!" All three captains turned their faces up. "Kor, I command your execution on the battlefield. I want you to lead strikes up the coast, ignore Renda Bay for now, as my shaman insists." He grunted with displeasure, but he would listen to Chalk. Chalk had never let him down.

"Take ten ships and the maps I will give you. Attack and plunder Larrikan Shores, Skald's Keep, anywhere you encounter, and if you do not fall in battle in those places, then I command you to attack Serrimundi. If you conquer that city without being killed, then move on to another city and another." Grieve leaned forward, lowering his voice. "You can delay your execution as long as you like, if you continue to be victorious."

Kor seemed stunned, as if he couldn't believe his fortune. "I will die as you command, my king. I'll do my best to die on the last day of the last battle, after the final city in the Old World has fallen to you."

Grieve stepped to the other two captains, who continued to avert their gaze. "Lars, you will do the same. Take ten ships of your own. You bear the same death sentence for the disgrace you have brought upon the Norukai. I command you to die fighting in my war of conquest for the Old World."

Finally, he stepped over to Yorik, lifted his foot, planted it on the man's chest, and shoved hard, knocking him backward so that he sprawled to the floor.

Chalk danced about with glee. "Yes, yes, it was in my dream! You knew, King Grieve, my Grieve! You knew."

"The serpent god must be appeased," Grieve said. "There are other prices we need to pay for the strength of our race. Yorik, the serpent god will drink your blood, even though it is contaminated by failure and cowardice. You'll be the sacrifice for us."

Yorik closed his eyes, and lifted his arms, lying on his back on the floor. "I will gladly embrace the serpent god."

King Grieve bellowed for warriors to rush into the Bastion's throne room, where they seized the unresisting Yorik, keeping him in his manacles while a smith was called to strike the chains from Kor and Lars, so they could prepare to die in battle.

CHAPTER 39

After miserable days of fighting through awful swamps and monstrous creatures, Maxim finally saw the thornbushes and razor grasses open into a normal marsh. It was still an unpleasant wilderness, but he was relieved to face a natural hazard rather than a predatory and malicious obstacle. Small wonder that no enemy had ever attempted to strike Ildakar from the direction of the swamps, although he had never envisioned that those defenses might hinder his own escape.

At least he had left the persistent Adessa far behind.

He was sore and hungry, and perspiration clung like grease to his skin. His fine garments, the stylish pantaloons and silk shirt open at the chest, had been through rough conditions. He had used his gift repeatedly to dispel the grime and freshen his clothes, but the rigors of the swamp now resisted even his powers of magic. How he longed for a pleasure party again in the grand villa!

So many centuries ago, he had given everything for the glory of his city, to protect it. He and Sovrena Thora were the heart and soul of Ildakar, but he had come to despise the wealth and obliviousness of the nobles. Endless ennui would do that to people. While sealed beneath the shroud of eternity, the society had rotted. Maxim recognized that, while Thora had merely grown blind to what was going on. It was only one of the reasons he had come to hate her.

Originally, Thora had been fresh and desirable, like his beautiful city, but like a fish left too long out in the sun, both had grown foul. Maxim had devoted much of the last century to planning how to tear down Ildakar. The people would destroy their own lives and their homes. It was so delicious!

He merely dabbled to amuse himself in the endless days, and he hadn't known exactly how to bring his plans to fruition, until the great shroud faltered, as magic itself weakened and then abruptly changed. Ildakar had been thrust back into the normal world, stripped of its protective barrier. The wizards had been able to erect the shroud again and again, through extensive bloodworkings, but it wouldn't last.

That taste of freedom and the outside world after fifteen long centuries had convinced Maxim to finally set the wheels in motion. Ildakar was doomed, and the revolt was inevitable. The downtrodden people needed to cling to hope and were so easily manipulated, like a cart loaded with boulders tilted downhill. Maxim simply provided the nudge, and let the slope and the weight of their oppression drive the city to its inevitable crash.

Maxim relished the thought of starting anew, creating another legendary city, a perfect society under his own terms. Once he found a new home, Maxim would be wizard commander again, without the shrewish Thora, but he hadn't really thought it through.

As he splashed along through the mud and grasses, he plucked at his garments, releasing more of the gift to freshen the color and dispel his unwashed body odor. His once neatly trimmed goatee had grown out and the stubble on his cheeks was long and scratchy. Bugs hummed around him, thirsty for his blood, and he used more of his gift to dispel them. It was exhausting and annoying.

With no trail to follow, he kept to hummocks of grass, working his way through reeds taller than his head. He easily vanished among them. He was surprised to find a path of trampled grasses on solid ground, a trail perhaps made by swamp boars or deer, but the path widened as he walked along. The reeds were too high for him to see far ahead, but the narrow streams led to larger pools of water where fish jumped—and he found baskets tied with cords and weighted down in the water. Animal traps of some kind? He saw footprints in the mud on the path.

He paused, wondering if these were Adessa's footprints, but he hadn't seen the morazeth leader in days, and he was sure he had lost her. No, this was something else, maybe a real settlement with dry homes and good food.

Maxim followed the trail through the reeds until it became an actual footpath, joining other paths leading from the scattered fishing ponds. Abruptly, the reeds opened up, giving him a view of the Killraven River, a calm oxbow on which stood a village of more than fifty reed huts, some structures extending out on stilts, with smaller huts built in the marshes. He saw racks of gutted fish angled over smoky fires, and his stomach grumbled with hunger. Villagers went about their daily business. Some took canoes through the waterways, while larger boats ventured out of the calm oxbow into the river's main current.

Seeing the settlement, Maxim felt true joy, not just at the thought of warm food, clean clothes, and a dry place to sleep. This was a real town with a fair number of people, and he needed people if he was ever going to build a new city for himself.

Maxim counted more than a hundred men, women, and even rambunctious children. Fishermen in canoes dumped their catch on wooden docks, while half-naked villagers sat on reed mats at the shore to gut the fish and cut the heads off, separating the meat and the offal into different buckets. Old women tended smoky fires to preserve the fish. Teenagers clustered together weaving reeds and marsh grasses into baskets, while groups of women pounded the reed fiber and twisted it into twine, with which they wove and strung nets. Women and men came in from foraging in the marshlands, carrying sacks of spiny seedpods or muddy tubers they'd pulled up from the soft ground. Small children lay on paddleboards in the mud near the shore, using little nets to scoop up crayfish, which they dumped into pots.

Maxim was pleased to see his new village thriving. Cleaning any last smears of mud off his face, grooming his dark hair, which had grown longer than he preferred, he walked out of the marsh. With the power of his gift, he could make these villagers think positively of him, see him as their new leader, believe every statement he made.

He'd used that power long ago to enchant Thora into becoming his lover. He'd been ready to give anything for her! He had wanted her so badly. By the Keeper's crotch, if only he could go back and tell himself not to waste the effort. There had indeed been some good times in their relationship, maybe a hundred years out of fifteen long centuries, but the best part was that he never needed to see Thora again.

He came into view with his arms raised, and as the villagers noticed him, their casual singsong chatter dropped into silence. They stared at the stranger in wonder and fear.

Seeing that he had their attention, Maxim released his gift with a flourish and made a boom of thunder echo through the cloudless sky. Then he put on a benevolent expression as he stepped forward. "I greet you with kindness. I am Maxim, the wizard commander of Ildakar." He waited for the name to sink in, and smiled more broadly as he released his gift, let a tingle of glamour flicker through the air, like a blanket smothering their uncertainty. "And I have even better news, because I am now your wizard commander, too! What is the name of this village?"

"Tarada," said an old woman at her fishing nets, plucking at the twine and tightening a knot. "We are a simple folk, and we have little. If you've come to steal, you'll be disappointed."

"I've not come to steal," Maxim said. "You have great

potential, and that is what matters. Who is your village leader, so I can meet my second-in-command?"

A broad-shouldered man in his midforties came forward, not looking happy. He had short gray-brown hair and was missing two fingers on his left hand. "I am Danner. I resolve disputes here, but Tarada doesn't need much more leadership than that."

"You have more leadership now. You have a wizard commander." Maxim released more glamour, and the people muttered, nodding, displaying uncertain smiles.

"We've never had a wizard commander before," Danner said.

"Then this is a great day for your village. I'll help you make changes. You are all my subjects, and we'll build Tarada into something much greater than it is. You've never before dreamed what was within your reach, but I'll help you make it happen." Maxim smiled at all of them, glad that he no longer needed to hide his face with a mirror mask. These people were already in the palm of his hand.

"First I'll need food, clothing, and a home appropriate to my station." He gestured to the town leader, who didn't yet understand that he no longer had any power here. "Danner, find me what I need. I'm sure the people will be happy to sort through their possessions and provide the necessary items for their wizard commander."

He scanned the women in the town, wistful for the beautiful noble ladies at his pleasure parties. When he had left Ildakar in turmoil and fled into the wilderness, he hadn't considered how long it would be before he had a woman in his bed again, to lay her down and stroke her, to hear her moan as she experienced the pleasure of being the wizard commander's lover.

The women in Tarada seemed plain and washed-out, looking older than their years from eking out a life with no luxuries. He did see some young ladies still barely in their teens. Maybe if they were cleaned up, he might find them attractive, and if Tarada was going to be the start of a new rule for him, he would have to grant these people at least some small reward. If the women pleased him, he would return the favor.

Men paddled in with their canoes, curious about the stranger that the rest of the villagers gathered around. Larger boats returned from the wide river, and Maxim greeted them all. He maintained the calming veil of his gift like a mist throughout the air. The village was already his, and he merely had to finish arranging the details.

W ithin several days, thanks to Maxim's efforts, Tarada entirely changed. Five of the smaller huts had been torn down, and the reeds, structural poles, and thatched roofing were used for a much larger building. It certainly wasn't a palace—anyone in Ildakar would have laughed at the very suggestion—but it did have a certain amount of grandeur in relation to the rest of the village.

Until now, life in Tarada had mostly concentrated on gathering food, and the people had succeeded well enough, but Maxim had far greater ambition, and he had to start his new empire somewhere. Even Ildakar had humble beginnings on the shores of the Killraven River in ages past. Once he established himself in Tarada, Maxim might move on to a grander place, maybe one of the bustling towns downriver. Tarada was a fine start, though, and he was pleased with his progress.

Danner proved to be quite skilled as his second-in-command. The man knew all the villagers and resources in Tarada. Under Maxim's glamour, he threw himself wholeheartedly into serving the new wizard commander.

Maxim chose two young women who were comely enough—one of them Danner's own daughter—and took them as his lovers, granting them that extra glow of importance. The village girls were inexperienced and unimaginative, but pleasurable, and Maxim could train them, or even try others who might catch his attention. He didn't want anyone in Tarada to feel left out. For the first time since he had abandoned Ildakar, Maxim saw a bright future.

Then Adessa arrived.

Over the last week, Maxim had prepared for the possibility of her coming and given the villagers instructions to sound a warning upon the approach of any strangers, but Adessa was fast.

A fisherwoman came running through the reeds, yelling at the top of her voice, "The morazeth is here! To arms!"

Moments later, Maxim emerged from his palatial reed structure to see a haughty Adessa stride into the village with her weapons drawn and a deadly gleam in her eyes. Under Maxim's spell, an older fisherman threw himself upon her, attacking with a boat hook, but Adessa chopped the wooden staff in half, then sliced her knife across his stomach. Not even slowing her pace, she kicked the man aside as he fell clutching at the ropy entrails spilling out of his stomach. "Maxim, I am here for your head! On orders from Sovrena Thora."

Knowing she was protected from his magic, Maxim cried out to the people, "Protect me! Stop her!" He used his glamour spell to nudge the villagers who were already wrapped around his finger.

Danner charged forward, lips drawn back in a grimace of anger and disgust. "We won't let you harm our wizard commander!" Two more fishermen joined him.

Adessa looked at them as if they were bothersome flies. The villagers clumsily swung makeshift weapons, as Maxim had known they would. He needed them only for a diversion. They slowed Adessa for a moment, but she cut the legs out from under Danner, stabbed the two fishermen, and kept moving forward at her inexorable pace.

With a wild shriek, Danner's young daughter bounded forward and threw a torn fishing net at Adessa, surprising her. The morazeth thrashed, tangling her short sword in the net, while other howling villagers rushed into the brief opening.

The mob struck the morazeth leader with sticks. A young child darted in with gutting knife to stab her rune-marked legs. Adessa kicked him aside and into the water. More villagers crowded forward with murderous intent, but Adessa slashed herself free from the net.

Now the morazeth took the attack seriously. Whirling as if she were in an exhibition for the Ildakaran combat arena, she slew the Taradan villagers as fast as they came within reach of her sword. A few of them managed to land blows, though Adessa ignored the pain. She killed them all, leaving the marsh path and the village littered with severed limbs and decapitated heads.

Maxim dispatched more villagers to come running to his defense, well aware that the morazeth would surely defeat them all, and as the villagers died, one after another, his own tenuous glamour frayed. Terror loosened his hold on the population, and they pulled away.

Maxim knew it was time for another tactic. This small fishing village would never have served as the capital of his new empire, he realized. It was just an experiment, a way-stop on his journey, and it was time for him to use the supreme power of his gift so he could escape unscathed.

His magic would not harm Adessa, but he was clever enough to put it to other use. He used his gift on the sluggish waters of the oxbow bend, pulling upon the current.

As Adessa hacked her way through the last villagers, Maxim hurled the river water in a wide smothering flood over Tarada. The sudden wave washed away his reed palace and the numerous huts. Adessa braced herself for the crash of the wave.

At the same time, Maxim unleashed more magic, triggering a surge of heat that exploded the curtain of water into hot steam. Searing vapor roared and whistled, scouring the village. Boiling water drenched the people and structures, and swept Adessa away in the hot rush. As more of the river exploded, the entire oxbow was engulfed in impenetrable fog.

It gave Maxim the perfect cover to escape. He had already found a boat, which he would take to the main river. From there, he could get far away.

CHAPTER 40

Left inside her lifeless cell, Thora was tired of waiting. She refused to let her captors determine her fate anymore, and she would not be blocked from the great city, *her* city. Ildakar had discarded her, shoved her into this dark corner where no one bothered to think about her anymore. Thora had reached her breaking point.

Her own husband had spread his poison, brought the city down upon itself, and then dashed off, laughing at what he had done. For a long time, Thora had felt a sneering indifference toward him, and now when she thought of how he had kissed her and stroked her skin, she felt nauseated.

High Captain Avery had been a far superior lover, so attentive, appreciating her for her beauty, not just her power. In the cell now, thinking of the handsome captain, Thora touched her arms, her breasts, let her fingers explore her thighs and between her legs, but what should have been a tingling erotic sensation was little more than a numb touch. Her body was more stone than flesh and could no longer experience pleasure.

How she hated Maxim, hated the duma members who had cast this petrification spell on her, the conspirators who had pronounced her guilty because they didn't understand what she had done for Ildakar. Everything for Ildakar!

She felt like the unloved stepchild of her mother city. The leaders dismissed her vision and ignored her powerful magic that had protected them for so many centuries. Her heart was broken for how her dreams had crumbled.

She returned to the doorway of her cell, where the rune-engraved stone blocks prevented her from using magic to escape. Thora ignited a light in her hand and set it afloat. The glowing ball hovered in the air, illuminating the stone walls. She studied the spiderwebbed fracture pattern where, in her fury at Lani's taunting, she had lashed out and damaged the block with her bare fist.

It was just a start. She knew she could do more.

Thora had to get out of this cell, had to see her city. No, she needed to *escape* this place. Much to her dismay and disgust, Ildakar was no longer her home. She understood that full well. Nicci and Nathan, the duma, the ungrateful lower classes who had revolted against Ildakar and killed her son Amos—they were no longer her people. No, Ildakar was not her city anymore, no matter how much she had given to it.

She bunched her fist, drew it back, and slammed against the stone above the cracked block. Her knuckles hit so hard that the blow resonated up her arm, sending a shiver of pain up to her shoulder. In a way, she was reassured that she could feel it.

But she hadn't managed to crack the next stone. She needed more.

Something about Lani's provocation had triggered the extra power in her. Now, when she thought about her dulled sensations, how she longed to feel the thrill of pleasure in that most intimate of places which was now dead to her, she felt anger again. It grew brighter than the flame that hovered nearby.

Ildakar had taken so much from her! Lashing out, Thora struck another resounding blow against the stone, and this time she felt the block fracture. Before she let her anger fade, Thora smashed again and again, building it into a wild frenzy. She recalled how much she had enjoyed pleasure parties, thought of her lover Avery who had been murdered by Mirrormask's rebels . . . murdered by her own husband!

After many repeated blows, Thora felt the damage to her hand, saw blood oozing from her chalky skin. If she'd been a normal human, Thora's fists would have been smashed to a bloody pulp. She didn't relent, but merely ignored the damage so she could keep going.

She continued battering the stone until the runes were finally destroyed. The blocks crumbled, the door sagged on its hinges, and Thora kicked hard against the heavy wooden barrier. Iron pins snapped from the hinges, and the crossbar clattered into the corridor. With a groan, the door broke free and crashed to the floor, leaving the way open for her.

Laughing, Thora stepped out of her cell. Once past the protective runes, she felt her gift swell within her. With an off-hand gesture, she flicked a bleeding hand down the hall, igniting all of the torches with magic. Glancing down at her mangled fists, which had begun to scream with pain, she restored herself, sealed the worst of the injuries. She was the sovrena, intact once more, although she was unable to drive away the slow permanence of stone that still infused her body.

She was free, and now at last she could do what needed to be done. Ildakar had forsaken her, but General Utros and his vast army might appreciate Thora's work, her magic. If she joined forces with him, she could help him overthrow this broken Ildakar and destroy the treacherous duma; then she could install herself as sovrena again and begin to fix things. Yes, that was how she could have her city back. That was how she could restore her dream, even if it meant she had to forge a terrible alliance with an ancient enemy.

She drove away the thought of what Utros and his armies would do to Ildakar once they surged through the gates, at least at first. It was for the best in the long run. She owed nothing to the city anymore, and she would rebuild it from scratch.

Thora knew her way around the dungeon levels. In her years as sovrena, she had sentenced many traitors to be killed in the combat arena, or she had simply used the petrification spell to turn them to stone. But some were sent to the dungeons, where she expected them to learn their lesson. Sometimes, she forgot about the captives long past the point where they had become contrite, then desperate, and then insane. After that, they rotted in the cells, leaving only moldering piles of bones for the rats to eat. Thora felt no sympathy for those victims, nor for her current jailers. She had her own priorities.

Freed, she strode along the passageways, searching for a way out into the open air. In a lit antechamber she startled two guards as they played a game with gambling sticks, bidding with stolen gold coins and jewelry. She recognized the two men who had treated her with such disrespect. As she strode into the antechamber, they lurched to their feet, astonished. "The sovrena's escaped!"

She called a fist of air that slammed one of the guards against the far wall, and when he was pinned there, she pushed, harder, feeling the delicious thrill as his ribs cracked, and blood poured out of his mouth and nose. She kept pressing, crushing his heart flat, pushing the breastbone all the way against the spine.

Yelling, the second guard tried to run, and Thora smacked him with her magic just as he passed through the door, knocking his skull like a melon against the wall. She slowly pressed harder, flattening his skull until his brain oozed out like pinkish-gray slime down the walls.

Moving onward, Thora crashed through doorways, scattering more guards. Some turned to fight, but she dispensed with them quickly. Others fled. She had full command of her gift now, unhindered by protective runes. No one would stop her. When she reached the barred doorway of the dungeon tunnels beneath the bluff, she bent and twisted the metal barricade, then hurled it at two guards who raced forward to stop her.

When she finally broke out to the landscaped streets and orchards, Thora paused to inhale, smelling freedom, smelling Ildakar. It was very late at night, the streets nearly deserted just before dawn. All the noble mansions were well lit, but she saw no one moving about. Above her, the shattered ruins of the sacrificial pyramid stood like an insult, where Nicci had thwarted the sovrena's plans to raise the shroud of eternity. So much had collapsed on that night. . . .

Thora needed to make changes, but she couldn't do it while Ildakar stood against her. No, the city had to be purged. She had to reshape Ildakar so that it could achieve the glory it deserved. She would use General Utros, the mortal enemy of Ildakar, but Ildakar had become its own enemy. She had to save her city from itself, and to do that, in order to surrender to Utros, she needed to get past the wall. She was sure the enemy camp would accept her.

She paused, feeling a chill of second thoughts, dreading how the victorious enemy soldiers would pillage Ildakar, punish the people for resisting the siege, for turning them to stone. They would destroy much of the splendor—

No, she banished those ideas. In the long term, if it was the only way Thora could become sovrena again, the results would be worth the terrible price.

Now that she had escaped, she needed to be careful. Before she could get past the main gates, Nicci, Nathan, and the duma members would stand against her, so she moved quickly, before news of her escape spread.

Down in the lower levels of the city, she heard a loud commotion and she saw many torches and gathering crowds. Something was happening at the main wall, and beyond the city she could see large fires spreading from the grassy hills down into the siege encampment.

In the chaos, maybe she would have her chance. Thora

made her way swiftly through the city streets, keeping hidden. She came upon a late-working gardener who pushed a small cart filled with night soil, tending the grapevine trellises for the vineyards long after dark. With a shovel he scooped his fertilizer into the plants, then looked up at her. "Good evening, my lady." Then he recognized her, reacted with surprise. "Sovrena Thora! I thought you were—"

She snapped his neck with a gesture, and he collapsed into the steaming brown load in his cart. She should have felt a flicker of guilt, since he was one of her subjects, but she didn't consider any of them her people anymore. They were just obstacles hindering her escape.

As she approached the towering wall, she heard shouts and a clamor of marching feet, whinnying horses, the jingle of armor. When she finally came within sight of the tall gates, she watched a battered and disorganized army returning from battle in the darkest hour before dawn, hundreds of fighters in mismatched uniforms, armor, and weapons. What had happened? Members of the city guard marched alongside arena slaves. She even saw several morazeth among them, which proved to her how much Ildakar had been corrupted. The fabric of her city was ruined!

She tried to put the pieces together from what she saw. Had Ildakar launched some kind of attack? Had this mismatched group of defenders attempted to challenge General Utros and his myriad soldiers? The returning fighters looked battered, sullen, and they didn't cheer or whistle as they might with a well-earned victory. Rather, they seemed badly bruised.

Then she saw the hated Nicci riding a bay charger with Nathan in the saddle behind her, trotting alongside Damon, with Elsa behind him. Even Oron, head of the skinners' guild, and Lady Olgya rode with the duma members, as if they belonged there. Lani strutted about, drunk with her own power. Returning fighters poured through the gate even as it crashed shut behind them.

Damon and Quentin extended their hands and worked a barrier spell, the locking magic that secured the towering doors. Thora realized she would never escape that way. All the gates would be likewise sealed. She would have to make it over the wall somehow and leave these people to their well-deserved fates.

Soon after the great gate sealed, she heard the monotonous pounding of Utros's hardened soldiers against the immense walls. Thora herself, just one person, had smashed her way out of her cell, and with countless thousands of hard fists battering the wall, she knew it had to crumble before long, no matter how many reinforcement spells the wizards used.

But she intended to be on the other side with the victors when the city fell.

As the returning Ildakaran army milled around the gate, Nicci was still shouting commands from her horse, while other duma members called upon subcommanders for reports. Suddenly, a group of shouting guards ran through the main streets, heading toward the duma members. With a cold trickle of fear, Thora realized what they were saying. "The sovrena has escaped! She smashed her way out of the dungeon."

Thora began to run, darting through back streets and dirty shadows, then becoming even bolder as she reached the steps leading to the watchtowers on the wall. After the nighttime attack the sentries would be on high alert, making it even more difficult to sneak past them. If she used her gift to unleash storm blows or a flare of fire, she could clear a way to the wall. If she climbed to the top, she could probably even jump and survive the landing with her stone-hardened body. That was her desperate chance. It would not be subtle, and her surprise would last for only a few moments, but it would be enough for her to get away.

Throwing aside all caution, Thora ran forward, gambling everything. As she burst into the well-lit open areas, several nearby soldiers saw her. "Here she is. Sovrena Thora is here!"

She knocked them aside with a blast of magic, but didn't waste time killing them. Right now, she just needed them out of her way. Clearing a path with brute force and magic, she ran to the stone steps that climbed the wall. The resonant booms of relentless pounding outside echoed through the faint dawn.

On the wall above, sentries shouted as they saw her ascending toward them. Several shot arrows at her. Most missed, but two shafts struck her arm, scratched a gouge, then clattered off. A thin line of blood welled up on her skin, but she would heal it later, after she escaped.

The uproar increased as more soldiers rushed to capture her. Thora kept climbing, dismayed again that her own people had turned against her. Below, she saw powerful duma members ride to the base of the wall, including Nicci and Nathan. The sentries above were shouting and the soldiers below rallied, rushing up the stone stairs after her. Thora kept climbing.

Nicci dismounted at the base of the wall, her black dress flowing around her. She came after her, like a vengeful storm. "We will stop you, Thora."

Thora put on a burst of speed. Almost there.

Reaching the top walkway, she blasted aside the sentries who confronted her, sending three of them over the wall to their deaths. Far below, lined up against the thick stones were hundreds of the enemy soldiers. If Thora could drop down there, she would present herself to them and demand to be taken to General Utros. She could help him bring down Ildakar and restore herself to power. She knew the city's weaknesses.

But it was a long way down, and she quailed. Even with her stone skin, she wondered if she would survive the fall. And when she landed, would those angry soldiers listen to her, or would they just kill her outright because she was from Ildakar? She hesitated as she looked over the edge.

Nicci strode toward her across the top of the wall. Her once-long blond hair was ragged and short. Thora lashed out with a blow of wind, much like the one she had used to hurl

Nicci out the high windows of the ruling tower during their previous duel.

But Nicci was obviously stronger now, and Adessa wasn't here to help the sovrena fight. Nicci blocked the blast and launched rippling wizard's fire—which no mere sorceress should have been able to use! Thora barely dodged in time, but the edge of the searing flames burned her skin, blackened her garments, reminding her that she could indeed be wounded. She peered over the sheer drop again, not sure she could survive the fall.

"You intend to kill yourself, Thora?" Nicci mocked, stepping closer. "If that's your wish, we can make it happen."

"I mean to save Ildakar!" Thora said. "You've all turned against me, and the only way to save my city is for Utros to win. When you are overthrown, we can rebuild Ildakar the way it should be!"

Nicci said, "So you mean to betray your city, just as Maxim did."

"Never! I love Ildakar." Appalled, she lashed out with a lightning bolt, and Nicci blocked it with lightning of her own.

Lani climbed up beside Nicci, followed by Nathan, Elsa, and Oron. "So you said in your cell, but now look at you, Thora. You try to justify your actions, but they aren't for the good of Ildakar. You're only saving yourself."

"I am the sovrena! *I am Ildakar*. Whatever I do—"

Nicci interrupted. "Whatever you do is not for these people. More than a thousand of them went out tonight, and hundreds gave their lives to test General Utros. Would they have done that for *you*?" She lowered her voice, sounding harder and more threatening. "Would you yourself have made that sacrifice for Ildakar?"

"I would never do anything to harm my city," Thora said.

Damon and Quentin reached the top of the wall, adding their powerful gift to the air as if the magic itself were alive and threatening.

"You truly meant to betray us to General Utros?" Elsa asked, shocked and saddened.

Thora's thoughts spun as she fought to deny it. She looked at Elsa, then Lani. She hated her rival sorceresses, but was it really for the "good of Ildakar" if she sold herself to the enemy army? If she allied herself with the very force that wanted only to conquer the city?

Thora glanced beyond the walls at the hundreds of thousands of fighters gathered across the plain, who had once been petrified by the wizards of Ildakar. They had been turned to stone for centuries, taken away from their own time. If she were to help them break through Ildakar's defenses, she knew they would exact their revenge. There would be fires, destruction, rape, and pillage, as conquering armies always did. How could she let that happen to her city? How could she? What was she doing?

Thora looked at all the besieging soldiers far below. She didn't dare aid the enemy. As Nicci and the other duma members closed in, preparing to fight her with powerful combined magic, she realized it was her last chance to throw herself over the wall. But she couldn't do it.

Instead, she turned to Nicci and the others facing her. "I would never do anything to harm Ildakar," she insisted, then lowered her voice. "I won't be like my husband."

She let her hands fall to her sides and bowed in surrender. The wizards came forward, and she didn't resist as they bound her.

CHAPTER 41

B annon couldn't remember what had happened to him, but the ache of his muscles and his bruised and battered skin gave him a dull awareness. Memories began to return, though they remained a blur. Previously, whenever he went into his blood-maddened state, he didn't remember what he had done.

Nevertheless, against all odds, he was still alive.

As he blinked his way back to consciousness, Bannon discovered that he was confined inside a wooden shack. Dim morning light filtered through gaps in the mismatched boards. When he drew a deep breath, he hissed in involuntary pain. He hurt everywhere, inside and out. He gingerly touched an egg-sized lump on the back of his head where someone had struck him a hard blow.

"He's finally awake," said a ragged voice.

A second, closer voice sounded forlorn. "Maybe they'll kill him first, but I know they'll kill us all."

Bannon turned toward the voices and winced. The aching throb turned into loud drumbeats in his skull. He saw Jed and Brock huddled against the wooden wall of the shack. They sat on the ground, knees drawn up to their chests. Their bright silken robes were stained and bloody, their eyes swollen, their faces covered with scabs.

"You survived, too!" Bannon said. "Where are we?"

"In the enemy camp, of course," Brock said. "Prisoners."

"Keeper's crotch!" Jed hung his head. "I suppose we should thank you for getting us captured instead of killed outright."

"He only delayed what's going to happen," Brock groaned. "It might have been cleaner to let them kill us out there. At least it would be over with."

Bannon pressed the swelling on the back of his head, felt dried blood in his hair. "I got us captured? How did I do that?" He touched his bruised eye, looked at the cuts on his arm, and decided not to take a complete inventory of his injuries. "I don't remember anything except fighting the soldiers."

"We knew we were going to die, but you battled like a madman," Jed said. "I've never seen anything like it. When you threw yourself on them, something changed. You went berserk."

"I . . ." Bannon shook his head, which made him grit his teeth from the pain. "Sometimes that happens. I lose myself in a fighting frenzy."

"You saved us, whatever it was," Jed said. "Brock and I tried to defend ourselves, but you—I think you killed a dozen of them before they finally took you down. The soldiers said you fought so well, they wanted to show you to General Utros. We surrendered, too. We had no other choice."

Brock added, "These silk robes showed that we are important people. That is probably why they saved us."

Trying to look outside, Bannon pressed his good eye against a gap in the wall boards. He smelled thick, pungent smoke. In the daylight he saw blackened hillsides and hundreds of warriors scurrying across the scorched area, putting out smoldering patches. As his thoughts came back to him, he recalled Lila and the morazeth fighting and Mrra tearing apart enemy soldiers. He remembered Nicci and the other gifted using wizard's fire and lightning, while he and the countless

Ildakaran defenders fought with more conventional weapons.

"Did we win?" Bannon asked. "Is the rest of the army safe inside the city?"

Brock made a rude noise. "We didn't win. It was never possible we would win. We killed plenty of them, and they killed a lot of our army."

"We caused some damage, though," Jed admitted. "More than Utros expected, I think."

The shack's door flung open and one of the pale soldiers stood there. "I am commanded to bring you to General Utros. You will come."

Bannon lifted himself to his feet. "Good. I was going to demand to see him."

"He'll kill us now," Brock groaned.

"The general will question you first," said the soldier. "Maybe he will kill you afterward. It depends on your answers."

The three captives were marched out into the open, and Bannon shrank from the bright morning light after the rank-smelling shadows of the shack. He saw the enemy soldiers working in the encampment, repairing damage. The hills still smoldered, but the conflagration had been stopped. Some of the swift flames had encroached on the great camp, burning tents and structures. The blaze had even approached the general's head-quarters, but a valiant effort had stopped the fire's progress in time. Ancient soldiers, some singed, glowered at the three young prisoners walking under guard toward the command structure.

Though his head throbbed, Bannon dredged up bravery from within. Jed was physically shaking, and Brock sniveled. The two noble boys had been so haughty when they were with Amos, but now they seemed broken and terrified.

Bannon had wanted so badly for them to be his friends, but Nicci often told him he was naive. He realized that he no longer had Sturdy, which was no surprise, though he didn't remember being disarmed. The loss of the weapon saddened him, but Bannon feared he was about to lose much more.

As the captives approached the rough headquarters, he recognized the legendary figure of General Utros. He was a big man, well muscled, wearing a leather vest that sported a stylized-flame symbol. Utros had a full beard, neatly trimmed, but the left side of his face was scarred from an ancient burn. His skin and hair were grayish white from the stone spell.

Two strange, beautiful women emerged from the dark interior of the command structure and took places on either side of Utros. They stared at him with predatory eyes. He realized they must be the sorceresses who had attacked Nicci with her own hair.

Jed and Brock fell behind Bannon as if hiding in his shadow, but he had learned a great deal about bravery. He moved closer to the general without being encouraged. "My name is Bannon Farmer. I'm a swordsman and a traveler. I came to Ildakar with my friends Nicci and Nathan."

Utros remained silent, then gave a respectful nod. "You are an exceptional fighter. You managed to impress even my invincible army." He took a step closer. "You are not of Ildakar, then? And you know the sorceress Nicci and the wizard Nathan, who came to parley with me?"

"Yes, I'm friends with Nicci and Nathan." He turned to his companions. "And these are Jed and Brock, from Ildakar."

The two young men scowled, as if they preferred to remain invisible and unidentified.

"I know they are nobles, possibly worth a ransom," Utros said. "They did not help you much during the fight, however."

Jed and Brock looked offended, and Bannon said, "They aren't fighters."

"Ildakar's defenders did surprisingly well," Utros said, in grudging acknowledgment, "but you cannot win. I have orders from Emperor Kurgan." He gazed over Bannon's shoulder, as if seeing something that wasn't there; then his focus snapped back to Bannon, like a raptor sighting prey. "Those two are useless, but you fight well, Bannon Farmer. Why not join my army? Be part of the victory."

Bannon was horrified. "I would never do that. I couldn't betray my friends."

"We're not useless," Brock said. "Even before your stone army woke up, we destroyed hundreds of your soldiers. That's more than anyone else in the city accomplished."

Utros flipped his attention to the young man behind Bannon, and his stiff features twisted in an expression of disgust. "You smashed statues? When we were helpless?"

Jed said defiantly, "We didn't know you'd ever wake up, but we damaged hundreds."

Brock said, "I wish we had destroyed all of you."

The twin sorceresses whispered in voices that hissed like serpents. Utros said, "Then I change my opinion. You weak nobles caused inexcusable damage."

Bannon squared his shoulders, facing the enemy general. "The people of Ildakar are not helpless. They have many powerful wizards, and Nicci and Nathan are the strongest of them all. Your siege doesn't have a chance of succeeding."

One of the painted sorceresses said, "How did Nicci survive our spell that possessed her hair?"

Bannon flared his nostrils. "We all fought together. I was there. Nathan and I helped cut her hair, and she used her own magic to break the bond. They're stronger than you think."

"So are we," Utros said.

Another ancient soldier rushed up to report to the general, interrupting their conversation. Utros listened to the whispered report, then called two guards. "Take them back into confinement. I will interrogate them further after I finish my work here." He turned a steely glare at Jed and Brock. "These two noble boys deserve painful questioning to reveal everything they know about the inner workings of Ildakar."

Chalky guards manhandled the three prisoners back toward their shack. As he was herded along, Bannon studied every detail of the camp, hoping to see some chance of escape.

CHAPTER 42

Nicci had seen the morazeth in action, knew the steel of their bodies, the anger that pulsed through their veins, but when a battered Lila came to her the morning after the sortie, Nicci saw something she had never expected. Lila looked defeated.

"I failed him," she said. "I let Bannon down. He is dead because of me."

The hazy sunshine of midday warmed the top of the plateau. Nicci stood outside the ruling tower with the shadow of the high structure stretching away from the river and the sheer bluffs. Drained from the battle the night before, Nicci had not allowed herself to consider all the emotional consequences yet. She intentionally blocked those feelings and tried to remain analytical. Her heart was hard, cold . . . black ice, and she clung to that.

"Hundreds of people died last night, not just Bannon," Nicci said. The more she tried not to think of the young man's face, his eager smile, his good nature, the more clearly she saw him in her mind.

Lila remained unconvinced. "True, many died, but *I* didn't

fail the rest of them. I did fail Bannon. His training must have been inadequate, and my protection faltered. I lost track of him when I fought beside my morazeth sisters, and the enemy soldiers swept in, cutting me off. I didn't even see him go down, so I don't know what happened to him."

Nicci had not seen it either. During the frenzied battle, the arena fighters, city guards, volunteers, and duma members had been on their own. "Bannon was a good fighter," Nicci said, and then her voice dropped and the words came out before she could even think about it. "He was my friend." Nicci found it strange to admit the fact, but there was no other word. Bannon Farmer had become more than just a temporary companion on their journey. "If you failed him, then so did I. There is nothing we can do to help him now."

The dead were still being counted. Oron had lost his son Brock during the battle, and Lady Olgya reported with more anger than grief that her boy Jed hadn't returned either. Nicci could not fully comprehend what a parent felt over the loss of a child, even worthless and disappointing sons such as Jed and Brock, but then she thought of the girl Thistle, and the heavy ache made her understand.

"Unless Bannon's not dead," Lila said, startling Nicci. "I will not give up hope until I know for certain."

Nicci hardened her heart, not wanting to waste time on unrealistic imaginings. "There is very little chance. You know that."

Lila crossed her arms over the black leather wrap. "Unless you want to surrender right now, we must cling to hope wherever we find it. All of Ildakar has very little chance, but we won't give up."

Nicci realized the young morazeth was right, and she knew that Richard Rahl would never simply give up, otherwise he would have surrendered to the Imperial Order before the first battles. "Hope may be our greatest weapon. Don't forget your hope." She looked into Lila's determined eyes. "Thank you for reminding me."

As the morazeth sprinted away, Nicci didn't ask what the young woman intended to do. Instead, she had her own decisions to make. General Utros and his army would be in turmoil after the attack, but Ildakar itself also rang with speculation, questions, and uncertainties. The defenders had struck a powerful blow, and the duma would revel in what they had accomplished, for a few hours at least. Neither side would be in any shape for a major operation, but only a fool would assume the siege would be over soon.

Thora was confined again, but in a different dungeon cell. She seemed changed now, as if something fundamental had broken inside her. Nicci still didn't trust her.

The duma members had gone back to their homes to recuperate before they met to discuss what to do next. When Nicci entered the quiet ruling tower, she found the main chamber silent, the thrones vacant and the stone benches unoccupied. The chamber echoed with her footsteps.

"Ah, I thought I might find you here, Sorceress," Nathan said, startling her.

She turned to see the wizard in his scuffed robes, his white hair tangled. She was surprised he hadn't cleaned himself and changed his garments since the night before. Nathan had always been vain about his appearance and his comforts, but the previous night's battle had shaken him.

"I wanted a place where I could contemplate," she explained.

Nathan came closer, his expression drawn. "I know. I grieve for the dear boy, too. It's a terrible loss."

Nicci didn't want to admit her own feelings. "There is no time for grieving or foolish hope. We need to consider our next actions while we have a brief respite. It might last only a few days." She glanced at the stairs behind the throne dais. "Come with me to the top of the tower, where we can get a broader perspective."

They ascended the spiraling stone steps and emerged onto the open rooftop, where the sunshine was bright and carefree larks flitted about. Even from up here, she could feel and hear the monotonous pounding against the walls.

Nicci lowered her voice, though there was no one but Nathan to hear. "It wasn't enough, and Bannon died to defend a city that wasn't even his own, on a foolish and arrogant strike that served little purpose. How long can Ildakar withstand this siege?"

Nathan raked his fingers through his long hair in a gesture that reminded her of Richard. "For as long as we must. I don't believe any army is invincible. Emperor Jagang and the Imperial Order fell. Sulachan and his undead army were defeated. General Utros will fall, too."

Nicci listened to the drumbeat of coordinated blows outside the wall. "A drip of water will eventually carve a bowl in solid rock. I don't think we have that much time, and Ildakar is only one target for General Utros." Together, they looked across the great valley. The rolling hills on the northern boundary were a blackened scar from the grass fires, and a low pall of smoke hung in the air, but even after the losses they had suffered, the enemy seemed infinite. "His army could threaten the whole world."

Nathan stretched out his hands, sketched a rectangle in the air, and pulled the air taut to create a new magnifying window. Many of the general's soldiers were working hard to rebuild the camp, but they also saw columns of soldiers, thousands at a time, splitting off in different directions, marching away from the valley like separate invasion forces, any one of which could conquer a whole city.

Nicci felt cold inside. Looming grief over Bannon wrapped her like a blanket that could not warm the black ice of her heart, but Utros posed a far greater threat. "If those expeditionary forces are meant to conquer more territory, then that ancient general can take over the land that Richard told us to save." She looked at him. "The danger goes well beyond Ildakar. Utros could conquer the entire Old World. And from there, what is to stop him from surging upward into D'Hara, just like Jagang and the Imperial Order? We have to stop him here."

Nathan stroked his chin where pale stubble had sprouted after the long night. She had never seen him so disheveled. "Now that we've shown him our fighting spirit, should we demand to speak with him again? Suggest that it is in his best interest not to pursue this war further?"

Nicci shook her head. "How could we convince him of that? He has already sent out many armies."

Through Nathan's magnifying window, they watched a group of the general's engineers working with tall trees, cutting the wooden trunks into components that included a long throwing arm. Working like bees, they assembled a single catapult, which they wheeled close to the towering gates.

"Even if they hurl boulders, the reinforcement spells will protect our walls and gates," Nathan said. "What is he up to?"

The sentries on the outer walls sounded an alarm, and the guards braced themselves as the catapult moved into position. Nicci narrowed her blue eyes. "I think he has something else in mind."

The two watched uneasily as the ancient soldiers cranked their ropes and ratcheted back the throwing arm. The catapult hurtled forward until it smacked the halting block and flung the cargo from its basket. A dozen corpses sailed through the air over the high wall and pelted the streets of Ildakar, landing on tiled rooftops and falling into water cisterns. The Ildakaran soldiers who had died during the nighttime raid. All of the heads had been chopped off, the bodies mutilated.

Even as the first rain of corpses fell across the lower levels of the city, the ancient warriors wound back the catapult again. Carts came forward, loaded with even more bodies.

Nicci set her jaw. "General Utros is not in a mood to negotiate."

She felt the coldness in her heart, the tingle of both Additive and Subtractive Magic. This fight was about more than just

319

Ildakar. She knew what she had to do. "All of the Old World and the entire D'Haran Empire must know about this threat. I will make my preparations." The breezes on top of the tower fluttered her close-cropped blond hair. "Tomorrow, I intend to use the sliph."

That night, trying to rest before she departed on her swift journey, Nicci again traveled with Mrra on the outside of the giant camp. The darkness looked different through the eyes of the sand panther, but she could see the devastation, smell the acrid char of the burned hills as well as blood from the great battle. Mrra had emerged from hiding among the trees in a distant hollow, but now she approached the army of General Utros. The big cat knew the ancient soldiers had weak night vision, even worse than most humans', and now she ventured even closer to the camp.

Nicci's thoughts guided the panther as she herself lay restless and half asleep in the grand villa. She was still disturbed by so many losses from the night before.

As they recovered throughout the day, the people of Ildakar tried to assess how much damage their attack had really inflicted on the enemy, but the mutilated bodies hurled by the catapults had caused great shock and dismay. The people struggled to find a sense of victory, but they couldn't help but count their own fallen, even though they couldn't identify the mangled corpses. Nicci didn't even know if Bannon's body was among them.

Through the sand panther, though, Nicci could now see the true damage General Utros had suffered. Many of the blazing fires were not bright campfires, as the Ildakarans assumed. Mrra smelled burning flesh, saw the piles of bodies, the charred skin and blackened bones falling into greasy embers. These were funeral pyres. Though the ancient warriors were hardened from the remnants of the stone spell, they still bled and they still died. Now the corpses burned, although it took a great deal of firewood.

In her partial dream state, Nicci guessed that the number of enemy dead was at least three to five times as many as Ildakar had lost, but even so it was not a cause for celebration.

Mrra moved like a shadow in the faint moonlight, circling the troops and funeral pyres, seeing the blasted trenches and the damage done. As she crept close to the general's headquarters, Nicci felt her senses heightened, all sounds and smells intensified tenfold. Mrra sniffed and discovered several large barrels that reeked of blood. Nicci didn't know why General Utros would store casks of blood, and Mrra didn't care. Blood did not frighten her.

Nicci memorized all the details as Mrra continued to move around the camp, observing even though the big cat didn't comprehend human warfare. But she had gleaned enough understanding through her association with her sister panther that she noticed something odd, familiar smells that didn't belong among the ancient army.

Though unable to approach closer due to the movement of ancient soldiers, Mrra spotted one wooden shack with no windows and a barred door. She heard stirring, low voices, smelled a different scent. Other humans were inside, not these dusty-smelling ones, but warm-blooded men. Captives, perhaps? Hostages that Utros would use as bargaining chips?

There was certainly no way to rescue them in the midst of the gigantic enemy camp.

Before she departed through the sliph the next morning, Nicci would report the news to the duma. Thanks to her feline spy, she had a great deal of new information to share.

CHAPTER 43

M any cities in the Old World had suffered under the Imperial Order, but the threat of General Utros's army was something entirely different from what they had experienced previously. Now that parts of his army were clearly on the move, Nicci had to spread the warning far and wide. She would travel to Tanimura, Serrimundi, Larrikan Shores, maybe all the way up to Aydindril or the People's Palace, if the sliph could take her that far. She would tell her story, sound the alarm, rally them in any way possible.

But she needed to have proof. They would not just accept her wild story.

The following morning, after Nicci had delivered her report to the duma of what Mrra had seen, and told them her plan to spread the alarm to other cities, Elsa joined her and Nathan outside the ruling tower. She wore clean purple robes, and she had pinned back her gray-shot hair.

The older woman smiled and nodded slowly. "I think I have just the proof you need, a way you can take the ancient army with you. You can show everyone how great a threat Utros is, and they won't be able to deny it." She held up a small pane of glass she had brought with her. "We can use transference magic."

With the sharp point of a dagger, Elsa scratched runes in each corner of the glass rectangle, then inspected her work. "I can transfer the image of what we see and capture it within the pane. The picture will live inside the glass."

While Nicci and Nathan watched, she lifted the rectangular glass and slowly turned it, holding it at arm's length and gazing through it to see the countless soldiers, the burned hills, the numerous tents, the immensity of the siege army. Then she touched the scratched rune in the lower left corner and handed the small pane to Nicci. "That should convince anyone who looks."

Nicci held the glass, amazed that it had captured the precise image of what they saw from the tower, an undeniable and frightening record of the great army gathered outside of Ildakar. "Yes, this will help a great deal." She wrapped the glass pane in a cloth. "Now I have to go to the sliph."

"And we are going along with you," Nathan said. "In case you need help."

Nicci flashed him a quick, skeptical glance but withheld her comment. As she walked purposefully down the steep streets with Nathan and Elsa following, she thought of the sliph. "Though I can travel great distances swiftly, I will not be able to bring any help back with me. Ildakar is still on its own."

Elsa took Nathan's arm. "We have been on our own for a very long time." She looked confident, even majestic as she walked along. "During so many centuries beneath the shroud, I did dream of the outside world. I read the histories of other cities, mining towns in the mountains, trade centers by the ocean. They seemed like magical places, and very few people in Ildakar remembered ever seeing them. If I'd known about the sliph and how easy it is to travel, maybe I would have explored." They descended through the merchants' district and into crowded residential levels where the lower classes lived. "But I suppose even the sliph couldn't pass through a bubble in time. Our shroud would have been impenetrable."

Nicci kept walking at a brisk pace. "That would not have been your primary problem. The sliph can only be used by someone with both sides of the gift, Additive and Subtractive Magic. Millennia ago, many wizards could access that magic, but now very few can use the Subtractive side."

"Then how are you going to use the sliph now?" Elsa asked.

"I was a Sister of the Dark, and I served the Keeper. I can use Subtractive Magic because of the terrible price I paid." She thought of the destruction she had caused, the people she had hurt, how she had tried to destroy Richard. Though she had forsaken that darkness, the scars were still within her, as was that poisonous strength. "I will be able to travel."

They reached the lowest levels of Ildakar, and Nicci went directly to the low stone building that held the hidden sliph well. The door was open and unguarded, but people avoided the place. Though some had peered inside, the eerie darkness and the chill kept them away.

Nicci ducked and entered the enclosure, igniting a ball of light to drive away the shadows. Elsa and Nathan followed close behind. The air inside smelled like stagnant water and mold, with an undertone of rot. Green moss grew on the stone floor, but otherwise the chamber was empty, no furniture, no ornaments, no symbols.

Nicci knew how to summon the sliph. She had used the strange method of transportation before, sometimes uneventfully, while other journeys had turned into ordeals. Now she saw no other way to spread her warning so widely and so quickly.

Her feet whispered along the smooth floor as she walked to the low circular well. With all the places the sliph could travel, she considered where to go, how she might best sound the alarm to other cities, whom she could rally. The people across the Old World would have to prepare their defenses, gather for war. As proof, she had Elsa's cloth-wrapped rectangle of glass, which she secured next to one of the daggers at her hip. But she didn't know if it would be enough.

Nicci looked into the bottomless well in front of her, a hollow blackness that exuded cold and utter silence. "Sliph! Sliph, I summon you. I wish to travel." When she sensed no response, she shouted louder. "Sliph, I command you to awaken! I wish to travel." She looked back over her shoulder at Nathan and Elsa. "I will need your help."

"Are you sure the creature is still alive?" Elsa asked.

"Oh, I'm certain she lives, although she may have gone dormant after so much time," Nathan said. "They are not natural beings. We must call her again."

"I traveled within the sliph not long ago," Nicci said. "It's how we got back to the People's Palace in time to fight Sulachan's hordes." Determined, she reached out with her gift, called with her mind and heart as well as with her voice. "Sliph, you know me. I need your services."

The sliph was a woman who had been altered by ancient wizards in preparation for their war. She remembered the original sliph, a former whore transformed into a magical creature who existed to carry travelers from destination to destination, deriving great pleasure from doing so.

But the other sliph that had rescued Nicci and her companions when they were trapped within the cliff city of Stroyza was an entirely different creature, one who remembered her name as Lucy. That sliph had been less passionate, less desperate to serve, and far less cooperative, but Richard had convinced her to whisk them all away.

Nicci didn't know which one dwelled here.

Nathan and Elsa stood beside her at the cold stones surrounding the well. "Reach out with your gift," Nicci urged. "Call to her. Ildakar is far from any other sliph well we know, and we need to make her remember this one."

She focused her thoughts, extending lines of magic like a

fisherman trolling in the water. She sent her thoughts into the infinite black well, while Nathan and Elsa concentrated hard, straining with everything they had. Nicci shouted in her mind at the same time she shouted aloud. "Sliph!"

Finally, a faint, gurgling echo came from far below, like water dripping down a very long pipe. Nicci sensed a churning sound that grew louder and closer, a waterfall charging straight toward them from the depths of the world.

Nathan and Elsa recoiled in alarm, and Nicci stepped back from the edge of the low wall, but stood straight as a turbulent froth of silver roiled up like a geyser about to explode. She didn't flinch as the quicksilver liquid boiled just to the edge of the well and stopped, perfectly smooth like a razor edge of ice. A shape formed in the mirrorlike surface, rising up until its features sharpened into the hard and beautiful form of a woman.

This sliph looked different from the original, eager one and the less compliant Lucy. This sliph had long locks of hair like molten metal, blank mirror eyes, thin lips that showed no hint of a smile. Her cheekbones were high and her face was wide. She would have been a beauty in life.

"You wish to travel," the sliph said, a statement rather than a question. Her voice sounded cold, impatient, certainly not solicitous. "It has been a long time, but I know no time."

"Yes, I wish to travel," Nicci said. "I have urgent business. I must go to some of the cities in the Old World to spread news of a war."

The sliph's expression grew more animated. "I exist to serve the cause. I was created to help deliver our faithful spies and saboteurs to fight the wizards of the New World. I am disappointed that the war isn't already won." She looked at Nathan and Elsa. "You all wish to travel? You all serve Sulachan?"

"Dear spirits," Nathan said. "I don't think—"

Nicci quickly held up her hand to silence him. "Is a war ever over? We must continue to fight. If you serve the cause, then you will help me travel." She shot a quick glance at the wizard, who understood the danger of revealing too much.

"I serve the cause. Once, Emperor Sulachan even traveled within me. I still have his taste as part of me." She turned those eerie silver eyes to Nicci. "How will you taste? You must be within me and I within you, then we will travel."

Troubled, Nathan lowered his voice. "Sorceress, maybe we should reconsider."

"I need to present our report, and quickly." She faced the sliph. "It is vital that I deliver my intelligence. Others are waiting. The cause may depend upon my report."

"I sacrificed everything for the cause," the sliph said. "We will travel. Where do you wish to go?"

Now Nicci was at a loss, because sliphs could go only where they had been before, where a counterpart well existed. After so many centuries, she suspected the names of many cities had changed, so how would the sliph know? Getting her warning to Richard was Nicci's priority, though. "Do you know the People's Palace near the Azrith Plain? Or perhaps Aydindril?"

"I do not know the People's Palace, but Aydindril?" the sliph asked. "The Wizard's Keep? You wish to go into enemy territory? It is too dangerous. I was never allowed to go anywhere in the New World. I was only required to go where our spies and operatives have business."

"Where is the last place you went?" Nathan asked. "Perhaps we know that."

"Tanimura was the farthest boundary, although I delivered many faithful fighters to Serrimundi, Larrikan Shores, Orogang."

Nicci quickly formed her plans. "Tanimura is acceptable." She knew that city from her time at the Palace of the Prophets, and she would find a way to dispatch a message from there to Richard's capital.

"Then come, I will deliver you," said the sliph. "The mission must not wait. You will help us achieve victory against the enemy wizards of the New World."

Nicci didn't respond, deciding not to tell this sliph that millennia had passed, that the ancient wizard wars were long over, and that Sulachan had been defeated, not once, but twice.

"Be careful, Sorceress," Nathan warned.

She turned to him and Elsa. "I won't be gone long. Meanwhile, keep looking for ways to defend the city." She flashed a hard smile. "I'd be very displeased if I returned from Tanimura only to find Ildakar destroyed." Nathan chuckled weakly. Nicci faced the sliph. "I'm ready. We must travel."

"You will breathe." The sliph loomed higher, rising up like a molten sculpture. "Breathe in me and come with me."

The silvery figure enfolded Nicci in a wave of cold liquid metal. The froth boiled all around her, engulfing her, and Nicci fell forward into the well. The sliph embraced her, pressed harder. In her mind, Nicci heard the command. *"Breathe!"*

She inhaled the silvery essence of the strange being, felt the sliph fill her mouth, her throat, her nose, her lungs. Her heart kept beating, but she was drowning.

The sliph carried her down and down and far away.

CHAPTER 44

After Nicci was swallowed by the silvery sliph and pulled down into the well, Nathan stared uneasily into the darkness, smelling the metallic dampness in the air. He glanced at Elsa, who was amazed at what had happened.

"Perhaps it's a good thing I am unable to travel in that manner," she said.

Nathan turned back toward the daylight outside, confident in Nicci's abilities. "I'm sure she will be safe, my dear. But while Nicci is off to save the rest of the world, we have the far simpler task of protecting only one city."

Elsa's full lips turned down in a frown. "I never know when you're joking, Nathan."

"I insist on looking at difficult challenges from a certain perspective. It helps me consider extraordinary solutions, and it's preferable to wallowing in despair, don't you agree?"

Elsa gave him a wan smile as she followed him out of the enclosure. "My Derek was always a cheerful person, too. It was infectious."

"Then let me infect you." He extended his elbow, and Elsa slid her arm through his. He could see how beautiful she must have been as a young woman. He corrected himself: she was still beautiful now, as well as admirable and intelligent. "Now let us find a weapon powerful enough to destroy the army of General Utros."

Elsa brushed against him. "That sounds awfully ambitious."

"Since you helped me restore my gift, how can I be anything but ambitious?" Nathan suddenly winced with a flicker of unexpected pain as his thumping heart tripped over a beat. He rubbed his breastbone, feeling the long thin scar there.

Elsa looked at him with concern. "Is something wrong?"

"Just a bit of indigestion." He wondered if a faint remnant of Chief Handler Ivan remained within the muscle of his new heart. Before she could press further, he said, "Come along. I have an idea I'd like to show you."

Elsa would undoubtedly be alarmed by what he intended, and his suggestion was extremely dangerous, but he thought his idea was their best chance to hit General Utros hard.

They passed the huge combat arena and the larger noble homes, heading toward Fleshmancer Andre's mansion. Giant sandstone blocks lay strewn about the streets where city buildings had been brought down. Workers had cleared some of the rubble since the night of the rampant destruction, but debris still clogged a few streets. Stonemasons loaded the broken rock in carts and wheeled them down to the outer wall, where the sentries used them as missiles to pelt the enemy warriors below.

Elsa paled as she realized where he was taking her. "This is a terrible reminder of what happened that night. And how you saved me."

Nathan patted her arm. "Saving you from that gigantic Ixax was exactly the right incentive for me to find my gift again." He led her up the street. "Just keep an open mind."

She held his arm more tightly. "For you, I will."

He took her through the piles of rubble, collapsed columns, and fallen walls of the fleshmancer's studio. She looked around in concern. "Do you expect to find some of Andre's chemicals or writings still intact? How can they possibly be helpful to us now?"

"Not his writings or chemicals." Smashed stones rattled underfoot as they worked their way through the collapsed entryway toward the rear wing. "I believe these two may save Ildakar after all."

He stopped in front of the Ixax warriors.

Elsa's eyes went wide, and she withdrew her arm from his. "You saw what one of them did to our city! That thing almost killed both of us."

"Almost, Elsa. Remember that word—'almost.'" He looked up at the towering brutes that had once been human. From what Andre had told him, those starry-eyed young men hadn't been coerced to become the Ixax warriors. They had volunteered themselves, offering everything to save Ildakar.

Elsa appeared nervous as she stared at the colossal warriors. "But the fury they contain," she whispered, gesturing toward the rubble all around. "When Mirrormask awakened only one of them, it killed our most powerful fleshmancer and brought down this entire villa, wrought havoc in the streets of Ildakar, tried to kill both of us."

Nathan turned to look at the pair of motionless warriors. "Remember what Andre did to those poor creatures. He held them frozen here in maddening boredom for centuries upon centuries. He taunted them, drove them to murderous rage. But they still know why they were created. I believe they still have Ildakar in their hearts." He lowered his voice. "We just need to help them remember."

With her expression of consternation, Elsa reminded him of Prelate Ann, with whom he had spent so much time after the two of them had escaped from the Palace of the Prophets. He had at first resented Ann because she was responsible for holding him prisoner all those centuries. She had been his nemesis, but he'd gradually come to respect her, even love her.

He knew that Elsa was special from the start, though. Among all the gifted duma members, she had been the most compassionate, the most understanding of his plight, and she had helped him get his gift back.

Elsa made him remember how he had fallen in love with Ann, who was killed by Sisters of the Dark in service of Jagang. Before that, he'd been smitten with young Clarissa, another romance that ended tragically. Love had left Nathan with many scars, and by now he should have been embittered by the capriciousness and pain associated with it. But that was the thing about love. It was always accompanied by hope and the confidence that next time would turn out right.

"I have been coming here for days, just talking to them, reading to them, keeping them company. They are quite an attentive audience."

Nathan took a few steps closer to the titans. He raised his voice and spoke directly to them. "I've come to tell you more stories from history, and some of my own exploits. I'm sure you are not familiar with the Imperial Order and the Emperor Jagang. Let me tell you what the world has been doing since Ildakar vanished beneath the shroud."

Speaking in a raised voice, he explained about the evil dream walker who tormented and controlled people through their nightmares. "Jagang was a brutish man who enslaved the Sisters of the Dark, including Nicci herself." He smiled. "Ah, let me tell you about Nicci. So many stories, we could talk for hours." Nathan stroked his chin and glanced at Elsa. "In fact, I think I will. You'll find it a welcome diversion."

He sat on a toppled column. "Afterward, I'll need to tell you about Richard Rahl, his D'Haran Empire, and how he defeated not only Darken Rahl, but Jagang as well. He even sealed the veil to the underworld and ended prophecy for all time." He chuckled. "I wish dear Richard were here now. He would certainly help save Ildakar."

Nathan studied the glowing yellow eyes of the armored

warriors. "You both were created to do just that, to save Ildakar." Had the hatred begun to dull? He seemed to have their attention. "I know how terrible it has been for you to be trapped like this, unable to serve your purpose, but the time may soon come, I promise."

Elsa blurted out, joining the conversation as she primly took a seat beside Nathan, "I am Elsa, one of the duma members. I just . . ." She shook her head. "I want to say I am sorry for what Andre did to you." She gestured with her open hand toward their towering forms. "I honor your sacrifice. I am proud of you, and I deeply apologize in the name of Ildakar. Andre is dead now. Please don't hold it against all of us."

The colossal figures remained unable to move, unable to speak. Nathan continued in a congenial voice. "There's so much more to tell, and I can keep coming back to entertain and enlighten you. Just before I traveled to the Old World, our most recent war was against the resurrected Emperor Sulachan. You might have heard of him, because he used Ildakar as one of his bases during the wizard wars three thousand years ago. He led a huge army of half people from the Dark Lands. They surged out of the Third Kingdom to destroy D'Hara."

He mused, his eyes twinkling. "I wish we could have turned you two loose to fight on that battlefield. You'd have smashed thousands of the undead. Just look at you!" Nathan was sure the blazing light in their eyes was softening. Soon, he might consider them ready to be unleashed.

CHAPTER 45

From inside the dusty shack where he, Jed, and Brock were held, Bannon listened to the distant pounding on the walls of Ildakar. He didn't know how much damage the ancient warriors were causing, but the monotonous drumbeat would set the city on edge. Imprisoned here, Bannon had more important things to worry about.

"How soon do you think they'll kill us?" Jed asked. "I expected they would torture us by now."

"Are you in a hurry? Keeper's crotch!" Brock huddled against the rickety wooden wall.

"I don't think it will be quick," Jed groaned. "They want to make a spectacle of us. They'll probably cut us to pieces in front of the city gates where everyone can watch."

Brock knotted his fingers together. "My father had no business forcing me to fight like a common foot soldier. I'm a noble!"

"You are a captive," Bannon corrected him, "and your time would be better served if you considered ways to escape instead of how painful it'll be when you die."

"Escape?" Brock squawked.

Bannon shushed him for his outburst. "Be quiet! The soldiers out there will hear you."

The young man didn't lower his voice at all. "Yes, thousands of soldiers! Who cares if they hear us? How are we supposed to fight our way through them?"

"Think of some way to break free that does not involve fighting." Pressing his face against the wall, Bannon peered through the crack in the boards. It was late afternoon and the sun had already set behind the mountains. Long shadows crept across the plain. "Wouldn't you rather die trying to escape than be murdered as a showpiece? Remember how you wanted me to die in front of an audience, for your entertainment?" Bitterness edged his voice. "I'm done with that."

He turned away from the wall and looked at the other two young men. "I was never your slave, yet you and Amos arranged for me to be sent to the combat pits. I am free now." He pounded on the wooden wall, and the boards rattled. "Even here, I'm free. And if you want to be free, you'd better start thinking about how we can get out of here."

He knew that Jed and Brock would be useless. It was going to be up to him.

He expected Utros to use them as hostages, hauling the three in front of the gates and threatening to execute them unless the city surrendered. Even though Jed and Brock were the sons of powerful nobles, he knew they weren't that important. And Bannon didn't believe for a minute that Nicci, or even Nathan, would sacrifice Ildakar to save him.

"We've got to get out of here," he muttered to himself. Jed and Brock still weren't his friends, and he knew who they really were in their hearts, but Bannon was better than that. The two young men were human beings and fellow captives, and they were all in the same dire situation. He would at least try to help.

He pressed his eye against the crack, trying to see details in the shadows as twilight fell over the camp. Fires were lit, comrades gathered together. Like soldiers in every army far from home, they talked and boasted with one another. Some sang, while others gambled. Because of their invincible numbers, the warriors wouldn't be overly worried about their prisoners. Only a fool would attempt to escape.

Bannon had no choice but to do the foolish thing, though. What other option did he have? He stared through the crack in the shack's wall and pondered, struggling to find ideas. His heart leaped as he saw a flash of tawny fur just barely flickering into his view, far from the fires. He spotted the movement again. Yes, it was Mrra!

Two of the ancient warriors walked past, blocking Bannon's view. The sand panther ducked into the darkness, and when the chalky-gray soldiers were gone, Bannon couldn't see her anymore. He whispered through the crack. "Mrra! I'm here! It's me."

He didn't know what the big cat could do to help, but knowing she was out there gave him hope. He rattled the wall boards, testing them. This confinement structure had been built quickly with makeshift tools and rough-sawn lumber. The boards had been sunk into the ground, but they were loose. Bannon pushed on them and managed to get his fingers through the crack. Splinters dug into his knuckles when he pulled.

Neither Jed nor Brock bothered to help him. "They'll probably interrogate us before they kill us," Jed said. "General Utros will want to know all details about Ildakar."

"I'm not going to tell him anything," Brock said.

Bannon kept working at the boards, wiggling the gap wider.

"Yes, you will, and you know it," Jed said. "Once they shatter your knees and peel off your nails with tongs, you'll talk. You saw those two sorceresses. What if they ignite your fingers like candles, one at a time, until your flesh drips like wax off your finger bones, down to the knuckle?"

Brock began to whimper.

Gritting his teeth, Bannon wobbled the board back and forth. He would have demanded their help, but there wasn't room for more than one set of hands anyway. He had to do this himself. When the wood creaked, grinding against the adjacent board, Bannon froze at the noise. The gap was wider now, and he could see better out into the camp.

None of the soldiers paid attention to them. The nearest campfire was at least sixty feet away, and Bannon saw shadows beyond. That was where Mrra had vanished. Maybe if he and the other two captives could get out of the shack unseen, they could slip away into the darkness. He had noticed that the ancient soldiers had difficulty seeing in the darkness, so maybe they had a better chance than he had at first thought. How he wished he had his sword!

Even the slimmest chance was better than no chance at all. As he wiggled the board, it squeaked again, much looser now. The camp was settling down for the night, and the moon rose over the hills. He saw the silvery light as a disadvantage, washing away some of their cover.

The squeaky board moved more freely now. With a hard shove he could knock it loose and probably fit his body through the gap, when the time was right. Bannon nodded to himself. "We'll wait until midnight, and then we run."

"We'll be caught," Jed said. "And killed."

"Or you can stay here and be killed. I'm trying to help you! Sweet Sea Mother, have you never had to do anything for yourselves in your entire lives?"

The two indignant young men didn't answer.

The hours crawled by as he listened to the movement in the camp, the activity slowing. The soldiers did not bed down, because unlike normal men, they didn't need to sleep or eat. He wondered if they ever let down their guard. He had to hope so.

Gradually, much later, the night grew quieter. He kept staring into the darkness, searching for Mrra, just to build his confidence. He got ready to make his move one way or another.

He was surprised to see a flicker of gray and black, a shadow that moved and rippled. He realized it was a human figure, a woman covered in a mottled silk cloak the color of shifting shadows. As the figure trotted on light footsteps toward the shack, Bannon pressed the loose board sideways, widening the gap. She approached, using the painted shadows of her silk cloak for cover. Reaching the wall, the cloaked figure pulled back the camouflage.

"Lila!" he gasped in a whisper.

She held a short sword in her left hand and a full-length sword in her right. It was Sturdy! She had retrieved it somehow. "Come, boy. I'll get you out of here."

He wiggled the board and uprooted it like a rotten tooth. He called over his shoulder to the other two, "Come on, we've got to go now."

"You are insane, farm boy," said Jed.

Brock lunged to his feet. "I'm going to run."

Lila helped pull the board away and set it aside. Bannon thrust his shoulder into the opening, scraping his chest as he wriggled through the narrow gap. She grabbed his arm, and as he emerged, she handed him the sword. "I found this in the debris outside the camp. I thought you might want it back."

He gripped the leather-wrapped hilt with a shiver of excitement. "Thank you."

Brock worked his way through the gap, making the boards groan with his stockier chest. At his side, Jed pulled on the board, and with a loud snap the wood split, creating a greater opening. The sound, though, attracted attention.

"Now!" Lila whispered, tugging Bannon's arm. "We have to go."

Jed stumbled after Brock, and they were all outside the shack. The morazeth was already sprinting away, and Bannon followed her, calling to his companions, "Faster!" He could barely see the flickers of Lila beneath her special shadowy cloak. The other two ran after, heaving great breaths.

Then shouts resounded through the ancient army. "Prisoners escaping!" Soldiers ran to the fires, grabbed their weapons and firebrands. Their heavy footfalls thundered louder than their shouts. Three enemy warriors came in from different directions to cut off the escape.

Lila sprang forward with a hard kick, planting her foot in the center of one soldier's chest, knocking him back. More shouts erupted in the night. Torches came closer as warriors hurried to intercept the captives.

Jed and Brock saw the oncoming soldiers and panicked. "They'll catch us again," Brock said. "Split up! We've got to get away."

"No, we can all fight together," Bannon shouted. "Follow Lila."

The other two tore off in different directions, dodging the soldiers. Bannon kept up with the morazeth, ready with Sturdy to do as much damage as possible. The sword's edge was dulled and notched from his fighting during the nighttime battle. He couldn't remember his blood frenzy, but knew he must have killed dozens of Utros's soldiers. He would have to do that again tonight.

Hardened warriors closed in from opposite directions, and Bannon's heart sank. Lila threw off her cloak for greater freedom of movement. "At my side, Bannon. Show me how I taught you to fight."

"But Jed and Brock . . ." he said.

"They're lost. For now this is my fight and yours."

Two soldiers blocked Lila, and more came from other directions. He and the morazeth would have to battle their way through, but Bannon feared he would be captured again, and this time they'd have Lila, too.

A feline blur crashed into the soldiers from the side, knocking two of them flat. Mrra raked her claws across the face of an ancient warrior, tearing the man's jaw loose, then sprang away from him to attack another soldier.

Lila took advantage of the surprise and pounced on the next fighter, stabbing and hacking with such force that she killed him.

Bannon saw his chance, too, and chopped down on the hard armor and stony skin of a fourth opponent. Their unexpected fury cleared a gap.

"Run, boy!" Lila sprang between the fallen soldiers as Mrra continued to attack. The morazeth raced into the shadows toward the charred hills, and Bannon fled after her, burning all the energy he had left, running for his very life. Mrra knocked down another pursuing soldier and crushed his throat in her jaws. Bannon and Lila ran without looking back, although the young man could think only of Jed and Brock still trapped. Maybe they had gotten away. Maybe . . .

Lila's voice was rough and raw. "To the wall. There's a low side door we can use to get back in."

Bannon didn't waste breath answering her, just kept up.

Because they were fleet and the half-petrified army was sluggish, they put distance between themselves and the rallying enemy forces. When they were safe, Mrra bounded off on her own, heading into the hills, where she could hide. When Lila slowed her frantic pace to a trot, she flashed Bannon a smile. "I am pleased to see that you survived, boy. It would have been a disappointment to me if you had been killed."

"To me as well." Bannon felt a rush of relief as they ran toward the high walls under the moonlight. He didn't even criticize her for not using his name.

After the clamor died down, General Utros learned that one of the three prisoners had escaped, although the other two—the weak ones—were recaptured. He was disappointed to lose the young swordsman who had so impressed him with his fighting abilities.

First Commander Enoch reported, "They had assistance, General. Someone slipped in and helped them break free."

"And there was a sand panther," reported another soldier. His armor had been mangled, and one gray-white arm showed raked furrows from where the claws had injured him. "One of the combat animals from the Ildakar arenas."

Utros was not impressed. "And we had hundreds of thousands of soldiers, who somehow couldn't stop them."

He ordered the two prisoners to be brought forward among the ranks. The young men, both bloodied, were dragged closer, weeping. Their wrists had been broken, intentionally, and they moaned in pain. Their bloodstained silken robes were tattered, and both reeked of urine from soaked patches on their pantaloons. Helpless, they looked at their broken wrists, lifting up their arms in disbelief to see their hands flop uselessly.

"We surrendered," said Brock. "We won't try to get away again."

"The problem is, you are worthless to me," Utros said, "and we have no food for captives."

The two young men stood shivering as Utros paced before them. "But you can serve another purpose. You can pay for the damage you did, the malicious harm you inflicted upon my army when we were helpless."

The captives looked up in pain-fogged confusion.

Utros said, "You were so brave when we could not move to defend ourselves or see who was attacking us. Do you even think about the horrors you have done? Do you understand the conditions in which you left some of my loyal soldiers? What you did was . . . evil."

Utros issued a command, and shuffling figures were led forward, some of them guided by soldiers, others carried on blankets. The two captives, swimming in a sea of their own pain, looked up in horror as the mutilated ones came to face them. One man's face was a slab of pounded meat, without a nose or eyes, just ripped skin and a smashed mouth. Others had limbs broken off completely, ears torn away, fingers snapped off to leave only chalky, meaty stumps. Several had no faces at all, and they made wet sucking sounds when they inhaled through holes in the battered ruins of their heads.

"No!" cried Jed.

"Behold what you did. These are the mangled ones, but they are my soldiers. They still want to fight the enemy." He glanced from one whimpering captive to the other. The second boy pissed himself again. "You are both helpless now, just as they were helpless. You mutilated them when they could not fight back. Now, I will give them the same opportunity." Utros turned to the mangled soldiers. "You can have them."

The intact warriors stood in a great circle, crowding closer to watch while the two young men wept and wailed for mercy.

The mangled ones closed in on them and practiced mutilation of their own.

CHAPTER 46

Though the siege of Ildakar would continue for some time, Utros could think only about his beloved Majel, who was separated from him by time and death itself. He also needed guidance from his emperor, for whom he had sworn to conquer the known world. Did his orders even still exist?

The two sorceresses had given him a new chance, and they were ready.

Utros clung with childlike hope to the possibility that he might speak with both Kurgan and Majel again. His loyalty and passion were at odds as much as two warring armies, but in his rational mind, he compartmentalized those conflicting desires before they could drive him insane.

After the damage from Ildakar's unexpected attack had been mitigated, he commanded Ava and Ruva to begin. The twins admired the barrels filled with the blood of innocent children from Stravera. They caressed the staves, pressed down on the intact lids, sensed the red liquid inside and the power it represented.

"We have enough, beloved Utros," Ruva said.

Ava added, "But we need the other raw materials to forge the lens, ash and sand to make the glass."

"You shall have everything." Utros summoned First Commander Enoch. Manpower was the one thing he did not lack.

In the initial part of the siege, his soldiers had dug great trenches, diverted and dammed the wide streams that rolled across the open plain to feed the aqueducts of Ildakar, although the city could still draw water from the river below. Now, what he needed was not water, but sand from the stream banks. His men brought wagonload after wagonload of sand, while the sorceresses cleared a working area near the headquarters structure.

They collected iron taken from Stravera, as well as rusted scraps of armor and thick old chains recovered from the ancient battlefield. Ava and Ruva used their magic to heat and shape the metal, forging an enormous basin seven feet across, which they lined with insulating clay, thus creating a huge glassmaking crucible. They filled the crucible with clean sand from the streambeds, while another contingent of soldiers filled a cart with bitter-smelling ash from the burned grasses, as well as coals from the countless campfires.

Once the ash was mixed with the sand, Ava and Ruva joined hands and used their gift to create a constant flow of heat until the material softened, flowed, and melted. The women took turns stirring their molten mixture for hours.

Utros watched impatiently, smelling the acrid tang, studying the silver-white pool of hot glass. "I can sense the power there," he said.

Ava flashed him a thin smile. The paint covering her cheeks and shoulders had begun to flake with the sweat of her effort. "This is merely glass. We haven't yet made it special."

For half a day, the glass mixture heated, became smoother, purer, until it was ready. Ruva glanced at the barrels filled with innocent blood and responded with a broad smile.

Utros watched but offered no advice, asked no questions. His sorceresses knew what they were doing. Soldiers carried the stained barrels to the crucible, where heat waves shimmered in the air. Their half-petrified skin was able to withstand the searing temperature.

The sisters went to the barrels, caressed the lids. "We'll need it all, just to be sure." When they cracked open the barrels, Utros smelled the change in the air, a sour and portentous coppery tang.

Ava and Ruva watched with delight as burly soldiers lifted the barrels to the edge of the crucible with its roiling molten glass. The sorceresses muttered spells, called upon their gift, shifted the material structure of the mixture. At a signal, the soldiers tilted the kegs and poured the dark red liquid into the lake of glass. The screech of evaporating burned blood sounded like the wails of countless slain children. The red stain swirled in the molten slurry as Ava and Ruva used their gift to churn it like a thick stew of dark magic.

When it was done, both women let out a long sigh of relief. "The mixture is complete," Ruva said. "The glass and blood can now become the lens. The innocent spirits have left their mark, and when the lens is finished, the invisible traces of their former lives will let you see through the veil."

In the back of his mind Utros heard a hint of Majel's voice, her laughter, whispered endearments she spoke to him after they had enjoyed each other. "How soon will it be ready?"

"Several steps remain," Ava said. "We still have to pour and set the glass."

In the dirt outside the command structure, they had fashioned a shallow crater six feet across. Releasing a trickle of power through the palms of their hands, they had fused the dirt and clay into a hard impenetrable mold. Now, the sisters broke open the drain in the giant crucible and guided the viscous blood-tinted fluid out, letting it pour into the hardened crater until it became a pool of solidifying glass.

Utros stood beside the two sorceresses, admiring the molten glass. The substance shimmered as it wrestled with its heat and its new shape.

"Even with our magic, it will take a day to cool, beloved Utros. Then we can perfect its surface, raise up the lens, and activate the final spell."

Utros sighed and pushed back his anticipation. "I've waited fifteen centuries already, but one more day will seem like an eternity."

The sorceresses stroked the general's arms, pressing their cold, hard flesh against his. "We will help you through it," Ruva said.

"Soon," Ava whispered. "Soon, you will see through the veil."

The next sunset, the clouds over the mountains grew crimson, as if the blood of children had been added to the sky, too. Utros watched, restless, his heart torn. He was ready to face the spirit of his emperor, ready to see his beloved Majel again.

A normal lens of such size would have taken weeks to cool gradually, insulated and controlled so as to leave no flaws in the glass, but Ava and Ruva guided the process themselves, using their gift to stroke the internal crystalline structure, to calm it as it hardened and stabilized. When they declared the blank lens ready, they knelt over the solidified pond of glass and used their hands to smooth and shape the outer surface. They fashioned the precise curve they had seen in their minds when they designed it.

When the process was complete, thirty of the general's strongest soldiers attached ropes, used cloth-wrapped bars, and levered the hardened glass out of the crater mold, pulling it upright while the sorceresses formed a frame to hold the lens like a mirror, six feet high. The women went to opposite sides of the glass blank and worked with their hands, scrubbing, shaping, smoothing, making the lens transparent.

Utros was fascinated by every detail, but his thoughts were preoccupied with what he would say. As part of his long-standing

346

orders from Iron Fang, he had continued the siege on Ildakar, and he had no doubt the city would fall eventually, but his mission for his emperor extended beyond Ildakar. He had promised to conquer the entire world, and he wouldn't need all his thousands of warriors to maintain the siege here. He had already sent many armies out on important expeditions.

From his main palace in Orogang, Emperor Kurgan had wanted to rule the Old World. It was a fractured continent for the taking, and Utros had taken it. He had been shocked, but not surprised, when the emissary Nathan Rahl explained that the empire had swiftly fallen apart after Kurgan's death. The conquered territories required firm military control, but Utros did not dream of administering an entire continent. His orders were to conquer, not rule.

While his awakened army continued the siege, he made plans to recapture the lands that had once fallen under his military fist. Some of his dispatched armies would make their way to the coast, some would travel south, others would head into the hills and mountains to the north, or along the Killraven River. They would head as far as they could march, seizing territory in the near-forgotten name of Emperor Kurgan.

As soon as he spoke to his emperor's spirit, he would report great progress, even after fifteen centuries. If Kurgan could issue orders through the lens and continue to rule from the underworld, his empire could endure for eternity, and Utros could feel great satisfaction for having done his duty more thoroughly than any man in history.

But he felt a chill in his heart. Majel's spirit was also there beyond the veil. Nathan and Nicci had told him that Iron Fang was aware of his wife's betrayal with his own general. Did revenge survive fifteen centuries in the underworld? For a spirit, did time pass at all?

Utros stood before the blood-tinted lens. He was a brave and determined man, as history had shown countless times, but this might be his most unnerving encounter.

"Activate it now!" he demanded of Ava and Ruva. "I must see them."

"We need to stay so we can use our gift and make the connection through the veil," said Ruva, glancing at the uneasy spectators. "But these others . . ."

Ava looked at the nearby soldiers, who were troubled and frightened by the blood-tinted lens. "Yes, Utros. Perhaps privacy is best."

He turned to First Commander Enoch. "Send all troops away, clear the area. I will have a private conversation with my emperor."

"Understood, General." Enoch barked orders, drove off the soldiers, and then retreated as well, while Utros stepped up to the looming glass disk. He could show no fear or hesitation, not to his emperor, not to his soldiers. At least now, no one could overhear his words.

As the sunset sank into deep twilight, the sorceresses went to opposite sides of the lens. The glass gleamed like a moonstone, translucent, showing only shadows in its interior. Whispering to each other now that they stood alone with the lens, Ava and Ruva reached up to touch the round rim. They sketched designs with their fingertips, dipping into the softened crystal and drawing spell-forms that glowed with orange heat. The designs continued to shimmer as the twins made successive marks, indicating anchor points around the rim.

Ava reached upward and clockwise, while Ruva drew downward and in the opposite direction. They completed ten runes, and each woman finished her last mark at the same time. The runes continued to blaze as the sorceresses stepped back.

Warmth and energy rippled through the glass, making the lens transparent, and then intensely clear, to show images not of the opposite side, but magnified through the veil, swirled with hints of a greenish mist.

Utros stepped even closer until his face was only inches from the curved surface. He peered into the blood-soaked glass and saw shapes there, spirits, shadows, the echoes of countless people, millions of slain, millions who had died of old age, countless men and women who had lived since the dawn of time. The Keeper had so many in his possession, so many. . . .

Utros longed to find the ones he needed. Moisture formed in his eyes, but he didn't want to admit they were tears. "Majel," he called, glad that no one else could hear him. "Where are you? I didn't leave you. I still want you. We need to speak." He would find Majel first, and afterward he could make his formal report to Iron Fang. His heart demanded satisfaction before his mind did. "Majel, where are you?"

The spirits seemed to hear him through the lens. Shapes were distant and infinite, but they responded and found the one he sought.

Ava and Ruva stood back, barely breathing, but Utros could pay attention only to the curved glass in front of him. As a figure came forward, he recognized the way she moved. He knew her instantly, because he had given her his heart.

"Majel . . ." He remembered her beauty, her shining eyes, the softness of her skin.

As she approached the lens, the greenish mists cleared. "Utros, is it you?" He knew the voice.

But when her image sharpened, Utros could only stare, feeling his heart break.

Majel's face had been stripped away. Moving the raw red muscles of her jaw and her exposed, smashed teeth, she said, "I am here, my love."

CHAPTER 47

After an endless but brief journey immersed in the silvery froth of the sliph, Nicci emerged from a well nearly identical to the one in Ildakar. She couldn't see through the quicksilver behind her eyes, inside her mouth and lungs.

"*Breathe!*" the sliph commanded. "*Breathe now!*"

Nicci choked, coughed. She had been engulfed in that otherworldly presence, soaring along, but now that they had arrived at their destination, the sliph ejected her. Nicci tumbled over the low wall around the well.

She dropped to her knees and sucked in lungfuls of air, tried to assemble details, remembering where she expected to be. Tanimura! Dry branches, weeds, and twigs snapped under her knees and palms as she moved forward, then climbed back to her feet.

She saw an overcast night sky above, crisscrossed with forest branches. She heard the whispering sounds of night insects, the cry of a hunting bird, but she saw no sign of any city. "Where?" she coughed out, and turned to see the form of the hard-featured silver woman rising above the mirrored pool.

"Tanimura. As you commanded."

Nicci looked around. "This is a forest."

"The forest is outside of Tanimura. Because of our hidden plans in the war, we could not put the sliph well in the middle of the city where others might find it." The sliph looked at Nicci as if she were slow-witted. "You can walk to your rendezvous from here."

Nicci slowly recognized the Hagen Woods, a wilderness on the outskirts of Tanimura. "At least the well wasn't inside the Palace of the Prophets," she said. "It has been destroyed."

"Destroyed?" said the sliph, sounding surprised. "As part of a battle? Is it a great victory for our cause?"

"The palace was destroyed in a battle," Nicci answered cautiously, not wanting to give information that the sliph didn't need to know. "I have my mission. I will call you when I am ready to return."

The sliph's features showed nothing but determination. "I will be here. We must achieve victory against the evil wizards of the New World."

The strange creature settled back into her metallic pool like a candle melting in a puddle of wax. Nicci heard a rushing sound as the silver froth retreated into the depths.

The Hagen Woods . . . it made sense to her now. For centuries this dark forest had been a sinister place, supposedly haunted and dangerous. The gifted young men trained by the Sisters were warned never to go there, but Nicci and the Sisters of the Dark had performed numerous rituals in the woods. With a chill, Nicci remembered when she herself had been brought into the forest as a young convert, surrounded by grim Sisters who indoctrinated her into the service of the Keeper. The initiation had been horrific and painful. The other Sisters had watched with acid enjoyment as they tied Nicci down and summoned the Keeper's monstrous servant. She'd been forced to submit to the brutal caresses of the warty-skinned being who took her and took her again, as she writhed in pain, unable to fight. Nicci had wept but clenched her teeth, trying not to scream. It hadn't been rape because she had requested it. She surrendered her body and soul, and it had changed her forever.

Now she shuddered. No wonder the sliph well had remained hidden in the Hagen Woods for all this time. Few people explored here, and those who did seldom returned. Nicci wondered how long the rumors and warnings had existed about the dark forest. Maybe this had been part of Sulachan's insidious cause, too, a bastion of rumors spread to keep the woods empty so the sliph could transport spies whenever she wished.

After marking the location of the well so she could find it again, Nicci worked her way through the shadowy forest, finally coming upon a clearing from which she could see the delta of the Kern River and the lights of Tanimura. She knew where to go.

With the cloth-wrapped glass secured against her side, Nicci walked in her black dress through the underbrush. She made her way down to the city's outer districts by dawn. She had walked these streets for many years on business for the Palace of the Prophets.

In the port where sailing ships docked and unloaded their exotic cargo, she had served the Sisters for decades, arranging for supplies, negotiating with craftsmen, buying fabrics, commissioning garments to be made by seamstresses. Nicci remembered that Sister Hilda had been fond of preserved kraken meat, and she had often been dispatched to buy a crate of the fresh catch when the stinking, oily ships came in. No one but Sister Hilda could tolerate the rubbery meat that befouled the air of the palace kitchens whenever the chefs attempted to cook it. Hilda offered to share her delicacy, but none of the Sisters accepted her offer.

Nicci had also gone on dark missions for the Keeper, helping recruit for the Sisters of the Dark, assassinating victims identified by the Keeper, although she was never allowed to know why such people needed to die. Nicci didn't ask, suspecting it might just be a test to prove her unquestioning loyalty.

She walked into the streets of Tanimura as the sun rose and craftsmen emerged sleepy-eyed, building fires in their forges, filling cooling buckets from public wells. Tanners began scraping skins stretched on racks, potters added water to soft clay or brushed glaze on unfired pots they had fashioned the previous day and let dry overnight.

Barking dogs chased chickens into alleys. Children walked with their mothers, carrying dough for community ovens where the women would bake the day's bread and carry it home in baskets. Nicci walked among them, calling no attention to herself. She remembered Tanimura as a thriving place with markets, crowded dwellings, inns and brothels, glassblowers and leatherworkers. She wasn't a customer, though. She needed to find the D'Haran garrison.

Richard had begun to consolidate the new reaches of his empire. The first soldiers had come down to Tanimura by the time she and Nathan arrived here on their travels. Now she hoped the military had a significant presence in Tanimura so she could deliver her report about Utros's huge army.

Pausing at the stall of a man who made jaunty hats, she asked, "Where can I find the garrison? Surely there is a commander here."

"Of course!" the hatmaker said. "My, but they are excellent customers. Soldiers off duty love a fine hat for when they flirt with the ladies. My partner in the next block makes felt jackets and fur-lined cloaks. He and I are the ones who make the D'Haran army look so dashing."

"I don't care whether they are dashing," Nicci said. "They need to be warned. Where can I find them?"

The man straightened his hats on display, running his fingers along a dyed feather. "General Linden is in charge of the garrison, since General Zimmer and Prelate Verna took a large expeditionary force to the south."

"Verna?" Nicci asked, remembering Verna from the Palace of the Prophets. She was the one who had finally brought

Richard in so he could begin his training. "With the Palace of the Prophets ruined and prophecy itself eliminated, I'm surprised there are any Sisters who need a prelate at all."

"Oh, there are still Sisters, my lady, I don't know what the world would come to if there were no Sisters of the Light! Who would hold the Keeper at bay, I ask you?" He chuckled nervously.

"Who indeed?" Nicci asked, then added in a firm voice, "Tell me how to find the garrison."

It was midmorning by the time she worked her way around the bustling harbor, through market squares, to the district where the D'Haran garrison was. Because she had spent so much time in the city, some of the townspeople actually knew Nicci. Her dress was distinctive because she had always worn black, even among the Sisters who more often chose bright colors.

The D'Haran army had coopted several multistoried inns and warehouses. The buildings had been gutted and remodeled, and lumber from numerous sawmills brought in to erect barracks inside the compound. Soldiers wearing the armor of D'Hara marched on patrol. Tanimura would be a good beachhead for Richard's expanding empire. Even though the city might have seemed the southern limit of civilized lands, Nicci now knew there was far more to the Old World, including General Utros and his vast army.

As two soldiers walked toward her, side by side, nodding politely to passersby, Nicci was glad to see that the Tanimurans were not frightened by the soldiers, unlike the reaction when Jagang's army occupied a town. Nicci stepped in front of the pair, blocking their way. "Gentlemen, I need you to take me to your commander."

The two young soldiers blinked in surprise. "That's most irregular. I—"

"I am the sorceress Nicci. I fought with Lord Rahl."

"Nicci?" cried the other guard. His eyes ran up and down

her form. "I know your black dress, but your hair—what happened?"

"Are you soldiers or hairdressers? I need to speak with General Linden. I have news that Lord Rahl must learn immediately."

"Yes, Sorceress, of course!" The two men turned about and walked at a pace brisk enough to satisfy even Nicci.

They led her through the gates of the garrison, where soldiers were practicing swordplay in the yard. They all stopped and looked at her. Someone whispered loudly, "That's Death's Mistress." Nicci ignored the comment.

The headquarters building was a two-story wooden structure with open double doors. The three hurried up a staircase of fresh pine boards to the second level, where General Linden sat in his main office. He was busy at his desk, writing reports, folding them, dribbling red wax to seal them, and pressing the wax with the stylized "R" of Lord Rahl.

"Excuse me one moment," he said without looking at them. He folded another document, scribbled with a quill pen, then sealed it with more wax, which he set aside to dry. Then he glanced up.

The two soldiers stepped forward to report, but Linden turned his full attention to Nicci. He was obviously surprised by the intensity he saw in her. The thin officer was no older than his midthirties, with a port-wine splotch high on his left cheek. The crookedness of his nose implied that it had been broken at least once, but he seemed a calm man, not an embittered veteran.

"General Linden, this woman is . . ." The soldier's voice faltered.

Nicci stepped between them and approached the desk. She removed the rectangle of glass from her side, but kept the wrappings in place. "I am Nicci, companion to Lord Richard Rahl. On his orders, the wizard Nathan and I are exploring the Old World as his ambassadors."

Linden sat back in his desk chair and smiled. "Yes, of course.

I am honored to see you, and more than a little surprised. We received messages up from Renda Bay and a report from Cliffwall. Thanks to your message, General Zimmer and Prelate Verna took a hundred soldiers as well as the Sisters of the Light to protect the great archive there."

Nicci was pleasantly surprised. "I am glad to hear that. The knowledge in Cliffwall would be very dangerous if it fell into enemy hands. Now, it is more important than ever to keep the archive protected." She leaned across the desk and impatiently moved aside the document he had just signed. "General Linden, we must send word north to the People's Palace as well as make preparations throughout the cities of the Old World. A vast army from ancient times has reawakened, and they are on the move."

"Ancient soldiers?" Linden asked. "That sounds like a story told in the tavern."

"It's true, and they have laid siege to the city of Ildakar. So far, the wizards there have held them off, but now General Utros is dividing his forces, sending thousands of troops on exploratory missions. Sooner or later that great force will move north."

Linden looked at the papers on his desk as if one of them might contain instructions for a situation such as this. Behind Nicci, the two escort soldiers muttered in surprise.

"I can't emphasize the danger enough. Lord Rahl needs to know, and you must prepare. We have to fortify not only Tanimura, but all the cities up and down the coast. We need the D'Haran army." She unwrapped the cloth from the glass rectangle Elsa had created. "Here is the proof you need."

Nicci turned the magical window with its implanted images so Linden could see Utros's ancient army covering the plain.

"They have already begun to move, General, but you have the advantage of time and distance, so long as you begin your preparations now."

Linden stared at the images in the glass. "Dear spirits . . ."

CHAPTER 48

As the expedition departed from Cliffwall, Verna felt optimistic. The company included General Zimmer and half of his D'Haran soldiers along with the guard escort that had accompanied Renn on the journey from Ildakar. Captain Trevor and his men were pleased to be going home, although none of them relished the thought of another hard trek.

"A journey doesn't need to be difficult if you know your way," Verna said to the uneasy Renn, who was torn between his desire to go home and his wish to stay at the comfortable archive. He expressed his worries about getting lost, running out of supplies, fending off wild beasts, and countless other wilderness hazards. This time, though, they all rode horses from the D'Haran expeditionary force, and General Zimmer's men knew how to make efficient field camps along the way.

Riding along, the wizard looked over at Verna. "I much prefer this to walking on sore feet, although I may change my mind after several days in the saddle." He shifted his position, holding on to the reins of his ash-gray mare, and rubbed his already sore buttocks. "In Ildakar we have few horses. The city was bottled up for so many years, where would we ride? How would we feed them?"

"Didn't your nobles use carriages to travel about the town?"

"Oh, sometimes, but they live in the higher levels and rarely need to go down to the lower districts, since they have household servants to run errands for them." He rocked back and forth as the horses continued at a fast walk.

Verna stared ahead at the severe line of mountains that rose out of the great green bowl that had once been the Lifedrinker's Scar. The wizard seemed intimidated by the range ahead of them, remembering the hardships of their first crossing. The people of Cliffwall had spoken of the legendary beauty of Kol Adair, although Renn had an entirely different experience of the windy mountain pass. He had complained about the thin air, stumbling over loose rocks, fighting through willows in the tundra. He hadn't seen much beauty.

As they rode toward the rugged mountains, Verna tried to sound reassuring. "We'll guide you better this time, Renn. I am certain of it."

"I trust your word, Prelate, and when we reach Ildakar, I will return the favor and show you our hospitality." He lowered his voice. "After we give a cautious report to Sovrena Thora."

Verna said, "Nicci and Nathan will help, I'm sure."

Six of her fellow Sisters of the Light accompanied her and Amber, while four remained at Cliffwall to continue their studies with the other scholars. An additional dozen gifted scholars and students rode with the party, intent men and women who had studied the preserved records and learned much magic. They had been wisely afraid to exercise their abilities, having seen the previous mishaps caused by naive and uncontrolled amateurs, but Verna thought these earnest trainees could learn more by *doing* than by merely reading. This expedition might give them a chance to stretch their abilities.

Oliver and Peretta shared a horse. Looking ahead, they pointed out interesting landmarks to each other and also Amber, who seemed just as starry-eyed about her adventures since leaving Tanimura. The three young people had become fast friends, and Amber talked about her brother who had stayed behind to defend Renda Bay.

Verna listened to their conversation, but kept her thoughts to herself. She had traveled for much of her life, wandering with Sisters Grace and Elizabeth in search of Richard Rahl. Verna hadn't known at the time that her two companions were secretly Sisters of the Dark working for the Keeper. So many things had slipped beneath Verna's notice that she felt embarrassed and ashamed. She hoped that would never happen again.

By the good spirits, she was still here in another land and another situation. The Sisters of the Dark were gone, the veil to the underworld forever sealed, and the Keeper locked away. Magic had changed. Prophecy was gone. The Palace of the Prophets had been erased, but Verna was still prelate, even though their order had little meaning anymore.

For days they traveled into the hills, following Trevor's best guess of the route, though General Zimmer expressed gruff skepticism about trying to retrace the path of a party that had been lost and miserable in the first place. They could see the high mountain pass ahead, and Peretta had memorized descriptions of Kol Adair from the ancient records. The party camped at night with cook fires, tents, and warm blankets.

Renn sat at the main campfire next to Zimmer, Verna, and Sisters Rhoda and Eldine. The wizard helped himself to a second plate of mashed beans. "Ah, I remember when Lani and I would have the servants prepare feasts for only the two of us, and we would enjoy calm conversation long into the night. She was such a wonderful woman." He smiled. "Did I mention that Lani could call songbirds? They would flutter and sing around us. We'd sit outside and the larks would provide better music than any minstrel."

"She sounds very nice," Verna said. "Was she a sorceress? What happened to her?"

"Thora turned her to stone." Renn's expression darkened. "Once a person has been frozen with the petrification spell, nothing can revive them. Even the wizard commander said he couldn't reverse the magic." He glanced away.

The group climbed higher into the mountains, and the days and nights grew intensely cold. General Zimmer looked at the rugged ridgelines ahead, where a relatively clear path for the horses switchbacked up the slopes. "We should push ourselves hard so we can be over the pass before sunset. If we can get back down to the tree line, we will have a much warmer camp tonight."

"And plenty of firewood," Trevor added.

The soldiers hunched down on their saddles, wrapped in cloaks as they rode into the cold wind. Oliver and Peretta huddled closer to each other in the saddle, warm and content as they wrapped one blanket around the two of them.

The horses plodded along, climbing to the summit of the pass, where the vista suddenly unfolded before them, a world full of black, glacier-hung mountains. The group paused to marvel at the peaks, the frozen waves of ice that slid down the crags, the waterfalls of snowmelt running down sheer gorges, the jewel-like lakes, the lush hanging valleys.

As the sun dipped lower in late afternoon, shadows spread out in the bowl beyond Kol Adair. Renn gestured toward the vista. "You see what I told you? Imagine picking your way over those mountains, down into the valley, then back up over this pass. What a nightmare!"

Peretta drank in the view, filing every detail in her memmer's mind. Oliver marveled at what he saw, though his eyesight was poor.

Zimmer spotted the path that zigzagged down the slope on the opposite side of the pass, but the shelter of the tree line seemed a long way below. "I'll send scouts to reconnoiter the best way. With the steep rocky trail, I don't want the horses to break a leg, and we certainly don't want to pick our way down in the dark."

Amber stared across the valley toward the glaciers clinging

to the black rocky slopes. "What is that over there? It looks like people—lots of people."

Oliver shaded his eyes, squinting, but his expression remained blank. He shook his head. "I can't tell."

Verna and Zimmer tried to discern what the young novice's sharp eyes had spotted. "I see it now. It looks like a significant force of troops at the base of the cliffs on the next ridge. It's a huge camp, but where are their tents? Their campfires?"

Beside her, Peretta squinted. "It's thousands of people, maybe as many as ten thousand, like a whole moving city."

"Not a city," Zimmer said. "An army."

After dismounting, Renn stood in his maroon wizard's robes, hands on his hips. The wind blew his hair. "But where would such a military force come from? Even Ildakar doesn't have an army that size."

Captain Trevor looked pale and uneasy. "That is the direction we have to go. How will we get past them?"

"Maybe they're friendly," Amber said.

"An army of many thousands is not likely to be friendly," Zimmer said.

"The only giant army near Ildakar was turned to stone," said Renn. "And they couldn't possibly . . ." His voice trailed off.

Trevor also looked concerned. "Where else would they come from?"

"We have to know." Zimmer blew cold air through his lips. "Right now, we'd best remain hidden. Our force isn't large, but we are exposed up here on the pass. We need to get into the trees. Alas, we can't build campfires tonight, because they might be spotted."

Verna continued to stare, disturbed. "Whoever it is, they're marching in the general direction of Cliffwall."

Shaken by what they'd seen, the expedition hurried down off the exposed pass, painstakingly picking their way down the stony slope. Riders in the lead had identified the best way to get into the shelter of the trees below. When they reached the forest cover in the last glow of twilight, the soldiers spread out to set up a rudimentary camp. Renn looked forlornly at the plentiful fallen wood, but no one built a warm, cheery fire. Verna, however, assigned several Cliffwall scholars the task of using magic to boil water so they could at least make hot soup or tea. The Sisters also generated heat to warm rocks, which made the camp much more comfortable.

General Zimmer met with several of his best D'Haran scouts. "We need to know what that army is. Their camp is large, but not permanent, so they haven't been there long. I want some answers before they begin to move again. A force that size will take some time to pack up and set off."

Trevor seemed anxious. "Let one of my people accompany your scouts. If they travel under cover of darkness, they could get close enough for a good view. My men might recognize those soldiers, if they did come from Ildakar."

Zimmer agreed and dispatched three men into the deepening dusk to investigate the unexpected army.

Verna sat next to the general on a fallen log. "It will take hours for them to bring back a report. We should get some rest in the meantime. It's going to be a long night."

Shortly before dawn, the three scouts returned, their faces scratched from branches. They had made their way around the curve of the hanging valley to the edge of the encamped army, where they had indeed gotten a good view.

"We saw thousands of armed warriors, General," the first man reported. "I don't know how to explain it. They have no campfires, blankets, tents, or food that we could see. They are simply on the move, thousands of them, but they stopped for the night. The terrain is too rugged to cross in the darkness."

The second scout said, "And their armor looks ancient. Some of them bear standards with a flame symbol on it."

"It is the mark of Emperor Kurgan," said the Ildakaran guard who had accompanied them. He sounded certain. "I have seen it before on the petrified army outside of our city."

"We saw two of their sentries as they passed close to us on patrol," said the first scout. "They moved sluggishly, and they were not very alert." He glanced at Verna, then back to his commander. "General, sir, their skin was grayish, like stone."

Renn and Captain Trevor looked appalled. "I was afraid of this," the wizard groaned. "By the Keeper's beard, it's the ancient army, the soldiers of General Utros. They are somehow awake and on the move."

Verna heard the news with a chill. "And they are marching toward Cliffwall."

CHAPTER 49

The Norukai serpent ships were at last ready, and King Grieve felt the hot blood singing in his veins. Each day his people moved with energy and determination as they made preparations for war. Their voices grew louder as they shouted boasts and pounded drums. Grieve had seen it before. The Norukai called it raiding fever, but this would be more than just a raid.

Accompanied by his pale and shivering shaman, the king went down to the harbor and watched all the serpent ships sail in from outlying islands. He had gathered a navy of truly breathtaking scope. In addition to the forty ships they already used in their depredations, another fifty new war vessels had been completed by the island shipwrights, and dozens more were under construction. When his fleet set off to conquer Ildakar, it would be remembered as the greatest raid in Norukai history, one that would give his people a whole continent to squeeze.

The disgraced captains Kor and Lars would each have ten ships of their own to crush and conquer the large coastal cities. The world was about to feel the strong Norukai fist.

Out in the open water beyond the main island, his warships waited. Long oars protruded from the hulls, and the muscular crew pulled, guiding the serpent ships through the dangerous labyrinth of reefs. The vessels were well supplied already, and they would find towns to raid and provisions to seize along the way, until his fleet reached the estuary and sailed up the Killraven River to seize Ildakar.

Ready to embark on their suicidal missions, Kor and Lars had gathered the surviving members of their defeated crews and encouraged volunteers to join them. Their raiders were an unruly lot, mostly Norukai who had committed crimes and wanted to purge their sentences; others had huge gambling debts. When Kor and Lars put out the call for fighters, Grieve announced that anyone who joined the expeditions could erase everything with their own blood. The crimes would not be forgotten, but the Norukai would regain their honor. They would kill, pillage, and destroy until such time as they themselves fell in battle. If they did conquer the world for King Grieve, then all would be forgiven.

From the harbor, he looked back up the slick, sheer cliffs dotted with moss to the walls of the looming Bastion. That was his ancestral home, where he had ruled for years, where his father had lived and died, and where so many other Norukai kings had ruled. Grieve realized he might never return here if Ildakar was all Kor said it was, but he also knew that the king of the world could not be isolated on an island.

Before the separate fleets could launch, however, important sacrifices needed to be made. The Norukai knew how to guarantee victory.

Squat Norukai women stood together at the rim of a drum five feet across, pounding with clubs on the stretched skin of a scaly serpent. The drums boomed out, echoing along the cliffs and shuddering in the water, louder even than the waves crashing against the black rocks. Around the corner of the harbor cliffs, a second group of summoners clanged on the cylindrical iron bells that dangled on chains from the rock walls.

Beside him, Chalk bounced from one foot to the other,

energized by the drums, though his movements didn't follow the rhythm. When the shaman grinned, his scarred lips twisted and his pockmarked face wrinkled. "My Grieve! And the serpent god! Serpent, serpent, serpent! And blood for our war."

"We will feed the serpent god," Grieve said, "and he will feed our bravery and our strength."

Captain Kor waited at the end of the dock. Ten serpent ships were tied up in the harbor, making final preparations for his own raid, and Lars had a similar group of vessels, while the rest of the Norukai navy was anchored well beyond the reefs, ready to sail for Ildakar.

Kor presented himself before Grieve, stiff and formal. "I am honored to watch the sacrifice at your side, my king. The serpent god will empower my raiding party as well as your fleet."

Grieve opened his mouth wide, exposing his teeth all the way back to the molars, and he let out a loud hiss, imitating the serpent god. Chalk laughed, delighted at the exhibition.

Grieve said, "The serpent god will empower me and my warriors, but he must forgive you and your weakness. Do you think Yorik has enough blood to buy both of those things for us?"

"Yorik is a powerful man. The serpent god will be pleased."

Crowds gathered down at the harbor to watch from a safe distance. Norukai women brought their wide-eyed children out for the ceremony. Grieve saw that some of the boys were old enough to undergo the scarification. A few young men had their cheeks slit all the way back to the hinge of the jaw, but their scars were still red and angry. Others still had bandages wrapped around their faces. The young men watched the war preparations with shining eyes. Some of their mothers, also well armed, would go along for the battle, leaving the children in the care of trusted slaves.

Grieve looked at his people, and they stared back at him in admiration. They all feared him, but it was a healthy fear. He had led them to great glory and wealth, but he himself had remained in the Bastion for far too long. He was ready to feel hard bone and vulnerable flesh against the blade of his axe, the hot spray of blood across his face. Yes, it had been too long.

But before they could go, he had to receive the strength and blessing of the serpent god.

Leaving the crowds in the safety of the harbor, Grieve strode alongside Chalk and Kor on the narrow rock path above the tide line. This way led around the protective point to a deep, rough cove open to the sea, where the great serpents could come.

They followed the edge of the cliffs to where they could look across at pillars of stone erected on the reef rock, from which manacles dangled. This was the place of sacrifice, safely far from the ships anchored out beyond the reefs. Eager Norukai from the fleet set out in small coracles, paddling around the harbor and keeping close to the jagged shore, where they didn't need to fear the great serpent when it came. Some of the large raiding ships also rowed closer so their crews could watch the spectacle.

The iron bells and loud drums thundered around the cliffs, sending a relentless call through the water. The serpent god would hear and respond to the summons.

Kor's voice was hoarse. "We must prepare." He stared at the stone posts and the empty chains hanging from them. "Quickly."

"Prepare!" Chalk shouted. "My Grieve, King Grieve!"

A large coracle came into the cove and approached the stone pillars from the deep water. Two burly Norukai warriors rowed the coracle, while Yorik rode in the front, hunched down. He did not look panicked. Instead, he stared at the twin pillars and the chains waiting for him; then he gazed out to sea, knowing that was where the monster would come.

Kor watched him, his face expressionless.

Chalk cried out, "Serpent, serpent, serpent! I've seen it! Blood, and war, and victory." Then he lowered his voice, tilted his head, and snickered. "But who will win? Who will die? The serpent god will feast."

"Quiet, Chalk," Grieve chided. "This is a solemn occasion. It is important for our future."

"Our future! Ildakar! Ildakar will be gone after we arrive."

"Ildakar will be ours," Grieve said, and turned to Kor. "And if your raiders do their jobs, so will the cities along the coast."

"Lars and I will attack them all, King Grieve," Kor said. "Those cities have never seen anything like the Norukai."

The guards rowed the coracle up to the stone posts and threw a grappling hook to anchor the small boat against the rocks. They prodded Yorik, but he needed no encouragement. Naked, he stood up from the boat and stepped onto the shore, willingly taking his place between the posts with the chains. His body was muscular and scarred, covered with tattooed curves and stripes along his ribs, shoulders, buttocks, and the backs of his legs. Watching him, Grieve thought Yorik was a proud man despite his unforgivable failure.

Kor said, "The serpent god will devour him and consume his weakness, leaving the rest of us stronger."

"You have to consume your own weakness, Kor," Grieve grumbled.

"I know. My shame will sharpen my sword and strengthen my battle-axe. I can only pray that enough blood will wash it away. Lars and his fleet will do the same."

The guards raised Yorik's arms and fastened the manacles around his wrists. Arms outstretched, Yorik hung between the two stone posts. His feet barely touched the slick rock where waves crashed against the base of the posts.

From where they stood on the opposite side of the cove, Chalk hungrily watched the sacrificial victim. Dangling there, Yorik stared out to sea. He didn't struggle. The drumbeats and the iron bells made a louder and louder clamor.

After placing the victim in chains, the guards climbed back into the coracle and rowed swiftly away, knowing the serpent god would come soon.

At the end of the path opposite from the sacrificial post hung a wide brass gong on a trunk of driftwood. King Grieve picked up the baton and shouted, "Serpent god, we have a sacrifice for you. We need your strength, and we give you ours. Help us share in the blood of conquest."

Like a warrior swinging a battle mace into an enemy's skull, Grieve smashed the gong, eliciting a thunderous crash, surely loud enough to be heard even in the greatest depths of the ocean. The sound of the gong reverberated around the island. Thousands of Norukai aboard the serpent ships let out loud cheers, as did the crowds in the sheltered harbor. Aboard the serpent ships, the raiders began stomping on the decks, rattling on the rails. The pounding on the iron bells and drums grew louder, more insistent.

Chalk snatched the baton from Grieve's large hands and swung it against the gong, clanging and clanging.

Isolated on the spit of rock, Yorik hung on his chains, watching the open water until a ripple formed on the choppy waves, a jagged, razor-edged fin that sliced the surface. Around the island and out in the ships, spectators cried out for the serpent god. Grieve wondered why their noise didn't distract the enormous creature, but the serpent god knew its intended sacrifice.

The snakelike form glided through the deep channel, approaching the island. Waves crashed against the reefs, boomed on the rocks and cliffs, echoed in the cove. From his chains, Yorik shouted, "Serpent god, I am yours!" The man let out a loud snarling growl which sounded of both challenge and surrender.

The shape grew larger, the shadow darker in the water, and finally the serpent god rose from the waves. The creature's head was long and angular, like a spear point. Frills of fins spread out like bloodred fans behind its head and under its jaw. Its scales were magnificent, blue and green. Each of its eyes was larger than a human head. As the great serpent sinuously lifted itself higher, rivulets poured from its jaws. It was far more fearsome and magnificent than the carving at the prow of any serpent ship.

The creature fixed its gaze on Yorik and opened its huge mouth, flicking out a long, forked tongue and releasing a deafening hiss.

King Grieve opened his own mouth as wide as he could and belched out his own hiss, trying to sound like the serpent god. Dangling from his chains, Yorik laughed and screamed and called out, struggling—not to break free, but to stretch himself toward the serpent god.

King Grieve shivered with awe and amazement. Seeing the great monster, he felt small, weak, insignificant. Kor fell to his knees, gibbering with amazement and terror.

From the boats anchored beyond the island, the Norukai crews yelled. The drums and iron bells continued, but Grieve saw only the serpent god as it glided into the cove toward the man who had been offered to it.

For a frozen moment the serpent towered above, regarding Yorik, who kept laughing insanely, squirming, flailing, challenging.

Grieve was suddenly terrified, wondering what would happen if the serpent god refused the sacrifice. If Yorik's flaws made him unacceptable, would the Norukai then be cursed? Would his war of conquest be doomed from the beginning?

The serpent flashed forward and engulfed Yorik, biting down hard and ripping its morsel away. One of Yorik's severed arms swung from the manacle, flopping against the stone post and splashing a mark of red there. With two snaps of its jaws, the serpent god consumed the sacrifice and turned about in a graceful rippling arc.

From the other side of the cove, the giant reptilian eyes regarded King Grieve, who managed to stare back. Chalk whimpered and hid behind his king, clutching the big man's waist. Grieve barely felt him. He stared at the serpent god and shared thoughts. The fires in his blood burned even hotter, and he swelled his chest and pounded a fist against his heart.

Satisfied, the serpent god submerged again. Long rippled fins cut the water as the monstrous form glided back out to sea.

After witnessing the sign, King Grieve knew that his Norukai were destined for greatness.

CHAPTER 50

Even after they got safely back inside the walls of Ildakar, Lila kept running as if they were still being pursued. Bannon panted hard, and his muscles ached. His shirt was torn, his trousers caked with mud and blood, but he was free!

When they reached a yaxen trough in the lower levels of the city, he dropped to his knees and wheezed, "Stop, I need to rest." He plunged his hands into the water and splashed his face. The cool liquid felt glorious, washing away sweat, grime, and blood. He let out a long sigh and kept his eyes closed as water trickled from his long tangled hair. He scooped up a handful and drank deeply.

Sweat shone on Lila's skin as she stood next to him, proud. He remembered when she had looked so imperious in the training pits, provoking him to fight harder. Now her gaze was strangely soft. Still unable to believe what had happened, he said, "You came back for me."

"I did." She put her hands on her narrow hips, touching the small cylinder of the agile knife that could inflict so much pain. She nudged him with her knee. "Come, we need to let the others know. After Nicci's sand panther spotted what might

371

have been a rude prison for captives, they didn't believe I had any chance of finding you."

Bannon levered himself to his feet. Without looking back, she set off at a brisk pace to the upper levels, expecting him to follow. Her hips swayed beneath her black waist wrap, and Bannon saw the rune-marked skin on her back over the landscape of taut muscles. He increased his pace to walk next to the morazeth, rather than behind her like a pet on a leash. "How many others were killed during our sortie? Was the surprise attack a success?"

Lila turned to him with her shadowed eyes. "We killed many of the enemy. Two morazeth died, but we made a good accounting of ourselves."

"Two morazeth? Which ones?" He had resented the women for how they treated the trainees, but now he felt a strange heaviness to learn that some were gone.

"Ricia and Marla. Genda was wounded, but she will recover." Lila showed no emotion when she recited the names. "When I lost you on the battlefield, I . . ." She had to struggle to get out the word. "I *apologize*. I will attend to you more closely from now on, if we ever find ourselves in a similar situation."

Bannon drew a shuddering breath, not wanting to think about what must have happened to Brock and Jed. "Let's hope it never happens again."

She paused. "General Utros and his army are still undefeated, and Ildakar is still under siege. Surely, there will be more battles."

Bannon gripped Sturdy's hilt. "I know. I just wasn't looking forward to it."

Dawn wouldn't come for another hour yet, and the street-lights still blazed, lit by transference magic. Lila led him directly to the ruling tower, though he couldn't imagine the duma members were meeting at such a late hour. He wondered how Nicci had reacted to the news that he'd been lost on the battlefield. . . .

As they reached the top of the plateau, he glanced longingly at the grand villa. Right now he wanted to sleep in his guest bed for days, but he had to report to the duma first. He followed Lila into the tower and up the waterfall of stone steps to the ruling chamber, which was lit by a warm fire and burning candles.

Elsa, Oron, Damon, and the chalky-white Lani were huddled over unfurled scrolls, studying a map of Ildakar, the winding streets and aqueducts that riddled the bluff. The duma members looked up at the disturbance, and Lila spoke before anyone could react. "I have rescued Bannon Farmer. He was exactly where Nicci's panther suspected prisoners might be held."

Nathan emerged from a side alcove carrying a thick book, which he dropped on the marble floor. "Dear boy, you're alive! So many died that we couldn't even tally their names, but you're alive!" Grinning, he bounded over, and Bannon could barely breathe as the wizard embraced him. "Dear spirits, you're alive!"

Bannon didn't know what to say.

Nathan released him and stepped back, just staring at him with sparkling eyes as if to convince himself the sight was true.

Regaining his balance, Bannon looked around the chamber. Duma members stared at him, their faces full of questions, but he didn't see Nicci. He wanted to tell her that Mrra was still prowling out in the hills.

"We fought hard. I . . ." He tried to organize his rattling thoughts. "I couldn't have done it without Lila. She came for me. For me, Jed, and Brock. I—"

Oron came forward, his long yellow braid hanging on the left side of his head. His face was stony, without sympathy, exactly the expression he'd worn when skinning the poor fur animals. "You were with Jed and my son? We thought they died on the battlefield."

"Yes, we were all prisoners, and General Utros was going to interrogate us. When Lila and Mrra came, though, we broke free. We all ran . . ." Each word felt heavier as he spoke it.

Oron stood waiting for a full report. "And?"

Lady Olgya came up to stand beside him, also concerned. "What about Jed?"

Bannon glanced at Nathan for support, but knew he would have to say what he needed to say. "Before we got far, the alarm was sounded. W-We ran as fast as we could, but the enemy soldiers closed in. I called for Jed and Brock, but they . . . they thought they'd have a better chance if we split up. While Lila and I fought our way through, those two ran in different directions. I never saw them again. I don't know if they were captured or killed."

Oron considered this for a long moment as the other duma members remained silent and sullen. Finally, he frowned and turned back to the stone tables. "My son was worthless anyway. What is worse, to be killed in battle, or to be captured?" He made a disgusted sound. "*Twice?*"

Olgya shivered, closed her eyes, and when she opened them again, her expression was like iron. "I already accepted that my son was dead several nights ago. Come, we have business to do and an entire city to save."

Nathan gave Bannon another paternal hug. "You look quite a mess. Go clean yourself up, eat, rest. When you have recovered, the duma will want a full report of what you saw inside the enemy's camp."

Bannon nodded sheepishly. "Where is Nicci? I should let her know that I'm alive."

Nathan paused. "She has gone away."

For an instant, Bannon's heart failed, fearing that the beautiful sorceress had been killed on the battlefield.

"By now, she is in Tanimura, I hope," Nathan continued. "She traveled in the sliph to spread a warning about General Utros and his army."

Still protective, Lila placed a firm hand on Bannon's shoulder, guiding him from the duma chamber. "We can discuss this later. Bannon Farmer is weary and hungry. I will see to his needs."

The young man was relieved, not sure he could think straight after all he'd been through. He swayed on his feet as he followed the morazeth.

They headed toward the grand villa that had, until recently, been the lavish home of Maxim and Thora. Many of the rooms had been taken over by household servants who had worked there. Leading Bannon, Lila called out to two women who stood in the corridors under the open trellises. "Bring food. This man needs nourishment. He is a brave fighter for Ildakar."

The women recognized Bannon and hurried off. When he reached his chambers, he looked at the broad bed with its silken sheets, the small table, a wardrobe for his garments, a pitcher filled with fresh water, a bowl with overripe and moldy fruit that had been there for days. Two tangerines were still intact, despite their hard, dry rinds. Bannon grabbed one and worked at the peel, but Lila took it from him and sliced it in quarters with her dagger. He slurped the sweet citrus fruit and felt a rush of energy. He let his eyes flutter closed as he let out a long sigh.

Lila moved about the room, businesslike. She found a soft cloth, moistened it with water from the pitcher, and began to scrub the dried blood from his face, rubbing hard as if she could wipe away the freckles as well. She dabbed at a scab on his mouth, then washed his neck. Her intent eyes seemed to be studying a specimen or preparing him for sale to some discriminating merchant.

"I just want to lie down and rest," he said, feeling uneasy.

"Not yet. You have been through a difficult challenge, as hard as combat in the arena. You're sweaty, your muscles are hard and knotted. You are not ready for sleep yet."

The two servant women appeared, carrying platters with grapes, cheeses, a couple of hard rolls, and sliced yaxen meat. Bannon's mouth watered. The tangerine hadn't been enough. "Maybe I'm not ready for sleep just yet." The women hovered, asking if he needed anything else, but Lila shooed them away.

Bannon ravenously tore into one of the rolls, then ate

cheese and a handful of juicy grapes that he barely chewed before swallowing.

As he ate, Lila tugged at his shirt, but the fabric stuck to scabs on his back, and crusted dirt and blood made the cloth stiff. With a grunt of frustration, she used her dagger to slice the shirt down the back. He yelped in surprise, but she tugged the cloth away. "It was ruined anyway." She tossed it into a pile on the floor.

Bannon chewed a slice of meat, tasting the savory juices. It was all he could concentrate on.

With the shirt gone, Lila used the wet cloth to rinse his back, then his chest, and Bannon relaxed. Only hours ago, he had been sure of being executed. He slid away from the tray of food and sat on the edge of the bed. After she finished washing his chest, she went behind him and kneaded his shoulders, then worked her way down his back. Morazeth trainers usually inflicted extravagant pain, but this was exactly the opposite.

"You have skills beyond combat, Lila. I'm glad."

"I have many skills." She placed her hand on his chest and pressed him abruptly backward onto the bed so she could remove his boots. "As you well know."

"What are you doing? I'm tired and sore."

"You had a great battle," she said. "I . . . worried about you, and I am pleased you were not killed. I want to show my gratitude."

"Thank you, but it's not necessary."

Lila had never accepted no for an answer. "Honor demands it." After his hard days of training in the combat pits, she had claimed him as her lover, granting him a "reward" of physical pleasure, whether or not he wanted it. She had demanded it for herself and gave him no choice. "Do you have the strength to resist me?"

"I am not your prisoner anymore," he said.

"You are still a man." Her voice was gruff. With a gesture so swift he barely saw her move her fingers, she unfastened the wrap around her breasts and let the leather strip drop to the floor. "I no longer need to force you."

Bannon felt the cool sheets under his bruised back, looked up at the naked Lila as she leaned forward, climbing on top of him. He remembered the three beautiful acolytes from Cliffwall, Audrey, Laurel, and Sage. They had been his first lovers, and they had given him amazing nights of pleasure, one after another, but the twisted magic of Life's Mistress had turned those three beautiful women into monsters.

Could the opposite happen? A hardened morazeth turned into a soft and sensuous woman? As Lila bent closer to him and he felt her warm skin, smelled her musky feminine scent, he remembered how ruthless she had been, a steely trainer who forced him to do what she demanded. She had terrified him. When he looked at her now, she seemed warmer. Something had changed. She touched him with a hint of tenderness.

Tentatively, he reached up and brushed the bare skin of her back, feeling the mysterious symbols marked on her skin. As he ran his palms down her spine, he felt as if he might be reading an arcane book by touch alone.

"I did save your life, boy," Lila said. "You owe me a reward."

Bannon couldn't argue with that.

CHAPTER 51

As Utros stared through the blood-tinted lens, he couldn't tear his eyes from his beloved Majel, the woman he had longed for since leaving Orogang. He had vowed to conquer the world for her husband, but his heart belonged to her. He remembered her pointed chin and delicate nose, the full lips he had kissed so many times.

Now, she was a horror, her entire face peeled off, her eyes intact, but with the lids flayed away so she could watch what her husband did to her body. Her jaw muscles were leathery red strips. As she spoke, her teeth clacked together, exposing her meaty tongue. "Utros, my love! You called for me."

He stared through the lens, stricken. Even Majel's spirit was mutilated, an eternal reminder that Kurgan had personally imposed this punishment upon her.

"Utros, why don't you speak to me?" she pleaded, coming closer to the other side of the glass. "You called me through the veil."

Despite the shocking wounds, he could see Majel in her eyes, the woman he had caressed and loved, and it was still her voice calling to him. "Oh, Majel . . ." he said. "Keeper and spirits, what has he done to you?"

"The form of a spirit doesn't matter," she said. "What counts is the heart and soul."

Ava and Ruva stood back watching this conversation, fascinated by the shadowed souls lurking in the greenish mists behind the lens.

The general's focus remained on his beloved, and he heard the wisdom in her words. "It's been so long, Majel," he said, in a quiet voice. "I left Orogang and conquered many lands, as I swore to do. We swept across the Old World and sent reports back to the capital. I did what Iron Fang commanded . . . but I missed you so much."

"By then I was already dead," she said. "And so was my husband. Your battles were for nothing."

"No battle is for nothing. Because of . . . us, I had to prove that I was also loyal to my emperor." The words pained him as he spoke, and he forced himself not to turn away from her horrific visage. "I didn't mean to be gone so long, my love. The centuries must have been agony for you in the underworld, but I was stone. I could not help. I could not join you."

Majel looked at him with her raw, naked eyes. "Time has no meaning here beyond the veil. My death was like yesterday, or maybe it was forever ago. I have missed you, Utros, and that makes even an instant seem like an eternity."

He extended his arms, but didn't touch the glass. He wanted to embrace her, wanted to remember her. Perhaps the only way to join Majel was with his own death, if the Keeper would allow them to be together.

She looked alarmed as she saw him more clearly. "Your face, Utros! What happened?" The question seemed a great irony to him, considering what she had endured.

He reached up to touch his cheek, felt the long-healed scar there that ran from his temple, around his eye, and down his cheek to vanish into the patchy area of his beard. "It is a burn from dragon fire," he said, lowering his head. "We captured a silver dragon and meant to unleash it on Ildakar, but the dragon turned on us instead. I was burned badly, but my sorceresses healed me. Others did not recover, and the dragon escaped."

Utros didn't want to talk about past history or tactical mistakes. He longed to tell Majel how he wanted to bring her back through the veil, but that was impossible. Ava and Ruva reaffirmed what Nicci and Nathan had said. The veil was forever sealed, and he would have to content himself with seeing her, hearing her. They were separated by an impenetrable wall between life and death.

"I love you," he said.

The flayed spirit answered, "I love you too. I long for you. I did everything for you, Utros, and I lost everything for you. But I . . ."

Another voice, grating, deep, and shudderingly familiar, emanated through the lens. "But she is mine."

A second form appeared out of the greenish mist, a bulky copper-skinned man with oiled black hair tied in dozens of thin braids. He had a heavy brow, a hooked nose, a strong jaw. Emperor Kurgan, *his emperor,* was an imposing man who had gone to fat after years of hedonistic life. When he spoke, he exposed his teeth, showing one hooked iron fang on the left side of his mouth. "Just as you are mine, General Utros. You swore your loyalty to me, as did Majel. That vow cannot be broken. Loyalty is stronger than love. I command that you remember it now!"

The response was automatic. Utros placed a fist against his heart and bowed. "My liege."

Kurgan pressed closer to the lens, standing next to Majel. From his actions he still considered her his wife, his possession, his symbol. "You betrayed me. You both betrayed me." His eyes blazed with more than just anger. "You swore. You cut your hand and poured blood into a goblet, which I drank. Majel also gave me her blood. We were bound forever. You think the Keeper ignores such vows? I demand your loyalty, both of you!"

Utros dropped to his knee in front of the lens. "I betrayed

you, my liege. I have no excuse, other than that I loved her. You have already inflicted your punishment on Majel." His voice was raw with horror. He was glad his army could not see or hear this.

"I need no apologies, no groveling, no explanations," Iron Fang said.

Inside, Utros felt as if wild horses were ripping apart his heart. "I remain loyal to you, my emperor. I conquered many lands in your name. My military force still numbers in the hundreds of thousands. I have laid siege to Ildakar as you commanded and dispatched other armies to reconquer the cities and lands that have been lost over the centuries."

"What is taking so long?" Kurgan demanded. "If you had been swifter in your conquest, I would have had wealth and power, and my people would never have turned on me. I would have been the greatest emperor in history, yet you left me in Orogang with this treacherous woman who pretended to love me. But now I know that when she gave me her body, she was imagining *your* kisses, *your* caresses." He turned his glare upon the mutilated woman who stood beside him in the spirit world.

"Loyalty is stronger than love," Majel said, as if he had drummed it into her for fifteen centuries. "I am loyal to you, my husband." Her voice cracked. "And I'm sorry for you, Utros."

The words resonated in the general's mind. He muttered, repeating them. *Loyalty is stronger than love.* That was how he had been raised and trained. That was what he had held dear, until Majel changed his heart.

"You say that?" Utros asked her. "Even after what he did to you?"

"I remain loyal to my husband," Majel said meekly, "to Emperor Kurgan."

"And I still command you, General Utros," Iron Fang said. "Your original orders stand, now that I can communicate with you from the underworld. You must pay your price. You must do as you promised and hope for forgiveness."

"I will, my emperor," Utros said, still kneeling. "A great deal has changed over the centuries, but I will regain the lands I once conquered for you."

Kurgan sounded annoyed, impatient. "Why don't you have Ildakar yet? With an army of hundreds of thousands, surely you are strong enough to defeat one city."

He knew Emperor Kurgan was capricious, volatile. He issued orders that thousands of followers worked to implement, only to change his mind before the task was completed, while General Utros was a steady and rational commander. His soldiers followed his orders, but Utros had always done his best to do as Iron Fang instructed. Now, even though death separated them, the general vowed he would do no less.

"My armies continue to press our siege, but the wizards of Ildakar are powerful. I don't know if I have the weapons necessary to tear down the city just yet." He climbed to his feet and stood as a military commander should. "But I will find a way to conquer Ildakar."

Kurgan spoke in a harsh voice. "If your army is too weak and you don't have the proper weapons, then get more powerful weapons." He snorted. "I know of the silver dragon you captured. Another failure of yours! You should have used the dragon to destroy the city, to grind those people under fire and terror. Don't fail me again. If you are as great a general as you claim, why not capture another dragon? That shouldn't be impossible."

Majel turned away. "Loyalty is stronger than love."

Utros swallowed and forced himself to repeat her words, for Kurgan's benefit: "Loyalty is stronger than love." His thoughts began turning as other parts of his mind pondered tactics, possibilities. "I will discuss the matter with my sorceresses. I had not considered calling another dragon, but that might be possible."

He had to try. Maybe at long last he would achieve his victory over Ildakar.

CHAPTER 52

"We cannot defeat them," said Damon, sounding so reasonable. He seemed more relaxed with Nicci gone. "We have known this for fifteen centuries."

The wizard stood before the duma members, pacing restlessly back and forth on the blue marble tiles. The long mustaches on either side of his mouth drooped with a stylish affectation, each one tipped with a ruby bead knotted through the thin hairs. "When we sent out our best strike force against General Utros, we massacred many of the enemy, but we also lost nearly a third of our fighters." He gestured generally toward the high windows that looked out upon the distant battlefield. "And untold numbers of the enemy remain."

Still seated, Nathan frowned in consternation, disappointed. He knew that Nicci would have scolded the wizard for his defeatist attitude. He cleared his throat and spoke up. "What you say can't be denied, Damon, and I understand the uneasiness in your hearts." Subconsciously, he rubbed the scar on his breastbone. "But the same could have been said about the Imperial Order, or Sulachan's undead army, and yet they were both defeated. You can't give up."

On the seat beside him, Elsa gave him an appreciative smile and patted his arm. "Ildakar does not give up. We can be stronger than ever."

The duma members were exhausted, having slept little in recent days, and despite their endless discussions, they had found no ingenious solution. Nathan considered the Ixax warriors again, but he didn't think the titans were ready yet.

Quentin left the stone table to join his fellow wizard in the speaking area, showing solidarity with Damon. "We have to face facts, even if we don't like what they reveal. The soldiers are constantly pounding on our walls, and although our reinforcement spells continue to hold, they cannot last forever. Our defenses may have seemed invincible when we built them thousands of years ago, but even the stone must eventually crumble. We can't hide here forever."

"We defeated General Utros before," Oron pointed out. "Is our city weaker now?" In annoyed distraction, he picked at a plate of sweetened pastries, selected one, and took a small bite.

"Of course we are weaker!" Damon snapped. "During our greatest days, imagine what the wizards of Ildakar did. They raised this city high above the river, created the cliffs, flooded the swamps and filled them with monsters. We petrified the entire army. Could any of us do that now? Our gifted nobles are not what they once were."

"But Ildakar is free," interjected Rendell, who usually didn't speak during the meetings. The other wizards scorned him and ignored his comment.

"We no longer have the wizard commander," Quentin said. "Maxim was one of the most powerful wizards in our history, and he is gone. *He* developed the petrification spell that saved us before. Andre is dead. Ivan is dead. Renn is gone. Even Nicci has left us!"

"Well, my friends, you do have me," Nathan said with a wry smile. "My gift is strong. Let us not give up hope."

"And Renn might come home soon," Lani said. She now

wore a blue silk robe over her pale, hard skin. "If he found Cliffwall, maybe the archive there will offer something even more powerful than a petrification spell. We can use it against General Utros."

"I like the man well enough," Olgya said with a frown, "but Renn always struck me as somewhat, ah, lackluster. I'm not convinced he managed to find Cliffwall at all."

Lani looked ready to defend the wizard she loved, but Elsa broke in. "Renn left Ildakar before the stone army awakened, so he has no idea about our crisis. He wouldn't know what to look for."

Rendell spoke up again. "Ildakar will fight together in ways it never did before, but we need to know how. We have a large population, and many are willing to join our defenders if we give them armor and weapons. But we can't simply throw fighters against the siege force. No matter how brave we are, we would lose!"

"We would die," Oron corrected.

"That is a valid definition of losing," Nathan said in an acerbic tone.

An unexpected female voice came from the doorway. "You have *me*."

With a rustle of armor and heavy boots, two Ildakaran guards led a slender woman in a dress of flowing green silk. Her stiff hair was done up in an elaborate sculpture of braids and ringlets. Her skin was as pale as Lani's.

Nathan and Elsa lurched to their feet, but Damon turned to greet Thora, extending his arm in a welcoming gesture. "Quentin and I asked for the sovrena to be brought here."

"She is no longer the sovrena," Lani said.

"She is still a very powerful sorceress, regardless," Quentin said. "We should not underestimate her powers. We need all the help we can get."

Thora walked two paces ahead of the guards, as if leading them. Her hands were bound with thick ropes and chains, but the restraints were merely for show. Thora had proven that she could easily break free with magic if she so chose.

"When I let myself be captured at the wall, I vowed that I would fight for Ildakar. This is my city. My heart is the heart of Ildakar." She entered the open speaking floor without a glance at her now-empty throne. "When I escaped, my anger caused a kind of madness in me. I did consider joining General Utros to betray Ildakar, and I am ashamed. That will never happen." She looked at them with her green eyes, strong and confident. "But my gift is powerful, and I can help."

"Help with what?" Nathan tried to control his uneasiness. "Please explain."

Elsa's face was flushed with anger. "You think you can return to our good graces? Damon, Quentin, and I sentenced you because of your crimes against Ildakar."

"Ildakar is in a different situation now," Quentin said, embarrassed. "A desperate one."

Damon cleared his throat and said to the duma, "We have an idea to propose, something we have to consider as our circumstances grow worse."

Quentin continued in what was obviously a rehearsed presentation with his friend. "We attacked General Utros and stung him like a wasp, but that wasp will be swatted. He is bound to attack us. We bother him so little that he has dispatched a quarter of his army on other conquests. He knows he will crush us, given time. Will we just wait for it to happen?"

Olgya snorted. "And how exactly do you suggest we use Thora to defeat him?"

The former sovrena turned her gaze to all the duma members. "That is a mistaken assumption. We don't have to *defeat* Utros to keep Ildakar safe. The solution has been right in front of us all along." She raised her voice. "How did we stay safe for fifteen hundred years?"

"The enemy army was turned to stone," Lani said. "But we cannot restore that spell on such a scale."

"No, not that." Quentin sniffed impatiently. "Ildakar would be saved if we just raised the shroud of eternity again. The city could retreat safely into time as we did so many centuries ago. Then it wouldn't matter what General Utros did."

The proposal left the ruling chamber in sudden silence. "But the pyramid is destroyed," Elsa said. "All the apparatus is gone."

Damon said, "I'm a shaper, and I could re-create the equipment. We know how to do the blood magic."

Oron pondered. "That might work. We could hide for a few centuries, and by then the general's army would be long gone. None of our concern."

Rendell was aghast at the suggestion. "But . . . all that bloodshed!"

"We just returned to the world," Elsa said. "We would be trapped again."

"We would be *safe*," Damon insisted.

"Dear spirits, that would not be a good idea at all," Nathan said. "You have to consider more than just this city. If Ildakar vanished, that huge army would range across the entire continent and wreak havoc on city after city."

"But Ildakar would be safe and intact," Quentin said with a satisfied smile. "The rest of the world has to defend itself."

Nathan was appalled. "But all the blood sacrifices! That might be a massacre greater than any attack we could expect from Utros."

"Yes, it would take a tremendous bloodworking, just as it did before," Thora said. "Thousands of volunteers. Think of how many people will die if the walls fall and Utros ransacks the city! We cannot let that happen. Better to spend the blood of the people to *save* the people. I know that enough devoted citizens would make the right choice. Let them decide."

"And you will need my help to accomplish it." Thora lifted her delicate wrists to show the heavy bindings there. "I swore I would do what was necessary to help my city. I meant it."

Nathan heard muttering around the chamber. He looked in

alarm at Elsa, who had gone pale. Lani said, "But we have to wait for my Renn to come back."

"We will wait until it is truly the last resort," Quentin replied, sounding reasonable, just like Damon. "But for the good of Ildakar, we have to consider our options. Rather than let this city fall into enemy hands, we know what we have to do. Unless someone can think of another way to defeat General Utros?"

"I don't like this," Nathan muttered. "Dear spirits, I don't like this at all." Maybe when Nicci returned from Tanimura through the sliph, she would bring hopeful news, and they could have a different discussion.

"There is no reason we can't prepare," Damon suggested in a smooth voice. "We will spread the word throughout the city, start the people thinking about who is willing to become heroes to save our city by shedding their blood."

Oron stood. "That is enough discussion for now. We all need food and rest. We are not thinking straight anymore."

Lani said in a hard voice, "Thora can't be allowed to remain free, no matter what she promises. Take her back to her cell."

"At least for now," Olgya said.

Uneasy about the duma's considerations, Nathan went back to visit the Ixax warriors. This time, he carried a disturbing book he had discovered in Andre's library, an old diary. In the destruction of the villa, the shelves had collapsed and the volumes were scattered, but Nathan had read the journal with widening eyes.

He understood far more about these towering invincible warriors and everything they had sacrificed to become the Ixax.

As he walked into the chamber where the colossal figures stood, Nathan placed a calm smile on his face. He knew the two giants were watching him, and he wanted to keep them at ease. They focused on him each time he came to converse with them. For many days he had told the silent figures stories, regaling them with legends, even exaggerating some of his own exploits. The armored warriors knew Nathan Rahl as a person now, and he hoped the Ixax also remembered who *they* had been as humans.

Andre's diary emphasized the fact with even more poignancy than anything Nathan had told them before. He held up the old journal with its brittle, brown pages. "I know who you are now. This is a diary written centuries ago in the hand of Fleshmancer Andre himself. It is from when the army of General Utros first laid siege to Ildakar, when the wizards were desperate for any means to save the city. Do you remember?"

He sat on a broken pillar of marble and flipped the discolored pages, skimming the scrawled handwriting. "Let me read you some of what he wrote. 'I fear our city will fall. All of Ildakar is in panic. The wizards seek a way to fight back against this enormous horde. Our walls are strong, and our magic is strong, but the army of General Utros is like a swarm of locusts. Even if all our people go out and fight to the death, it will not be enough. We need stronger warriors, and I can create them.'"

Nathan smiled up at the armored giants. He tapped the words with his fingertip. "You were afraid too, weren't you? You knew you had to protect your families, and when the desperate call went out, three of you agreed to give up your lives and your loved ones for the sake of Ildakar." Though neither of the Ixax moved at all, he imagined that they nodded.

Nathan turned the pages, summarizing the words. "Andre says he chose you from more than a dozen volunteers to become the mighty Ixax. Do you remember your names? Do they sound familiar?" He looked up. "Jonathan, Rald, and Denn. You were young men, talented fighters. Andre says that you were the pick of your commanders, that you all excelled in personal combat."

Nathan didn't know which one of the three he had killed, which two remained, but he was sure all three volunteers had known each other well. "Jonathan had a wife named Maria and a daughter who was sick. As part of the agreement, the wizards agreed to heal the little girl once he volunteered to become an Ixax." He looked down at the pages, at the descriptions. "Rald had a sweetheart, but he broke off his relationship because he believed this was a greater duty." Nathan felt a lump in his throat. "And Denn came from a large family with four brothers and three sisters. He was the youngest, a recruit for the army of Ildakar. His family was so proud of him."

He looked down again at the pages of Andre's diary. The fleshmancer had viewed Rald, Jonathan, and Denn as mere specimens, test subjects, not as tragic human beings. He had ignored their bravery and everything they were giving up. Nathan decided not to read that part of the diary aloud to them.

The fleshmancer described the transformative magic he had used, how he unleashed energy to make the young men's bones grow like trees, their muscles swell and expand, their bodies becoming giants through a combination of fleshmancy and metallurgy. Andre had reinforced their bones with bronze, added armor to their flesh in order to turn the warriors into something more than human. But Nathan knew they were still human inside.

"You agreed to fight for Ildakar," he said. "But you never got your chance. Andre was an unkind, heartless man. I know that, as do you. He tormented you needlessly." He brushed his pale hair away from his cheek and closed the book. He knew what was written there, but he didn't want to read any more of the fleshmancer's petulant complaints against the old duma for not letting him unleash his monstrous warriors.

"Your reasons were pure," Nathan reminded the giants. "I know that your hearts remember. Even though your families, your sweethearts, your children are long gone, Ildakar still needs you. If the time comes, I hope you remember the real reason that you gave up so much. There are good people here, just as you were good people."

Nathan waited in silence for a long moment, then stood. "I will come back, I promise. I'll tell you more stories."

CHAPTER 53

As the cold dawn washed over the mountains, Verna shaded her eyes. Because of the ancient army camped beneath the glaciers, she no longer saw the beauty of Kol Adair. She now knew that the enemy soldiers weren't quite human, and they were on the move from Ildakar, thousands of them. The army had no visible tents, fires, or supplies, just a powerful force moving through the mountains. The prelate could only imagine how much destruction they would cause as they crossed the Old World.

"It is not natural," General Zimmer said. His face was ruddy, and beads of perspiration stood out on his brow. "The D'Haran army is sworn to fight the enemies of Lord Rahl, and there's no doubt it is an invasion force."

"But where are they going?" Verna asked. "Who is their commander?"

"They have gone away from Ildakar," Renn said. "Maybe that is a good thing, from a certain point of view?"

"There is nothing good about this." Captain Trevor shook his head. "What can we do to stop them? We are only a handful against thousands."

Amber continued to stare, her face flushed. "What if they find Cliffwall?"

As the early-morning light spilled over the crags, the enemy army began to stir. Verna said quietly, "We need to hurry, General, whatever we do. Right now, they are vulnerable. They don't suspect we have seen them."

"Why should they care about a few dozen people anyway?" Renn asked. "We are insignificant."

"We're not insignificant," Verna said, "and neither are you, Renn. You are a wizard of Ildakar. I am a Sister of the Light. Even young Amber knows some basic magic, as do these Cliffwall scholars." She gestured to the wide-eyed scholars and memmers who had accompanied them from the canyon archive. "They wanted to learn how to use magic. Now the time has come, and we can't wait."

"You want to attack thousands of ancient soldiers with magic?" Renn sounded skeptical. "What would you suggest? Do you have spells that can wipe out an army of half-petrified warriors? I would love to learn them!"

"It would be folly to attack an enemy army of that size with a handful of spells," Verna said. "We must try something else."

"What did you have in mind, Prelate?" Zimmer asked. "Give me a viable battle plan."

Sheltered by the sparse trees, she looked to the cliffs above the large encampment, where morning sunlight dazzled on the snow hanging on the steep slope. "We don't fight the army directly." She narrowed her eyes as she pointed up. "We use the glaciers as our weapon."

Renn chuckled. "That might indeed have sufficient force. Good idea, Prelate. I see that Nicci is not the only woman with a ruthless imagination when faced with a powerful enemy."

Verna sent word among the rest of the Sisters of the Light, Oliver and Peretta, and the gifted and studious scholars from Cliffwall. They all hurriedly gathered around, knowing they would miss their chance once the army moved.

Renn rubbed his chubby hands together in the brisk morning chill, his eyes bright. "Fifteen centuries ago, General Utros laid siege to Ildakar, and this is my chance to strike a real blow. At last I can be a true hero to my city."

General Zimmer was all business. "What do you need from my soldiers, Prelate?"

Verna considered the high wall of packed snow and ice that had collected above where the thousands of enemy soldiers had gathered. As the army made preparations to pack up camp, she knew all those fighting men would cross Kol Adair and march down to the high desert plains. With their sheer numbers, some scouting expedition would surely discover the hidden canyon, where they would find and overwhelm the Cliffwall archive.

"They are in a perfect position now. We have to stop them before they move out," she said. The rising sun sparkled on the glacial ice fields. "General, have scouts take all our gifted up near the glaciers without being seen." She glanced at Renn's rich maroon robes. "Is there a way you can be less obvious?"

He frowned at the lush fabric he wore. "If you insist." He released his gift, and the deep maroon shifted into a mottled gray and white that would be invisible up in the tundra. "Not my preference, but it will do."

The soldiers were ready to help in any way possible. Captain Trevor stepped up to Zimmer. "My men and I wish to fight for Ildakar."

"You'll have your chance, Captain," Renn said, with a glance at Verna, "but right now it is time for a wizard. Leave it to the prelate and me."

At a fast pace, D'Haran scouts led the way around the bowl and up the slopes to the ice fields. Verna and Renn, the Sisters and the gifted scholars picked their way among the forest deadfall, climbing through sparse trees and over boulders, higher into the rocky cliffs. Below, as the day warmed and illuminated the rugged valley, the ancient army began to form ranks for the next march. Although Verna was out of breath, she urged the climbers to greater speed. "If we don't get to the glacier soon, we will miss our chance."

Scouts raced ahead, finding the easiest routes. "That way ends in a blind cliff," one man said, gesturing them back. "We have to go down to that spine of rock and then up into those adjacent bands. See where it picks up?" Some of the Cliffwall scholars muttered in dismay, but Verna pressed on.

Renn was breathing hard in the thin air. "I hope I have the strength to use my magic once we get there."

"You will," Verna replied, "you have to."

Finally, the scouts guided them through huge talus boulders covered with patches of old snow. Ahead, they looked at the broken hummocks of the glacier field. Each winter the snowfall in the mountains covered the peaks, and even high summer didn't melt it completely, leaving layers that built year after year. Now, heavy glaciers hung poised above the bowl where the army was breaking camp.

Verna's heart skipped a beat. "Hurry! We need to use our magic."

Sister Rhoda's brow was furrowed with concern. "Now that we're here, Prelate, how do we shove this mountainside of ice and snow down on them?"

"Consider the problem in smaller pieces," Verna said. "We can't move all of the snow, but we can release heat. We melt pockets at the bottom, flash the snow into steam, release loose sections. The water itself will lubricate the higher layers of the glacier." She gestured to large fissures. "It's already just waiting to slide down in an avalanche."

She fell silent and closed her eyes. "You can sense the power here. We just need to nudge it. Once it starts, the steam will widen the fissures, and the rest will take care of itself." She smiled, showing grim confidence. "Nature wants to move this glacier down the steep slope. We merely have to encourage it."

Renn smiled. "By the Keeper's beard, I see what you're saying. We can do it."

Oliver nodded. "We learned how to boil water for tea, so we will do the same thing but on a larger scale."

Amber stared across the ice field and pointed upward. "Start with that section up there, near the edge. When the cornice comes down, the rest of the glacier wall should fall behind it."

"Then let's not waste time," Renn said. He gestured with his hands, closed his eyes, and released his powerful gift with a sizzle in the air.

Below in the hanging valley, Verna could hear the loud voices of enemy soldiers as they prepared to move out. She extended her gift into the piles of packed snow and ice and let her magic go into the widening cracks in the blue ice. She released her heat, felt the water melt.

The Cliffwall scholars did the same. The Sisters of the Light pushed, releasing waves of warmth that crisscrossed the glacier field like hot knives. Pockets of steam boiled up, expanding weak voids. Puffs of white vapor coughed out of softer pockets in the snow.

Like a shattering tree creaking and cracking, the glacier wall spread apart. Beneath it, warm water mixed with boulders and glacial debris to form a soup of mud and melted snow.

Verna felt a thrill of excitement. Nearby, Renn clenched his left hand into a fist and gestured in the air, as if the motion helped him hurl his magic with greater force. With a booming crack, the piled cornice of snow on the high cliff shuddered free and slid down the rock face.

That was just the beginning.

Mists of steam curled from the sliding glacier. Sheets of ice shifted and slid forward to crash into the next section of ice, knocking it loose. The Sisters and their trainees concentrated on the front wall, heating the dark boulders trapped inside the ice so that they, too, created pockets of steam, melting more ice.

In the bowl beneath the glacier, thousands of enemy soldiers saw the frozen mountainside shifting and sliding toward them like a living thing. Their outcry echoed into the air as loud as the avalanche.

Verna continued to release her gift, melting more sections of the ice underneath, and soon the entire glacier shoved itself forward, picking up momentum as it rumbled down the mountain with a catastrophic roar.

Beside her, Amber squeezed her eyes shut, clenched her hands, and rhythmically pounded the ground, trying to melt more and more of the snow. Verna touched her wrist, stopped her. "That's enough, child. We've done it."

Amber opened her eyes and turned to watch as the nightmare of snow blocks and ice slabs brought half the mountain down with it. The roar was deafening. Steam and snow spray poured up like a thunderstorm into the air.

The stone army was trapped in the hanging valley, and the glacier buried them in an avalanche that was centuries in the making.

Long after the expeditionary army had been inundated, Verna sat back, shaking, not from exertion, but from the realization of what she had done.

Renn seemed delighted. "Oh, that was magnificent! Exactly what a wizard of Ildakar should do."

Verna watched as the snow and ice continued to settle, as rocks pattered down from the now-naked patch of cliff. The invasion force was entirely buried. "It was what we needed to do," she said.

CHAPTER 54

As the most powerful sorceress in Lord Rahl's army, Nicci was feared and respected. She had once murdered a wizard and stolen his abilities, had learned the Subtractive side of magic through her dark service to the Keeper, and she had become known as Death's Mistress.

Thus, when she presented her warning about Utros and his vast army, the D'Haran garrison believed her. General Linden brought in military scribes to take down her report in detail, and within hours copies were dispatched by two separate riders racing north to the People's Palace. Nicci could crush petty dictators and slave masters, but defeating hundreds of thousands of warriors went beyond what she could deal with alone.

But she didn't have to do everything alone. It had taken her a long time to realize that.

General Linden gathered a succession of his line officers, foot soldiers, cavalry riders, and scouts, so she could show them the terrifying images preserved in Elsa's glass. "I want them all to know," Linden said. "The more our army understands the scope of this threat, the better prepared they'll be to face it."

Nicci walked slowly along the lines of soldiers gathered inside the garrison walls, showing them the images, and she saw that she had struck fear—not gibbering terror, but a genuine respect. By nightfall she had accomplished what she needed to do and decided it was time to return to Ildakar.

She had to make sure the walled city was still safe against the siege. If so, Nicci would travel through the sliph to other large cities along the coast and continue spreading her warning.

Because it was already after dark, Nicci would not enter the dense and trackless Hagen Woods in the hope of finding the isolated sliph well. Instead, she informed Linden, "I will sleep in the barracks and leave at dawn."

"It must be a long journey to Ildakar," Linden said. "Do you need supplies? A military escort?"

"I have other means of travel."

He found her a private room in the officers' quarters, which were redolent of fresh sawdust and green pine. The sweet wood fragrance contrasted with the fishy-smelling kraken-oil lantern that burned on the writing desk. Nicci opened the window shutters to let the cool night breeze drift in. With a flick of her fingers, she snuffed out the lantern from the other side of the room and settled back on the straw mattress. She needed no further comforts. As Nicci drifted off, she cleared her thoughts of strategy, concerns about Ildakar's defenses against General Utros, and the loss of Bannon Farmer. She would sleep.

When she descended into resistant dreams, she felt an animal presence waiting there, a feline awareness that was bound to her. Mrra. Though Tanimura was far on the other side of the Old World, the sand panther remembered Nicci in her dreams.

They ran together. Her wiry muscles pulled her along as she bounded with her hind legs to land on her wide front paws, feeling the curved claws dig into the turf. Nicci felt the joy of being part of the big cat's fine, muscular body. She was exerting herself to her wild limits, fiercely running.

She quickly realized that Mrra was not hunting, and the

cat's pounding heart was more than just the joy of racing free. She was terrified.

Monstrous predators were pursuing the sand panther. Mrra ran along the hills, each leap a desperate attempt to escape. Her long tail thrashed, her claws tore up the dirt. She leaped over a fallen tree as she raced along the black fringe of the burned grass. Her sharp ears heard panting and slavering behind her, like the bellows in a blacksmith shop.

Two huge creatures ran after her, each as large as a small horse, dripping saliva from yellow fangs. They were ferocious and intent on tearing her apart. Mrra ran with all her might. Behind her, the creatures thundered along, their jaws and fangs ready to rip her flank, tear out her throat.

Mrra glanced back, and her golden eyes saw the pursuers, huge wolflike beasts with rounded ears, long heads, and tan fur that made them hard to see among the dry grasses. They snarled, springing forward. Mrra put on another burst of speed, and Nicci offered her own energy, driving the panther faster. But Mrra was exhausted, nearly ready to collapse.

Nicci could only guess what those beasts might be. She'd heard Richard describe heart hounds, vicious creatures that guarded the misty boundaries and the veil to the underworld. The more Nicci recalled his stories, the more convinced she became that these *were* heart hounds. Had they somehow slipped through the veil? But Richard had sealed it! The walls of the underworld should never have allowed such monsters to return.

Mrra dashed into a thicket of scrub oak. She clattered through fallen branches and leaped over a lichen-mottled boulder. The heart hounds rushed into the thicket after her and kept drawing closer.

Nicci knew Mrra couldn't elude them, whether in the forests or in the grassy hills. Heart hounds had senses so acute they could hear a victim's heartbeat even from a distance. Richard had also said the monsters would tear out the heart of their prey and devour it first as a bloody prize.

Nicci rode inside Mrra, pushed her, helped her, but she was in far-off Tanimura, and she couldn't extend her gift through the big cat. She could only use the big panther's body.

Running would not be enough.

There was no place to hide in the grassy hills, even in the darkness.

The heart hounds kept coming.

Nicci stirred in her sleep in the barracks room, but her thoughts stayed with the panther. The big cat's instincts told her to do what any fleeing animal would do, but if she did that, Nicci knew, she would lose.

Listen to me, sister panther, Nicci thought. The heart hounds will run you down. You can't fight both of them. They will wait until you are exhausted and weak.

She felt Mrra growl as she ran. The grassy slope opened up, and Mrra bounded along unhindered, but the heart hounds picked up speed, too.

You've got to do the unexpected, Nicci told her. You have to fight them anyway, so fight on your terms. Our terms. Now! Turn and fight!

The panther spun and, instead of leaping away, used all the power of her hind legs to launch herself into the oncoming beast like a battering ram of claws and fur. Mrra struck just beneath the jaw of the slavering monster, slammed into its barrel chest. Her claws raked along the curved lines of its ribs. Using the heart hound's own momentum, she ripped open the tan fur, gouged into bone, and split the creature's chest. As it crashed down upon her, she clamped her long fangs around its throat, bit down hard, and pulled back. Blood sprayed.

The heart hound collapsed, gurgling, unable to make much sound now that its throat was destroyed. Mrra's instinct was to stay with her victim, rip open the belly and dig out the entrails, but the monster was already as good as dead. Nicci knew that.

Instead, Mrra yanked herself free as the heart hound twitched and bled, impotently snapping its long yellow teeth.

The second beast skidded past, taken by surprise, and over-shot its quarry even as Mrra brought down the first victim. As the other monster scrambled to turn, Mrra abandoned the bleeding carcass and, using all her remaining energy, sprang into the air to land on the second beast's back. The heart hound was already off balance from turning so abruptly in its full-hearted charge. Mrra's weight knocked it down on the grassy ground, and the beast struck out with its paws, trying to throw her off.

But Nicci and Mrra bit down hard, using the big cat's powerful jaws to crunch the back of the heart hound's neck, biting hard enough to sever its spinal cord. With one blow, one deep bite, the second heart hound was paralyzed. When it collapsed, the lower half of its body couldn't even twitch. A steaming puddle of urine pooled out from between its hind legs. In an instant, both enemies were dead.

Mrra stepped back, covered in blood. She padded away from the two dying beasts, her senses still alert. She pricked her ears and listened to the night, making sure there were no other heart hounds howling in the hills.

Even from her bed in the Tanimura barracks, Nicci tasted the hot iron blood in her mouth, felt her pulse pounding from the chase. She and her sister panther had defeated these two creatures that shouldn't have been here at all. Had someone meddled with the veil after Richard's star shift? How could these monsters have escaped from the outskirts of the underworld?

Nicci broke the spell bond, letting Mrra return to satisfy herself with ripping the heart hounds to shreds. Nicci drifted back into her own sleep, but it was far more troubled than before.

CHAPTER 55

The lens to the underworld had faded to misty green opacity, but rumors spread throughout the camp. General Utros withdrew into his headquarters, lost in thoughts and questions. He felt the weight of history, responsibility, and his iron-hard betrayal.

The ancient army continued its daily routine, maintaining the siege. Scouts worked their way through the hills and forests, mapping the landscape and marking towns to be raided or conquered. They delivered summaries to First Commander Enoch, who kept the information to himself until such time as the general requested it.

Even the sorceresses left Utros to his intense concentration. Ava and Ruva had always given him advice, offered ideas, but now he brooded in his headquarters, so deep in thought he seemed to have become a statue again. He sat with shoulders hunched on the sturdy wooden bench, leaning close to the smoldering brazier. Smoke curled around his scarred face, fumes burned his eyes and nose. Without interrupting his thoughts, the twins added various substances, black mineral powders that stung when he inhaled, but made him light-headed. Utros sat in silence, feeling his heart torn, his mind separated into opposing vows, obligations, and desires.

Loyalty is stronger than love.

But, he loved Majel! He still heard her voice, remembered her touch, though he had seen her face and knew what Iron Fang had done to her, and that was the emperor Utros had sworn to obey! Yet, Majel had broken her sacred vow, too, just as he had. Not only had the general torn his loyalty to shreds, he had also stolen the love of his leader's wife. What punishment was too great for that?

Utros hunched over the brazier smoke, closed his eyes, and pressed sharp fingernails against his face, feeling the scar from the dragon burn. Maybe he deserved to be flayed alive, too. What if Emperor Kurgan demanded that of him?

Loyalty is stronger than love.

He sat up, reaching a firm decision, a tactical decision. He was General Utros. That was why Iron Fang considered him so important, and that was why he needed to succeed here at Ildakar. It was the only way he could atone for his great betrayal.

The two sorceresses sat in silence on the other side of the room, so close to each other that their pale bodies touched, the matching scars on their thighs close, as when they had been fused as children. Though the twins had been cut apart, their hearts, their thoughts, and their magic still connected them.

When he looked up at the sisters with a decision clear on his face, Ava and Ruva could see that their beloved general had come back to them. His cool and rational military mind had returned.

"Our emperor made his wishes clear," he said. "You heard him speak from beyond the veil. My charge, *our* charge, is still to bring down Ildakar. Our entire army is duty-bound to make that happen." The two women sat motionless, meeting his flinty glare. "Iron Fang commanded me to find a way to summon a dragon. For that, I will need your help."

General Utros respected magic, treated it as one would handle a poisonous viper, and he let Ava and Ruva do their work. The twins spoke in whispers, sharing ideas, finishing each other's sentences. Moving in eerie synchronicity, they talked about how to find a dragon.

Even fifteen centuries ago, the majestic and terrifying beasts had been extremely rare. On the march toward Ildakar, he had sought out a silver dragon, because such dragons were the most warlike, the most destructive in battle. Silver dragons were also the most difficult to control. Finally, they had succeeded in capturing one of the creatures, a small one, but still a nightmare of metallic scales and fangs, belching fire and acid. Its huge wings could knock down tents and create a wind strong enough to sweep aside a cavalry charge. After they had chained the monster, Utros realized he could never tame it, not with time, nor magic.

The silver dragon had chewed through its chains and burst out of its confinement. In a vengeful fury, the creature had burned hundreds of his soldiers, scorching them to ash, before ripping up the camp. Utros had tried to challenge the dragon himself and force it back into captivity, and as a result the beast had burned the side of his face with a splash of its acid fire.

Now he reached up and ran his fingers across the healed scar that covered his cheek. Emperor Kurgan had commanded him to capture a dragon again.

Ava and Ruva came to him as he stood outside, contemplating the large milky lens to the underworld and dreading his next conversation with Majel or Kurgan. He turned to acknowledge them. "We found a way, beloved Utros," Ava said, her voice faltering. "We can summon a dragon."

Ruva smiled shyly. "It will be painful and dangerous."

His heart felt blank and empty. "As I expected, but pain and danger are our charge."

The two women stepped close like lovers awaiting an

embrace. Ava reached up to stroke his scarred cheek. "In order to find a dragon, we need a connection to dragons. They are distant and rare. The nearest one may be far, far away."

Ruva said, "But you are already connected with dragons, beloved Utros. When the dragon fire burned you and left the scar, it also left part of its essence in you. Dragons are bound to the heart of the world itself, intertwined with magic." She also touched the scar, next to her sister's fingers. "Part of that lingers here on your face. Your skin bears the faint residue of dragon fire, and dragon fire is connected to dragons themselves."

Ava added, "We can use that residue to send a summons that no dragon could resist, if any dragons remain in this land."

Ruva's eyes sparkled with tears. "We have everything we need, General, if you are willing to endure the sacrifice."

"Emperor Kurgan commanded me. I will sacrifice whatever is needed."

The sorceresses placed their delicate fingertips on his waxy flesh. "All we need is your skin, beloved Utros."

Inside the dark wooden structure, the two women built the brazier fires high. They had sealed the doors and windows so that not even First Commander Enoch could see what was happening, nor would any of the soldiers hear his screams.

With the lingering effects of the stone spell, the sensitive nerves on his face were dulled, but not numb enough. He felt the searing pain when the two sorceresses used a razor-edged knife to slice away the scarred half of his face.

He braced himself, sitting in the sturdy chair built out of logs lashed together, but as he clenched the arms, the thick logs creaked. His wrists had been tied to the chair, his chest also strapped to the back, rendering him immobile. He felt as if he might explode from the bonds.

"Just a few moments more," Ava said, being as gentle as she could.

"We are so sorry," Ruva whispered as the sharp dagger tip traced a deep cut under his eye, around his cheekbone, then over to his ear. She peeled down ever so delicately, while Ava tugged on the flap of waxy skin with another knife, pulling his cheek and half of his face away.

Utros groaned deep in his chest and realized that this was what Majel had endured, only her punishment had been far worse. Iron Fang had not only stripped one cheek, but all of her face, then her neck, breasts, back, and thighs, all the skin on her body. Majel had endured that, and she had still been alive when he fed her body to flesh beetles. Utros knew he could tolerate this smaller sacrifice.

Loyalty is stronger than love.

The sorceresses had a shallow basin filled with water next to the brazier. When they finally succeeded in cutting off all the skin that had been marked by dragon fire, they took the uneven scrap of flesh, held it up like part of a mask, and dropped it into the basin, gently washing it, letting the blood infuse the water.

"That is the first step, beloved Utros," Ava said.

When the skin was clean and the water tinted red, Ruva removed the thin scrap of his cheek and tossed it into the brazier, where it burned. Ava added crystalline powders that made the fires blaze brighter, consuming the scrap of skin. It shriveled and blackened like leather.

Using her gift, Ruva damped the flames so she could remove the charred skin. "Now it is ready," she said, dropping the remnants back into the basin with the blood water.

The burned skin crumbled, the ashes dissolving, and the two women peered down into the basin, swirling the water with their fingertips. They began to chant. The small chamber was filled with magic, pulsing and sparkling, as they sent out their implacable call to summon a dragon.

CHAPTER 56

In the duma chamber, while Quentin reviewed lists of names that his representatives had gathered from among the population, Nathan and Elsa worked side by side, sharing ideas in low voices. They had not yet openly raised the suggestion of the Ixax warriors to the duma.

Though the hour was late, Lani also joined them, her skin pale and hard. Nathan knew little about her, but she had challenged Thora for her rule, and that made Lani a decent person, as far as he was concerned.

Without explaining her actions, Lani walked up to the stone table and picked up the pitcher of water left for the duma members. Nathan looked up, curious. "I thought you didn't need to drink or eat?"

Lani looked down into the water in the pitcher. "This is a weapon. It's my own magic."

"I remember your scrying magic." Elsa smiled and turned to Nathan. "It is similar to my transference magic, but Lani has an affinity for water. She can call on it, use it as a conduit, like the aqueducts beneath Ildakar."

"That gift comes from within me. My blood is infused with

it." Lani caressed the curve of the pitcher. "Renn and I would share the things we read in obscure texts, and we discovered many forgotten legends and spells. Thora didn't much care about our studies. She considered herself at the pinnacle of her strength and did not need to learn anything else."

"One should always keep learning," Nathan said. "Even when I was stuck in the Palace of the Prophets for a thousand years, I continued to read and study." He stroked his chin. "Actually, my reasons weren't entirely altruistic. I was hoping to discover a way to escape my prison, so I could live my own life."

"I am glad you finally succeeded, Nathan," Elsa said. "I rather like having you here."

"I can help Ildakar, now that I have the heart of a wizard again."

"But is your gift powerful enough to stop General Utros?" Lani asked.

"Not alone, of course." He self-consciously brushed the front of his wizard's robes. "But surely with everyone joining their magic, we can defeat an old general and a half-petrified army."

"Only if we are aware of what the enemy is doing." Lani turned with the pitcher and surprised them by pouring the water in a spreading pool onto the blue marble.

Nathan yanked his feet up so the water wouldn't splash on his boots. At the opposite table, Quentin looked up from his list of names. He grumbled impatiently, then went back to his work.

Lani knelt next to the spreading pool on the polished floor. "I can use scrying magic to spy on our enemy. I can see what Utros is doing, if he has open water nearby." She sighed. "I wish Renn were here. He always gave me strength, but I will do it without him." She looked up and met Elsa's eyes. "I'll do it for him."

"He will return someday," Elsa said.

Lani held her hands over the water and called upon her gift, making images appear. Thora had used the same magic, scrying through the water basins in Ildakar as an illicit way to spy on her own people. "General Utros will not suspect. I just need to find water, close to him. . . ."

Lani closed her eyes, holding her chalk-white hands above the surface of the pool. She pulled on her gift and pressed her hands lower, until with the faintest of touches, her fingers met the still surface. The images sharpened, and she opened her eyes again.

Curious, Nathan could see shadows forming, and he recognized the place where he and Nicci had spoken to the general in their parley session. "That is his headquarters."

Lani narrowed her eyes. "This is what Utros is doing right now, what he is saying, what he is seeing. I am looking through a water basin in his quarters." Her voice dropped to a whisper, and her expression grew more intent.

The rippling images stilled, and the pool looked like a mirror on the floor. Through the water, Nathan saw Ava and Ruva, their heads shaved, their white skin painted with cryptic swirls and designs. The vision was tinged red, as if seen through stained glass.

General Utros loomed closer as the two sorceresses chanted, pulled with their own magic. Sitting close to the water on the floor, Lani gasped. She seemed frozen, but could not break the vision. She struggled, and the images grew more potent, more startling.

Utros had lost half of his face. Someone had cut the entire burn scar from his cheek, his mouth, beneath his eye. The wound was fresh and raw, dripping blood.

The sorceresses continued their chant, calling in an ancient tongue, then spoke to the general. "We are summoning the dragon. He must come."

Nathan and Elsa both recoiled in astonishment. "Dear spirits, how can they call a dragon?"

When Lani gasped again, the two sorceresses suddenly looked at the water, like eagles spotting a rabbit on the ground. Lani yanked her hands back from the pool, trying to break the scrying spell, but Ava and Ruva leaned closer on their side, throwing harsh magic into the water and following Lani's connection back to her.

"No!" The water on the blue marble floor roiled like soup in a cauldron. The scrying images shattered, but the water continued to writhe, pulling itself together. The liquid rose up in a translucent frothing column and flung itself at Lani's face. She lifted her hands, clawing at the water, which covered her like a smothering sheet.

Nathan and Elsa leaped over the stone table, running to help her. Quentin stood up from his books, staring in disbelief.

Lani thrashed, but could not tear away the water that covered her face, pushing into her mouth, her nose. She couldn't breathe, and the water forced itself inside her.

"She's drowning!" Nathan said. "We have to help her!"

Elsa scribbled a transference rune, tried to move the water. It pulled and squirmed like a jellyfish on Lani's face, pressing into her nose, her eyes. Lani couldn't breathe, but she fought back.

Nathan manipulated the air, creating a vacuum to suck the water away, but Ava and Ruva combined their gift and counter-attacked. He couldn't react swiftly enough.

The water pressed into Lani's sinuses, into her throat. Its force broke her jaw, ruptured her windpipe, shattered her cheekbones from the inside, and the smothering water filled her, flooding her head, her lungs.

Even as Nathan and Elsa frantically tried to help, Lani collapsed to the marble tiles. The floor was now dry, because all the water was within her. The visions were gone.

The sorceress lay dead, her face misshapen and flaccid now that all the bones that held her features had been pulverized. Her stiff skin folded in on itself, and in an evil irony, all the water flowed back out of her nose and mouth, running across the floor.

"Oh, Lani!" Elsa wrapped her arms around the dead woman's shoulders. "Oh, Lani."

Quentin stood behind them, appalled.

Nathan felt stricken and helpless. "I didn't know how to stop it. I could not save her. Dear spirits . . ."

"Dear spirits, indeed," Quentin said. He turned to Elsa and Nathan. "And now we should be even more afraid. We know that General Utros is calling a dragon."

CHAPTER 57

Lila never let herself relax, and Bannon suspected that she didn't know how. The young morazeth remained vigilant, muscles taut, reflexes alert. Even when she shared his bed and showed some small amount of tenderness, she remained a coiled spring ready to react.

Now, when she led him down steep streets to an arched gateway into the rough sandstone bluff, he knew she didn't just want to go for a walk with him.

"We should always be on our guard," she said. Since his escape from the enemy camp, she had occasionally stopped calling him "boy." Perhaps it was an indication of respect, or maybe Lila just forgot herself. "Ildakar's walls have protected our city for thousands of years, but our river defenses keep us safe as well."

In the merchants' district she stopped at an entrance to the supply tunnels within the sandstone bluff, and he followed her into the cool, torch-lit passages. Muscular workers rolled barrels or loaded carts with piled sacks of grain. Some carts were drawn by plodding yaxen, others pulled by broad-shouldered men. Lila walked along at a brisk pace, following the wide tunnel.

"Where did all these supplies come from?" Bannon asked. He had known of previous trade with villages in the hills, but the giant siege army had cut off those routes.

"When we were under the shroud, Ildakar had to be self-sufficient," Lila said. "Our stockpiles can supply us for many years, and that is why the general's siege will never succeed, no matter how long he waits."

Bannon paused at wooden tubs full of fish with drooping whiskers. Their sucker mouths gaped, and their eyes were glassy. "Those are fresh fish, not preserved," he said. "From the river?"

"Once the shroud came down, many villages upriver came to trade with us," Lila said. "We still receive plenty of supplies even with the army encamped on the plain."

As she led him along the tunnel, he spotted daylight ahead, which outshone the torches. Lila brought him to a wide opening that looked out upon the sheer cliff and the river below. She paused at the edge of the opening and peered down the bluffside.

Bannon joined her and saw that while the sheer cliff seemed as unassailable as the high city walls, a network of steps, ladders, platforms, and ramps let people enter and exit through numerous openings on the cliffside to receive deliveries from dock platforms on the riverbank. In the air in front of them, several crows chased each other high above the water.

Lila explained, "We take goods from the trading boats and bring them up here for delivery throughout the markets in the city."

Bannon remembered the three Norukai slaving ships that had come to the city. Kor and his companions must have led their numerous beaten captives up to the slave market by this route.

"We are secure," Lila said. "If anyone tried to attack us from the river, we could drop the platforms, disengage the docks, and isolate ourselves." She stepped right up to the edge and looked down, her feet less than an inch from the drop-off.

Bannon felt dizzy just looking at her. "We have never needed to take such extreme measures."

She stepped out onto the cliff face, finding cleverly hidden stairs in the sandstone. Without a rail or a rope, she began to descend toward a wooden platform twenty feet below them. When he hesitated, she called, "Come with me." She darted down the path carved into the rugged bluff.

Bannon refused to show fear and stepped after her, seeing wider walkways, wooden steps anchored into the rock so that haulers could carry crates, sacks, and barrels into other openings and holding areas. Lila waited for him on the platform below, and he realized she had been testing him. He joined her without comment or complaint. She hurried along steps to another platform, and they worked their way down the cliff.

When he reached a wide spot to spread his feet, he turned to look up. The bluff face was smooth and sheer, showing little natural weathering of the soft rock. Other pockmarks and cave openings led into a warren of tunnels within the uplift. More than a hundred feet below, the river looked blue-green and placid, and the top of the cliff was just as far overhead.

Two small flatboats had tied up against the receiving docks, where Ildakaran workers helped unload sealed barrels from one boat and quarried stone blocks and slabs of rock from the other. Workers used ropes and pulleys to lift the heavy crates along tracks in the cliff to a receiving cave. Other platforms levitated on their own, and Bannon realized that some gifted merchants were using magic to assist in the efforts.

Two levels below, as they climbed down a ladder, Bannon saw a smaller platform no more than four feet wide, which held two basins of fresh-caught river fish, still flopping. Workers high above pulled ropes to raise the tubs of fish to a different receiving cave. Even though their city was under siege, with thousands of enemy soldiers just outside the thick walls, the workers at the river called out in casual conversation, joking and laughing as if this were any normal workday.

Zigzagging along the sheer rock, he and Lila made their way down the sheer bluff. He held on to the sandstone, keeping his balance, and fixed his gaze on her bare back, not looking down. She went to the southern edge of the main bluff, where the stairs switched direction again, and showed him a stream of river water tumbling and gurgling along a wooden chute. Bannon was startled to realize the water was flowing backward, running *uphill* from the river into the aqueduct passages. It splashed and sprayed with the speed of its passage, until it plunged like a reverse waterfall inside the cliff. He saw spell runes carved into the rock.

Lila said, "General Utros blocked off the streams that normally provide water from the valley, but we have all we need from the river. We just bring it up into Ildakar. If necessary, we can also release the water. If invaders try to scale the cliffs, we can open the locks and let our cisterns and storage tanks flood the cliffside."

Bannon followed her to the river's edge, and they had to step aside as workers trudged up the stairs carrying sacks of grain on their shoulders. Finally, at the waterline, they walked out onto the wooden docks, where the two flatboats were being unloaded. Each had a captain and a handful of crew members.

Ildakaran merchants stood beside the flatboats, tallying up supplies and receipts, paying the captains with bags of gold coins and jewels. One city merchant puffed out his cheeks. "The grain doesn't cost any more to produce, and the fish are still fish. Why so expensive?"

The riverboat captain frowned. "Sorry for the increased prices, sir, but with your city under siege, our danger has increased. I have to pay my crew more to convince them to come here."

"War demands higher prices," said the second captain. "Your need is more desperate now, and if you're desperate, then prices go up. Simple commerce."

"We will pay the asking price," the merchant grumbled.

"Ildakar has no use for all this gold anyway. I'd rather have food to eat." He looked down at the last barrels, where the slippery forms still twitched. "And those are eels, my favorite! I'll eat half the cargo myself."

Bannon remained puzzled as he and Lila came forward. "But the siege is on the plains, and the soldiers can't make their way down to the river. Your work is no more dangerous now."

"Oh, there are dangers, young man," said the captain, and the man on the adjacent flatboat nodded as well. "Hanson there comes from downriver, which means he has to skirt the swamps, and if you want the stone he brings from the quarries, he has to take his boat past all those swamp dragons and killer snakes."

Hanson gritted his teeth and nodded again.

The captain continued, "One of the villages down there was destroyed, thanks to some wizard from Ildakar and a morazeth. There's almost nothing left of Tarada now."

Lila frowned at the information. "A morazeth and a wizard?"

The captain nodded. "Tarada was a fine town in a peaceful oxbow. They caused no one any trouble, but then a wizard made himself their new leader, and a morazeth attacked him— a woman just like you. All the villagers suffered, many were murdered, and most of their huts were ruined."

Hanson crossed his arms over his chest and grunted. "So if you want our goods and you ask us to face dangers like that, you can pay a little extra."

"We will pay, as I said," the merchant repeated, eager to be done with the transaction. He had his workers unload the containers of eels onto one of the lifting platforms.

Bannon was confused, looking at Lila. "How can there be a morazeth out in the swamps? Do you think the wizard was Maxim?"

"I have no doubt of that." Lila stared down the wide river toward the swamps, which looked like a festering scar of vegetation. "And I would wager the morazeth was Adessa."

CHAPTER 58

F ar downriver from Ildakar, the swamps finally gave way to normal terrain. Adessa had to worry about normal, natural hazards. And Maxim himself.

She continued her hunt for days after leaving devastated Tarada. She was still scratched and bruised, but she healed quickly, and the extra life energy from her absorbed baby continued to give her unparalleled strength, though she hated to squander the rare blood magic. When she finally cornered the wizard commander, she would need that strength to defeat him.

First, though, she had to find him.

Adessa kept tracking Maxim through the swamps, fighting low-hanging branches, splashing across shallow channels, trying to sense which direction he would have gone. After the explosion of steam and the wash of water that had obliterated Tarada, he had stolen a boat and gone miles downstream before working his way into the wilderness again. He couldn't hide forever, but he had a significant head start on her.

She narrowed her eyes in the waning light. The sun had already set, and orange light filtered through the forest. Frogs and night insects began their music even before darkness fell.

Adessa pushed through the tall grass, but when she heard rustling in the underbrush and the splash of a large animal, she decided to find a protected place to wait out the darkness. She wasn't tired. Her body had enough energy to go all day and night, but it would be a foolish risk to blunder ahead without being able to see. There were too many potential predators, and she could easily lose Maxim's trail in the dark.

Resigned, she found an ancient tree, a swamp oak that might have been growing since the early days of Ildakar. Its trunk was covered with moss and shelf mushrooms. Overhead, among dangling vines and the patchy beards of swamp moss, she saw a wide horizontal branch and decided that would be a good place to spend the night, high enough above the ground. Finding handholds in the cracked bark, she scampered up the trunk. When she reached the wide branch, she swung her legs over either side of it, feeling the rough bark on her bare thighs.

Darkness fell like a blanket tossed over the trees. Adessa didn't need a fire, since the air was warm and humid, and she had no food to cook anyway. Instead, she settled herself in a comfortable position, her back against the trunk, her legs drawn up on the thick branch. She tugged some of the nearby loose vines, snapped the twigs and air roots that held them in place, and lashed herself to the branch to keep her from falling while she slept.

For many nights she had lain awake, alert, resting her muscles but not her mind. Now, she felt secure enough that she could give her body what it needed. She channeled her breathing, felt her heartbeat, concentrated on her singular goal.

She repeated the words of Sovrena Thora in her mind. "Kill him. Leave the city, now, and hunt him down." The command was burned into her memory, and Adessa had accepted it. "Bring his head back to Ildakar. The people of this city must see that the wizard commander has met justice."

She imagined the moment when she would defeat the wizard commander and use her long combat knife to cut off his head.

Adessa's thoughts stopped there. She didn't let herself think of what she would do after she completed her mission. For now, there was no "after." Killing Maxim was the only thing in her life.

As she pressed against the trunk, she felt only a slight easing of tension in her muscles. Not quite relaxation, but it was enough. A morazeth didn't need much.

She thought about the women she had trained to fight at her side to serve the needs of Ildakar. No arena warriors were as great as the morazeth, and Adessa was the greatest of them all, but she had left her sisters, and she was here now, out in the swamps alone, tied to a tree above the ground in a dangerous night.

Adessa closed her eyes, touched her flat abdomen, and traced the fine rune brandings on the taut skin, but she thought of the unborn child that was no longer inside her womb. If she had let Ian's baby come to term, it wouldn't have been her first child. She'd let herself be impregnated by four other champions. Three daughters were now being raised by gifted nobles, and if they proved worthy, Adessa would take them as morazeth trainees. None of them knew their mother's identity, and she would not treat them differently. Her last child, a boy, was of no use to her. Apparently, he was a rambunctious young man who had difficulty learning his sums, and therefore posed problems for the merchant family that had adopted him.

Adessa inhaled the air redolent of rot and swamp flowers, closed her eyes.

Ian's unborn child was different. Ian had been a brave and strong young man, devoted to Adessa, until Bannon and the sorceress Nicci helped turn the entire city against the long-established order.

Ian . . .

She remembered how she had taught him to please her. When she took his body into hers, it was like a form of physical combat, and Ian had excelled at it. He was, after all, the champion.

She shut off those thoughts. Ian was dead because she had killed him. The child growing within her womb had served a different purpose, providing the magical strength she would need to defeat Wizard Commander Maxim. Nothing else mattered.

Adessa heard a rustling below and looked down from her high branch to see large creatures prowling along the ground on stumpy legs, gliding through the muddy water in search of prey, a pair of swamp dragons with jaws that could snap through the thickest thighbone. Adessa was high above, though, and the swamp dragons didn't even look up. She made no sound.

As an exercise, she considered dropping from the branch, thrusting her dagger into the backs of their skulls, and killing both of them. It would have been enjoyable and would have provided fresh meat, but Adessa remained where she was. She needed to rest. She needed to find Maxim.

She could slay all the swamp dragons she liked, once she had the wizard commander's head in a sack. *That* was the joy she anticipated most. Other forms of entertainment would wait.

She rested her head against the trunk, checked the vines holding her in place, and closed her eyes. Tomorrow she would continue the hunt.

The wizard commander would not elude her forever.

CHAPTER 59

As she left Tanimura, Nicci felt satisfied with the response from the D'Haran garrison, confident that General Linden would build up the defenses and alert the rest of Lord Rahl's army. She was already making plans for similar missions to major Old World cities, but after she had dream-witnessed Mrra's battle with the heart hounds, Nicci worried about Ildakar. She had to get back.

"Breathe!"

Returning via the sliph, Nicci rolled over the low wall inside the chamber in the lower levels of the city. She dropped to her knees on the hard floor, coughed up the silvery presence that filled her lungs, her heart and soul. The sliph was in her, but she forced it out.

In the shadows of the unlit chamber, Nicci summoned a light in her hand as she got to her feet. The glow filled her surroundings, and she smelled the damp rock and moss. She turned to find the sliph waiting in her well, gleaming, metallic, and beautiful.

"Tell me what you achieved for the cause," the sliph said. "Tell me about Sulachan and how our war fares." She was eager and intense. "I sacrificed everything long ago to achieve

421

victory against the wizards of the New World. I expect the same sacrifice from all our allies."

"What I accomplished is not your concern," Nicci said. She thought the sliph might be able to detect a lie, and she didn't want to answer at all.

The creature was incensed. "I need to know. I can travel from city to city, but I see only my well. It has been so long since I carried anyone else. Tell me news."

Nicci would need to use the sliph again to travel, but she was uneasy that the strange woman was so curious, so demanding. Placing her hands on her hips, Nicci faced the sliph. "Talking about secret missions is a sure way for the cause to fail. You took me to Tanimura, and I did what I had to do. You don't need to know what it was. Soon, I will require you to take me elsewhere for another mission. I expect you to cooperate."

"I will cooperate," the sliph said, sulking.

"Be satisfied to know that you are helping me."

"So long as you and I fight for the same cause," she warned.

Nicci felt a hint of suspicion in the creature's voice. Without answering, she went to the door of the low chamber and emerged into the daylight of Ildakar. Behind her the sliph remained, watching her for a long moment before she melted back into her placid pool.

Utros's half-petrified soldiers continued to pound on the walls. Ildakaran engineers had discovered alarming, hair-thin cracks within the ancient blocks, and gifted nobles used magic to reshape and solidify the stone before the cracks could widen.

With a gathering crowd of curiosity seekers around her, Nicci went to the ruling tower to report about her trip to Tanimura. When she walked into the chamber, Rendell was talking about all the work ungifted people did throughout the city, sharpening swords, fashioning armor, creating weapons, and generally keeping Ildakar functioning. The former slave's words faltered as soon as Nicci entered.

Nathan jumped to his feet. "Dear sorceress! I am glad to see you."

Her gaze swept around the room. "I informed the D'Haran garrison about Utros and his army, and Lord Rahl will soon be aware of the threat. We cannot expect reinforcements any time soon, though. Ildakar must defend itself. Have you made any progress? Found any new weapons?"

Olgya explained that the Ildakaran silk houses were working to create enhanced worms that spun even tougher silken armor. Before the woman could finish her report, Bannon dashed in, grinning, accompanied by a businesslike Lila. "Nicci! You're back."

Though overwhelmed with surprise to see the young man still alive, Nicci controlled her reaction. "I'm pleased to see that you survived. You are a good fighter, and I would not have wanted to lose you." He seemed overly exuberant as usual, and hurried forward, but reconsidered a welcoming embrace at the last moment.

Elsa added in a heavy voice, "We also have bad news. Lani is dead."

The conversation in the chamber became low and muted. Nicci asked, "What happened to her?"

Nathan stroked his long white hair. "She used her water-scrying magic to spy on General Utros, but his two sorceresses caught her and struck back."

"Lani was no match for them," Elsa said. "They killed her, right here. And we could not save her."

"That is a blow," Nicci said. "We need every gifted fighter, and Lani was strong."

Nathan said, "It gets worse, I'm afraid . . . dear spirits, it gets worse. Before she was killed, Lani learned that Utros and those two women were working a summoning spell. Something so powerful that it terrifies me."

"It terrifies all of us," said Quentin. "We should seriously consider our last resort of raising the shroud before the general can succeed. Sovrena Thora offered us her cooperation."

Nicci didn't want to hear about Thora. "What did Lani discover? What summoning spell?"

Nathan said, "Utros intends to summon a dragon. He has a connection, and the sorceresses drew upon it."

Damon's voice cracked, showing his fear and stress. "If a dragon joins that ancient army, our walls won't be able to protect us. The monster will wreak havoc on Ildakar. Countless thousands of lives will be lost, our homes destroyed."

Nicci understood the threat. "If General Utros can command a dragon, then we have to prepare."

Quentin said, "If a dragon comes, what can we do? We haven't found a sufficient weapon."

Nathan looked down at the stone table in front of him, then squared his shoulders. "I have been waiting for Nicci before even suggesting this." He looked at them all with his alert azure eyes. "Ildakar does have such a weapon, and now we truly have to consider it." Intrigued, Nicci waited for him to say more. Nathan rose to his feet. "Sorceress, come with me. You can tell me whether or not I'm mad even to suggest the idea."

In broken patches of sunlight in Andre's ruined studio, Nicci stared at the towering Ixax warriors. "You destroyed one of these yourself when you regained your gift," she said.

Nathan and Elsa were beside her, both uneasy. Nathan said, "Mirrormask unleashed it to cause chaos, and the Ixax was maddened by centuries of mindless inactivity." He lowered his voice, stroking his chin. "The fault lies squarely on Andre's shoulders."

Nicci looked at the two remaining titans. Behind the slits in their cumbersome helmets, she saw their yellow eyes staring straight ahead.

Nathan moved closer to them, as if to demonstrate his confidence. "These two have suffered the same endless waiting, but the souls of the original young men are still inside them—I know it. When Ildakar was first threatened, long ago, they volunteered to become these monstrous warriors. But they remember, and they know the city's need."

Nicci thought about the sliph, who had similarly volunteered to become something inhuman because of her fierce devotion to a cause. "Are you sure they remember their loyalty? Have you spoken with them? *Can* you speak to them?"

"I have been talking to them regularly, reading them stories, legends, and history," Nathan said. "I've explained what is happening now outside the walls, with the reawakened army. I am convinced they understand."

Elsa touched his arm. "We reminded them of their duty. The Ixax may not be able to defeat a dragon, but they are the most powerful weapon Ildakar has right now."

Nicci nodded slowly. "They were designed to slay tens of thousands of enemy soldiers. They would certainly cause much greater harm than our surprise attack the other night." She studied the giant warriors for a long moment. They would be devastating in their own way. "Yes, I think we should take the chance."

CHAPTER 60

Fighting stormy seas, the Norukai fleet sailed south from the jagged islands, heading to the wide mouth of the estuary where the Killraven River spilled into the ocean.

Fifty sturdy serpent ships, blessed by the blood of Yorik and the grace of the serpent god, pushed across the open water, their dark blue sails stretched tight by guiding winds. Whenever the breezes faltered, King Grieve would sound the drums, and his warriors extended the lines of oars to row the ships onward.

Grieve had always been a restless man. Sitting on his blocky throne left him impatient, so he tended to leave the Bastion walls and roam the island, hunting by himself or taking a small boat to one of the nearby islands. His people needed to see him, and they needed to fear him.

Wanting to fight, he would provoke clan leaders, yell at them, open his scarred mouth wide as if to bite their faces off. He insulted them, shamed them until they retaliated. Occasionally, some hotheaded fool got angry enough to challenge him for the rule of the Norukai, and those reluctant challengers always died. Grieve selected them carefully.

Now, the Norukai islands were half empty, since the bravest were with him aboard the serpent ships in his giant navy, while others had gone off in separate fleets with the disgraced Kor or Lars. Those others were misfits and lackluster warriors, mostly drunkards, those with exorbitant gambling debts, or cuckolds who couldn't face their fellow warriors without shame. King Grieve knew they would fight with wild abandon, but he was interested in blood and glory for himself. Ildakar was a legendary city with countless wizards and ancient defenses that had held for centuries, but no mere city could stand against a Norukai invasion.

He stood behind the serpent carving that roared from the prow of his ship. When he grew bored of staring at the waves and the spray, he stalked back along the deck. His shaman pranced alongside him, unable to contain his energy. "Sailing, sailing, sailing!" Chalk said. "We are sailing, and soon we will kill. I've seen it. We will kill! Ildakar will be *gone*! My Grieve, King Grieve! They'll all grieve."

"Yes, I'm your Grieve, and our enemies will grieve."

"We'll kill soon, I've seen it." The albino grinned with glee.

Grieve knew they were still far from the estuary. "What will we kill?" On the open sea they wouldn't find any ships, nor would they bother to attack small coastal towns, like Renda Bay. Not this time.

"Don't know, my Grieve." Chalk looked away as if he had failed his king. He stared into the sun without blinking, gazing for so long that Grieve thought he might go blind. He knocked the gangly shaman aside. Chalk rubbed his eyes. Back at the Bastion, he would stare at the flames in the large hearth and sort out his visions. Now without a convenient fire, he seemed to seek premonitions in the sun itself.

With a brisk wind, the water was rough and choppy. Even though Chalk had sailed with him from island to island, this was the longest ocean voyage the pale man had endured. For the first three days, Chalk was abominably sick, clutching his stomach with one hand and holding on to the rail with the other as he retched over the side, convinced that the serpent god had cursed him, that somehow Yorik's sacrifice hadn't been sufficient. In his misery, he threatened to throw himself overboard, but Grieve held him back.

"It is not the serpent god. It's just sickness from the sea. You know that others get it." Even brave Norukai with painfully scarred faces, warriors eager to bloody their hands and weapons on raids, could be struck with seasickness, for which they were mocked by the other Norukai.

Two raiders had snickered and insulted Chalk on this voyage, and King Grieve clubbed one of the men to death while he was guffawing. With the man's head leaking brains like a broken cliff gourd, Grieve heaved him over the side of the ship.

The second mocking man fell to his knees and bowed. "Forgiveness, King Grieve! Let me die in battle."

Grieve turned to Chalk. "It is your decision. Should he die?"

Utterly miserable, the shaman had shaken his head and staggered to the side of the boat, where he vomited again. Grieve made sure he drank enough water to keep himself alive. Finally, after three choppy days, the seas calmed and Chalk's queasiness retreated. Now that he was over the worst of it, the shaman was again full of energy, eager to see the coast, the river, and Ildakar.

As they sailed, the serpent ships dragged nets to catch fresh fish to eat. The food was considered an offering from the serpent god and far better than the preserved and salted stores. For himself, King Grieve had brought along the last of the yaxen meat from Ildakar, which he refused to share.

The raiding fleet sailed through gray waters. Chalk darted to the side of the ship, tugging on Grieve's muscular arm. "I've seen it. You'll see it, too! Look." He pointed, but Grieve couldn't see anything on the waves. "Killing!"

Hearing the excited jabber, other Norukai strode to the side of the vessel. A shout came from one of the adjacent serpent ships, and Grieve shaded his eyes. "There!" Chalk said. "I told you we will kill soon. Look!"

"Selka." The Norukai warrior beside him growled in his throat. "Look on the waves, my king."

Now Grieve did see bobbing figures, slick gray shapes swimming there, but they were not human. Grieve ground his molars together, felt his jaw muscles strain. "Selka . . ." He said the word as if spitting poison. "Why doesn't the serpent god just devour them all and rid the seas of their stain?"

He felt a blood fire in his gut. The selka were an undersea race of vicious monsters that might once have been human long ago. They swam together and served their cruel selka queen. The creatures attacked ships they considered trespassers. They would swarm up the hulls or tear holes below the waterline. The selka had iron-hard claws and rows of daggerlike teeth.

Despite their fearsome appearance, though, they could be killed. Grieve knew that for a fact, because he had killed many himself. Often the selka would overwhelm a Norukai ship with their numbers, and then leave the vessels adrift after murdering everyone aboard. Sometimes the wrecks were found on the open sea, the dark blue sails shredded, the masts broken, claw marks, slime, and blood all over the decks. Grieve hated the selka.

A succession of shouts rang out from the serpent ships. The Norukai gathered spears, axes, and harpoons, preparing for an attack from the water. They called out to the selka, taunting them, daring the creatures to come closer.

"Too many," Chalk said, shaking his head. "Too many."

"We will fight them," Grieve said. "I don't care how many there are."

"No, no, my Grieve. Too many *of us*. The selka are afraid. Too many! The Norukai would kill them all. They won't attack."

"Then they are wise," Grieve said, disappointed. He saw at least a hundred selka, but he had thousands of Norukai warriors. The creatures kept their distance, and Grieve glowered, challenging them.

One figure bobbed in front of the rest, brightly colored and vicious. He thought it was the selka queen. If so, he wanted to jam his fist in her mouth and break through her skull. He grinned at the thought.

From the stern of the ship, when the Norukai pulled the knotted ropes and raised the trolling nets to see what fish they had caught, the men shouted in surprise and triumph.

Chalk bounced up and down. "Told you, told you! Now we kill."

A selka was caught in the net. It had tried to slip in among the serpent ships for a treacherous attack, looking for a way to damage their hulls. How many others might be unseen below the surface? The entangled selka writhed and clawed at the net, almost breaking free, but the Norukai pummeled it with their clubs and axes.

"Don't kill it!" Grieve yelled. "Not yet."

The battered creature had large slitted eyes and a wide fishlike mouth that seemed a mockery of how Norukai scarred their mouths to look more like the serpent god, but Grieve knew these selka were no children of the serpent god.

Even cut, bruised, and bleeding, the selka snapped its jaws and slashed at them with its claws. Grieve strode forward, not fearing the thing. He balled his fist and punched the selka full in the face. The impact of his iron-reinforced knuckles made a squelching sound accompanied by a crunch of facial bones. The selka spewed blood from its flattened nostrils, leaking slime and saliva from its slack mouth.

Grieve said, "Tie a rope around its ankles and take it to the mainmast." He secured the thick chain-link belt around his own waist.

The Norukai dragged the stunned creature across the deck, leaving a trail of slime and blood as if a slug had curled its way across the boards. Grieve stood beside the tall mast. Gazing out at the water, he saw that more selka had gathered just beyond the reach of the serpent ships. Grieve could sense their anger, but the selka spy and saboteur was a prisoner of war. They had sent it here to attack, and he would treat it accordingly.

One of the Norukai climbed the mast with the other end of the rope, which he threw over the yardarm. Grieve seized the dangling end and pulled hand over hand, hoisting the captive selka up off the deck so that it swung head down. The rope remained tight around the creature's ankles, lashing its webbed feet together. As it hung high above the deck, the captive selka hissed and stirred, swaying like bait on a fisherman's hook.

Grieve tied off the rope on a deck stanchion. The inverted selka struggled but could find no purchase in the air. It bent its back, trying to reach the rope at its ankles, but to no avail.

Grieve bellowed out to the open water. "Selka queen! We have one of yours. Watch what we will do to all of you!" The big king climbed the mast, hand over hand, holding on to a rigging rope until he reached the yardarm from which the selka hung. The captive swung and clawed at the air, unable to reach Grieve.

From his high position, the king bellowed, "Watch, selka queen!" He pulled out his knife, whose hilt was carved from a sea-serpent skeleton that had washed ashore on one of the Norukai islands. With one hand, Grieve pulled the flailing creature close. With his other hand, as he balanced precariously on the yardarm, Grieve drew the razor edge across the selka's throat. The creature gaped and snapped with its jaws, but now its neck yawned open like a wide red gill slit. The selka shuddered as its blood sprayed out.

Below, Chalk bounded along on the deck, raising his pale hands to receive the spattering of red rain. Other Norukai joined the shaman, turning their scarred faces upward and letting selka blood fall on them.

From up on the mast, the king could see the gathered selka on the water, angry and vengeful, but wise enough not to attack the Norukai raiding force.

When the body was drained, Grieve cut the rope and let

the selka fall to the deck, where it lay cracked and broken. He worked his way down and jumped the last five feet to the boards. He bent over the selka body and used his big knife to hack off the creature's hideous head. It was slimy, covered with blood, its slitted eyes dull, but still open. Grieve decided to mount it on a spike behind the carved serpent head on the prow.

"I will keep this for my collection, but take the body. Keep the rope tied around its feet and drop it over the side. Drag it behind our ship so the selka can smell the blood in the water." He chuckled. "Maybe they will learn their lesson." He doubted it, though.

The Norukai cast the headless selka body overboard, and it drifted in their wake.

Less than an hour later, the rope tugged hard, and King Grieve wasn't surprised when his crew pulled the rope back in to find the body gone, the rope gnawed through by sharp teeth.

CHAPTER 61

With the dire possibility of General Utros summoning a dragon, the duma members were forced to make a swift decision, rather than indulge their penchant for endless debate. Once Nicci added her voice to Nathan's and Elsa's, the council voted unanimously. Ildakar would unleash the two Ixax warriors as a powerful weapon against the enemy.

Late at night, workers lashed together large wooden platforms mounted on heavy iron-shod wheels, creating a pair of carts sturdy enough to carry the Ixax warriors. Using ropes for balance, work teams pulled the armored titans, supporting them as they tilted the massive figures, while Nathan and Nicci used their gift to cushion the fall with air as the giants landed on the wagon beds.

With the Ixax warriors prone on the large carts, teams hauled them through the rubble of Andre's villa and out into the open. They led a nighttime procession through the streets of Ildakar, slowly guiding the Ixax wagons toward the walls and the main gate. Many people came out to watch under the glowing streetlights. Some cheered in foolish defiance of General Utros, while the wiser citizens were somber and frightened.

The city had fallen ominously silent hours before, when

the ancient half-petrified soldiers outside the walls ceased pounding and withdrew to the main army, without explanation. Nathan knew that was not a good sign. Utros must be planning something terrible. What if he had found a dragon? That alone was enough to spur them to greater speed. Now, the procession replaced the ominous silence with defiant noise as they approached the giant gate.

As Nathan and Elsa walked alongside the slow-moving carts with Nicci leading the way, the wizard looked at the enormous warriors lying back and staring upward at the starry sky through the slits in their helmets. Nathan realized this was the first time these titans had seen the stars in more than fifteen centuries. He thought again about what those innocent young men had sacrificed. Jonathan, Rald, and Denn.

The procession passed gathered crowds. Children looked wide-eyed at the colossal warriors rolling past, while parents, old men, merchants, and freed slaves watched uneasily. With forced good cheer, Nathan ignited a bright fire in his palm. "Why so sullen? Dear spirits, we must cheer for these heroes, our Ixax warriors! They will save Ildakar. Show how much you appreciate them. They have given everything for your city." He flared his hand torch brighter.

Elsa smiled, realizing what he meant. "Yes, everyone—cheer!" She let out a whistle and lit her own magical fire. "For the Ixax warriors, for the defenders of Ildakar!"

With a slowly building ripple, shouts rang out along the streets, and the congratulatory applause grew louder. Walking beside the armored head of one Ixax, Nathan bent close to whisper, "Listen to them, my friend. They know you and they appreciate you. Soon, you will finally get to do what you've waited to do for centuries."

Elsa's bright glow lit the other side of the groaning cart. After Nicci heard Nathan urge greater and greater cheers, she responded by sending up a column of fierce wizard's fire in a dazzling beacon that awed the crowd.

The heavy carts rolled down the streets, passing the now empty and shadow-filled combat arena, the merchants' district, warehouses, and workers' homes, to finally arrive on the broad lower levels in front of the high walls. Dawn was just breaking, a glow rising to the east behind the city. The towering gates were closed and barricaded, and the carts bearing the two Ixax warriors stopped just behind them.

"These Ixax warriors remember their hearts, their families, and their city," Nathan announced. "They will defend us, as they swore to do so long ago."

High Captain Stuart commanded his sentries to release the locking spells, roll back the gears, and ratchet the crossbars out of their sockets. With a mighty heave, dozens of workers hauled on ropes, slowly creaking open the gigantic gates of Ildakar.

Impatient with the ponderous barrier, Nathan waved his hand and added a push of magic. By now, the sky was brightening, and the sun was over the river behind the bluff. When the gates were open far enough, teams guided the two carts carrying the colossal warriors through the gap.

The general's army had withdrawn far from the walls, and the ancient soldiers stirred in their camp.

Concerned, Nicci said to Nathan, "Look at the army. Something is happening. General Utros is making his move."

"Then we must make ours," Nathan said. "Quickly now." He turned to Elsa and the duma members who had accompanied them. "No time for a work crew. Use your gift. Let us stand our defenders on their feet and prepare to set them free at last."

The newly constructed carts tilted down, placing the giant boots of the Ixax on the ground. Nathan released his gift. Nicci added her push. Oron, Damon, Quentin, and Elsa all used their magic, helping to raise the first warrior upright. He stood on his massive legs like a sentinel statue, half as tall as the huge city gates.

Working together, they raised the second Ixax warrior, so that the pair stood immobile but ready. Nathan could sense a difference in the giants, a tingling anticipation behind their armor, as if their blood was beginning to boil, trapped inside their encased forms.

"Soon," Nathan said to them, gesturing. "Soon! You can see your enemy now, that giant army out there." Though he wasn't sure the Ixax could shift their gaze, thousands and thousands of troops filled the plain before Ildakar. The sheer number of foes was breathtaking, but the Ixax seemed ready. Anxious.

"Those soldiers are a threat to Ildakar. They want to shatter the walls and ransack the city," Nathan said. The sky continued to brighten. "They plan to conquer Ildakar in the name of Emperor Kurgan, who has been dead for centuries. You can save us." He looked up at the giant warriors. "The two of you can save us."

Shouts came from the sentries on the walls above. General Utros was clearing a great area in his camp for some unknown purpose, and Nathan felt a growing dread. The other wizards looked around, also expecting something.

Nathan swallowed hard, and turned to Elsa. "Very well, my dear, let us prove ourselves right." He looked at the towering inhuman soldiers. "Remember who you are. Remember why you were created."

Elsa added, "Remember us. You have to remember us." Then she activated the embedded rune on the plates of the Ixax armor, illuminating the mark with a glow of magic, setting them free.

The symbol flared, brightened, and Nathan heard a cracking sound as the joints became unfrozen, long-hardened muscles thawing. The eyes in the helmets blazed brighter, bonfires of anger and frustration. In a flash, Nathan remembered the night he had almost died when he'd faced a single Ixax. He, better than anyone else, knew the danger and power these things represented.

Now he was unleashing them, on purpose.

Moving now, coming alive again, they swiveled their huge helmeted heads down to give a knowing look to Nathan. Then, with a groan of ancient, unparalleled power, the Ixax warriors began to move.

CHAPTER 62

It was a bright morning, a fateful morning, and the sun rose above Ildakar's bluffs, silhouetting the city. General Utros studied the haze in the air, the orange colors of brightening dawn, and he felt the magic around him strengthening—the magic that Ava and Ruva had released.

Because the spell was tied to the skin they had peeled from his face, Utros was part of the magic as well. When his sorceresses had burned the dragon-fire scar and mixed the ash with his blood in the water basin, a magical bond had been forged like a gossamer net cast throughout the gift. They knew it would take time. Finally, days later, in the darkness of the headquarters structure, all three of them had sensed . . . a dragon. Yes, their spell had found one of the magnificent ancient beasts, and caught it.

Even during Kurgan's original reign of conquest, dragons had been imposing, unpredictable beasts, and rare. Now, with the powerful spell Ava and Ruva cast, they had found one dragon. Only one.

"He is distant," Ava said in a hushed whisper. Ruva leaned closer, stroking Utros's cold, hard skin. They shared their body warmth, their magic, their presence with him. "But we will make him come to us, through you."

At midnight, Utros had withdrawn his lines of troops from the wall, where their unceasing pounding had begun to shiver Ildakar's defenses. He knew the unexpected silence would unnerve the enemy, make them cower because of the quiet as much as they feared the hammering.

Sooner or later the walls would come down. The wizards inside had reinforced the blocks with their spells, but it was only a matter of time, and after fifteen centuries as a statue himself, Utros wasn't worried about time. His emperor and his beloved Majel were already with the Keeper in the underworld. Utros wanted to succeed, *needed* to succeed to atone for his broken loyalty. Having seen Iron Fang's absolute fury and vengeance, Utros knew he would not be forgiven easily. Maybe if he conquered the entire world . . .

Ildakar was the first step.

Once the pounding soldiers retreated, the night had been left with resounding silence while Utros made final preparations.

After painstakingly removing any hint of hair from their bodies, the women had used fingertips and bright pigments to daub designs over each other's arms, necks, faces, breasts, each making her sister an exotic sensual masterpiece. With their bodies so colorfully painted, neither of the sorceresses needed clothes.

Utros knew they wouldn't fail him. During the initial workings of the spell, after they dissolved his scar and sent out their call, they had discovered the water-scrying sorceress from Ildakar, but Ava and Ruva had dealt with the spy. Now his enemies inside the city were likely aware of his plan, even though they could do nothing to stop it. How could even Ildakar prepare against a dragon in thrall to Utros?

After tense days of waiting, the time had come, and there was no sense in hiding their plan. Ildakar would burn, its walls would fall, its people would scream and try to surrender, though it would be far too late. Now, at the break of dawn, Utros walked with the twin sorceresses to the center of the plain. He had ordered his soldiers to clear a great open area in full view of Ildakar. It was time for Ava and Ruva to pull on the unbreakable spell chains and drag the giant dragon here to do the general's bidding.

The women walked naked alongside General Utros out to the summoning point. Ruva spoke in a husky whisper. "Daybreak is the cusp between darkness and light, a time when magic is at balance, when certain spells are easier."

Ava added, "It is not easy, beloved Utros, but my sister and I will give all we have. We will bring you the dragon."

Now that the sun was up, the twins were ready. Utros stood in his ancient uniform, leather armor with polished metal strips, the helmet with the imposing bull's horns. Around him, his army had erected banners to bring Iron Fang's flame emblem to the battlefield again. Utros touched the large sword at his side, squeezed the leather of his gauntlets, felt the tight bracer on his right arm.

Sunlight reflected off the beaten-gold mask that covered the left side of his face, where his skin had been cut away. Ava and Ruva had used magic to fashion a half mask out of raw gold, shaping rings, bracelets, and necklaces into a covering that fit precisely against his exposed flesh. It seemed more glorious than his old dragon scar. It made him feel legendary.

"From which direction will the dragon come?" Utros asked.

Ava and Ruva turned slowly. "He will come from the sky, but we can't know more than that. We have yet to call him."

Two soldiers had brought large drums to the center of the wide clear space, according to the sorceresses' commands. The women knelt, each facing a drum. With open palms and half-petrified hands, they began pounding a loud beat that resonated across the hushed army. The drumming was only part of the summons, though. They released their gift, and Utros could feel it tingling through his own body. Because of the scar and skin he had sacrificed to the spell, he and all dragons were joined by an invisible bond. Ava and Ruva sent the thrumming call through that bond, like a plucked string on a musical instrument.

Utros felt a lurch inside himself, like a trout struggling against a fishline, and then a surge of exhilaration. He knew the dragon was there, knew it was coming. He could feel the sheer power, the ancient reptilian strength, a creature whose very existence was tied to the bones of the world.

Ava and Ruva continued pounding the drums. The magic sparked like lightning through the air, cowing his thousands of soldiers. He no longer thought of the fires that had scorched the grass hills, or the separate armies he had dispatched on their own missions of conquest. All that mattered was this moment, this place, and the dragon that answered his summons.

With a thrill of never-forgotten fear, Utros recalled the wild silver dragon that he had captured long ago. That debacle should have made him terrified of dragons, but the general did not accept terror. He did know respect, however. With the bond through his skin, through the scar, Utros would command such a beast.

He heard a mutter of anticipation. He could feel the approaching dragon before any of his sentries caught sight of it. Ava and Ruva hammered the drums, sending loud reverberant thumps into the air and across the valley, like the frantic heartbeat of a doomed man.

The women stopped abruptly, sitting back on their heels and looking at the sky. Utros spotted a winged shape flying impossibly high, no more than a gray fleck against the blue. He felt it tugging against the bond, and then he saw the huge wings, the long sinuous neck, the lashing barbed tail.

Hushed gasps and outcries of amazement rippled across his countless soldiers. Once he sent the dragon against Ildakar, Utros wanted his entire army to attack as well, but even with his regimented tactical mind, Utros couldn't worry about details of the military operation. Not now. His awe was too great.

The dragon swooped in, indomitable and unbelievable. It was far more ancient and much larger than the wild silver dragon he remembered from long ago. This one was a gray dragon that radiated unbelievable age, immeasurable wisdom, and the bile of anger that twisted back through the magical bond, lashing at the general's heart.

With a bellows whoosh of hot air and a pounding of great weight, the dragon landed heavily before General Utros. Ava and Ruva stepped back from their drums as the general faced the creature. "You are mine," he said.

The dragon's head was as large as a horse cart, its jaws so wide and powerful they could snap a bull in two and swallow it in a single gulp. The yellow eyes burned with an inner fire, and smoke curled from its nostrils. Remembering the burn of the acid flames the silver dragon had spat at him, Utros knew this massive creature could incinerate him with a single breath.

The dragon's deep voice rumbled like a storm. "Why did you summon me from Kuloth Vale?" The black forked tongue lashed out like a weapon.

"I am your master," Utros said. "I command you to fight for me and my army."

The gray dragon curled its wide serpentine neck. "I am Brom, and I have no master."

In response, the general tugged on the magical bond, watched the dragon twitch in surprise. Ava and Ruva worked a spell, muttered incomprehensible words, and jabbed in perfectly synchronized motions. Brom flinched as if they had pierced him with hot slivers of metal.

"I am not yours to command!" Brom retorted. "I guard the bones of my ancestors." Smoke boiled out of his mouth and flickers of flame curled in the back of his throat as he spoke. "To my knowledge, I am the last of my kind."

Utros pressed his hand against the golden half mask. "You have a new loyalty now, a new mission. I call upon our bond. Fight for me. Attack and destroy Ildakar."

Brom thrust his great wings into the air, flapping twice with a burst of wind that forced Utros to anchor himself to keep from being blown flat. "I will not."

Utros stood firm. "You must! I command your service."

Ava and Ruva worked their magic, unleashing what they had planned so carefully. Utros had not expected the gray dragon to resist so fiercely, but the twin sorceresses were surprisingly strong. They struck hard with the magic that connected them.

Brom roared, thrashed his head from side to side, and belched a long ribbon of flame into the air. Ava and Ruva wore malicious, defiant expressions as they jabbed magic daggers of pain into Brom's brain.

"You will obey me!" Utros said again. "I command you to attack Ildakar."

The sorceresses continued to inflict agony, and the huge gray dragon shuddered as if struck repeatedly by lightning. Though Brom struggled and his yellow eyes flared with hatred and resistance, he finally lowered his immense head toward the ground in submission before the general.

Utros smiled with half a face.

CHAPTER 63

The avalanche that had thundered beneath Kol Adair had erased the ancient roads, so the expedition from Cliffwall took several days to pick their way around the debris and search through the rubble. Scouts climbed up mountainous slopes, worked their way through the tumbled ice chunks and boulders. They had to find a route suitable for the horses, and the path was so narrow the mounts had to go single file, plodding over the rocks.

They also searched for survivors from the annihilated army, to interrogate if nothing else.

In the avalanche path, they climbed over mounds of ice and rubble, discovering countless broken bodies. The deadly snow had buried the army, crushed their bodies, smashed and suffocated them. At the edge of the ice field, Zimmer's scouts dug out one of the bodies that had been partially exposed in the shifting snow. "Look, General!"

The ancient soldier had been crushed in the falling glacier. His neck was broken and his face was slack, his eyes open. Verna stared curiously at the dead warrior. "He looks so pale." She had seen corpses many times before, and they always had a grayish pallor, but this one's skin seemed unnaturally white.

Bending down, Renn poked at the dead soldier's cheek. "It's hard and stiff."

"Probably frozen," Oliver suggested.

"I don't think so. It is skin, but tougher, as if partly stone."

Zimmer looked down. "They still bleed, and they still die, but they might be more difficult to kill. But we have fought difficult enemies before."

Renn brushed more snow away to expose the dead man's chest armor. He sat back, disturbed. "That flame symbol. This man definitely belonged to the army of Iron Fang, just as the scouts thought."

"Emperor Kurgan," Verna said. "I have read the histories."

"The histories don't tell the entire story, because the great General Utros brought an army of hundreds of thousands of soldiers to lay siege to Ildakar." Renn poked the leather armor. "As I've told you, our great wizards turned them all to stone with a petrification spell, but something must have awakened them." He ran his fingers along his patchy beard. He had not shaved since they departed from Cliffwall, claiming that the whiskers would keep his face warmer. "Maybe only this part of the army came back to life and marched away from Ildakar to seek some other home in the mountains."

"And we killed them all," Amber said, sounding shaken. "We don't even know if they were an enemy."

"They were," General Zimmer said, looking down at the fallen soldier. "Ten thousand soldiers could not have been on a peaceful mission." He shook his head again, looking at the jumbled field in the aftermath of the avalanche.

Working her way up among the blocks of ice, wading through the loose snow, Verna came upon another half-buried figure, and she was startled when he stirred, groaned. "This one is alive! Dear spirits."

She brushed snow from the warrior's face, saw his expression wrenched with pain, his grayish skin smashed and leaking blood. He coughed. Verna knelt, helping to pull the body out of the snow as Renn and General Zimmer hurried closer. The ancient soldier's eyes were glazed.

"Should we help him?" Peretta asked. "Your gift can heal him, Prelate."

"He could tell us information," Zimmer said.

Verna could sense the man's terrible injuries, his smashed bones and crushed internal organs. The soldier groaned, and she was astonished he remained alive at all.

She looked at his square features, his eyes squeezed shut, the grimace on his face. She released enough energy to revive him. "He is . . . strange inside." She shook her head slightly. "He does not have long."

General Zimmer leaned close. "Who is your commander? What is your mission?"

The soldier coughed, and looked around, saw the prelate and the others bending over him, the unfamiliar uniforms of the D'Haran army.

"General Utros," the soldier said. "We serve Utros, in the name of Emperor Kurgan. We will conquer all the lands of the Old World."

Renn looked at the others nearby as his face went as pale as the dying soldier's. His voice grew urgent. "You were at Ildakar. Your army was stone. I saw it myself! How did the spell fade? What happened? Why were you marching?"

"We awakened. Utros will bring down Ildakar and we will also overwhelm the rest of the world. It is . . . our mission."

"Where is the rest of the army?" Renn demanded, sounding more distraught. "This is just a small fraction of the general's forces at Ildakar."

"We were marching . . ." The soldier stirred, but could not free himself from the snow packed around his lower body. "Other armies are marching, like this one. We will conquer whatever we find." His stiff face twisted into a pain-racked smile. "But the bulk of our army is still at Ildakar, to bring down the city."

Renn's face reddened. "Ildakar will never fall!"

The soldier choked out a laugh, which made blood spill from the side of his mouth. Verna felt her ability to keep the man alive dwindling away into the chill of the snowfield, but an angry Renn gestured, releasing his own gift, and a *crack* pushed down on the warrior's ribs and breastbone, snapping the fragile body. The soldier shuddered, then lay still.

Renn looked ill.

General Utros looked at Verna with a stormy expression. "As I thought, this was an invasion force, and if there are many more just like it marching across the Old World, we already have a war on our hands."

Amber stared down at the dead soldier. "But why? We don't even know them. Why do they want to conquer the world?"

Verna felt sorry for the innocent girl. After her centuries among the Sisters of the Light, the prelate was accustomed to misery. She had taught young wizards to control their gift, lessons that often required a great deal of pain and effort. She had seen incredible death and destruction when Emperor Jagang and his Imperial Order came through Tanimura. She had faced many terrible battles herself, including the heartbreaking fight that cost the life of her beloved Warren. Yes, she had seen death aplenty.

The fresh-faced young novice, though, was new to the violence the world could deliver. Her brother, Norcross, had seen bloodshed in the last war, but he was also very young. Verna knew, sadly, that violence and killing would age even an innocent young person far too soon.

Zimmer called his soldiers together, designating two of his best scouts. "I am dispatching you back to Cliffwall immediately. Tell them what we just learned and make sure they are prepared. Our soldiers are facing a much greater threat than we thought."

"It is not just Cliffwall, but the whole Old World," Verna said.

Renn's face was florid. "But the biggest threat stands against Ildakar, and that makes our mission more important than ever."

He brushed snow from his soggy robes and glanced urgently over at Captain Trevor. "There's nothing more to see here. We know what we did. Now, we should go back to our city as quickly as possible."

Verna saw the strain on his face. "Renn is correct, General. Have your scouts find the best way out of these mountains and on our way to Ildakar. Once we join forces with Nicci and Nathan, that should give the ancient army something to worry about."

CHAPTER 64

O ut on the battlefield, the great gray dragon bowed, snared by the magic of Ava and Ruva, but he did not look defeated.

Utros felt more awe than fear. Brom's enormous eyes flared, his wings arched upward in defiance. His growling exhale sent scorching wafts of brimstone and smoke toward the general, but Utros held the bond within him. He touched the burnished gold half mask to remind himself of the price he had already paid. "I need you to fight for me. My emperor commands it."

The dragon's voice was blunted by pain, but still exuded a clear threat. "You do not command me, human."

Ava and Ruva interlocked their fingers and joined their magic. Brom curled his head back as agony exploded inside his skull. He let out another roar.

"I do command you," Utros said calmly. "I need a weapon to defeat that city. Nothing is more powerful than a dragon."

Brom lurched back on his haunches. "I do not care about your petty wars. I am the guardian of Kuloth Vale, and I must return to my sacred duty." He flapped his wings, two huge strokes that lifted his reptilian body partly off the ground.

Utros called on the bond again. "No, you will destroy the city, defeat my enemies, and break this siege. I don't care where you go after that, but first you must obey me. Grant me my victory."

Brom loomed over the ancient general. "I am a scholar dragon. I know lore from thousands of years. I know the bones of my ancestors, and I guard their resting place. I am no one's weapon."

"You're a dragon!" Utros said. "Fly to Ildakar, unleash your fire. Terrify the people, knock down the towers and walls. Do that, and then you can go free."

Without waiting for the gray dragon to reply, the sorceresses worked their magic once more and hurled spears of pain into his chest.

Brom spewed fire into the sky. Snarling with frustration and anger, the dragon launched himself into the air and flew toward Ildakar.

With a deep groan, the colossal Ixax warriors began to move.

Watching them, Nathan felt a rush of fear and excitement. The iron armor screeched reluctantly as the Ixax lumbered forward, moving on their own for the first time in centuries. The turretlike giant waists turned with a creak. The Ixax swiveled their helmets, tilting down to look at Nathan. Though he was a great wizard, he felt insignificant when these warriors looked at him.

He remembered how the first one had pounded Andre into a smear of skin and crushed bone. If they became treacherous, these Ixax warriors could turn on him, rip down the gates of Ildakar, and wreak havoc throughout the city.

"Please . . ." Nathan whispered, not sure that they could hear him.

The Ixax straightened themselves to stare ahead at the

countless thousands of enemy troops and the dragon that had just landed in the general's camp. The titans plodded forward onto the battlefield.

"Back inside," Nicci shouted to the people around him. "Close the gates!"

Leaving the large empty carts outside the wall, the duma members, gifted nobles, and workers retreated into the city, and the enormous gates swung closed. Nathan, Nicci, and Elsa hurried to get a view of what the warriors would do. They raced to the top of the wall, where they joined the sentry guards and countless spectators.

Nathan watched the Ixax stride toward the huge army. "This is why they were created."

The Ixax warriors strode forward like battering rams on two legs. The ancient soldiers that filled the valley had focused on the arrival of the dragon, but now the front ranks turned to face the new threat as the Ixax warriors picked up speed.

The enemy soldiers formed a line, locking their shields in a barricade against the oncoming juggernauts. The giant warriors towered over them, and each Ixax held a sword in one gauntleted hand, its blade as tall as a man. They waded among the enemy ranks like wolves in a chicken coop.

Utros's soldiers were cleaved into pieces, dozens dying in a single stroke of an Ixax sword. Hundreds of the ancient soldiers converged around them, heedless of their own lives, rushing forward to thwart the giants. In response, the two colossal warriors slaughtered hundreds and moved deeper into the army camp.

From the high wall of Ildakar, the spectators cheered the unleashed Ixax. Nicci grabbed Nathan's arm and pointed toward the sky. "Look, the dragon! It's flying toward Ildakar!" Utros had apparently won his struggle to command the gray monster. She set her jaw. "I will go to the city's high point, where I can fight the dragon if I have to." She darted off without waiting for him to reply.

Nathan watched the titans release their fury. For countless centuries the Ixax had been unable to twitch, unable to react, and now all that pent-up anger was directed against a real enemy. The two giants swept their huge swords down lines of the half-stone warriors. They smashed with their massive gauntlets. Hundreds more enemies died, and the Ixax crashed deeper into the army, bashing heads, crushing dozens at a time.

Nathan had never felt sympathy for General Utros and his half-petrified army. He would have preferred that they saw reason and founded some new land of their own in the untamed vastness of the Old World, but now he knew they had to be defeated. Utros would never surrender. He had catapulted the mutilated bodies of fallen Ildakaran soldiers over the walls. His two sorceresses had attacked Nicci with her own hair and they had killed poor Lani.

This was a deadly game, and now the Ixax would knock all the game pieces off the board.

Their widening swath of destruction ripped through the enemy army. Thousands lay broken and dead as the titans crashed forward without slowing. Nathan felt great satisfaction at what he saw. The Ixax were as powerful as he'd hoped. And they were following their mission to protect the city. But they still had many thousands more to defeat, and Nathan feared that even those gigantic fighters didn't stand a chance.

Meanwhile, the gray dragon flapped its enormous wings, flying fast toward Ildakar.

As the dragon soared away from Utros, First Commander Enoch galloped up on his warhorse, shouting, "Thousands down already, General! We have to fight those giants."

Utros had seen the behemoths emerge from the gates of Ildakar, but forcing his will on Brom had demanded all his attention. At another time, he would have found the two huge warriors terrifying and impressive.

But he had a dragon.

The old veteran's craggy face was drawn, his gestures frenetic when he heard no response. "We need to fight them, General! We need all the magic we can summon. Your sorceresses must blast them."

Utros turned to Ava and Ruva, who looked diminished after their recent effort. "I require all their strength to maintain control on the dragon. We don't dare let it turn on us, and they have expended so much magic already."

"But look at those giant warriors, sir! We'll lose much of our army."

Utros watched the towering inhuman giants careering through the ranks of his soldiers. They seemed unstoppable. He regarded Enoch through his golden half mask. "Then turn all of our army against them, overwhelm them with sheer numbers. We have more thousands than they can imagine."

With cold detachment, he admired the sheer power unleashed by the armored monstrosities. His own soldiers flew in all directions like scattered coins, and fell broken. Utros drew a deep breath, adjusted the horned helmet on his head. "Yes, that is what we must do. Gather our fighters. Those giants may seem invincible, but we have only two targets, two enemies, and countless ranks to throw against them." He smiled with his hardened face. "I am confident we will be victorious."

As the battle raged outside the walls, Nicci raced to the top of the plateau, where the ruling tower rose high and the broken pyramid marked the night when the old order of Ildakar had begun to fall.

Beyond the wall, the Ixax warriors continued to mow down countless enemy soldiers, but Nicci turned her attention on the dragon flying high above. She could see few details, except for how huge it was. With a beat of powerful wings, it swooped down, spewing an orange trail of flame in the air. The beast torched long patches of vineyards, ignited olive groves, burned the roofs of warehouses. In the city below, people rushed to find shelter wherever they could, but neither inner rooms nor root cellars would protect them from a barrage of dragon fire.

When Nicci reached the top of the plateau, she raised her hands to the sky and let out a resounding shout. "Dragon! Come face me." Using her gift, she unleashed black and white lightning that skittered across the sky, demanding the creature's attention.

She began to run up the steps of the broken pyramid, choosing that structure intentionally, since the stone blocks would not catch fire, and there were no other people or homes around. Nicci alone would face the beast.

The dragon circled toward her and bellowed from the sting of her lightning bolts. Seeing her scramble up the broken steps of the pyramid, it swooped closer.

The beast seemed familiar to her, and as it filled its chest to exhale deadly flames, Nicci called out its name: "Brom!"

The dragon faltered, flapping his enormous wings and circling again.

"Brom, guardian of Kuloth Vale. Why did you abandon the bones of dragons? You should be protecting them, not fighting us."

The gray beast snorted, but seemed curious. Nicci remembered the ancient and decrepit dragon, his wings tattered, his ribs showing. Even in his aged, weak condition, Brom had fought to defend the graveyard of dragons. Nicci, Nathan, Bannon, and the girl Thistle had gone to Kuloth Vale because they needed a dragon's rib bone to defeat Life's Mistress. When they had battled the ancient gray dragon, Nicci's magic had inadvertently rejuvenated him, giving strength and energy to the feeble creature.

Now Brom was enormous and frightful, a true monster. Backflapping his wings, he landed on the uneven rubble of the pyramid, where Nicci stood before him.

With her uneven blond hair still growing out, she didn't know if Brom recognized her. Maybe the dragon considered all humans identical. She felt her gift boil within her, ready to be unleashed. She shouted bravely, "I fought you before when you were much weaker, Brom. I will fight you again, if you force me."

The gray dragon poised on the broken pyramid, crackling with intelligence and energy. He sniffed, drawing in a loud hollow snort. Smoke curled around his scaled face. "You are the sorceress. I remember."

"We met at Kuloth Vale," Nicci said. "You granted us one rib bone for our needs, and my magic reignited the fires in your heart. I gave you strength and burned away some of your age."

"Yes, you did. And I gave you the bone you needed. I no longer have any debt to you."

"I am not calling in a debt," Nicci said. "I am only appealing to your common sense. You are a wise dragon, an ancient scholar. Is a wise dragon drawn into a war that means nothing to him? Why do you fight for General Utros? Why would you care?"

"I do not care. And I do not care about you."

"Then why do it?" she asked.

Brom snorted. "He has bound me with magic from a dragon-fire scar on his face. We are joined, and his sorceresses forced me to do his bidding. This once, and then he says I will be free of him."

"How can anyone force such a powerful creature as yourself?" she asked. "I know where his scar came from. You are not the silver dragon who fought him a long time ago."

"The connection is weak," Brom agreed, "but I cannot break it. His sorceresses inflict pain. Utros told me I must destroy Ildakar and burn you all before I can return to guard my ancestors. That is all I care about."

Nicci put her hands on her hips. "Then you will force me to fight you, and you already know that I, too, can inflict pain."

Brom opened and closed his immense jaws. "I do not want this fight."

"I am the one who helped you in Kuloth Vale, gave you back your strength, while General Utros binds you, forces you, hurts you. He is your true enemy."

Brom thrashed. "I must burn Ildakar, or I will never be free."

Nicci extended her gift, felt the powerful presence of the gray dragon. With her own Han as well as the aura of magic that throbbed through the city of Ildakar—especially *here,* at the pyramid itself—she could see the faint gossamer thread that strung out from Brom. "His sorceresses bound you, but only with a weak chain. They used a piece of his dragon-burned flesh to call on any dragon. You just happened to be closest."

Brom snorted fire, blasting at the air to release his fury. "I know! I am a wise dragon. Do not think you can fool me."

"I'm not trying to fool you. I am stating the obvious, and my magic is greater than the magic those sorceresses wield. I killed a wizard once, and I have his power as well as my own." She studied the tenuous line between Brom and Utros. Reaching out, she seized it, and used her gift to sever the link, just as she had cut the single key strand from her hair when Ava and Ruva attacked her.

When the invisible bond broke, Brom reeled. He flared the scaly plates at the back of his head, drew himself up tall, and spread his wings wide. Huge and terrifying, he loomed above the damaged pyramid.

"Choose whom you wish to fight," Nicci said. "I set you free. You may go back to Kuloth Vale if you like." She smiled. "But I have placed a new debt upon you. If you attack General Utros and his army, however, we will be even again."

Brom thrashed his barb-tipped tail. "With pleasure." He launched himself into the air again.

Energized and angry, the dragon flew above Ildakar and plunged back toward the enemy army.

CHAPTER 65

The screams of slaughtered soldiers, the crunch of bones, the splash of blood filled the battlefield, but the Ixax warriors uttered no sound. The titans covered a dozen paces with every stride. Their iron-shod boots crushed multiple opponents at a time, grinding enemy soldiers underfoot. Their swords decapitated ten at a time. A single blow from a gauntleted fist knocked down steadfast defensive lines.

The Ixax destroyed hundreds, then thousands, and set their gaze on thousands more. They moved in tandem as countless enemy soldiers rallied against them, attacking with spears and swords, battering their impenetrable armor. The Ixax destroyed anyone who engaged them.

First Commander Enoch rode up on his chalky-gray warhorse, raising his sword and yelling to the troops. "Rally! All soldiers of General Utros, rally! We have strength in numbers. Make your stand!"

Messengers raced among the farthest ranks, and the invincible army pulled together like a living creature, tens of thousands falling into ranks and running in lockstep, perfectly trained.

The Ixax warriors smashed forward, as if wading through waves of flesh and bone. Many opponents fell with each blow, but the ancient army did not scatter. Enoch knew they wouldn't. He had spent his life with these men, and he'd trained them for decades. Now they were all joined by a brotherhood of blood, their families dead, lost from time. The only thing remaining to them was the victory that Utros promised, and they had faith in him.

Battle horns sounded, and desperate orders spread like wildfire. "For the general, whatever it takes!" Enoch shouted, and thousands of voices echoed the resounding response. "For the general!"

Two companies locked their shields together, pointed their spears, and formed a pair of phalanxes. They marched forward with precision in the face of the chaos caused by the colossal Ixax. More hardened soldiers threw themselves upon the giants, and they were summarily slain, but more came in their wake to continue the attack. And then more.

Enoch was horrified by the casualties he saw. In the past half hour, more of his comrades had been killed than General Utros had lost in all of his military campaigns combined. But the general's army would not retreat, nor would they surrender. Judging by the uncontrolled destruction caused by the two giants, Enoch knew the Ixax would never give up, either. He couldn't tell whether these titans were intelligent and aware, or just mindless fighters with one purpose. The massive armored warriors would continue to fight until they had killed every enemy soldier.

The only choice was to destroy them, no matter how much blood it cost. General Utros felt the same.

Another fanfare sounded, and half-stone soldiers closed in from all directions, tightening the net. The two phalanxes struck the giant warriors, and when the Ixax shattered the point of the formation, the soldiers closed up and pushed ahead, jabbing with spears. The enraged giants flattened the formation, but the numbers that flooded in were becoming overwhelming. Around them, bloody, broken bodies of slain soldiers piled up like mountains.

Astride his warhorse, Enoch bellowed orders, but the mayhem of the battlefield was simply too loud for anyone to hear him. Even so, the soldiers knew what to do. "For the general!" they cried, their voices scattered and overlapping, and as they repeated it, their shouts fell into a pattern, a rhythmic chant. "For Utros, for Utros!"

The Ixax warriors took down more and more of the ancient soldiers, but General Utros had hundreds of thousands of fighters, all well trained and well armed, each man ready to give his life to cause even a flicker of damage against the titans. Even Enoch, who had relayed the order, stared in breathless disbelief.

The soldiers reminded him of a swarm of ants trying to take down a much larger insect. They came forward by the thousands, throwing themselves upon the Ixax warriors. Their bodies piled up in barricades of bloody flesh, broken bones, and severed limbs, but they pressed closer to overwhelm the Ixax.

Then more came.

And then more.

G roans of dismay rippled among the spectators on the high walls as they watched the Ixax falter against the overwhelming resistance. Nathan unconsciously wrapped an arm around Elsa's shoulder, folding her closer to him. Even as the gray dragon circled over Ildakar under some kind of command from General Utros, Nathan watched the vast army switch tactics and close in on the two juggernauts, oblivious to their own casualties. "Dear spirits, they are like locusts."

"More like wasps," Elsa said, "swarming to sting their enemy."

At the city's high point, the gray dragon circled, blasting fire in the air, and Nathan suddenly recognized Brom from the ancient graveyard of dragons. Nicci stood in her black dress, challenging him from the ruins of the pyramid.

Out on the battlefield, the Ixax warriors kept slaughtering company after company of the half-stone warriors, but as the numbers turned against the two titans, Nathan's hope began to dwindle. Enemy soldiers threw themselves upon the giants in an endless wave. They piled more and more upon the bodies of their own comrades and then began to overwhelm the two Ixax, covering them with sheer numbers.

Fleshmancer Andre had claimed that his Ixax could each single-handedly slay a thousand or more of the enemy, and these two had done far better than that. Ten thousand, possibly even twenty thousand lay massacred. But it wasn't enough.

Utros's army hacked at them with their weapons, swarming, climbing, fighting, dragging. Finally, they brought down the inhuman fighters like great lumbering beasts. The two crashed, still struggling, unable to move. The maddened ancient warriors swarmed over them, eventually pulled them to the ground, and chopped them to pieces, a thousand cuts at a time.

Trembling on the battlements as he watched in horror, Nathan whispered, "I am so sorry for what was done to you." His azure eyes filled with tears as he watched their end. "I hope you can find peace now. You did better than anyone could have asked."

His army did exactly what the general expected them to do. The soldiers surrendered their lives without question for the cause of Emperor Kurgan and for Utros himself. First Commander Enoch unleashed their combined strength, which proved invincible, as always.

Utros turned now to face the impregnable city walls, wanting to see Ildakar burn under the attack from the dragon. Brom had unleashed fire as he flew above the buildings, and seeing smoke in the air, Utros knew that some parts of Ildakar were ablaze.

But not enough. The city should be an inferno by now.

Next to him, Ava and Ruva both collapsed backward as if stabbed with invisible knives. They clutched their chests, their hearts, and Utros felt the thread of magic that bound Brom to him suddenly severed. Shortly after the army toppled both Ixax warriors, the dragon came surging back to the battlefield.

The enormous gray beast soared toward their army. Utros braced himself, feeling disbelief build within him. "The dragon is free now. How did he break free?" He whirled to his sorceresses. "Get him back! I need that dragon."

Ava and Ruva frantically tried to restore their magic, but they could not. Ava said, "Your scar was only enough to create the one bond, and because Brom was not the dragon who injured you, the hold was tenuous from the start."

Ruva said, "Someone broke the bond." They looked at each other, and said simultaneously, "Nicci. The sorceress Nicci must have done it."

The angry dragon thundered toward the huge besieging army. With beating wings that looked like axe blades in the air, Brom swooped away from Ildakar and cruised low on an attack flight. He unleashed a river of fire upon the scattering ranks of the general's army. Columns of half-petrified soldiers turned into smoking debris. Entire companies were flattened as if by a giant hot cudgel.

Utros had already withdrawn toward his headquarters, planning to activate the blood lens so he could announce his victory to Iron Fang in the underworld. But now the gray dragon came for them.

Brom flew over the giant knot of soldiers who had converged to bring down the Ixax warriors. With blasts of acid flame, the monster ignited countless screaming men, demonstrating his might and punishing Utros and the sorceresses for what they had done.

The dragon angled up into the air again, filling his lungs so he could dive down and unleash another incinerating assault.

He was searching for Utros in particular, but because the bond was now broken, all the human forms down below looked the same. The dragon blasted rows of tents, exploding shacks and storehouses, searing the blood-soaked ground.

The general stood near the tall oval lens crafted with the blood of innocent children. "We can't let him damage this!" Utros yelled. "Ava, Ruva, protect it!"

Brom swept closer, opening his jaws wide. Spotting Utros and the blood lens, he dove and unleashed a powerful gout of flame directly at the general. With a shriek, Ava and Ruva clasped each other's hands and raised a protective wall, shaping the air into an impenetrable shield around the three of them as well as the lens. Flames washed over them, and Utros felt the searing heat in spite of his mostly numb skin.

The invisible shield diverted the fire to either side. Behind them, the command structure erupted in flames, the wooden walls crumbling to ash within seconds. The magical shield held, though, and they were spared. The lens to the underworld remained intact.

The dragon flew past, gushing out more fire before Brom exhausted his anger and vengeance. The ancient gray dragon had made his point.

Utros collapsed backward to the ground. The smell of burning wood, grass, and flesh rose all around him. He stared into the sky as Brom bellowed his defiance one last time, flew high into the air, and turned north toward the mountains and Kuloth Vale.

CHAPTER 66

Beyond the walls of Ildakar, the siege forces reeled from the devastation. Nicci could see that the Ixax warriors and the gray dragon had struck a ringing blow to the confident enemy army, and for the first time, General Utros tasted the bitter and very real possibility of defeat.

Returning to the ramparts near the towering main gate, Nicci looked out at the scorched enemy camp. She saw rivers of blackened soil where soldiers had been obliterated by Brom's fire, the mounds of bodies slain by the Ixax warriors. She doubted Utros could recover from this.

"Now is the time to press our case and demand that the general end this siege," she said.

Nathan stroked his chin. "I agree, although with such a defeat, he may not be in a mood for a gentlemanly discussion."

High Captain Stuart, standing with them on the top of the wall, was glad to see the vast army in turmoil. "As captain of the city guard, I will ride out and deliver a message to General Utros. I will insist that he negotiate an end to these useless hostilities."

Damon and Quentin were pleased with the suggestion, though

Oron seemed skeptical. "I'd rather just kill the general once and for all. Will we be able to trust him, whatever he negotiates?"

"We have to try, at least," Elsa said. Olgya agreed.

Stuart's eyes were flintier after the surprise nighttime attack in which so many of his city guard had been killed, but now he had hope again. He took a horse, and the duma members wished him good luck as they opened one of the small gates. Sitting tall in the saddle, the high captain rode out to the enemy army, and Nicci watched as several of the half-stone soldiers met him and escorted him deeper into the damaged camp.

Quentin said, "While we wait, let us discuss what terms we might suggest. We have to be prepared when General Utros responds."

Rather than convening inside the ruling tower, Nicci suggested that they gather at the pyramid, where they could watch the gates and see when Stuart returned. At the top of the plateau, the duma members worked their way up the damaged steps to the third tier. Nicci brushed dust off her black dress and stared across the burned grasslands. So many soldiers remained out there, Utros still posed an enormous threat, and he had already dispatched tens of thousands in separate exploratory armies across the Old World.

Damon sat on the stone blocks, looking pleased. He released his gift to shift some of the rubble back into place. "We will restore Ildakar to its glory, now that we have the chance."

Quentin assisted, and soon the gifted duma members had cleared the rubble from where the sacrifices had been held.

Elsa slipped her arm through Nathan's as they climbed higher to where they could look out over the city. "We are all exhausted," she said. "We have used so much magic to defend ourselves, but it was worth the effort. Now General Utros has to discuss terms with us. He knows how powerful we are."

Quentin clapped his hands as if expecting slaves to rush in at his summons. "We should have a feast! Call a day of remembrance here in Ildakar."

Nicci looked at the duma member with sharp annoyance. "This is not the time for celebration. Look out there!"

Nathan sketched a rectangle in the air and created his magnifying window so they could have a better look at the row after row of powerful ancient warriors, still ready to fight, no matter how many had just been slain.

"Look at them," Nicci said. "We unleashed the two Ixax, the most powerful fighters the wizards of Ildakar ever created. They killed tens of thousands of the enemy, but they are gone now. The dragon fought on our behalf, and his fire incinerated thousands more, but he is also gone." She narrowed her blue eyes. "Yes, we should be proud of the damage we just caused, but we have used our greatest weapons, and Ildakar is still under siege. By my guess, two-thirds of the enemy army still remains." She jabbed at Nathan's expanded view, feeling her anger. "No, it is not a time for celebrations, until the general capitulates." The duma members were cowed into silence as she continued, "We will maintain our defenses and stand against the siege, but Ildakar isn't just one city holding firm against an army. The whole continent is at stake."

"This is the greatest city in history," Oron said with a snort. "No one is stronger than the wizards of Ildakar. If we can't stop Utros, what chance does the rest of the world have?"

Nicci regarded him coolly. "My point exactly. Ildakar has greater defenses than any other city, yet General Utros has us at a stalemate. That army is still more powerful than we can defeat." She felt hardness in her heart and determination in her mind. "Ildakar cannot do this alone."

"I doubt even the D'Haran army could stand against a regimented force like the general's," Nathan muttered.

Quentin said with a sigh, "I had hope after seeing so much destruction, but now I realize we are in just as much danger as before."

"High Captain Stuart will convince the general to talk," Elsa said. "We need to make him see that there is no reason for his war anymore. There must be a way to bring peace, and then we can all thrive."

Nathan shifted his magnifying window toward a commotion near the center of the camp. Stiff soldiers were leading the high captain's horse back toward the city walls. Perched on the saddle like a shocking trophy, Stuart's head stared forward with glassy, open eyes. His mouth was slack, as if he'd been decapitated in the middle of issuing his invitation to General Utros. The enemy soldiers led the horse and its gruesome reply toward the gates of Ildakar.

Elsa began to weep as Nathan dissolved the aperture of air.

Nicci stared with her hard, blue eyes. "Now I am even more determined that Ildakar must not stand alone. Utros will not give up."

With a pack of possessions, clean traveling boots, black dress, and the wrapped pane of glass with the preserved image of the siege army, Nicci stood in front of the damp-smelling well. "Sliph, I summon you!" She had lit two glowing balls of light, which hovered in the air, creating sharp shadows inside the enclosure. After her voice died away, she called again. "Sliph, I wish to travel."

The murder of High Captain Stuart had galvanized the duma members to find some other means to attack the wounded enemy army, and Elsa had raised the possibility of grand-scale transference magic that could impact the entire army. She had an idea that might cause as much destruction as the dragon.

Quentin and Damon fell into frenetic preparations, their eyes showing the ragged edge of panic. In an uncertain voice, Damon said, "Maybe we should consider releasing Thora again. She is a powerful sorceress."

"She's also not to be trusted," Nathan said.

No one could argue with that, and yet the suggestion hung in the air like the rumbling echoes of thunder.

More than ever, Nicci knew she had to rally the rest of the Old World, and she decided she would swiftly travel to other cities with her warning. Simply rallying Tanimura wouldn't be enough. She had to form an alliance with the other lands that would be threatened by General Utros. She had turned her back on the duma, no longer interested in their endless deliberations. "I have my own mission."

She had gone to the isolated well hidden in the low building, and now she shouted again, impatient. "Sliph! I wish to travel."

Finally, the sound of bubbling silver roiled upward until the mirrorlike surface filled the well. The feminine shape emerged. "You have another mission for the cause? I demand to know whether your other work succeeded. Are we winning the revolt?"

Nicci didn't lie outright. "We continue to face many challenges."

"Where is Emperor Sulachan? Why have I not seen Lothain? I do not know you."

"You know me. I have traveled in you, and I must travel again. Take me to Serrimundi. I need to find our allies there and prepare them for war."

She knew the sliph would hear what she wanted to hear, but the silvery woman still seemed doubtful. "And they will fight for Emperor Sulachan?"

"That is not your concern. Do you know Serrimundi? I need to travel there."

"I know many places, but I exist only to serve our cause. Tell Emperor Sulachan that he should travel in me. I will take him where he needs to go. I will carry him to victory."

"Emperor Sulachan does not take orders," Nicci said.

The sour-faced sliph's form shifted and reshaped, reflecting the magical light in the air.

"Take me to Serrimundi," Nicci said again.

Clearly angry, the sliph lurched up to engulf her. "*Breathe!*" she commanded, then dragged Nicci under.

CHAPTER 67

The camp was devastated, as was the general's heart. As a military commander he felt the pain and anger as he considered how many soldiers he had lost in one day. Killing the smug emissary from Ildakar had done almost nothing to assuage the pain. Nevertheless, Utros had made his answer clear.

Ildakar would fall, under his terms.

All these men had sworn their loyalty to him centuries ago. Without a qualm they had offered their lives in service, but none of them knew when they marched away from Orogang that they were giving up their homes, their sweethearts, their children—forever. Now their comrades were all they had.

Utros stood outside his makeshift new command tent, a large structure stretched across support beams. The fabric was stained with soot, salvaged from a scorched wagon that soldiers had dragged away from the flames. A gray drizzle had extinguished any fires that still smoldered, but the smell of bitter ash lingered in the air.

Though the recent attack was incredibly devastating, he suspected that it was the worst that Ildakar could produce. Perhaps the great city was now mostly defenseless. The giant warriors had been destroyed, and Ildakar surely had no more of them, or they would have turned them loose during the battle.

The dragon had also wrought a terrible amount of damage—damage that should have been inflicted on Ildakar. Iron Fang had commanded him to summon the monster, but Utros had experience with the capricious and vicious nature of dragons. In hindsight, he wasn't surprised at what Brom had done.

In the aftermath he had to report his failure to Emperor Kurgan. He had lost tens of thousands of men to the Ixax warriors and the dragon, without a single stone being knocked from the city's walls. Sadly, Utros would also have to confess his failure to Majel, which made his heart and mind heavy.

In the smoky daylight he stepped up to the blood lens, staring at its curved surface like a man gazing into a mountain tarn. The murky glass did not reflect back at him, nor could he see through the greenish mists, but Ava and Ruva touched the markings around the lens and called upon their gift to illuminate the runes. Energy sparkled through the glass, then clarified until the veil to the underworld became transparent.

Iron Fang and the raw, red form of Majel were there waiting for him on the other side of the lens. "I am ready for your report, General," Kurgan said, showing off his sharp metal tooth. "Did you follow my commands?"

"Yes, my emperor. My sorceresses worked their spell. We summoned a dragon as you commanded." Utros felt the words like hot lead in his mouth. He chose his revelations carefully, but he was only delaying his shame.

Kurgan was delighted by the news, but Majel's skinned face bore no readable expression. Iron Fang roughly grabbed his wife's peeled shoulder and squeezed the exposed meat. "You see, your lover hasn't failed me. Tell us, General Utros! Have you finally broken Ildakar? Is the city now conquered in my name?"

Utros lowered his gaze. "I am afraid not, my liege." The two sorceresses stepped back, their faces drawn with concern. This was his battle to face. "The dragon came and was bound to me. I forced it to attack the city."

"Then Ildakar should be a smoking ruin by now!"

Majel breathed out a long, low sigh. "Oh Utros, what happened?"

"The dragon broke its bond and turned on us instead. Someone in Ildakar was powerful enough to disrupt the magic, and the monster killed thousands of my soldiers." Utros squared his shoulders. "The wizards of Ildakar also created two giant warriors, which they unleashed against my army. More than thirty thousand of my fighters were killed before we destroyed them."

Kurgan was furious. "And you allowed this? You call yourself a great commander!"

Utros had never boasted about being a great commander, although he did his best to be one. From the emissary Nathan, he knew that history had painted him as a hero, as a genius. In the past, his victories might have warranted such a characterization, but after the recent losses and tremendous setbacks, historians might describe him differently.

"I will continue to do my best, Emperor Kurgan. Our siege will break the city, but it may take time."

"Time," Kurgan said with a rude snort. "You have already had fifteen centuries. Should I wait another hundred years? A thousand? You are a failure and a disappointment, General Utros. You marched off with my invincible army to conquer the world, but you took too long. Because you were gone from Orogang, my people turned against me. If you had been there, my reign would not have ended. My empire would have endured."

His words came out fast and angry, dripping with venom. Kurgan pressed closer to the lens so that his image filled a large portion of the glass. He sneered. "Then again, if you had been there, then you would have betrayed me with my wife, again and again in your tent or in my own imperial bed."

He glowered at Majel, who stood woodenly, her torn face quivering.

Kurgan reached out and stroked her slick cheek, where he had carved the skin off her face with a filleting knife. Utros clenched his fists, wanting to reach through the lens to grasp Kurgan around the throat.

"But she loves me now," Iron Fang said. "Here in the underworld, poor Majel understands her error. The Keeper has left her physical form like this, so she can always remember what she did to me."

Majel also caressed Iron Fang. Her voice wavered. "Yes, my husband." Utros had heard that voice so many times whispering in his own ear. "Loyalty is stronger than love."

"I am so sorry, Majel," Utros said, a groan deep in his throat.

"My wife is none of your concern," Kurgan snapped. "You are my general. You could have had any whore in your camps, yet you chose the one woman sworn to your emperor."

"I am yours now, my love," Majel said to Kurgan, not looking at Utros, whose heart felt stony, his emotions broken. Iron Fang kept staring through the lens at him, impatient and annoyed, and he slapped away the fawning caresses of the mangled woman. "Swear your loyalty to me again, Utros. Promise that you will defeat Ildakar and then finish conquering the Old World. For me."

"I swore it to you a long time ago," Utros said. "That hasn't changed."

He knew that Majel was just speaking the words, forced to stay with the emperor in the underworld. Could a spirit feel pain? Physical pain? Certainly emotional pain—he could read it in her face. But something had changed deep within her. She had not forgotten him, but maybe her love had died when her physical body did.

"Majel . . ." he whispered.

Kurgan shoved her away, and Majel's bloody form fell out of view. Iron Fang's image filled the entire glass oval. "You are my general. You are my servant. You are my slave. Even from the underworld, I am still your emperor. Swear to me that you will conquer the continent, as you were meant to do."

Utros clenched and unclenched his stony fists. "Yes, I swear it." He could no longer see Majel's mutilated form, but Kurgan was even more hideous in his own way.

Utros did not make empty vows. He had spoken the words many times. He knew that loyalty was stronger than love, and his hundreds of thousands of soldiers were entirely loyal to him. His soldiers had often told him so, but he was blinded by his own loyalty to a petulant leader who did not deserve it. His every victory was for the glory of Iron Fang, while the soldiers in his army did it for *him*.

If Utros did tear down Ildakar and conquer the Old World, maybe he should do it for his own purposes, rather than for the unworthy emperor. Such a man did not deserve to rule. Such a man was dead because his own people had torn him apart.

Such a man should no longer be issuing orders to General Utros.

Perhaps it had been a mistake to create this lens. Emperor Kurgan no longer had anything to say that Utros needed to hear. The general didn't bow, didn't speak another word to his emperor, whose face still filled the lens.

Instead, with a sweep of his hand, he smothered the magic in one of the glowing runes, and the images faded back into impenetrable green mists.

CHAPTER 68

Inside her villa, Elsa sat in the courtyard next to her peaceful fountain. The sound of the running water helped inspire her, and Nathan felt the same. She had sheets of paper and a stylus on which she drew experimental designs, spell-forms, and connecting runes that she could activate using transference magic.

Nathan had taken several old volumes from Renn's cluttered library, tomes of magical lore that the wizard had shared with Lani. Nathan felt a pang for what had happened to the sorceress. He rubbed the scar on his chest, feeling occasional slivers of phantom pain in his heart.

General Utros had no idea how weakened the wizards of Ildakar had become, so many powerful duma members gone. Nathan was determined to find some other unexpected defense before the ancient general recovered enough to make a new move. "Dear spirits, how do we do this ourselves?" he muttered, but Elsa was too deep in concentration to hear him.

She bit her lower lip as she scribbled small designs and added connecting lines. "Transference magic is usually a stage-to-stage spell, one spell-form connected to a counterpart, using the magic in an even exchange, but in order to increase the power, maybe we can segregate, then amplify it." She tapped her stylus on the paper where she had drawn eight smaller runes in a circle and connected them like the spokes of a wheel. "Through a central point, we can widen the flow, like a pipe delivering water." She glanced over at her fountain. "If the pipe is only as wide as your finger, that limits the amount of water you can transport. But if we widen the conduit to a foot in diameter, imagine the water we could deliver." She scribbled on her paper, then glanced up at Nathan, who was looking at her with admiration.

"I see what you mean, my dear," he said. "Are you suggesting it might be possible to flood the entire plain and wash away the siege?"

"That might do, but it's not necessarily destructive enough," Elsa said. "I was thinking of a flood of magic. Let me keep developing this."

Glad to be in the other woman's company, Nathan paged through the books. He saw notations Renn had made in the margins, but the portly wizard had not been in the mind-set for war when he did his research. He'd been looking for ways to combine wind chimes and fountains for his own villa.

After several hours of his fruitless searching, while Elsa expanded her transference runes, they both needed to rise and stretch. "Let's go see what Olgya is doing in the silk spinners' guild," Elsa suggested. "We shouldn't dismiss any possible advantage. Maybe she has come up with something."

"I am curious about the weaving operations myself," Nathan said. He had cleaned his white robes and admired the cool and comfortable silk. "Her new enhanced fabrics are nearly as good as armor. If you will lead the way?"

They walked through the nobles' district, passing citrus orchards and lush flower beds. The trees along the next boulevard had darker leaves and were manicured into rounded shapes, but some were entirely stripped of leaves. Workers stood under the trees with baskets, plucking leaves in a swift methodical motion. "What are they doing?" Nathan asked. "Are the leaves used for food? Medicine? Spices, maybe?"

"They are mulberry leaves." When she realized he didn't understand the significance, Elsa added, "Silkworms prefer to eat mulberry leaves."

Ahead, Nathan saw a large open structure with tall support beams and cross braces over the roof. Smaller open storehouses were stacked with bolts of colorful cloth, one on top of the other, like rolled rainbows.

Dozens of people moved in and out, including workers with baskets full of dark leaves. Doorway curtains breathed in and out as a pair of men hurried along with a bolt of bright red silk. Nathan heard the voices of workers inside the building, along with another sound . . . rustling, rattling, whispering. Elsa pushed aside the gray doorway curtain and led him into the cavernous warehouse.

Nathan felt as if he had fallen into the web of a tunnel spider. The walls and rafters were covered with meshed webs, sheets of silken strands that extended for twenty or thirty feet. Drooping banners hung down like the sides of a sagging tent. He smelled a sweet resinous scent that clung to the fibers.

Workers dumped baskets of leaves into wide troughs, and Nathan saw green worms as long as his forearm, chewing and squirming. With their blind, flat heads, they gorged themselves like maggots on rotted flesh. Men and women bustled about, stepping around Nathan and Elsa.

Olgya stood near several rattling and clacking looms where workers fed in the raw silk threads and created sheets of the marvelous fabric. She quickly finished her instructions to the weavers, then turned to Nathan and Elsa with a frown. "Is this duma business? We are working as swiftly as we can."

"We just wanted to have a better understanding of your efforts," Nathan said. "I have never seen silk weaving before."

"The worms make the silk strands," Olgya said. "We make

the fabric." Tense with her desperate work, she was a wiry mass of energy. Her silk robes were patterned with beautiful designs, primarily green and blue with a flash of red and orange. Her many ribboned clumps of hair looked somewhat disheveled. "The worms eat and eat, and they mature in only a few days, thanks to fleshmancy, and they no longer go into a pupa. They used to mature over time and then spin their cocoons, which we unraveled for the silk, one cocoon per worm. These altered worms are different, larger, and they produce large, furry cocoons that provide all the silk we need, and they remain worms for at least ten cycles. They spin a cocoon and then go back to eating until they're fattened up, and soon spin another cocoon."

Green, quivering worms crawled out of the troughs, finding a perch in a network of dowels and false branches, where they extruded glistening strands from spinnerets. Even as the cocoons hardened, workers detached an anchor line of the threads and then rolled the fibers onto wooden batons, which they took over to the looms.

"And this silk will help in the war effort?" Nathan asked.

Olgya showed them the magical loom, a clattering wooden machine with metal hinges, wires, and cross wires that held the emerging fabric. Runes carved in the wood glowed a pale blue, and the silk fibers absorbed some of that glow as the cloth grew inch by inch. Weavers used their gift to guide the process.

"The new silk is highly protective." Olgya took them to the far end of the loom, where the fabric emerged. "Special pigments further enhance its strength, but this is already ten times stronger than normal silk and it can protect our people against the blows of enemy soldiers, like fine mesh armor." She gave Nathan a challenging glance, noting the ornate sword he wore at his side. "Try to cut this silk with your blade. Thrust the point right through."

Nathan withdrew his sword. It felt good to hold the weapon, and he poked the sword into the silk, but the sharp point didn't cut through.

"Harder!" Olgya commanded.

He stabbed downward so that the fabric belled out, showing the pointed shape of the tip, but he couldn't pierce the cloth.

"Harder!"

Nathan pulled back and thrust with all his strength, jabbing and jabbing as if the cloth represented his most hated enemy, but he still couldn't pierce it. The cloth remained rigid enough to stop most of the damage to the skin of its wearer. "I must say I am impressed."

"Enemy arrows or blades cannot penetrate it. Our soldiers will be safe, although it was not enough to protect my Jed." Her firm voice suddenly cracked. "That boy did not want to fight, and he paid the ultimate price. I never thought to raise him as a soldier, since he was the son of a gifted noble. Why should he ever have to worry about being killed in battle?" She shuddered, and then her expression became stony again. "We all have to fight. We all do our part, even the silkworms." She looked at the thick cobwebs of fresh silk fiber. "We are driving them to burn their energy, and some of them don't survive."

Three silkworms drooped over the edge of a trough and fell, flaccid and limp. Workers plucked the soft bodies and cast them into a basket full of dead worms, while others dumped in more mulberry leaves for the thriving worms to devour.

Nathan listened to the chitter and rustle of the voracious creatures as they ate leaves and spun their cocoons, as the loom rattled and clacked, as the workers rolled the fresh silk fabric and carried it to the storehouse.

"We each do our part," Elsa repeated. "Because if we fail, Ildakar fails, and then we all die." She turned to Nathan with an incongruous grin on her face. "But I have just realized exactly what to do with my transference magic, and how I can smash a good portion of the siege army. I think this will work!"

CHAPTER 69

Thora remained locked in the dungeon cell, bored and frustrated, but this time the prison was of her own making. Although protective runes were again chiseled in the stone blocks around the door, she knew how to break free. She could smash her way out of the cell any time she chose, and her captors knew that. But she refused.

How odd, Thora thought, that the people who had betrayed her, the people who considered their own sovrena to be a danger to them, would grant her such a measure of trust. Yet, she had surrendered, and she did indeed want to save her city. She remained in the cell, bound by chains of her own guilt. For Ildakar.

Though she sat quietly, her thoughts never rested. For hours at a time, she would ignite a bright glow that illuminated the bare stone walls. Other times, swallowed by black thoughts, Thora preferred darkness and she would sit surrounded by possibilities.

Previously, when she escaped, a kind of blindness had convinced her to abandon Ildakar. She had actually made up her mind to aid General Utros, the true enemy. Thora realized now that she had been mad. Despair and frustration had twisted her thoughts, tangled them like a mass of tentacles, and she almost made a terrible mistake, worse than any mistake she'd ever made.

Something had broken inside her, though, when she stood on that wall, ready to throw herself to the ancient army. Her heart had undergone a metamorphosis, like one of Olgya's enhanced silkworms that was finally allowed to enter a cocoon after a lifetime of exhausting service. Thora knew that Ildakar would endure. It was still her perfect city, and she had to help preserve it, if the duma members ever allowed her to do so.

She was different from Maxim. Her treacherous husband had done everything possible to destroy Ildakar, not for any grand purpose, but simply because he was bored. She would not be like him. Yet she remained isolated here, as if sealed in a tomb.

When she heard whispering voices in the corridor, the rattle of the lock, she drew herself up, straight-backed and proud. She faced the door and shielded her eyes against the sudden flood of light as two men in wizard's robes greeted her.

"Sovrena, we need to speak with you." The gruff voice belonged to Quentin.

Though she had been contemplating possibilities in the dark, she summoned the bright glow again to light her chamber. Damon stood next to Quentin, looking uncertain, even frightened.

She narrowed her eyes. "You have come alone. No one else knows you're here?" The two men looked skittish, like the larks Thora had kept in cages. "Where is Lani?" she demanded when they didn't answer. "Why isn't she here to taunt me?"

"Lani is dead," Damon said, his frown enhanced by the long mustaches. "The general's sorceresses killed her when she used a scrying spell to spy on them. She drowned in her own scrying water."

Thora fought to hide her satisfaction. "And now you need me. How can I help? I want to fight."

"Ildakar needs you." Quentin scratched his round cheek as he and Damon explained the recent battle, how they had unleashed the two remaining Ixax warriors, how the dragon had come.

"But we have no more significant defenses, and the ancient army is still impossibly powerful," Damon said. The bangs on his forehead nearly reached his eyes and he subconsciously brushed them out of the way. "We have to use every possible means to save the city."

Thora was surprised. "And what of Nicci? I thought she was so powerful she could single-handedly save the world. Isn't that what Nathan Rahl's life book predicted? That she would save the world!" She snorted, but controlled her anger. She had been isolated so long she needed to hear whatever these two wizards could tell her.

"Nicci abandoned us again to go rally other cities, and she may never come back," Quentin said.

"Why should she?" Damon asked. "It is only a matter of time before Ildakar falls. The other duma members are digging through magical lore and testing obscure spells. Elsa believes she has an innovative transference rune to present to the duma, but that plan is not certain and seems desperate."

"It will never be enough," Quentin interjected with a groan. "That is why we have to be realistic. That is why we came to you."

Damon swallowed audibly. "Quentin and I have concluded there is only one sure way to protect Ildakar for all time, a way that we never need to worry about General Utros or any enemy again."

Quentin nodded. "We have to raise the shroud of eternity again. And we will need your help, Sovrena, if you are willing."

Thora had already guessed where the conversation would lead. "When I surrendered at the wall, I vowed to you that Ildakar was sacred to me, that I would do anything to save my city, if only you would let me. I meant that."

Damon and Quentin looked at each other, relieved. "We

can do much of the preparation work ourselves. In fact, we've already begun. While Nicci is gone and Nathan and Elsa are making plans for her transference-rune scheme, we have spread the word secretly among the citizens. We are collecting names. Some are volunteers, some are . . . suggestions."

Thora touched her hard, cold cheek, feeling the infusion of stone there. "You understand how terrible the cost will be? How much blood will be required? You will need a great many people, and gifted blood is the strongest."

"We know," Quentin said. "So does everyone, but they can also see the enemy army outside. They think of their families. They think of the future. They know that if the general breaks down our gates, the city will be laid waste. Nothing will remain but rubble. All their families will be slaughtered. Even some rebels have offered to be sacrificed."

"Rebels?" Thora scowled. "They broke down our traditions and the boundaries of the classes. Why would they help?"

Damon shrugged. "They wanted to be free. Now they need to understand the cost of freedom. If everyone wants to be equal in their new Ildakar, then they must accept equal responsibility."

Damon's voice cracked. "And they are agreeing! They understand. Some even quote the words of Mirrormask, vowing to fight and die for the future of their families and friends."

Thora was surprised. "My husband was never sincere in his words. He made them up."

"They were good words, no matter his motivations," Quentin said. "What is important is how his followers heard them, not what was in the wizard commander's heart."

Thora wondered if he was still alive, since Adessa had been hunting him for some time now. She pointed out, "The pyramid is destroyed, the blood channels and spell-forms gone, the apparatus ruined. How will you work so much blood magic?"

"I can remake the equipment," Damon said, "and we don't require the pyramid. We just need a place for the sacrificial victims to gather."

Quentin added, "And we need executioners to shed all that blood to work the magic and raise the shroud."

Thora remained dubious. "Even with the best of intentions, I'm not certain you will find enough volunteers."

"As I said, we have a large list of names," Quentin said. "And we've compiled a second book of people we can take by force, if we need more blood. We can mandate one sacrifice from each family."

Thora felt warm inside, a glimmer of pride for her city. "Then maybe Ildakar can be saved after all. I will help in any way I can. Come to me when your plans are ready."

CHAPTER 70

M axim found just the place to rest and hide while he gathered his strength, a cozy cottage in the forested hills above the Killraven River. He had traveled a great distance, covering his tracks all along the way. He'd abandoned his small stolen boat from Tarada at another river town and then moved on.

He had encountered many settlements on the banks, since the widening river provided food and work for so many people, but Maxim didn't want to live in a town again, not yet. He did intend to build a new empire greater than Ildakar, but that would come in time, and Maxim had plenty of time.

His mistake at Tarada was that he'd been in too much of a hurry. He had waited nearly a thousand years for the downfall of stagnant Ildakar, and by now the city was surely destroyed by the stone army he had awakened. He couldn't expect to create a comparable city in only a year or two.

Here, up in the hills above a small river town called Gant's Ford, Maxim settled in to a time of impatient peace, maybe for months. The isolated cottage was spacious, with a main area and hearth. A large bed for the mother and father was blocked off by a hanging leather curtain, while a smaller room off to the side had three narrow beds for the children. In the fireplace, an iron hook held a cauldron for a pot of soup, as well as iron skewers for roasting fish brought up from the town market, or squirrels or hares caught in the forest.

In the larder behind the cottage, the father had hung strings of venison sausages. Chickens ran about in the yard, pecking at beetles and worms, taking care of themselves. Maxim, the former wizard commander of Ildakar, was not a man to tend barnyard fowl.

Someday when he built a grand city again, he would have uniformed guards, servants to attend to his every need, practitioners talented in the art of massage after he luxuriated in a perfumed bath, young women for his bed. He would have clothiers create magnificent garments for him out of the finest fabrics, the softest weaves, the warmest furs. His jewelry would be crafted by the most skilled smiths in his domain.

He sighed, missing Ildakar more than he'd thought he would.

For now, this cottage was an acceptable home. The forest silence was comforting, enhanced by the sound of rushing spruce boughs in the breezes. The man and his wife had cut down the tallest trees, leaving stumps in the front yard. Blocks of firewood were stacked against the cottage, and an axe rested next to one of the stumps that served as a chopping block. When he ran out of split firewood for the hearth, though, Maxim didn't deign to swing the ax, but used his gift to expand cracks in the logs, shattering them into pieces the fireplace could accommodate. He was resourceful, even self-sufficient.

After fleeing through the swamps for days, avoiding predators as well as the maddeningly determined Adessa, he was glad to have a safe and quiet place to reside. He knew she wouldn't give up, although if Adessa had any sense at all, she would realize she could never defeat a wizard commander! The protective branded runes would save her from an overt attack of magic, but she had no powers remotely comparable to his own. He'd been shocked at how strong the morazeth was when she tried to kill him, and he wondered where that enhanced strength came from. Had Thora found a way to trigger some manifestation of the gift in Adessa? It was annoying.

As he moved through the silent home, he plucked at the clean linen shirt that had been the husband's. The trousers were too large, and he needed a rope belt around the waist to hold them up, but that was part of his disguise. His Ildakaran garments had been beyond repair, and he'd discarded the gray robes he had worn as Mirrormask. At Tarada, he'd been forced to flee so swiftly he had been unable to bring extra clothes. At least he no longer looked like a beggar.

After he used a small glamour spell, people in Gant's Ford gave him what he needed. He just had to lie low for now, like a bear hibernating for the winter, and eventually he would emerge with detailed plans to conquer the world. The solitude was the hardest part. After living for so many centuries in Ildakar, Maxim was not accustomed to being alone.

Once every two or three days he would make the hour walk down the forest path to the river town. He called no attention to himself in his rough-spun clothes, and people assumed he was one of the many woodcutters, farmers, and hunters who lived in the wild. Maxim ate food from the inns, and he especially liked the catfish pie. Sometimes he spent coins he'd found in a jar inside the cottage, while other times he just worked a forgetting spell and left without paying. He drank the town's sour ale and grimaced, even tried some wine that came from barges upriver. Once, he asked if the tavernkeeper possessed any bloodwine from Ildakar, and the portly man had just laughed at him, explaining that bloodwine was an extravagance no one in town could afford.

Maxim convinced himself that he was getting to know the poor people, the hardworking ungifted types. When he played his role as Mirrormask, he had pretended to understand the plight of the lower classes. He had learned the right words to say and watched how easily people reacted to his promises. He could incite them with honeyed words about freedom, although the people in Gant's Ford were already free, and they knew their lot in life would never change for the better.

Later, after he had his fill of people, Maxim would walk back up the path to his cottage in the hills, where he continued to dream of greater conquests.

One afternoon, the silence and boredom weighed heavily on him, and he left the cottage. Out in the yard the wild chickens clucked and fled, though he had no intention of killing them. That would be too messy, too much work.

The family kept a garden plot with onions, beans, and a squash plant whose vines sprawled across the ground. Behind the cottage, a line of brambles held sweet berries. He had enough food to last a while, but he was growing impatient with all this waiting.

He strolled past the garden patch and saw the five stone figures, exactly where they had been since he first arrived here. The broad-chested husband, and his wife who was not old, but not pretty either. Her petrified hair was tied back, covered with a scarf. A drab skirt hung from hips widened by childbirth. The mother held the hand of one of her children, a boy of about eight. The father grabbed the smallest one, a girl no more than five. An older boy of eleven ran between them. Their expressions had turned to panic when they realized how much danger Maxim posed. They had tried to sneak away into the night, but hadn't gotten far. Maxim had emerged from the door and saw them running. Without bothering to call out, he released his petrification spell. They froze in midstep, their skin and bones hardening into stone. They would always keep that expression of fear, their eyes wide, but they would never take another step. He regretted his impetuous move, because now they couldn't help him, couldn't serve him, and Maxim needed someone to do the work around the cottage.

When he first arrived, the family had welcomed him as a

traveler, fed him, let him spend the night, but they became frightened when he forced them to do things, and he'd been too tired to use much finesse.

Now he walked past the statue family, looked at the mother and father, whose blind, staring eyes didn't move, didn't see him. Sarcastically, he wished them a good day, since he had no one else to talk to.

He walked along the hilltop, listening to the whisper of tall spruces, until he reached an overlook from which he could see the Killraven River far below. He stood on a rock promontory, drinking in the view, seeing the noon sun sparkle on the current. Gant's Ford filled the bank, the tiny people going about their daily business.

Then he spotted the ships on the river, a large and imposing fleet of at least fifty sturdy vessels with lines of long oars, midnight-blue sails, and a fearsome carved serpent at each prow. Maxim stared. The Norukai!

This was no simple trading fleet, not a ship or two delivering slaves in exchange for bloodwine and yaxen meat. This was a full Norukai invasion. In the past, the raiders had come to Ildakar pretending to be simple merchants, but now that he saw the dangerous fleet pressing upriver, he understood their goal. This wasn't just a raid or two on vulnerable river villages. He smiled as he began to imagine how much havoc those fierce warriors would unleash upon Ildakar.

When the Norukai attackers arrived, Maxim had no doubt that the city would fall, if Ildakar wasn't already destroyed in the aftermath of what he himself had done. He drove away a twinge of remorse and just watched for the next hour as dozens of serpent warships sailed upriver toward his former home.

CHAPTER 71

Even though Bannon didn't have the gift, he wanted to help protect Ildakar. After being captured, he was less than enthusiastic about running out to face hordes of enemy soldiers with his sword, but when he learned that Elsa needed physical labor for her giant plan to unleash transference magic on the battlefield, he volunteered.

Crews gathered at the top of the sheer bluff above the river. The sky held a smear of dull clouds that hung like leftover dragon smoke, carrying a persistent drizzle. The air was cold, wet, and miserable, which made the cliffs treacherous. When Bannon looked uneasily down at the dangling ropes, the narrow wooden platforms and scaffolding, the workers climbing down with buckets of fresh paint, he almost lost his nerve. "Sweet Sea Mother." But he sucked in a deep breath and nodded to Elsa. "If I can fight a thousand warriors, I am brave enough to paint a cliff."

The older sorceress nodded. "If we succeed here, young man, this giant transference rune will defeat more enemy soldiers than a thousand Ildakaran swords."

"Then it is worth a bit of vertigo," he said. Lila had taken him down the narrow stairs, the wooden ledges, and the hanging platforms to the river below. He knew he could do it. Elsa's giant rune needed to cover the entire cliff face, an intricate design painted across the open sandstone, with no gaps, no errors.

The sorceress peered over the edge, studying the rock surface. "See that section over there, near the water sluice? No one is working that part of the cliff. It would be a good assignment for you."

It seemed a very long way from any of the stable platforms or stairs. "I will have to anchor a rope from the top of the cliff here."

"Either that, or you need to fly." Elsa gave him a quirk of a smile. "Ropes are probably more reliable."

"Need more paint down here!" called a deep male voice.

Below, Bannon saw a potbellied man standing alone on a rickety platform. He waved a thick brush so that droplets of red paint spattered his bare shoulders. Two workers from a nearby access tunnel tied a rope to the handle of a full bucket of paint and lowered it swiftly, hand over hand. The bucket swayed, spilling a little, but the potbellied man reached up and caught it. He set the bucket on the boards at his feet and began painting again.

On top, at the cliff's edge, Bannon tied a harness around himself, assisted by other workers, who secured the knots and double-checked them. Elsa paced the edge of the bluff, watching the crews below.

She had crafted her intricate spell-form with numerous curling loops and connecting cross lines. She had tested the rune until she was sure she had perfected the design. While the duma members planned the desperate charge out onto the battlefield to complete the other half of her transference spell, according to her plan, Elsa had rallied more than forty volunteers who were willing to paint the anchor design across the sheer cliff face. Including Bannon.

Most of the painters were cargo loaders and river workers

accustomed to moving along the steep stairs, platforms, and ladders. Standing at the top of the bluff, Elsa had used a different sort of transference magic. In the misty rain, she held the sheet of paper on which she had drawn her intricate rune and used her gift to magnify and project the image onto the rock, where it remained clearly visible. Up and down the cliff face, the precariously suspended workers could see the exact lines to paint.

As Bannon roped up, Elsa showed him the spell-form drawn on the damp sheet of paper. "If other wizards can lay down smaller boundary runes around the enemy army, as well as a central anchor rune, I can link all of them to this much larger design painted on the cliffs. Then I can transfer from the bluffs and the Killraven River right out to the middle of the general's forces."

"Transfer what?" Bannon asked. "Water?"

"The river and the stone have something far more destructive than just water." Her eyes twinkled. "*Heat*, a great reservoir of heat. I could drain all the heat from the river for as much as a mile in either direction, and I can suck the heat from these rocks and dump it all into the middle of the battlefield from the anchor point of the connected runes. But first we need to have the primary spell-form painted large and bold. That's the important part for now. We need to be ready in a day or two for the main assault."

Bannon had never understood or attempted magic, but always fought with his sword. Right now, though, he would continue the battle with a paintbrush.

"Over the edge with you, young man," Elsa said once he had all the ropes tied around him. "As soon as this is completed, we will hit General Utros again. Their army is in shambles, and after the terrible thing they did to High Captain Stuart . . ." A stormy expression crossed her face. "We are not inclined to show them much mercy."

Bannon checked the rope again. In the drizzle, the thick

cord was wet in his hands, but the knots were tight. He backed toward the edge of the sheer drop-off holding a bucket of paint in his right hand. "I will do my part."

"Just paint the lines you see. So long as the projection magic keeps the design in place, the rune is clearly marked. You won't have any trouble."

The cold mist clung to him like a sheen of sweat. Determined, he lowered himself over the edge, taking care not to spill the paint. He found small handholds and footholds in the sandstone, then a narrow carved walkway.

After a quick glance at the dizzying drop, he focused on the rock in front of him. The rain picked up, but he kept descending toward the obvious mark of Elsa's giant rune. He was glad Lila wasn't watching him today. Instead, she was continuing to train prospective swordfighters for the charge of separate strike forces that Elsa's plan would require.

Dangling on the rope, he reached the proper position near the sluice chute where river water flowed upward into the aqueducts. The shimmering design hovered on the rock. Bannon dipped the brush into the bucket and smeared a wide line of red paint on the sandstone. The paint was thick enough to stick to even the rain-wet rock, and Bannon covered the appropriate spot. He swung like a pendulum, back and forth, to reach more of the design. He dipped the brush into the bucket and slapped red along the projected line.

Across the cliff face, he watched his fellow volunteers hanging in their cradles, standing on narrow platforms, gripping rickety rails so they could lean out and paint farther along the lines. Many parts of the grand design were already coming together.

One of the workers leaned too far and slipped on the rain-slick wood. He yelped, and his bucket tumbled over the edge, splashing red paint like blood as it fell toward the river. The man managed to hook his arm around the scaffolding, while the rest of his body dangled free. He kicked his legs and flailed his other arm, but no one was close enough to help him. After a few tense seconds, the man levered himself back onto the scaffold, where he hunched on his hands and knees, panting to recover.

From above, Elsa looked down, her face filled with concern. When it was clear the man was safe, she yelled, "None of the paint got on the cliff. The spell-form is intact!" She called into the loading tunnels. "Bring that man another bucket. We need to finish."

Bannon checked the knots on his harness and anchored his foot on a hard lump of rock for greater stability. He held the wet rope with one hand and brushed more paint with the other.

That night, knowing that the giant rune would be completely painted within the next day, Elsa met with Nathan and the leaders of six separate groups of volunteers who believed in her plan. She joined them in the torch-lit ruling chamber, making them gather around the stone tables where she drew on a large unrolled sheet of paper. "Here is how we will use transference magic to hurt General Utros."

Nathan smiled at her in encouragement, admiring the scope of her plan. With precise instinctive motions, she described the complex spell-form on the cliff and the unique design of the boundary runes she had developed for this exact purpose. "*This,*" she said, tapping the paper. "Burn it into your minds." It was a circle with internal loops bounded by a triangle. "With transference magic, each rune, each spell-form, has a certain grammar, a kind of punctuation that must be exact. I won't explain what every curve and line means. Just know that you cannot make a mistake."

Oron, Olgya, and three other gifted nobles would lead the satellite teams. Julian was one of Olgya's primary silk merchants. The second gifted volunteer, Leo, was a short, effeminate man who managed two yaxen slaughterhouses and who had a remarkable control over his own magic. The third, Perri, was a meek-looking, middle-aged woman. She was a shaper, like Damon, and she manipulated the vines in the bloodwine vineyards to produce a larger harvest. These five team leaders had all sworn to use their skills to help Elsa's plan.

"You will each be responsible for drawing one of these satellite runes—five boundary spell-forms—and they must be exact." Elsa looked at each gifted leader to make sure they understood. "Your boundary runes will encircle the zone of destruction. Each of your teams will have a fighter escort to lead you to your respective positions around the valley. Nathan will accompany me, because we will face the hardest fighting to place the anchor rune in the center of the camp." Her voice cracked. "We will mark the center point to connect the boundary runes. This complex of symbols will magnify and draw from the single huge design painted on the cliffs above the river."

Nathan said to her softly, "I have no doubt you will save us all."

Knowing the risks, the duma had decided not to send out *all* of their wizards, however. If Elsa's attempt met with disaster, then no one would remain to defend the city. Damon and Quentin had offered to stay behind. Nathan also knew that he would find a way to keep Bannon safe behind the walls. The young man would want to volunteer to become part of a strike force, and he had certainly proven his mettle on the battlefield, but he had already been captured and nearly killed by the ancient army. Nicci wasn't here, and Nathan would see to it that the young man remained inside the walls. Elsa's plan had more than enough volunteers, and he knew he could convince Lila to keep Bannon safe. The morazeth wouldn't risk him either.

As he thought of the upcoming mission, Nathan forced good cheer, more for Elsa's benefit than for anyone else. He looked at the gathered volunteers, the powerful wizards who believed in her proposal. He brushed his hands together. "When Nicci returns, I will be quite pleased to tell her that we managed to defeat General Utros while she was gone."

CHAPTER 72

Serrimundi sprawled across low hills surrounding a harbor that was crowded with tall sailing ships and fishing boats. Closely built homes lined the slopes that had been forested at one time. Serrimundi was an ancient city, and all that remained of the untamed woods were spacious parks. Wide canals guided water between the hills and into the bay. Boatmen poled shallow vessels along the canals, delivering supplies or ferrying people.

From a high point in the hills as Nicci stared across the rolling streets, the dark tile roofs, the whitewashed buildings, she acknowledged that Serrimundi was indeed a beautiful city. And entirely vulnerable.

When she emerged from the sliph, Nicci coughed and sucked in a deep breath. She realized that the sliph had not admonished her to "Breathe!" As she regained her balance, she turned to see the silvery figure staring at her with a hard expression. Without even acknowledging that she had delivered her passenger, the moody creature dropped back into her well and retreated into the unfathomable depths.

Nicci found herself in the open sunlight on a hill above the harbor. The sliph well was part of an unoccupied open-air temple with fluted support pillars. Tall urns filled with fresh-cut flowers were arranged across the tiled floor. A platter of overripe fruit sat on an altar, an offering to some god or goddess that had apparently gone unheeded for days. Dry leaves skittered across the floor, and birds chirped in the vines overhead.

Nicci turned to see a statue of a revered woman with long, flowing locks of hair, like the waves on the sea. Her hands extended as if calling supplicants. Nicci had seen a similar statue before, a giant carving on a cliff at the mouth of Serrimundi Harbor. The Sea Mother.

On Chiriya Island, Bannon had been brought up to worship the Sea Mother, and the religion was common along the coast of the Old World. It was generally compatible with the prevalent belief in spirits and the underworld, which Nicci knew to be true because of her direct experience with the Keeper. She decided this must be an isolated temple to the Sea Mother.

Strangely, the goddess bore a striking similarity to the sliph. Nicci wondered if some gullible observer, thousands of years ago, had seen the quicksilver woman emerge from the well, delivering travelers who secretly served Emperor Sulachan. Could that have been the inspiration for the Sea Mother's appearance and the huge statue on the cliff?

Though empty, the temple was obviously still used. Supplicants to the Sea Mother generally made their sacrifices in the open ocean, but if the original sliph well was up here, someone would have built a temple to mark that spot. Gardens spread out beyond the temple, and stone footpaths wound in haphazard directions, as if supplicants were expected to walk a contemplative path before they arrived at the altar.

Nicci heard voices and saw figures passing among tall hedges, approaching the open temple. Since she didn't want to explain where she had come from, she departed down a different path, making her way toward the residential buildings closer to the harbor.

She reached the crowded streets where women sat outside sewing garments and men toiled at craft benches. Some of the people acknowledged her as she walked past. The inhabitants of Serrimundi were not suspicious, not even curious about the stranger. Nicci's black dress was different from the style of their own clothes, but she realized that the bustling harbor city must see many foreigners.

She had been here once before, when she and Nathan sailed south from Tanimura aboard the *Wavewalker*. Back then, they were simply traveling the Old World as emissaries for the D'Haran Empire. Nicci had briefly met the harborlord, a man named Otto, when Captain Eli Corwin took on more supplies. She decided to start with the harborlord and deliver her warning.

She walked along one of the canals until a boatman drifted by and offered her a ride. Nicci didn't mind walking, but she was in a hurry, and so she accepted. As she balanced on the boat while the man poled them along, she scanned the hills, buildings, commercial districts, orchards. Serrimundi was open, thriving. They would be entirely unprepared if General Utros's invading army crashed into the city.

Serrimundi had been mostly unscathed by the Imperial Order, and now she could see they were too complacent. She would have to change their mind-set.

Eventually, she reached the offices of the harborlord, near the water's edge. Clerks inside the harborlord's office kept detailed ledgers of all ships that entered Serrimundi Harbor, along with notations of their captains, their primary cargo, and their ports of origin. Three older men with nearly identical fringes of short white hair around their bald skulls sat squinting over their books.

One of the men glanced up at Nicci, squinted as if she were more difficult to see than the notations in his leather-bound ledger. "Harborlord Otto isn't here, miss. He went down to meet a ship. His daughter's just been betrothed to Captain Ganley."

"Which ship?" Nicci asked. "I will find him on the docks."

"The *Mist Maiden*," said one of the other men. "He should be there."

Nicci set off along the harbor's edge, carrying the cloth-wrapped rectangle of glass that showed the vast ancient army. She passed a foul-smelling krakener, whose hull was permeated with the slime of the tentacled sea creatures they hunted. One ship had just pushed off from its dock and drifted away from the crowded piers, heading toward the mouth of the harbor, where waves crashed against a rock outcropping that stood like a sentinel. A towering female figure had been carved there, a woman bursting from the raw rock, the Sea Mother. Again, Nicci recognized the familiar features of the sliph.

The *Mist Maiden* was a three-masted cargo ship, even larger than the *Wavewalker*. Its sails were tied up, and thick hawsers lashed the hull against the largest pier in the harbor. The ship's crew had already disembarked except for a handful of men still lounging aboard on the open deck. Large crates of cargo had been stacked while workers and carters hauled the goods away. Merchants squabbled over the division of the shipment.

Nicci recognized Harborlord Otto as he strolled down the gangplank of the *Mist Maiden*. He walked with a spring in his step, adjusting his floppy leather hat that she remembered from before. On the deck of the *Mist Maiden*, she saw a young woman talking to the bearded captain and guessed it might be Otto's daughter, Shira. The young woman had lost her husband, Captain Corwin, when the *Wavewalker* was wrecked by the selka. Soon, Shira would be marrying a new husband, Captain Ganley.

The harborlord was hearty, good-humored, and well respected in Serrimundi. If Nicci could enlist Otto as an ally, he would help spread the warning and prepare the city's defenses.

She called out in a brisk, businesslike voice. "Harborlord, I need to speak with you."

He turned his caramel-colored eyes to her. "How may I help you?"

"You can help me spread a warning throughout Serrimundi."

He frowned. "A warning about what?"

"An enemy army, a huge force of ancient soldiers that may eventually move against the Old World. They are far away, laying siege to Ildakar, but Serrimundi must be prepared. Luckily, there is time, if you act."

Harborlord Otto seemed more puzzled than alarmed by the suggestion. "An enemy army? Do you mean the Imperial Order? We heard that Emperor Jagang is dead and his entire force defeated. What is there to worry about?"

"Yes, Jagang is dead." Nicci didn't point out that she herself had killed him. "This is another army, one that served Iron Fang fifteen centuries ago. They were under a spell, but now they are reawakened."

Otto chuckled. "I've heard sailors tell many stories about sea monsters, selka, and krakens. You are having a joke on me."

Nicci unwrapped the glass and showed him the image of Utros's army. "It is true. The legendary city of Ildakar is besieged, and regardless of whether they survive or fall, General Utros is likely to continue his conquest. He will eventually come to the coast and Serrimundi. You need to build up your defenses."

Otto chuckled again. "But Ildakar is on the other side of the world, if it even exists! No one has heard of it in centuries."

"Ildakar exists, and is not as far away as you might think. The D'Haran Empire has been alerted, and Lord Rahl's soldiers will be moving south from the Tanimura garrison. Serrimundi needs to help as well."

The harborlord scoffed. "We don't fear any invasion. We survived the Imperial Order, miss." He narrowed his eyes, scrutinizing the glass. "How did you get this image?" He tapped the pane with his fingernail as if expecting the figures to dissolve. "Did you come by ship? Which vessel were you aboard?"

"I am a sorceress, and I came by other means," she said. "You and I met briefly some months ago, when I arrived aboard the

Wavewalker. Afterward I sent a message by courier that the ship had been sunk by selka."

He hung his head, suddenly serious now. "Yes, we received that news. It was tragic." Otto struggled to recall a name. "You are . . . Nicci?"

"Yes." She held up the glass again. "And you need to listen to me about this army. General Utros has a force as great as the Imperial Order. Sooner or later you will be under attack."

He frowned as he struggled to recall a conversation. "Now that you mention it, I heard secondhand from a fishing boat that came in this morning, something about one or two coastal villages being destroyed, Effren and one other. But I have no further proof, and I don't think we should overreact until the news has been verified. Is that what you mean? Is this enemy army attacking the coast?" He pointed toward her pane of glass.

"No. General Utros is far inland, but he will be moving. I promise you, this is a threat. You must prepare." She could see that her words were not getting through to him.

He nodded distractedly. "Thank you, I will make note of it, but Serrimundi has no standing army. Our harbor is busy, as you can see. Our population is healthy and prosperous. Everyone trades with us. We are not on a war footing."

"That's why I came to warn you." Even though Elsa's pre-served images proved what Nicci said, the sheer distance from Ildakar to Serrimundi made the threat seem a small one, but Utros had already dispatched large portions of his army. If those forces continued marching, needing no supplies of food or water, they could cross the continent more swiftly than anyone expected. "You don't comprehend the danger, Harborlord. This is not an army to be ignored."

Otto paused to consider the glass again. "The Sea Mother will protect Serrimundi as she always has. We need not fear an attack."

Growing frustrated, Nicci wrapped the cloth over the glass, covering the image. "Remember that I warned you."

As if he didn't give her a second thought, Otto adjusted his leather hat and strolled down the dock, still smiling. From the deck of the *Mist Maiden,* his daughter waved and wrapped her arm around the other captain, her fiancé.

Hoping she would have better luck if she spread the word around the harbor, Nicci made her way along the piers where sailors lounged about, waiting near their ships. Some whittled scraps of wood or kraken-horn ivory. Three deeply tanned and unshaven sailors passed around a bottle of wine. She showed many others her pane of glass, talking to merchant captains, kraken hunters, fishermen. To little use.

She came upon four shirtless, arrogant young men who lounged on a pile of sailcloth as if someone had placed it there for their bed. By the strings of tattoos across their chests, she recognized them to be wishpearl divers. The similar divers she had met aboard the *Wavewalker* were unpleasant, self-important men who refused to do work aboard the ship. They had poisoned her, diminished her powers, tried to rape her. They hadn't succeeded. When the selka killed all of them, Nicci had not grieved.

She regarded the divers with a scowl as they roused themselves, curious about her attention. She asked, "If Serrimundi were under attack from an enemy force, would you lift a hand to defend it? Or are you as worthless as the other wishpearl divers I've met?"

Angrily, the four shirtless men climbed to their feet and sneered at her. One man said, "I might lift a finger if you came to my bed."

"Then I might lift a finger to crush all of your bones into little pieces," she said. "Mark my words, the threat is coming, an army that could destroy this city."

"What army?" asked one of the other divers. "We've heard of no army."

"I am telling you so you can prepare, if you know how to fight."

"We know how to swim," said one of the divers, chuckling.

None of them took her seriously. She showed them Elsa's image on the glass, which they found interesting, but unconvincing. "That is an army in the mountains. We have no mountains here."

"Armies can cross mountains," Nicci said. "They are on the move."

"If they are far away, then I'm not worried yet," said one diver.

"I don't even believe there is an army," said another, squinting closer at the preserved pane. "It's just a trick. There is magic in that glass. She could be showing us anything."

"Heh, I know something I'd like her to show me," said the lecherous diver.

Nicci was of a mind to burst his testicles right there, which would certainly gain his attention, but she hadn't expected to earn any support from wishpearl divers in the first place, and they didn't disappoint her. After a long day she had hoped to rouse the people of Serrimundi, though she knew it would be a more difficult task than convincing General Linden and the D'Haran garrison. These people did not know her. Not yet.

As the wishpearl divers laughed, mocking her story about the great army, she heard shouts raised across the harbor. A lookout on the *Mist Maiden*'s tall mast was casting dried bread to screaming gulls, but he suddenly dropped his basket and began hollering at the top of his lungs. Around the harbor, other ships picked up the alarm. Loud ship's bells rang.

Beyond the rocky promontory at the mouth of the harbor, Nicci saw smoke in the sky. A ship was sailing into the harbor, engulfed in flames. It bobbed and yawed without guidance, its sails ablaze, a krakener riding low in the water. She saw several sailors dive overboard. Two of them were caught in the current and swept up against the outcropping beneath the carving of the Sea Mother. The burning ship continued to drift into the crowded harbor.

"Ship on fire, ship on fire!" The outcries spread among the vessels. The krakener listed to one side as the flames grew more intense. Harbor workers scrambled about, afraid that the fire would spread to other vessels. Several fishing boats rapidly set sail away from the docks to get clear. The krakener took on water as it began to sink near the mouth of the harbor.

Nicci shaded her eyes, wondering what could have set the ship ablaze. It was like a warning torch thrown at the city of Serrimundi. Soon enough, she had her answer. They all did.

With midnight-blue sails fully stretched and line after line of oars extended, a Norukai serpent ship cruised around the promontory, coming in from the sea and entering Serrimundi Harbor, following the krakener they had set ablaze.

Behind the first Norukai serpent ship came another, and another, a line of ten raiders. Frantic shouts roared among the dockworkers, and the harbor bells clanged. Nicci had never seen so many Norukai ships, and they were coming to invade Serrimundi.

This was not the army she had warned them about, but it was a threat just as deadly.

CHAPTER 73

The mists on the wide river did not obscure the cold, miserable morning. Rain fell gently on the decks of the Norukai ships, and King Grieve stood in the open in his sharkskin vest, his massive bare arms slick from the rain. He stared ahead as if he could penetrate the fog with the power of his gaze, but he saw only the gray shadows of tangled trees on the nearer shore.

The treacherous swamps had gone on for miles as the Norukai fleet sailed upriver. The opposite shore was lost in the gloom and rain. In places, the Killraven River was so wide it seemed like the sea. Grieve didn't like close banks and narrow shores, which made him feel confined.

Water lapped against the hull of his serpent ship, and the dark sails stretched, pushed along by the directed breeze. Grieve wanted to increase their pace, so Norukai crewmen extended their oars and drove the fleet onward, like a slow sword thrust against the current.

The fog muffled all sound. Drummers on each foredeck pounded out a steady rowing beat as the ominous vessels moved along. The rhythmic pounding would strike fear into any weak villagers huddled on the banks watching the ships pass.

A large trout leaped up, startled by the passage of such

immense vessels. Chalk pranced over, gripping the rail and lurching himself up on spindly arms. He peered over the edge, squirming, watching the ripples in the brown current. Grieve grabbed his bony shoulder and pulled him back so he wouldn't fall overboard.

"A fish, my Grieve, King Grieve! A king fish!" He grinned with lopsided lips on his pocked face. "Ildakar is a fish. We will catch it and gut it, and roast it over a fire."

"Yes, we will catch it and gut it," Grieve said, "but we can't destroy it, because it is mine. It will be the capital of my new empire."

"They'll all grieve!" Chalk looked over the railing again, searching for more fish.

Another trout leaped, and the pale shaman grinned, but a different form cruised through the water, unseen. A swamp dragon lunged, and its jaws snatched the trout. Holding the fish in its teeth, the reptile submerged and swam away with barely a ripple.

The drumbeats continued, the long oars stroked, and the Norukai ships moved up the river.

Mounted on a spike at the prow was the hideous head of the selka. The slimy creature had sagged, the rubbery skin falling slack along its cheekbones and jaws. The yellow eyes had turned to jelly, and the crew had repeatedly chased away ravens that tried to peck at the delicacy. The sea creatures would not bother them now that the Norukai ships were far up the Killraven River.

Out in the ocean, the angry selka had followed the fleet, threatening, but unable to attack. The Norukai raiders had jeered and taunted them, throwing harpoons on ropes, trying to stab the outlying creatures, but missed. The selka followed them all the way to the estuary, raising their ugly heads above the water, hissing unintelligible curses. The Norukai responded by emptying the foul-smelling bilges into the water behind the ships.

The rain had started on their third day moving upriver. The Norukai ships sailed past villages on the banks, small fishing and trading towns. Previously, Norukai slavers might stop and raid the weaker villages just to replace any walking meat that died during the voyage.

This time, the fifty serpent ships were on a military conquest, not a mere raid, but Grieve's fighters were restless. He allowed a few vessels to pull ashore and let the fighters slosh to the banks, where they could kill townspeople, set homes on fire, rape women, and leave a mark of terror. If King Grieve was going to wrap the entire continent in his iron fist, he needed the people to fear him. But he wanted to get to Ildakar.

Shivering, Chalk wrapped his scrawny arms around his bony chest. "Fire. I wish we had fire. So cold."

"I gave you a blanket," Grieve said. "Wrap yourself in it."

"Fire. I want a fire. Like the big hearth in the Bastion."

"We can't have a big fire on a ship. Use the blanket."

Chalk hunched down, and his teeth chattered loudly enough to be heard over the drumbeat the rowers used to keep time with their oars. "Cold. Ice. Snow."

Grieve felt sorry for his eccentric and stubborn friend. Chalk always seemed to be chilled, even on the main island. The shaman spent half his days near the roaring fire, but he chose to wear no more than a loincloth. He didn't want to hide the countless bite marks that covered his skin, but he looked so miserable now.

"You will have your fire in Ildakar," Grieve said. "We can burn part of the city and that will keep you warm enough." When Chalk didn't answer, he nudged the shaman. "At least get out of the rain. Take shelter in the back cabin or belowdecks."

"Snow and ice," Chalk moaned. "Everything so cold. The river frozen!"

"It's just rain. Soon the sun will come out."

Forgetting his physical discomfort, Chalk sprang to his feet again. "The sun will come out, my Grieve! Yes, late in the morning, and we will see Ildakar! Our fish, King Grieve. They'll all grieve."

"They'll all grieve." He recognized the cockeyed intensity in Chalk's expression. "Is that a dream?"

"Yes, Ildakar. We are almost there, but the cold and ice . . ." Chalk shook his head and huddled around himself again, shivering. "And snow!"

"You don't even know snow," Grieve said. "You have never seen it."

"Cold!" Chalk insisted.

The drums pounded, and the oars sloshed in perfect coordination. The serpent ships glided past the swamps. Grieve had listened to Captain Kor's report of the previous expedition to Ildakar, and he knew they were nearly at their destination.

An hour later, the rain slackened and the mists grew more diffuse as weak yellow light burned through the river fog. Grieve hunched over the prow, sick of waiting, and stared into the brightening light. Chalk relished the faint sunshine.

Finally, around midmorning, exactly as the shaman had predicted, the sun broke through, so the Norukai king could look ahead. He saw the sandstone cliffs, the uplift the ancient wizards had created. At last he saw with his own eyes the ancient city of Ildakar towering above the river, its white buildings and tall towers shining in the distance. The city alone was larger than the main Norukai island. Grieve's fifty ships would be enough to conquer it, though. Of that he had no doubt.

Chalk jabbed a bony finger at the sight. "They'll all grieve. Our fish! They'll all grieve."

The Norukai king touched the soft smelly head of the decomposing selka. He squeezed the oozing flesh of its cheeks and turned the creature so its runny eye sockets pointed toward the vulnerable city. "There," he said, in a low voice, "I want you to see our next victory."

CHAPTER 74

The expedition from Cliffwall pushed through the mountains, where the air was thinner and the cold air blew harder. Verna looked behind them, imagining the desert canyons they had left far behind, then turned in the direction of Ildakar. That was their destination, and she couldn't wait to see all the wonders Renn had promised. By now, the road was more apparent, recently trampled by the large, half-stone expeditionary force that had marched away from the legendary city.

On his warhorse, General Zimmer led the group. Oliver and Peretta made notes of their travels and exchanged stories with young Amber. The other scholars looked sore and dirty, tired of the long journey. None of them had ever left their isolated canyon before.

Within days, the terrain transitioned to forested foothills, winding down to a watershed where streams provided all the drinking and bathing water they needed. They toiled up the next ridge, reaching the rounded top only to see another ridge ahead of them.

Verna began to lose hope that they would ever find their

destination, but Renn grew excited as they climbed the next line of hills. "This is it, I think. The plains of Ildakar are just ahead." He inhaled deeply, as if the air smelled different to him. "It will be so good to be home."

Verna would be glad to see Nicci and Nathan again, to talk with them, and she would trust their assessment about Ildakar.

"I smell smoke," Oliver said as they worked their way through the trees. A drizzle had continued throughout the morning, and Verna was wet. Her gray-brown hair hung limply against her skull, and she tried not to look as miserable as she felt.

"How can you smell anything in this?" Peretta asked.

"I have always had a keen sense of smell."

General Zimmer and the scouts crested the ridge and rode out of the sparser pines. Ahead, they saw grass-covered hills and a broad open valley. Renn pushed forward to get a better view. "It's Ildakar. That is the plain. That's—"

Zimmer raised a hand, commanding them to stay within the shelter of the trees. "We don't want to be seen."

Verna, Amber, Peretta, and Oliver crowded forward. Renn stood with his arms at his side, his mouth open. "By the Keeper's beard!"

The grassy hills to the north of the great valley were scorched black. Out on the plain Verna saw a huge army, thousands upon thousands camped in rows with a few tents dispersed among the troops. The soldiers were moving, marching, forming precise groups, a military force vastly greater than the invasion army they had buried under the avalanche.

"That looks as big as the entire population of Tanimura," Amber said in a trembling voice.

Verna looked beyond the countless warriors. Ildakar rose up like a beautiful island covered with tiers of buildings, layers of neighborhoods piled up to the summit of the plateau. It was indeed a magnificent city, and it was under siege.

Tears leaked down Renn's cheeks. "General Utros is awake. Look what they have done to Ildakar!" He shaded his eyes, scanning the high, protected upwelling of the city. "I can barely make out the top of the plateau in this drizzle. I see the ruling tower, but I can't find the pyramid. It seems to be gone."

Peretta narrowed her dark eyes. "I see a pyramid, but it is broken. What did it look like before?"

"Something happened in my city," Renn said. "Something terrible. We've got to help. We need to fight for Ildakar."

The seven other Sisters of the Light gathered, waiting for the prelate to issue orders, but Verna wasn't sure she had anything to offer. "We have several gifted with us. My Sisters and I can use some magic. You, Renn, are also a wizard, but this won't be like creating the avalanche. Look at the size of that army."

"I have only a handful of soldiers," said Zimmer. "What can we possibly do against an enemy force like that?"

Renn groaned. "Ildakar is full of gifted men and women at least as powerful as I am. We have to figure out how to sneak through the walls, so I can rejoin the duma. They will need my help."

As Verna looked at the entrenched army that stood between them and the city, she had no answer for him.

CHAPTER 75

Elsa's transference magic was ready, after several days of work. The huge painted rune covered the sheer side of the bluff above the river, and they were ready for their risky foray out to the encamped enemy army. "I cannot imagine or plan a greater release of energy," she said. "After the dragon and the Ixax warriors, this might be the final blow that breaks them."

"If we all do our parts," Nathan said.

He saw tension on her face. Drawn lines chiseled her fine features, and the crow's-feet had deepened around her eyes. He'd always admired her as a brave, determined, and talented woman. The transference magic she had developed during centuries of isolation in Ildakar was impressive, and he had helped her create this marvelous and risky counterstrike. Elsa didn't seem anxious or doubtful, but dread wrapped around her like a burial shroud.

"It will succeed, my dear, and I will do everything I can to help you. Over the past two days we gathered a powerful force and they are well trained and well motivated to protect the six strike forces. We have to be swift and focused. They all know what to do to help you, and they all know what is at stake." He smiled. "We're ready to move."

Elsa reached out to squeeze his hand. "Truly, it would not have been the same without you, Nathan. I'm glad you will be by my side for this."

"Be brave. Dear spirits, we will do what we need to do." He stroked his chin and frowned. "Are you certain you don't want to wait for Nicci to return? The sorceress is more powerful than any of us."

"No," Elsa said abruptly. "We don't know when she might come back, and we are ready. The rune is painted. The six teams are armed and trained." She straightened, but still seemed edgy. "It has to be now. I've made up my mind."

Nathan squeezed her hand in response. "I understand. We can be just as impressive without Nicci."

Today, Bannon and Lila were preoccupied on the bluff, adding finishing touches to the enormous transference rune, though the giant design had been completed the night before. Nathan had sent Bannon, tasking him with guaranteeing that every detail was correct. That would keep the young man away from their desperate charge, though he would not like it. It was very possible the fighters and protectors would not survive the desperate ride, and Nathan knew this last battle against Utros would be decided by magic. More than enough fighters would guard the separate gifted parties assigned to scribe the proper boundary runes.

Under gray skies, he and Elsa hurried along the wet streets toward the long wall where the separate strike forces were gathering. The horses were saddled, the fighters wearing their armor and holding swords and iron-tipped clubs. It would be another surprise operation, but unlike the first testing foray, this one had a clear goal. Elsa's transference magic would do the bulk of the work, provided that the gifted designates completed their runes on the battlefield.

Nathan whispered close to Elsa's face. "I trust your abilities implicitly."

The largest concentration of fighters had gathered here at

the main gates to accompany Nathan and Elsa on their charge to the heart of the camp to lay down the central rune, but five other teams, led by Oron, Olgya, Justin, Perri, and Leo, had been dispatched to secondary gates up and down the wall. They would all rush out at the same time, each with a very specific destination and assignment.

Olgya had presented each of them with a new cloak made of the impenetrable armor silk to serve as both protection and camouflage. The worms in her warehouse had spun themselves into exhaustion, but they had produced countless bolts of the special cloth. All of the escort fighters were likewise protected.

Nathan and Elsa wrapped their silk cloaks around themselves, sashed tightly at their waists. Nathan had his ornate sword at his side, with his black pants and traveling boots. He felt like an adventurer and a wizard, as well as Elsa's protector.

The ranks of the city guard, infuriated by the brutal execution of High Captain Stuart, had supplied many of the volunteers for the escorts. "For Stuart!" the guards called, raising their swords.

Each of the teams also had two morazeth warriors. The women had sworn their lives to protect the gifted team leaders while they marked the spell-forms.

"We have to be fast," Nathan called out. "Our purpose is not to engage the enemy and fight. Each team must get to its position and lay down the boundary runes." He smiled. "Then Elsa will do the rest."

The older sorceress sat silent and preoccupied on her chestnut gelding, which she had agreed to ride because they required speed. Nathan sat astride a sturdy gray horse close to her. The escort fighters gathered around their respective teams at the different gates, hard-bitten arena veterans as well as uniformed city guard. Not long ago, these groups had been bitter enemies. Now they would all go out to fight together.

"So much has changed," Nathan muttered to Elsa. "Amazing how facing a common enemy can form fast friendships."

She looked over at him, her face filled with emotion. Tears

sparkled in her eyes. "Thank you for being my friend, Nathan. I am glad you came to Ildakar, and I am glad I got to know you. You're the first man since Derek who has truly warmed my heart."

"I hope I continue to do so, my dear. But now it is time. We should be off!"

Elsa nodded, biting her lower lip.

Nathan saw the freed slave Rendell among the fighters, a man who had served Mirrormask and then become the first member of the lower classes to have a seat on the duma. Rendell raised an iron club in salute to Nathan. "I am fighting as well, Wizard. I may not have magic, but I have a sword arm and my anger is as great as anyone else's."

"We will celebrate together afterward," Nathan said.

They had decided not to blow defiant war horns, but would simply ride out unexpectedly into the morning rain under the gray skies. Even a few minutes of surprise might make a great difference.

The main gates began to open, and the tense guardian soldiers pressed closer around Nathan and Elsa. They all held their swords ready to charge.

Elsa carried a large bladder of bright red paint, identical to the pigment used to mark the giant rune on the cliff wall. When it came time, she would snip the corner and draw a spattering line across the ground to outline her anchor rune. Oron, Olgya, and the other three gifted nobles had similar sacks of paint to draw boundary runes in the proper places. After they all sent up a signal to indicate they had completed their work, Elsa would connect the boundary runes with the anchor rune, and transfer all the heat stored in the cliffs and the river right into the midst of the ancient army.

Nathan gave Elsa a confident smile as gates opened up and down the main wall of Ildakar. "We are off, my dear! Let us go see what victory feels like."

He kicked his gray horse, which galloped ahead with Elsa

racing beside him. The rest of the escort fighters charged, ready to battle to the death for this desperate plan. Nathan was already calling lightning with one hand, while summoning wizard's fire in the other. He planned to make quite an impact.

"For Ildakar!" he cried. The words echoed from countless other throats.

CHAPTER 76

All the flatboat pilots, fishermen, and river traders had been warned away from Ildakar as soon as the giant transference rune was painted on the bluffside. When Elsa activated the towering spell-form, the backlash would be dangerous for anyone in the vicinity.

Lila stood with Bannon at the edge of one of the tunnel openings, peering down the network of ramps, stairs, and cargo platforms to the river below. Considering the huge painted design, the morazeth frowned. "I should not have allowed you to hang from a rope while you painted. It was a risk, and I promised to keep you safe."

"There are different ways of fighting the enemy." Bannon gestured with pride at the prominent design, which stood out bright and red on the cliffs. "And I needed to help."

She scoffed. "You could have fallen."

"I'm not clumsy." He was exasperated with her attitude. "Neither of us needs protection here. The battle is on the opposite side of the city, and I am worried about the strike teams, and Nathan. By now they should be ready to ride out to place the boundary runes on the battlefield, and that is far more dangerous than anything I've done here." He looked behind him into the tunnels and the city beyond. "Nathan tricked me. I wish he had let me go along with him."

"Your wizard friend wanted to protect you, and he gave me instructions to do the same. I intend to obey them," Lila said. "My morazeth sisters are out there with the teams. Therefore, the mission will succeed."

Bannon touched Sturdy, which he kept comfortably at his side. "What if they fail because one more fighter would have saved a wizard or a sorceress at a critical time? What if Nathan needs me?"

"I don't dispute your concerns," Lila finally said, sounding wistful. "I would have liked to go along as well."

Doing a final check, four painters on separate scaffoldings touched up sections of the design that had washed thin in the rain overnight. "Hurry!" Bannon called to them. "The attack will launch any minute now. When Elsa triggers her transference magic, you don't want to be out here."

The cocky young painters swung on the ropes, with no fear of heights. They completed their work, called to one another, then lowered themselves to the wooden platforms. After securing their half-empty buckets of paint, they ducked into the entry tunnels. Rainwater trickled out of small drain outlets from gutters in the streets, streaming down the cliff to the river.

Bannon felt a strange premonition when he saw the water running out of the drain holes. It looked as if Ildakar were weeping rivulets of water, like tears pouring through the painted spell-form and down the cliff.

He thought of the enormous statue of the Sea Mother that towered over Serrimundi Harbor and remembered that he'd felt a similar strange dread when the *Wavewalker* sailed past. Bannon wondered if that had been an early warning about the selka attack that had destroyed the ship not long afterward. Nathan and Nicci had told him time and again that prophecy was gone, that Lord Rahl had changed the underpinnings of magic. The young man didn't think he possessed some previously undiscovered gift that let him glimpse the future. He decided the shiver must have been caused by the damp chill in the air.

Lila stood practically naked with only the thin leather wrap around her waist and chest, sandals laced all the way up her calves. Moisture glistened on her skin, highlighting the rune markings. "Aren't you cold?" he asked.

"No. Never."

From the tunnel overhang, Bannon and Lila watched the fog lifting off the river as the day brightened. He heard the whisper of the sluggish current, the stir of turgid swamps; then in the distance he heard an eerie, muffled thumping, like a steady heartbeat.

Alert, Lila leaned out over the edge. "Those are drums. Many drums." The sun broke through, warming the air, dissipating the mists as the approaching drums grew louder. "Something is coming."

Straining to see through the thinning fog, Bannon felt an ominous change in the air. Unconsciously, he moved closer to Lila.

Together, they watched in horror as a shape appeared on the wide river below, dark sails, a frightening sea serpent head carved at the prow. The ship glided forward as the drums continued their steady threatening beat, oars raised and lowered, pushing the vessel against the current.

Bannon remembered the Norukai slave traders who had come to Ildakar to sell their cargo of walking meat, and he felt angry.

Behind the lead ship came another, then another—dozens of vessels, with even more trailing off in the remaining fog. Ice spiked through his veins as he realized this was no small merchant expedition. "Sweet Sea Mother, those aren't Norukai traders. This is an invasion!"

Bannon's hatred for the Norukai remained unbounded. He had slain many in a blood rage at Renda Bay, and he had loathed them when they came to trade in Ildakar. When he'd foolishly challenged three Norukai near the yaxen pens, he was battered and thrown into the training pits.

The drums pounded louder, and the serpent ships drifted close to the docks at the base of the cliff. Bannon could hear the shouts of challenge from hundreds, thousands, of Norukai as they closed in on the city.

He grabbed Lila's arm. "We have to raise the alarm, jettison the docks below, and guard these tunnels. Ildakar is under attack!"

After Elsa and the five other strike teams rode out on their mission into the huge army camp, Damon and Quentin remained in the ruling tower. The two wizards made plans, afraid they might have to launch their final solution after all. They had to be ready. Although Nicci had traveled through the sliph to spread her dire warning across the Old World, Damon knew she would never bring reinforcements here. Ildakar had to save itself.

After discussing with Sovrena Thora the possibility of restoring the shroud, the two wizards had proceeded to lay the groundwork without consulting the rest of the duma. As a shaper, Damon had worked with metals, fusing and forming a new crucible, mirrors, and guidance channels exactly like the ones used on the stair-stepped pyramid. While the other wizards of Ildakar were preoccupied with their own desperate plans, he and Quentin were pragmatic about what would truly save Ildakar. They knew their scheme would work, even if everything else failed. Elsa's dramatic plan with transference magic would cause tremendous harm, if it succeeded, but the risk was high. And even if it worked, the destruction might not be sufficient. Again.

He and Quentin were realists.

Suddenly, Bannon burst into the ruling tower, flushed and

breathless. "It's the Norukai! Dozens of serpent ships, thousands of warriors. We have to mount a defense on the cliff."

Lila ran beside him. "The boy is correct. The Norukai are not here to trade. They've come to conquer. We are under attack."

Turning pale, Damon looked at his companion. Both wizards knew that this was why they had remained behind, while Elsa and the others rode out to place the boundary runes.

Quentin pressed a hand to his chest as if in a sudden bout of indigestion. "I always found the Norukai disgusting."

"You should never have traded with them in the first place," Bannon growled. "They are monsters, and they mean to kill us all. Their warriors will storm us from the river. We've got to stop them. We need you and your wizard's fire. We need to activate the traps that were built into the cliffs—and we need them now." As thoughts circled and tangled in Damon's mind, Bannon snapped at his hesitation, "Sweet Sea Mother, can't you hear me? There are thousands of them! They will attack the city."

"Sound the alarms," Quentin ordered.

Damon wiped perspiration from his brow. "Call the city. We need every remaining fighter to drive back the Norukai."

But he had another thought. Was this not proof that they needed to raise the shroud and isolate the city? It was the only way to be certain. When the alarm bells rang through the streets, he thought they sounded like the call to the old blood-workings at the pyramid.

Lila took Bannon's arm, and they sprinted back to the bluff so they could fight. Remaining behind, Damon looked at Quentin and saw the same realization in his friend's wide brown eyes. "Even if Elsa's plan works, General Utros will retaliate. He will stop at nothing to break down our walls." He shook his head. "And now the Norukai are swarming to our cliffs. If they get inside, the city will fall—unless we do what we must. You know we have no choice, Quentin."

His companion nodded. "We will send out the call and

summon the volunteers to the arena, and the city guard can round up as many more as we need. Gifted blood is strongest, so if they can find a few useless nobles, that would be even better. This is no time for delicacy. We have to start immediately. Shedding so much blood might take more time than we have left."

CHAPTER 77

Prelate Verna and her companions stared in disbelief at the vast army encamped in front of Ildakar. Renn groaned, "A handful of us can't do anything against that." He hid behind a tree and seemed to be holding himself back. "I looked out upon that stone army for so many centuries, but I never expected them to be a threat again."

"Our avalanche took care of thousands of them," Zimmer said. "But from what I see down there, I doubt General Utros would even notice the loss of that expeditionary force."

Scanning the ancient army, the burn scars on the hills, the damage done to the plain, Verna tried to imagine what had happened here. "The city fought hard against them, that's for certain. And it looks like they have had some success."

Captain Trevor looked pale and distraught. "We need to get inside Ildakar and find out what's happened."

General Zimmer heaved a great breath. "I know you want to make your way back to the city, but unless you can find a way for us to fly, wizard, we will not get through that army. Is your gift that strong?"

Renn scratched the beard stubble on his cheeks. "No."

The gray drizzle and the clouds overhead muted the details,

though the sun struggled to come out. As they watched, Verna saw the distant gates of Ildakar open, and six separate groups of fighters, like individual strike forces, rode outward in a brash and foolish sortie. "Look, they're launching an attack."

"Such small strike forces! Are those all the defenses Ildakar has left?" Renn said in disbelief. "They will be like tiny darts against a bull yaxen."

They all watched the small parties race recklessly away from the walls. The six parties galloped in separate directions, heading toward different points. Reacting to this unexpected and unimpressive incursion, the large ancient army began to stir. At the lead of each Ildakaran strike force rode a gifted fighter who called up roaring winds and flashes of lightning, using magic to sweep aside the defensive lines. The six parties rode at full speed, intent on some clear goal.

"That cannot be a full-scale attack," Zimmer said, crossing his arms over his chest. "Most of the groups are skirting the edge of the big camp, riding the perimeter. Are they trying to get away? It makes no sense."

"Yes, it does," Verna said, pointing. "Each of those groups has a specific target. They know where they're going."

The six teams galloped at breakneck speed, flailing with swords and magic, clearing away the half-petrified soldiers who closed in to stop them. Verna could tell they were avoiding direct engagement for the sake of speed. Two of the groups rode to the boundary hills along the southern edge of the valley, and two other teams went north, riding along the edge of the blackened grass.

Another strike force circled around and cut through the sparsest part of the camp toward the far end of the valley, where Verna and the others lay hidden. The gifted leader of that group formed a wedge of air, like a plow through the defending soldiers.

The last of the six teams headed straight into the heart of Utros's army, cutting their way into the thick of the soldiers.

Fierce lightning lanced out from all the groups, striking clustered enemy soldiers, blasting divots in the ground. Verna struggled to understand what they hoped to accomplish.

Oliver and Peretta stood together, staring, and Novice Amber said, "Can't we do something to help? They don't even know we're here."

Oliver gave a determined nod. "When we called down the avalanche, we all worked together, and look what we achieved." He looked behind him at the gifted scholars in their party, along with the D'Haran soldiers, the handful of guards from Ildakar, and Verna's Sisters of the Light. "We can do something. We know some spells."

"But we don't know what their plan is," Sister Rhoda pointed out, "or how we can assist them."

"We know that we should help Ildakar, no matter what," Peretta said. "We know what side to choose."

Renn's voice cracked with dismay. "That's Ildakar. If we can take action, then we must."

The strike forces galloping along the northern and southern hills were heading swiftly to some predetermined position. One group on each side of the valley stopped halfway along the boundary hills. The defenders formed a circle around a gifted leader in the center, who began some sort of activity. Other strike forces continued riding even faster along the hills, farther from Ildakar.

The strike force closest to Verna and her hidden companions faced fierce opposition, though. The enemy ranks closed up as they charged forward, blocking the team and curtailing their progress, though they all kept fighting.

"Look, there is our chance! We have to help." Renn pointed. "We can surprise the enemy from behind. Nobody knows we're here!"

"Dear spirits, yes." Verna looked back at Amber, Rhoda, Eldine, and the other Sisters who had followed her from Cliffwall. "We will use our magic now, all of us."

Their expedition got ready to move, even though the odds were against them. "If we are going to make a difference, we'd better head out." General Zimmer mounted his warhorse. "Come on!"

Drawing upon his glory as a wizard of Ildakar, Renn swirled his hand in the air, and the thick clouds overhead pooled like an eddy in a gray river. At his summons, rain began to pour heavily out on the battlefield.

As she mounted her horse, Verna directed her comments to the eager apprentices from Cliffwall. "Remember what you learned. We taught you many spells already, and we will need every trick you can think of."

As they spurred their mounts into motion, Renn shouted in a hoarse voice, "For Ildakar!"

Ahead, the nearby strike force had stalled, surrounded by half-petrified fighters who battered them. The Ildakarans fought furiously, seemingly protected by unusual silken cloaks. The wizard who led the group summoned lightning to blast the enemy ranks, clearing an area and knocking the ancient soldiers back, but it bought him only a small amount of time. He got immediately to work.

The enemy fighters regained strength and pressed forward again toward the trapped strike force, while the defenders made a last stand, encircling the central wizard to give him room to complete his task. He lifted a sack and dribbled a red liquid on the ground, drawing some kind of large pattern.

Utros's fighters pummeled the defenders, trying to reach the wizard before he completed his work.

"Faster!" Verna said, as they raced forward.

In the downpour, Renn surprised the enemy attackers by blasting lightning from behind them, incinerating twenty of the hardened soldiers. A roar of astonishment swept through the ranks as they turned to face the unexpected attack from the rear.

Verna leaned forward, grasping the horse's mane with one hand while clenching her other into a fist and pounding the air in front of her. Her magic sent a rumble of wind that slammed into the enemy line surrounding the trapped strike force. Amber and the other six Sisters used the same magic, blowing the stiff warriors out of their way.

The wizard at the center of the strike force did not fight back with his own magic, did not break his concentration as he painted an intricate design on the ground. He had long grayish-yellow hair that hung in a thick braid at the side of his head, and he worked swiftly, ignoring the bedlam all around him. Verna realized that he must be making some kind of spell-form with the red paint.

Renn called as he rode forward, "That man looks like Oron, using magic to shield it from the rain, a wizard from the skinners' guild!"

All eight Sisters of the Light blasted with more wind. Verna released a jagged bolt of lightning that vaporized a tall warrior in leather armor. General Zimmer rode hard with his sword raised, as did the D'Haran soldiers behind him. Captain Trevor and the city guards kept up, flushed and determined to fight as well. They crashed through the besiegers around the strike team.

"We will help you, Oron!" Renn yelled.

Despite the mayhem all around her, Verna saw that the other strike forces had formed pitched battles at generally equidistant points around the hills, like a loop that enclosed nearly a quarter of the ancient army. Verna still didn't know what they were doing, but the groups anchored themselves and fought hard to allow their gifted commander to create a spell-form on the ground, similar to what Oron was doing.

The protectors around Oron fell back in a last desperate defense, but the Cliffwall expedition crashed into the enemy soldiers, scattering them and giving the wizard all the room he needed. Verna and Renn rushed up to him. The rune drawn on the ground was unlike anything Verna had ever seen.

"That looks like transference magic," Renn said.

Oron squeezed the last droplets of red on the trampled

dirt and finished his pattern. He looked up, his face serious, showing no surprise or welcome. "Renn, it is about time you came back. We need more wizards to help in the fight."

"I brought these others with me. They can help, too."

Exhausted, Oron looked at the design on the ground and spread his palms above it, as if warming his hands over a fire. He pressed down, meeting some invisible resistance, and a shimmering transparent glow covered the paint. "There, the rune is preserved and intact, and Utros will not be able to damage it until Elsa can finish her work." He swiped perspiration from his forehead. "If her plan succeeds, we might not need another army of our own."

He glanced around the valley and saw the other strike forces also completing their work. He quickly explained about the five squads, each led by a gifted noble, like himself. "The teams are each laying down a boundary rune, while Elsa and the wizard Nathan are pushing into the heart of the camp, where Elsa herself will anchor the transference magic and then trigger it. We might destroy a significant portion of the enemy army."

"All the more reason for us to help," Renn said.

Oron jabbed his hand toward the sky and released a bright fireball that rocketed higher and higher, like a flare. "Now they know my rune is in place." Thousands more enemy soldiers began to close in, rebounding from the unexpected attack. Oron tossed his thick yellow braid over his shoulder. "I would like to live long enough to see the effect."

By the time Bannon and Lila rushed back to the bluff's edge, the first five Norukai ships had slammed against the docks below. Bannon ground his teeth together. "I can smell them from here. They stink of blood, pain, and ugliness."

Lila flashed him a grin. "I would have enjoyed killing them regardless, but if you tell me there is even more reason to hate them, I will enjoy the fight all the more."

The raiders threw ropes, tied their serpent ships to the pier at the base of the bluff, and swarmed off the decks. The river behind the hideous fighters was crowded with serpent ships, all converging on Ildakar.

On the cliff face, more than a hundred city fighters appeared at the openings of various access tunnels, holding weapons ready to defend against the assault from the river. As he stood at the opening, Bannon glanced at the intricate transference rune he had helped paint on the sheer stone. Above, on top of the bluff, though, he didn't see the duma members he expected. "Where are Damon and Quentin? They should be here fighting! We need their magic."

The Norukai began swarming up the platforms and carved stone steps like a line of army ants. Beside him, Lila had a short sword and a dagger, but she slid both weapons back into their sheaths at her side. "I will fight with those later."

Instead, she picked up a barrel of flour from among the supplies stored in the tunnel and hurled it straight down. The cask crashed into two of the Norukai climbing the lower steps, knocking them both loose. Blood sprayed from their broken heads mixed with the cloud of white flour, and they tumbled down the bluff, knocking down other raiders who climbed behind them. Bannon liked the idea and did the same, tossing a small cask down to smash more Norukai.

In the other tunnels the Ildakaran fighters did likewise, grabbing sacks, rocks, even a crate of old fish that they dumped down the bluff face, pelting the oncoming Norukai. But raiders continued to swarm up from their ships, ignoring their losses as they climbed the cliff.

At last, waves of magic from above whooshed down the sandstone wall with a snap and a shudder. Bannon craned his neck and saw several figures in silken robes unleashing their gift from the top of the bluff.

"Now we have some help," Lila said.

The docks anchored at the river's edge disengaged from

the rock, making the lashed serpent ships grind together, their hulls creaking. With an outcry of dismay, the Norukai still on the decks clambered over one another, some diving into the river as their ships shifted.

But the Norukai kept coming. More raiding vessels crashed together, clogging the river, piling up until the raiders tied their hulls together to form a boarding ramp and they ran from ship to ship to reach the cliff face.

The wizards on top of the bluff released more magic, and spouts of water thundered out of the cliff face. Drainage from the streets and sewers gushed out upon the swarming Norukai. Although the cliff was already wet from the morning's rain, the effluent drenched the attackers.

Bannon lugged a heavy barrel over to the opening. "Sweet Sea Mother, is this thing full of rocks?" He only cared that it was heavy. With a lurch, he tossed the barrel out the opening and watched it tumble and smash into one of the platforms far below just as the Norukai tried to climb up.

Lila seemed to be enjoying herself. "Let us each do that a hundred more times. Even so, we may still have to face the rest of the Norukai with our swords." She grinned at him. "Then the real fun will start."

Thora rose to her feet inside her dungeon cell as the heavy door crashed open. Quentin and Damon stood there, sweating and terrified. "It is time, Sovrena! If we don't work the blood magic now, Ildakar will surely fall."

"Has General Utros breached the wall?"

"The other duma members are out battling his forces now, trying to implement Elsa's transference magic," Quentin said.

Damon interrupted, "And a Norukai attack fleet just arrived on the river! Fifty serpent ships and thousands of raiders are attempting to breach the city through the bluffs. We cannot survive both attacks."

Thora raised her eyebrows. "So, you have decided to raise the shroud once and for all?"

Quentin nodded quickly. "It has to be now. Any duma members who would speak out against the action are on the battlefield, and Nicci is still gone. That means we can make this happen, if we move quickly. We have to do something before Ildakar falls."

Damon clasped his hands together. "Please, Sovrena, we need your help. You are the most skilled at bloodworking. You've raised the shroud before."

"I promised I would help," she said, moving toward the doorway.

Quentin hurried her along. "We have already dispatched guard teams throughout the city. They have the names of volunteers and will round them up."

Damon added, "Along with the provisional lists."

Galvanized, Thora followed them at a brisk pace through the stone-walled corridors, following the bright torches that lit the way. "It is a sacrifice we must make to save Ildakar. Those brave volunteers will rescue us."

"Eight hundred are being brought now," Damon said as they ran along the corridors.

"We will need at least a thousand for a bloodworking of this magnitude," Thora said. "And nobles, if you can find them. Gifted blood is powerful. That would decrease the number necessary."

"But the ungifted are easier to catch and kill," Quentin said. "The guards are gathering great numbers of candidates. Since the murder of High Captain Stuart, they have grown much more bloodthirsty."

They passed under the stone archway and emerged into the open outside air. Thora looked up into the gray sky and scanned across the top of the plateau. "The pyramid is destroyed. Where will we perform the magic?"

"We don't need the pyramid," Damon said. "We just need the spell-forms and the apparatus."

"And the blood," Quentin said. "We had to find a place that could hold so many people."

The city was in a panic as word of the Norukai invasion spread. Citizens ran through the streets, some rushing for shelter, others grabbing weapons and racing toward the bluffs to help fight the raiders. Soldiers ran to defend the main gates and the outer walls in case General Utros should retaliate in response to the strike teams outside.

When Thora saw where the two wizards were leading her, she was pleased. Quentin and Damon took her through the high entrance to the huge combat arena. A buzz of frightened conversation echoed among the large crowds that had already been herded here. City guards roughly rushed people through the entrances, deaf to their pleading. Many of the men and women were weeping, while others walked in a daze. One older couple stared ahead and held hands, walking with grace as they willingly entered the sacrificial arena.

Inside on the combat field, Thora saw that Damon had re-created the silver crucible, the metal channels and troughs to hold the blood, the great mirrors that reflected the wan sunlight and directed it toward rotating prisms of quartz. Across the raked fighting field, Quentin had drawn the complete spell-form.

"It is just waiting for all the blood it needs," Damon said.

As more and more people were herded into the arena waiting to die, Thora nodded. "We should start immediately."

CHAPTER 78

Ten Norukai ships smashed into Serrimundi Harbor, skirting the wreck of the kraken hunter, like wolves ignoring prey they had already killed.

From the docks, Nicci shouted, using her gift to manipulate the air so that her voice boomed out. "The Norukai will destroy the harbor. Prepare to fight."

The wishpearl divers forgot about their lewd laziness. "The woman isn't lying."

A second diver looked appalled at what he witnessed. "We have seen Norukai before. They are animals. They don't care about money or wishpearls, just flesh."

"I heard just this morning that Effren was burned to the ground, everyone slaughtered by Norukai raiders. I didn't believe it."

Nicci narrowed her eyes. "Believe it. Are you going to help fight now?" She was surprised the men actually lurched to their feet.

The burning krakener sank slowly at the mouth of the harbor. Sailors raced back to their ships from the city streets and dockside taverns. Once aboard, crew members climbed the rigging, unfurled sails. Several ships anchored in the open water prepared to set sail, though Nicci doubted they could get past the Norukai vessels blocking the exit to the sea.

Farther down the wharf, Captain Ganley of the *Mist Maiden* yelled for his sailors to return. "We need to get to open water, where we can defend ourselves!" Half of his sailors obeyed, crowding the deck to fight for their ship, while the less brave ones bolted into side streets to hide in the fish markets and warehouses. Other Serrimundi residents fled into the hills.

The ten serpent ships pressed into the harbor in search of easy targets. A volley of flaming arrows set a cargo ship alight, and as its sails caught fire, many of the crew dove overboard to escape. A Norukai vessel careened against its hull with a crash and crack of splintering wood. Scarred raiders leaped over the rails wielding axes, swords, and clubs to slaughter the remaining sailors on the cargo ship.

Harborlord Otto ran down the dock with his daughter in tow. Seeing Nicci, he cried out. "Sorceress, you warned us! I'm sorry. Now we have to fight. What should we do?"

"You should have maintained defenses all along," Nicci said in a harsh voice. "Did the Imperial Order teach you nothing?"

Otto was flushed. "Emperor Jagang spared us because we had no navy. We paid him heavy taxes, and his armies moved up the coast without wasting blood or effort on conquering us. We thought Serrimundi was safe."

"The Norukai are not interested in a tithe or your surrender. They are here to destroy. I watched them burn Renda Bay. Serrimundi is just a bigger target to them." She wondered how many other coastal towns the raiders had already struck.

Nicci stared at the oncoming serpent ships and the coordinated rows of oars that propelled them forward. Two of the ominous vessels closed on either side of a cargo ship that lumbered toward the mouth of the harbor. They crashed into the helpless ship, boarded it, and methodically killed every sailor aboard in a very short time.

Otto squeezed his daughter's shoulder and gave her a push toward the city and the hills. "Go to the old house, Shira. Find your children and hide. Barricade the doors in case the Norukai make it into the city."

The young woman's eyes filled with tears. "I can't leave you, Father. I can't leave my fiancé." She gestured back to the *Mist Maiden*.

"You must not leave your children," he said. "Now, go!"

Nicci added, "If the Norukai get into the streets and ransack the city, then that means your father and husband are already lost." She turned her hard gaze to the harborlord. "We can't let that happen." She regarded all the vessels tied up to the docks, including the *Mist Maiden*. "We need to make use of these ships. They cannot just wait here to be burned and they cannot try to flee. Look—you have a navy here, and it is ready to launch, if the captains and crew are willing to fight."

"They are—or they will be."

With booming drums, the serpent ships pressed into the harbor, attacking any vessel that attempted to get away. The Norukai launched volleys of fire arrows. Most of them fell short, but some struck the extended piers of Serrimundi, while others hit smaller fishing vessels. The flames started to spread.

Nicci held out her hands, called upon her gift, and pushed, sending a focused whirlwind to scour and whip past the ships. The wind snuffed out the small fires before they could catch hold, and she hammered again with an even stronger wind, raising whitecaps that rocked the foremost Norukai vessel.

After Shira ran off, Otto turned to Nicci. "Now that I know she is safe, what do we do?"

Nicci saw that the *Mist Maiden* was almost ready to depart, with Captain Ganley shouting orders. His sailors untied the hawsers from the docks. "That will be our flagship. You know the captain. Will he follow orders?"

"He will know he has to save sweet Shira and her children."

As Nicci turned to run with the harborlord toward the

three-masted ship, she called to the four wishpearl divers, "You want to fight? I have a job for you. Are you brave enough?"

With a haughty retort, the man who had made the lewd comments said, "Don't insult us."

"Then don't give me reason to. Come!"

The shirtless men sprinted after her to the *Mist Maiden*, running up the gangplank. Captain Ganley bellowed to the crew members who had stayed with him to defend the ship. His well-practiced sailors moved the webs of lines, stretching the sails, and Nicci used her gift to nudge the sailing ship into motion. Other vessels nearby were also setting their sails. The crews armed themselves with boat hooks and staves.

Harborlord Otto ran to the *Mist Maiden*'s bow and shouted to the other ships. "We have to drive off the invaders or they will burn Serrimundi. Fight for our city, fight for our families!"

Captain Ganley said, "Many of those ships don't even hail from Serrimundi, Otto."

"Then they will fight for their own lives," Nicci said. "That should be enough reason for anybody."

She pushed with the wind, assisting the sails, and the *Mist Maiden* pulled away from the docks, accompanied by three nearby ships. At the edge of the harbor, near the stone figure of the Sea Mother, the krakener had dwindled to a mere curl of smoke, its blackened hulk submerged.

The attacking Norukai rowed swiftly, and the first serpent ship careened into the outlying piers. Raiders swarmed off the decks, and the townspeople rushed to defend the city, but Nicci couldn't help them, not yet. Right now, she guided the naval attack against the other serpent ships.

"I will try to destroy five of them," she said to Captain Ganley and Harborlord Otto. "For a start."

"What are we supposed to do? How do we help?" demanded one of the wishpearl divers. "We didn't come aboard just to watch." His companions grumbled as well.

Instead of answering, Nicci turned to Ganley. "I need glass

bottles with stoppers, one for each of these men. They will be carrying deadly weapons."

Frowning, the captain turned to Otto. "What does she—?"

"Do as the sorceress asks. She warned us we might be attacked, and I refused to listen. I will heed whatever she has to say now."

That was enough for Captain Ganley. He barked orders, and soon his first mate returned with four brown glass bottles from the galley. He uncorked the stoppers and poured the contents over the side, then handed the empty bottles to Nicci. She smelled the pungent tang of spiced liquids, pepper oils, and vanilla tinctures. "These will do."

Ganley stood on the foredeck and shouted orders as the *Mist Maiden* moved forward, driven by Nicci's magic. The serpent ships closed the distance, propelled by pounding drums and lines of razor-edged oars.

Nicci reaffirmed in her own mind how she would destroy five of them. She turned to the surly wishpearl divers. "You have strong lungs. Can you truly hold your breath for a long time?"

"That's why we bear these marks!" The men indicated the tattoos on their chests.

"Then I need you to swim—deep," she said.

Carefully, using great dexterity with the gift, Nicci conjured a small ball of wizard's fire no larger than a grape and dropped it into the first brown glass bottle, suspending it with another spell to keep the destructive force bottled and ready. She pushed the cork into place, and the brown glass container blazed like a lantern. "This is what you need." She handed it to the first diver, and created another ball of wizard's fire to put into the second bottle, and then made two more, so that all four wishpearl divers had one.

"The raiders are closing in!" Ganley yelled.

With booming drums, the serpent ships approached the *Mist Maiden*. The crew cried out in defiance, building their anger in a desperate attempt to overcome their fear.

Otto turned to Nicci. "We are ready to fight, Sorceress. I hope your plan works."

"Fight them and kill them," Nicci said. "That is the plan."

The Norukai aboard the approaching ships rallied an even louder cheer. With their mouths slashed and cheeks tattooed like serpents, the raiders looked like an inhuman army, but Nicci wasn't so easily terrified.

"Overboard, now!" she told the wishpearl divers, after explaining what they needed to do. "You can win half the battle for us, if you succeed."

Clutching their blazing glass bottles, the divers agreed upon their targets and plunged overboard, swimming deep.

Nicci looked over the rail and saw the bright lights submerging like glowing night wisps, which then began to move toward the serpent ships.

At the rim of the harbor, Nicci watched two more serpent ships crash among the docked vessels that had not yet managed to set sail. The Norukai threw torches to light the ships and piers on fire, and the blaze would surely spread to the warehouses. Serrimundi could become an inferno.

But before Nicci could fight that battle, she had to destroy these other attacking ships.

The crew of the *Mist Maiden* waved staves, swords, boat hooks, harpoons. Nicci targeted the carved serpent at the prow of the foremost ship and released a blast of wizard's fire. The searing flames turned the serpent figurehead to ash.

The Norukai roared their outrage, and Nicci used wind to deflect the oncoming lead ship, shoving it aside so that instead of ramming them, it barely grazed the *Mist Maiden*. Even so, the ships were close enough that the Norukai men and women leaped across the gap, swinging axes, spears, and swords in mad bloodlust.

Nicci recognized their leader in his sharkskin vest and the implanted fang that protruded from his bald scalp. It was Captain Kor, one of the traders who had come to Ildakar to sell slaves. As his crew swarmed aboard the *Mist Maiden,* Kor sprang onto the deck. His hard boots landed with a thud. Screaming loudly, more raiders came across, ready to slaughter Captain Ganley's crew.

The *Mist Maiden*'s sailors rushed to meet the enemy. Nicci strode forward, her ragged blond hair drifting in the wind, her black dress rippling as she built up her magic. She faced the Norukai captain, ready for blood.

CHAPTER 79

Along with the clash of blades, the thudding of hooves, and the shouts of pain and fury, the Ildakaran strike team fought their way deeper into General Utros's camp. Nathan hurled more wizard's fire ahead of them, clearing the way so he and Elsa could keep moving toward their destination. The blazing ball engulfed fifty enemies, but within seconds more ancient soldiers filled the gap, closing in.

"We will not make it much farther," Nathan said, breathing hard as he and Elsa rode deeper into the camp. "This may be the best we can do. Is it good enough?" Somewhere, she needed to draw her large anchor rune in order for the transference magic to work.

As a half-petrified soldier ran toward the sorceress, Nathan swept out with a rumble of air, throwing the man aside. Under his breath, he said, "I really should have had Nicci show me how to stop a human heart. I never wanted that type of power because it seemed unfair against an enemy." His long white hair hung in sweaty clumps, dusty and spattered with blood from the warriors he had already killed. "I forgot that in war, everything is fair."

After Elsa pulled her horse to a halt in a clear area with churned-up mud, she slid out of the saddle. "This place will have to do. I had hoped to set the anchor deeper into the camp so the circle would engulf more of the army." Her voice was ragged, filled with heartache.

Many of their guardians had already fallen in their push to get this far, but the two morazeth and Rendell were still with them, along with about a dozen others. They didn't look as if they expected to survive.

"I hope this is worth the price. Oh, Nathan, I hope it's worth it." Elsa held her red paint and moved about frenetically, spilling bright lines, creating an intricate design across the cleared space. Her frightened horse galloped off, but she didn't seem to care.

The morazeth, Thorn and Lyesse, battled furiously to give Elsa room to work, as did many surviving Ildakaran fighters. The toughened silk robes offered some protection against the wild enemy blows. Together, the defenders kept fighting, keeping Nathan and Elsa safe. She just needed time to finish.

As the older sorceress continued drawing her powerful rune on the ground, Nathan sent out a furious shock wave that spread in concentric circles, knocking the enemy soldiers back and keeping them away from Elsa. She moved with swift steps along the perimeter, drawing her lines, while the remaining Ildakarans used all their energy to keep the attackers away.

Nathan dismounted to protect Elsa, and within moments he had lost his horse as well. Elsa was gambling everything on this attempt, and Nathan could tell that her thoughts had narrowed down to the singular pinpoint of her task. He had to give her the chance.

But their success depended on the other five teams as well. Without the boundary runes in place, the transference magic would fail. Nathan looked up with a thrill of excitement to see a bright fireball shoot straight into the sky from the farthest of the two southern teams. "Another one, Elsa! Four of them finished!"

His distraction lasted only a moment before a burly warrior riding a half-stone horse thundered toward him, charging into the circle where Elsa was marking her rune. Nathan pulled up a wall of dirt like a rope from beneath the ground. The dirt slammed into the horse and sent the beast sprawling. The warrior tumbled out of the saddle, and Nathan leaped upon him with his ornate sword. He plunged the blade down, breaking through the soldier's hard skin into his chest. He turned with the sword in one hand and wizard's fire in the other. He threw another flaming ball to knock back twenty more enemy soldiers, but he felt his gift waning. He didn't have much strength left.

He watched the signal flame flicker out in the sky. Against all odds, four of the boundary runes were drawn and preserved. He turned to scan the burned hills. "Still one more."

He saw flurries of the ancient soldiers closing in where the last group needed to mark their design. Gray clouds and then lashing snow and ice came down in a pillar, harsh weather blasting the enemies away. The gifted leader of the last strike force was using magic to complete his task, while the other four successful groups were now fighting to survive as they retreated to safety.

Elsa worked, breathing hard and sweating as she finished her large design. On foot, the two morazeth battled like wild animals, and Rendell fought clumsily but vehemently with his iron-tipped club.

Elsa had a fierceness Nathan had never seen before. As more enemy soldiers broke through and tried to attack, closing in around them, Nathan remained close to her, fighting to keep her safe, and he saw that she was crying as she drew her lines.

When she activated the transference rune and drew all the heat from the Killraven River and the sandstone bluffs, the effect would kill countless enemy soldiers. Nathan tried to reassure her. "They are enemies, and sometimes enemies deserve to die."

"But not friends," she said. "Not dear friends."

Nathan didn't know what she meant. When several more soldiers charged forward, spears extended, he unleashed another hammer of air. A spear point caught in his enhanced silk covering, but couldn't pierce the fabric. Nathan struck hard with his sword.

A hundred yards away, he saw General Utros himself wearing a mask of beaten gold across half his face and thick leather armor that bore the flame symbol of Iron Fang. His two painted sorceresses stalked along with him, pushing forward to face Nathan and Elsa.

"Dear spirits, I don't know how long we can last against two sorceresses and all these soldiers. Please hurry, Elsa!"

Then he saw a flaming arrow climb into the air from where the fifth strike force had been marking their rune. The bright light soared high, then arced down, sputtering out and leaving a trail of smoke. It wasn't magical fire, but he knew what it meant. "The last signal! The final boundary rune is done, but they did not use a fireball." He knew that no gifted person would simply send an arrow. "That means . . ."

Elsa squared her shoulders. "That means whoever made the boundary rune is now dead, but the pattern is finished." She braced herself. "We are ready. I have just one more connecting line here." She held up her sack of red paint. "And then I can activate the transference. It will be glorious, Nathan. I hope it saves Ildakar." Her tears flowed more freely now. "I am so glad to have known you. You are such a dear, dear friend."

His heart felt a chill. "What do you mean? Prepare your rune, so we can escape and celebrate together."

"This is the anchor rune, the center of the spell," she said. "It needs to be activated here. It will draw the transference magic from the five boundary runes, pull it all together, and connect the lines. Anything enclosed will be in the target zone." She drew a deep breath. "And I have to be at the center."

Nathan recoiled. "No, I won't let you. Come!" He extended

his hand to grab her, but Elsa surprised him. She called up a surge of air. He hadn't even known she could be so strong in that type of magic. Billowing waves of wind yanked him off his feet, bore him up into the sky like a piece of chaff. The two morazeth, Rendell, and all the rest of the escort fighters flew up with him.

"Stop!" Nathan cried. "Come with me."

He flailed, putting up a shield to block her magic, but Elsa flung him on a rushing river of air with the speed of a quarrel shot out of a crossbow. He lurched out, tried to find something to hold on to, but he was a projectile, catapulted over the enemy soldiers, along with the rest of his party.

All by herself in the large cleared circle where she had drawn her rune, Elsa squeezed the last droplets of red that connected the remaining line in her pattern. Hundreds of ancient soldiers pushed closer, now that the defenders were gone. They would engulf Elsa, who looked so small and all alone.

She completed her spell-form and triggered the transference magic.

The heat arrived all at once, and the plain blazed with the heat of the sun.

S pouts of water gushed through drainage holes in the bluff, streaming down upon the Norukai on the ramps and ladders. Bannon had run out of barrels and crates to throw, but other volunteer fighters continued pelting the invaders with rocks, bricks, large pieces of pottery.

The snarling Norukai tried to dodge the barrage. Many died, falling down the cliff into the masses of raiders, but their numbers seemed inexhaustible. Bannon felt a familiar fire burning through his veins. Unable to control his rage, he leaned out of the overhang, waving Sturdy as he shouted, "We will cut you to pieces."

Lila gave a confident nod. "When they come, you and I will

keep score. I might soon consider you an equal, instead of an apprentice." Even with her terrifying smile, he found her beautiful and alluring. "If you do well enough, boy, I might reward you again."

He let out a brief laugh. "I thought you said I was rewarding *you*."

"Do they have to be separate things?"

From the top of the cliff above, gifted nobles hurled conventional fire, rolling flames that struck the misty rocks. Some burned the hideous raiders, but the Norukai kept climbing even when their skin was smoking.

Though caught up in the battle, Bannon saw the giant painted rune on the cliffside begin to glow, throbbing and pulsing. The scarred raiders cried out, startled. The Ildakaran defenders halted their barrage and retreated into the tunnels, suddenly fearful.

"It's the transference magic!" Bannon said.

Lila swept an arm across his chest and knocked him back into the shelter of the overhang. The giant rune brightened, and Bannon felt the breath rush out of his lungs. The drizzle in the air turned into tiny frozen diamonds, like grains of sand. With a sound like a thousand bones breaking at once, the sheets of water on the cliff froze into a glass of ice. The flow thundering out of the sluices solidified as all the heat was sucked out of the cliff stone.

With a shattering roar, the Killraven River itself froze solid, heaving up in sudden slabs. Like deadly cold fists, the river ice crushed the Norukai ships, splintering the hulls as if they were no more than toys.

With angry curses, the raiders began to fall, slipping from where their handholds had turned to ice. Some Norukai warriors had frozen solid, covered by sheets of ice, but others broke away from the cliff and toppled to splatter on the rock-hard river. The platforms and ladders shattered in seconds.

Astonished, the Ildakaran defenders poked their heads out

from their tunnels and cheered. Bannon's breath steamed out of his mouth and nose, and he laughed in triumph, turning with delight toward Lila.

But even the sudden storm of cold did not deter the Norukai raiders for more than a few moments. Many had tumbled from the bluff and lay dead or broken on the river ice, but some still clung to the frozen cliffs, used their daggers to chip away at the ice, and began to haul themselves up again.

There were fifty serpent ships, and countless more Norukai, who hadn't even begun to fight.

Bannon leaned over to look down the glazed wall. Long icicles hung like fangs, but the hideous raiders showed no fear. By the hundreds, they swarmed up, and Bannon prepared to fight for his life.

CHAPTER 80

Two more reckless Norukai ships plowed into Serrimundi Harbor. The raiders tossed torches onto the wooden docks and into the rigging of commercial ships tied up to the piers. The burly attackers abandoned their oars, leaped onto shore, and ran forward, striking down terrified dockworkers who tried to defend their city.

The Norukai men and women were unstoppable, letting out wordless screams to terrify their victims. They lunged forward, hacking with axes, twirling and smashing with heavy battle hammers, thrusting with bone-tipped spears. They raced along dock boards slippery with blood, leaving mangled bodies strewn about.

The dockside fires began to spread into the warehouses and marketplaces. Families evacuated, taking small boats up the canals or running into the hills. Serrimundi had been sure of its peace and prosperity for far too long.

Slowly, though, the frightened people began to turn like a wave that breaks on the shore. After sending their families off to hide, brave citizens returned to the harborside, carrying household weapons. Some old veterans managed to find armored chest plates, heirloom swords, shields that had been used for decoration, and dented helmets from near-forgotten conflicts in the past.

Even with three serpent ships piled against the damaged docks, the landed Norukai numbered less than two hundred, and Serrimundi could call many more defenders. The tide turned as the city awakened.

From the deck of the *Mist Maiden,* Nicci saw the clash on the docks, but she focused on the five nearest ships. Her own makeshift navy was crowded with determined but frightened sailors to stand against them, and they also had Nicci.

As the lead serpent ship caromed off the *Mist Maiden*'s hull, its charred snakelike figurehead still smoked. The barbaric Norukai leaped onto the deck with bare arms, wearing engraved metal bracers, spiked collars on their necks, rings and chains that made both the male and female warriors look more like demons than humans. When they let out ululating war screams, their jaws gaped wide from sliced-open cheeks.

The *Mist Maiden*'s first mate gripped his sword with both hands. He held the blade up to defend himself, but a Norukai bone-tipped spear plunged into his chest. Choking blood, he dropped his sword and fell to his knees. The armed crew of the *Mist Maiden* moaned at seeing the first casualty, but they had no time to wait. Dozens more raiders landed on their deck, charging forward with a forest of sharp weapons.

Nicci couldn't help the first mate, but she reached out with her gift and focused on the Norukai who had thrown the spear. The broad-shouldered woman stood crowing in triumph, but Nicci concentrated, found the woman's heart, and used her gift to crush it. The Norukai woman fell with a thud in front of one of her running comrades, who tripped and sprawled over the body. Nicci shifted her focus to the man, and as he lurched to his feet, Nicci found his heart and stopped it as well.

The ship's deck became a flurry of screams and deadly weapons. Three more *Mist Maiden* sailors fell. Harborlord Otto used a large staff to smash skulls and break arms.

Captain Ganley had a ceremonial sword, but it was dull, and he was unpracticed. As two Norukai closed in on him, he swung the sword, then dropped it and grabbed a boat hook instead, with which he seemed more familiar. He swung with all his strength, raking one Norukai's face with the curved hook. The second Norukai thrust in viciously, but Ganley caught him with the point of the boat hook and shoved it into his abdomen. The raider grabbed the slick shaft of the weapon and stared at it, apparently offended to be killed so early in the battle. The ship's captain, ashen but determined, shoved hard again, pushing the dying Norukai backward until he fell off the end of the boat hook.

After landing on the deck, Captain Kor roared, urging the raiders on. "Norukai! King Grieve ordered you to die, but you are not allowed to die until we secure our victory for the serpent god." He held a long-handled axe in one hand, a sword in the other. "We ransacked five villages so far, but now we take on an entire city!"

After Renda Bay, all Norukai were her enemies, but Nicci would take great pleasure in killing this particular one. She already loathed the man from having seen Kor beat slaves in Ildakar and laugh at the pain he inflicted. She held up her hand, felt the gift building, eager to be released. She could stop Kor's heart. She could throw wizard's fire at him. She could knock him overboard with a blast of wind.

But when he saw her and recognized her, his words made Nicci pause. "The sorceress from Ildakar! I thought King Grieve would kill you there in his invasion, but now the pleasure falls to me."

Nicci had no time to parse his words as she faced him. "I don't know your King Grieve, but I will be happy to kill you first." She had to dispatch the Norukai captain swiftly, so she could defend the other sailors. She raised her hand, felt the magic surge in her grasp to annihilate him—

Just then, the adjacent serpent ship exploded. An intense flash of light speared upward through the hull below the waterline, shattering the deck and erupting in a spray of fire. Wizard's fire. Wherever the spattering flames caught the Norukai, the deadly fire burned through their flesh and bones and kept burning. The serpent ship groaned and listed to one side, taking on great amounts of water from below, filling the hold. The raiders who had boarded the *Mist Maiden* spun and howled in outrage, astonished by what had happened.

A second Norukai ship burst into flame, more wizard's fire spewing upward from below, cracking hull planks, shattering the keel, turning the vessel into a burning wreck. The Norukai wildly searched for this unexpected enemy.

Nicci saw the remaining pair of glowing spheres below the waterline, where the last two wishpearl divers were delivering glass bottles filled with magical fire. Two more Norukai ships suffered the same fate, wizard's fire shattering out of the glass bottles and ripping upward.

Within minutes, the four wishpearl divers broke the surface, treading water and sucking in gulps of air.

As the battle continued aboard the *Mist Maiden,* Nicci called more wizard's fire with her hand, but she wouldn't risk unleashing it here. Kor's raiding vessel was smashed up against the ship, and the fire would surely spread.

Realizing that Nicci was somehow responsible for the explosions, Kor sprang forward, swinging his heavy axe. She ducked, felt the blade swoop just above her head, and he followed through with a swift jab of the sword in his other hand.

Nicci spun away, but the sharp blade sliced her black dress and laid open a gash across her ribs. She slammed him backward with her gift, but Kor planted his feet and shoved forward, swinging both weapons. Nicci reached out to stop his heart, but he moved too quickly, spitting, attacking, and she couldn't spare an instant to find the right point.

The Norukai attackers were more frenzied after seeing four of their ships wrecked. They became suicidal, attacking without any thought of surviving the battle. It reminded Nicci of when she saw Bannon consumed with his uncontrollable blood rage.

"You will all die!" Kor said. "And you'll all grieve, just like everyone in Ildakar right now." He swung his battle-axe and struck the deck boards, gouging out large chunks. "The whole world will know King Grieve, but Serrimundi will never forget Captain Kor."

Nicci was about to crush his spine, but she needed to know. "What do you mean Ildakar is under attack? How?" She had traveled through the sliph, left the city to face the siege of General Utros, but she had not considered a Norukai invasion.

"Fifty ships, Sorceress. King Grieve has thousands of Norukai warriors." Kor chuckled. "I have told our king everything he needs to know to take the city. Ildakar will be his capital when he conquers the Old World."

Nicci imagined a force of ships five times greater than what was now attacking Serrimundi. Could Nathan and the gifted duma members handle such attacks from two sides, the Norukai and Utros?

"I will go back and help them defeat King Grieve as soon as I have eliminated you," Nicci said. "I will tell your king how you died."

Kor sneered at her. "I'm already dead. Grieve ordered me to fight until I died in battle, and I intend to do so. But I will see you dead before I fall." He charged toward her, his eyes blazing.

Since he wanted to die here, she granted Kor his wish. She summoned her focus, shaped the air, and slammed it together, crushing his skull from all sides. She caved in the bone and turned his brain into a pulp.

Even as the Norukai captain collapsed, Nicci turned to the remaining raiders, anxious to defeat them and save Serrimundi. She saw the ships in the harbor and the warehouses in flames. Hundreds more Norukai fought their last battles, but the people had rallied and were driving the scarred warriors back.

Nicci drew one of her daggers in her right hand, and called up magic in her left. For now, she devoted herself to this battle. She had killed hundreds before, and she would do it again today. She got to work.

CHAPTER 81

After the transference magic activated, Bannon hoped Nathan and Elsa had survived out on the plain, which must now be an inferno. The magic left only bitter cold on the cliffs and the frozen Killraven River.

Wearing nothing but her scant leather wrap, Lila showed no reaction to the cold, although the breath steamed out of her mouth when she spoke. "They are coming. Be ready, boy."

Despite the suddenly frigid temperature, Bannon felt sweat running down his skin. He steeled himself. "My name is Bannon."

Even though all the Norukai vessels had been locked in fists of river ice, the raiders were not deterred. Ignoring their dead who had toppled from the bluff, they brought out their own siege ladders from the decks and braced the long narrow constructions against the glazed sandstone.

The unstable ice continued to crack and pop as shards broke loose and fell down the cliff like frozen spears, but the Norukai kept climbing toward the cargo platforms and tunnel openings.

Ready to fight, Bannon and Lila watched the raiders ascend,

level by level, using axes and daggers to chop handholds in icy rock. "Sweet Sea Mother," he said, clutching his frigid sword, "we can't just wait for them to overwhelm us."

"Agreed," Lila said. "Let's go down and stop them from climbing higher." She swung out of the overhang to the narrow ledge that led down to the next loading platform. The footing was precarious in the best of conditions.

Bannon gasped, "The ice—"

"The ice is in patches. Hold on to the solid rock and follow me down to this scaffold." She glanced up at him. "Unless you want to stay up there and watch me fight alone?"

"I'll fight at your side." He sheathed his sword in order to use both hands as he made his way after her.

Ildakarans poked out of sheltered tunnels, breathing steam in the bitter-cold air. They redoubled their efforts to throw any remaining debris they could find. At the top of the plateau, the three gifted nobles had come back after the abrupt wave of transference magic. Now they used the gift to dislodge ice chunks and send them tumbling down the frozen rock. Bannon couldn't understand why Damon and Quentin hadn't responded to the urgent alarm, since they were far more powerful wizards. Ildakar needed them!

Now that Elsa's transference spell was done, the sandstone began to warm rapidly under the bright sunlight, and veils of mist whispered all around, like a smoke screen. Bannon saw at least ten Norukai warriors slip and fall, screaming, but more kept climbing. The largest Norukai led the charge, a big man with bone spikes implanted in his shoulders and iron plates grafted onto his fists. He was accompanied by a spiderlike albino creature whose skin was pocked by what looked to be countless bite marks.

"My Grieve, King Grieve!" the creature cried as he scuttled upward, finding tiny handholds. "Cold, snow, ice! I told you, I dreamed it. Cold, cold!"

The Norukai king glared down at him. "You were right,

Chalk, but you also dreamed a victory. I don't care about ice. I care about Ildakar."

Bannon dropped down to an icy wooden platform that was used to raise and lower crates. Anchored to the cliff, the platform had frozen in place, the supporting ropes iron hard, but it was wide enough for Bannon to make a stand. Lila sprang beside him onto the wood, and the two of them watched the first Norukai climbing closer to them.

Bannon braced himself, feeling the anger heat his blood. He pulled Sturdy out of its scabbard and held it ready. Beside him, Lila grinned, holding her short sword and dagger. She spat down at the enemy. "These Norukai may be uglier than Utros's soldiers, but I think they should be easier to kill."

The sounds of battle grew louder as more invaders climbed the rocks and reached loading platforms and ledges scattered across the sandstone bluff. On one of the narrow wooden shelves, three defenders—Bannon recognized the young painters who had put the finishing touches on Elsa's giant rune—fought with sticks and knives. Their platform blocked one of the main entrances into the bluff. They whacked at the clutching hands of the Norukai, but they were overwhelmed.

One of the young fighters was stabbed through the side, and a female Norukai tossed his body from the platform. She and two other raiders climbed up, gripping the edge of the scaffolding. The remaining two young men fought with knives, hacking off Norukai fingers, and three of the raiders fell to their deaths, but it wasn't enough. Six more Norukai gained the platform, and the young men were doomed. They looked at each other, and Bannon saw a silent, fatalistic understanding pass between them. With the last of their strength, the two bloodied Ildakaran defenders used their knives to slash the ropes holding the platform. The ice-slick scaffolding broke free, dumping the two young men as well as the climbing Norukai down the cliff to the frozen river below.

Seeing this, Bannon let out a moan. "I am not waiting

anymore!" He left the safe platform and scrambled down a slippery ladder, not even thinking about the sheer fall. Instead, he dropped to the next shelf and reached another scaffolding platform that dangled against the bluff. Lila scrambled after him.

Nearby, King Grieve and his freakish white companion climbed up, batting away defenders. Bannon saw him and knew his enemy, the leader of the loathsome slavers. "I will kill you, King Grieve," he shouted.

The Norukai ruler looked at Bannon as if he were an insect, and grinned with his hideously scarred mouth. He shifted his ascent, climbing to the platform where the young swordsman stood ready. Bannon's body was covered with sweat. He felt the fire inside of him, and he wasn't afraid of the battle at all.

The wood on the platform was still slick. Ignoring the cold and the treacherous ice in crannies, Grieve clung like a beetle to the rocks. Intent on Bannon, he moved along the narrow incised path, climbing stone stairs that were smaller than his boots.

Bannon recalled how the Norukai had tried to capture him when he was a boy, dragging him to their long boats, and poor Ian . . . a life lost, tormented. He also thought about how many raiders he had killed at Renda Bay, and he looked forward to killing more, here and now.

"Look out, boy!" Lila landed on the platform next to him.

He heard a grunt just beneath him, and he spun to see a hefty Norukai lurching to the other side of the platform, reaching up to grab him from below. The Norukai opened his sliced mouth wide, and Bannon's boot heel caught him full in the lower jaw with a vicious kick. Flesh tore, facial muscles snapped, and the Norukai's entire lower jaw ripped off, leaving the man gurgling, his tongue dangling like a flap of raw meat from his open throat. Flailing, the raider grabbed at Bannon's foot, but the young man kicked again, caught his enemy full in the forehead, and sent him flying out into open air.

Two more raiders crawled up the side of the bluff, and Lila thrust at them with her short sword.

King Grieve had not forgotten Bannon's challenge, though. He worked his way over with his pale shaman scampering after him. He seized the edge of the platform, hauling himself closer. Bannon swung Sturdy, and Grieve blocked it with a muscular arm, catching the sword blade against one of his metal bracers. Sparks flew. Grieve grunted from the blow and let out a serpentlike hiss of challenge. He swung himself off the icy stone path and landed heavily on the wooden platform.

Grieve had a thick, cruel blade that Bannon wasn't sure he could have lifted with two hands, but the Norukai king held it in a single palm. He reached out to grab the young man, who swung a wide stroke with Sturdy. The king threw himself backward and the blade missed his broad chest.

As his emotions built up for this vital battle, Bannon began to see red at the edges of his vision. He smashed with the sword and sliced a crimson line across Grieve's chest, but the Norukai king didn't twitch. He hammered back with his huge curved sword, catching Bannon unawares. The young man barely managed to deflect the blow.

Lila decapitated a Norukai who had climbed up the other side of the platform. The ice-encrusted ropes groaned with the extra weight.

As the sun continued to warm the bluffs and the fog faded, more chunks of ice shattered and slid like broken glass down the cliff face. The Norukai had thrown up additional siege ladders, building makeshift platforms so they could climb higher. Some raiders had already reached the lower tunnels. Below, the river was beginning to creak and crack as the current backed up, flooding the banks. The thick surface ice broke apart.

All Bannon could see was Grieve, king of the Norukai, the leader responsible for so many brutal raids, for causing such incredible pain and misery. Had this man been king when Ian was captured as a boy a dozen years ago? Even if not, Grieve's predecessor would have been just like him. All Norukai men and women were just like him. Bannon felt a black heat growing hotter and darker within him.

If Nicci or Nathan were here, they could have used wizard's fire to annihilate all of the attackers at once, but Bannon was just as happy to do this with his own blade. He would draw the blood of the vile raider king.

"You're the one who will grieve," Bannon said. In a blinding, surprising rush with Sturdy, he pummeled Grieve, driving the big king to the edge of the platform.

The gangly shaman jumped onto the platform next to him. "My Grieve!"

Barely able to see through his red haze, Bannon swung his sword, intending to chop off the Norukai king's head, but Grieve ducked. Instead, Sturdy's sharpened edge sliced through the thick rope that held up one corner of the platform. Suddenly, the wooden base lurched and dropped. Grieve stumbled, let out a rough cry, and slipped. He barely managed to grab the edge as he fell. His nails bit into the wood, holding on to the icy surface. His jaw muscles clenched with the strain, widening the flap of scarred skin on his cheeks.

Bannon slipped, scrambling for purchase as his feet slid out from under him. Grieve grabbed his boot, clutching his ankle with a grip like the jaws of a wolf. The young man kicked and kicked again, catching King Grieve full in the face. The platform swayed.

Lila cried out and slashed with her sword, cutting the throat of yet another Norukai who climbed onto the now-unbalanced platform.

More icicles pattered down the cliff, booming into other chunks and starting an icefall. Water from the frozen sluice began to spray out again as the backed-up current pushed through the blockage.

Bannon smashed his foot into Grieve's face again. "Die!"

The king's crushed nose spurted blood, but his eyes blazed like firebrands.

"My Grieve!" Chalk screamed, and clawed his way forward, barely able to hold on to the sliding, tilted platform. He grabbed for Grieve, but Bannon swept one leg out to dislodge him, and the scarred shaman tripped and fell over the edge. He shrieked as he dropped toward the lower platforms.

In that instant, Grieve let out a shocked, anguished scream: "Chalk!"

Bannon struck him again, kicking so hard that Grieve's head snapped back. His grip on Bannon's boot loosened, and he, too, fell, roaring in anger.

Bannon scrabbled on the icy wood of the tilted platform, trying to hold on. Not far below, he heard a crash as Grieve and the pale shaman slammed into one of the other platforms and the swarms of climbing Norukai. Bannon clawed at the wood, dropping his sword, which slid and clanged off the platform and plunged down the bluff. His hands squeaked on the ice, and wood splinters tore open his fingers, but he couldn't hold on.

Lila lunged down for him. She seized his wrist, and he grasped her, holding on with all his might, but his hand was covered in blood and water. His skin was slick. She anchored herself by holding one of the ropes, trying to maintain her grip. "Hold me!"

Bannon squeezed, but his fingers slipped. His bloody palm slid through hers, and gravity pulled at him. He couldn't hold on. He snatched at the edge of the platform as he slid the last few inches.

Lila's eyes were wide, her face filled with shock and horror and a long, whispered "Nooooo!"

Bannon fell, his fingertips just touching hers for a last instant. He tumbled from the platform, falling past the rough sandstone cliff, seeing the ice, the openings. He tried to grab for something, anything. For a second, he caught the edge of another walkway, but his fingers slipped again and he tumbled through the air.

Unexpectedly he crashed on his back among dozens of bodies—murdered Ildakaran defenders, as well as dead Norukai piled on one of the wide lower platforms. But some of them were still alive, their fall cushioned by the soft flesh. King Grieve was there, as was the white shaman, both of them climbing to their feet. Bannon flailed about, looking for his sword.

Grieve bellowed, "Take him."

The Norukai closed around him and swallowed him up in a mob of hideous faces.

CHAPTER 82

The arena at the heart of Ildakar had become a slaughter-house, but this was the only chance for the city to survive. Sovrena Thora knew it.

As the battle against the Norukai invaders continued and the fires of Elsa's transference spell raged across the ancient army in the valley, Quentin and Damon pressed forward with their massive bloodworking. They didn't have much time, and Thora urged them on.

Determined, the city guard marched lines of volunteers onto the open sands, many of them weeping. These brave people had come forward in a time of Ildakar's great need, had offered their blood, their lives, convinced they must do something for their beloved city. But now the time had come, and the real sacrifice required more bravery than just writing down their names in a book.

Thora watched hundreds and hundreds of people with their throats slit, spilling their blood into the spell-form troughs fused into the arena sands. It was what Ildakar required, and these people had to meet their obligations.

Damon had shaped the troughs with his gift and added

gathering magic, so that the blood pooled where it was necessary, not a drop wasted. The spell-form was broad enough and deep enough to hold the quantity of blood necessary to raise the shroud again.

It was what Ildakar needed. It was what *Thora* needed. She knew more than ever that she was the heart of her city. In her own veins flowed the true blood of Ildakar. She still felt a lingering heaviness of stone throughout her body, where the petrification spell hadn't entirely worn off. Because Maxim had created the spell, and presumably canceled it to awaken the stone army, she guessed that meant he was still alive, which angered her. Otherwise that last magical thread would have been severed and she would have been restored to flesh again.

Adessa had failed, but Thora had to think of Ildakar now. Nothing was more important than Ildakar.

Damon and Quentin were sweaty and covered with blood, like butchers in a yaxen slaughter yard. The pair of wizards grabbed one victim after another, wrapped an arm around the chest and made a quick cut with their sacrificial blades before tossing the dying body to the edge of the trough, and reaching for the next dazed volunteer. They had killed hundreds already, and the two men were shuddering with the endless effort. But they moved mechanically, killing one more, then one more, then one more.

Thora knew it needed to be faster.

She extended a finger toward the shivering sacrifices lined up in front of the blood troughs. She used her gift to create a razor edge of air and slashed her fingernail in a line. Her invisible knife sliced deep, cutting through the throats of the victims, ten at a time. They were astonished as their necks unexpectedly yawned open and blood gushed out. They toppled forward, pouring their lifeblood into the channels, paying the necessary price. Everyone had to pay the price.

Watching the vicious but extremely effective slice of the sovrena's magic knife, Damon and Quentin looked startled and disturbed, but they nodded. More victims groaned and shuddered as they were dragged forward. Suddenly, ten of the captives lost their nerve and broke free. The city guards gave chase and stabbed the victims in the back, driving them down to the sand like fighters in an arena exhibition.

Alarmed, Thora shouted after them, "Cut their throats before it's too late! Don't waste the blood."

The guards lifted the heads of the dying cowards and bled them into the channels of the spell-form.

Now that they had begun the bloodworking, Thora felt fully alive again. Her true dream had returned, and she was saving Ildakar as she had always promised to do. History would remember Thora, *Sovrena Thora,* and she would no longer be disgraced. Her name would not be spoken with shame. She was the person fundamental to this final bloodworking to save the city.

Best of all, Nathan and Elsa were outside the city walls, and even treacherous Nicci was gone. They would not be saved. After the city was safely hidden beneath the shroud, Ildakar would have a real chance to become the perfect society she had always envisioned. Despite her normally implacable attitude, Thora felt a warm joy as she watched more victims fall and more blood flow.

Using her invisible knife again, she caught others unawares, cutting their throats and using a shove of magic to knock their dying forms toward the troughs. The blood flowed together in streams, but Thora knew the spell needed the lives of at least a thousand. The tedious, gory task would take hours more, unless they could find powerful, gifted nobles to give their lives.

"It's not fast enough," she groaned, looking up at the gray skies.

Seeing the sovrena coldly kill dozens at a time, some of the volunteers in the arena quailed, grabbed their families, and pushed their way toward the upper arched entrances, trying to escape.

Thora glared as she saw citizens shirking their responsibilities. "Stop them!"

The panic was spreading. Many weren't actually volunteers, merely people the guards had rounded up against their will. Thora had suspected the lists of volunteers would not be enough, and many who were brave on paper would renege on their commitment when the time came to actually pay the price. So they had to be forced. Those reluctant sacrifices sat bound and struggling at the base of the killing sands, but they fought against the guards.

In the struggle many unarmed sacrificial candidates were struck down away from the spell-form, where their deaths served no purpose, their blood spilled uselessly onto the sands. The cowards outnumbered the guards, who were mobbed, relieved of their swords, and killed. Swiftly, the volunteers began a mass exodus.

"But this is for Ildakar!" Thora cried. "If you don't die here, then the whole city will fall." She wondered if the Norukai had breached the tunnels yet, or if General Utros had returned to smash the gates after Elsa's transference magic.

The people weren't listening, though. They simply ran for their lives, taking their spouses, joining their friends. It had been a brave thing to do when they signed the ledger Damon and Quentin offered, but most hadn't believed the time would actually come. The guards barricaded the arena entrances, fighting those who tried to push free. Outside in the streets, guards were indiscriminately rounding up anyone they could find.

Such cowards didn't deserve Ildakar. Their blood would be too weak to serve the magic. She used her knife of air again, swinging it hard, expending a great deal of magic. The blow was so sharp that she completely severed the heads of thirteen sacrifices. They toppled, spouting jets of crimson from the stumps as their heads rolled.

Damon and Quentin kept cutting, but now their victims

fought back. Hundreds were leaving like panicked sheep. Thora knew they had killed only about half as many as were needed to raise the shroud.

"No!" She felt like weeping.

Another contingent of guards raced into the arena, and Thora was relieved to have reinforcements, but they had not come to help fight. Instead, they looked stricken, terrified. "The Norukai are climbing the cliffs! Many have already penetrated the tunnels. Soon there will be thousands within our walls."

Thora wanted to scream. "There's not enough time!"

If the shroud wasn't raised within the next few minutes, if the protective invisible walls didn't whisk her beautiful city out of the flow of time, then all would be lost. Her hopes were dashed.

"More, kill more of them!" She struck again with her magical knife, butchering others who tried to flee. She had nearly exhausted herself.

Damon and Quentin were frantic. They slashed throats and then simply began stabbing victims nearby. The towering quartz prisms slowly rotated, spattered with blood, and hazy sunlight shone down on the curved mirrors, drawing magic and energy into the curved silver crucible from which the lines of blood magic extended.

Thora howled at the evacuating crowds. "Why won't you save Ildakar? Why won't you do what your city needs?" These cowards didn't deserve her beautiful, perfect city. She hated them.

All around, the air smelled of fear and the sour iron of blood mixed with the stink of death. Bodies were piled high, like a siege wall of human corpses.

Thora felt despair. "Why won't they pay the cost? There must be some way."

Damon and Quentin turned to her, exhausted, soaked with blood. She was so furious she failed to notice the desperate gleam in their eyes. With hardened expressions, the two wizards approached her, holding knives in their slick red hands. "There is a way, Sovrena, and you know it yourself," Damon said.

"Everyone must pay the price," Quentin said.

"We can complete the bloodworking," Damon added with a glance at his partner, who nodded. Both of them closed in on Thora. "And you know the magic it requires. We have already sacrificed hundreds, and the magic is building. It only needs the nudge to push the bloodworking over the limit."

"It's not enough," Thora said, shuddering with anger and frustration. "You know it's not enough."

"But *you* can do the rest," Quentin said. "You said it yourself. Gifted blood is so much more powerful. You are the sovrena, the most powerful sorceress in Ildakar, and the blood magic is stronger in you than in hundreds of ungifted victims."

Damon added, coming even closer with his knife, "You can finish this. One sacrifice. You said we must each be willing to pay the price."

Thora felt cold inside. "You are fools if you think you can do this without me."

"Not without you. We *need* you. We need your blood," Damon said. His mustaches were caked with gore that had splattered his face.

Quentin tried to sound reasonable as he also closed in with his knife. "You were found guilty and disgraced. You said you wanted to buy your way back into history. In this way, you can atone for everything."

Thora lashed out, calling upon her gift. She sliced through the air with another invisible razor, but both Damon and Quentin raised shields and blocked her. "You are powerful, Sovrena, but we are both wizards, and you aren't strong enough to fight two of us." Damon lunged with the sacrificial knife, and she drew upon all her strength to blast him backward, a fist of air mingled with threads of lightning.

The blow knocked Quentin reeling, but Damon, the shaper, summoned the soft arena sand at her feet, which writhed up around her legs and waist like a smothering blanket, trapping her. Thora flailed, glared poison at him. "Stay back!"

Quentin pushed toward her. "Your blood can save the city. You know it. Don't fight us—we have no more time."

"No!" she shouted as both wizards rushed her with upraised knives. With her gift, Thora shattered the sand that cemented her legs, but a blast from Damon knocked her backward. She collapsed into the blood-soaked sands, paralyzed as she tried to get up.

Quentin and Damon fell on her, using their gift to hold her down despite her struggles. She was almost powerful enough to hurl them away—almost—but Damon stabbed the point of his knife into her throat, pushing hard, breaking through her tough skin.

She clawed at his hand, tried to drive the dagger away; then Quentin's blade also cut into her neck, sawing. Her scream was muffled, then drowned out in a gush of blood—the potent, gifted blood they needed.

As her vision faded, she saw the red river flowing toward the center of the symbol. Though her rage built hotter even as her life faded away, she knew with smug satisfaction that her powerful blood would indeed be enough. The warm spray spilled into the channel, completing the spell-form.

With her last thought, Thora felt the bright and triumphant magic surge in the air.

D amon stood exhausted. He had already seen so much blood and death today, but this was the last. This was the most important.

"Hurry!" Quentin said. He grabbed Thora by the shoulders, tilting her head, bending her limp body forward so the last of the crimson liquid gushed into the trough. It flowed together, filling the giant pattern, and pooled like oil crawling toward the central point.

Normally, all the members of the wizards' duma would be here. Damon had hoped that Thora herself would guide the magic, but he and Quentin knew what was required. When the blood of the powerful sorceress mingled with the other sacrifices, they called upon the magic scattered in the air, through the lines that ran throughout the city of Ildakar.

Still fleeing, many of the volunteers paused, staring up into the sky as the air shimmered. The wave of magic flowed out of the arena, rocketing upward from the crucible and the rotating prisms. The expansive and complex spell-form glowed across the blood-soaked sands.

"The shroud!" Damon said, his voice an awed whisper.

"The shroud . . ." Quentin repeated.

The air around them changed as the entire city folded out of the flow of time into a protected bubble of its own, away from everyone and everything.

CHAPTER 83

With the release of transference magic, the inferno swept toward them across the battlefield. The thunderous explosion of heat appeared out of nowhere, and General Utros threw his arm in front of his gold half mask, but the concentrated blaze was more intense even than dragon fire. Utros sucked in a breath to shout his defiance, refusing to believe that he would lose so completely, so abruptly.

Ava and Ruva flung themselves on him, wrapping around him, each holding out a hand. Their scream was a raw sound of desperation in unison. The sound rippled the air, and their magic formed a shell of emptiness like molten glass, a curved shield that covered them at the last instant. The bubble clamped down and sealed with a suddenness that made the general's ears pop, but even so, a tendril of superheated air was trapped inside with them. A single gasp of breath scorched his mouth and lungs.

Utros crouched beneath the fire that rolled as if someone had poured a crucible of molten iron over the top of them. He fell to his knees, squeezed his eyes shut, and clenched his fists. As the heat thundered on and on, Ava and Ruva strained next to him, weeping, their lips drawn back to expose their teeth.

They clutched at each other as if each twin had to steal energy from her sister just to survive.

He didn't understand what had happened. When he had seen the six small groups that rode out from the gates, each led by a gifted wizard or sorceress, he knew the Ildakarans had some desperate plan. Utros had stayed by his command tent, assuming this was another foolish sortie that could be easily defeated.

When they saw what the Ildakaran groups were doing, though, Ava and Ruva had grown frightened. Ruva said, "They are laying down runes! This is part of a larger spell. Look at the positioning!"

Ava pointed out the knots of fighting, then the flare signals sent into the sky from where the gifted raiders made their mark. "It is a spell-form of some sort! They could encircle and cut off a large part of our forces."

After the destruction caused by the Ixax warriors and the gray dragon, Utros knew he had to stop the Ildakarans. "Keeper and spirits, come with me. We will block that foremost group." After he armed himself and wore his horned helmet, Utros had marched brusquely through his troops to meet the nearest strike force. He saw the wizard Nathan among them, as well as an older sorceress wearing purple robes.

Nathan and numerous fighters defended the sorceress while she marked a prominent rune on the ground. Utros had rushed toward them, but before he could get there, the older woman used her gift to blast Nathan and all the other defenders into the air, flinging them far away and leaving her to stand alone.

"What is—" Utros began to say as the sorceress completed her magic, triggering the spell. Transference magic.

Ava and Ruva screamed and held up their hands. So much fire came out of nowhere. . . .

W hen the inferno finally died down, Utros pushed himself to his feet again and stared through the rippling haze of the protective shield. The air was hot and scorched inside the bubble. He desperately needed to see what remained of his camp, his army. "Set us free. Let me out there!"

"We are not safe, beloved Utros," Ava said. "I don't know if anyone is left alive in our army."

"I need to see!" he demanded. "Now." He pressed the gold half mask against his face.

Exhausted, Ava and Ruva sagged. When they allowed their magic to dissipate, the transparent shell flickered away, and Utros stared out upon a nightmarish landscape so hot that the ground had turned into glass. Lumps of rock smoldered, still glowing dull orange. Smoke fouled the air like black blood-stains. Nearby, the landscape was a forest of blackened bones, curved ribs, charred skulls exploded as the brains boiled in the flash of heat.

He and the twin sorceresses were the only ones alive nearby. The entire front ranks of his gigantic army had been wiped out.

Utros had always segregated his thoughts, walling off emotions from logic, tactical plans from historical knowledge, but now those compartments in his mind began to crumble with the horror of what he saw. Staring at the vacant black scar that had recently been crowded with loyal troops, he guessed that at least thirty thousand men had been caught in that instantaneous funeral pyre.

As he stared at the roasted world and thought of all those soldiers who had unquestioningly followed his command, he let out a bellowing roar toward Ildakar, demanding revenge.

And as he watched, the city itself shimmered and disappeared before his eyes.

Nathan tumbled through the air, heartsick as he watched the inferno rush across the battlefield, enclosed by the boundary runes the other teams had inscribed. Safe beyond the flames, he crashed onto the grass and rolled.

Other Ildakaran defenders tumbled beside him: Rendell, the two morazeth, the soldiers and arena fighters who had kept Elsa safe while she completed her magic. Elsa had used her last energy to hurl them all to safety. Lyesse and Thorn sprang to their feet and prepared to fight without even bothering to brush themselves off. Nathan, Rendell, and the others gained their feet and prepared to face the ancient soldiers.

But the outburst of fire from the transference magic was overwhelming. Nathan saw that this one blow, this one spell, had killed tens of thousands of the enemy.

And one dear Elsa.

In his anger at seeing the half-stone soldiers on the perimeter still moving toward them, Nathan flung out more wizard's fire, destroying any enemies who dared to come close. The blast gave him and his companions a moment to catch their breath. "We have to get back into the city," he called in a hoarse voice. "Fall back to the gates."

They turned toward the towering city of Ildakar, their only safe haven now. They had all sacrificed so much to defend it. But before they could move to rush back home, the entire city flickered, then vanished entirely.

"Dear spirits!" Nathan cried. He knew what had happened.

Rendell's jaw dropped open in disbelief. "Our city! Ildakar is gone."

The other survivors stared in dismay. "Our homes!" cried one of the city guard, who bled from a long gash down his left arm.

The two morazeth were still ready to kill, but their faces were stricken. "Our Ildakar . . ."

With the shroud restored, the city and much of the uplift were simply erased. The beautiful buildings, the orchards, the layered gardens, the merchants' district, the craftsmen's district, the warehouses . . . everything was gone, as if it had simply been shaved off the plain, leaving a drop-off to the river, but no city.

Ildakar had vanished again, sealed away in time.

Nathan groaned. He remembered the first time he had seen Ildakar from the high mountain pass of Kol Adair. His life book had guided him here, and he had indeed found what he needed, the heart of a wizard—Chief Handler Ivan's. He felt pain in his chest now and knew it was in response to the shock of seeing that the city was gone.

But the same prediction in his life book had declared that the sorceress would save the world. He didn't even know where Nicci was.

The "sorceress" . . . Had the foretelling meant *Elsa*?

"The shroud may be permanent, or it may be temporary," Nathan said to his shocked companions as they picked themselves up. Standing just outside the blackened devastation, he suddenly felt vulnerable. "Either way, Ildakar will give us no protection now. We have to get away from the battlefield, and swiftly, before Utros issues commands—if he survived. Either way, I imagine they will want revenge."

Though his soul ached from the loss of Elsa, he knew she would have been satisfied with what she accomplished. Her transference magic had dealt a terrible blow to the enemy army. Even now, General Utros's forces were barely recovering.

Nathan knew it was time to move. Now.

He looked in the blackened grasses, saw the other surviving strike teams, and realized they would be rushing for shelter, too. He drew his ornate sword and tossed his soot-smeared white hair behind him. "There may not be many of us, but we have to find a way to fight what remains of the army."

"We cannot fight them all," said the morazeth Thorn. "We are the only ones left."

"Not the only ones," Nathan said. "It is not over yet."

Still, there was no city left to fight for.

Their group raced around the well-defined edge of the burn and reunited with Olgya and her surviving fighters. Their larger group kept moving westward to the rugged foothills, in the direction of the mountains and Kol Adair. They also reunited with Perri's contingent, as well as Leo's, farther down the valley. When they encountered the bedraggled remnants of the group that had shot the fire arrow, Nathan learned that Julian had been killed, but not before finishing the boundary rune.

Together they continued to withdraw from the unsettled and stunned enemy army. Nathan thought the wilderness in the direction of the mountains would offer them the best chance. Nicci was gone through the sliph, presumably far away in Serrimundi. How could she ever come back now? He doubted he would ever see her again.

And poor, dear Bannon. He had hoped to keep the young man safe in the city, which was now whisked away. Nathan gritted his teeth. In a thousand years, he had made many bad choices, and he had to live with them all. He would find a way to live with this one.

"Come, we have to survive," he said. The remnants of all six strike force groups, the outcasts of Ildakar, also raced to the hills. The reeling enemy army was unable to count their dead, struggling to recover from what had happened. Was Utros even still alive? Nathan had seen the general and his two sorceresses well within the boundary of the inferno, but he couldn't be sure. If Utros was dead, then who would lead what remained of this gigantic force? He could always hope the ancient army would break apart and disperse.

In the foothills, the Ildakaran defenders converged, tired, frightened, and confused. They had all seen their city vanish, and they knew they were cut off from their homes and families forever, stranded in the wilderness. As the refugees gathered in the hills, they came upon the fifth group of fighters, who had drawn the last boundary rune.

Nathan was surprised to see a familiar face—one he had never expected to see again. "Prelate Verna! Dear spirits, I cross half the world and the Sisters of the Light are still following me." He had broken her jaw the last time she had caught up with him.

Verna looked wrung out. Her face was smeared with dust and dirt, her gray-shot brown hair a tangled mess. She had seven other Sisters with her, along with General Zimmer and a small group of D'Haran soldiers. He saw the wizard Renn, who had been sent away from Ildakar, and the two young scholars, Oliver and Peretta, whom Nathan and Nicci had dispatched as messengers from Cliffwall. "What are you all doing here?"

"We're exploring the world," Peretta said, "and committing all the details to memory. That is our mission as scholars."

Verna said, "You and Nicci sent these two from Cliffwall and they made it to Tanimura, where they told us of the great archive. General Zimmer sent an expeditionary force to help protect that magical lore, and we met Renn. He was leading us to Ildakar with news of Cliffwall."

"What . . . what happened here?" Renn combined a thousand questions into that one statement. He nodded toward the devastated plain where smoke wafted into the air, toward the emptiness where Ildakar had been.

"We will have a long time to tell stories," Oron said in an impatient voice. "First we have to get to safety and survive."

Olgya sounded lost. "Are we all that remain of the wizards of Ildakar?"

"We may still be wizards," Renn said, "but Ildakar is gone."

From the shelter of the trees in the hills, Nathan looked back at the army far below and the emptiness where Ildakar had been.

As he stood wiping sweat from his brow and feeling the misery in his heart, he heard a stirring in the underbrush. Beside him, Verna, Renn, and the other refugees turned. When a rune-branded sand panther crept out from among the scrub oak and tall grasses, the Cliffwall scholars backed away in fear. General Zimmer and his soldiers warily raised their swords, preparing to fight off the predator.

Nathan felt a rush of relief, though. "It's Mrra." He turned to the others. "No need to worry. That is Nicci's sand panther."

"Where is Nicci?" asked Rendell, sounding miserable. "She left us when we needed her most."

The big cat twitched, and her lips curled back to show curved fangs. She sniffed the air, obviously upset with all the fire, blood, and smoke in the air, too much death. Nathan held up a hand, trying to calm the big cat. "Mrra, you know me. You know our friends."

Everyone in the party remained hushed, feeling the tension. Mrra's long tail twitched, rustling the underbrush. Her golden eyes flashed and she turned her head as if hearing a distant sound.

"You are with us now, Mrra. Ildakar's gone," Nathan said, trying to sound soothing. "I don't know where Nicci is."

The sand panther made a low growl, then suddenly pricked up her ears. She looked up at the sky and curled about, as if she had sensed something, a connection. With a brief roar, Mrra bounded away, running into the hills to vanish in the deepening twilight. Nathan wondered what calling the panther had felt, but he had no answer. He couldn't begin to guess where Nicci might be.

Nor did he know what he and his small band of surviving fighters could do against the gigantic ancient army.

CHAPTER 84

After weeks of searching, Adessa finally found the wizard commander. Maxim had been quiet, hiding, keeping a low profile, but the morazeth doubted he would grow complacent. Neither had she.

Maxim surely must know that she would continue to follow him to the end of the world and the end of time. He was smart and powerful, but sometimes he was also a fool, and Adessa was no fool.

Over the long and hard pursuit, she realized that what had started out as a simple hunt was much more than that. This was an actual war between her and the wizard commander, with battles, tactics, and an ultimate goal.

She had lost his track for twenty days, but she kept moving down the river, sure that was where Maxim would go. In certain ways, he had little imagination, and he had no more knowledge of the river's geography than she had. They both knew the Killraven eventually widened into the estuary, then spilled into the great sea. She simply needed to find him.

With such mastery of the gift, Maxim could have claimed a place to hide, even created a small protective shroud to hide himself from time, and if he just waited long enough, Adessa would never track him down.

But the wizard commander was arrogant and lazy. Although he had grown impatient with Ildakar's hedonistic extravagances, he was not a rugged man, and he preferred his comforts. That was why Adessa knew he would find some other town, a cozy shelter where he could force someone to take care of him, as he had done at Tarada.

As she approached a river town named Gant's Ford, she decided to inquire about him there. In her distinctive black leather wrap and with countless protective runes branded on her bare skin, Adessa would be too memorable, and she didn't want to be recognized, didn't want word to reach Maxim, if he was indeed here.

She watched and waited, keeping to the reeds at the riverside as she observed the traffic coming into Gant's Ford. As dusk turned to deep purple, a lone man wearing a patched hooded cloak paddled past her in a canoe. A wicker basket filled with crawfish was balanced in the back of the canoe.

Adessa was already standing in the water, knee deep. As he approached, not seeing her in the twilight shadows, she waded out into the current and pounced on him as he paddled by. The man yelped as if afraid she were a swamp dragon attacking him, but she was worse than a swamp dragon.

Adessa dragged the man out of the canoe and into the water, wrestling him. She punched the nerve cluster on the back of his neck, rendering him helpless. Immobile, he looked terrified as she dragged him into the mud and reeds. There, she stripped off his hooded cloak, knowing it would be a good disguise she could use. She hung it on some tall reeds, then bent over him.

He shivered. "Who are you? I have nothing for you to steal."

"I am not a bandit," she said. "But I am the one who's asking questions."

He squirmed and choked, and she was losing patience. Holding him down in the soft mud, she removed the black handle of her agile knife and poked the sharp, stubby point into his thigh. It was a minor wound, but when she released the magic, agony careened through his body.

He arched his back and cried out, but his scream was swallowed up in the palm of her hand clamped over his mouth.

She let the surge of pain continue for a moment, then yanked the agile knife out. "I can do more of that, and I can do it all night, unless you tell me what I need to know."

His body shuddered with sobs. Tears ran down his face. "Y-You haven't even asked anything yet!"

She described Maxim, explained that he would have been a stranger only recently arrived in the vicinity. The canoe man was so desperate he would have told her anything she wanted to hear, though Adessa also knew how to identify lies. Fortunately, he had indeed seen someone who might have been Maxim.

"He comes into town every two days or so. He lives up in the hills. I think . . . I think the Farrier family took him in. Farrier is a woodcutter, and they have a cottage, but I haven't seen them in weeks."

She leaned closer. "What does this man do when he comes into town?"

"He . . . he eats. He drinks ale at the tavern. He listens. He is a friendly sort, but strange, won't tell anyone where he's from."

Adessa imagined that Maxim was simply biding his time, building alliances and making plans. "This has been most helpful, but I can't allow any word of my presence to whisper out."

His eyes widened, and she killed him as quickly and painlessly as she could, then rolled his body into the reeds, where a swamp dragon would find him soon enough and dispose of the evidence. She made a small cook fire and ate a meal of the crawfish in his basket. Then she developed her plan.

Disguising herself in the cloak, Adessa glided into town, listening, watching for Maxim to appear. While she waited in Gant's Ford, she learned as much as she could about his habits, the frequency of his visits. She learned the location of the Farriers' stone cottage in the hills above the river, a small home surrounded by tall spruce. She stole a long, sturdy rope that she calculated she would need.

Yes, she could have challenged the wizard commander right there in the open, but she'd done that before and he had escaped from her each time. No, she would have to trap him, ambush him, and kill him.

As a morazeth, she preferred a straight-up, face-to-face fight against an enemy. Maxim was a powerful foe, and Adessa didn't want to squander the powerful blood magic that still burned within her. She would have a final confrontation with him, and she would use up all of that power to defeat him.

But she had to be smart. Adessa did not dismiss the threat posed by the wizard commander. Maybe she couldn't outmatch him in a direct battle with magic, but she could be more clever than he was.

Although Maxim was in hiding, he was neither a loner nor self-sufficient, and he often liked to sit in a tavern, complain about the local ale and the food, and play dicing games. She learned that he was likely to come into town that evening because the river inn was serving their catfish pie, one of his favorite meals. Adessa didn't ask too many questions. She already had the answers she needed, and she already had her rope.

She waited discreetly until dusk, when she saw a man come into town and head directly for the inn. With just a glance she knew it was Maxim, and he walked without a care in the world. He worked his charm, grinning, adding a glamour spell so that people welcomed him, while she remained in the shadows.

Though she wanted to lunge out and kill him there, Adessa controlled herself, knowing that would likely fail. Instead, she knew Maxim would be in town for several hours drinking his fill of ale, and she would use that to her advantage. She had just enough time to make her preparations.

In the gathering dark, Adessa slipped away from Gant's Ford and into the hills, following the dirt path. Knowing where Maxim lived, she approached the dark and empty cottage that a woodcutter had built for his wife and three children. She found the whole family as statues in the yard, petrified in the act of fleeing. Adessa stared at them, reaffirmed in her determination to complete her mission. Thora had ordered her to kill the wizard commander, and she would take his head before the night was over.

She might have waited until Maxim was asleep, then broken into his home and fought him with all her strength, but that would have been messy and uncertain. She didn't doubt he would have left wards all around the cottage. He would know if she was coming. No, she had to be more devious than that.

Moving swiftly, Adessa carried her rope and circled the cottage, through the spruce forest, searching for what she needed. To one side, she found a large heavy log that had toppled to the ground, which the woodcutter hadn't yet chopped into firewood. Augmented by her blood magic and the rope, Adessa had enough strength to lift it into place, planning ahead.

When she had completed her preparations, Adessa discarded the stolen cloak she had used as her disguise and stood to fight in only her morazeth leather. When she faced Maxim, she wanted him to recognize her before she killed him. She tucked her dagger and short sword into her waistband. She would not need them, or the agile knife. In the darkness, the wind continued to stir the spruces, some of which creaked more loudly than others, as if groaning in pain.

She waited in the forest shadows for hours, until Maxim at last strolled back up the path, well satiated from his catfish pie and a tankard or two of ale. He whistled to himself, oblivious to any danger. Using his gift from a distance, he ignited the lamps inside the cottage, and light shone through the windows. He strolled up to the cottage.

Adessa stepped out of the shadows, placing herself in

exactly the right position. The dark spruces were dense and close, swaying back and forth. Maxim stumbled to a halt, staring at her. "You are damned persistent."

"I made a promise to kill you."

She felt a rippling defensive shield he manifested in front of him, but the markings on her skin protected her against any magic he tried to use against her.

"This is Thora's doing, isn't it? Do you know if she is even still the sovrena?" He sniffed. "By now, I suspect that Ildakar has fallen, one way or another." He quirked a smile. "I ended the petrification spell and freed the army of General Utros. And I saw an entire Norukai invasion fleet sailing up the river. Maybe you should have stayed to fight for the city instead of chasing me through the swamps?" He raised his eyebrows.

"I keep my promises." She braced herself. The wind grew louder, the trees rushed and creaked.

"This is tedious," Maxim said. "I do not fault your determination, but your power is no match for mine."

"I trust in what I can do," Adessa said. Leaving the short sword in its sheath at her side, she drew her dagger. "This knife is all I need to kill you."

He had a maddening smile. "And how do you expect to accomplish that?"

Although wizards had powerful magic and numerous defenses, they could be killed in a normal manner, so long as they were taken by surprise. Adessa had the most tremendous surprise.

Raising the dagger, she kept her gaze locked on Maxim's, and flung the blade to the side with perfect aim. The sharp knife sliced through the rope she had used to tie down one of the tall, supple spruce trees. Using her strength and the blood magic within her, she had bent and anchored the trees, and then fastened the heavy log, which hung on a cradle of the rope, dangling like a battering ram. The trees trembled like a strung bow, straining to be loosed, and Adessa's thrown knife cut the rope.

The coiled energy within the bent spruces suddenly released, and the supple trees surged upward and released the suspended dead log. Maxim had just enough time to turn and see the log hurtling toward him like a ram powerful enough to smash the gates of Ildakar. He heard the thrash of pine boughs, the creak of ropes, the groan of wood. He had only an instant to raise a shield before the log slammed into his chest with such force it shattered his torso.

As the log swung back into its relaxed position on the ropes, Maxim lay sprawled on the ground in a pool of blood, his face filled with astonishment. His chest was crushed, his ribs were splintered like a thistle, but he was still alive, spasming, choking. Even with his great magic, though, the wizard commander couldn't heal himself from this.

Adessa loomed over him and slid her short sword out of its scabbard. "Sovrena Thora commanded me to bring back your head, and it gives me great pleasure to do so."

She touched her flat stomach, thought of the child that was no longer there, felt the shadow of Ian's presence in her, and she convinced herself that the sacrifice had been acceptable. She'd had enough power to kill the wizard commander. Only that mattered.

Maxim lay gurgling, coughing blood. "I am a wizard . . . cannot kill me so . . . easily."

"It was not easy, but I will kill you," Adessa said.

His fingers curled, and light flickered in his hand as he tried to summon scraps of magic, but his chest was shattered, his life fading away. She had to hurry. "Oh no, Maxim, I am not going to let you simply die. I have to be the one to kill you."

He groaned, tried to form words: "I will still . . . be . . ."

She hacked down on his neck, cutting through the muscles and neck bone, until she lifted his dripping head by the beautiful dark hair. When she killed Maxim, a rushing glow flowed out of his body and whipped through the now-still spruces. She felt a shudder in the magic as if some last threads of an ancient spell were finally severed, although nothing touched her rune-protected body.

Maxim was hers. She stared at his slack face, his dull and open eyes. She would deliver the trophy back to Ildakar, back to Thora. It would be a long, hard journey home, but with the wizard commander's head, Adessa would have all the companionship she needed.

CHAPTER 85

Even after the conflagration burned the front ranks of his army, General Utros was not willing to admit defeat. But with Ildakar entirely gone, he no longer had a city to conquer. Despite his losses, he still had more than a hundred thousand brave fighters. They stood on an empty, burned plain without an enemy to face.

He stared at the remnants of his stunned army and knew that he needed to give them a new goal, another reason to exist. His separate expeditionary armies were already on the march to find other lands to conquer. Utros had hoped to use those victories to get back into Kurgan's good graces, yet he had less and less respect for the man to whom he had sworn his loyalty and his life.

Loyalty is greater than love. Was that even true anymore? Majel, his love, had been destroyed, and his loyalty toward her murderer was frayed and full of questions.

Utros returned to his makeshift command tent beyond the fringe of the great fire, where the tall oval lens to the underworld stood out in the open. Ava and Ruva were with him, determined to support him, whatever he should decide to do.

First Commander Enoch had also miraculously survived, much to Utros's relief, but he would never know the names of all the dead. A good commander owed that much to his fallen soldiers, but there were too many. Far too many.

The first commander sat on his warhorse, bowing to Utros. "The soldiers await your orders, General. They will follow you wherever you may lead."

Utros stared across the empty plain, still unable to believe that the city had simply vanished. Without Ildakar, the orders Iron Fang had given him were no longer valid, though in truth the emperor had never understood the situation on the ground, had never grasped his own empire. Iron Fang knew how to make people fear him, but he didn't know how to rule. He was a pompous, self-absorbed man who achieved power only through others, like Utros.

The general didn't know how he had been so blind before. No wonder Majel had sought love in someone else's arms. If it hadn't been Utros, would it have been another man? She had been so beautiful, so perfect, yet even after Kurgan had inflicted his horrific punishment upon her, she had gone back to him. Utros couldn't understand it, nor did he need to. His duty was to his hundreds of thousands of soldiers. He was their leader, their general, not some spirit that spoke only through a bloodstained lens.

Utros stopped in front of the scorched but still functional lens to the underworld. At his command, the sorceresses activated the glowing runes, and the greenish mists cleared, letting him see through to the realm of the spirits. Utros stood bravely before the glass, staring at the ravaged landscape of the dead, which looked all too similar to the blasted landscape of his own camp.

Emperor Kurgan appeared before him again, grinning to show his hooked iron tooth. Majel was beside him, her face a raw mask. Her brown, lidless eyes stared at Utros, but now he saw her more clearly. No love remained there for him.

"You summoned me again, Utros," Kurgan said. "If you have finally conquered Ildakar, then I am ready to issue my first orders. Execute all those who defied me, and when they come here to the underworld, we will punish them further." He seemed to relish the idea.

"Ildakar is gone," Utros said. "Vanished."

"Gone?" Kurgan was taken aback. "How do you lose a city?"

"How do you lose an empire?" Utros retorted, allowing the harsh tone to erase all the awe and respect he had once held for this man. "How do you lose your wife, the most beautiful woman in the world? How do you squander all the lands I conquered for you, while I continue to fight for your foolishness?"

Kurgan was outraged. "I forbid you to speak to me like that. I am your emperor."

"You are dead. You are no longer my emperor, and I no longer follow your orders. Neither loyalty nor love is strong enough. *I* am strong. *I* have my army, and *I* will conquer the Old World for myself. My soldiers are loyal to me, and we will create a new empire, a worthy empire. You corrupted everything you touched." He lowered his voice as the emperor snarled, unable to form words. Utros shifted his gaze and spoke to the other image inside the lens. "Majel, I did love you, but our love was doomed from the start. I should have been wise enough to know that. Maybe I could have saved you, but I will not mourn for what happened fifteen centuries in the past. Instead, I will make my own future without you." He turned back to Kurgan. "And without you, Iron Fang."

Leaving the emperor fuming behind the veil to the underworld, General Utros stepped back from the lens. He picked up a heavy war hammer he had taken from one of his soldiers, a weapon that felt solid in his hand, real and heavy and deadly. With a cry that encompassed all his rage and despair, Utros swung the weapon and smashed the center of the blood lens.

Golden magic crackled and flared around the fissures that shot through the glass. The central impact left a white crater, and the cracks spread, branching out toward the edge. He heard a final echoing howl of Iron Fang's rage before the blood lens shattered, crumbling into chunks of glass that fell in a pile on the scorched ground.

Ava and Ruva smiled at him with satisfaction and relief. First Commander Enoch pressed a fist to his heart in a salute and then shouted, "For General Utros!" The twin sorceresses took up the cheer, as did thousands of voices from his army.

Suddenly, unrelated to the shattering of the lens, Utros felt a strange force vibrate through the air like a magical lightning storm, a distant shock wave that rang through the fabric of the world. He instinctively clutched his chest, and his half-stone skin crawled.

Ava and Ruva stared at each other, then spun to him for answers. First Commander Enoch grasped his arm, touched his face, grimaced. The soldiers began to mutter. Some cried out, staring at their hands, bending their waists, flexing their arms.

Utros felt a shudder, and his skin tingled, warmed. The feeling was similar to what he remembered when he had reawakened from the nothingness of stone. But now he felt restored, even more human. The stiff petrification faded away.

His skin softened. His muscles loosened. With a sigh, he felt the dust go out of his lungs. He reached up to touch the gold half mask on his face, then ran his fingers over his other cheek. His beard was softer than before, silky. He looked at Ava and Ruva and saw that their pale, chalky skin had become warm flesh once more.

"The stone is gone from us!" Ruva said, holding up her delicate hand.

The twins touched each other, stroked their skin, caressed their faces. Ava said, "The spell is broken. Completely."

Utros listened to the rising murmur of wonderment

throughout the camp. One soldier leaped into the air and kicked his legs in joy. "We are human again!"

Whatever wizard had created the ancient petrification spell centuries ago was gone now, likely dead. There were no lingering remnants of the spell. They were free again, completely free.

Utros raised his hand, clenched his fingers into a fist. "We're alive!" A resounding roar rippled across the hundreds of thousands of armed men camped on the burned plain.

The general allowed himself a moment of satisfaction and tried not to let them see the deep concern on his face. They would realize it themselves soon enough, and come to the same conclusion.

More than a hundred thousand warriors were camped in the middle of a vast, burned plain, far from the nearest city. They had no supplies at all, no Ildakar to defeat, and all those mouths to feed.

With gnawing dread, General Utros realized that he was *hungry*.

CHAPTER 86

The Norukai raiders caused tremendous damage to Serrimundi. Even though the people had succeeded in defeating the serpent ships, Nicci wished she could have prepared them better. But there had been no time.

Peace and prosperity left entire cities vulnerable because they let down their guard, but Nicci never underestimated the potential for hatred and evil in the world, since she herself had caused so much harm.

When she had left the People's Palace on her mission with Nathan, Nicci had been convinced that Richard's heartfelt code of freedom and independence throughout the D'Haran Empire would bring a true change for the world. But in her travels it had not taken long for her to see that the world was still a dangerous place.

She and Nathan had encountered many worthy men and women who would fight for what was right, hardworking farmers and craftsmen, even warriors who wanted a good life and a better world. But there were also many enemies, and it was Nicci's job to fight them, to make a safe haven for those good people, and smother the ambitions of would-be conquerors, like the Norukai.

King Grieve's large invasion fleet was out there, supposedly attacking Ildakar. Captain Kor had revealed the grandiose plans of the Norukai, and now Nicci knew she had another great enemy in addition to the threat of General Utros and his half-stone army.

Harborlord Otto and Captain Ganley had brought the damaged *Mist Maiden* back to the wharf, where final mopping-up operations were under way. Thousands of evacuated Serrimundi citizens returned from the hills and helped extinguish the dockside fires. The emboldened citizens also stood against the last of the raiders. The stranded Norukai showed little concern for their own lives and simply kept fighting until they were brought down by archers launching volley after volley of arrows.

Aboard the bloodstained decks of the *Mist Maiden,* angry and shaken crew members heaved Norukai corpses overboard into the harbor for the fish to feast on. The bodies of their own dead crew members, though, were lined up with great reverence, their arms and legs straightened, their faces smoothed, as the harborlord intoned the blessings of the Sea Mother upon them.

Nicci stood at the prow of the ship, covered with blood, her blond hair caked with red. She faced Harborlord Otto as the *Mist Maiden* tied up to the damaged docks and shouting people raced along the harbor's edge. Captain Ganley waved as he saw his betrothed running toward him, laughing with relief. The harborlord looked as if he might burst into tears at seeing his daughter.

When they disembarked to a triumphant crowd of merchants and dockworkers, Nicci raised her voice. "I came here to warn you of an enemy threat, but the threat is even greater than I imagined. I hope you believe my warning now." She gestured out to the harbor to indicate the burning ships, the bodies of the Norukai, and the Serrimundi dead that crew members solemnly carried off the decks of the returning ships. "Prepare yourselves for worse. It is not over."

"Didn't we defeat them?" asked a gruff and lanky man in

stained captain's clothes. His face looked similar to Harborlord Otto's.

"This was just a raiding expedition, ten serpent ships," Nicci said. "The Norukai have an empire, which has decided to go to war."

Otto said, "This is my brother, Jared. He captains a kraken-hunting ship, like the one that burned at the mouth of the harbor."

Jared scratched the back of his head. "We know how to kill tentacled monsters in the open sea, but we don't usually worry about pirates. No one comes close to a krakener."

"Maybe it's the smell . . ." Otto joked.

"The Norukai will burn any ship they find," Nicci said.

Jared shook his head. "They are not going to burn mine. From now on, all of my crew will be armed. The Norukai are just a different sort of monster to kill."

"Every ship must be prepared to fight," Nicci told the harborlord. "Spread the news throughout the harbor and to all the outbound ships so they can carry the word as well. Other towns have been preyed upon by the Norukai. Open trade will no longer keep you safe. Even if you have a strong city, someone will want to take it.

"I have already delivered a warning to Tanimura and asked Lord Rahl for his help. An entire D'Haran expeditionary force will be ready to march, but Serrimundi and all the cities along the coast will have to help themselves. The Norukai may have already struck several targets. Send messengers far and wide, even to the cities inland, because the armies of General Utros might be coming as well. Be watchful and ready. Build up your defenses."

The people made promises. She could tell they wanted to be reassured that all would be well. Nicci couldn't afford to let them grow complacent again. She unwrapped the pane of glass she had carried with her. "This is another enemy that awaits you, a vast army awakened from fifteen centuries ago.

They have laid siege to Ildakar and already sent out satellite armies to ravage and pillage. They will conquer the lands in the mountains, then make their way to the coast."

She needed to return to Ildakar if the Norukai were attacking, as Kor had boasted. She had to let the people of Serrimundi build up their own defenses without her. "I might not come back here for some time, so I leave the task to you. Rally the Old World."

She turned slowly, showing them Elsa's pane of glass, in which the image of Utros's army had been imprinted. "This is proof of the enemy that is coming for you. Show everyone." She intentionally dropped the pane onto the hard boards of the pier, and when it struck, the glass broke into eight uneven pieces. Each of the shards contained an identical image. She picked up one of the fragments and handed it to Harborlord Otto, handed a second one to the kraken hunter Jared, then distributed the remaining pieces among those who might spread the word.

"It is up to you now," Nicci said. "I have to go back to Ildakar. You must all unite as part of the D'Haran Empire. Fight for your lives and your freedom."

Seeing the look in their eyes, she knew she had gotten through to them. They would do as she asked. Nicci felt confident as she left the harbor and made her way back into the hills, where she would find the ancient temple of the Sea Mother and the sliph well.

At twilight, the temple was silent and peaceful, abandoned. After the Norukai attack on the harbor, the people of Serrimundi were picking up the pieces and putting out the last fires. There were hundreds of wounded to be tended. Nicci could have used healing magic to help them, but Serrimundi had many doctors and gifted healers. She was no longer needed here.

If the Norukai were attacking Ildakar, she was certainly needed there.

"Sliph, I want to travel. Now." Nicci was sore, weary, and worried for her friends. She stood at the edge of the well and waited.

The shrubs and vines rustled in the evening breezes, and she smelled the gentle scent of blooming nightshade, but she heard nothing from the bottomless well. "Sliph, come!" She pushed out with her gift, felt along the threads of magic, the throbbing power deep within the well.

Somewhere infinitely far away, the intractable quicksilver began to move, roiling up the passage. Nicci was impatient, concerned about what might be happening in Ildakar right now. She had left Nathan and the duma members searching for a way to fight General Utros. How could they possibly battle King Grieve as well as a full Norukai invasion at the same time?

She shouted into the well. "Sliph, I require your services. I need to travel!"

Finally, the quicksilver surged to the top, like metallic acid boiling in a cauldron. The sliph's face looked angry. "I serve the cause. I do not serve you."

Nicci retorted, "You were created to transport travelers, and I need to travel." She had no time to cajole the sliph. Lucy, the sliph that Richard commanded in Stroyza, had also been moody and petulant, but in the end Lucy had done as she was told. Nicci put one foot on the edge of the well. "Carry me back to Ildakar."

"How will that serve Sulachan?" the sliph demanded.

"Sulachan is gone," Nicci snapped. "We fight a different battle now. The cause has changed."

The sliph recoiled at the revelation, and Nicci reached out with her gift, using Subtractive as well as Additive Magic. The sliph required both, and now Nicci proved that she was strong, her new master. "Take me to Ildakar."

The sliph looked devastated. Her face distorted as the quicksilver re-formed itself. "Sulachan . . ."

Nicci released more of her gift, hammering hard to assert her dominance over the sliph. "Take me to Ildakar. I command it."

"Ildakar!" The sliph lunged forward like an attacking wave of molten silver. "Breathe!" she commanded, then engulfed Nicci and pulled her down into a bottomless cold pit. . . .

CHAPTER 87

As the river thawed again and great chunks of ice drifted apart, the numerous serpent ships broke free, caught in the current, their hulls cracked. Drifting in the slush-choked water were hundreds of dead Norukai men and women who had tumbled from the bluffs or been killed by the defenders of Ildakar.

Bound and bloody, his body bruised from the fall and his head still ringing from a cracked skull, Bannon couldn't break free from the hideous raiders. Stunned, he couldn't think straight, but he knew where he was.

The young man had fought with every ounce of energy, fully expecting to die, and when he had tumbled from the platform to crash among the bodies below, he had never expected to awaken. Though he could feel several cracked ribs and blood running down the side of his face, Bannon was worse than dead. He was a prisoner of the hated Norukai! His captors dragged him along with dozens of other Ildakaran prisoners toward the crowded serpent ships in the river. Some of the captives were unconscious, some sobbing, and only a few made halfhearted efforts to escape, which were severely beaten back.

Bannon couldn't make sense of what he was seeing. From the river, he looked up the bluff where he should have seen the towering city above.

Ildakar was gone. *Gone!*

The entire city had simply been erased, as if the top of the plateau had been shaved off, leaving the lower portion of the bluff intact but the upper levels sheared away.

Though Bannon's thoughts were scrambled, he recalled the first time he, Nathan, and Nicci had approached Ildakar. They had seen only an empty plain, because the city was hidden beneath the shroud of eternity, a bubble that erased it from time. Had the wizards done the same thing again, whisking Ildakar away and leaving anyone outside to fend for themselves?

What about Nathan and Elsa and the raiding party out in the plain? What about the rest of the people of Ildakar? And where was Lila?

The defenders in the tunnels beneath the bluff had been abandoned, left behind to face the Norukai, who were even now ransacking the tunnels, dragging out prisoners and slaying any who resisted.

Ildakar was gone. Bannon was on his own.

As his captors shoved him across a wooden plank and onto the deck of a serpent ship, Bannon relived a horrifying nightmare from his childhood, when the scarred raiders had come to Chiriya Island, clubbed him and captured him in an isolated cove. Now, all these years later, Bannon was in the clutches of the same monsters again.

King Grieve and Chalk had also survived the fall, and that only increased Bannon's despair. Now, as they stood among the surviving raiders, Grieve bellowed to his countless fighters, "Search every tunnel. Find what is up there. Climb the cliff and reach the top of the plain."

The albino shaman laced his knobby fingers together. "Yes, the plain and the whole world! Out there is our destiny, my Grieve, King Grieve. They'll all grieve!"

The Norukai king snorted. "I don't know how much to believe you anymore, Chalk. Your visions are flawed."

"No, my Grieve! I saw the battle. I saw cold, snow, and ice. Remember? Remember, my Grieve? Cold, ice, cold!" He gestured to the thawing river, the ice chunks sliding down the bluff wall. "Ildakar did not win, and you have what is left. It's yours, my king, my Grieve. Ildakar is gone! I said so!"

"That is not what I expected."

"Never what you expect," the shaman said. "But I know it's true in the end. Go to the plain, and you will see how to take over the whole world."

Bannon struggled against his bonds. "You'll fail." His voice was a harsh croak. "The Old World will rally against you, and Lord Rahl has the entire D'Haran army to defeat you."

Grieve smashed the side of Bannon's head with his iron-plated knuckles. The young man collapsed, barely keeping a thread of consciousness. He fell backward onto the icy, blood-slick deck. He blinked, trying to look up and down the river, disoriented.

He could make out the Norukai ships and the countless raiders swarming into the tunnels, to climb up where the city had vanished. He saw the crumbling rocks, the river, and thick brush along the banks. At the edge of his vision, he thought he caught a glimpse of a slender woman wearing only black leather wrappings. Lila? Before he could focus, she darted into the shadows, hiding among the low trees.

Grieve said, "If we are going to take over the world, we will need many more captives, slaves, workers." With his broad chin he gestured toward the boats as he shouted orders to the other Norukai. "For now, kill as few as you have to. We need to launch a hundred more raids to fill our ranks and take captives, though I expect we'll have to kill quite a few just to make our message clear."

Bannon struggled as they dragged him among the shuddering captives. Ignoring him for now, the Norukai king gestured toward the bluff. "Let us make our way up through the tunnels, Chalk. I want to see what awaits us on the plain."

When she emerged after the timeless journey, Nicci spilled out of the well as if thrown in disgust. She crashed to the ground and rolled, gasping in air and trying to expel the intangible essence of the sliph. Something was wrong. She felt weakened and strange, and her ears rang.

Rather than finding herself in a dank, stone-walled enclosure in Ildakar, Nicci was in the open, late at night, sprawled on broken flagstones. Around her, she saw fallen stone pillars the size of massive oak trees. Great slabs of marble lay tilted at various angles, as if the ancient city had been shaken apart. On the far side of the plaza, a statue of a man as large as a dragon lay toppled, the colossus shattered into pieces.

From behind high patchy clouds, the moon shone down to illuminate the ruins of a vast city where grand towers had crumbled into rubble and majestic archways were overgrown with vines and moss. The jagged silhouettes of nearby mountain peaks hovered behind the haunted, silent buildings. Other than the stars, the only lights she saw were tiny fireflies swirling about like intermittent meteors.

She saw no campfires, no lamps in windows of the dwellings, no sign of life whatsoever in the extensive ruins. She turned back to the sliph, who hovered in the round enclosure. "Where am I? This isn't Ildakar." She felt suddenly dizzy, nauseated. "What have you done to me?"

Like an angry spirit, the sliph loomed out of her well. Her quicksilver form shifted and melted, as if she had trouble maintaining her shape. "Ildakar no longer exists. I cannot take you there. I tried, but I . . . ricocheted. The city is gone."

"What do you mean it's gone?" Nicci stepped back toward the well. "We came from there. I need to travel. Take me to Ildakar."

"I refuse. Ildakar is gone." Her expression roiled with anger. "And I am not your slave. If Sulachan is dead, then the cause is lost. I have no purpose. You have deceived me, and I will not help you."

Nicci realized how lost she was. She could be stranded, and this creature was her only connection, her only way of getting back. "No, sliph! If you can't take me to Ildakar, then return me to Serrimundi." She looked around at the abandoned metropolis. "Do not leave me here."

"You will never travel in me again." The sliph's voice held a dangerous finality. "I must recover."

Nicci rushed to the edge of the well, but it was too late. The sliph vanished, plunging back down into the bottomless well with a rushing, fading sound.

Nicci stood silent, all alone in the empty wreck of an ancient city, completely cut off from her friends and everything she knew.

Utros's returning scouts rode back at a fast gallop from the empty site of Ildakar, where the bluffs dropped off to the river. The first man had an unexpectedly alarmed expression on his face. "General! Warriors are climbing up from the Killraven and emerging onto the plain. Thousands of them!"

"They are armed and furious," said a second man, his skin warm and flushed. "Uglier than any humans I have ever seen."

First Commander Enoch stepped forward. "Another army? Where did they come from? Do they mean to fight us?"

Utros stared toward the river, where he saw the unruly lines of figures moving toward them. Even though his army was shocked and damaged after the inferno, they clearly outnumbered any possible enemy force. And yet the other warriors kept coming over the top of the cliff. Utros gritted his teeth and nodded to Enoch. "First Commander, go meet them with a party of armed soldiers. Find out who they are. I will want to speak with their leader."

With a brisk nod, the hardened veteran gathered fifty men and rode off to the raiders coming up from the river.

Utros ignored the unfamiliar pangs of hunger in his stomach. He remembered when he had tried to eat the roasted yaxen shortly after awakening, and he had vomited up the meat. Now, his stomach wanted food. All of his soldiers would feel the same way.

Before long, the first commander returned leading ten hideous warriors with scarred faces. One man, larger and more powerful than the rest of them, had bony spikes implanted in his shoulders and iron plates on his knuckles. He was accompanied by a pale man whose skin was covered with a forest of scars.

"We are the Norukai, and I am King Grieve," said the large man, striding forward to face Utros. "What have you done to Ildakar?"

Utros gestured to his surviving soldiers that spilled across the plain, restless in their makeshift camp. "We laid siege to the city. My army has been waiting here for fifteen centuries to bring it down."

Grieve interrupted with a loud laugh. "The statue army! Yes, my spies told me about the stone warriors. But you are awake now."

The general didn't flinch, showed no weakness. "We have been fighting to break down the city walls, but Ildakar just vanished before our eyes. I do not know what happened."

Grieve grumbled. "Yes, the city has done that before. Maybe Ildakar will return, maybe it won't. But I have all my Norukai navy, and my warriors need to fight." He leaned closer. "Maybe we should attack your army."

"Only if you wish to die," Utros said. "Do you not see the numbers of my troops? What would be the point? Do you think war is nothing more than a sport?"

Grieve shrugged. "Sometimes."

Ava and Ruva came close, their eyes bright, and he knew they were ready to attack with magic. The twins stared curiously at the scarred albino shaman.

The two men were both massive, and if Utros had still been hardened from the lingering effects of the stone spell, he could have crushed the king. But now he was flesh and blood again, with all the inherent weaknesses of a mere human. As he faced the Norukai king, Utros was both offended and fascinated by the scarification, the slashed mouth, the implanted bone spines, the tattoos on his skin. Even more hideous was the shaman whose skin was covered with bite marks.

"Destiny," said the albino. "Destiny, my Grieve, King Grieve! There will be war, a big war." He jabbed a finger at Utros. "But not with him."

The Norukai leader's expression showed a reckless challenge, but Utros remained calm. They had both attacked Ildakar, but from different sides.

"We have the same enemy," Utros said. "I assume you had your reasons to attack the city."

Grieve said, "To conquer it."

Utros saw thousands more Norukai ascending from the river below, and his scouts had reported numerous warships on the water. "Ildakar is no longer there. Are you going to make yourself my enemy? You and all your fighters?" He kept his voice calm and gestured to the countless ranks across the scorched and damaged field. "My army can easily defeat yours. It makes no sense for you to fight us."

"The Norukai always fight," Grieve said. "We raid, we pillage, we conquer."

"Admirable goals," Utros said, "so long as you choose the right target. And the right ally."

The shaman came close, curious to look at the twin sorceresses. He sniffed and shifted his gaze back and forth from Ava to Ruva. "Magic," he said. "Powerful magic! But they don't see what I see, my Grieve. I see a huge army! I see Norukai ships. I see Utros and his soldiers." He grinned. "I see a powerful force to sweep across the whole land."

General Utros was curious. "I once served Emperor Kurgan. Now I serve my own goals. I have no emperor."

"I am king," Grieve said. "King of the Norukai."

"You may be king of the Norukai, but I am general of my troops. The Old World is vast. How can you help me conquer it?"

Offended, Grieve puffed himself up as if ready to attack Utros. Ava and Ruva coiled, prepared to unleash their magic. With a single bolt of lightning, they could turn King Grieve into a smear of ash.

But the albino shaman jumped between them, frantically waving his hands. "This is what I saw, my Grieve, King Grieve! Allies. You and General Utros, a giant army! A great war."

"I have hundreds of ships," Grieve boasted. "Many down on the river, others raiding the coast, and more being built among our islands. It is a navy unlike any that history has ever seen."

"They'll all grieve!" the shaman cried.

Utros pondered how many soldiers he had just lost, and his new determination after forsaking his loyalty to Emperor Kurgan. He said in a calculating voice, "I have my army, but to overwhelm the entire land, a navy would be useful as well, and many more fighters. If your Norukai can fight."

Grieve spat on the ground, as if the answer were disgustingly obvious. The king described his great war fleet and his countless raiders, ruthless Norukai men and women, and powerful serpent ships. He told of the numerous Norukai islands filled with warriors who had not yet set off in battle, but were restless and eager to launch their own attacks. A war, a full war, to conquer the entire Old World.

Utros decided that, given time, he could wipe out these Norukai, if necessary, but for now he did not need another war for his displaced troops. Perhaps these warriors would be useful.

"Together, our armies can conquer the world," Grieve said. "If we fight together."

"They'll all grieve!" the shaman repeated.

Ava and Ruva leaned closer, whispering in eerie unison, "With a whole continent to conquer, beloved Utros, surely there is enough to carve out two empires."

He considered, then spoke to the Norukai leader. "With your ships and your raiders, and all my soldiers, we could overwhelm the land. King Grieve and General Utros."

The Norukai king opened his exaggerated mouth and clacked his teeth together. "I agree."

Smiling with satisfaction, Utros reached out to clasp Grieve's massive hand.